WITCHBLADE

✦ ORIGINS
VOLUME 2

Witchblade created by:
Marc Silvestri, David Wohl,
Brian Haberlin and Michael Turner

published by
Top Cow Productions, Inc.
Los Angeles

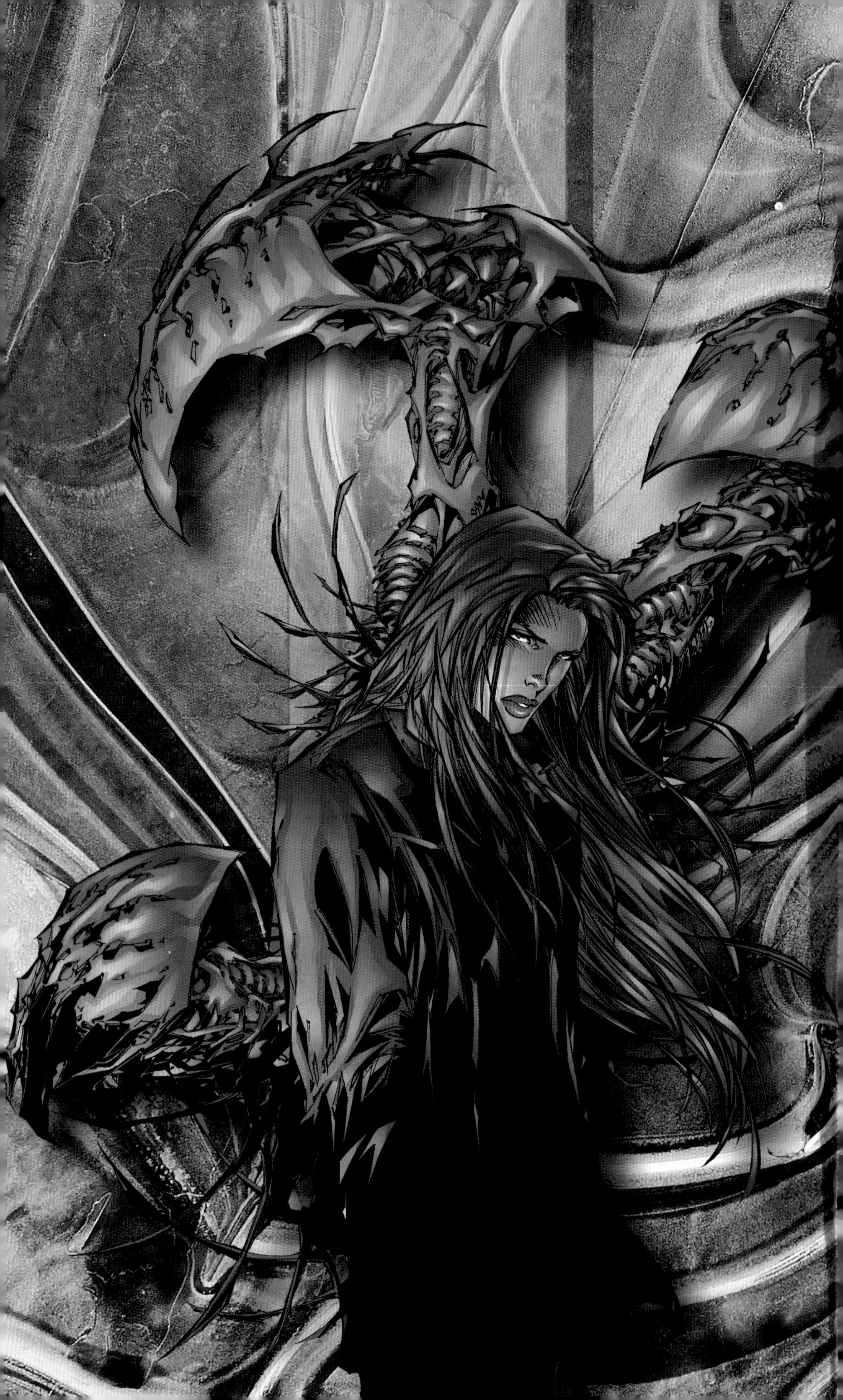

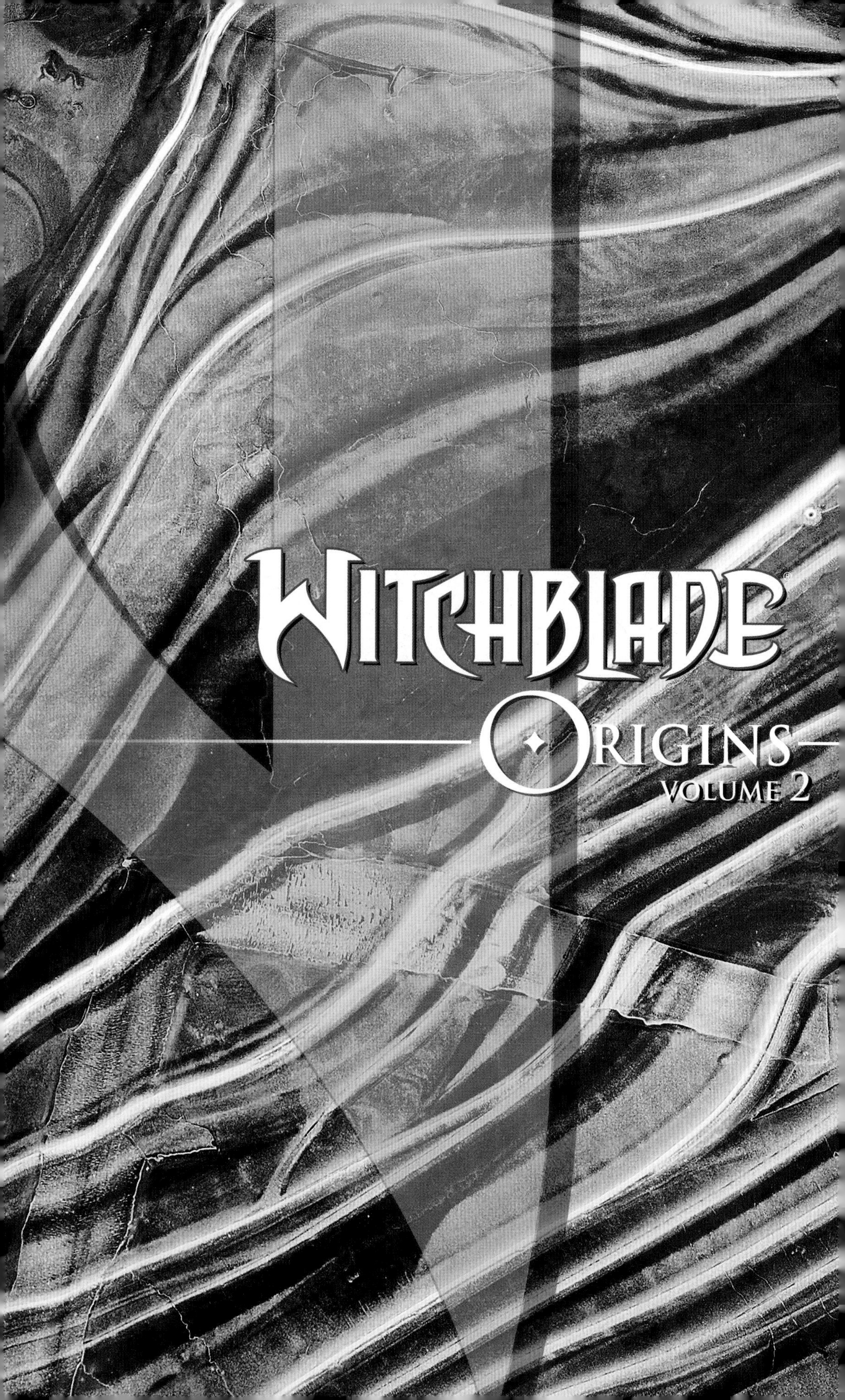
WITCHBLADE®
ORIGINS
VOLUME 2

WITCHBLADE

letters for all issues in this edition by:
Dennis Heisler

For Top Cow Productions, Inc.:
Marc Silvestri - Chief Executive Officer
Matt Hawkins - President and Chief Operating Officer
Filip Sablik - Publisher
Chaz Riggs - Graphic Design
Phil Smith - Managing Editor
Alyssa Phung - Controller
Adrian Nicita - Webmaster
Scott Newman - Production Lead
Jennifer Chow - Production Assistant
Rob Levin - Consulting Editor

For this edition
Cover art by:
Michael Turner, D-Tron
and JD Smith

For this edition
Book Design and Layout by:
Phil Smith

for *image* comics
publisher:
Eric Stephenson

to find the comic shop
nearest you call:
1-888-COMICBOOK

Want more info? check out:
www.topcow.com and **www.topcowstore.com**
for news and exclusive Top Cow merchandise!

Witchblade: Origins volume 2 Trade Paperback
May 2008. FIRST PRINTING. ISBN: 978-1-58240-902-3
Published by Image Comics Inc. Office of Publication: 2134 Allston Way, Second
Floor Berkeley, CA 94704. $14.99 U.S.D. Originally published in single magazine
form as WITCHBLADE 9-17. Witchblade © 2009 Top Cow Productions, Inc. All rights
reserved. "Witchblade," the Witchblade logos, and the likeness of all characters (human
or otherwise) featured herein are registered trademarks of Top Cow Productions, Inc.
Image Comics and the Image Comics logo are trademarks of Image Comics, Inc. The
characters, events, and stories in this publication are entirely fictional. Any resemblance
to actual persons (living or dead), events, institutions, or locales, without satiric intent,
is coincidental. No portion of this publication may be reproduced or transmitted, in any
form or by any means, without the express written permission of Top Cow Productions,
Inc. PRINTED IN CHINA.

ORIGINS
VOLUME 2

TABLE OF CONTENTS

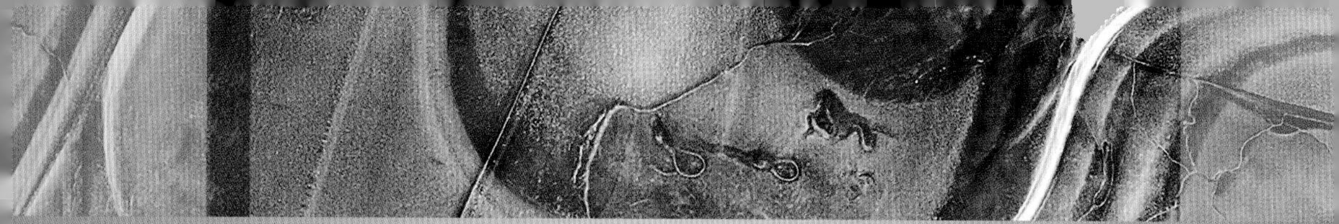

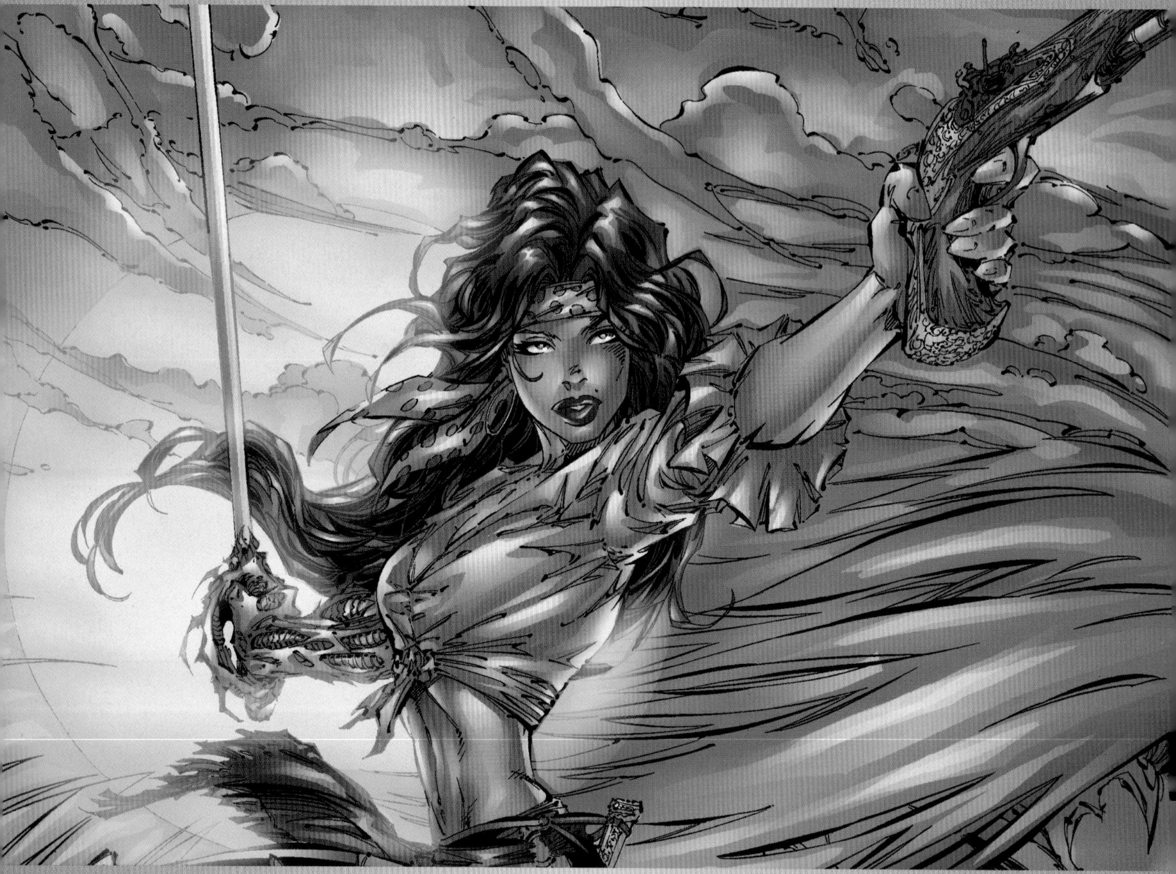

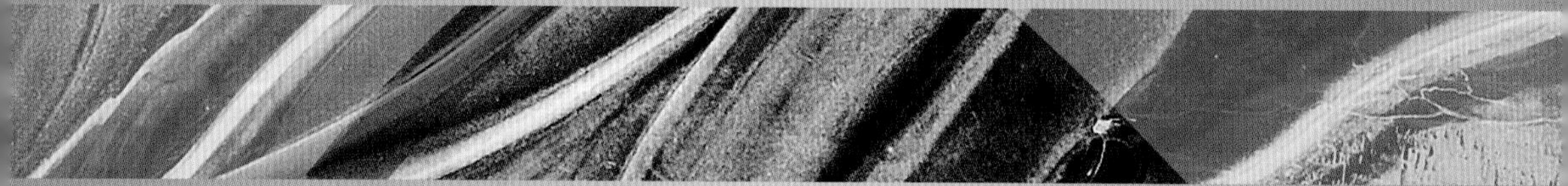

issue #9

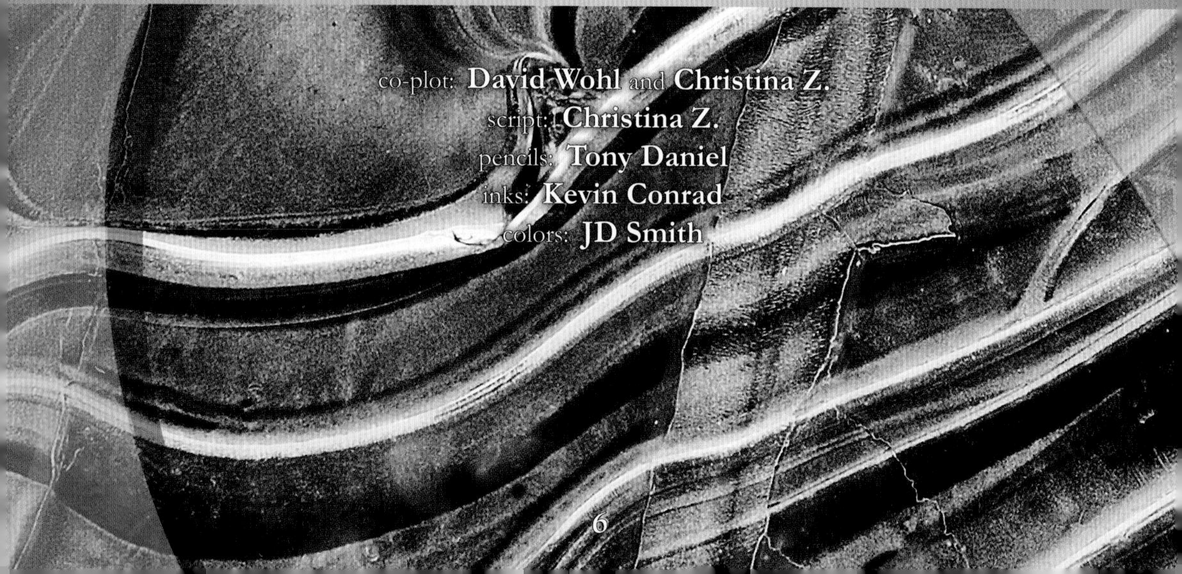

co-plot: **David Wohl** and **Christina Z.**
script: **Christina Z.**
pencils: **Tony Daniel**
inks: **Kevin Conrad**
colors: **JD Smith**

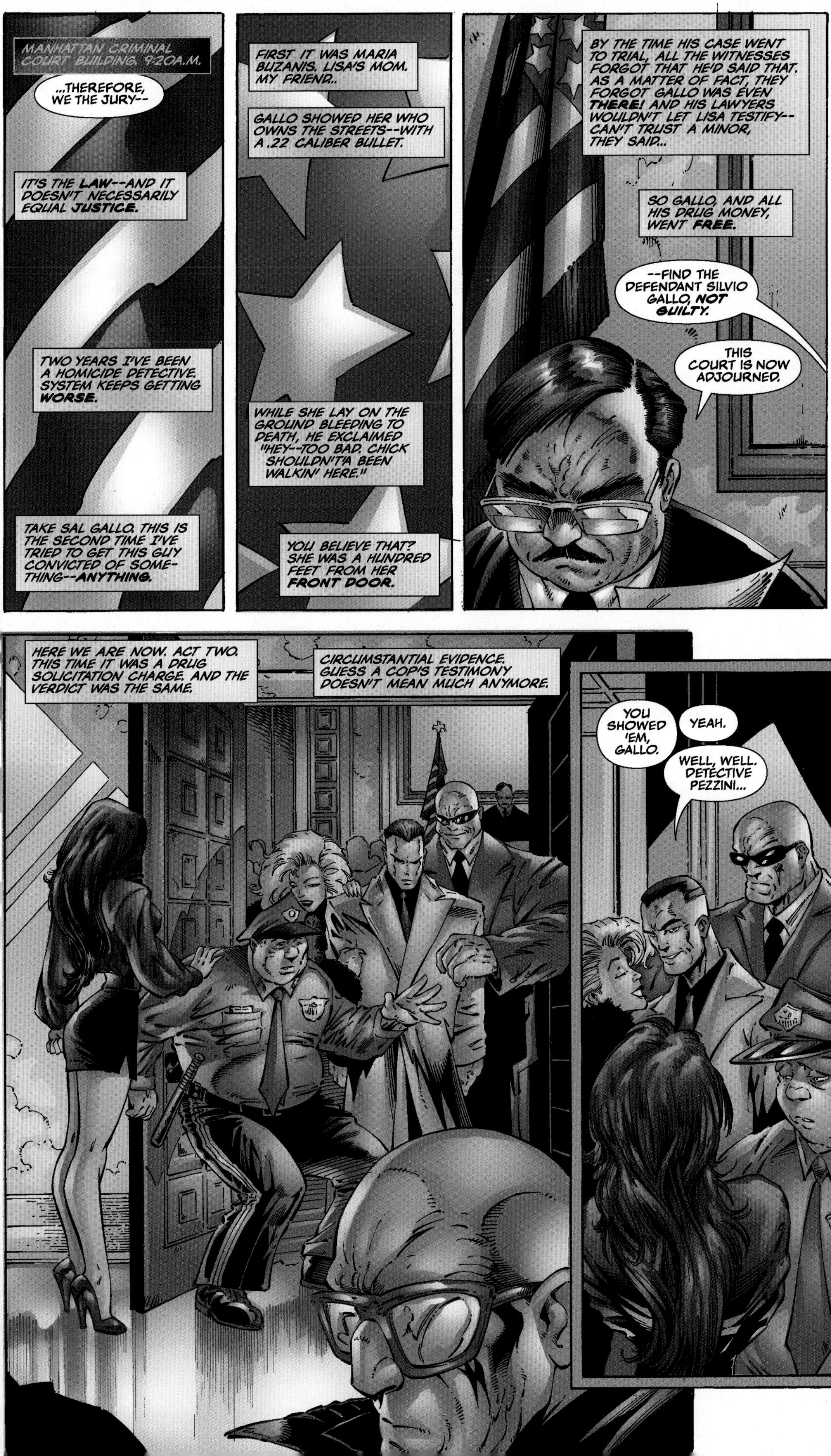
MANHATTAN CRIMINAL COURT BUILDING, 9:20A.M.
...THEREFORE, WE THE JURY--
IT'S THE LAW--AND IT DOESN'T NECESSARILY EQUAL JUSTICE.
TWO YEARS I'VE BEEN A HOMICIDE DETECTIVE. SYSTEM KEEPS GETTING WORSE.
TAKE SAL GALLO. THIS IS THE SECOND TIME I'VE TRIED TO GET THIS GUY CONVICTED OF SOME-THING--ANYTHING.
FIRST IT WAS MARIA BUZANIS. LISA'S MOM. MY FRIEND..
GALLO SHOWED HER WHO OWNS THE STREETS--WITH A .22 CALIBER BULLET.
WHILE SHE LAY ON THE GROUND BLEEDING TO DEATH, HE EXCLAIMED "HEY--TOO BAD. CHICK SHOULDN'T'A BEEN WALKIN' HERE."
YOU BELIEVE THAT? SHE WAS A HUNDRED FEET FROM HER FRONT DOOR.
BY THE TIME HIS CASE WENT TO TRIAL, ALL THE WITNESSES FORGOT THAT HE'D SAID THAT. AS A MATTER OF FACT, THEY FORGOT GALLO WAS EVEN THERE! AND HIS LAWYERS WOULDN'T LET LISA TESTIFY--CAN'T TRUST A MINOR, THEY SAID...
SO GALLO, AND ALL HIS DRUG MONEY, WENT FREE.
--FIND THE DEFENDANT SILVIO GALLO, NOT GUILTY.
THIS COURT IS NOW ADJOURNED.
HERE WE ARE NOW. ACT TWO. THIS TIME IT WAS A DRUG SOLICITATION CHARGE. AND THE VERDICT WAS THE SAME.
CIRCUMSTANTIAL EVIDENCE. GUESS A COP'S TESTIMONY DOESN'T MEAN MUCH ANYMORE.
YOU SHOWED 'EM, GALLO.
YEAH.
WELL, WELL. DETECTIVE PEZZINI...

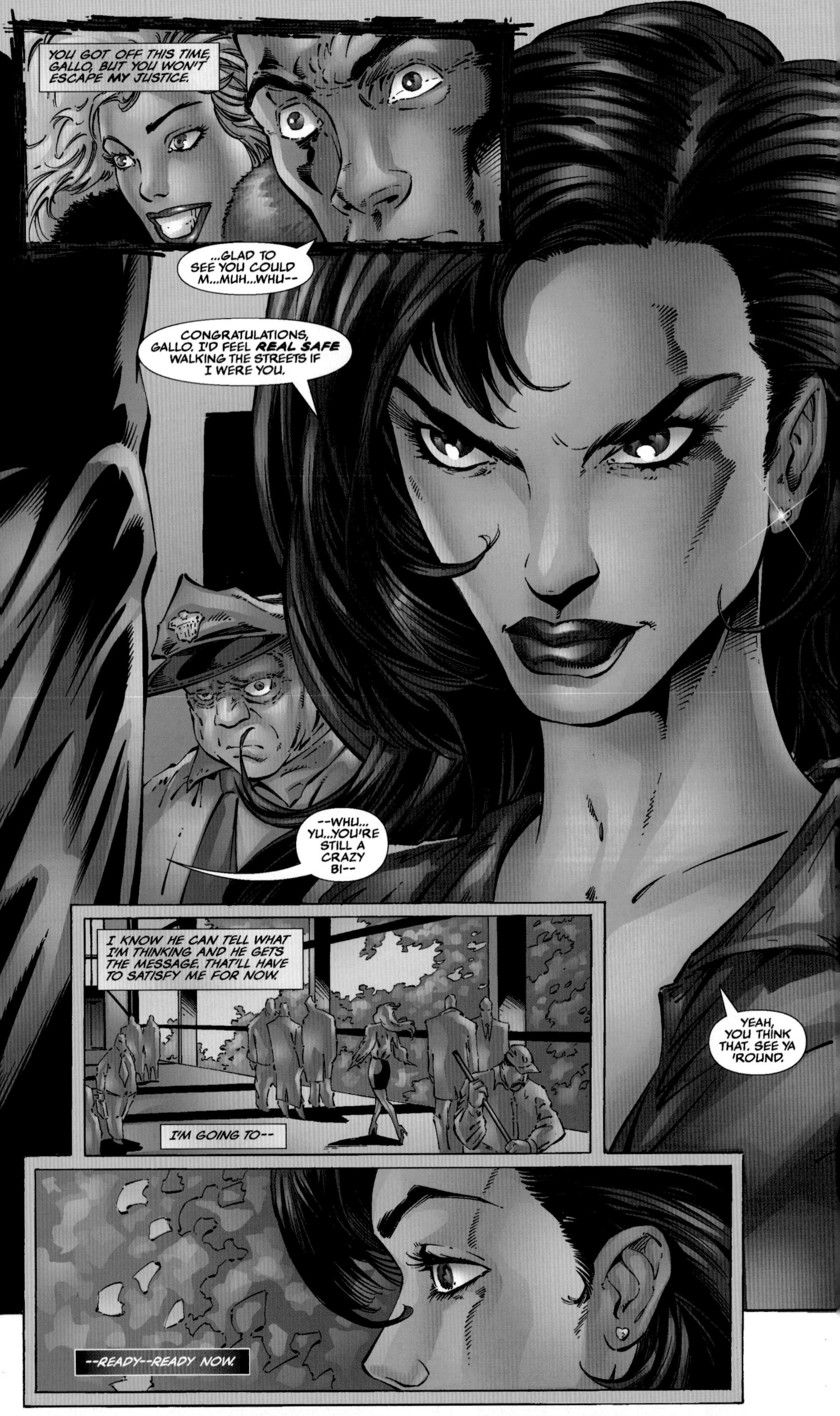
YOU GOT OFF THIS TIME, GALLO, BUT YOU WON'T ESCAPE MY JUSTICE.
...GLAD TO SEE YOU COULD M...MUH...WHU--
CONGRATULATIONS, GALLO. I'D FEEL REAL SAFE WALKING THE STREETS IF I WERE YOU.
--WHU... YU...YOU'RE STILL A CRAZY BI--
YEAH, YOU THINK THAT. SEE YA 'ROUND.
I KNOW HE CAN TELL WHAT I'M THINKING AND HE GETS THE MESSAGE. THAT'LL HAVE TO SATISFY ME FOR NOW.
I'M GOING TO--
--READY--READY NOW.

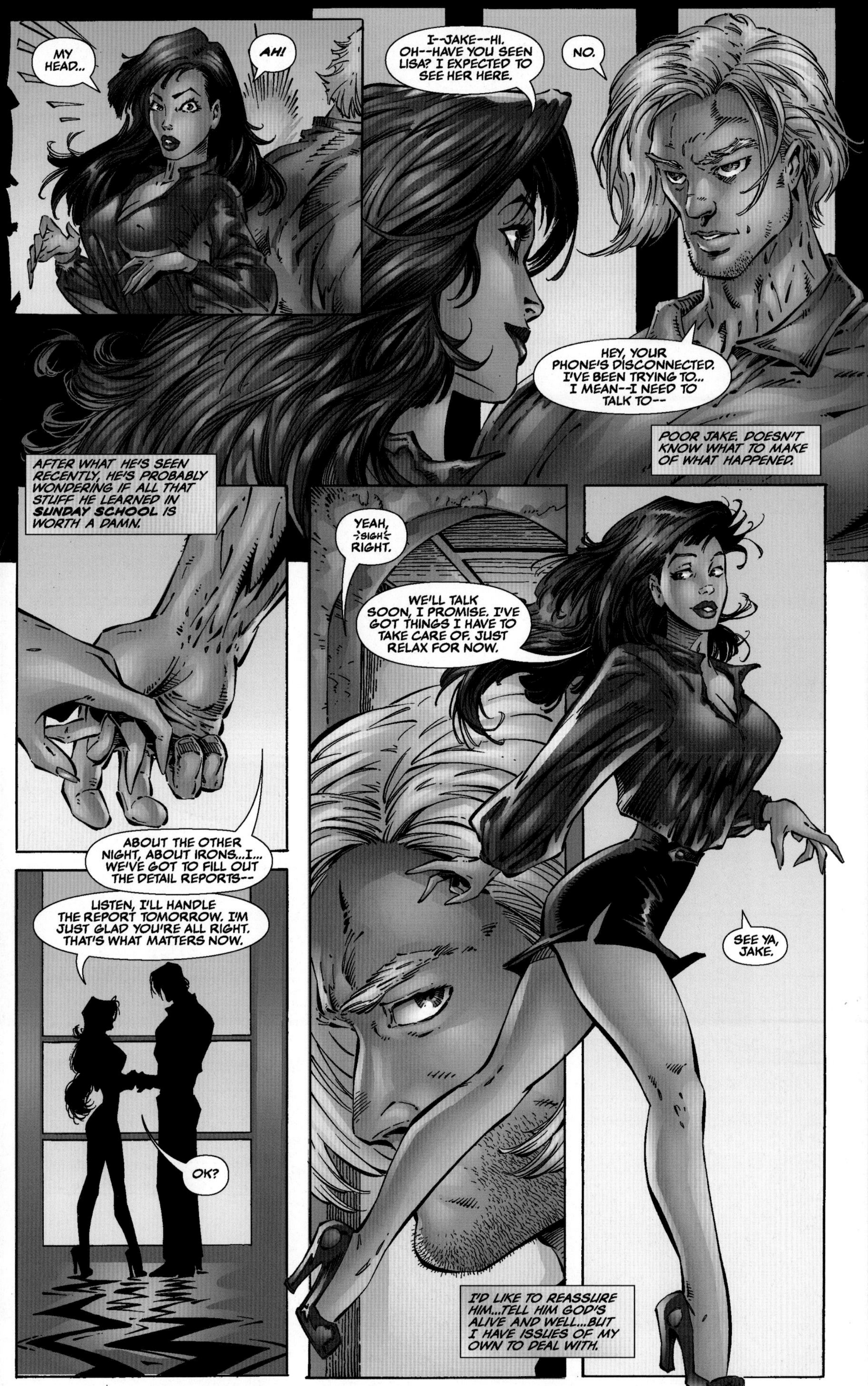
MY HEAD...
AH!
I--JAKE--HI. OH--HAVE YOU SEEN LISA? I EXPECTED TO SEE HER HERE.
NO.
HEY, YOUR PHONE'S DISCONNECTED. I'VE BEEN TRYING TO... I MEAN--I NEED TO TALK TO--
POOR JAKE. DOESN'T KNOW WHAT TO MAKE OF WHAT HAPPENED.
AFTER WHAT HE'S SEEN RECENTLY, HE'S PROBABLY WONDERING IF ALL THAT STUFF HE LEARNED IN SUNDAY SCHOOL IS WORTH A DAMN.
ABOUT THE OTHER NIGHT, ABOUT IRONS...I... WE'VE GOT TO FILL OUT THE DETAIL REPORTS--
LISTEN, I'LL HANDLE THE REPORT TOMORROW. I'M JUST GLAD YOU'RE ALL RIGHT. THAT'S WHAT MATTERS NOW.
OK?
YEAH, SIGH RIGHT.
WE'LL TALK SOON, I PROMISE. I'VE GOT THINGS I HAVE TO TAKE CARE OF. JUST RELAX FOR NOW.
SEE YA, JAKE.
I'D LIKE TO REASSURE HIM...TELL HIM GOD'S ALIVE AND WELL...BUT I HAVE ISSUES OF MY OWN TO DEAL WITH.

NEAR CITY HALL. 10:50 A.M.

UGH--THAT JUST *KILLS* ME!

GALLO--AND EVERYONE ELSE WHO THINKS THEY *RULE* THE STREETS. SOMETHING'S GOTTA--

--NEVER STOP--

--WE WILL NEVER STOP--

500 DOLLARS THEN!

MOM?

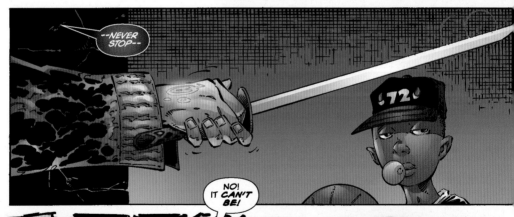

--NEVER STOP--

NO! IT *CAN'T* BE!

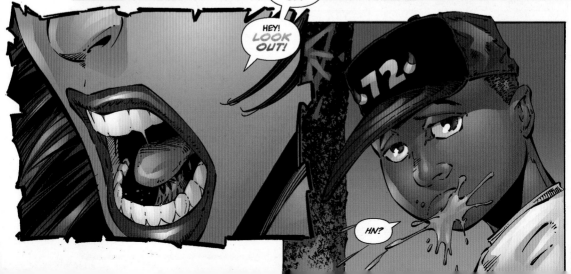

HEY! *LOOK OUT!*

HN?

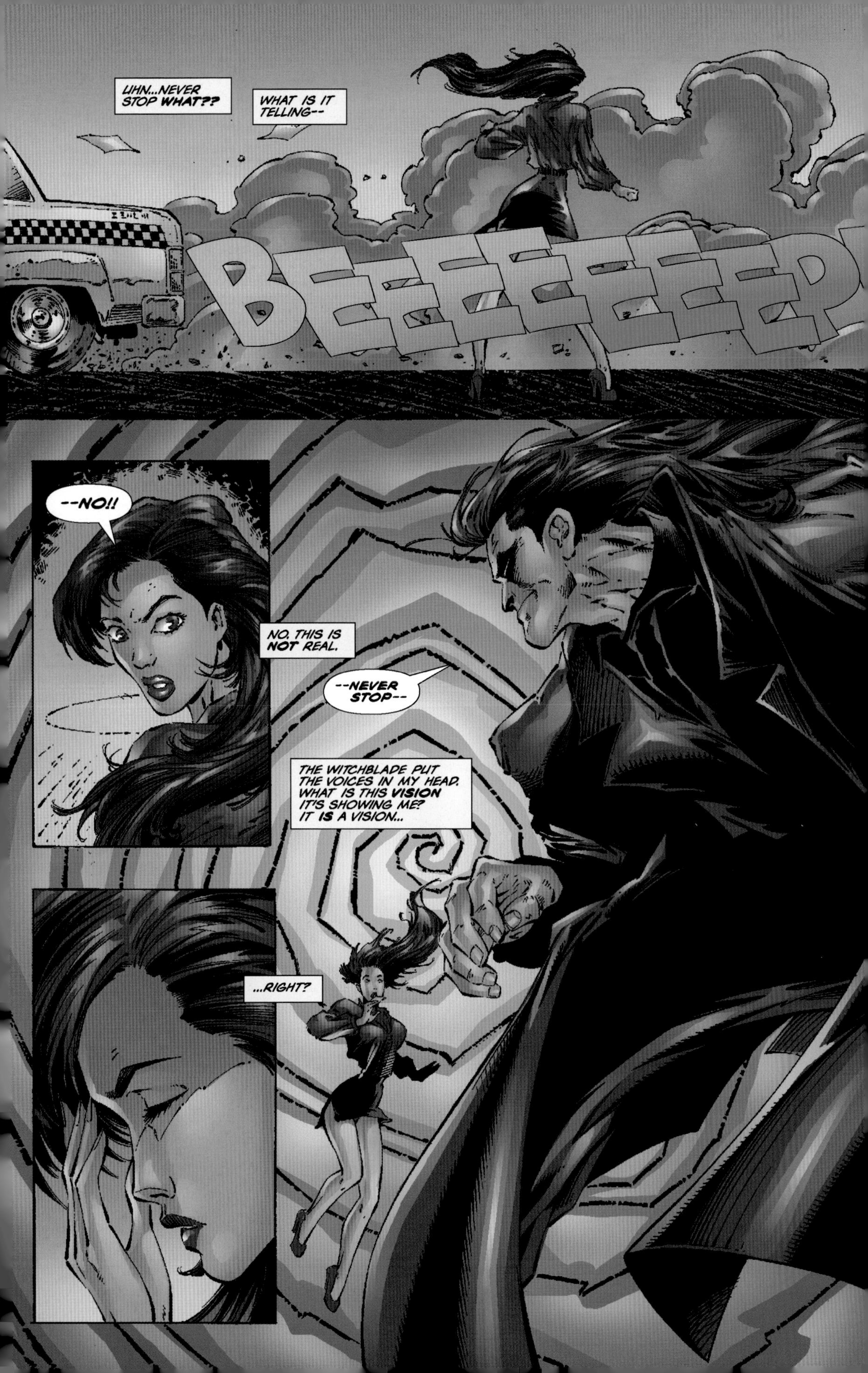
UHN...NEVER STOP WHAT??
WHAT IS IT TELLING--
BEEEEEEEEP
--NO!!
NO. THIS IS NOT REAL.
--NEVER STOP--
THE WITCHBLADE PUT THE VOICES IN MY HEAD. WHAT IS THIS VISION IT'S SHOWING ME? IT IS A VISION...
...RIGHT?

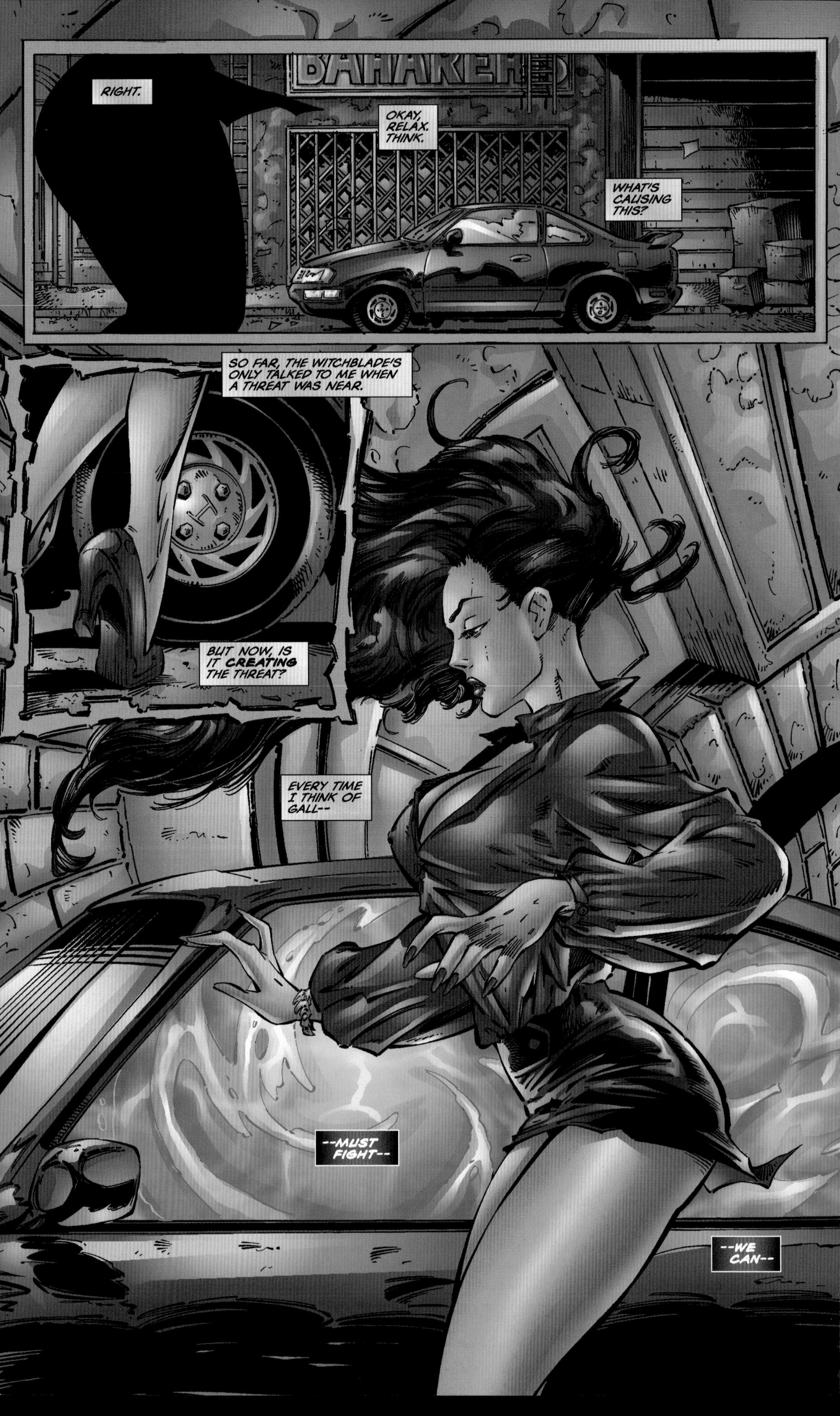

BAHAREH
RIGHT.
OKAY, RELAX. THINK.
WHAT'S CAUSING THIS?
SO FAR, THE WITCHBLADE'S ONLY TALKED TO ME WHEN A THREAT WAS NEAR.
BUT NOW, IS IT CREATING THE THREAT?
EVERY TIME I THINK OF GALL--
--MUST FIGHT--
--WE CAN--

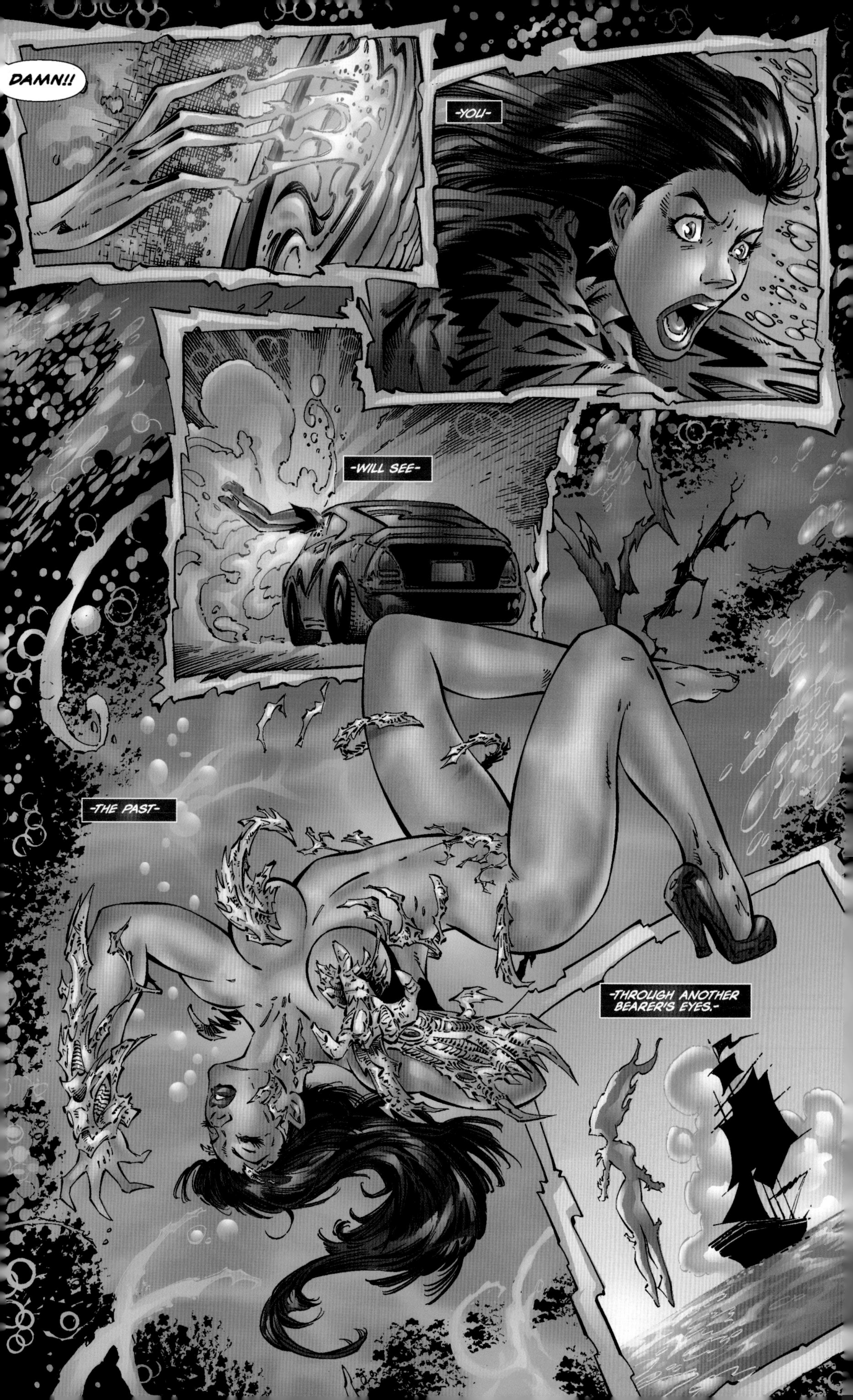

DAMN!!
-YOU-
-WILL SEE-
-THE PAST-
-THROUGH ANOTHER BEARER'S EYES.-

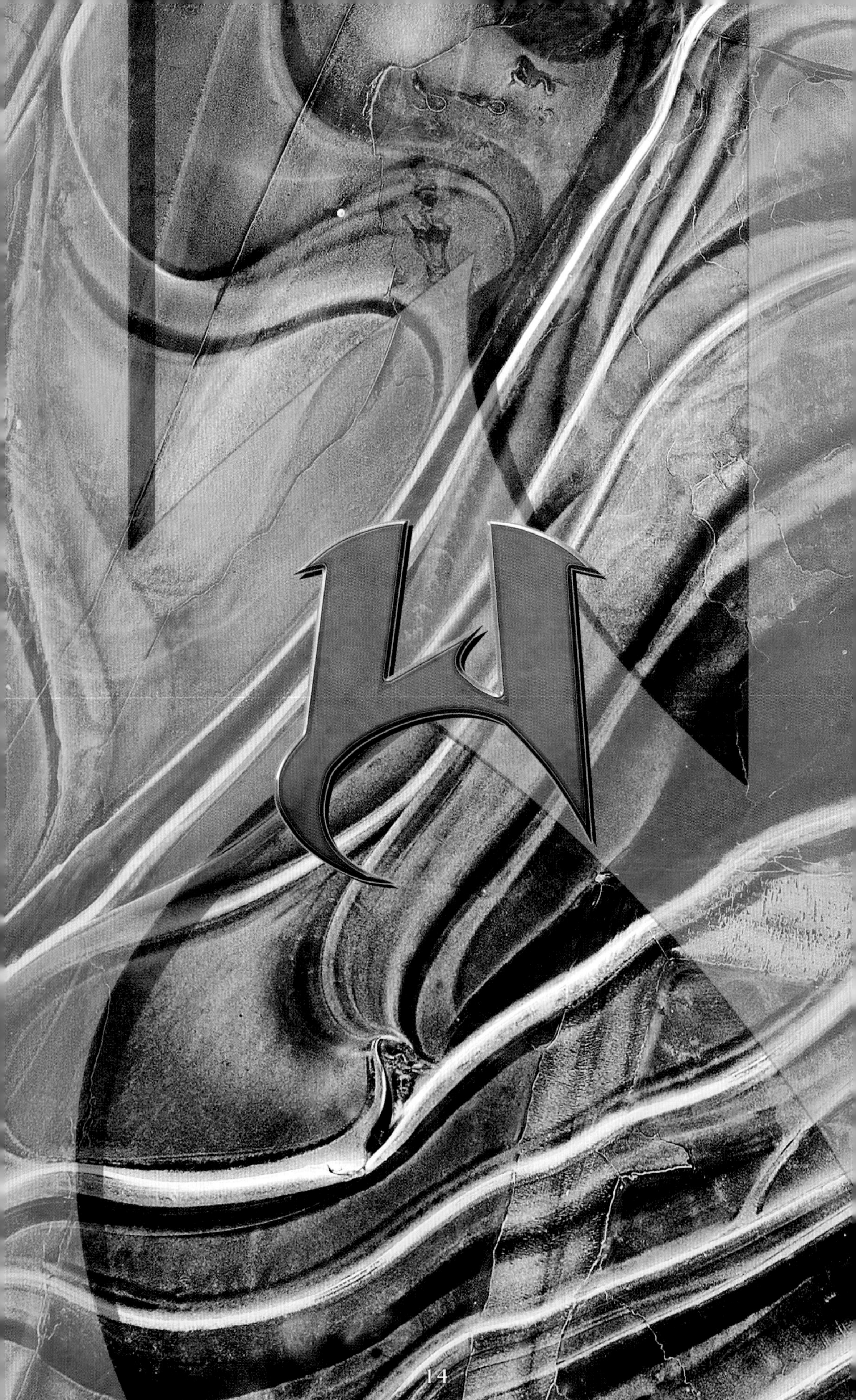

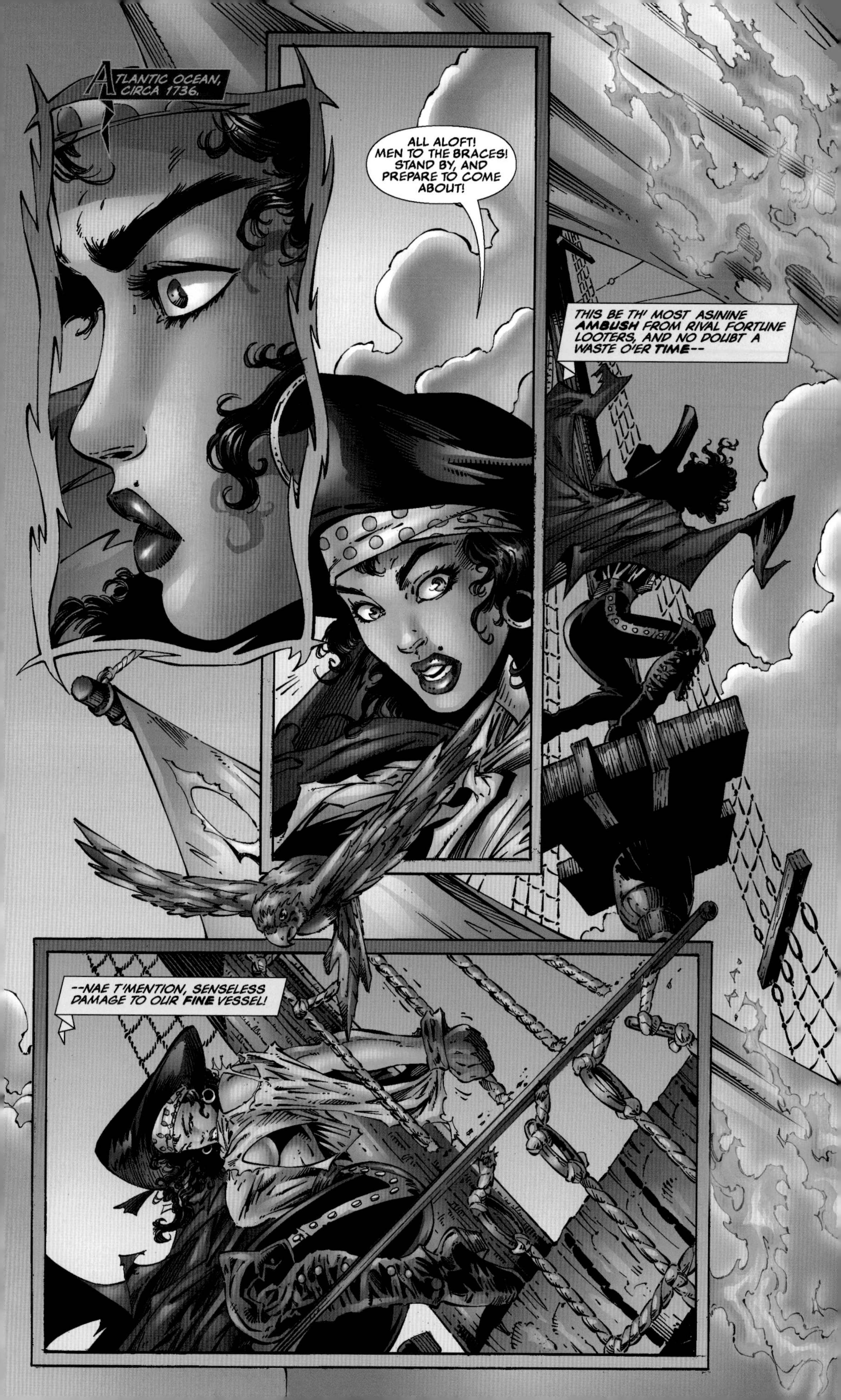
ATLANTIC OCEAN, CIRCA 1736.
ALL ALOFT! MEN TO THE BRACES! STAND BY, AND PREPARE TO COME ABOUT!
THIS BE TH' MOST ASININE AMBUSH FROM RIVAL FORTUNE LOOTERS, AND NO DOUBT A WASTE O'ER TIME--
--NAE T'MENTION, SENSELESS DAMAGE TO OUR FINE VESSEL!

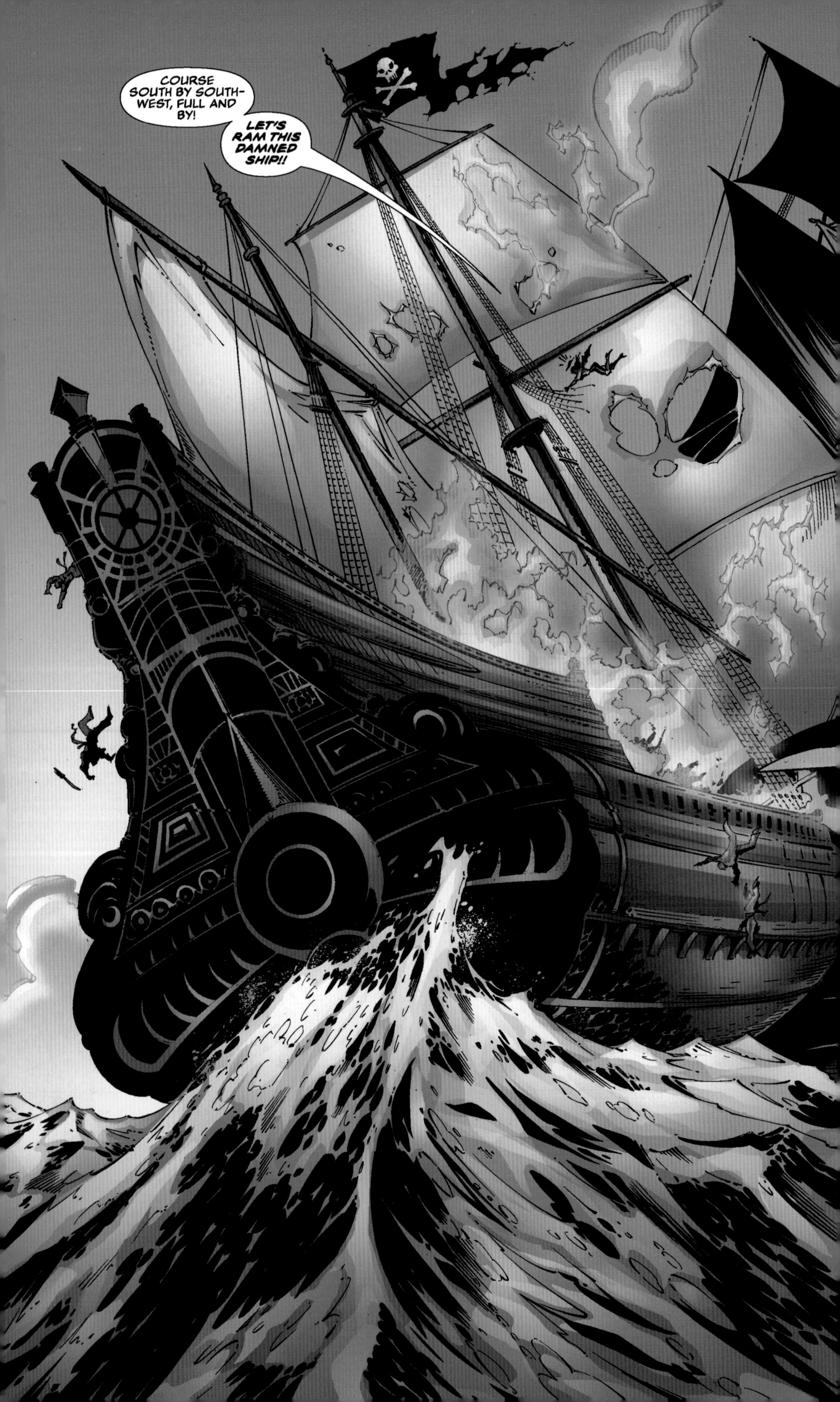
COURSE SOUTH BY SOUTH-WEST, FULL AND BY!
LET'S RAM THIS DAMNED SHIP!!

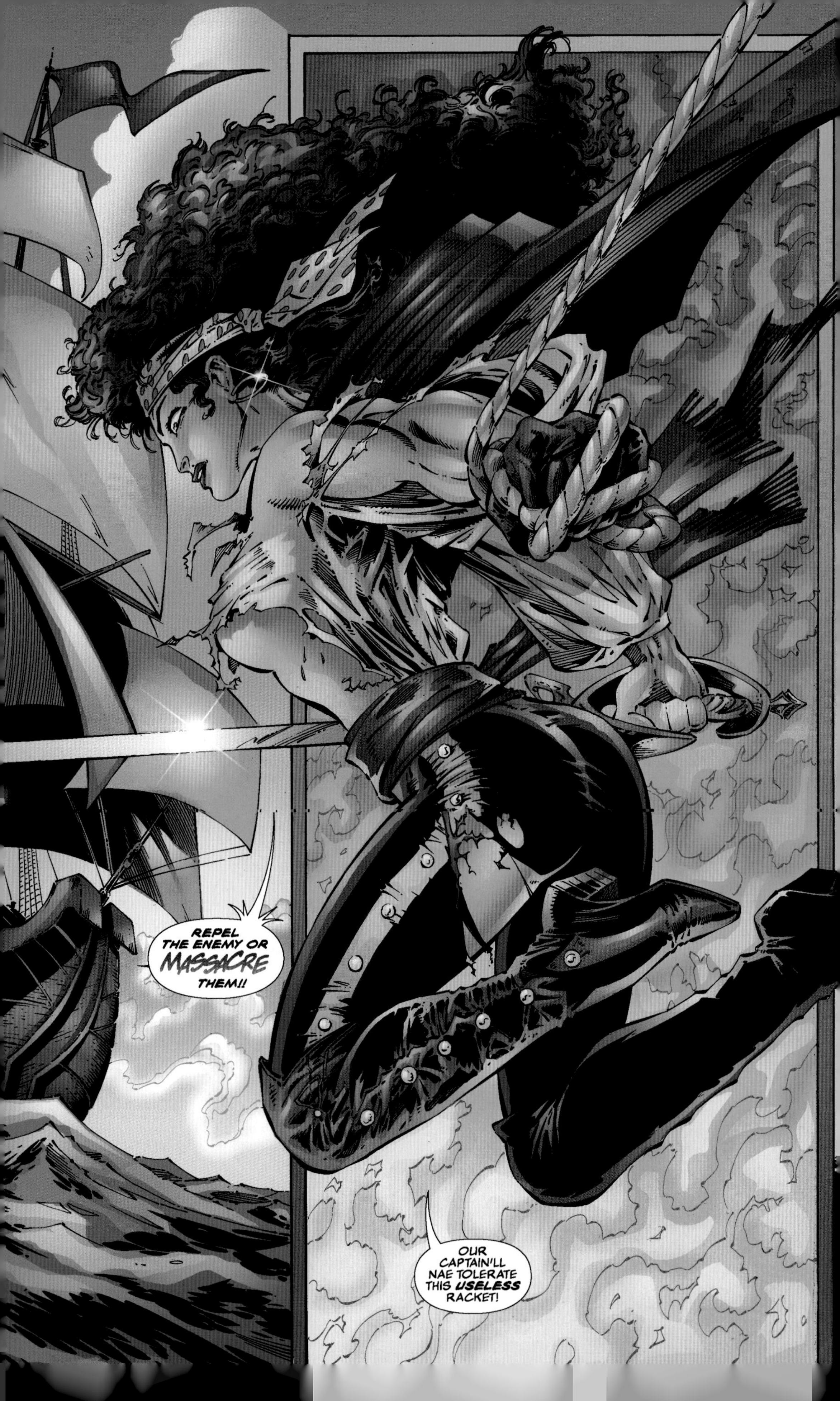
REPEL THE ENEMY OR MASSACRE THEM!!
OUR CAPTAIN'LL NAE TOLERATE THIS USELESS RACKET!

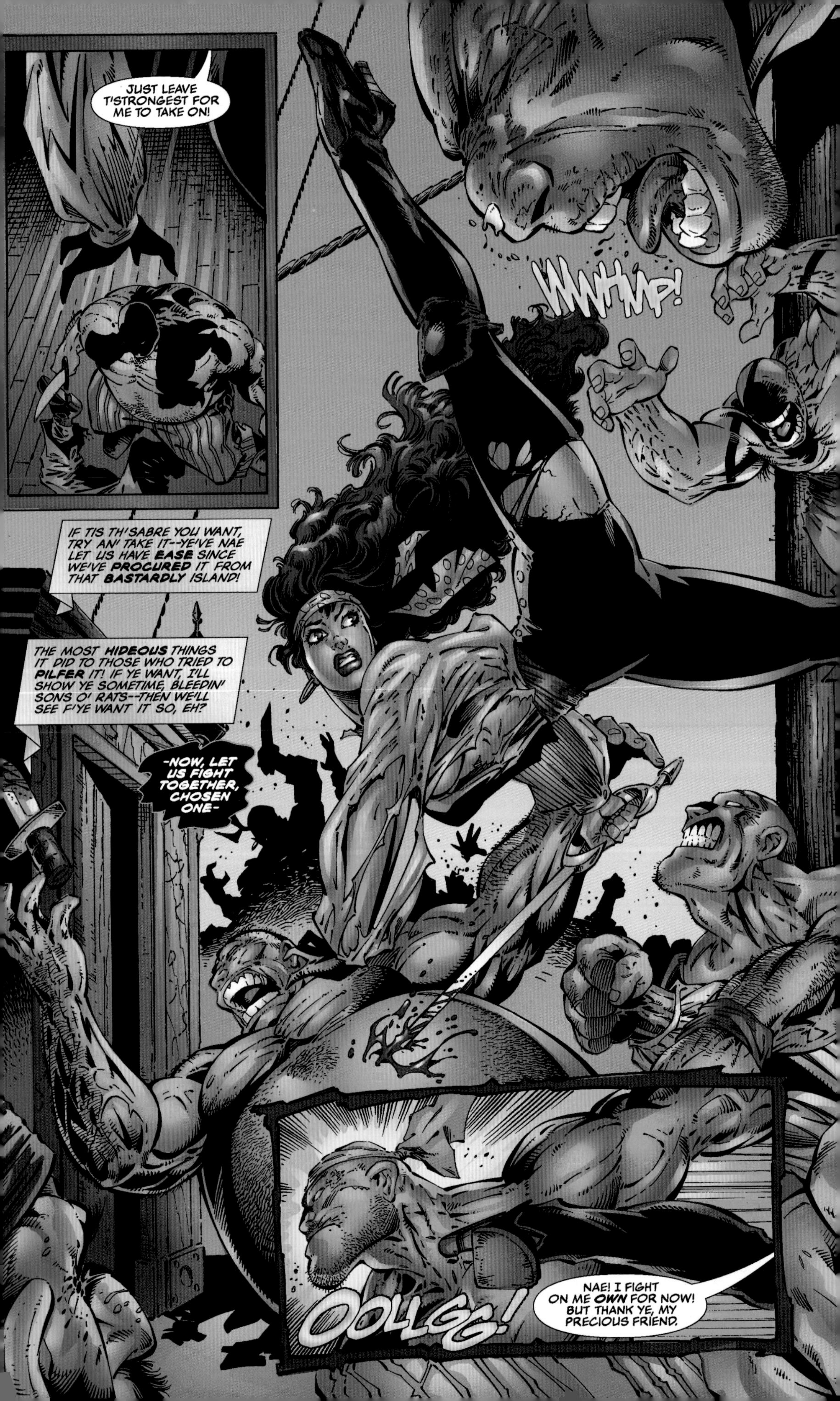
JUST LEAVE T'STRONGEST FOR ME TO TAKE ON!
WHHMP!
IF TIS TH'SABRE YOU WANT, TRY AN' TAKE IT--YE'VE NAE LET US HAVE EASE SINCE WE'VE PROCURED IT FROM THAT BASTARDLY ISLAND!
THE MOST HIDEOUS THINGS IT DID TO THOSE WHO TRIED TO PILFER IT! IF YE WANT, I'LL SHOW YE SOMETIME, BLEEDIN' SONS O' RATS--THEN WE'LL SEE F'YE WANT IT SO, EH?
-NOW, LET US FIGHT TOGETHER, CHOSEN ONE-
OOLLGG!
NAE! I FIGHT ON ME OWN FOR NOW! BUT THANK YE, MY PRECIOUS FRIEND.

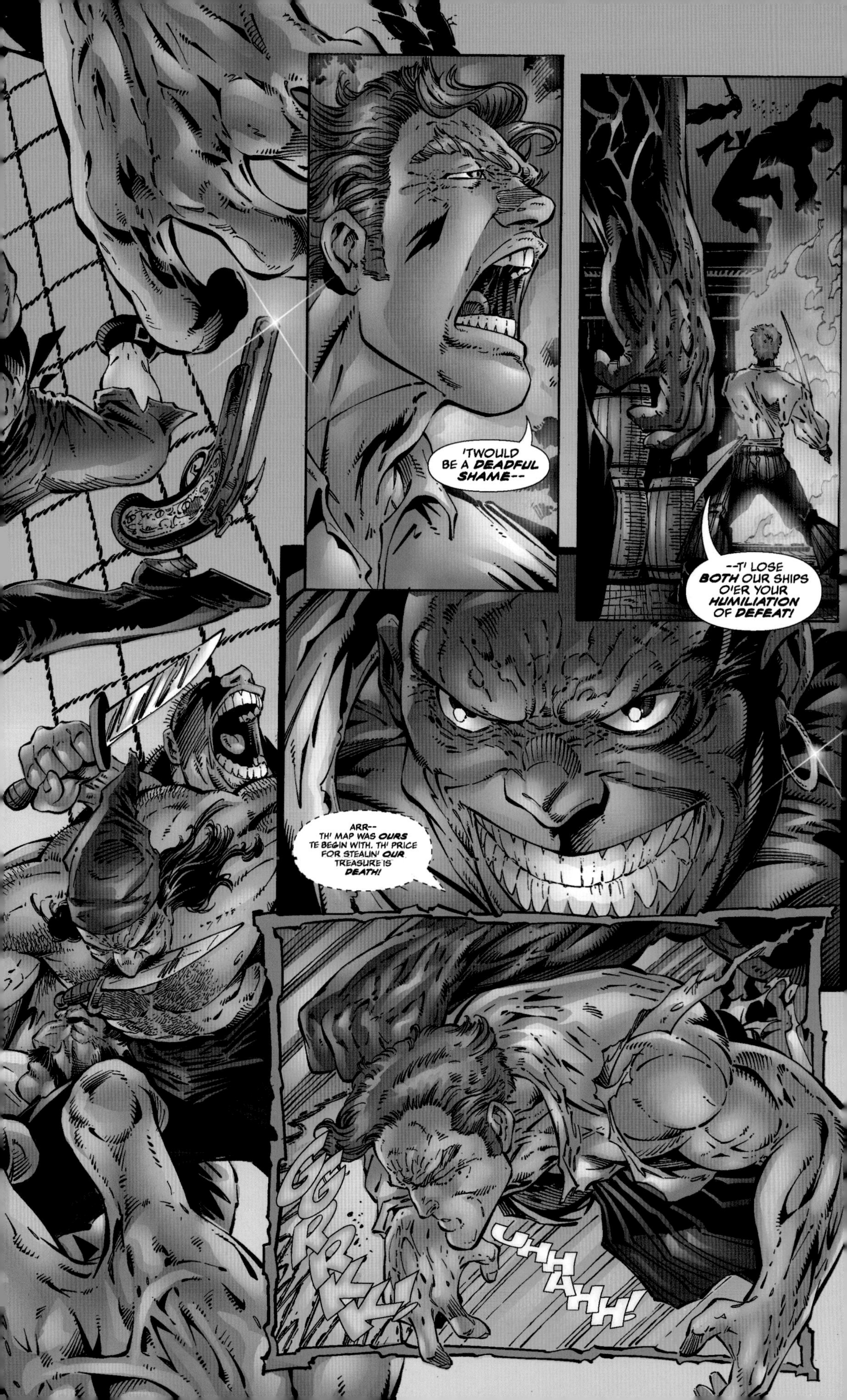
'TWOULD BE A DEADFUL SHAME--
--T' LOSE BOTH OUR SHIPS O'ER YOUR HUMILIATION OF DEFEAT!
ARR-- TH' MAP WAS OURS TE BEGIN WITH. TH' PRICE FOR STEALIN' OUR TREASURE IS DEATH!
GGRRKK!
UHHAHH!

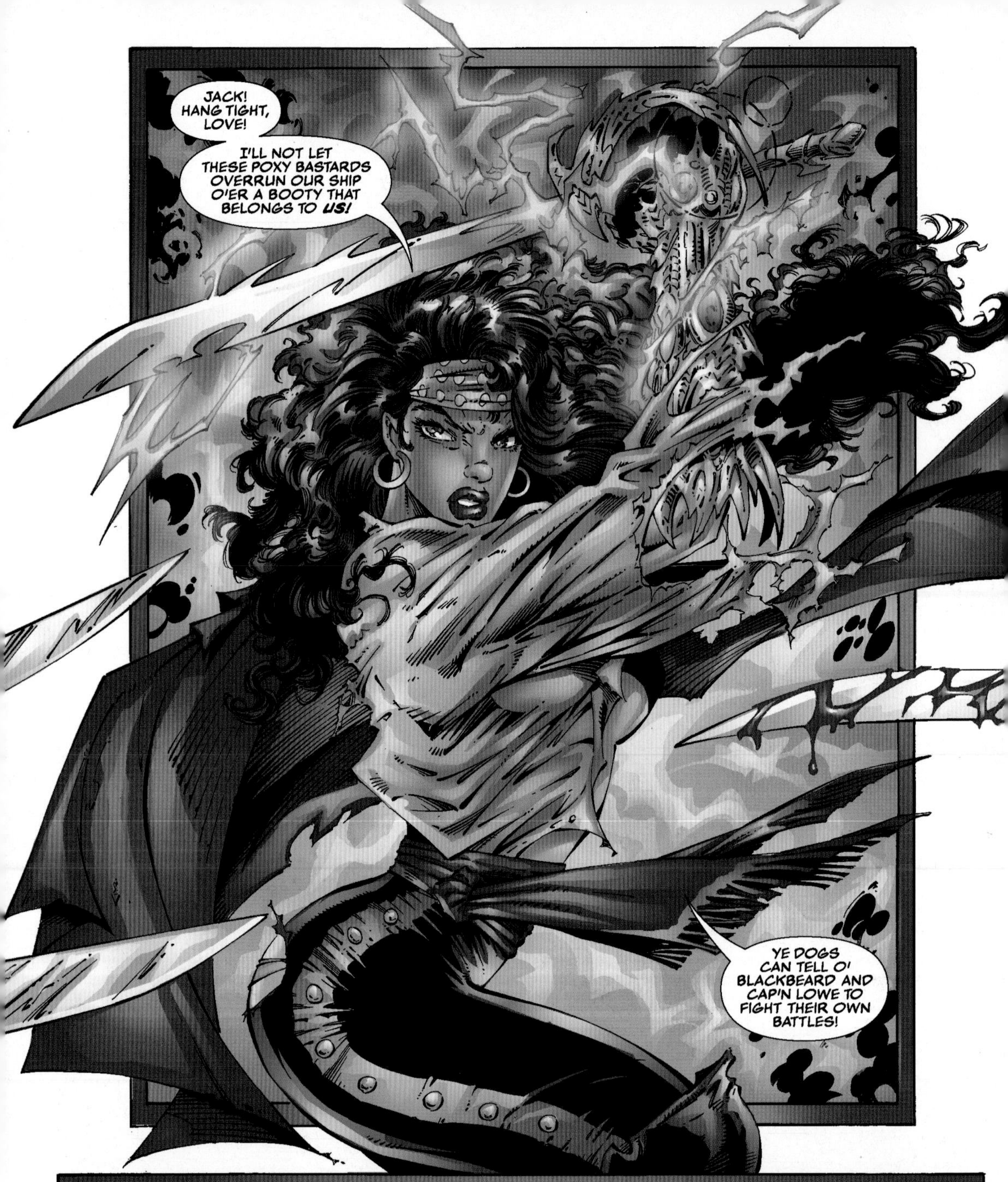
JACK! HANG TIGHT, LOVE!
I'LL NOT LET THESE POXY BASTARDS OVERRUN OUR SHIP O'ER A BOOTY THAT BELONGS TO *US!*
YE DOGS CAN TELL O' BLACKBEARD AND CAP'N LOWE TO FIGHT THEIR OWN BATTLES!

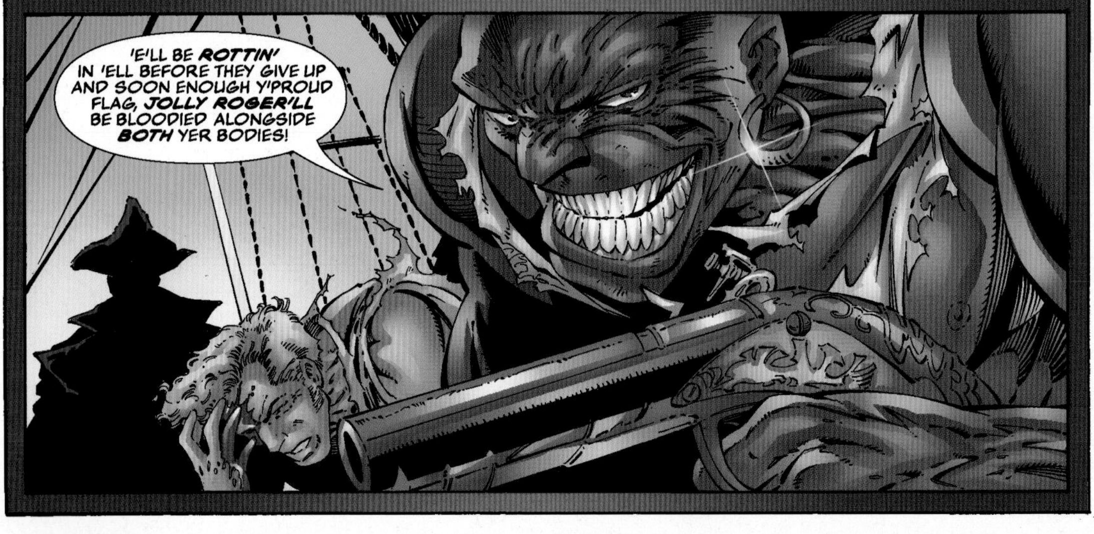
'E'LL BE *ROTTIN'* IN 'ELL BEFORE THEY GIVE UP AND SOON ENOUGH Y'PROUD FLAG, *JOLLY ROGER'LL* BE BLOODIED ALONGSIDE *BOTH* YER BODIES!

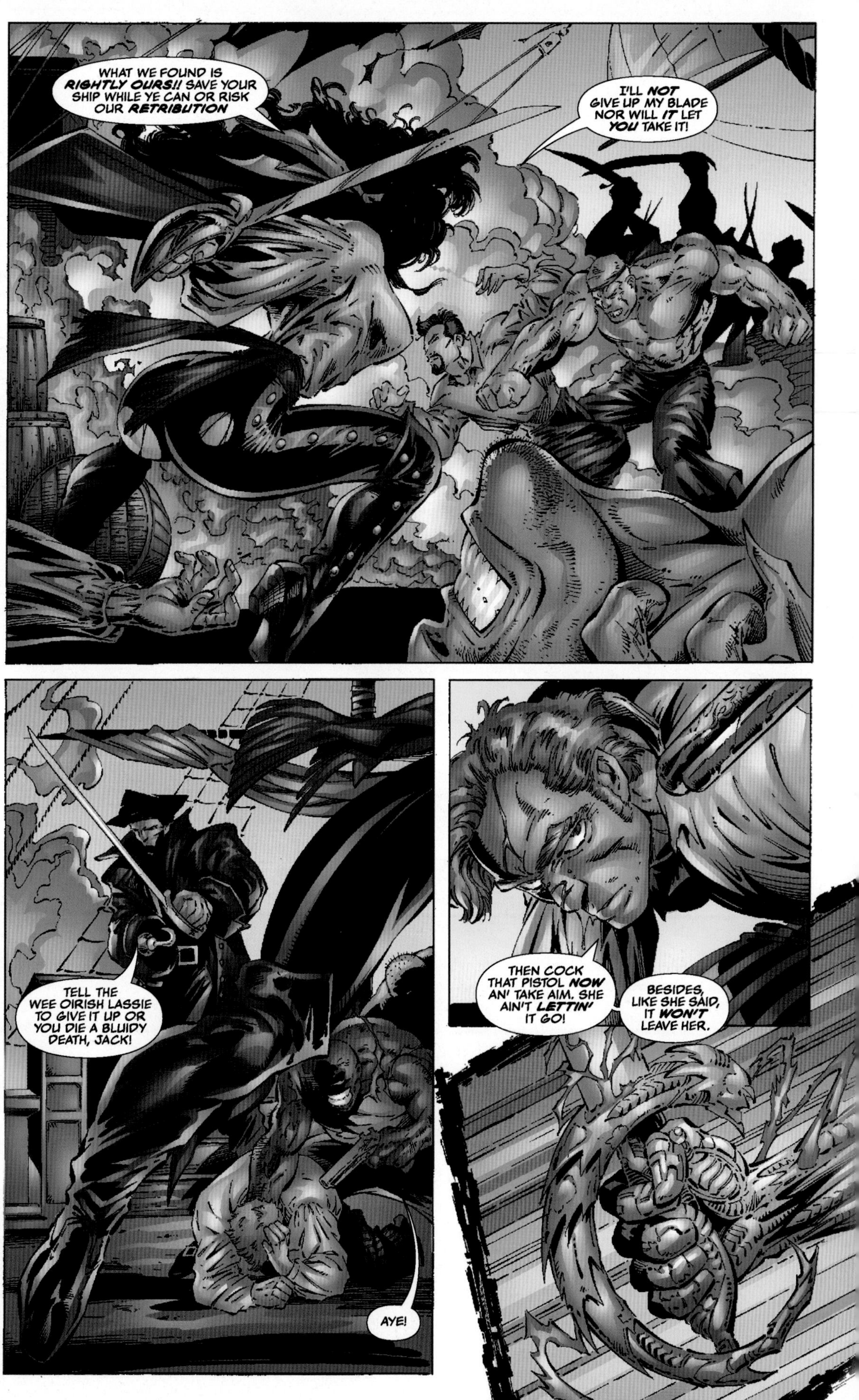
WHAT WE FOUND IS RIGHTLY OURS!! SAVE YOUR SHIP WHILE YE CAN OR RISK OUR RETRIBUTION
I'LL NOT GIVE UP MY BLADE NOR WILL IT LET YOU TAKE IT!
TELL THE WEE OIRISH LASSIE TO GIVE IT UP OR YOU DIE A BLUIDY DEATH, JACK!
AYE!
THEN COCK THAT PISTOL NOW AN' TAKE AIM. SHE AIN'T LETTIN' IT GO!
BESIDES, LIKE SHE SAID, IT WON'T LEAVE HER.

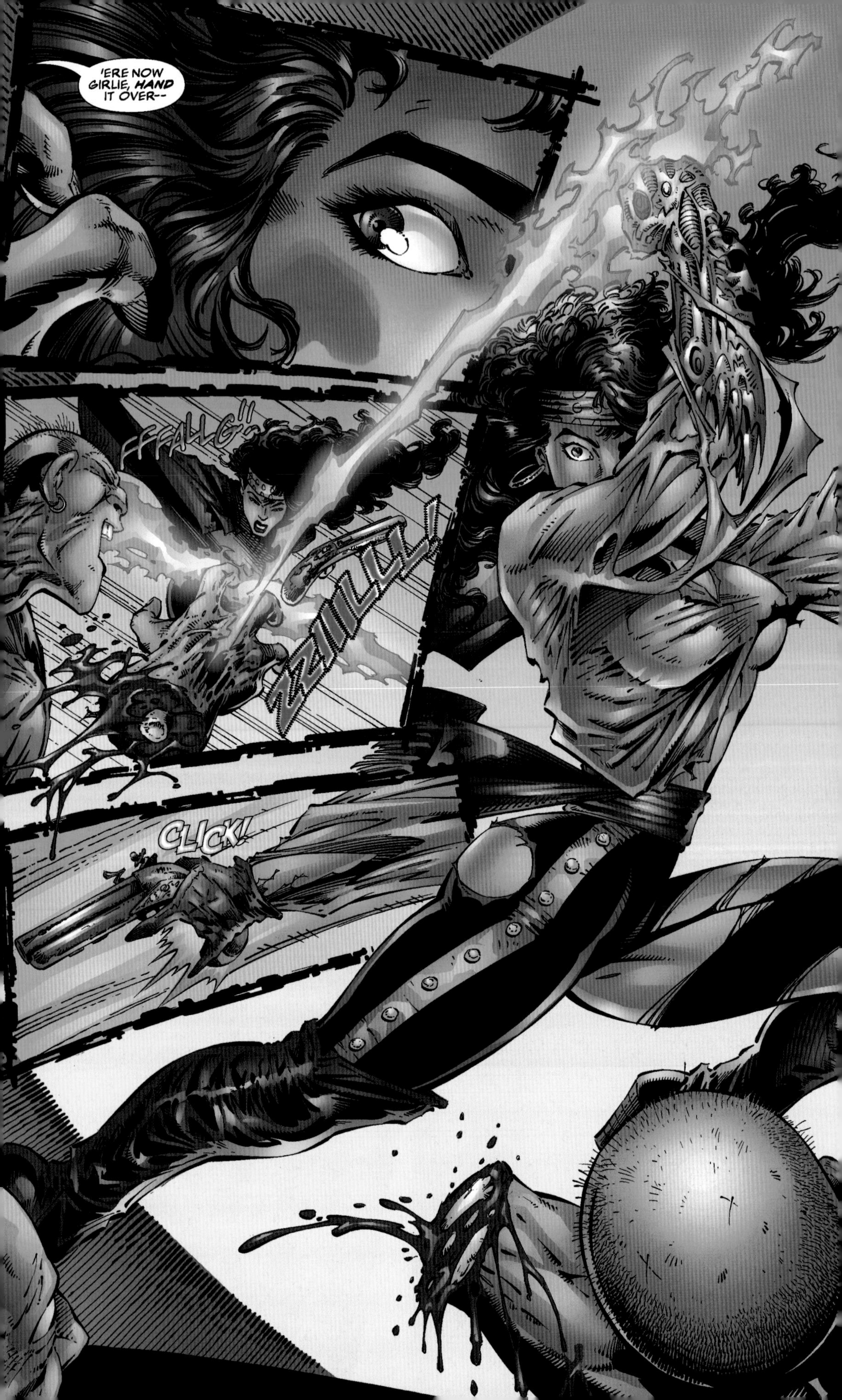

'ERE NOW GIRLIE, HAND IT OVER--
FFFALLG!!
ZZIIILLL!
CLICK!

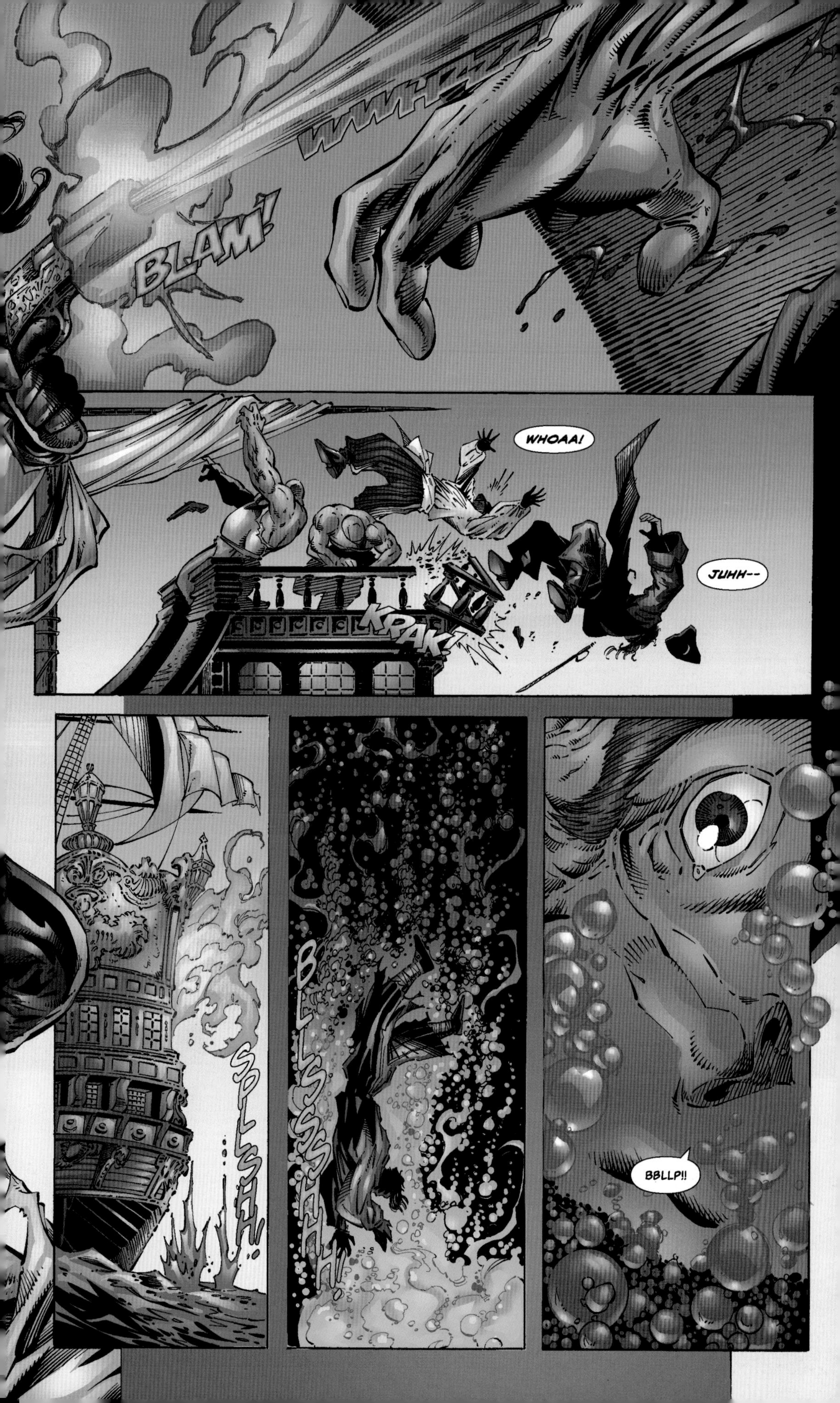
WWHZZZ
BLAM!
WHOAA!
JUHH--
KRAK!
SPLSHH!!
BLSSSHH!!
BBLLP!!

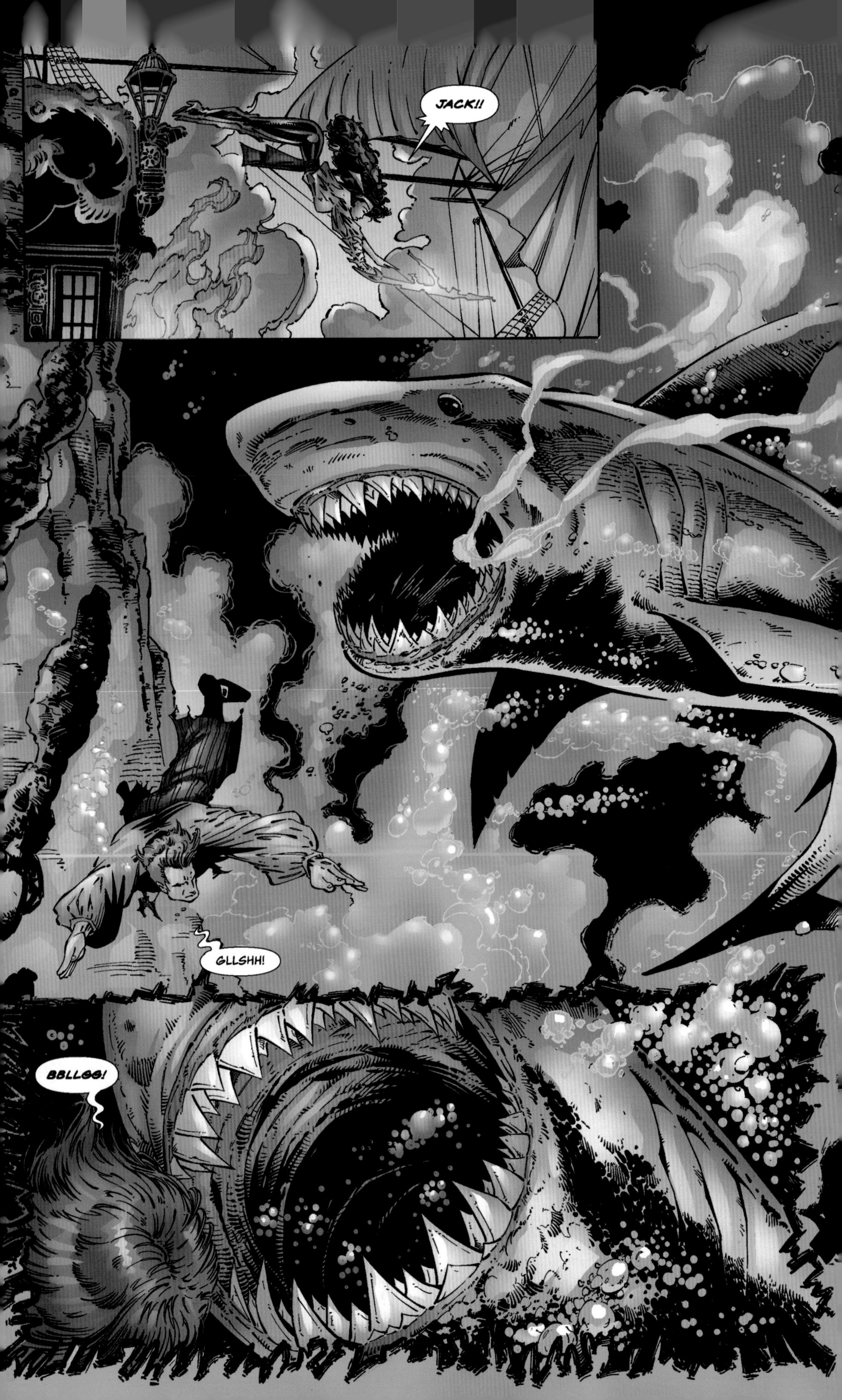
JACK!!
GLLSHH!
BBLLGG!

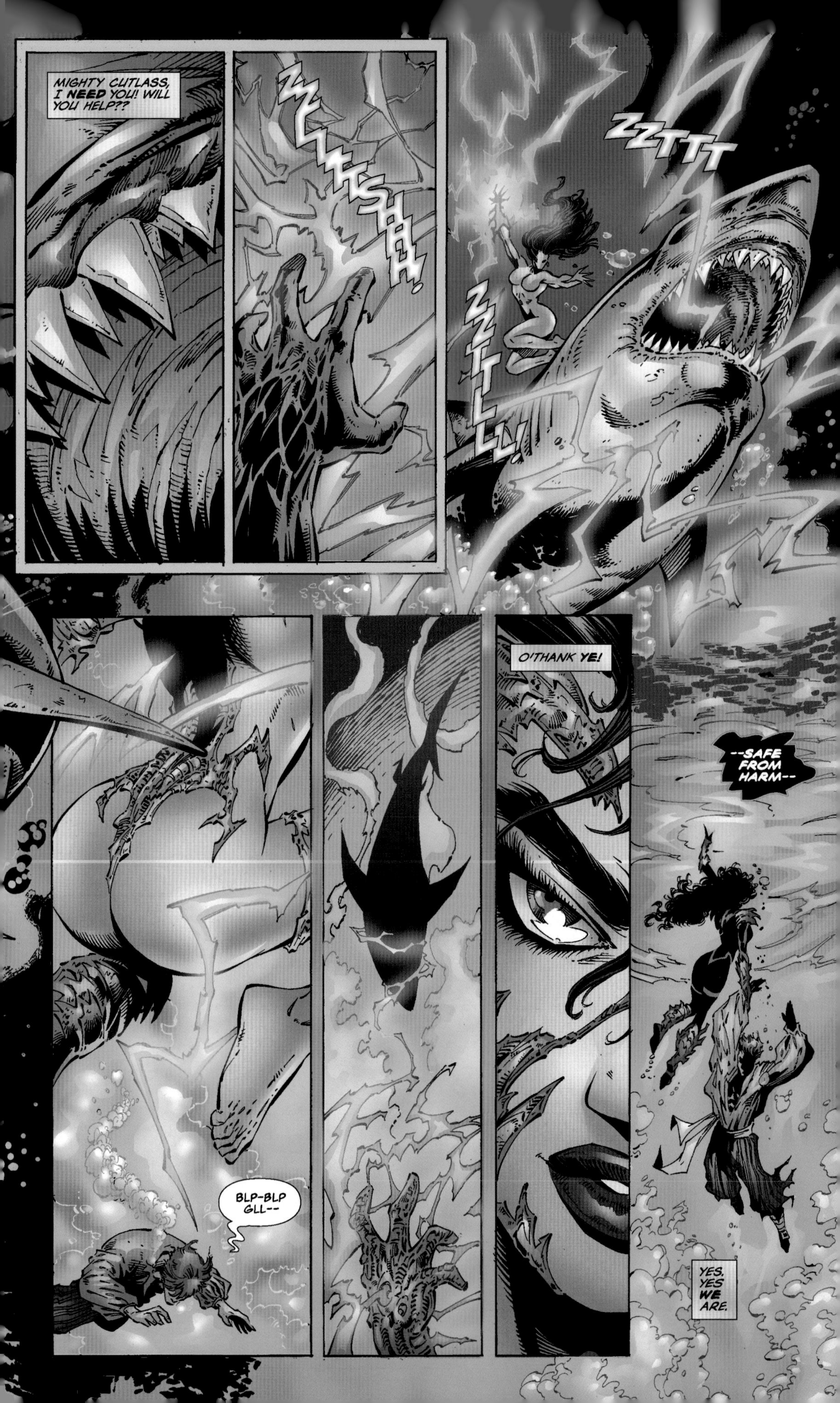
MIGHTY CUTLASS, I NEED YOU!! WILL YOU HELP??
ZZZTTSHHH!
ZZZTTT
ZZZTTLLL!
O'THANK YE!
BLP-BLP GLL--
--SAFE FROM HARM--
YES. YES WE ARE.

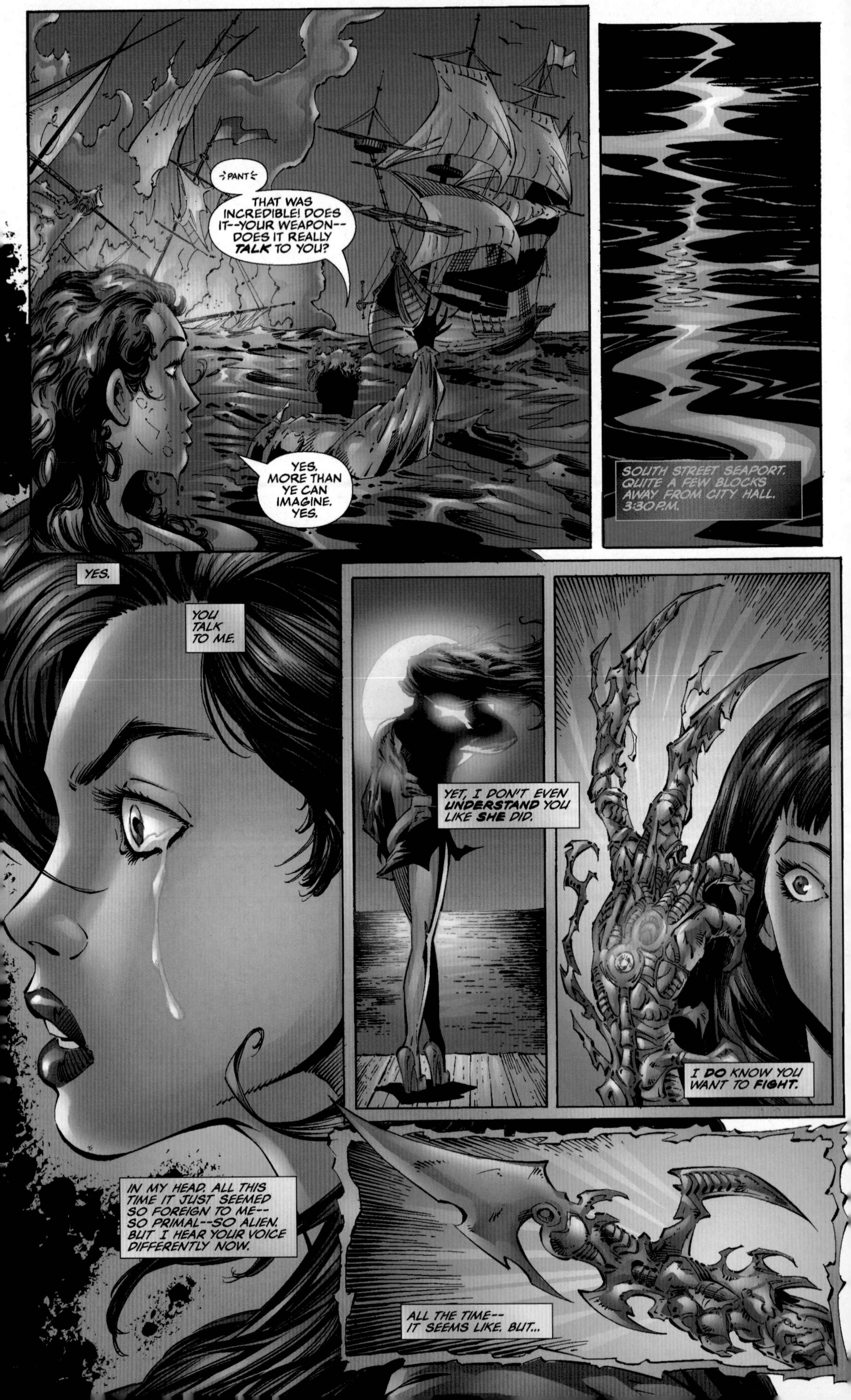

PANT
THAT WAS INCREDIBLE! DOES IT--YOUR WEAPON--DOES IT REALLY TALK TO YOU?
YES. MORE THAN YE CAN IMAGINE. YES.
SOUTH STREET SEAPORT. QUITE A FEW BLOCKS AWAY FROM CITY HALL. 3:30 P.M.
YES.
YOU TALK TO ME.
YET, I DON'T EVEN UNDERSTAND YOU LIKE SHE DID.
I DO KNOW YOU WANT TO FIGHT.
IN MY HEAD. ALL THIS TIME IT JUST SEEMED SO FOREIGN TO ME--SO PRIMAL--SO ALIEN. BUT I HEAR YOUR VOICE DIFFERENTLY NOW.
ALL THE TIME--IT SEEMS LIKE. BUT...

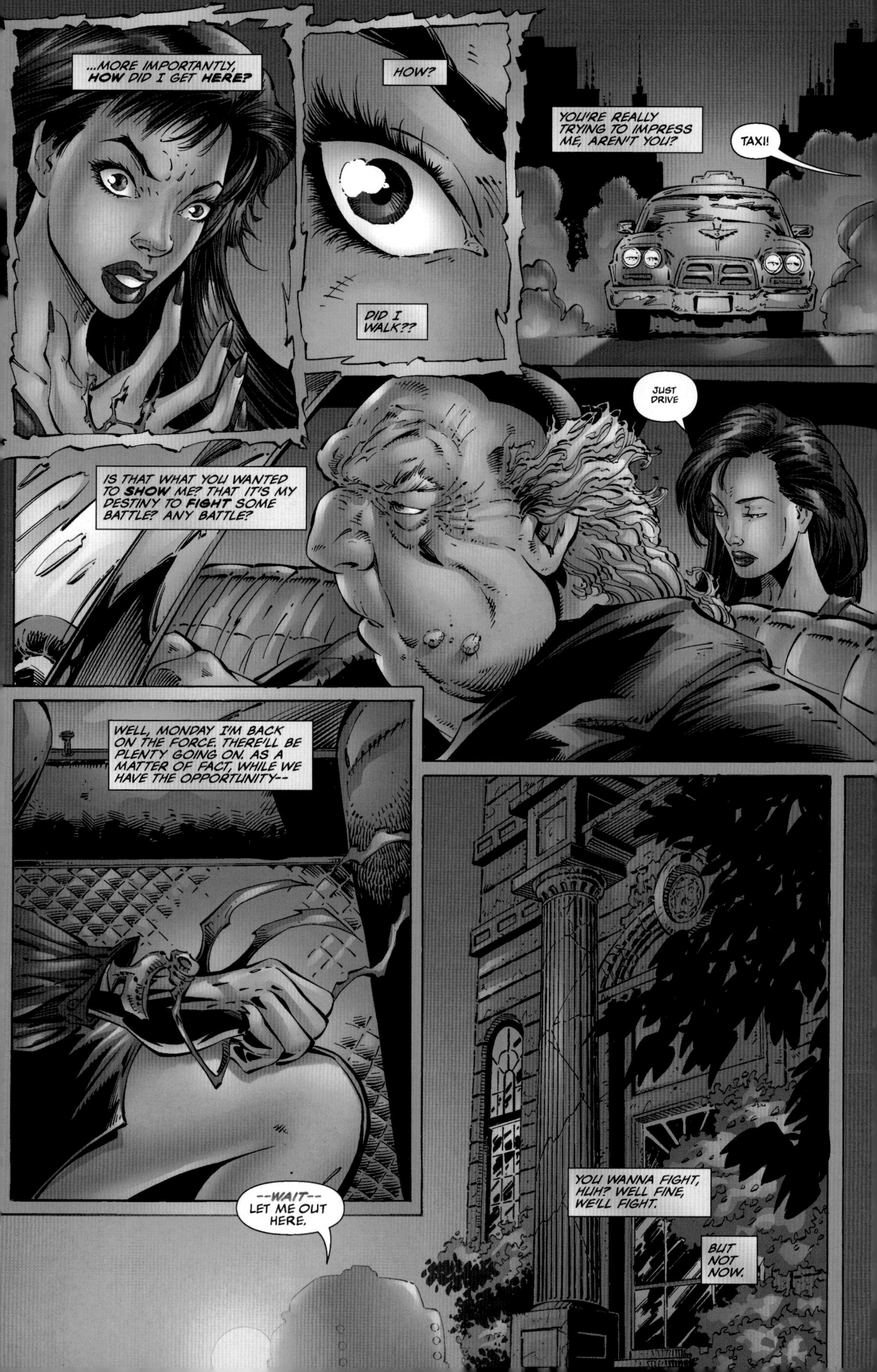
...MORE IMPORTANTLY, **HOW** DID I GET **HERE?**
HOW?
DID I WALK??
YOU'RE REALLY TRYING TO IMPRESS ME, AREN'T YOU?
TAXI!
JUST DRIVE
IS THAT WHAT YOU WANTED TO **SHOW** ME? THAT IT'S MY DESTINY TO **FIGHT** SOME BATTLE? ANY BATTLE?
WELL, MONDAY I'M BACK ON THE FORCE. THERE'LL BE PLENTY GOING ON. AS A MATTER OF FACT, WHILE WE HAVE THE OPPORTUNITY--
--*WAIT*-- LET ME OUT HERE.
YOU WANNA FIGHT, HUH? WELL FINE, WE'LL FIGHT.
BUT NOT NOW.

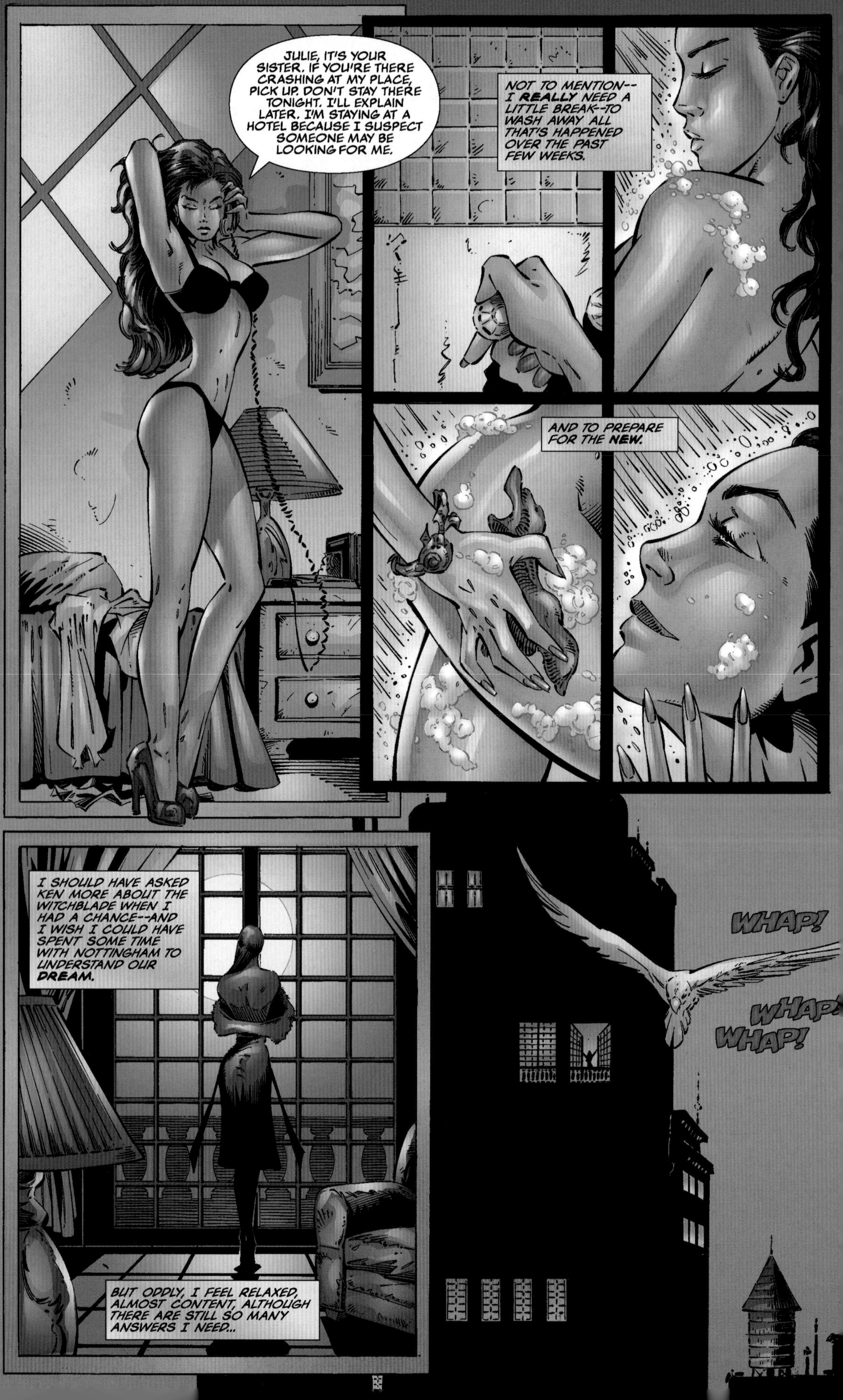
JULIE, IT'S YOUR SISTER. IF YOU'RE THERE CRASHING AT MY PLACE, PICK UP. DON'T STAY THERE TONIGHT. I'LL EXPLAIN LATER. I'M STAYING AT A HOTEL BECAUSE I SUSPECT SOMEONE MAY BE LOOKING FOR ME.
NOT TO MENTION-- I REALLY NEED A LITTLE BREAK--TO WASH AWAY ALL THAT'S HAPPENED OVER THE PAST FEW WEEKS.
AND TO PREPARE FOR THE NEW.
I SHOULD HAVE ASKED KEN MORE ABOUT THE WITCHBLADE WHEN I HAD A CHANCE--AND I WISH I COULD HAVE SPENT SOME TIME WITH NOTTINGHAM TO UNDERSTAND OUR DREAM.
BUT ODDLY, I FEEL RELAXED, ALMOST CONTENT, ALTHOUGH THERE ARE STILL SO MANY ANSWERS I NEED...
WHAP!
WHAP!
WHAP!

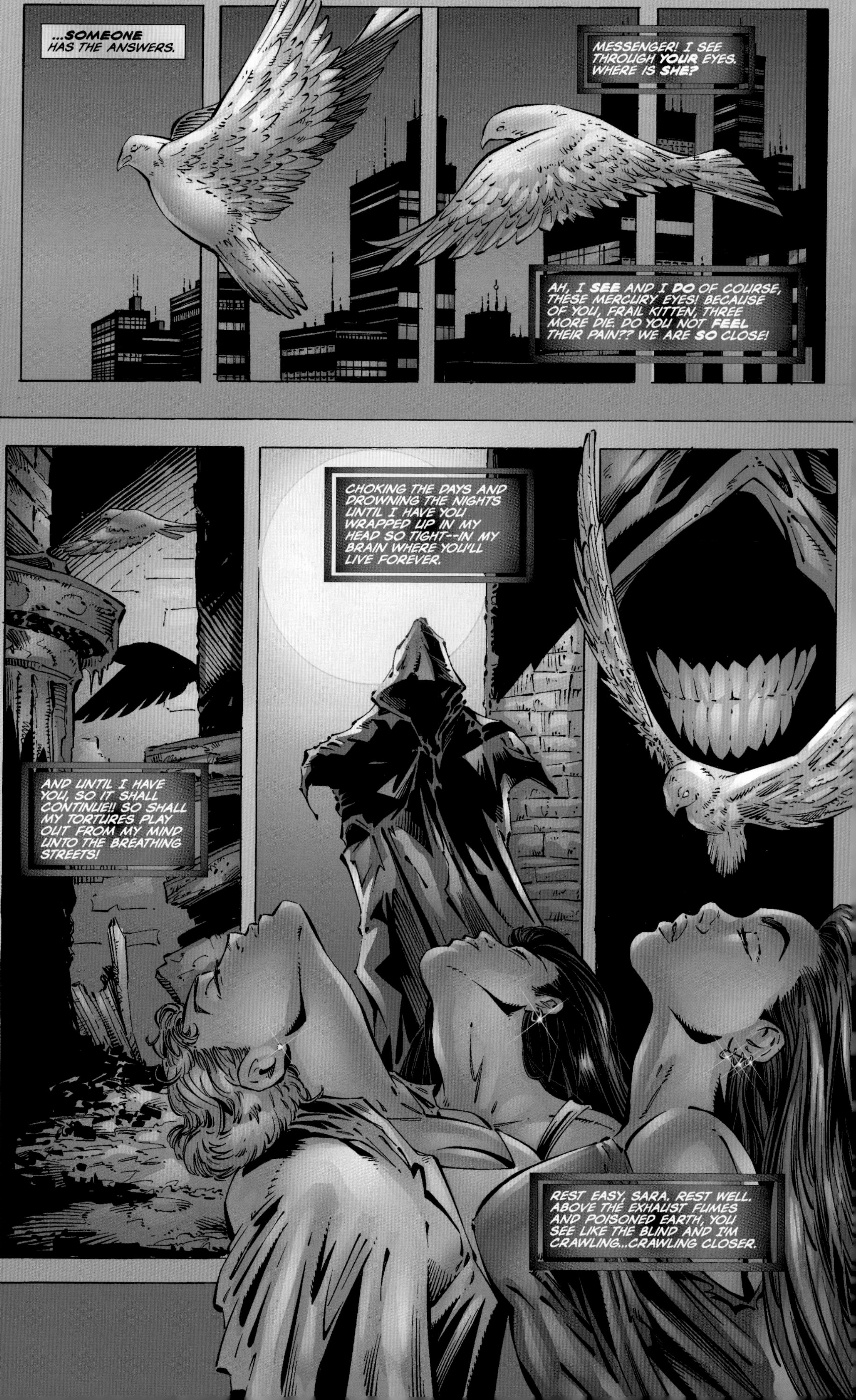
...SOMEONE HAS THE ANSWERS.
MESSENGER! I SEE THROUGH YOUR EYES. WHERE IS SHE?
AH, I SEE AND I DO OF COURSE, THESE MERCURY EYES! BECAUSE OF YOU, FRAIL KITTEN, THREE MORE DIE. DO YOU NOT FEEL THEIR PAIN?? WE ARE SO CLOSE!
CHOKING THE DAYS AND DROWNING THE NIGHTS UNTIL I HAVE YOU WRAPPED UP IN MY HEAD SO TIGHT--IN MY BRAIN WHERE YOU'LL LIVE FOREVER.
AND UNTIL I HAVE YOU, SO IT SHALL CONTINUE!! SO SHALL MY TORTURES PLAY OUT FROM MY MIND UNTO THE BREATHING STREETS!
REST EASY, SARA. REST WELL. ABOVE THE EXHAUST FUMES AND POISONED EARTH, YOU SEE LIKE THE BLIND AND I'M CRAWLING...CRAWLING CLOSER.

ISSUE #10

story: **David Wohl** and **Christina Z.**
pencils: **Michael Turner** pg. 1-6 and 11-22
pencils and co-plot: **Marc Silvestri** pg. 7-10
inks: **D-Tron** pg. 1-6 and 11-22 and **Matt "Batt" Banning** pg. 7-10
colors: **JD Smith**

ink assists: **Jose "Jag" Guillen, Viet Trong** and **Jeff Crumpler**

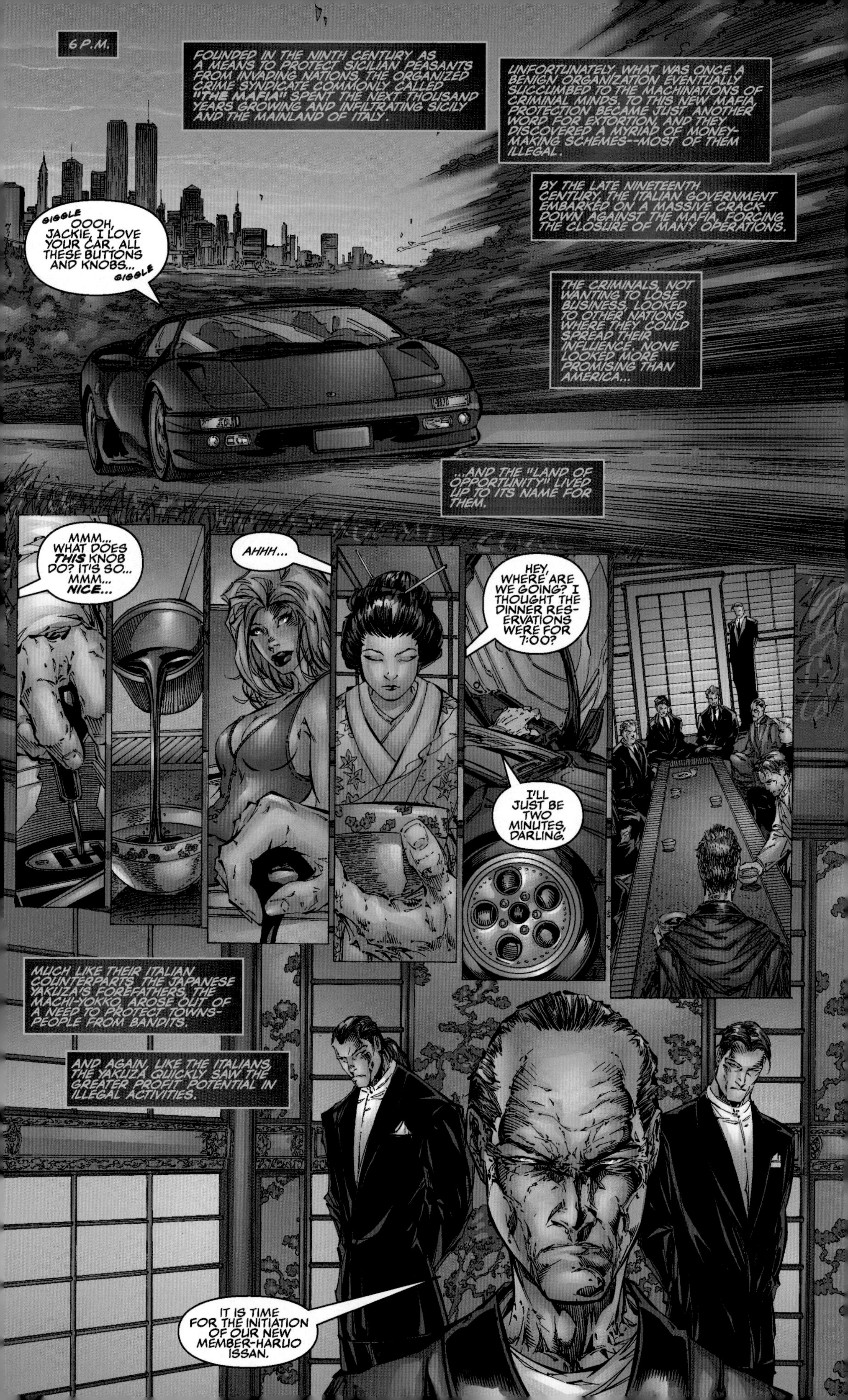
6 P.M.
FOUNDED IN THE NINTH CENTURY AS A MEANS TO PROTECT SICILIAN PEASANTS FROM INVADING NATIONS, THE ORGANIZED CRIME SYNDICATE COMMONLY CALLED "THE MAFIA" SPENT THE NEXT THOUSAND YEARS GROWING AND INFILTRATING SICILY AND THE MAINLAND OF ITALY.
UNFORTUNATELY, WHAT WAS ONCE A BENIGN ORGANIZATION EVENTUALLY SUCCUMBED TO THE MACHINATIONS OF CRIMINAL MINDS. TO THIS NEW MAFIA, PROTECTION BECAME JUST ANOTHER WORD FOR EXTORTION, AND THEY DISCOVERED A MYRIAD OF MONEY-MAKING SCHEMES--MOST OF THEM ILLEGAL.
GIGGLE OOOH, JACKIE, I LOVE YOUR CAR. ALL THESE BUTTONS AND KNOBS... GIGGLE
BY THE LATE NINETEENTH CENTURY, THE ITALIAN GOVERNMENT EMBARKED ON A MASSIVE CRACK-DOWN AGAINST THE MAFIA, FORCING THE CLOSURE OF MANY OPERATIONS.
THE CRIMINALS, NOT WANTING TO LOSE BUSINESS, LOOKED TO OTHER NATIONS WHERE THEY COULD SPREAD THEIR INFLUENCE. NONE LOOKED MORE PROMISING THAN AMERICA...
...AND THE "LAND OF OPPORTUNITY" LIVED UP TO ITS NAME FOR THEM.
MMM... WHAT DOES THIS KNOB DO? IT'S SO... MMM... NICE...
AHHH...
HEY, WHERE ARE WE GOING? I THOUGHT THE DINNER RES-ERVATIONS WERE FOR 7:00?
I'LL JUST BE TWO MINUTES, DARLING.
MUCH LIKE THEIR ITALIAN COUNTERPARTS THE JAPANESE YAKUZA'S FOREFATHERS, THE MACHI-YOKKO, AROSE OUT OF A NEED TO PROTECT TOWNS-PEOPLE FROM BANDITS.
AND AGAIN, LIKE THE ITALIANS, THE YAKUZA QUICKLY SAW THE GREATER PROFIT POTENTIAL IN ILLEGAL ACTIVITIES.
IT IS TIME FOR THE INITIATION OF OUR NEW MEMBER-HARUO ISSAN.

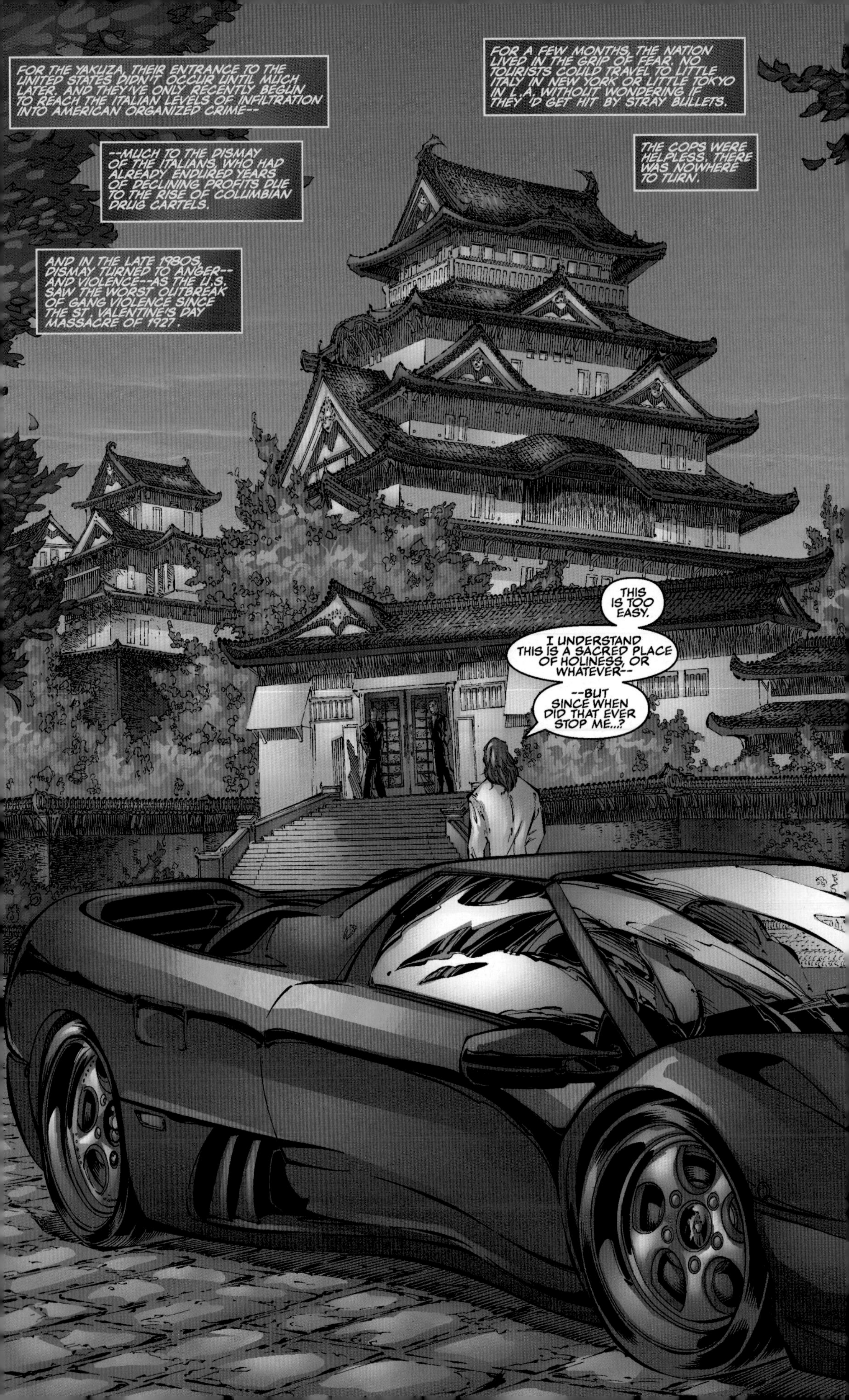

FOR THE YAKUZA, THEIR ENTRANCE TO THE UNITED STATES DIDN'T OCCUR UNTIL MUCH LATER, AND THEY'VE ONLY RECENTLY BEGUN TO REACH THE ITALIAN LEVELS OF INFILTRATION INTO AMERICAN ORGANIZED CRIME--
--MUCH TO THE DISMAY OF THE ITALIANS, WHO HAD ALREADY ENDURED YEARS OF DECLINING PROFITS DUE TO THE RISE OF COLUMBIAN DRUG CARTELS.
AND IN THE LATE 1980S, DISMAY TURNED TO ANGER--AND VIOLENCE--AS THE U.S. SAW THE WORST OUTBREAK OF GANG VIOLENCE SINCE THE ST. VALENTINE'S DAY MASSACRE OF 1927.
FOR A FEW MONTHS, THE NATION LIVED IN THE GRIP OF FEAR. NO TOURISTS COULD TRAVEL TO LITTLE ITALY IN NEW YORK OR LITTLE TOKYO IN L.A. WITHOUT WONDERING IF THEY'D GET HIT BY STRAY BULLETS.
THE COPS WERE HELPLESS. THERE WAS NOWHERE TO TURN.
THIS IS TOO EASY.
I UNDERSTAND THIS IS A SACRED PLACE OF HOLINESS, OR WHATEVER--
--BUT SINCE WHEN DID THAT EVER STOP ME...?

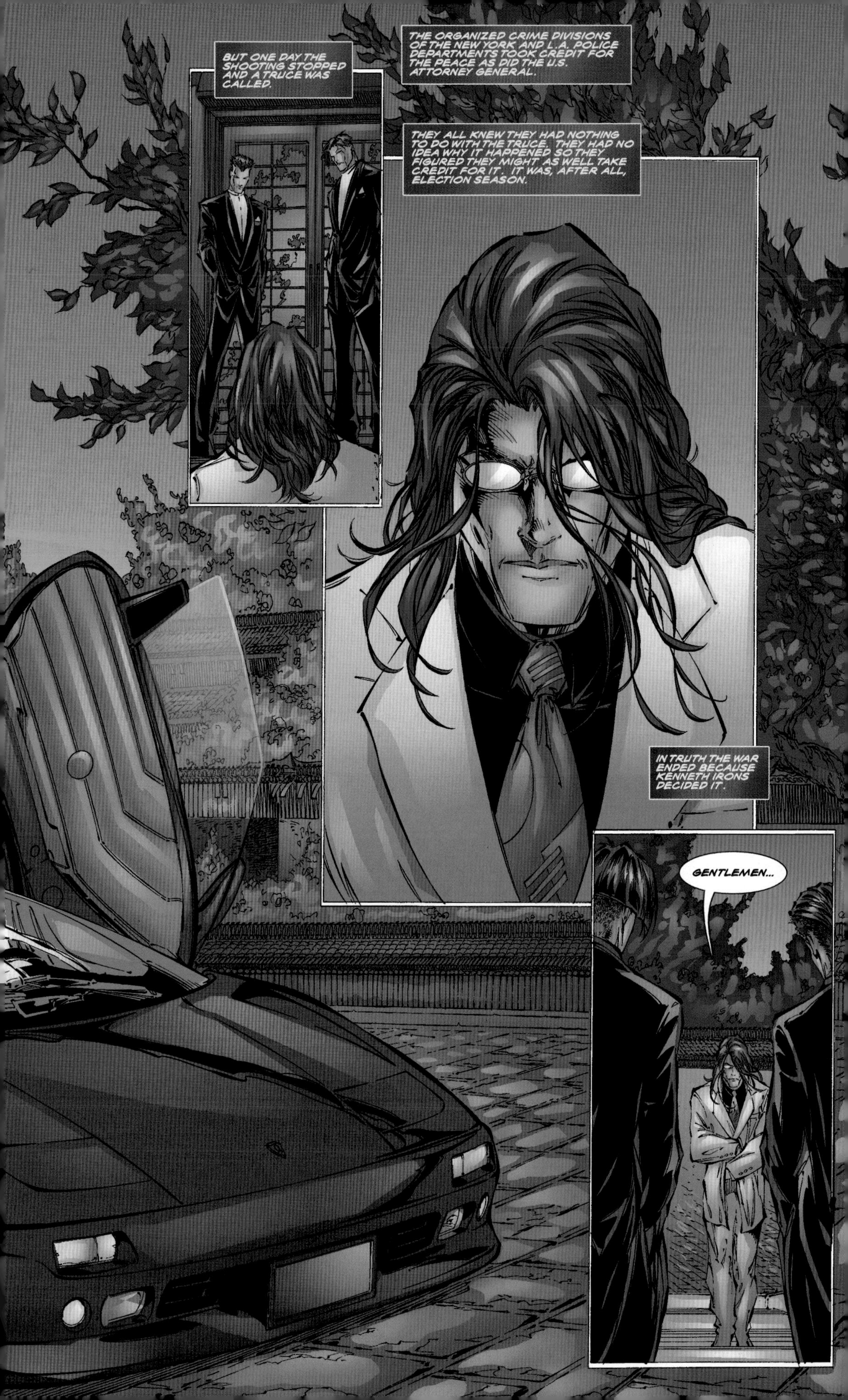
BUT ONE DAY THE SHOOTING STOPPED AND A TRUCE WAS CALLED.
THE ORGANIZED CRIME DIVISIONS OF THE NEW YORK AND L.A. POLICE DEPARTMENTS TOOK CREDIT FOR THE PEACE AS DID THE U.S. ATTORNEY GENERAL.
THEY ALL KNEW THEY HAD NOTHING TO DO WITH THE TRUCE. THEY HAD NO IDEA WHY IT HAPPENED SO THEY FIGURED THEY MIGHT AS WELL TAKE CREDIT FOR IT. IT WAS, AFTER ALL, ELECTION SEASON.
IN TRUTH THE WAR ENDED BECAUSE KENNETH IRONS DECIDED IT.
GENTLEMEN...

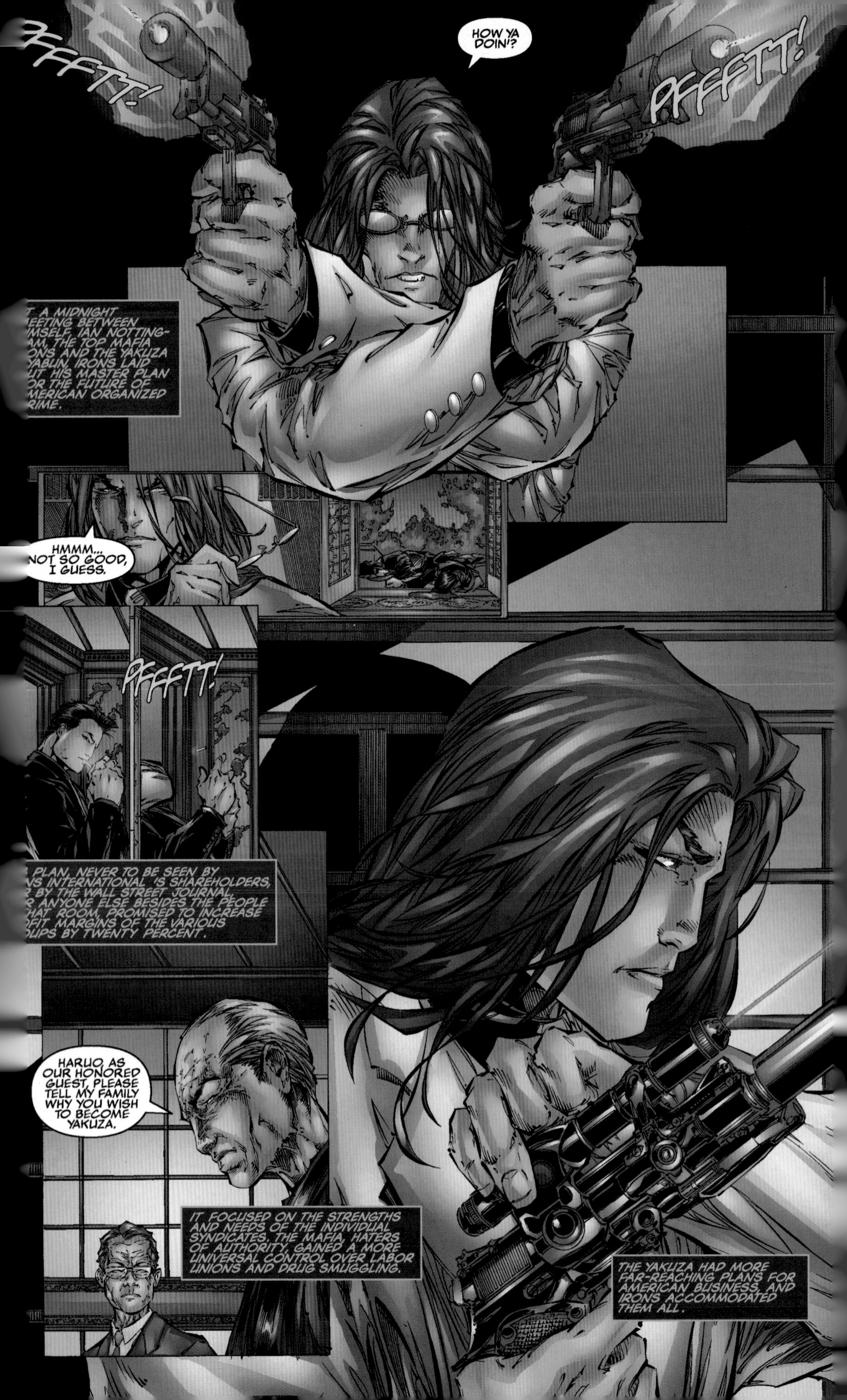
FFFTT!
HOW YA DOIN'?
PFFFTT!
T A MIDNIGHT MEETING BETWEEN IMSELF, IAN NOTTING-AM, THE TOP MAFIA ONS AND THE YAKUZA YABUN, IRONS LAID UT HIS MASTER PLAN OR THE FUTURE OF MERICAN ORGANIZED RIME.
HMMM... NOT SO GOOD, I GUESS.
PFFFTT!
E PLAN, NEVER TO BE SEEN BY ONS INTERNATIONAL 'S SHAREHOLDERS, R BY THE WALL STREET JOURNAL, R ANYONE ELSE BESIDES THE PEOPLE THAT ROOM, PROMISED TO INCREASE OFIT MARGINS OF THE VARIOUS OUPS BY TWENTY PERCENT.
HARUO AS OUR HONORED GUEST, PLEASE TELL MY FAMILY WHY YOU WISH TO BECOME YAKUZA.
IT FOCUSED ON THE STRENGTHS AND NEEDS OF THE INDIVIDUAL SYNDICATES. THE MAFIA, HATERS OF AUTHORITY, GAINED A MORE UNIVERSAL CONTROL OVER LABOR UNIONS AND DRUG SMUGGLING.
THE YAKUZA HAD MORE FAR-REACHING PLANS FOR AMERICAN BUSINESS, AND IRONS ACCOMMODATED THEM ALL.

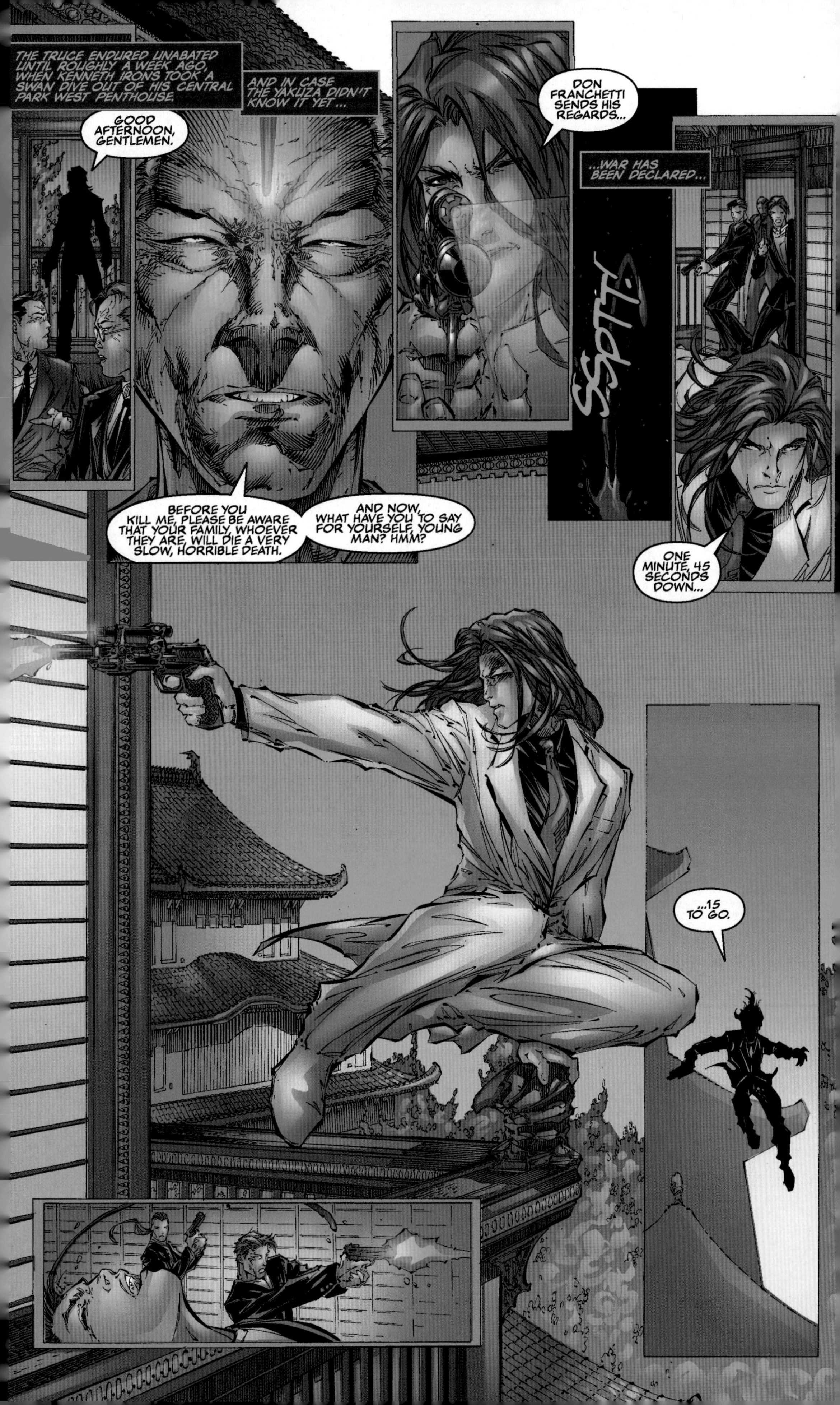

THE TRUCE ENDURED UNABATED UNTIL ROUGHLY A WEEK AGO, WHEN KENNETH IRONS TOOK A SWAN DIVE OUT OF HIS CENTRAL PARK WEST PENTHOUSE.
AND IN CASE THE YAKUZA DIDN'T KNOW IT YET...
GOOD AFTERNOON, GENTLEMEN.
BEFORE YOU KILL ME, PLEASE BE AWARE THAT YOUR FAMILY, WHOEVER THEY ARE, WILL DIE A VERY SLOW, HORRIBLE DEATH.
AND NOW, WHAT HAVE YOU TO SAY FOR YOURSELF, YOUNG MAN? HMM?
DON FRANCHETTI SENDS HIS REGARDS...
...WAR HAS BEEN DECLARED...
SPLT
ONE MINUTE, 45 SECONDS DOWN...
...15 TO GO.

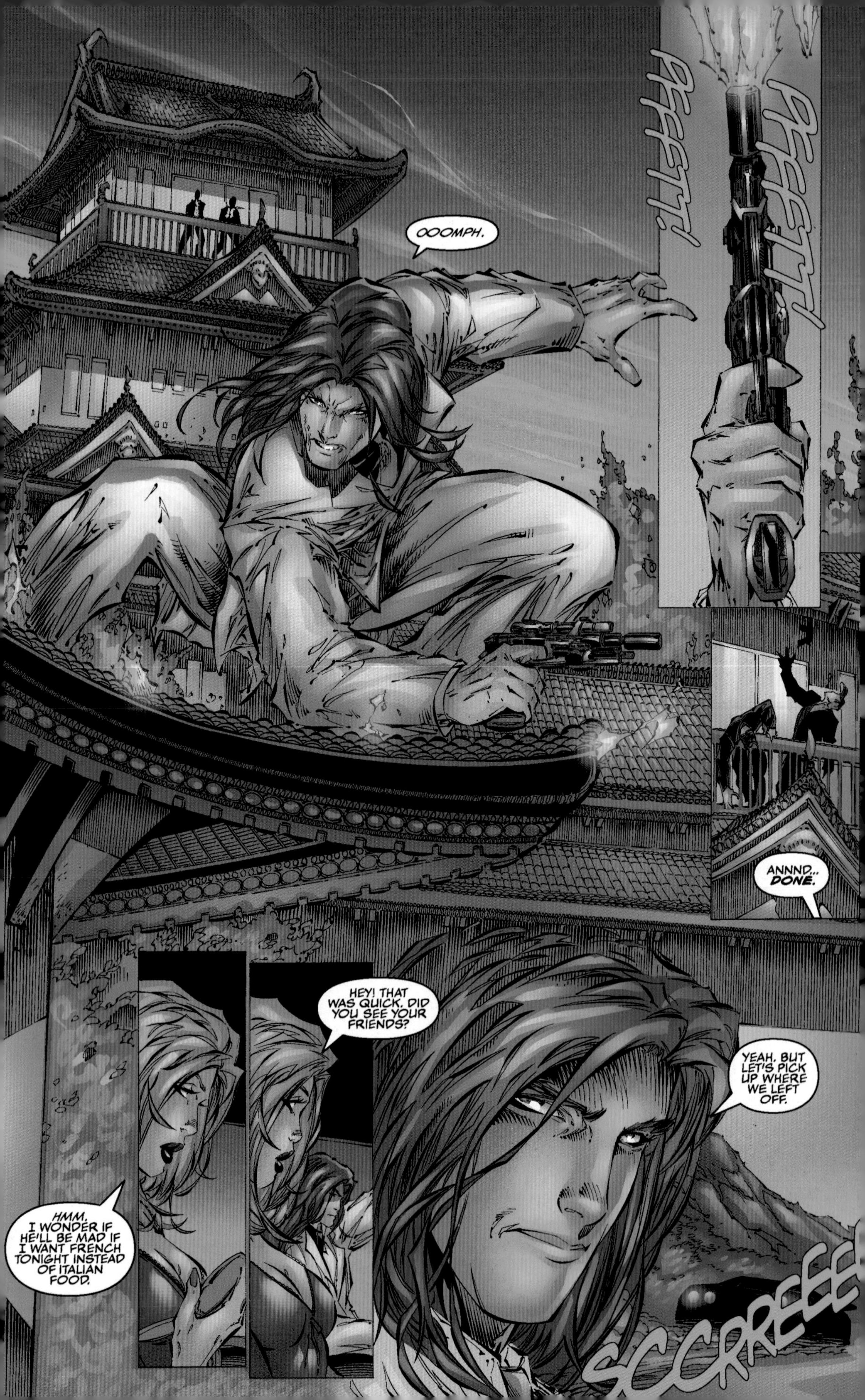

PFFFTT! PFFFTT!
OOOMPH.
ANNND... DONE.
HEY! THAT WAS QUICK. DID YOU SEE YOUR FRIENDS?
YEAH. BUT LET'S PICK UP WHERE WE LEFT OFF.
HMM. I WONDER IF HE'LL BE MAD IF I WANT FRENCH TONIGHT INSTEAD OF ITALIAN FOOD.
SCCRREEE

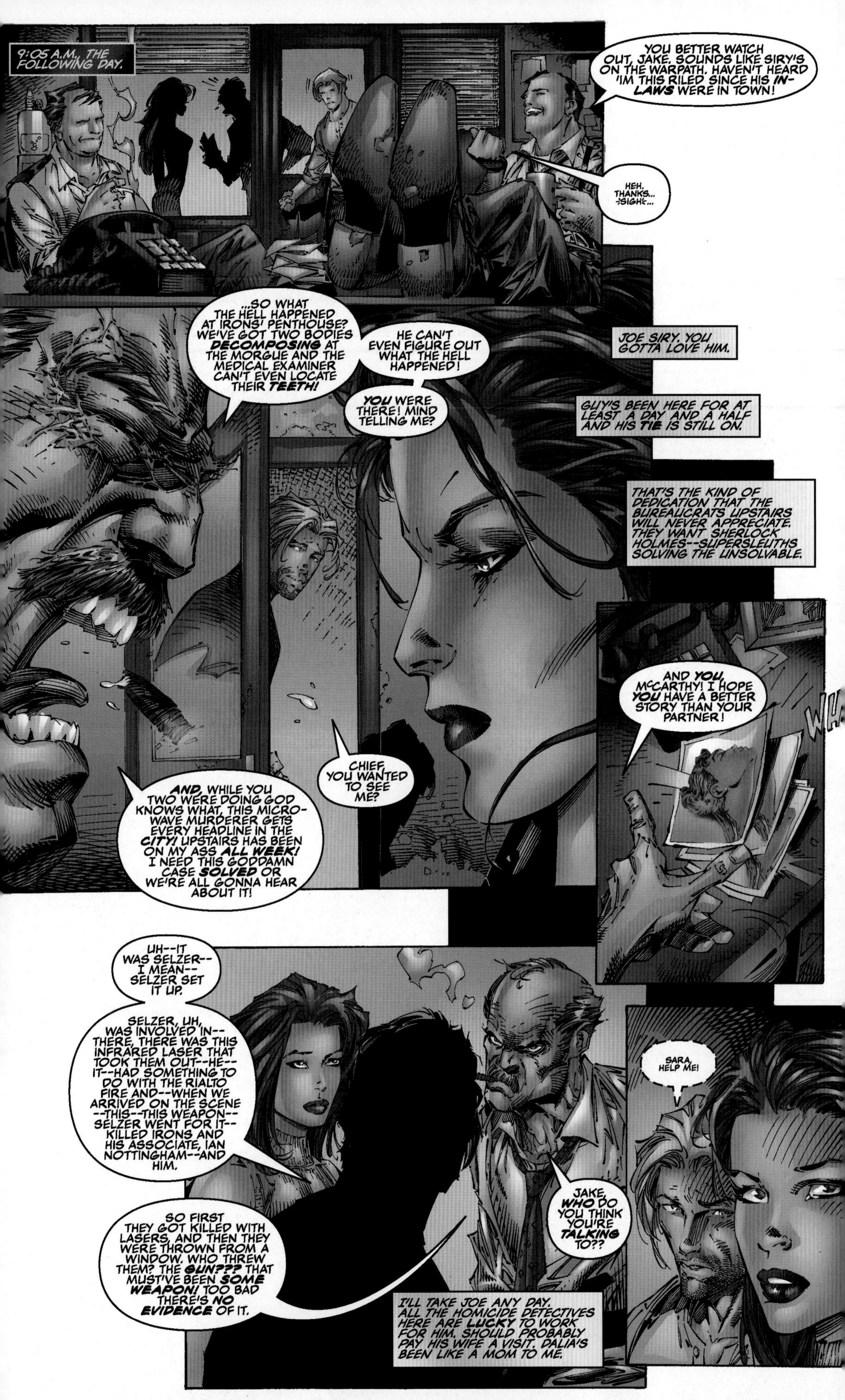
9:05 A.M. THE FOLLOWING DAY.
YOU BETTER WATCH OUT, JAKE. SOUNDS LIKE SIRY'S ON THE WARPATH. HAVEN'T HEARD 'IM THIS RILED SINCE HIS IN-LAWS WERE IN TOWN!
HEH. THANKS... *SIGH*...
...SO WHAT THE HELL HAPPENED AT IRONS' PENTHOUSE? WE'VE GOT TWO BODIES DECOMPOSING AT THE MORGUE AND THE MEDICAL EXAMINER CAN'T EVEN LOCATE THEIR TEETH!
HE CAN'T EVEN FIGURE OUT WHAT THE HELL HAPPENED!
YOU WERE THERE! MIND TELLING ME?
JOE SIRY. YOU GOTTA LOVE HIM.
GUY'S BEEN HERE FOR AT LEAST A DAY AND A HALF AND HIS TIE IS STILL ON.
THAT'S THE KIND OF DEDICATION THAT THE BUREAUCRATS UPSTAIRS WILL NEVER APPRECIATE. THEY WANT SHERLOCK HOLMES--SUPERSLEUTHS SOLVING THE UNSOLVABLE.
CHIEF, YOU WANTED TO SEE ME?
AND, WHILE YOU TWO WERE DOING GOD KNOWS WHAT, THIS MICRO-WAVE MURDERER GETS EVERY HEADLINE IN THE CITY! UPSTAIRS HAS BEEN ON MY ASS ALL WEEK! I NEED THIS GODDAMN CASE SOLVED OR WE'RE ALL GONNA HEAR ABOUT IT!
AND YOU, McCARTHY! I HOPE YOU HAVE A BETTER STORY THAN YOUR PARTNER!
WH
UH--IT WAS SELZER--I MEAN--SELZER SET IT UP.
SELZER, UH, WAS INVOLVED IN--THERE, THERE WAS THIS INFRARED LASER THAT TOOK THEM OUT--HE--IT--HAD SOMETHING TO DO WITH THE RIALTO FIRE AND--WHEN WE ARRIVED ON THE SCENE --THIS--THIS WEAPON--SELZER WENT FOR IT--KILLED IRONS AND HIS ASSOCIATE, IAN NOTTINGHAM--AND HIM.
SARA, HELP ME!
SO FIRST THEY GOT KILLED WITH LASERS, AND THEN THEY WERE THROWN FROM A WINDOW. WHO THREW THEM? THE GUN??? THAT MUST'VE BEEN SOME WEAPON! TOO BAD THERE'S NO EVIDENCE OF IT.
JAKE, WHO DO YOU THINK YOU'RE TALKING TO??
I'LL TAKE JOE ANY DAY. ALL THE HOMICIDE DETECTIVES HERE ARE LUCKY TO WORK FOR HIM. SHOULD PROBABLY PAY HIS WIFE A VISIT. DALIA'S BEEN LIKE A MOM TO ME.

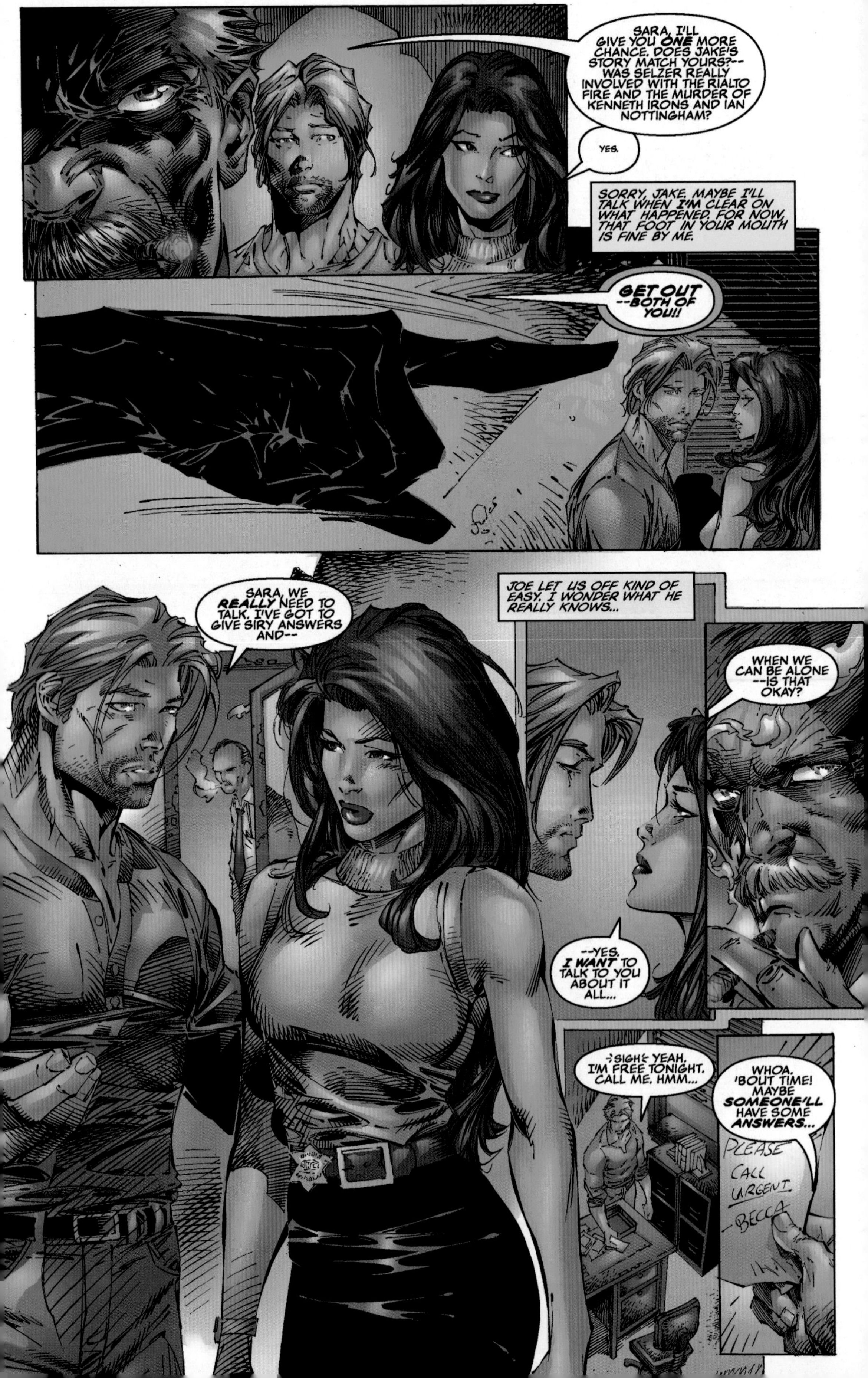
SARA, I'LL GIVE YOU ONE MORE CHANCE. DOES JAKE'S STORY MATCH YOURS?--WAS SELZER REALLY INVOLVED WITH THE RIALTO FIRE AND THE MURDER OF KENNETH IRONS AND IAN NOTTINGHAM?
YES.
SORRY, JAKE. MAYBE I'LL TALK WHEN I'M CLEAR ON WHAT HAPPENED. FOR NOW, THAT FOOT IN YOUR MOUTH IS FINE BY ME.
GET OUT --BOTH OF YOU!!
SARA, WE REALLY NEED TO TALK. I'VE GOT TO GIVE SIRY ANSWERS AND--
JOE LET US OFF KIND OF EASY. I WONDER WHAT HE REALLY KNOWS...
WHEN WE CAN BE ALONE --IS THAT OKAY?
--YES. I WANT TO TALK TO YOU ABOUT IT ALL...
SIGH YEAH. I'M FREE TONIGHT. CALL ME. HMM...
WHOA. 'BOUT TIME! MAYBE SOMEONE'LL HAVE SOME ANSWERS...
PLEASE CALL URGENT. -BECCA

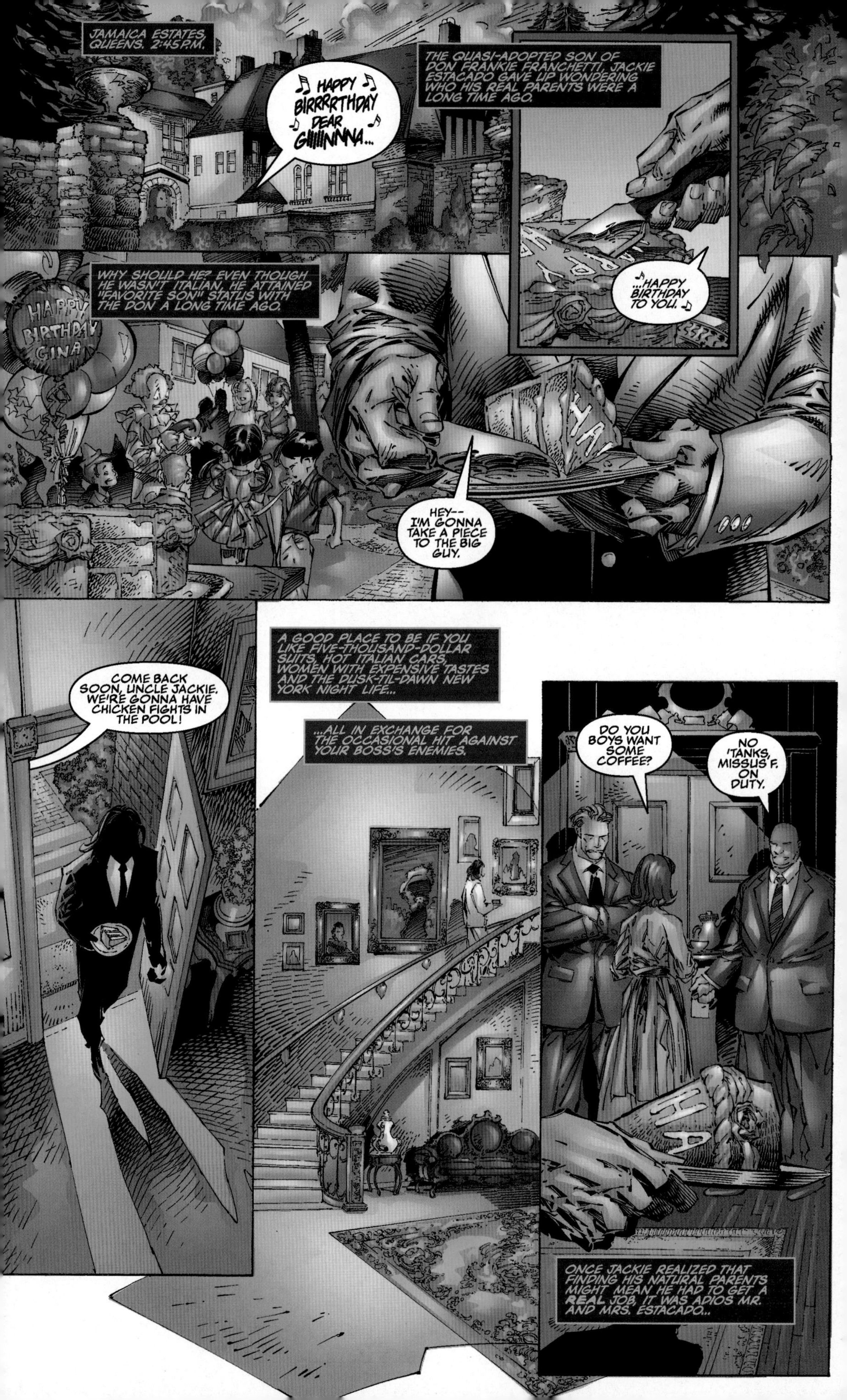
JAMAICA ESTATES, QUEENS. 2:45 P.M.
♪ HAPPY ♪ BIRRRRTHDAY DEAR ♪ GIIIINNNA... ♪
THE QUASI-ADOPTED SON OF DON FRANKIE FRANCHETTI, JACKIE ESTACADO GAVE UP WONDERING WHO HIS REAL PARENTS WERE A LONG TIME AGO.
♪ ...HAPPY BIRTHDAY TO YOU. ♪
WHY SHOULD HE? EVEN THOUGH HE WASN'T ITALIAN, HE ATTAINED "FAVORITE SON" STATUS WITH THE DON A LONG TIME AGO.
HAPPY BIRTHDAY GINA
HEY-- I'M GONNA TAKE A PIECE TO THE BIG GUY.
COME BACK SOON, UNCLE JACKIE. WE'RE GONNA HAVE CHICKEN FIGHTS IN THE POOL!
A GOOD PLACE TO BE IF YOU LIKE FIVE-THOUSAND-DOLLAR SUITS, HOT ITALIAN CARS, WOMEN WITH EXPENSIVE TASTES AND THE DUSK-TIL-DAWN NEW YORK NIGHT LIFE...
...ALL IN EXCHANGE FOR THE OCCASIONAL HIT AGAINST YOUR BOSS'S ENEMIES.
DO YOU BOYS WANT SOME COFFEE?
NO 'TANKS, MISSUS F. ON DUTY.
ONCE JACKIE REALIZED THAT FINDING HIS NATURAL PARENTS MIGHT MEAN HE HAD TO GET A **REAL** JOB, IT WAS ADIOS MR. AND MRS. ESTACADO...

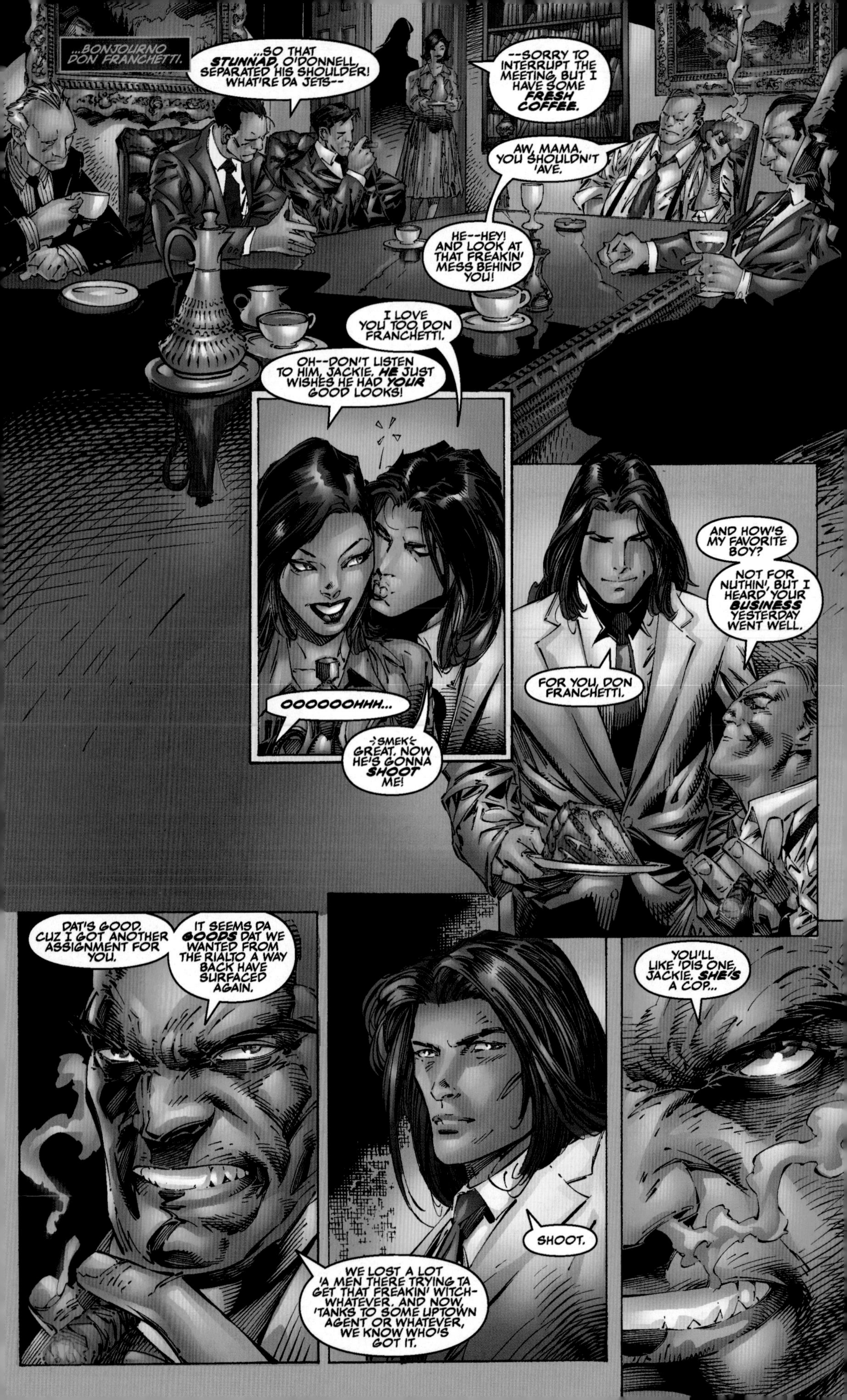
...BONJOURNO DON FRANCHETTI.
...SO THAT STUNNAD, O'DONNELL, SEPARATED HIS SHOULDER! WHAT'RE DA JETS--
--SORRY TO INTERRUPT THE MEETING, BUT I HAVE SOME FRESH COFFEE.
AW, MAMA, YOU SHOULDN'T 'AVE.
HE--HEY! AND LOOK AT THAT FREAKIN' MESS BEHIND YOU!
I LOVE YOU TOO, DON FRANCHETTI.
OH--DON'T LISTEN TO HIM, JACKIE. HE JUST WISHES HE HAD YOUR GOOD LOOKS!
OOOOOOHHH...
SMEK
GREAT. NOW HE'S GONNA SHOOT ME!
AND HOW'S MY FAVORITE BOY?
NOT FOR NUTHIN', BUT I HEARD YOUR BUSINESS YESTERDAY WENT WELL.
FOR YOU, DON FRANCHETTI.
DAT'S GOOD, CUZ I GOT ANOTHER ASSIGNMENT FOR YOU.
IT SEEMS DA GOODS DAT WE WANTED FROM THE RIALTO A WAY BACK HAVE SURFACED AGAIN.
WE LOST A LOT 'A MEN THERE TRYING TA GET THAT FREAKIN' WITCH-WHATEVER. AND NOW, 'TANKS TO SOME UPTOWN AGENT OR WHATEVER, WE KNOW WHO'S GOT IT.
SHOOT.
YOU'LL LIKE 'DIS ONE, JACKIE. SHE'S A COP...

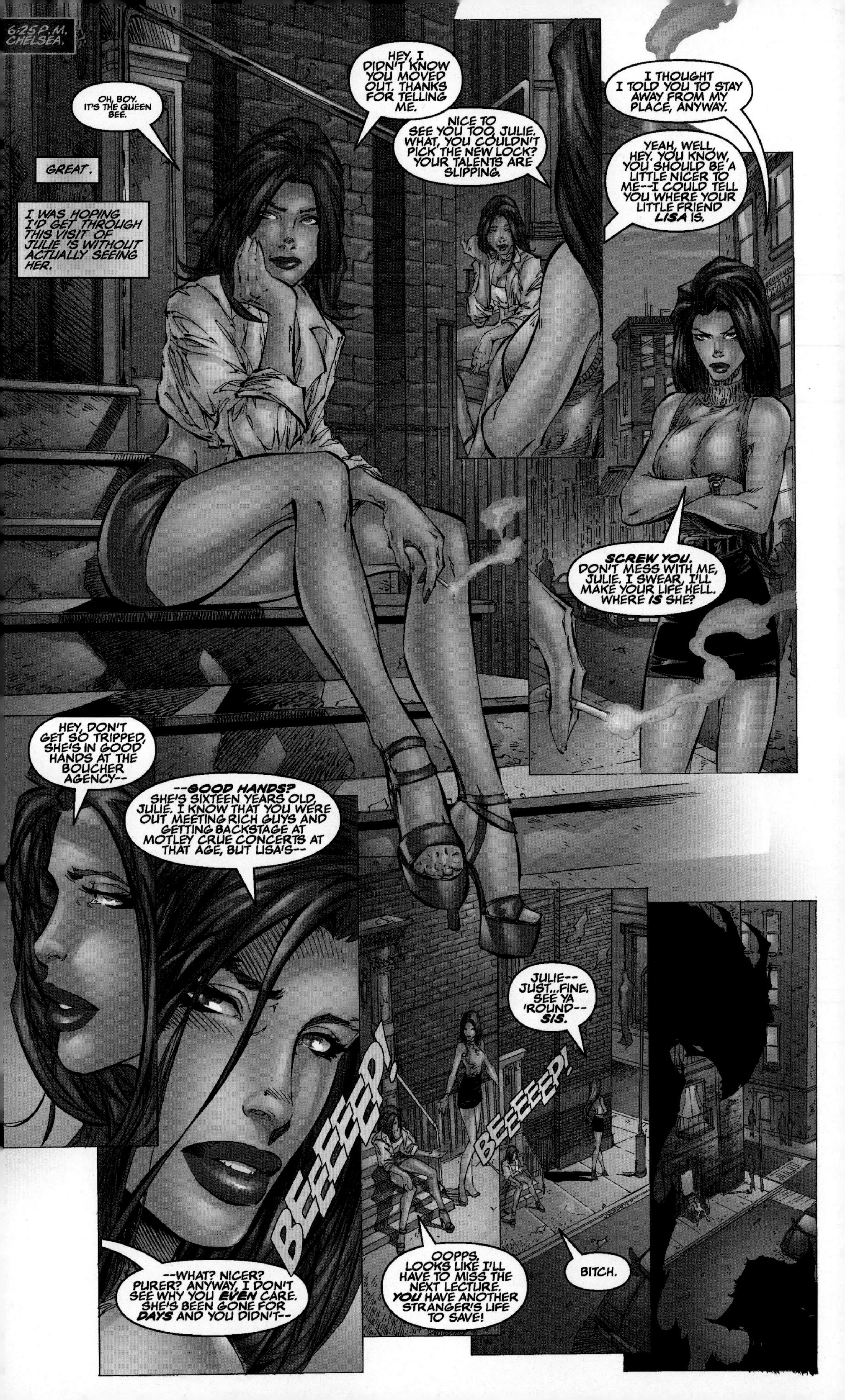
6:25 P.M.
CHELSEA.
OH, BOY. IT'S THE QUEEN BEE.
GREAT.
I WAS HOPING I'D GET THROUGH THIS VISIT OF JULIE'S WITHOUT ACTUALLY SEEING HER.
HEY, I DIDN'T KNOW YOU MOVED OUT. THANKS FOR TELLING ME.
NICE TO SEE YOU TOO, JULIE. WHAT, YOU COULDN'T PICK THE NEW LOCK? YOUR TALENTS ARE SLIPPING.
I THOUGHT I TOLD YOU TO STAY AWAY FROM MY PLACE, ANYWAY.
YEAH, WELL, HEY, YOU KNOW, YOU SHOULD BE A LITTLE NICER TO ME--I COULD TELL YOU WHERE YOUR LITTLE FRIEND LISA IS.
SCREW YOU. DON'T MESS WITH ME, JULIE. I SWEAR, I'LL MAKE YOUR LIFE HELL. WHERE IS SHE?
HEY, DON'T GET SO TRIPPED, SHE'S IN GOOD HANDS AT THE BOUCHER AGENCY--
--GOOD HANDS? SHE'S SIXTEEN YEARS OLD, JULIE. I KNOW THAT YOU WERE OUT MEETING RICH GUYS AND GETTING BACKSTAGE AT MOTLEY CRUE CONCERTS AT THAT AGE, BUT LISA'S--
--WHAT? NICER? PURER? ANYWAY, I DON'T SEE WHY YOU EVEN CARE. SHE'S BEEN GONE FOR DAYS AND YOU DIDN'T--
BEEEEEP!
OOPPS. LOOKS LIKE I'LL HAVE TO MISS THE NEXT LECTURE. YOU HAVE ANOTHER STRANGER'S LIFE TO SAVE!
BEEEEEP!
JULIE-- JUST...FINE. SEE YA 'ROUND-- SIS.
BITCH.

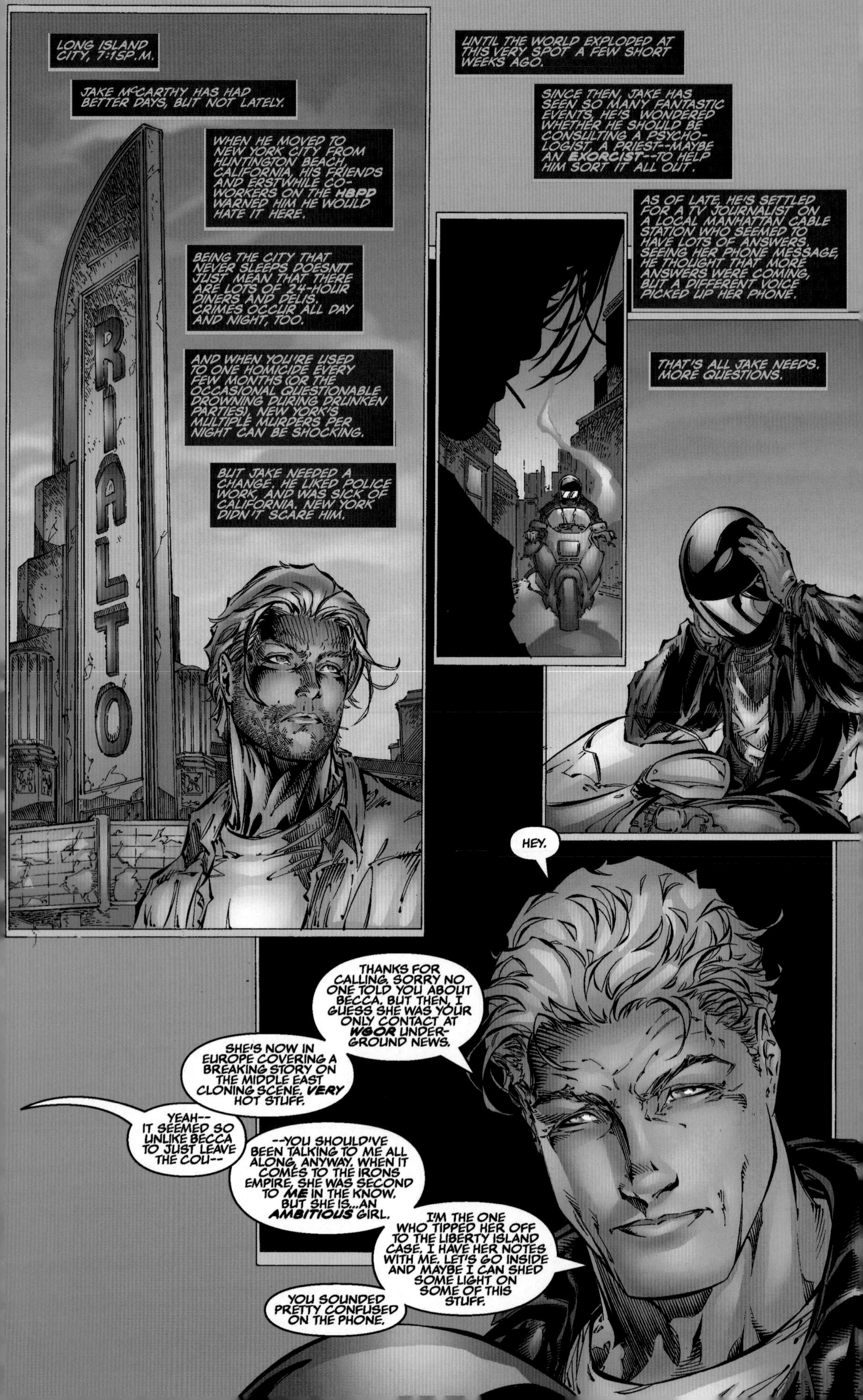

LONG ISLAND CITY, 7:15P.M.
JAKE McCARTHY HAS HAD BETTER DAYS, BUT NOT LATELY.
WHEN HE MOVED TO NEW YORK CITY FROM HUNTINGTON BEACH, CALIFORNIA, HIS FRIENDS AND ERSTWHILE CO-WORKERS ON THE HBPD WARNED HIM HE WOULD HATE IT HERE.
BEING THE CITY THAT NEVER SLEEPS DOESN'T JUST MEAN THAT THERE ARE LOTS OF 24-HOUR DINERS AND DELIS. CRIMES OCCUR ALL DAY AND NIGHT, TOO.
AND WHEN YOU'RE USED TO ONE HOMICIDE EVERY FEW MONTHS (OR THE OCCASIONAL QUESTIONABLE DROWNING DURING DRUNKEN PARTIES), NEW YORK'S MULTIPLE MURDERS PER NIGHT CAN BE SHOCKING.
BUT JAKE NEEDED A CHANGE. HE LIKED POLICE WORK, AND WAS SICK OF CALIFORNIA. NEW YORK DIDN'T SCARE HIM.
RIALTO
UNTIL THE WORLD EXPLODED AT THIS VERY SPOT A FEW SHORT WEEKS AGO.
SINCE THEN, JAKE HAS SEEN SO MANY FANTASTIC EVENTS, HE'S WONDERED WHETHER HE SHOULD BE CONSULTING A PSYCHOLOGIST, A PRIEST--MAYBE AN EXORCIST--TO HELP HIM SORT IT ALL OUT.
AS OF LATE, HE'S SETTLED FOR A TV JOURNALIST ON A LOCAL MANHATTAN CABLE STATION WHO SEEMED TO HAVE LOTS OF ANSWERS. SEEING HER PHONE MESSAGE, HE THOUGHT THAT MORE ANSWERS WERE COMING, BUT A DIFFERENT VOICE PICKED UP HER PHONE.
THAT'S ALL JAKE NEEDS. MORE QUESTIONS.
HEY.
THANKS FOR CALLING. SORRY NO ONE TOLD YOU ABOUT BECCA. BUT THEN, I GUESS SHE WAS YOUR ONLY CONTACT AT WGOR UNDERGROUND NEWS.
SHE'S NOW IN EUROPE COVERING A BREAKING STORY ON THE MIDDLE EAST CLONING SCENE. VERY HOT STUFF.
YEAH-- IT SEEMED SO UNLIKE BECCA TO JUST LEAVE THE COU--
--YOU SHOULD'VE BEEN TALKING TO ME ALL ALONG, ANYWAY. WHEN IT COMES TO THE IRONS EMPIRE, SHE WAS SECOND TO ME IN THE KNOW. BUT SHE IS...AN AMBITIOUS GIRL.
I'M THE ONE WHO TIPPED HER OFF TO THE LIBERTY ISLAND CASE. I HAVE HER NOTES WITH ME. LET'S GO INSIDE AND MAYBE I CAN SHED SOME LIGHT ON SOME OF THIS STUFF.
YOU SOUNDED PRETTY CONFUSED ON THE PHONE.

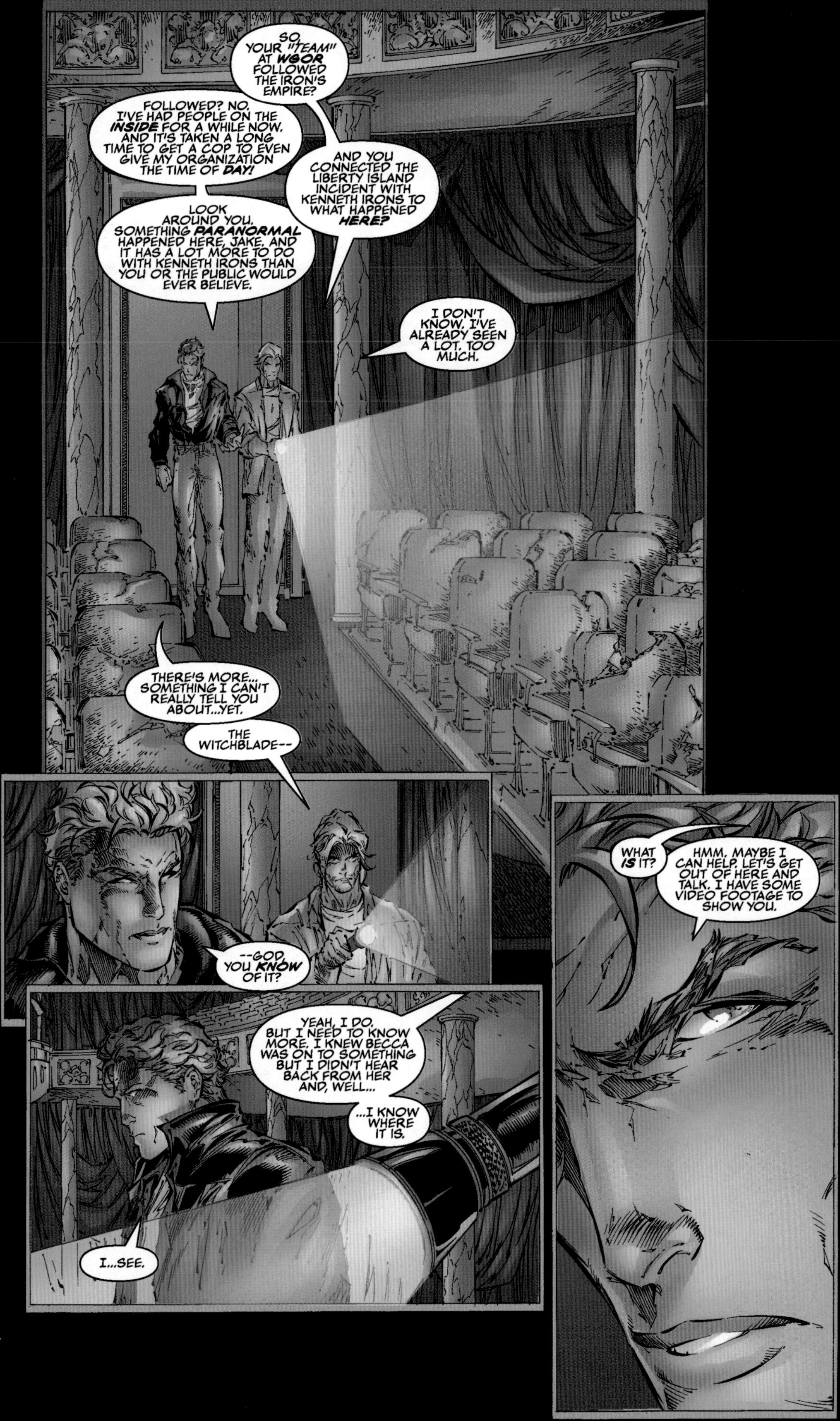
SO, YOUR "TEAM" AT WGOR FOLLOWED THE IRON'S EMPIRE?
FOLLOWED? NO. I'VE HAD PEOPLE ON THE INSIDE FOR A WHILE NOW. AND IT'S TAKEN A LONG TIME TO GET A COP TO EVEN GIVE MY ORGANIZATION THE TIME OF DAY!
AND YOU CONNECTED THE LIBERTY ISLAND INCIDENT WITH KENNETH IRONS TO WHAT HAPPENED HERE?
LOOK AROUND YOU. SOMETHING PARANORMAL HAPPENED HERE, JAKE. AND IT HAS A LOT MORE TO DO WITH KENNETH IRONS THAN YOU OR THE PUBLIC WOULD EVER BELIEVE.
I DON'T KNOW. I'VE ALREADY SEEN A LOT. TOO MUCH.
THERE'S MORE... SOMETHING I CAN'T REALLY TELL YOU ABOUT...YET.
THE WITCHBLADE--
--GOD, YOU KNOW OF IT?
YEAH, I DO. BUT I NEED TO KNOW MORE. I KNEW BECCA WAS ON TO SOMETHING BUT I DIDN'T HEAR BACK FROM HER AND, WELL...
...I KNOW WHERE IT IS.
I...SEE.
WHAT IS IT?
HMM. MAYBE I CAN HELP. LET'S GET OUT OF HERE AND TALK. I HAVE SOME VIDEO FOOTAGE TO SHOW YOU.

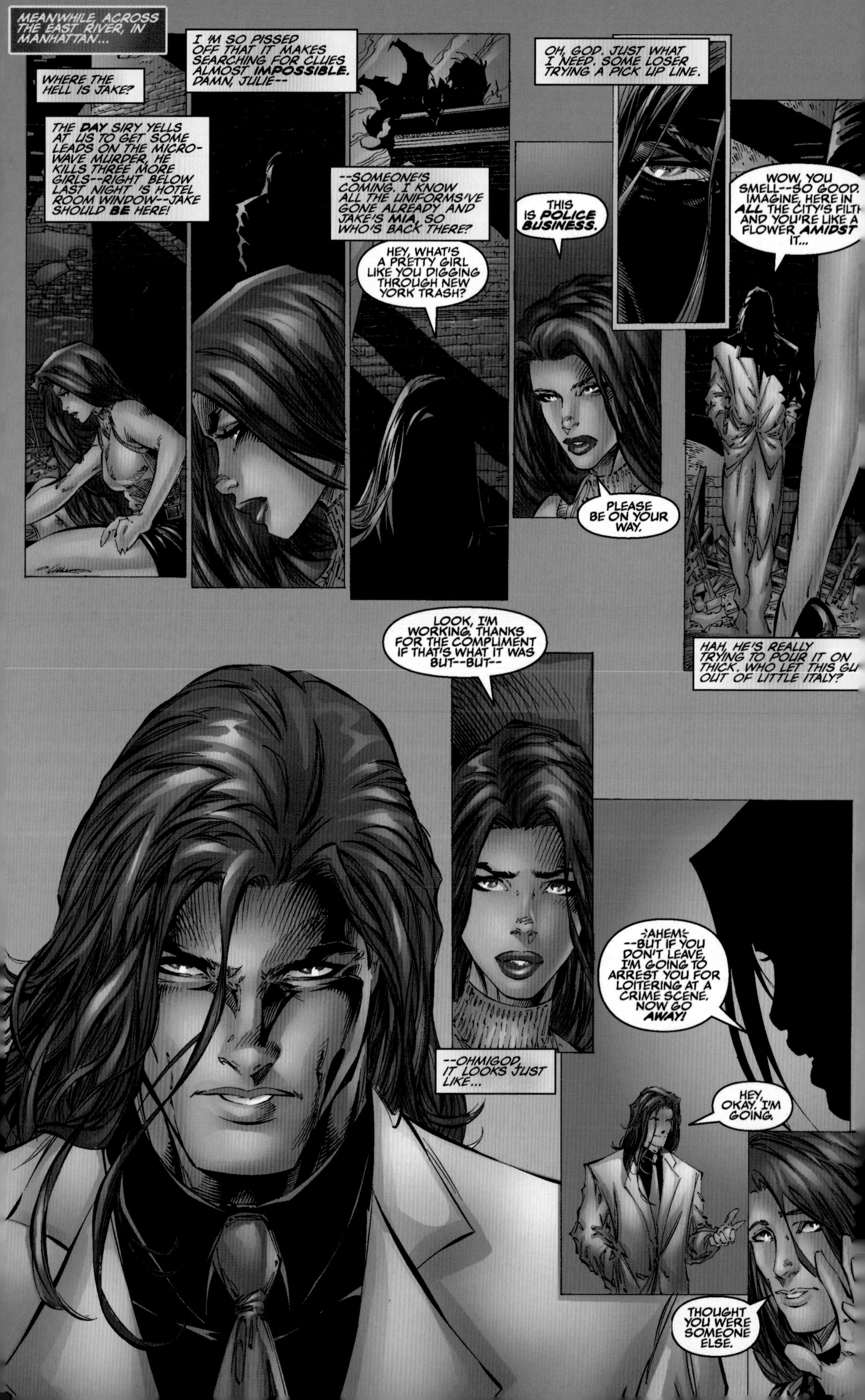
MEANWHILE, ACROSS THE EAST RIVER, IN MANHATTAN...
WHERE THE HELL IS JAKE?
THE DAY SIRY YELLS AT US TO GET SOME LEADS ON THE MICRO-WAVE MURDER, HE KILLS THREE MORE GIRLS--RIGHT BELOW LAST NIGHT 'S HOTEL ROOM WINDOW--JAKE SHOULD BE HERE!
I 'M SO PISSED OFF THAT IT MAKES SEARCHING FOR CLUES ALMOST IMPOSSIBLE. DAMN, JULIE--
--SOMEONE'S COMING. I KNOW ALL THE UNIFORMS'VE GONE ALREADY AND JAKE'S MIA, SO WHO'S BACK THERE?
HEY, WHAT'S A PRETTY GIRL LIKE YOU DIGGING THROUGH NEW YORK TRASH?
THIS IS POLICE BUSINESS.
PLEASE BE ON YOUR WAY.
OH, GOD. JUST WHAT I NEED. SOME LOSER TRYING A PICK UP LINE.
WOW, YOU SMELL--SO GOOD. IMAGINE, HERE IN ALL THE CITY'S FILTH AND YOU'RE LIKE A FLOWER AMIDST IT...
HAH, HE'S REALLY TRYING TO POUR IT ON THICK. WHO LET THIS GU OUT OF LITTLE ITALY?
LOOK, I'M WORKING. THANKS FOR THE COMPLIMENT IF THAT'S WHAT IT WAS BUT--BUT--
--OHMIGOD, IT LOOKS JUST LIKE...
AHEM
--BUT IF YOU DON'T LEAVE, I'M GOING TO ARREST YOU FOR LOITERING AT A CRIME SCENE. NOW GO AWAY!
HEY, OKAY, I'M GOING.
THOUGHT YOU WERE SOMEONE ELSE.

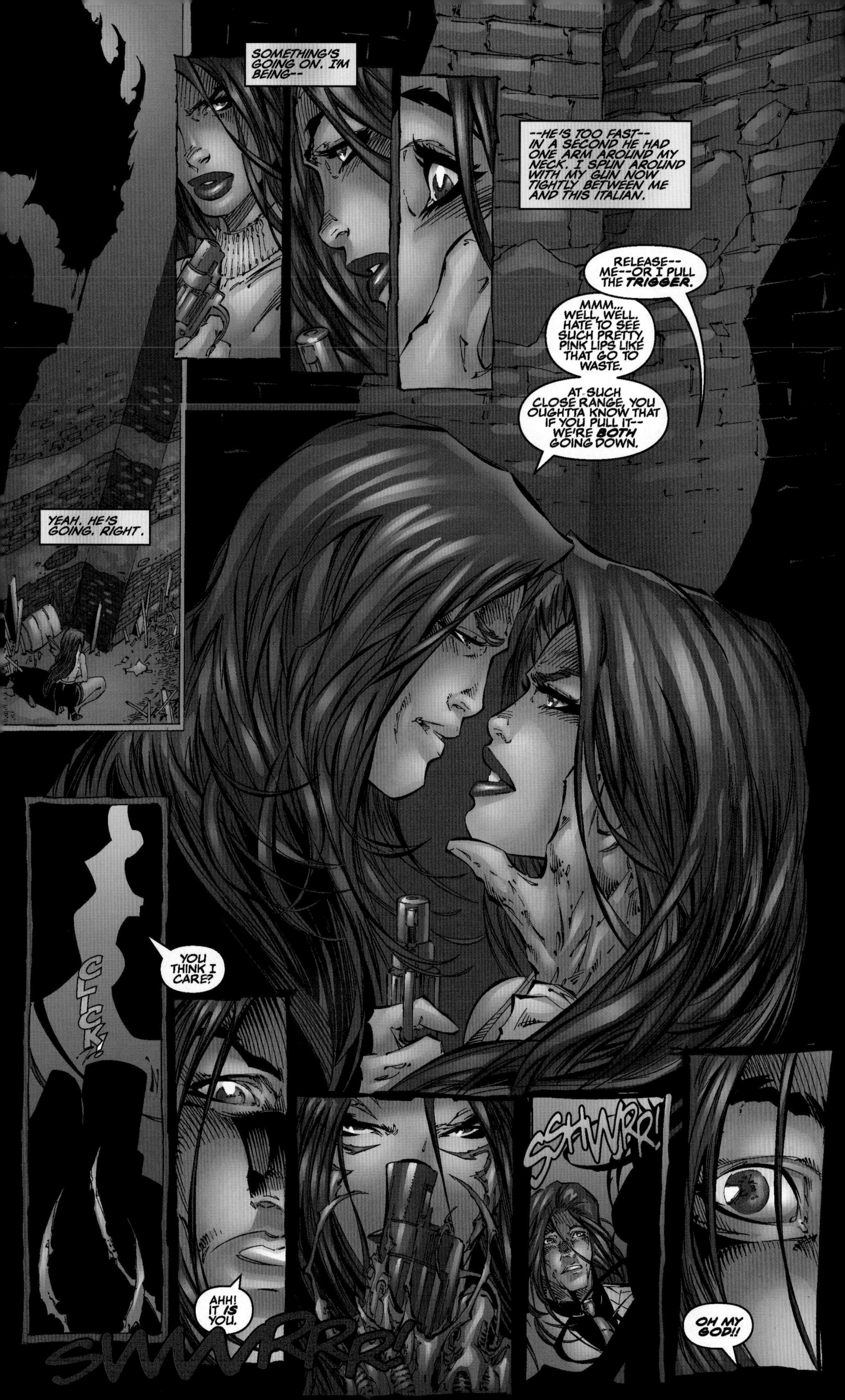

SOMETHING'S GOING ON. I'M BEING--
--HE'S TOO FAST-- IN A SECOND HE HAD ONE ARM AROUND MY NECK. I SPUN AROUND WITH MY GUN NOW TIGHTLY BETWEEN ME AND THIS ITALIAN.
RELEASE-- ME--OR I PULL THE TRIGGER.
MMM... WELL, WELL. HATE TO SEE SUCH PRETTY, PINK LIPS LIKE THAT GO TO WASTE.
AT SUCH CLOSE RANGE, YOU OUGHTTA KNOW THAT IF YOU PULL IT-- WE'RE BOTH GOING DOWN.
YEAH. HE'S GOING. RIGHT.
YOU THINK I CARE?
CLICK
AHH! IT IS YOU.
SHWRR!
OH MY GOD!!
SWWARRR!

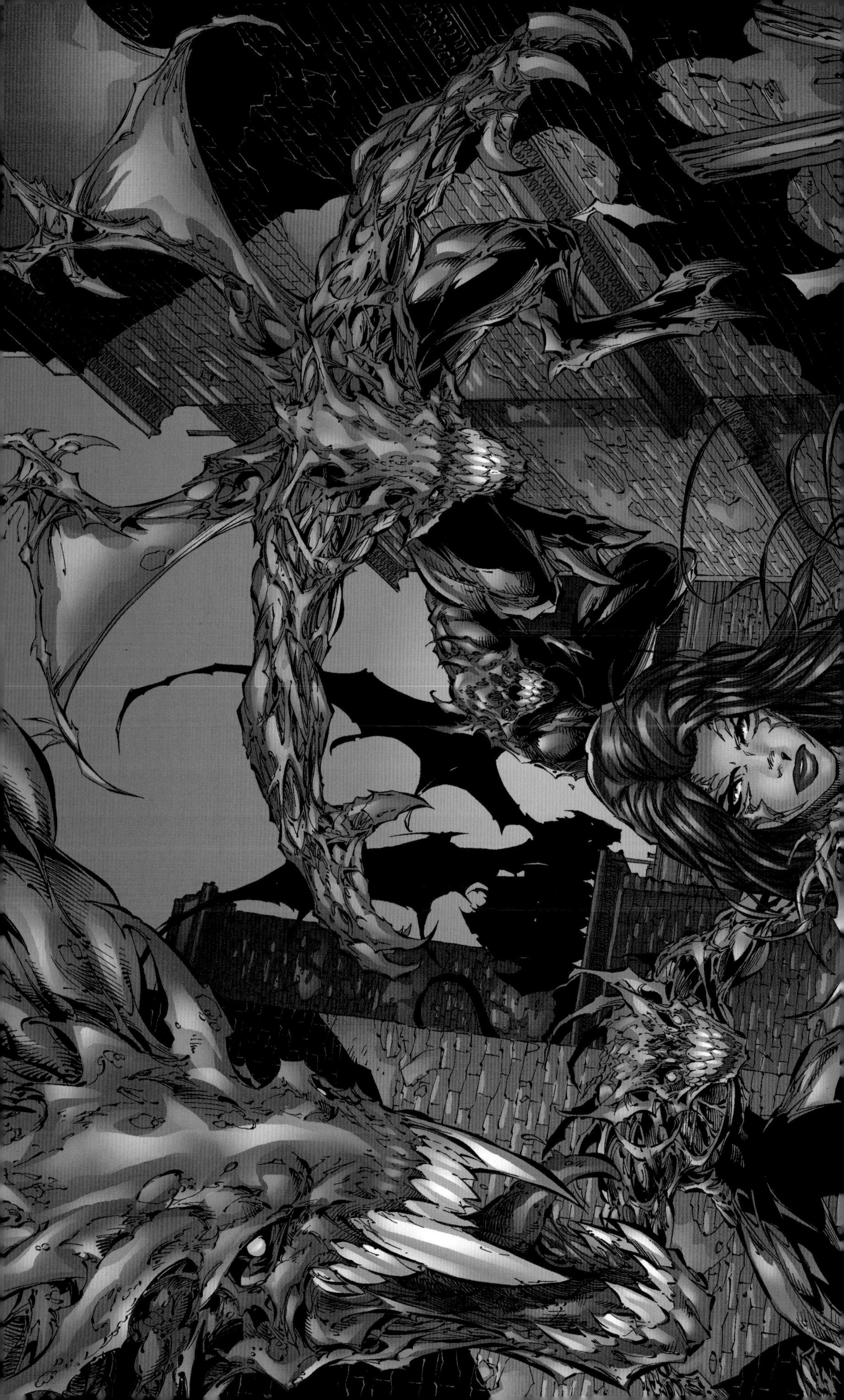

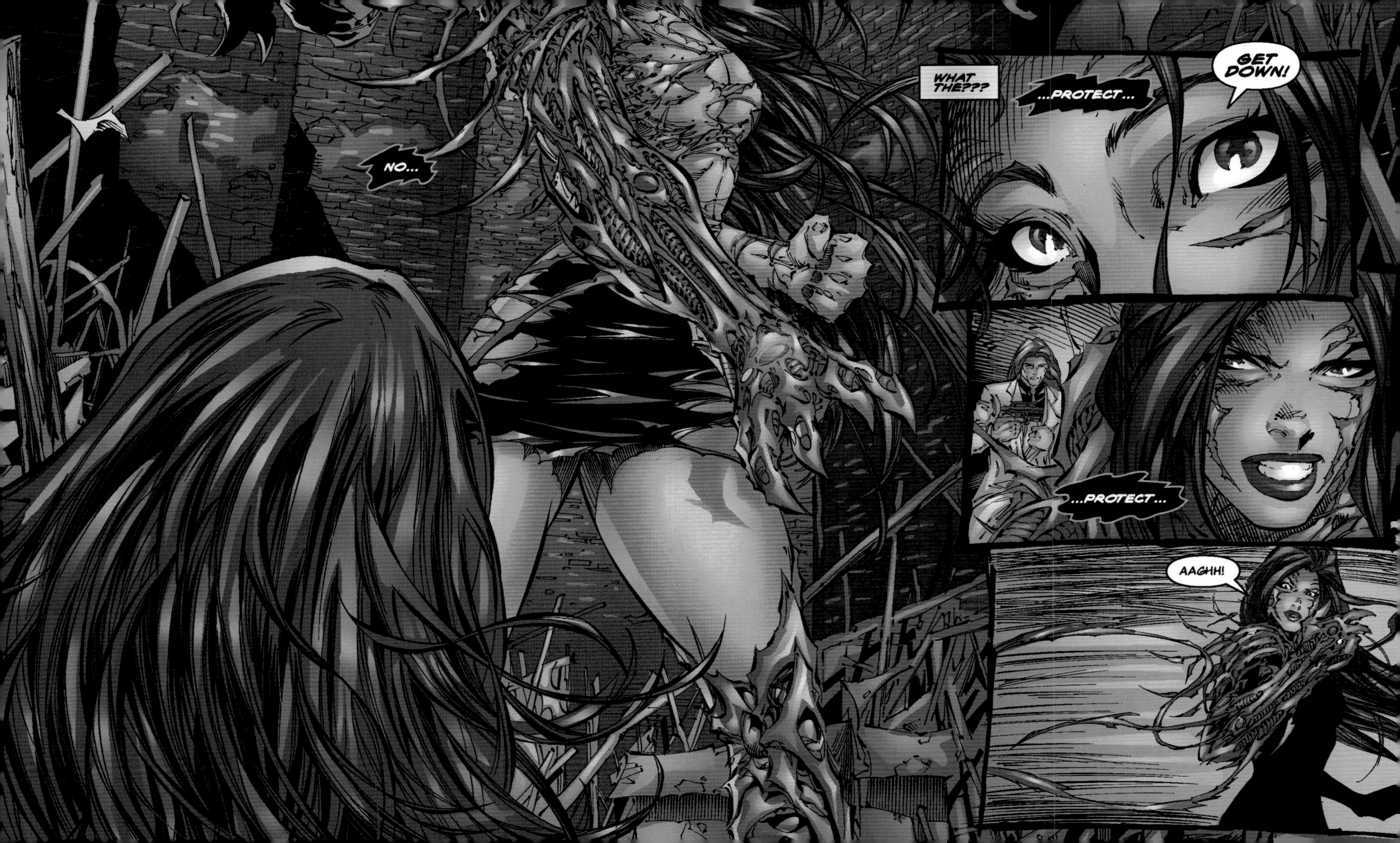
NO...
WHAT THE???
...PROTECT...
GET DOWN!
...PROTECT...
AAGHH!

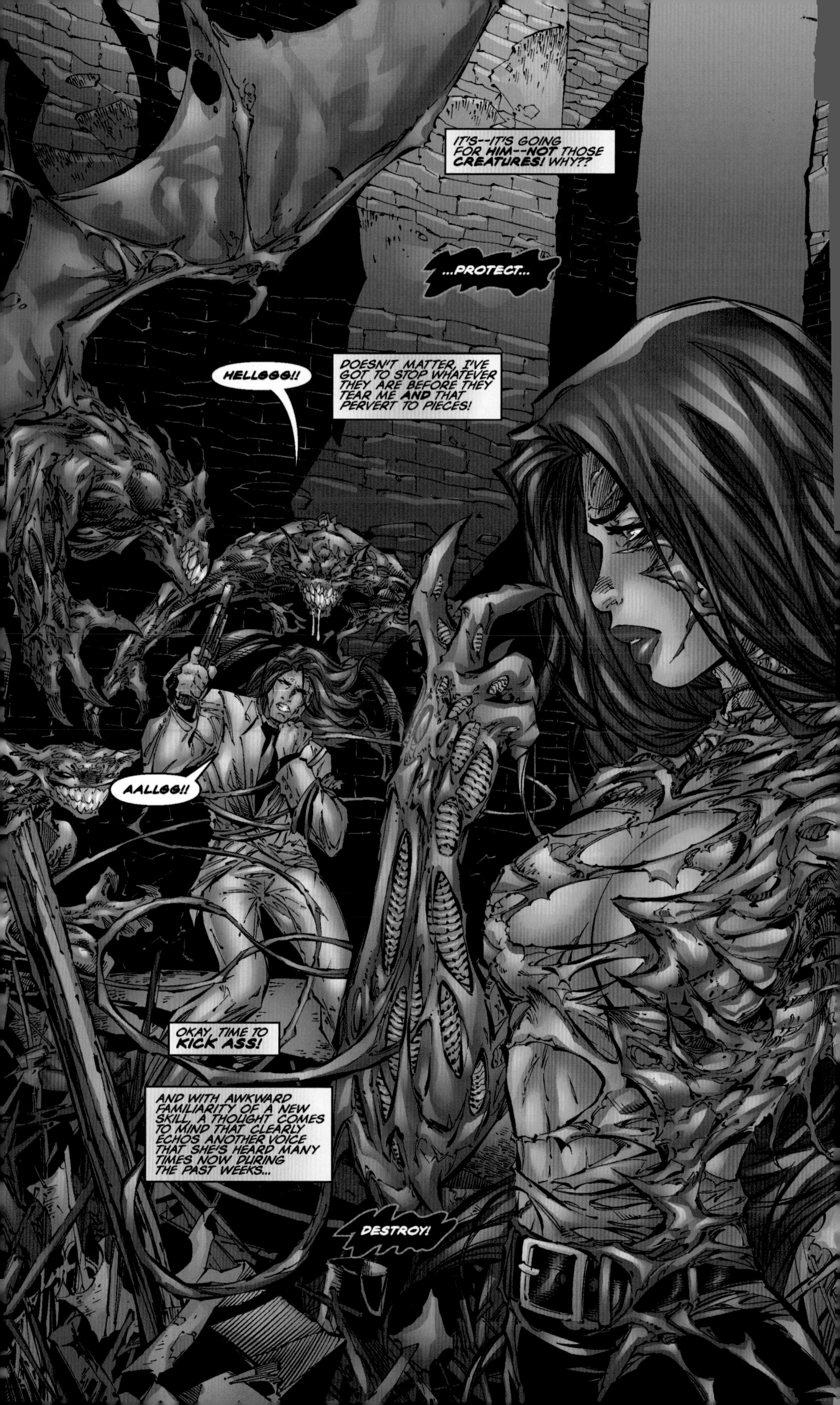

IT'S--IT'S GOING FOR HIM--NOT THOSE CREATURES! WHY??
...PROTECT...
HELLGGG!!
DOESN'T MATTER, I'VE GOT TO STOP WHATEVER THEY ARE BEFORE THEY TEAR ME AND THAT PERVERT TO PIECES!
AALLGG!!
OKAY, TIME TO KICK ASS!
AND WITH AWKWARD FAMILIARITY OF A NEW SKILL, A THOUGHT COMES TO MIND THAT CLEARLY ECHOS ANOTHER VOICE THAT SHE'S HEARD MANY TIMES NOW DURING THE PAST WEEKS...
DESTROY!

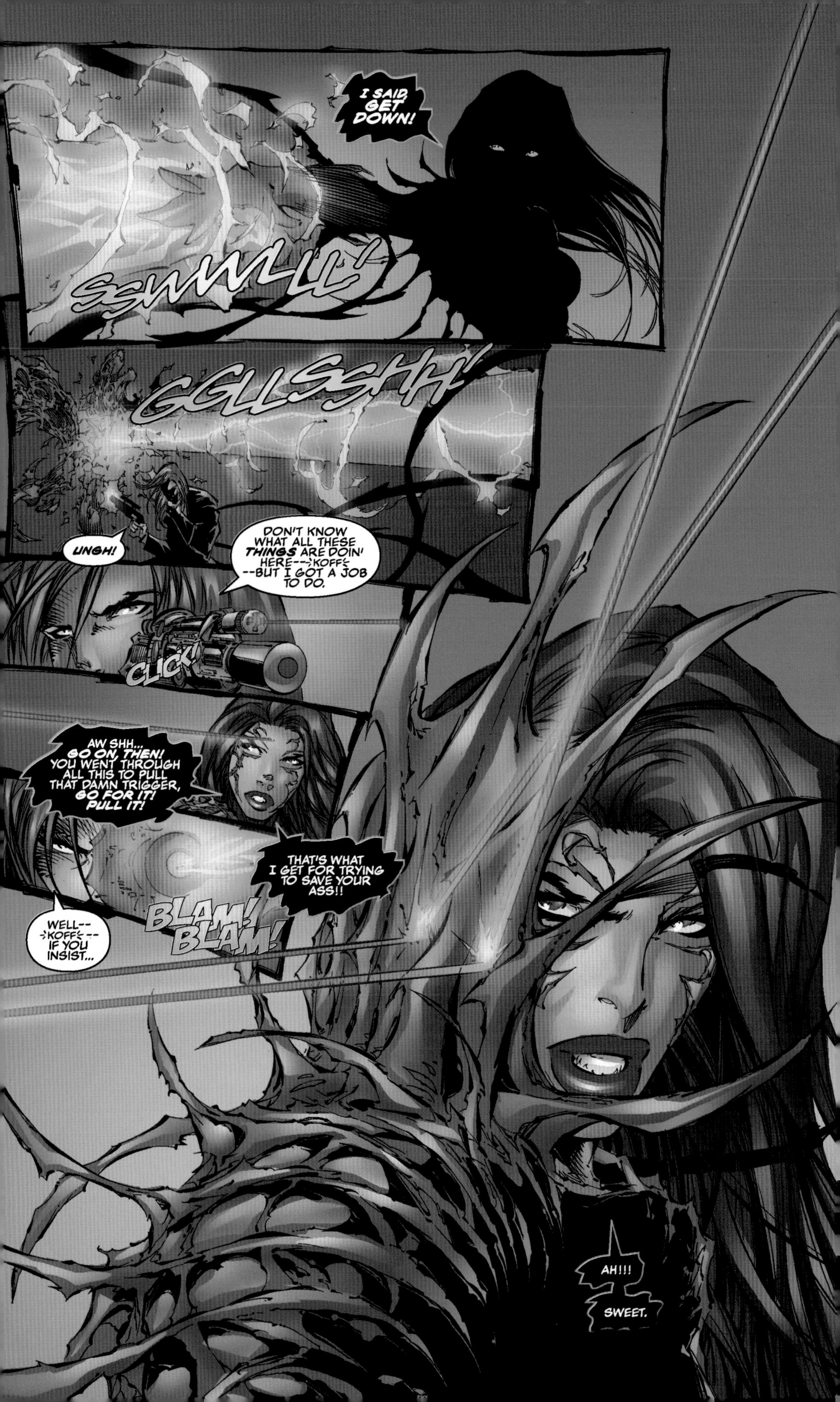
I SAID, GET DOWN!
SSWWLLL!
GGLLSSHH!
UNGH!
DON'T KNOW WHAT ALL THESE THINGS ARE DOIN' HERE--*KOFF*--BUT I GOT A JOB TO DO.
CLICK!
AW SHH... GO ON, THEN! YOU WENT THROUGH ALL THIS TO PULL THAT DAMN TRIGGER, GO FOR IT! PULL IT!
THAT'S WHAT I GET FOR TRYING TO SAVE YOUR ASS!!
WELL--*KOFF*--IF YOU INSIST...
BLAM! BLAM!
AH!!!
SWEET.

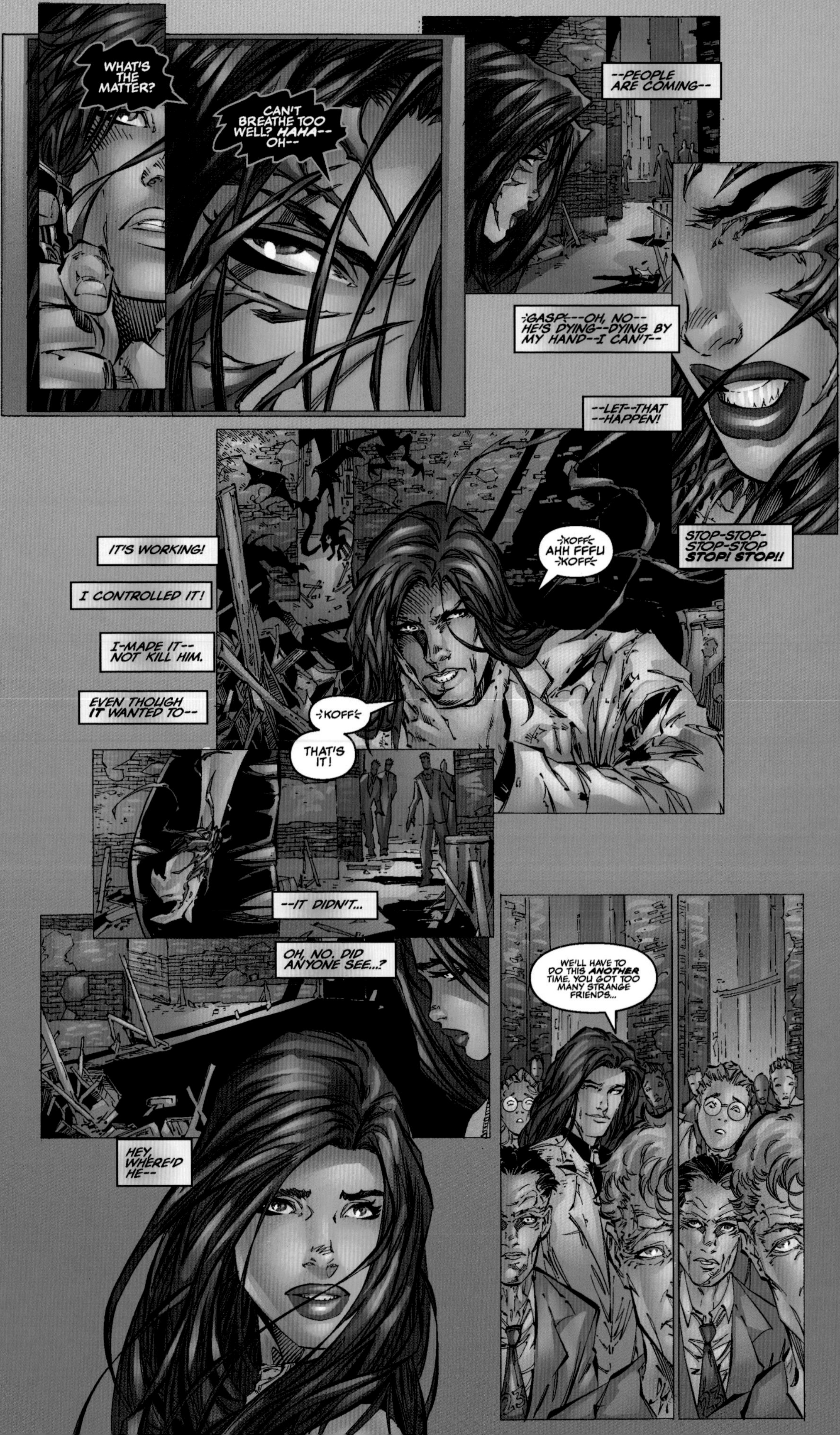
WHAT'S THE MATTER?
CAN'T BREATHE TOO WELL? HAHA-- OH--
--PEOPLE ARE COMING--
GASP--OH, NO-- HE'S DYING--DYING BY MY HAND--I CAN'T--
--LET--THAT --HAPPEN!
STOP-STOP-STOP-STOP STOP! STOP!!
IT'S WORKING!
I CONTROLLED IT!
I-MADE IT-- NOT KILL HIM.
EVEN THOUGH IT WANTED TO--
KOFF AHH FFFU KOFF
KOFF
THAT'S IT!
--IT DIDN'T...
OH, NO. DID ANYONE SEE...?
HEY, WHERE'D HE--
WE'LL HAVE TO DO THIS ANOTHER TIME. YOU GOT TOO MANY STRANGE FRIENDS...

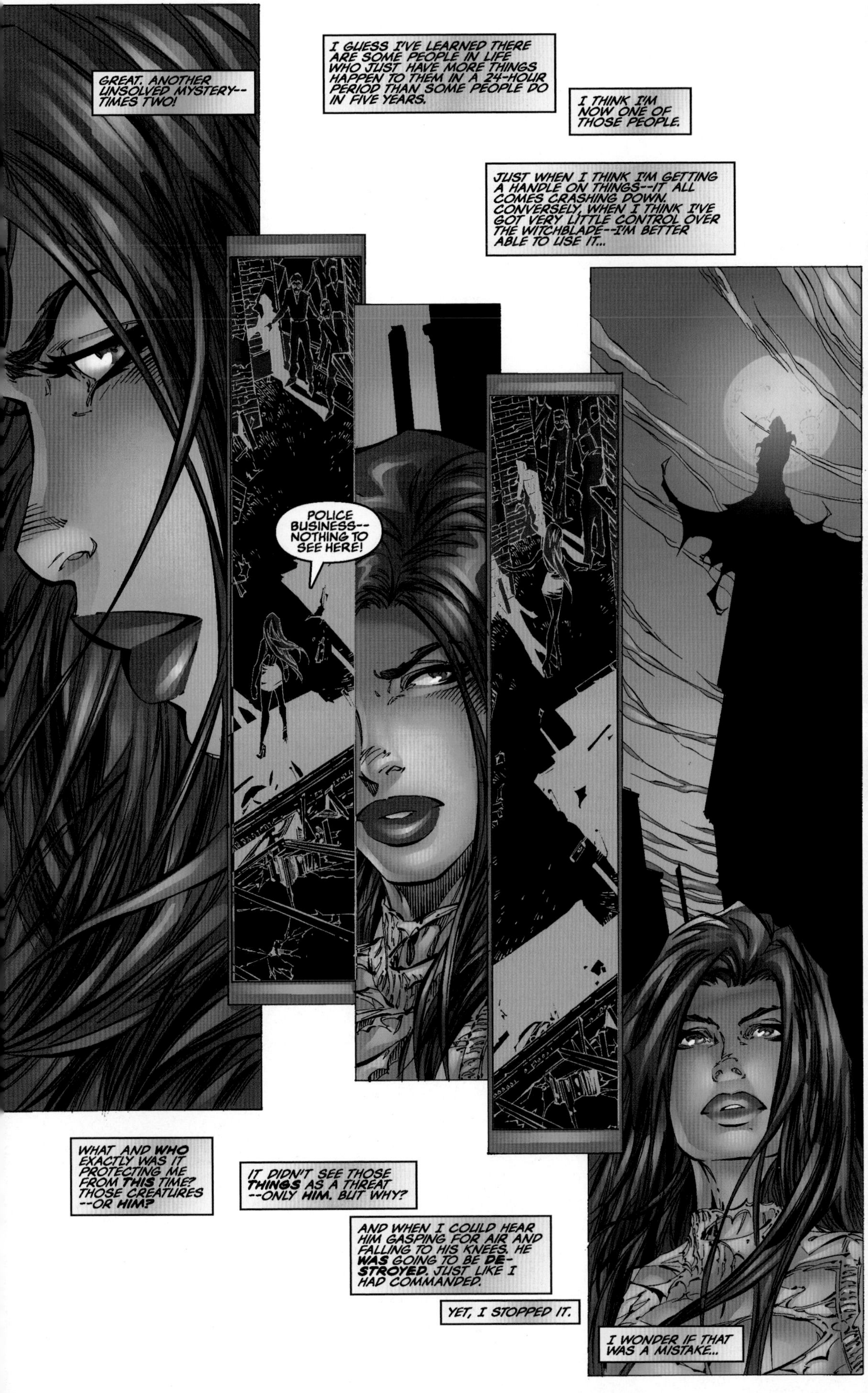
GREAT. ANOTHER UNSOLVED MYSTERY-- TIMES TWO!
I GUESS I'VE LEARNED THERE ARE SOME PEOPLE IN LIFE WHO JUST HAVE MORE THINGS HAPPEN TO THEM IN A 24-HOUR PERIOD THAN SOME PEOPLE DO IN FIVE YEARS.
I THINK I'M NOW ONE OF THOSE PEOPLE.
JUST WHEN I THINK I'M GETTING A HANDLE ON THINGS--IT ALL COMES CRASHING DOWN. CONVERSELY, WHEN I THINK I'VE GOT VERY LITTLE CONTROL OVER THE WITCHBLADE--I'M BETTER ABLE TO USE IT...
POLICE BUSINESS-- NOTHING TO SEE HERE!
WHAT AND WHO EXACTLY WAS IT PROTECTING ME FROM THIS TIME? THOSE CREATURES --OR HIM?
IT DIDN'T SEE THOSE THINGS AS A THREAT --ONLY HIM. BUT WHY?
AND WHEN I COULD HEAR HIM GASPING FOR AIR AND FALLING TO HIS KNEES. HE WAS GOING TO BE DE-STROYED. JUST LIKE I HAD COMMANDED.
YET, I STOPPED IT.
I WONDER IF THAT WAS A MISTAKE...

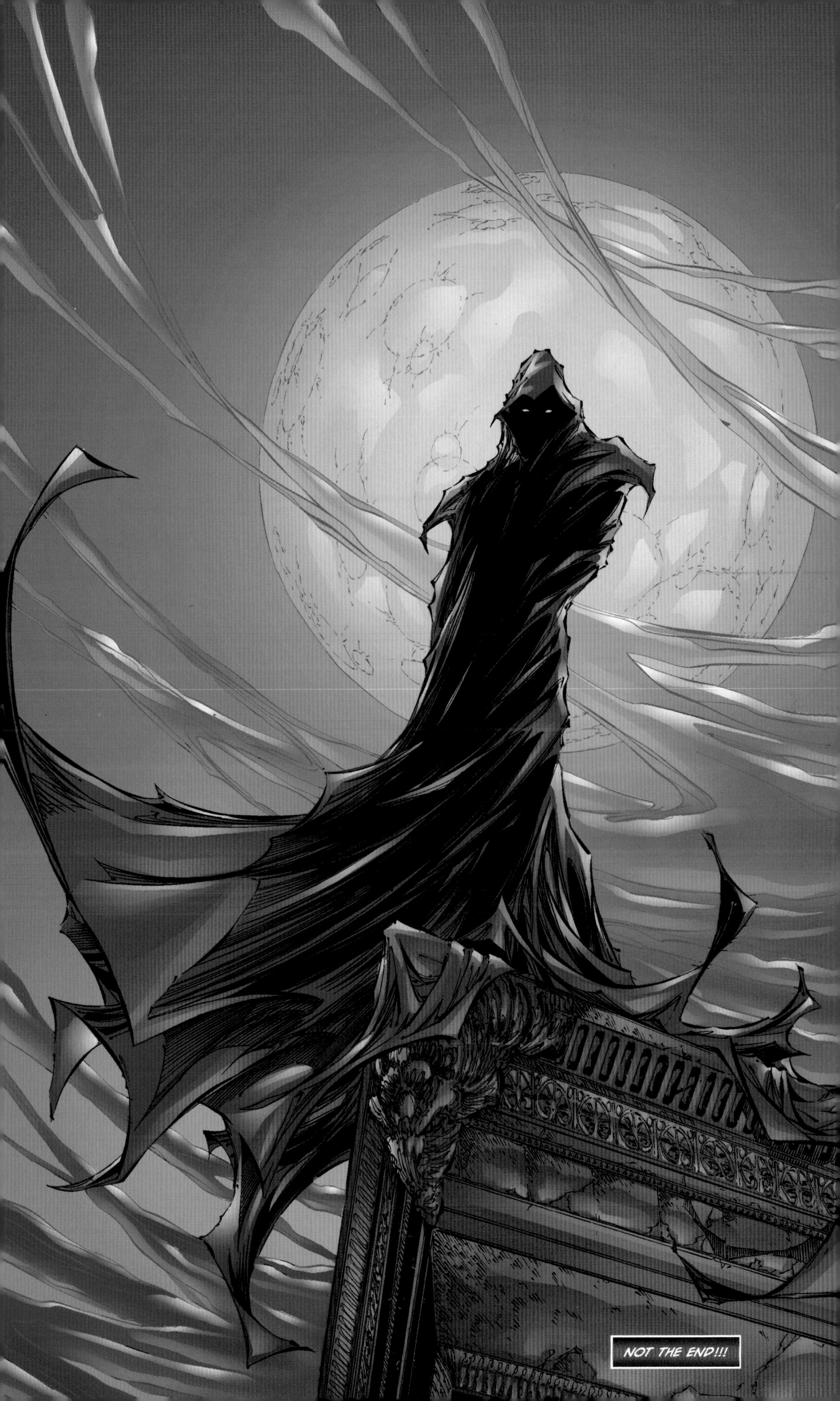
NOT THE END!!!

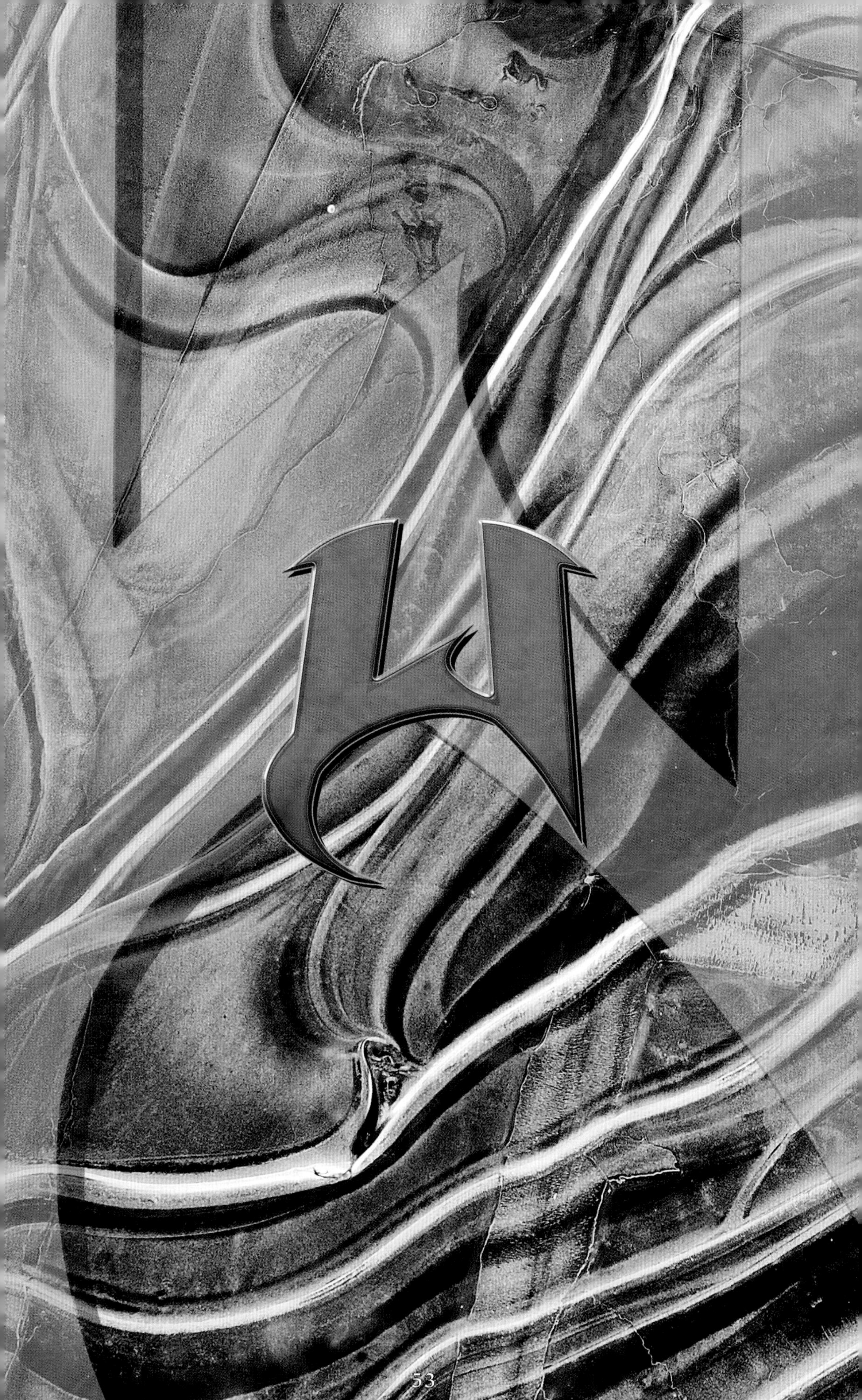
4

#11
ıssve

story: **David Wohl** and **Christina Z.**
pencils: **Michael Turner**
inks: **D-Tron**
colors: **JD Smith**

ink assists: **Jose "Jag" Guillen, Jeff Santo, Andy Kim** and **Viet Trong**

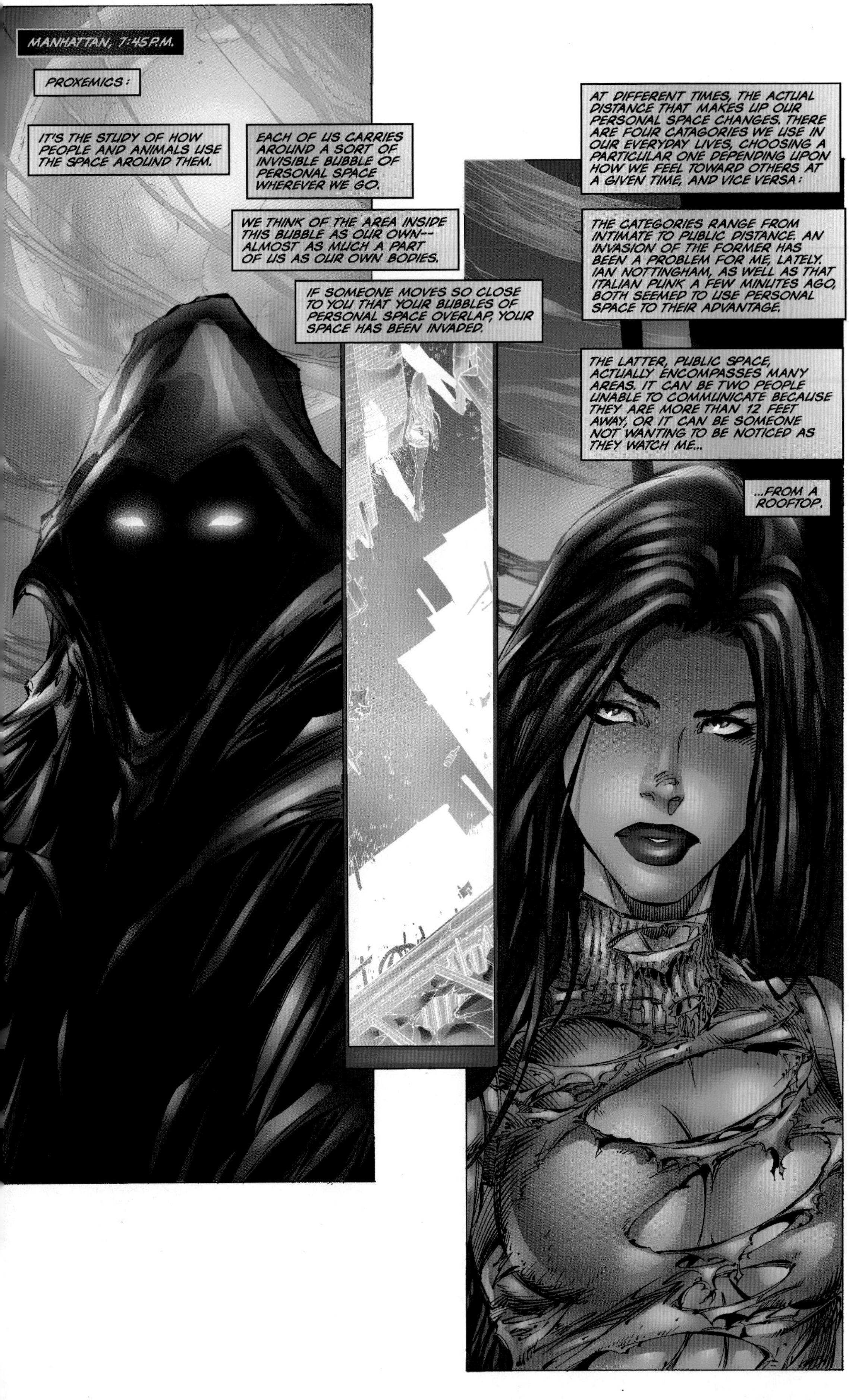

MANHATTAN, 7:45 P.M.
PROXEMICS:
IT'S THE STUDY OF HOW PEOPLE AND ANIMALS USE THE SPACE AROUND THEM.
EACH OF US CARRIES AROUND A SORT OF INVISIBLE BUBBLE OF PERSONAL SPACE WHEREVER WE GO.
WE THINK OF THE AREA INSIDE THIS BUBBLE AS OUR OWN--ALMOST AS MUCH A PART OF US AS OUR OWN BODIES.
IF SOMEONE MOVES SO CLOSE TO YOU THAT YOUR BUBBLES OF PERSONAL SPACE OVERLAP, YOUR SPACE HAS BEEN INVADED.
AT DIFFERENT TIMES, THE ACTUAL DISTANCE THAT MAKES UP OUR PERSONAL SPACE CHANGES. THERE ARE FOUR CATAGORIES WE USE IN OUR EVERYDAY LIVES, CHOOSING A PARTICULAR ONE DEPENDING UPON HOW WE FEEL TOWARD OTHERS AT A GIVEN TIME, AND VICE VERSA:
THE CATEGORIES RANGE FROM INTIMATE TO PUBLIC DISTANCE. AN INVASION OF THE FORMER HAS BEEN A PROBLEM FOR ME, LATELY. IAN NOTTINGHAM, AS WELL AS THAT ITALIAN PUNK A FEW MINUTES AGO, BOTH SEEMED TO USE PERSONAL SPACE TO THEIR ADVANTAGE.
THE LATTER, PUBLIC SPACE, ACTUALLY ENCOMPASSES MANY AREAS. IT CAN BE TWO PEOPLE UNABLE TO COMMUNICATE BECAUSE THEY ARE MORE THAN 12 FEET AWAY, OR IT CAN BE SOMEONE NOT WANTING TO BE NOTICED AS THEY WATCH ME...
...FROM A ROOFTOP.

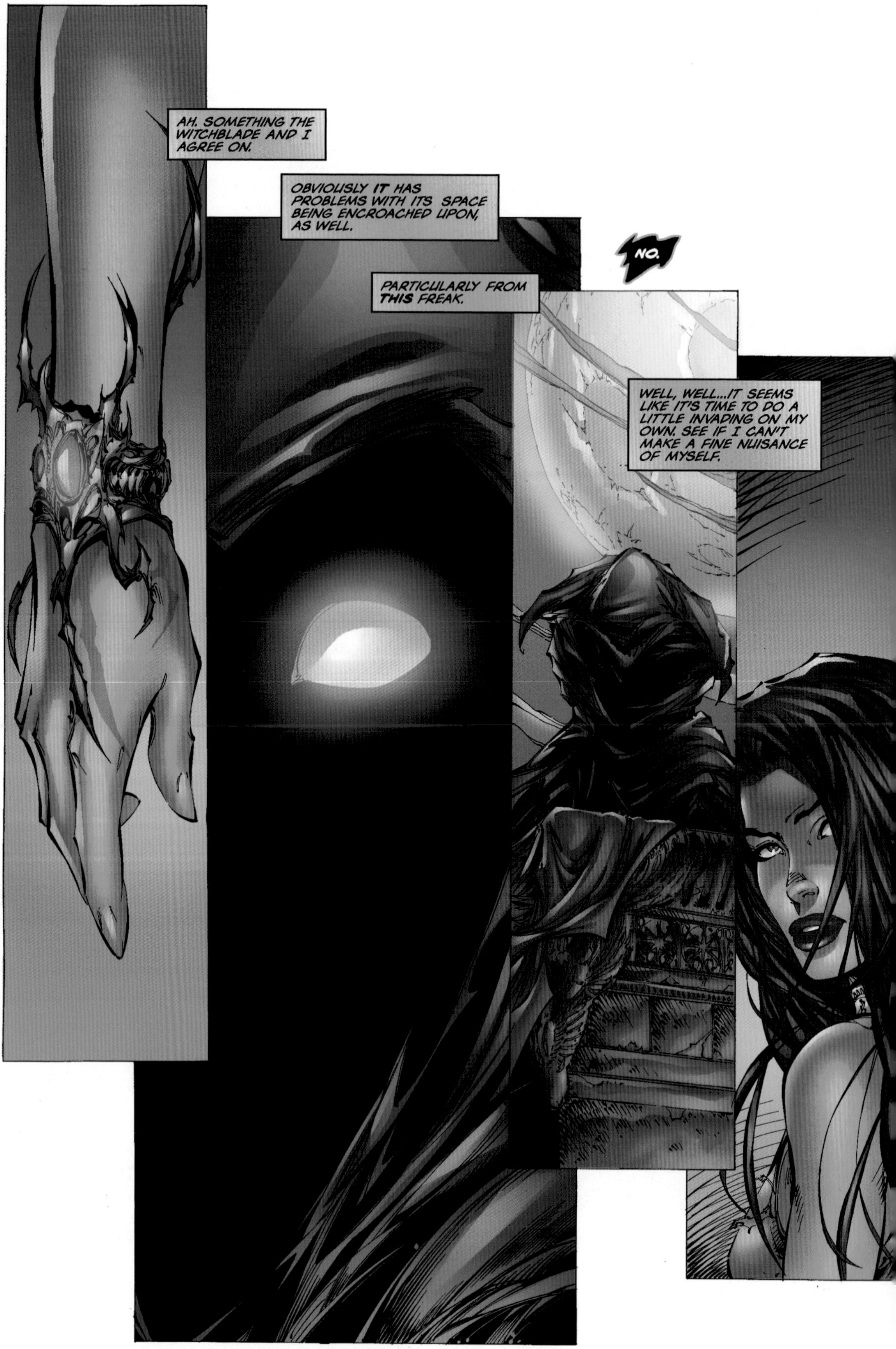
AH. SOMETHING THE WITCHBLADE AND I AGREE ON.
OBVIOUSLY IT HAS PROBLEMS WITH ITS SPACE BEING ENCROACHED UPON, AS WELL.
PARTICULARLY FROM THIS FREAK.
NO.
WELL, WELL...IT SEEMS LIKE IT'S TIME TO DO A LITTLE INVADING ON MY OWN. SEE IF I CAN'T MAKE A FINE NUISANCE OF MYSELF.

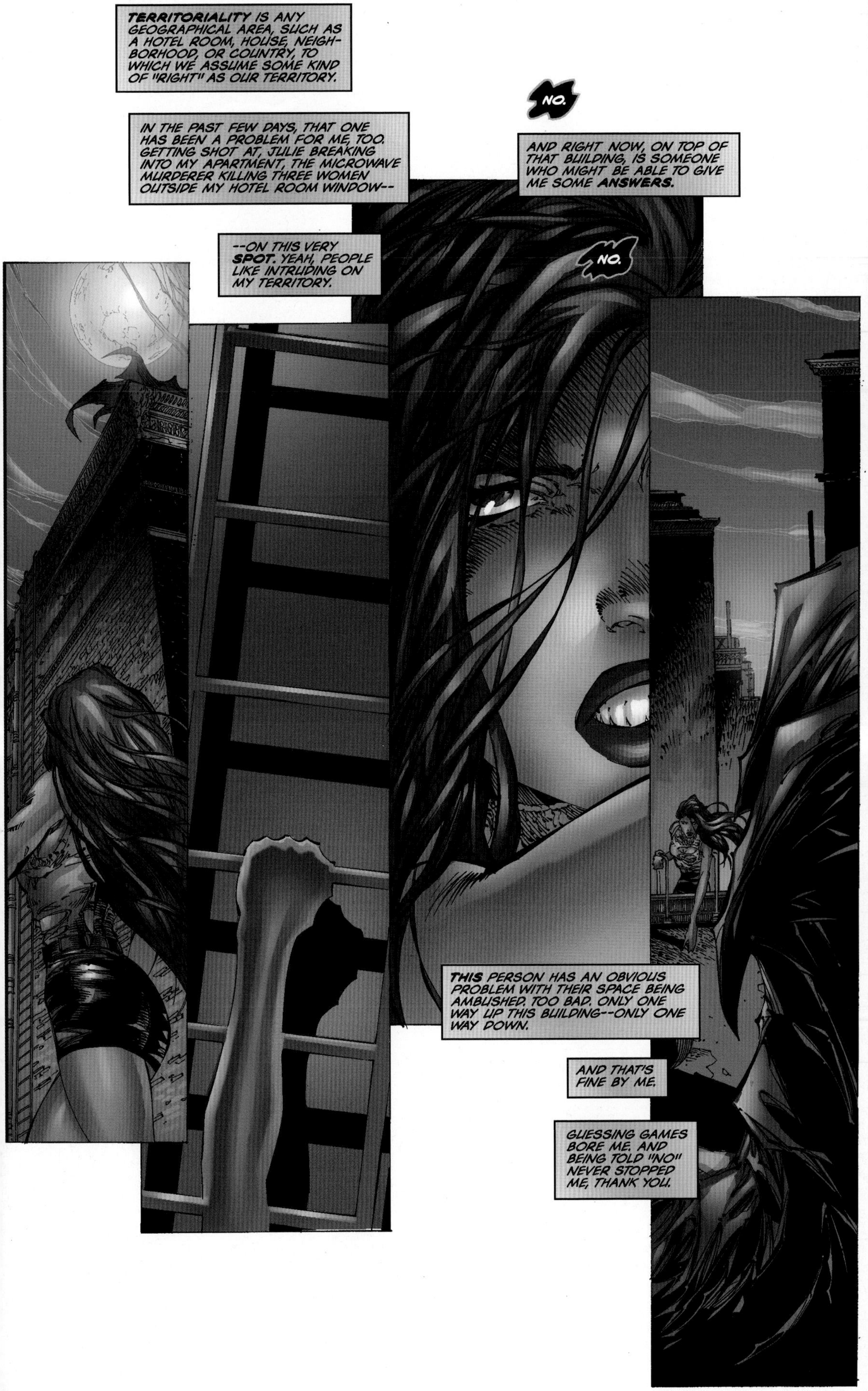
TERRITORIALITY IS ANY GEOGRAPHICAL AREA, SUCH AS A HOTEL ROOM, HOUSE, NEIGHBORHOOD, OR COUNTRY, TO WHICH WE ASSUME SOME KIND OF "RIGHT" AS OUR TERRITORY.
IN THE PAST FEW DAYS, THAT ONE HAS BEEN A PROBLEM FOR ME, TOO. GETTING SHOT AT, JULIE BREAKING INTO MY APARTMENT, THE MICROWAVE MURDERER KILLING THREE WOMEN OUTSIDE MY HOTEL ROOM WINDOW--
--ON THIS VERY SPOT. YEAH, PEOPLE LIKE INTRUDING ON MY TERRITORY.
NO.
AND RIGHT NOW, ON TOP OF THAT BUILDING, IS SOMEONE WHO MIGHT BE ABLE TO GIVE ME SOME ANSWERS.
NO.
THIS PERSON HAS AN OBVIOUS PROBLEM WITH THEIR SPACE BEING AMBUSHED. TOO BAD. ONLY ONE WAY UP THIS BUILDING--ONLY ONE WAY DOWN.
AND THAT'S FINE BY ME.
GUESSING GAMES BORE ME. AND BEING TOLD "NO" NEVER STOPPED ME, THANK YOU.

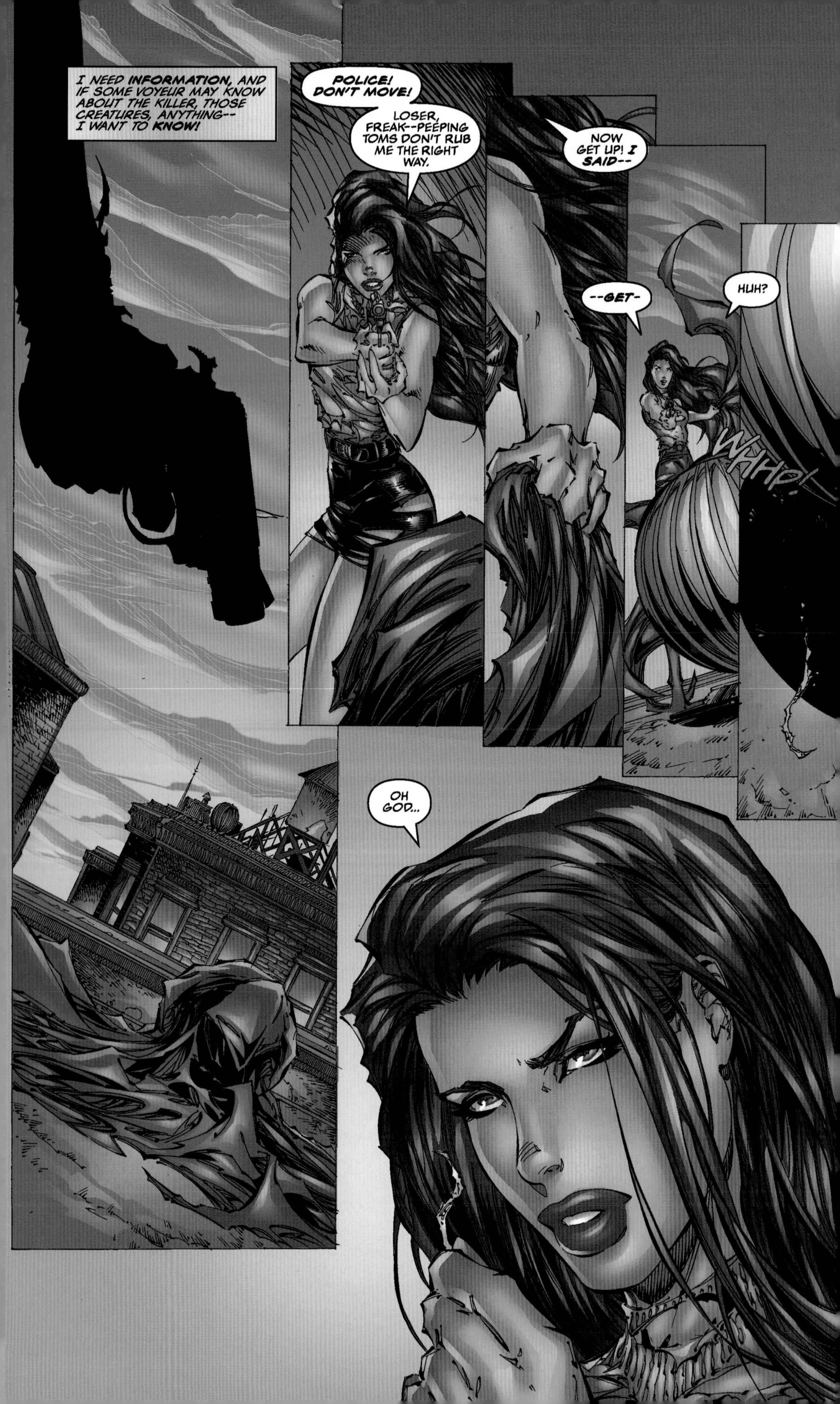
I NEED INFORMATION, AND IF SOME VOYEUR MAY KNOW ABOUT THE KILLER, THOSE CREATURES, ANYTHING-- I WANT TO KNOW!
POLICE! DON'T MOVE!
LOSER, FREAK--PEEPING TOMS DON'T RUB ME THE RIGHT WAY.
NOW GET UP! I SAID--
--GET-
HUH?
WHHP!
OH GOD...

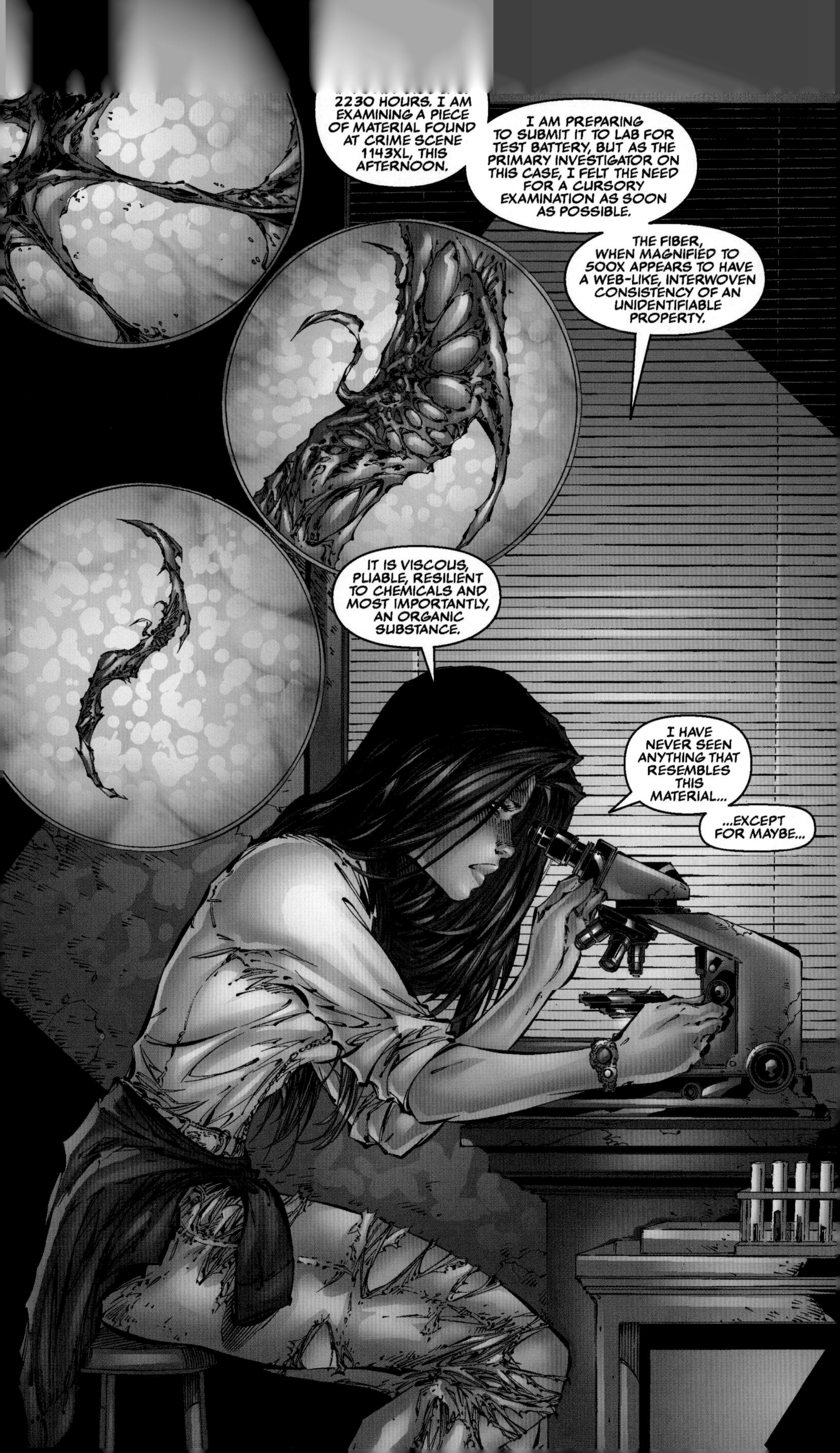
2230 HOURS. I AM EXAMINING A PIECE OF MATERIAL FOUND AT CRIME SCENE 1143XL, THIS AFTERNOON.
I AM PREPARING TO SUBMIT IT TO LAB FOR TEST BATTERY, BUT AS THE PRIMARY INVESTIGATOR ON THIS CASE, I FELT THE NEED FOR A CURSORY EXAMINATION AS SOON AS POSSIBLE.
THE FIBER, WHEN MAGNIFIED TO 500X APPEARS TO HAVE A WEB-LIKE, INTERWOVEN CONSISTENCY OF AN UNIDENTIFIABLE PROPERTY.
IT IS VISCOUS, PLIABLE, RESILIENT TO CHEMICALS AND MOST IMPORTANTLY, AN ORGANIC SUBSTANCE.
I HAVE NEVER SEEN ANYTHING THAT RESEMBLES THIS MATERIAL...
...EXCEPT FOR MAYBE...

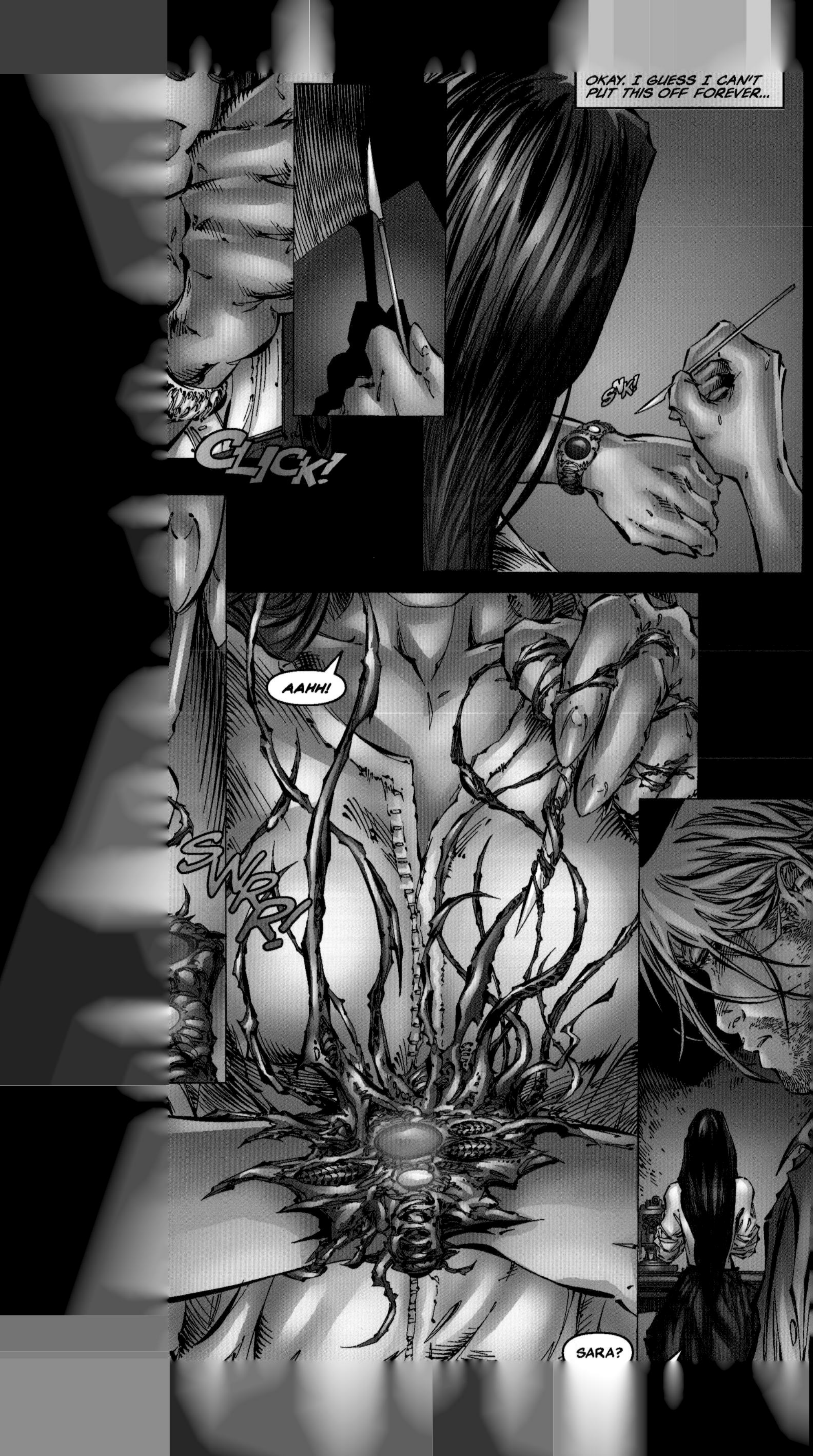

OKAY. I GUESS I CAN'T PUT THIS OFF FOREVER...
CLICK!
SNK!
AAHH!
SWRR!
SARA?

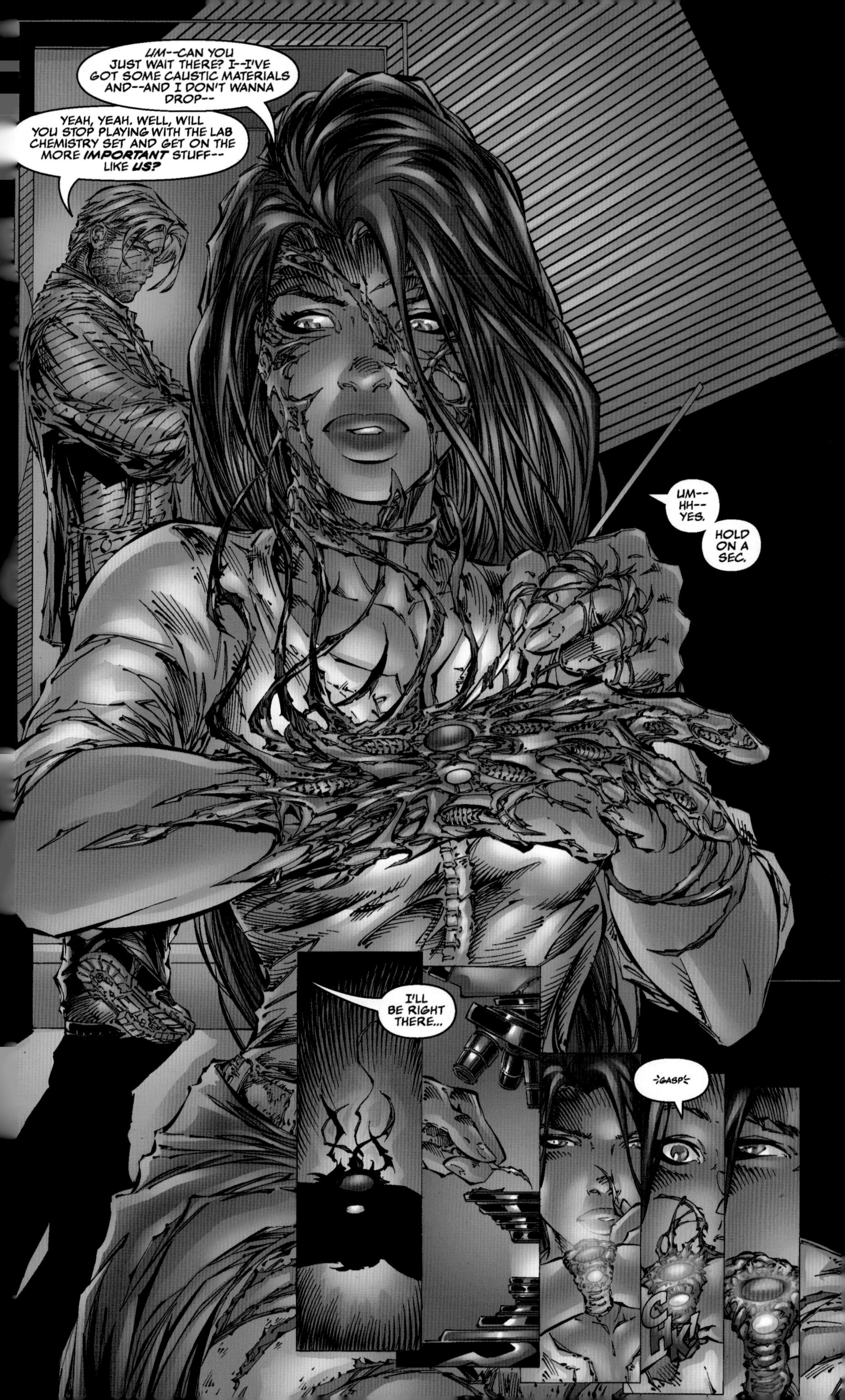
UM--CAN YOU JUST WAIT THERE? I--I'VE GOT SOME CAUSTIC MATERIALS AND--AND I DON'T WANNA DROP--
YEAH, YEAH. WELL, WILL YOU STOP PLAYING WITH THE LAB CHEMISTRY SET AND GET ON THE MORE IMPORTANT STUFF-- LIKE US?
UM-- HH-- YES.
HOLD ON A SEC.
I'LL BE RIGHT THERE...
GASP

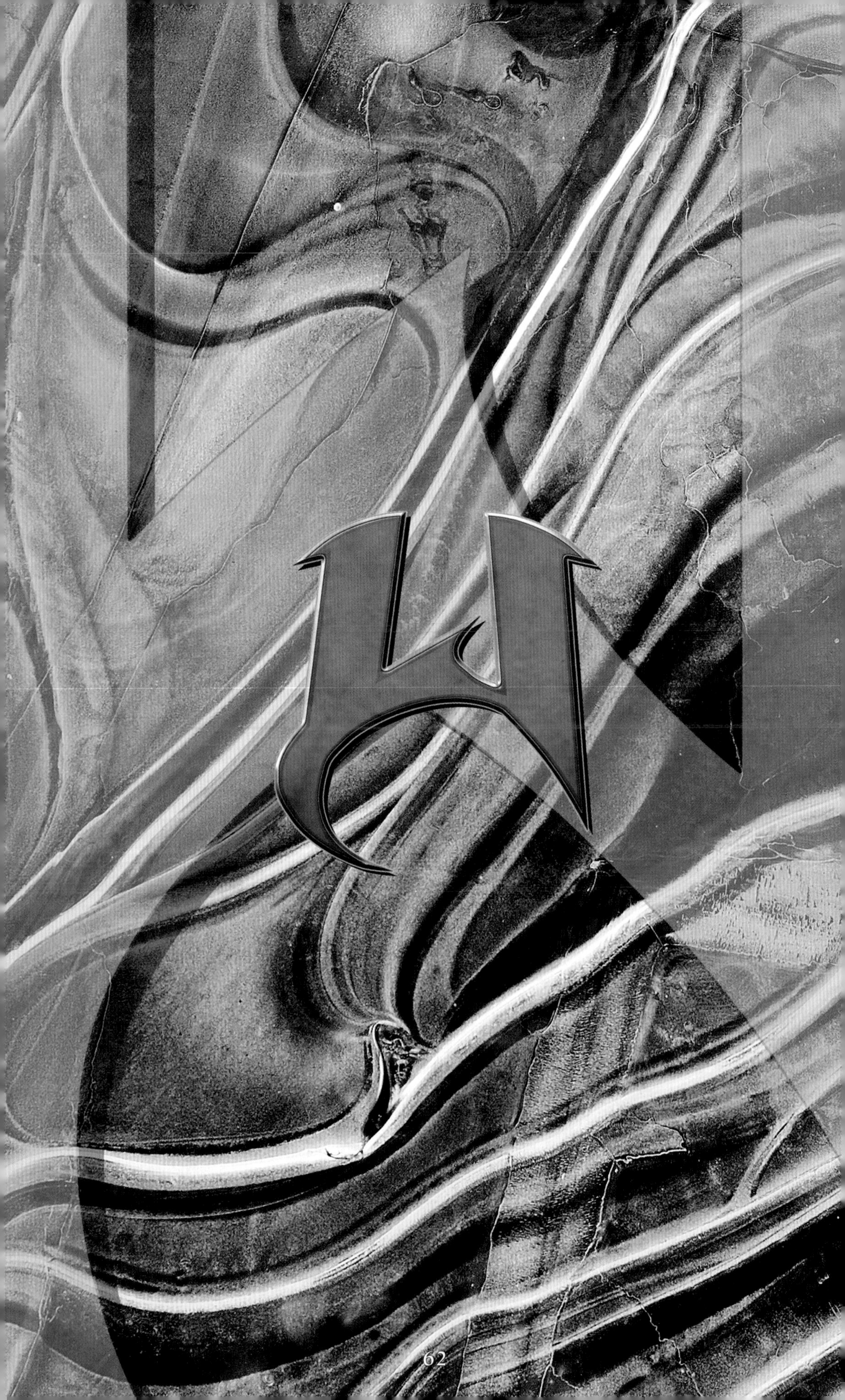

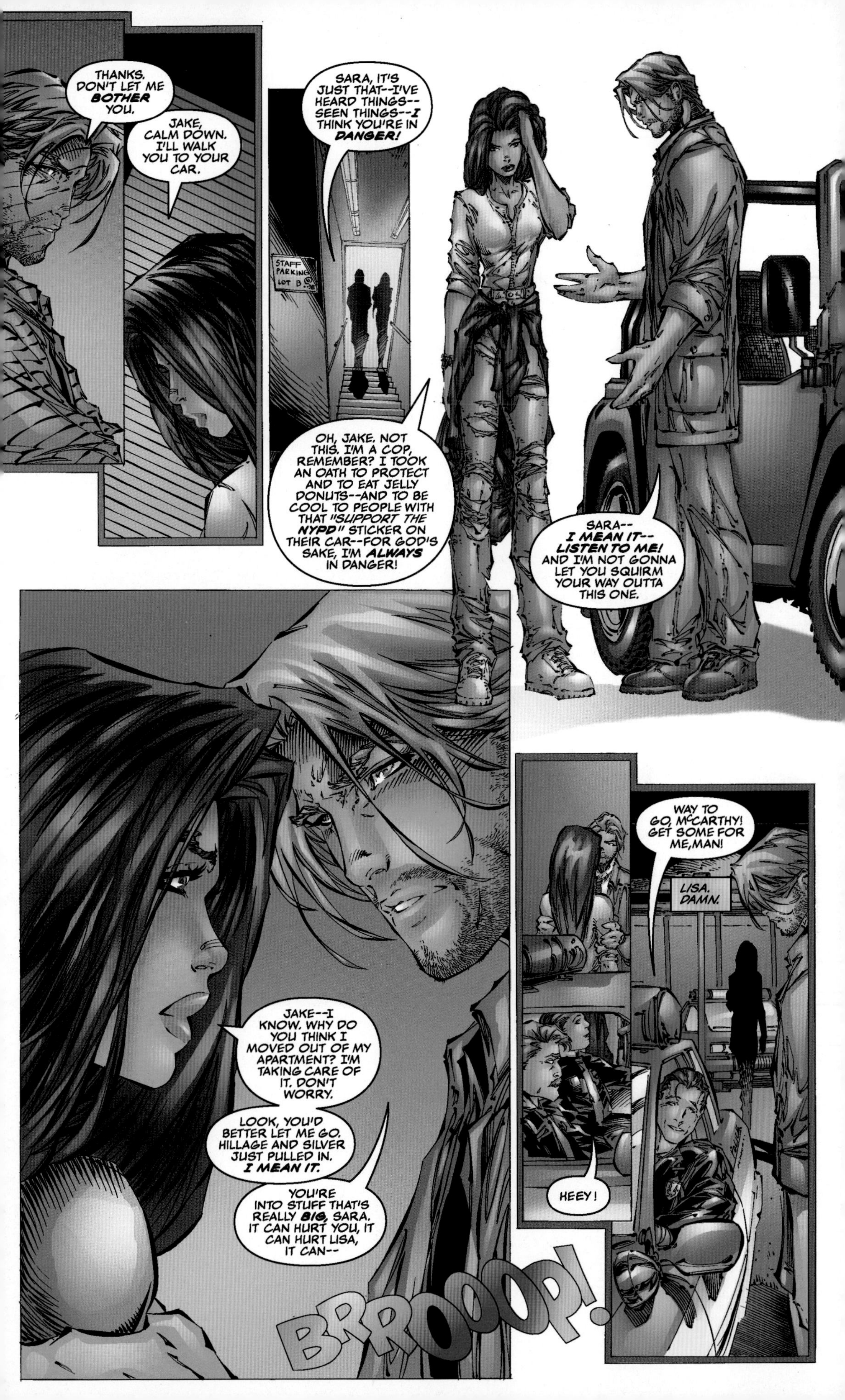
THANKS. DON'T LET ME BOTHER YOU.
JAKE, CALM DOWN. I'LL WALK YOU TO YOUR CAR.
SARA, IT'S JUST THAT--I'VE HEARD THINGS--SEEN THINGS--I THINK YOU'RE IN DANGER!
STAFF PARKING LOT B
OH, JAKE. NOT THIS. I'M A COP, REMEMBER? I TOOK AN OATH TO PROTECT AND TO EAT JELLY DONUTS--AND TO BE COOL TO PEOPLE WITH THAT "SUPPORT THE NYPD" STICKER ON THEIR CAR--FOR GOD'S SAKE, I'M ALWAYS IN DANGER!
SARA-- I MEAN IT-- LISTEN TO ME! AND I'M NOT GONNA LET YOU SQUIRM YOUR WAY OUTTA THIS ONE.
JAKE--I KNOW. WHY DO YOU THINK I MOVED OUT OF MY APARTMENT? I'M TAKING CARE OF IT. DON'T WORRY.
LOOK, YOU'D BETTER LET ME GO. HILLAGE AND SILVER JUST PULLED IN. I MEAN IT.
YOU'RE INTO STUFF THAT'S REALLY BIG, SARA. IT CAN HURT YOU, IT CAN HURT LISA, IT CAN--
WAY TO GO, McCARTHY! GET SOME FOR ME, MAN!
LISA. DAMN.
HEEY!
BRROOOP!

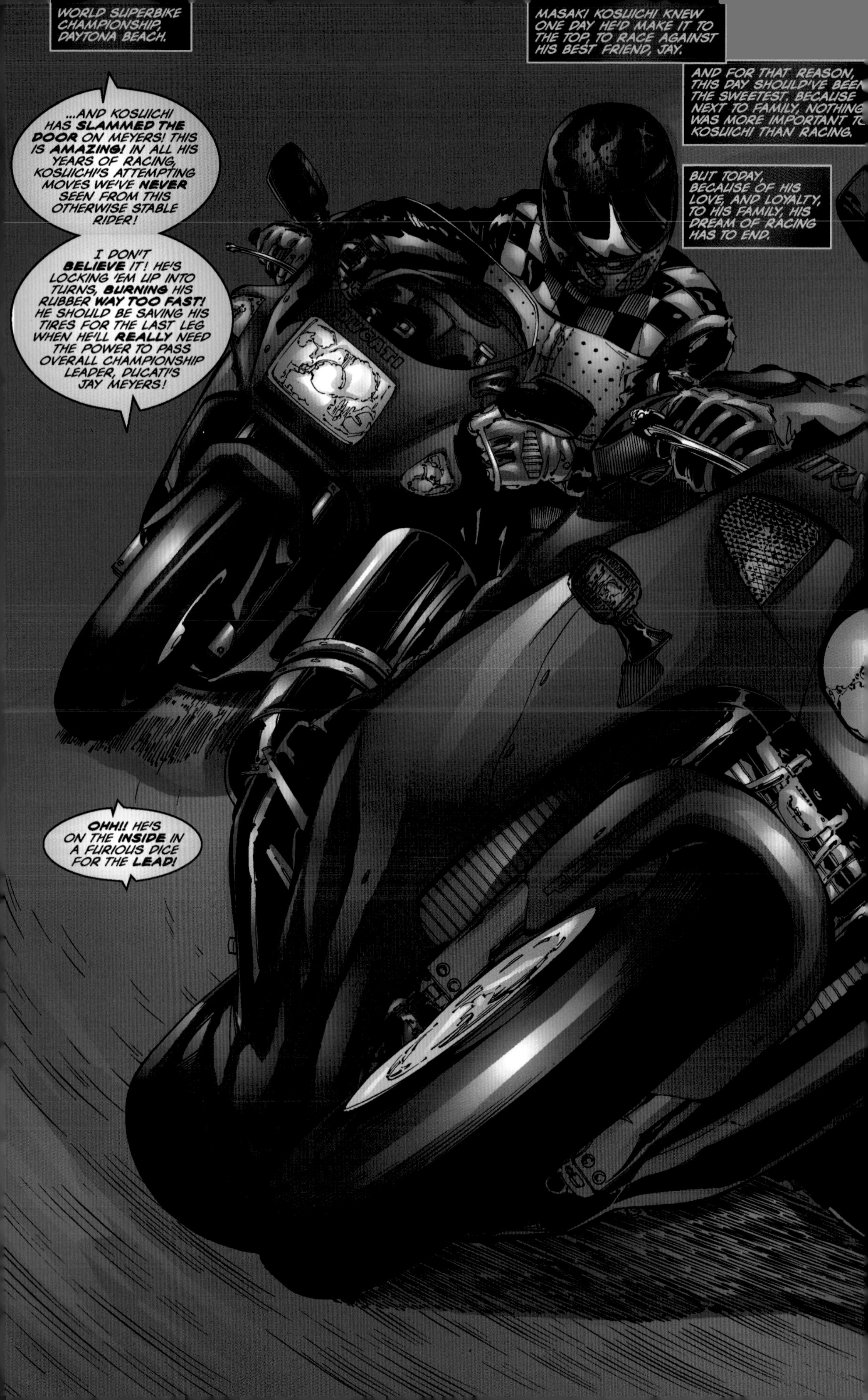
WORLD SUPERBIKE CHAMPIONSHIP, DAYTONA BEACH.
MASAKI KOSUICHI KNEW ONE DAY HE'D MAKE IT TO THE TOP, TO RACE AGAINST HIS BEST FRIEND, JAY.
AND FOR THAT REASON, THIS DAY SHOULD'VE BEEN THE SWEETEST. BECAUSE NEXT TO FAMILY, NOTHING WAS MORE IMPORTANT TO KOSUICHI THAN RACING.
BUT TODAY, BECAUSE OF HIS LOVE, AND LOYALTY, TO HIS FAMILY, HIS DREAM OF RACING HAS TO END.
...AND KOSUICHI HAS SLAMMED THE DOOR ON MEYERS! THIS IS AMAZING! IN ALL HIS YEARS OF RACING, KOSUICHI'S ATTEMPTING MOVES WE'VE NEVER SEEN FROM THIS OTHERWISE STABLE RIDER!
I DON'T BELIEVE IT! HE'S LOCKING 'EM UP INTO TURNS, BURNING HIS RUBBER WAY TOO FAST! HE SHOULD BE SAVING HIS TIRES FOR THE LAST LEG WHEN HE'LL REALLY NEED THE POWER TO PASS OVERALL CHAMPIONSHIP LEADER, DUCATI'S JAY MEYERS!
OHH!! HE'S ON THE INSIDE IN A FURIOUS DICE FOR THE LEAD!

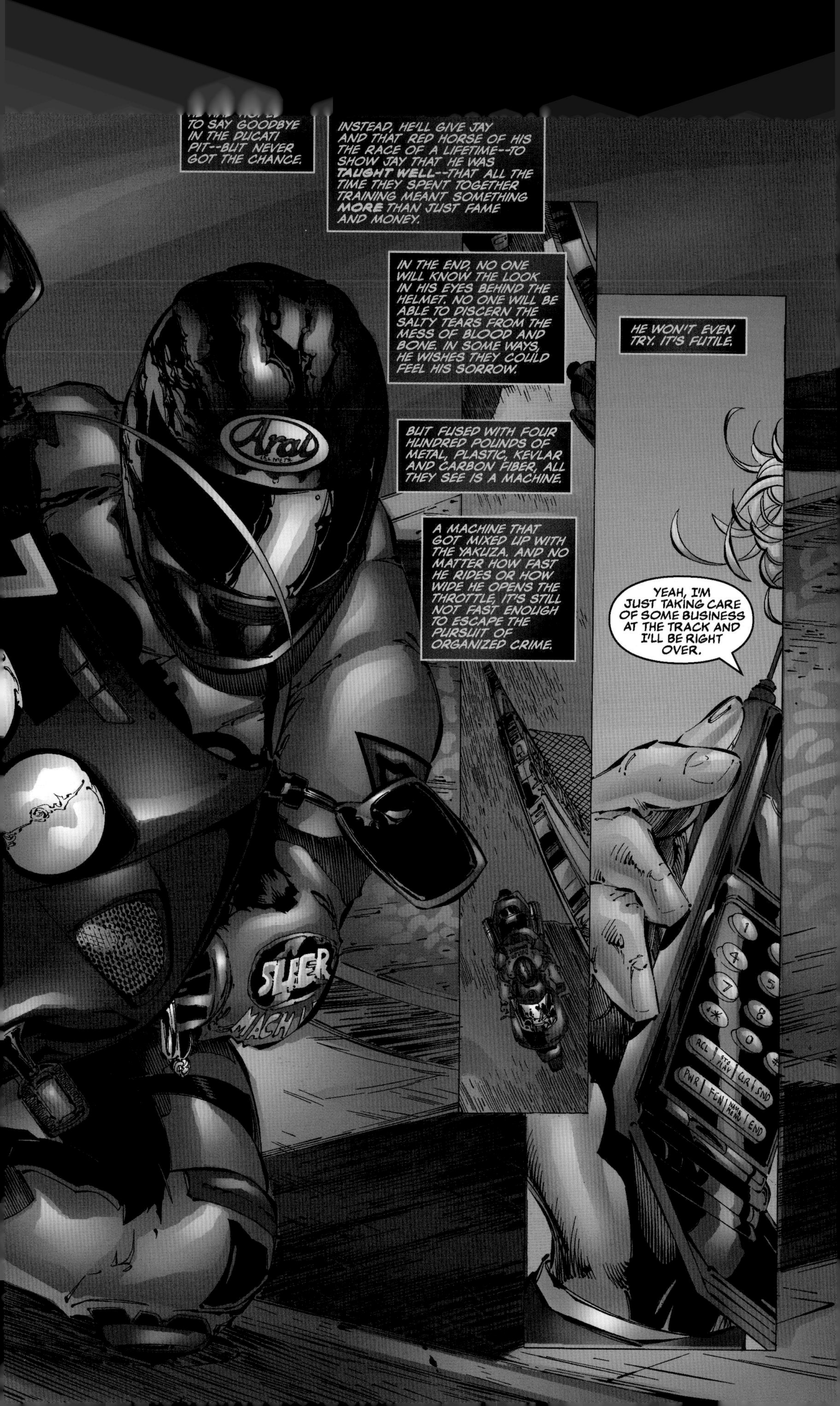

TO SAY GOODBYE IN THE DUCATI PIT--BUT NEVER GOT THE CHANCE.
INSTEAD, HE'LL GIVE JAY AND THAT RED HORSE OF HIS THE RACE OF A LIFETIME--TO SHOW JAY THAT HE WAS TAUGHT WELL--THAT ALL THE TIME THEY SPENT TOGETHER TRAINING MEANT SOMETHING MORE THAN JUST FAME AND MONEY.
IN THE END, NO ONE WILL KNOW THE LOOK IN HIS EYES BEHIND THE HELMET. NO ONE WILL BE ABLE TO DISCERN THE SALTY TEARS FROM THE MESS OF BLOOD AND BONE. IN SOME WAYS, HE WISHES THEY COULD FEEL HIS SORROW.
BUT FUSED WITH FOUR HUNDRED POUNDS OF METAL, PLASTIC, KEVLAR AND CARBON FIBER, ALL THEY SEE IS A MACHINE.
A MACHINE THAT GOT MIXED UP WITH THE YAKUZA. AND NO MATTER HOW FAST HE RIDES OR HOW WIDE HE OPENS THE THROTTLE, IT'S STILL NOT FAST ENOUGH TO ESCAPE THE PURSUIT OF ORGANIZED CRIME.
HE WON'T EVEN TRY. IT'S FUTILE.
YEAH, I'M JUST TAKING CARE OF SOME BUSINESS AT THE TRACK AND I'LL BE RIGHT OVER.

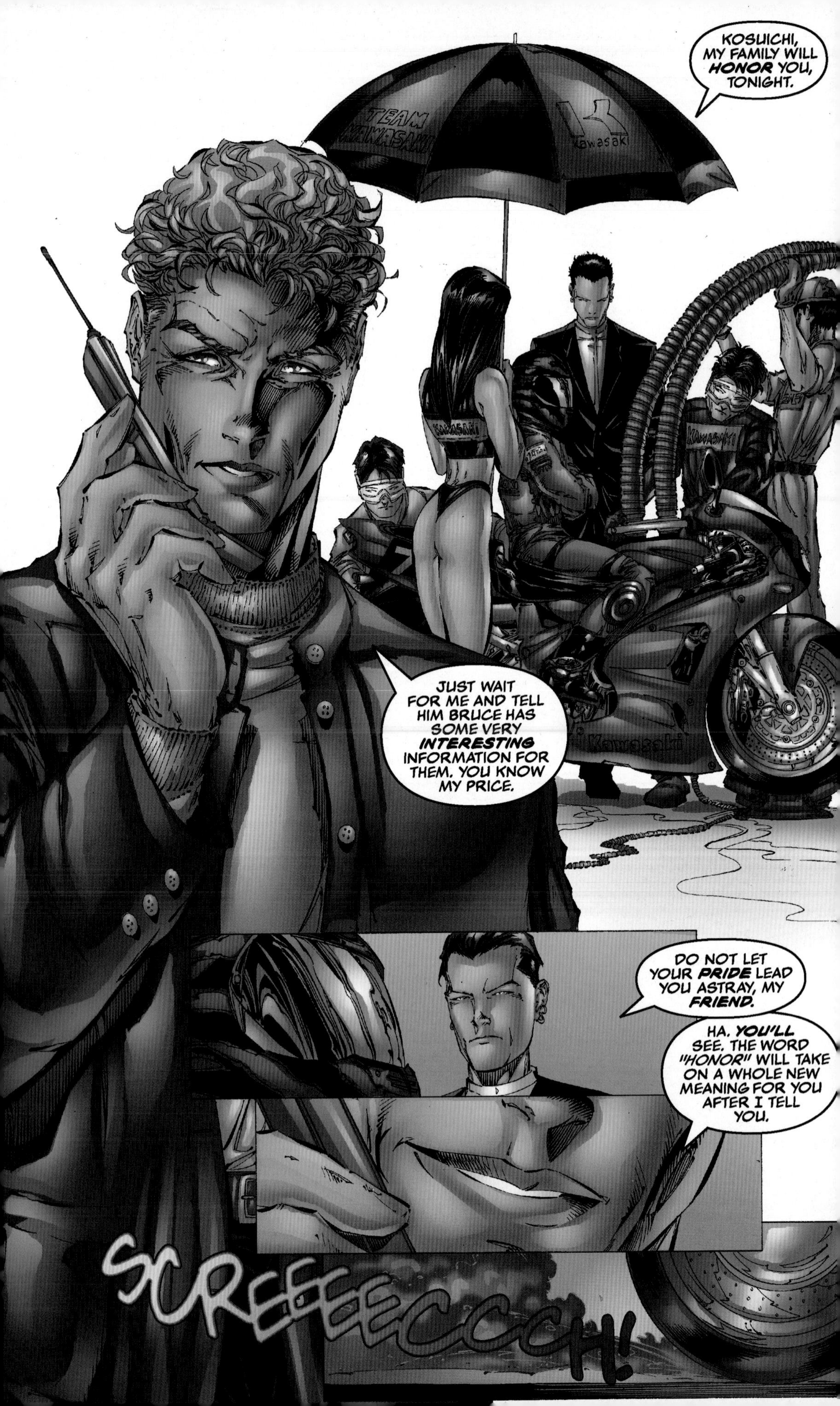
KOSUICHI, MY FAMILY WILL HONOR YOU, TONIGHT.
JUST WAIT FOR ME AND TELL HIM BRUCE HAS SOME VERY INTERESTING INFORMATION FOR THEM. YOU KNOW MY PRICE.
DO NOT LET YOUR PRIDE LEAD YOU ASTRAY, MY FRIEND.
HA. YOU'LL SEE. THE WORD "HONOR" WILL TAKE ON A WHOLE NEW MEANING FOR YOU AFTER I TELL YOU.
SCREEEEECCCH!

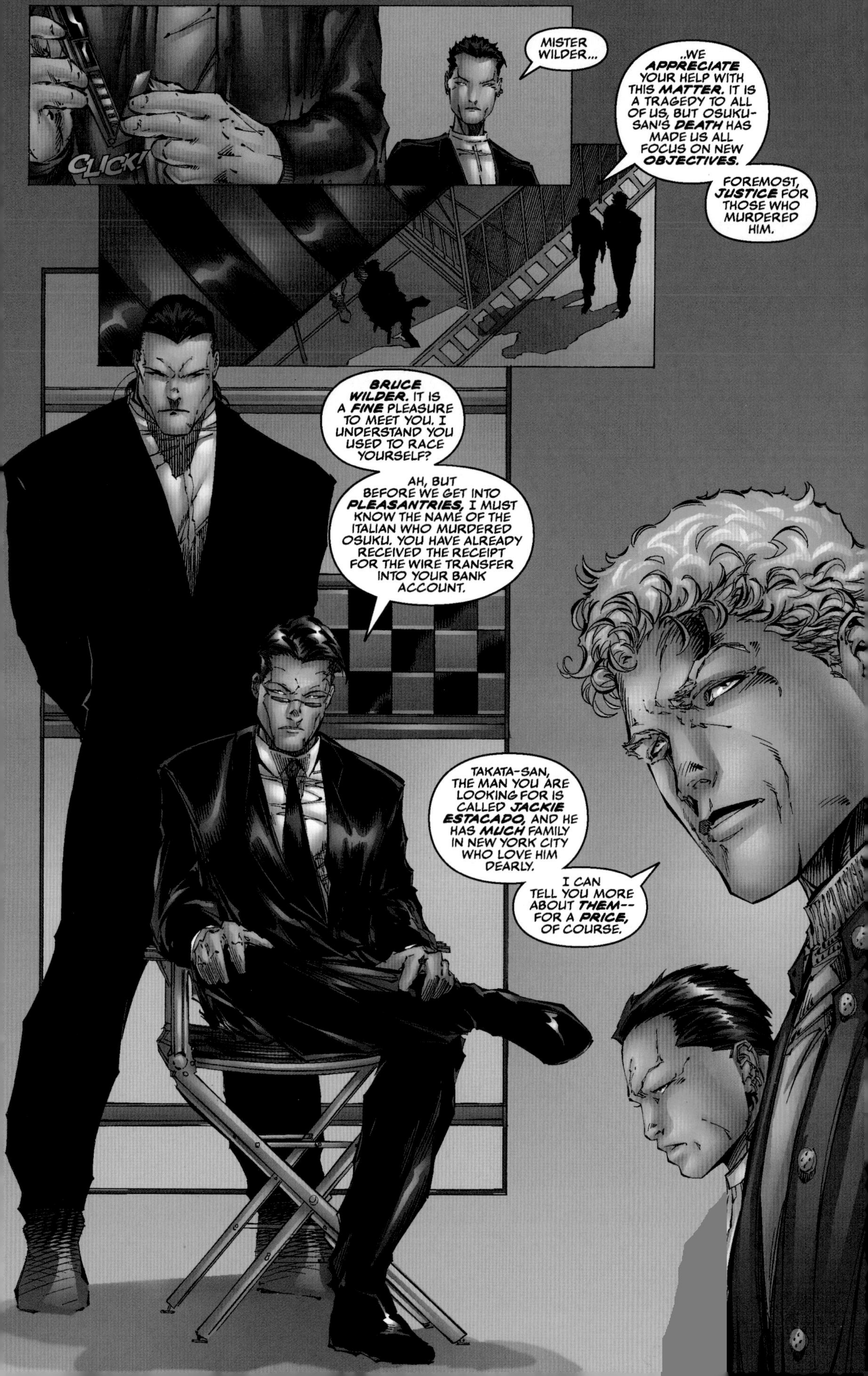
CLICK!
MISTER WILDER...
..WE APPRECIATE YOUR HELP WITH THIS MATTER. IT IS A TRAGEDY TO ALL OF US, BUT OSUKU-SAN'S DEATH HAS MADE US ALL FOCUS ON NEW OBJECTIVES.
FOREMOST, JUSTICE FOR THOSE WHO MURDERED HIM.
BRUCE WILDER. IT IS A FINE PLEASURE TO MEET YOU. I UNDERSTAND YOU USED TO RACE YOURSELF?
AH, BUT BEFORE WE GET INTO PLEASANTRIES, I MUST KNOW THE NAME OF THE ITALIAN WHO MURDERED OSUKU. YOU HAVE ALREADY RECEIVED THE RECEIPT FOR THE WIRE TRANSFER INTO YOUR BANK ACCOUNT.
TAKATA-SAN, THE MAN YOU ARE LOOKING FOR IS CALLED JACKIE ESTACADO, AND HE HAS MUCH FAMILY IN NEW YORK CITY WHO LOVE HIM DEARLY.
I CAN TELL YOU MORE ABOUT THEM-- FOR A PRICE, OF COURSE.

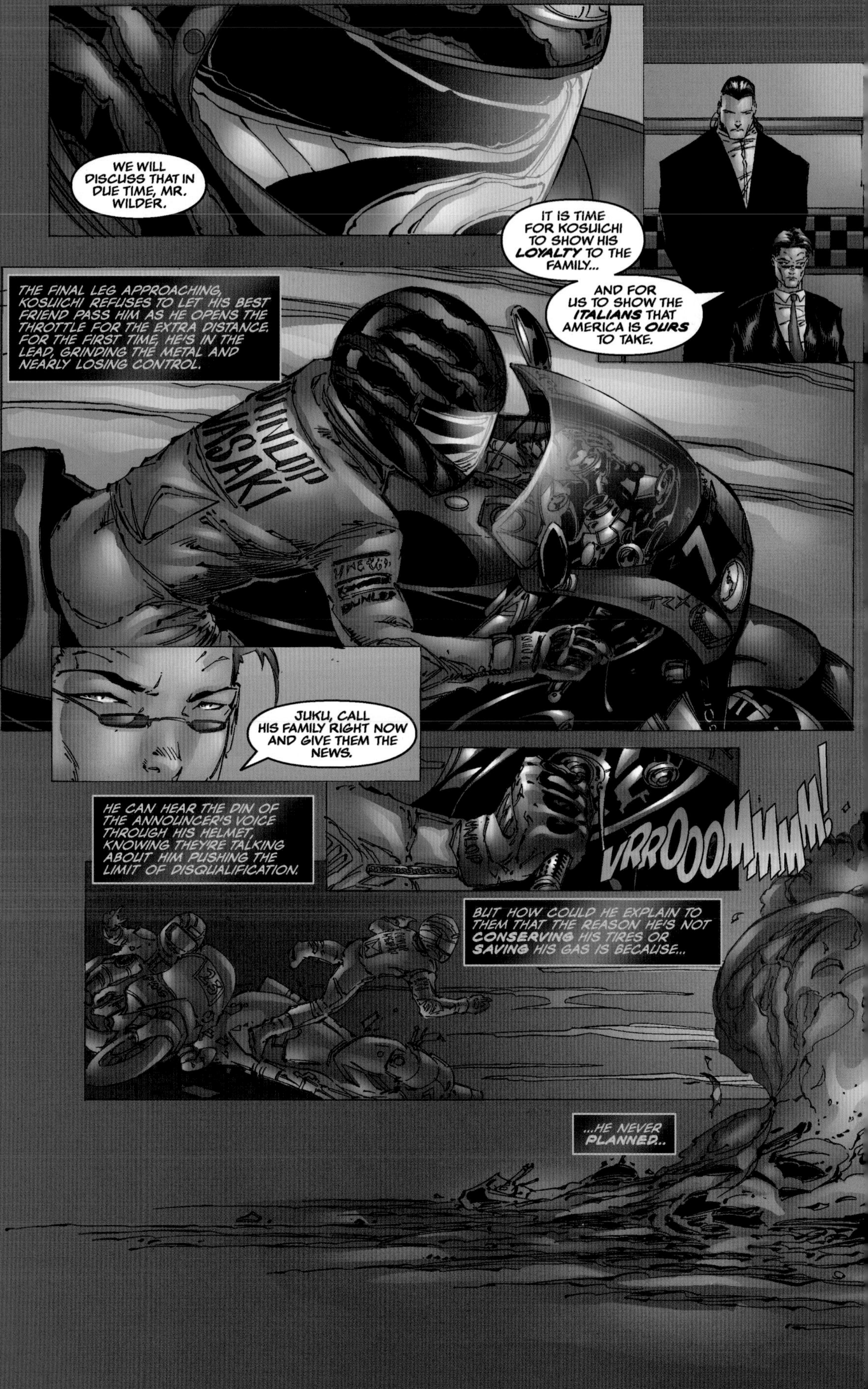
WE WILL DISCUSS THAT IN DUE TIME, MR. WILDER.
IT IS TIME FOR KOSUICHI TO SHOW HIS LOYALTY TO THE FAMILY...
AND FOR US TO SHOW THE ITALIANS THAT AMERICA IS OURS TO TAKE.
THE FINAL LEG APPROACHING, KOSUICHI REFUSES TO LET HIS BEST FRIEND PASS HIM AS HE OPENS THE THROTTLE FOR THE EXTRA DISTANCE. FOR THE FIRST TIME, HE'S IN THE LEAD, GRINDING THE METAL AND NEARLY LOSING CONTROL.
DUNLOP
KAWASAKI
JUKU, CALL HIS FAMILY RIGHT NOW AND GIVE THEM THE NEWS.
HE CAN HEAR THE DIN OF THE ANNOUNCER'S VOICE THROUGH HIS HELMET, KNOWING THEY'RE TALKING ABOUT HIM PUSHING THE LIMIT OF DISQUALIFICATION.
VRROOOMMMM!
BUT HOW COULD HE EXPLAIN TO THEM THAT THE REASON HE'S NOT CONSERVING HIS TIRES OR SAVING HIS GAS IS BECAUSE...
...HE NEVER PLANNED...

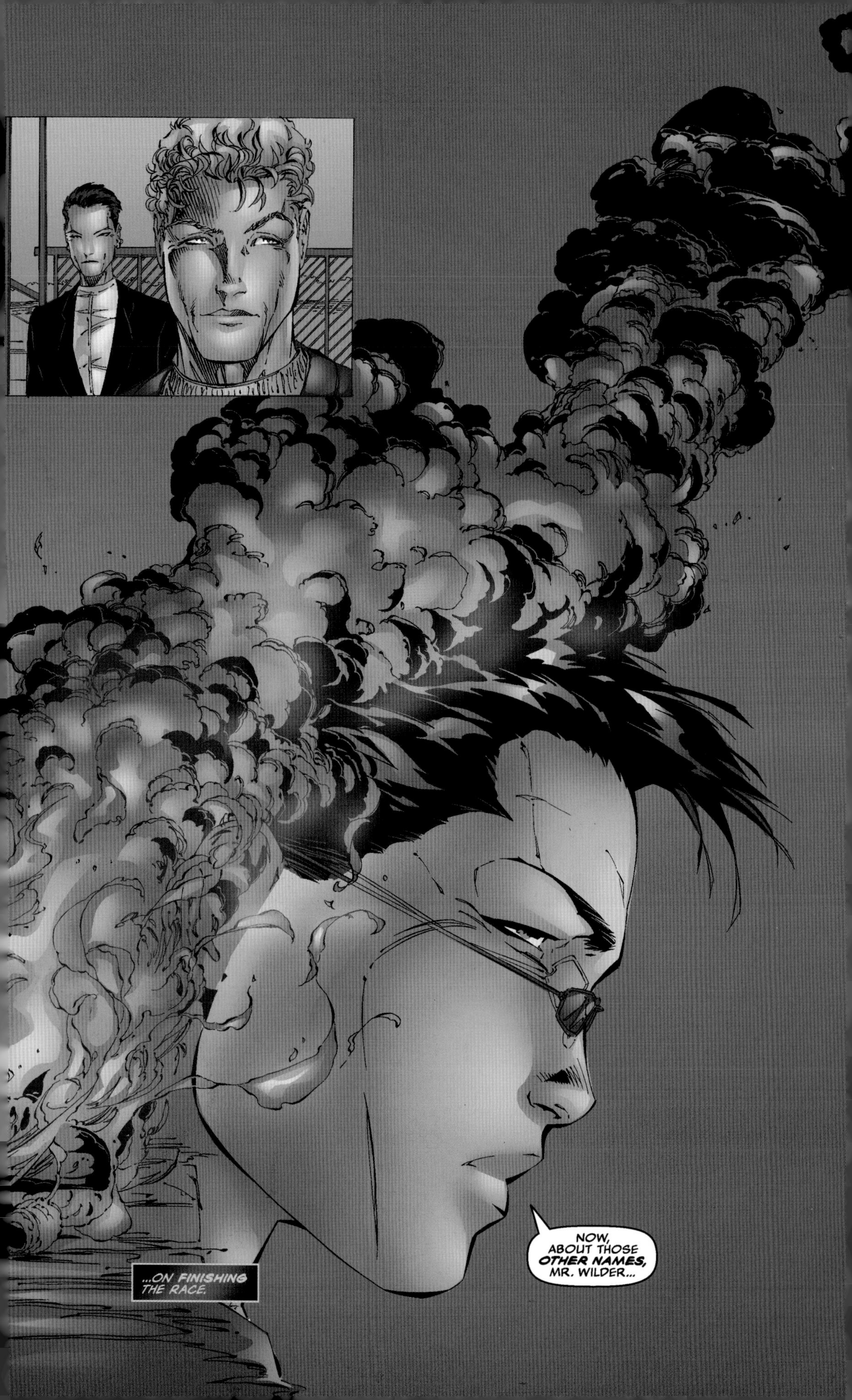
...ON FINISHING THE RACE.
NOW, ABOUT THOSE OTHER NAMES, MR. WILDER...

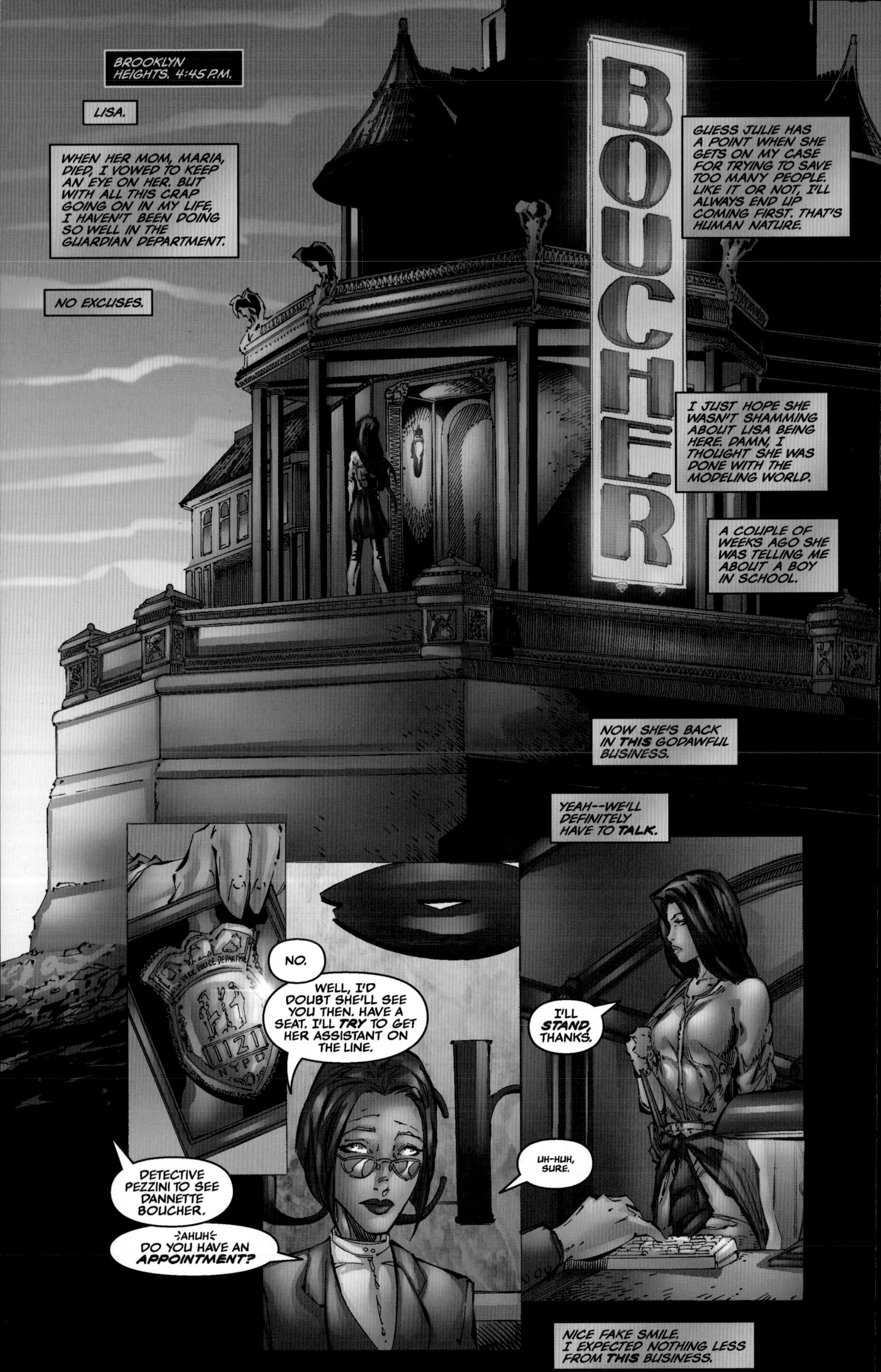
BROOKLYN HEIGHTS. 4:45 P.M.
LISA.
WHEN HER MOM, MARIA, DIED, I VOWED TO KEEP AN EYE ON HER. BUT WITH ALL THIS CRAP GOING ON IN MY LIFE, I HAVEN'T BEEN DOING SO WELL IN THE GUARDIAN DEPARTMENT.
NO EXCUSES.
BOUCHER
GUESS JULIE HAS A POINT WHEN SHE GETS ON MY CASE FOR TRYING TO SAVE TOO MANY PEOPLE. LIKE IT OR NOT, I'LL ALWAYS END UP COMING FIRST. THAT'S HUMAN NATURE.
I JUST HOPE SHE WASN'T SHAMMING ABOUT LISA BEING HERE. DAMN, I THOUGHT SHE WAS DONE WITH THE MODELING WORLD.
A COUPLE OF WEEKS AGO SHE WAS TELLING ME ABOUT A BOY IN SCHOOL.
NOW SHE'S BACK IN THIS GODAWFUL BUSINESS.
YEAH--WE'LL DEFINITELY HAVE TO TALK.
DETECTIVE PEZZINI TO SEE DANNETTE BOUCHER.
AHUH
DO YOU HAVE AN APPOINTMENT?
NO.
WELL, I'D DOUBT SHE'LL SEE YOU THEN. HAVE A SEAT. I'LL TRY TO GET HER ASSISTANT ON THE LINE.
I'LL STAND, THANKS.
UH-HUH, SURE.
NICE FAKE SMILE. I EXPECTED NOTHING LESS FROM THIS BUSINESS.

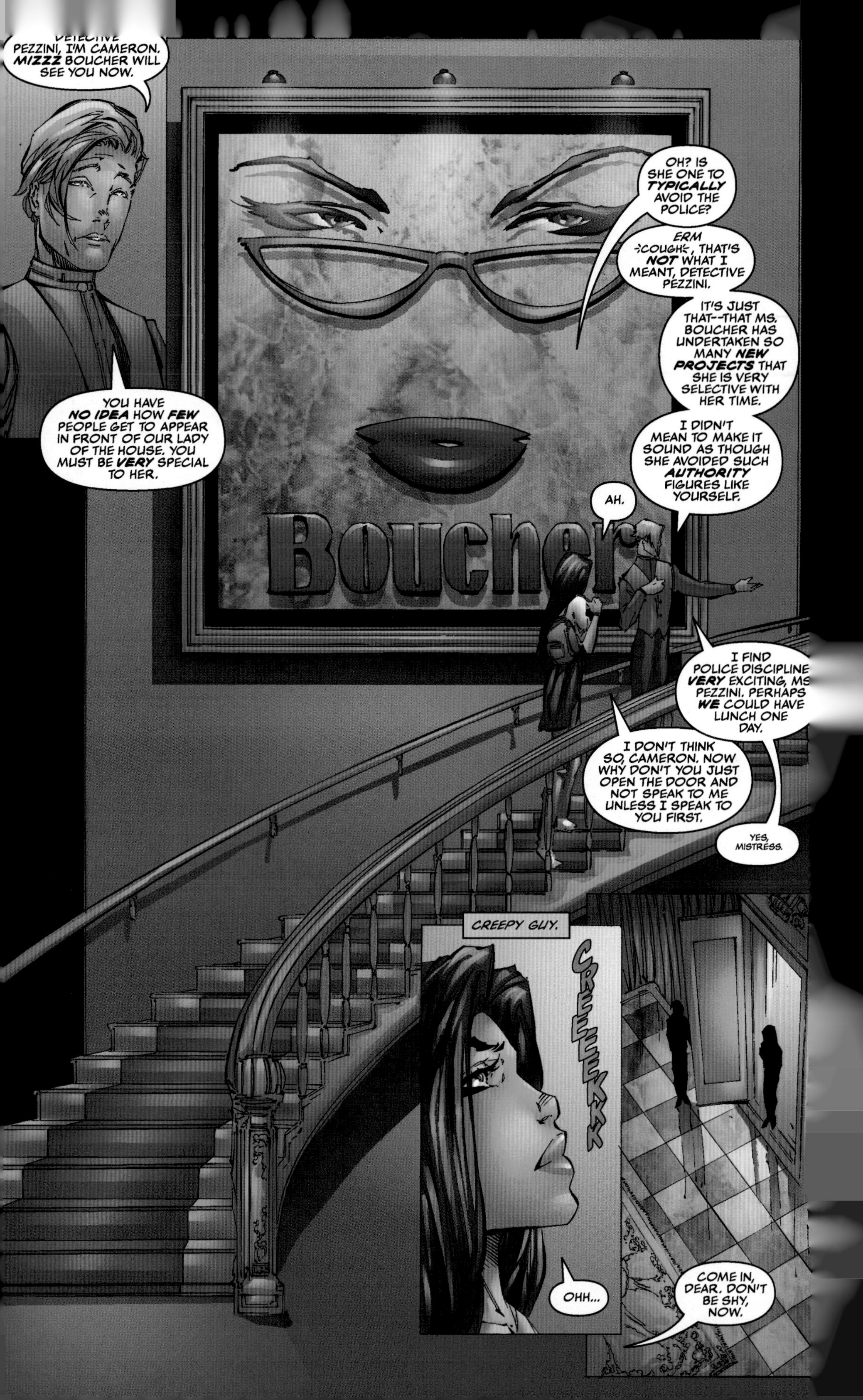
DETECTIVE PEZZINI, I'M CAMERON. MIZZZ BOUCHER WILL SEE YOU NOW.
YOU HAVE NO IDEA HOW FEW PEOPLE GET TO APPEAR IN FRONT OF OUR LADY OF THE HOUSE. YOU MUST BE VERY SPECIAL TO HER.
Boucher
OH? IS SHE ONE TO TYPICALLY AVOID THE POLICE?
ERM *COUGH*, THAT'S NOT WHAT I MEANT, DETECTIVE PEZZINI.
IT'S JUST THAT--THAT MS. BOUCHER HAS UNDERTAKEN SO MANY NEW PROJECTS THAT SHE IS VERY SELECTIVE WITH HER TIME.
I DIDN'T MEAN TO MAKE IT SOUND AS THOUGH SHE AVOIDED SUCH AUTHORITY FIGURES LIKE YOURSELF.
AH.
I FIND POLICE DISCIPLINE VERY EXCITING, MS. PEZZINI. PERHAPS WE COULD HAVE LUNCH ONE DAY.
I DON'T THINK SO, CAMERON. NOW WHY DON'T YOU JUST OPEN THE DOOR AND NOT SPEAK TO ME UNLESS I SPEAK TO YOU FIRST.
YES, MISTRESS.
CREEPY GUY.
CREEEEKKK
OHH...
COME IN, DEAR. DON'T BE SHY, NOW.

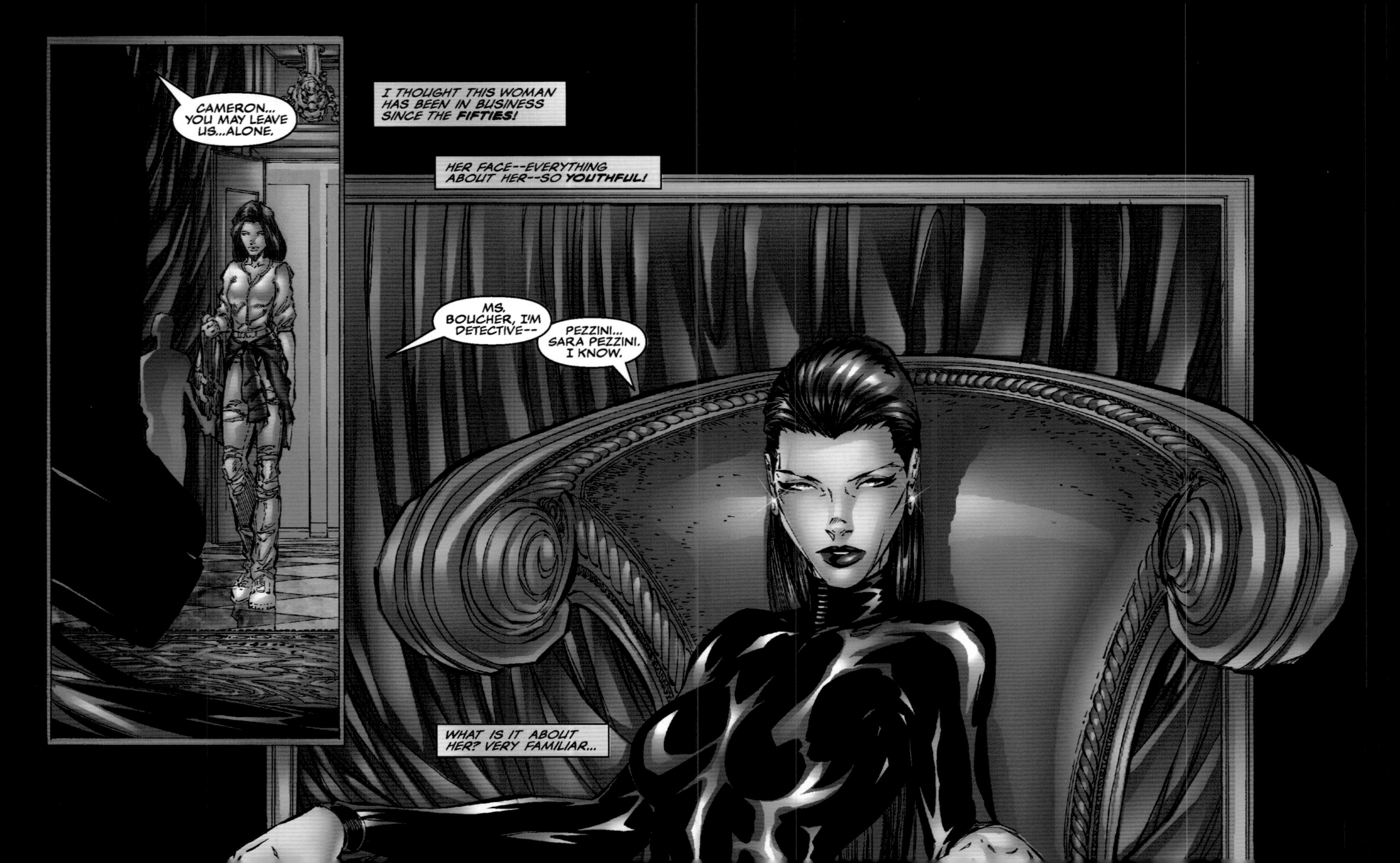
CAMERON... YOU MAY LEAVE US...ALONE.
I THOUGHT THIS WOMAN HAS BEEN IN BUSINESS SINCE THE FIFTIES!
HER FACE--EVERYTHING ABOUT HER--SO YOUTHFUL!
MS. BOUCHER, I'M DETECTIVE--
PEZZINI... SARA PEZZINI. I KNOW.
WHAT IS IT ABOUT HER? VERY FAMILIAR...

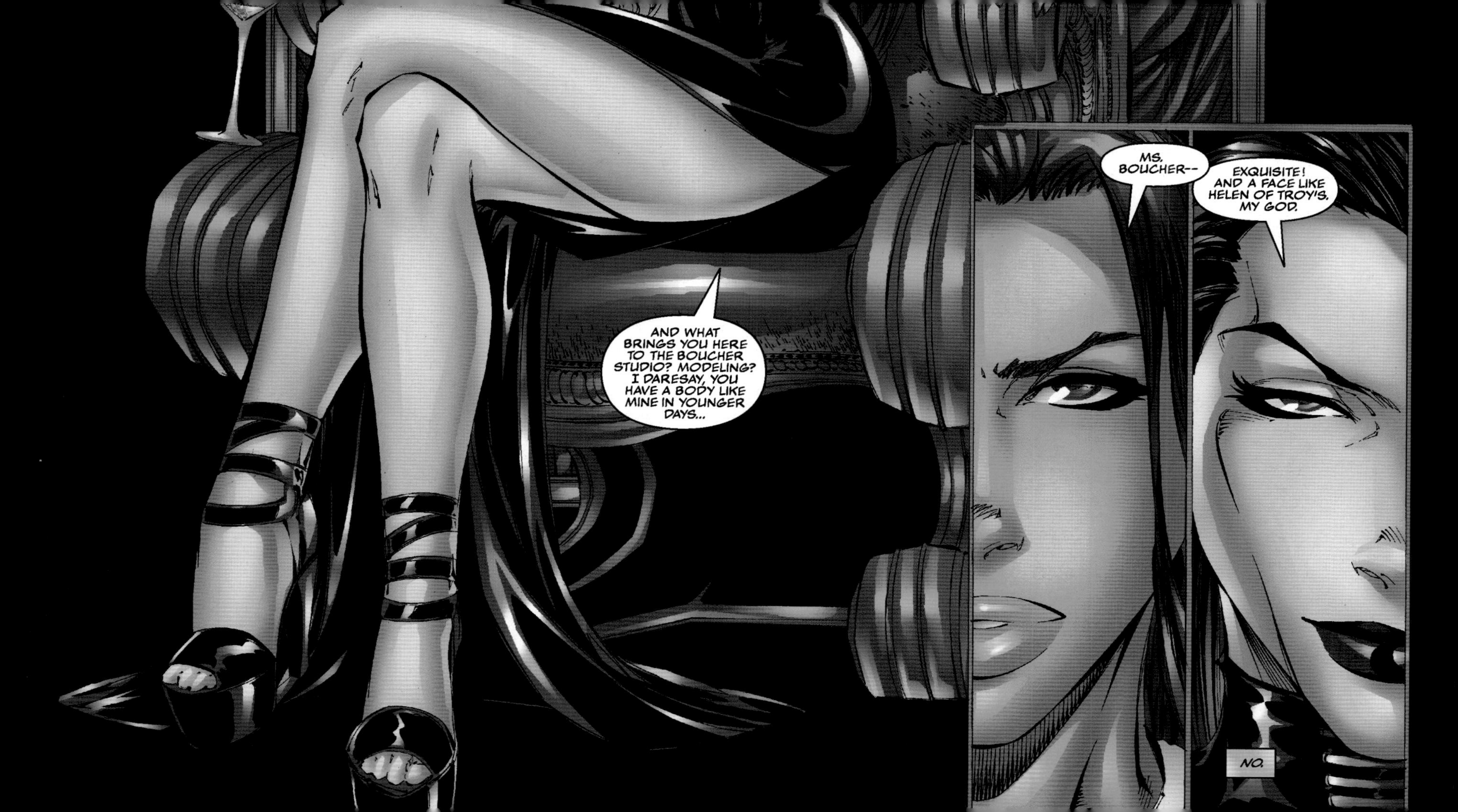
AND WHAT BRINGS YOU HERE TO THE BOUCHER STUDIO? MODELING? I DARESAY, YOU HAVE A BODY LIKE MINE IN YOUNGER DAYS...
MS. BOUCHER--
EXQUISITE! AND A FACE LIKE HELEN OF TROY'S. MY GOD.
NO.

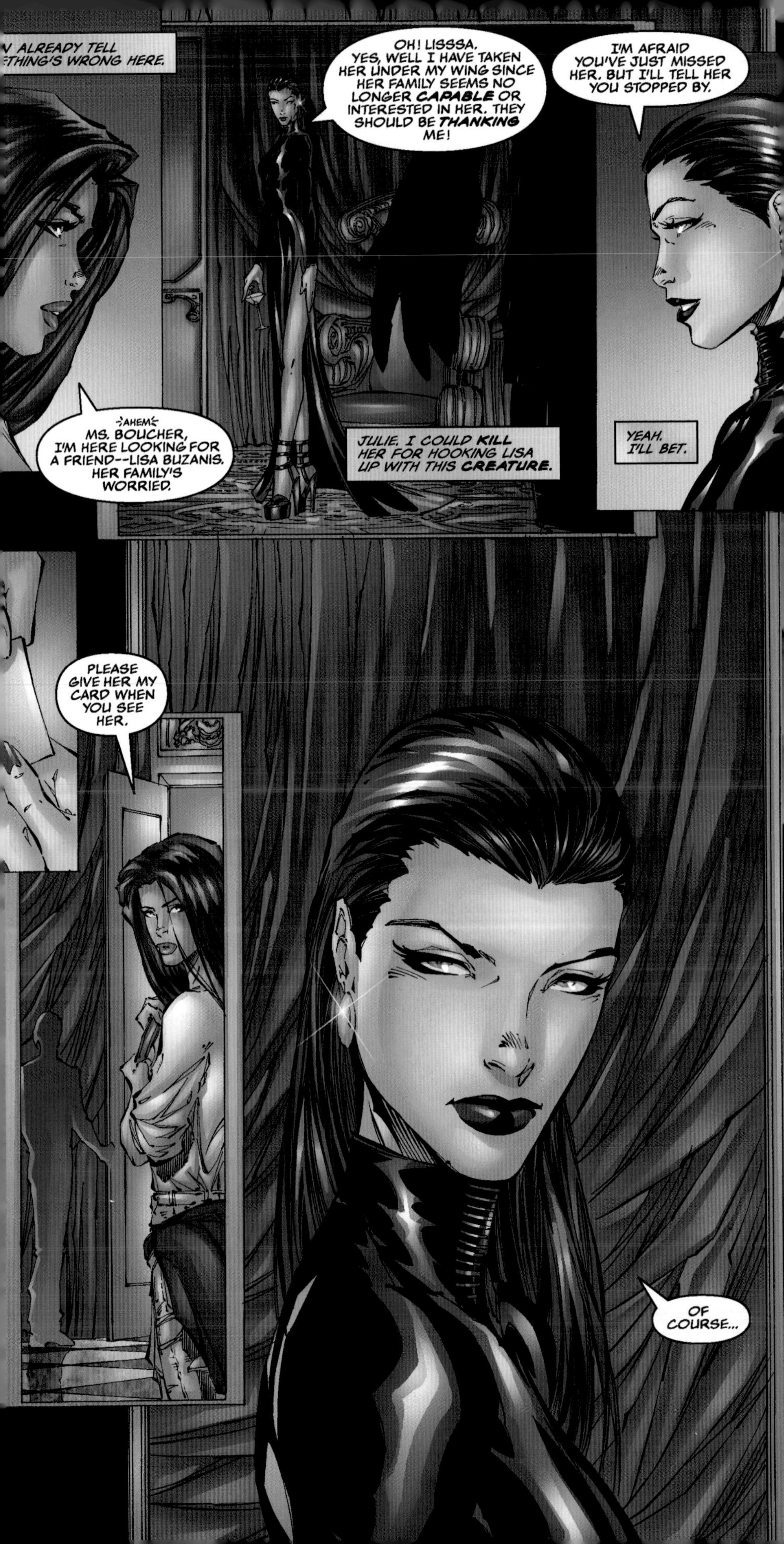
...N ALREADY TELL ...ETHING'S WRONG HERE.
OH! LISSSA. YES, WELL I HAVE TAKEN HER UNDER MY WING SINCE HER FAMILY SEEMS NO LONGER CAPABLE OR INTERESTED IN HER. THEY SHOULD BE THANKING ME!
I'M AFRAID YOU'VE JUST MISSED HER. BUT I'LL TELL HER YOU STOPPED BY.
AHEM MS. BOUCHER, I'M HERE LOOKING FOR A FRIEND--LISA BUZANIS. HER FAMILY'S WORRIED.
JULIE. I COULD KILL HER FOR HOOKING LISA UP WITH THIS CREATURE.
YEAH. I'LL BET.
PLEASE GIVE HER MY CARD WHEN YOU SEE HER.
OF COURSE...

‹AHM› HAVE A **WONDERFUL** DAY, DETECTIVE.

RIIIIGHT.

OKAY, THIS IS IT. GOTTA MAKE MY MENTAL **TO DO** LIST. TO START WITH, I HAVE TO TRACK DOWN LISA.

OH, AND DEAL WITH JAKE SOON, CHECK WITH THE M.E. ABOUT IRONS' AND NOTTINGHAM'S AUTOPSIES, TALK TO SIRY, WHO'S BEEN ACTING REALLY **TORQUED** ABOUT ALL THIS, PUT JULIE IN THE **ROUND FILE**--AGAIN...

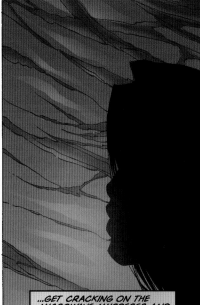

...GET CRACKING ON THE MICROWAVE MURDERER AND FIGURE OUT WHY IT HAD A PIECE OF THE WITCHBLADE, DO SOME RESEARCH ON DANNETTE AND BE ON THE LOOKOUT FOR ITALIAN HITMEN AS WELL AS LITTLE MYSTERIOUS CREATURES THAT SEEM TO ATTACK FOR NO REASON.

SIMPLE ENOUGH...

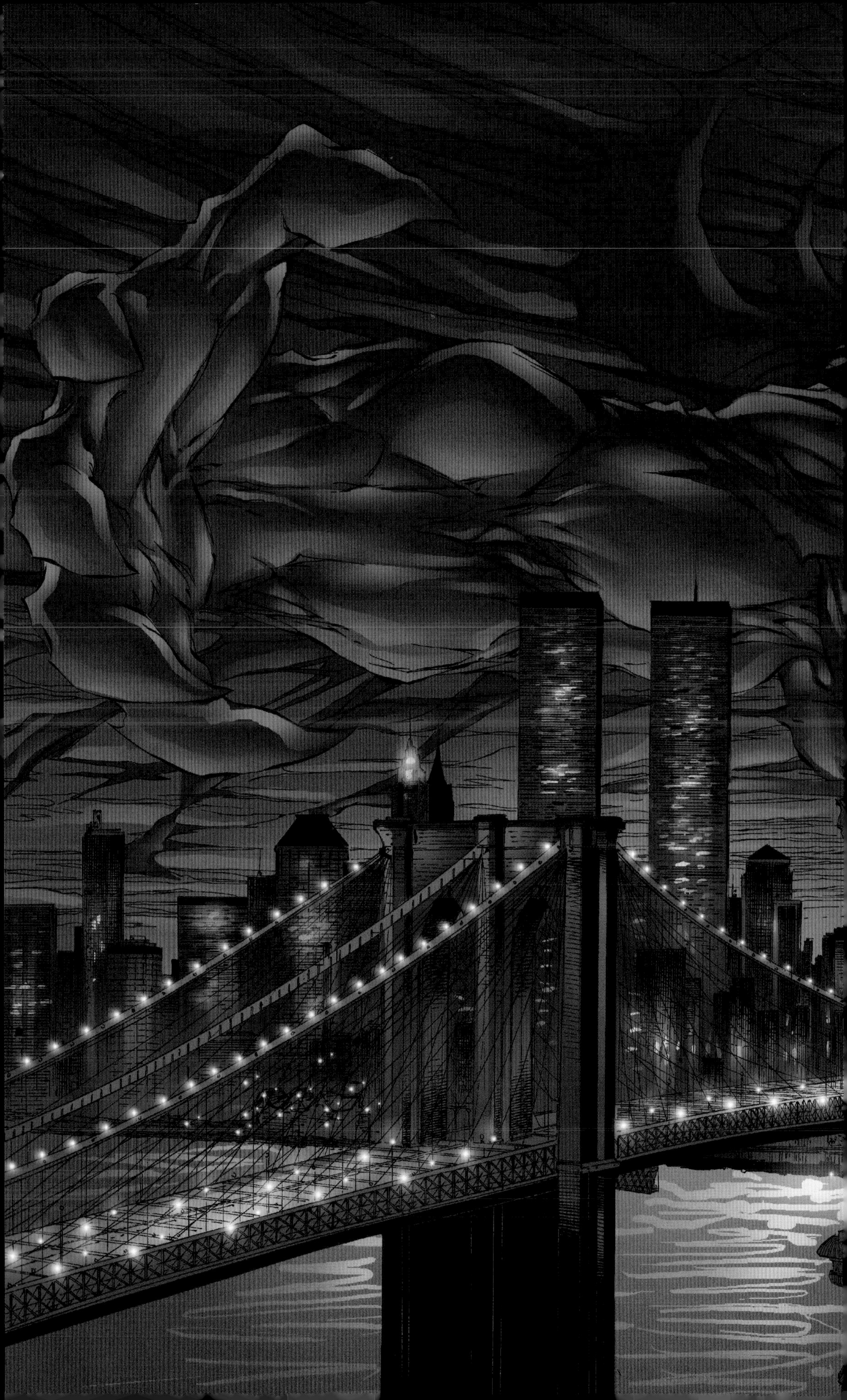

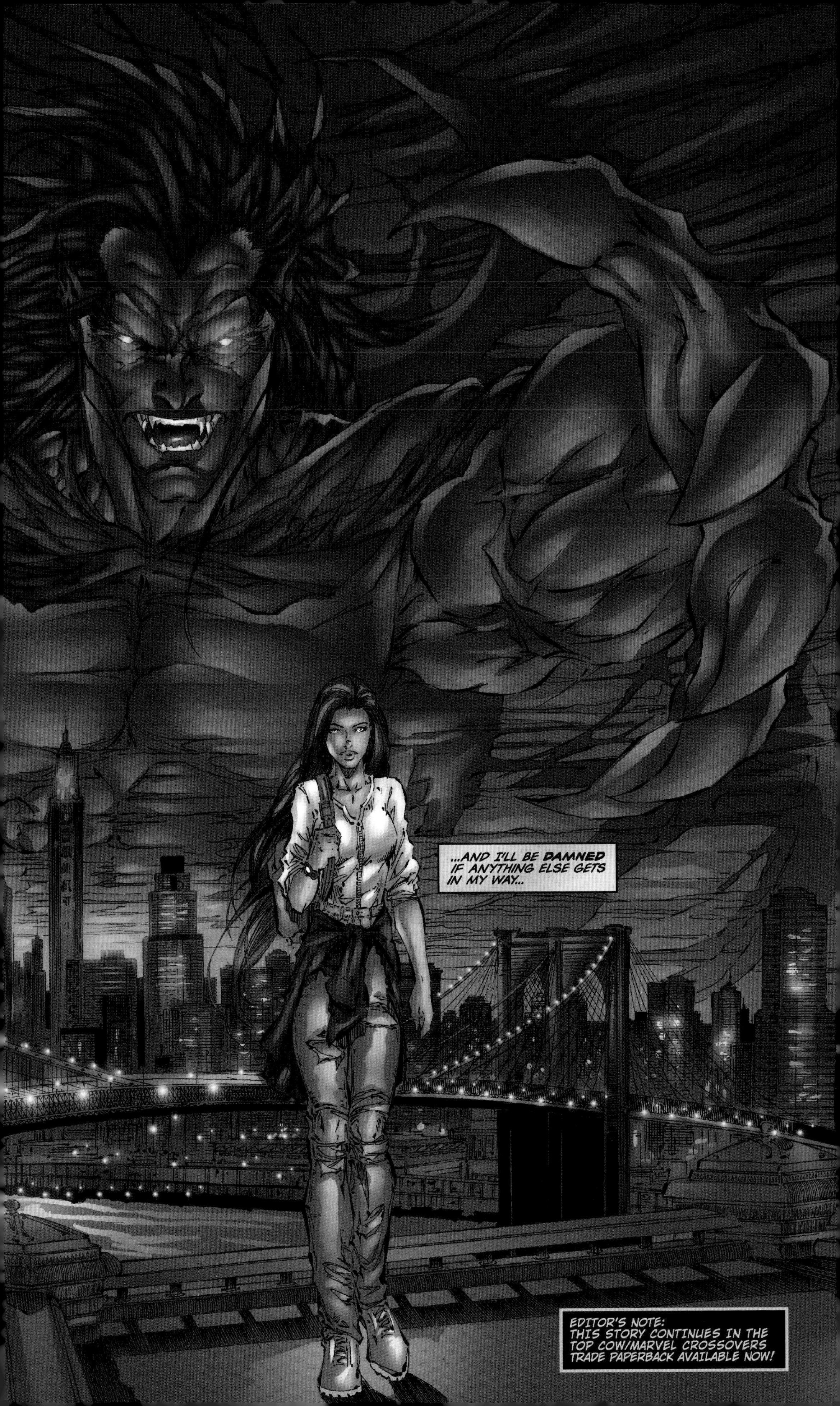
...AND I'LL BE DAMNED IF ANYTHING ELSE GETS IN MY WAY...
EDITOR'S NOTE: THIS STORY CONTINUES IN THE TOP COW/MARVEL CROSSOVERS TRADE PAPERBACK AVAILABLE NOW!

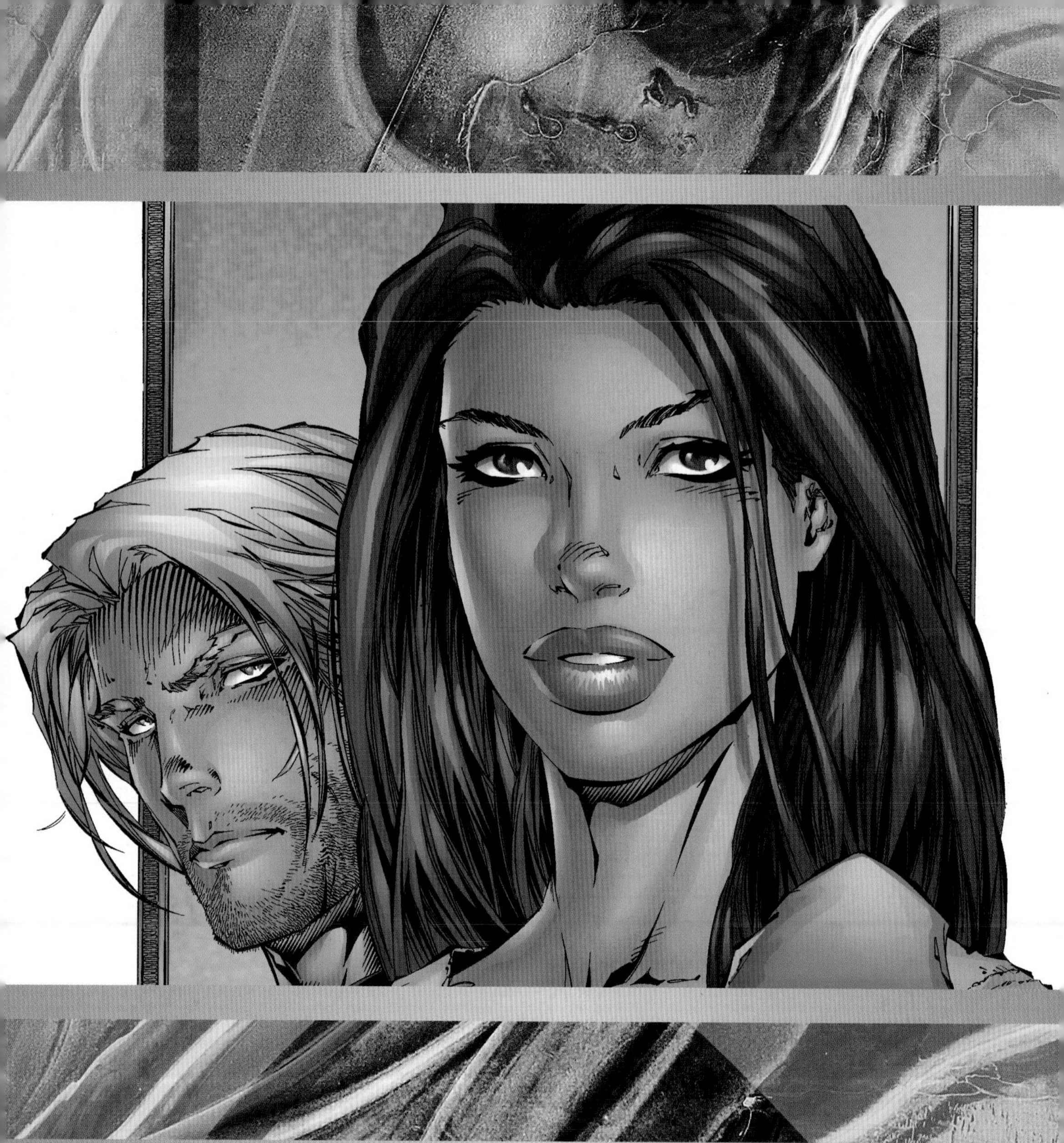

issue #12

story: **David Wohl** and **Christina Z.**
pencils/co-plot: **Michael Turner**
inks: **D-Tron**
colors: **JD Smith**

ink assists: **Jeff De Los Santos, Jose "Jag" Guillen, Andy Kim, Viet Trong** and **Marsha Chen**

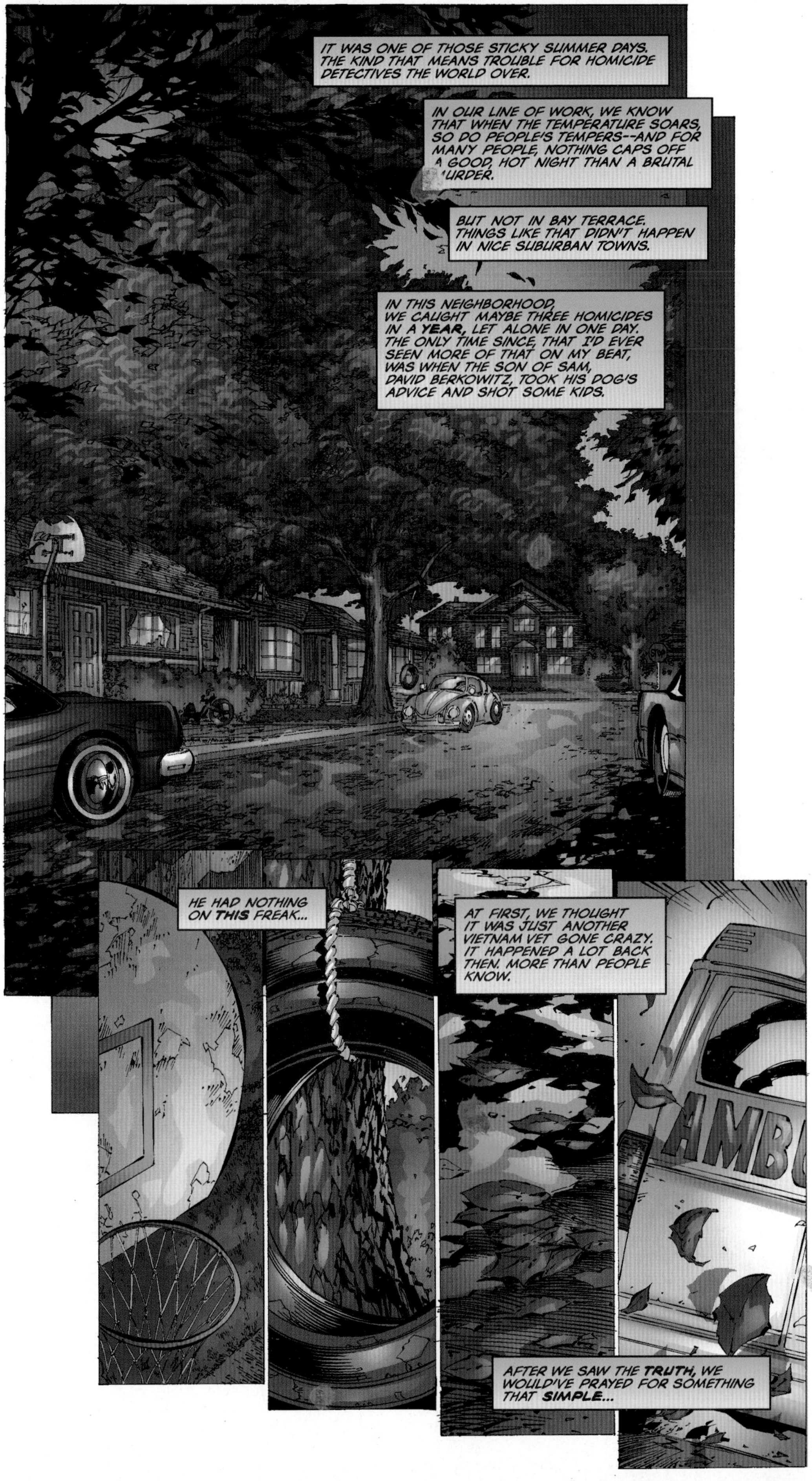
IT WAS ONE OF THOSE STICKY SUMMER DAYS. THE KIND THAT MEANS TROUBLE FOR HOMICIDE DETECTIVES THE WORLD OVER.
IN OUR LINE OF WORK, WE KNOW THAT WHEN THE TEMPERATURE SOARS, SO DO PEOPLE'S TEMPERS--AND FOR MANY PEOPLE, NOTHING CAPS OFF A GOOD, HOT NIGHT THAN A BRUTAL MURDER.
BUT NOT IN BAY TERRACE. THINGS LIKE THAT DIDN'T HAPPEN IN NICE SUBURBAN TOWNS.
IN THIS NEIGHBORHOOD, WE CAUGHT MAYBE THREE HOMICIDES IN A YEAR, LET ALONE IN ONE DAY. THE ONLY TIME SINCE, THAT I'D EVER SEEN MORE OF THAT ON MY BEAT, WAS WHEN THE SON OF SAM, DAVID BERKOWITZ, TOOK HIS DOG'S ADVICE AND SHOT SOME KIDS.
HE HAD NOTHING ON THIS FREAK...
AT FIRST, WE THOUGHT IT WAS JUST ANOTHER VIETNAM VET GONE CRAZY. IT HAPPENED A LOT BACK THEN. MORE THAN PEOPLE KNOW.
AMBU
AFTER WE SAW THE TRUTH, WE WOULD'VE PRAYED FOR SOMETHING THAT SIMPLE...

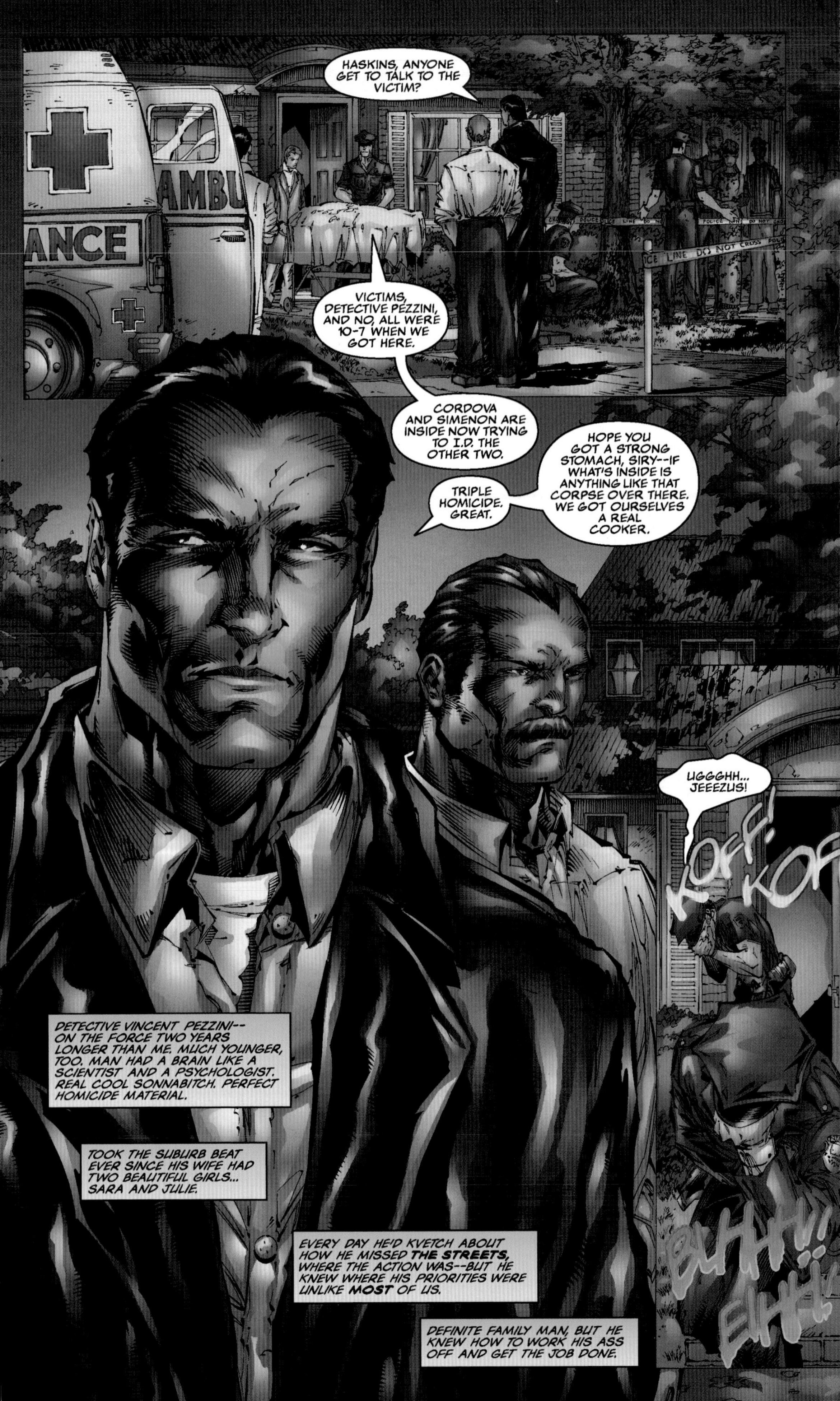
HASKINS, ANYONE GET TO TALK TO THE VICTIM?
VICTIMS, DETECTIVE PEZZINI, AND NO, ALL WERE 10-7 WHEN WE GOT HERE.
CORDOVA AND SIMENON ARE INSIDE NOW TRYING TO I.D. THE OTHER TWO.
TRIPLE HOMICIDE. GREAT.
HOPE YOU GOT A STRONG STOMACH, SIRY--IF WHAT'S INSIDE IS ANYTHING LIKE THAT CORPSE OVER THERE. WE GOT OURSELVES A REAL COOKER.
UGGGHH... JEEEZUS!
KOFF! KOF
DETECTIVE VINCENT PEZZINI--ON THE FORCE TWO YEARS LONGER THAN ME. MUCH YOUNGER, TOO. MAN HAD A BRAIN LIKE A SCIENTIST AND A PSYCHOLOGIST. REAL COOL SONNABITCH. PERFECT HOMICIDE MATERIAL.
TOOK THE SUBURB BEAT EVER SINCE HIS WIFE HAD TWO BEAUTIFUL GIRLS... SARA AND JULIE.
EVERY DAY HE'D KVETCH ABOUT HOW HE MISSED THE STREETS, WHERE THE ACTION WAS--BUT HE KNEW WHERE HIS PRIORITIES WERE UNLIKE MOST OF US.
DEFINITE FAMILY MAN, BUT HE KNEW HOW TO WORK HIS ASS OFF AND GET THE JOB DONE.

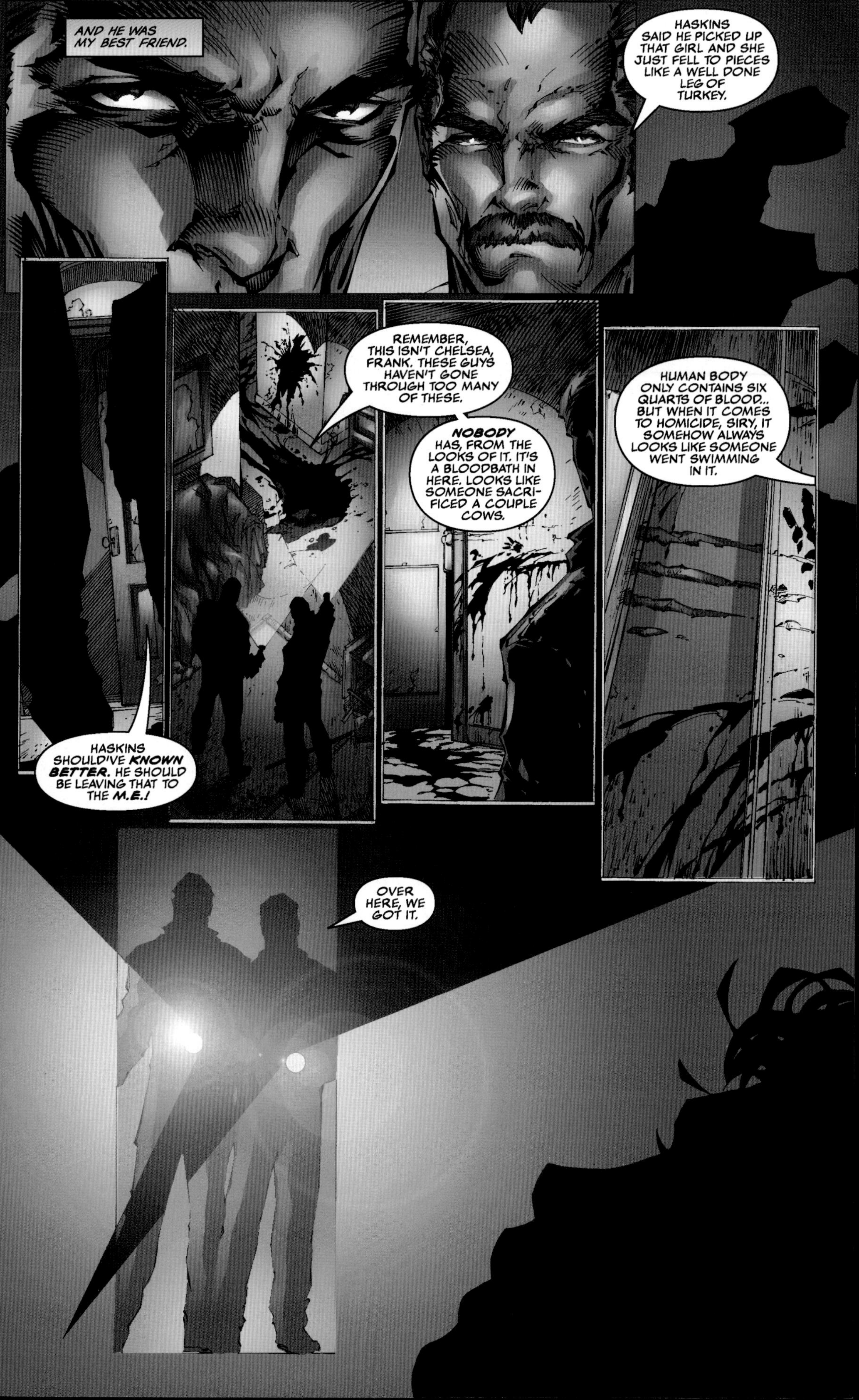
AND HE WAS MY BEST FRIEND.
HASKINS SAID HE PICKED UP THAT GIRL AND SHE JUST FELL TO PIECES LIKE A WELL DONE LEG OF TURKEY.
HASKINS SHOULD'VE KNOWN BETTER. HE SHOULD BE LEAVING THAT TO THE M.E.!
REMEMBER, THIS ISN'T CHELSEA, FRANK. THESE GUYS HAVEN'T GONE THROUGH TOO MANY OF THESE.
NOBODY HAS, FROM THE LOOKS OF IT. IT'S A BLOODBATH IN HERE. LOOKS LIKE SOMEONE SACRI-FICED A COUPLE COWS.
HUMAN BODY ONLY CONTAINS SIX QUARTS OF BLOOD... BUT WHEN IT COMES TO HOMICIDE, SIRY, IT SOMEHOW ALWAYS LOOKS LIKE SOMEONE WENT SWIMMING IN IT.
OVER HERE, WE GOT IT.

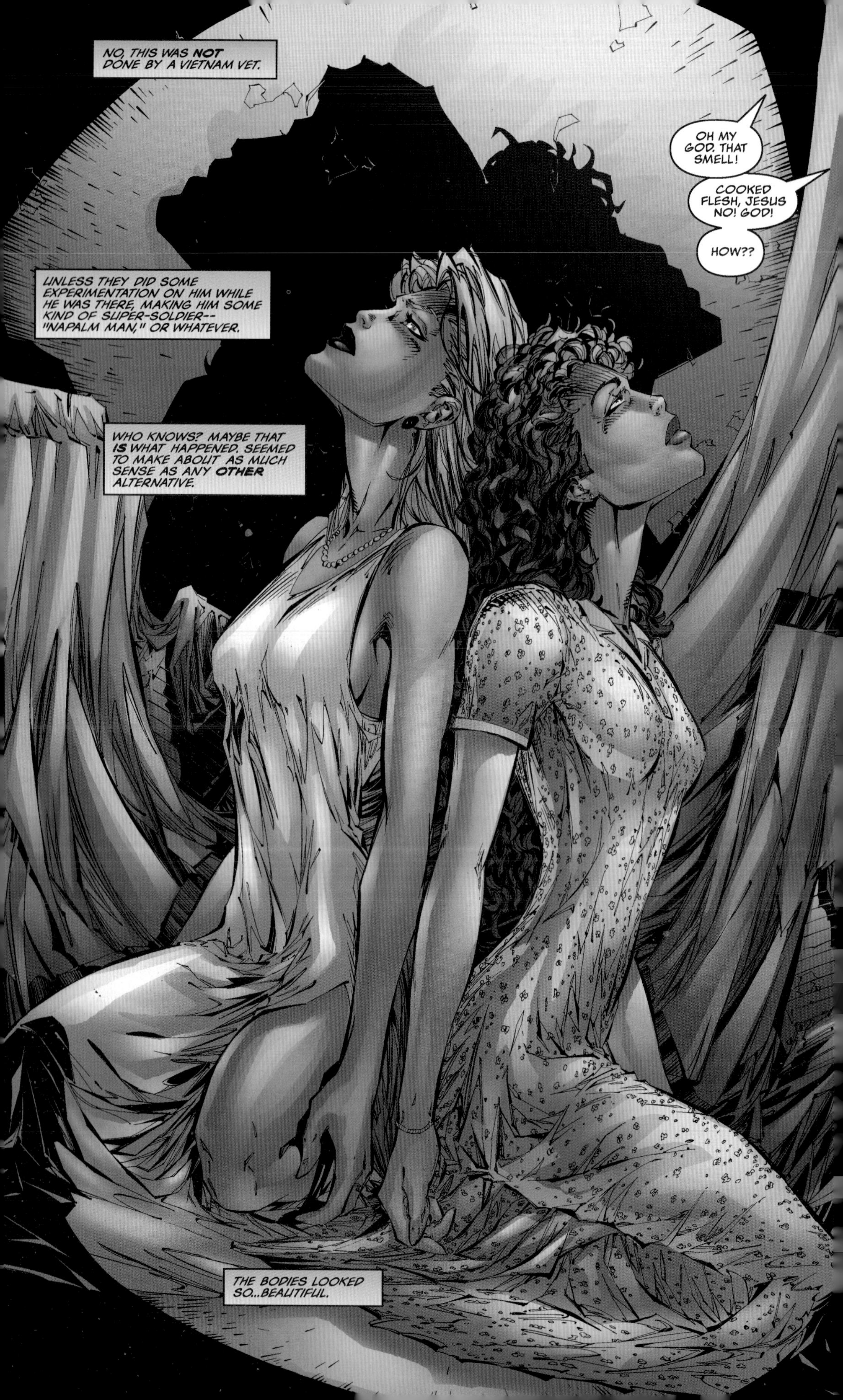

NO, THIS WAS NOT DONE BY A VIETNAM VET.
OH MY GOD. THAT SMELL!
COOKED FLESH, JESUS NO! GOD!
HOW??
UNLESS THEY DID SOME EXPERIMENTATION ON HIM WHILE HE WAS THERE, MAKING HIM SOME KIND OF SUPER-SOLDIER-- "NAPALM MAN," OR WHATEVER.
WHO KNOWS? MAYBE THAT IS WHAT HAPPENED. SEEMED TO MAKE ABOUT AS MUCH SENSE AS ANY OTHER ALTERNATIVE.
THE BODIES LOOKED SO...BEAUTIFUL.

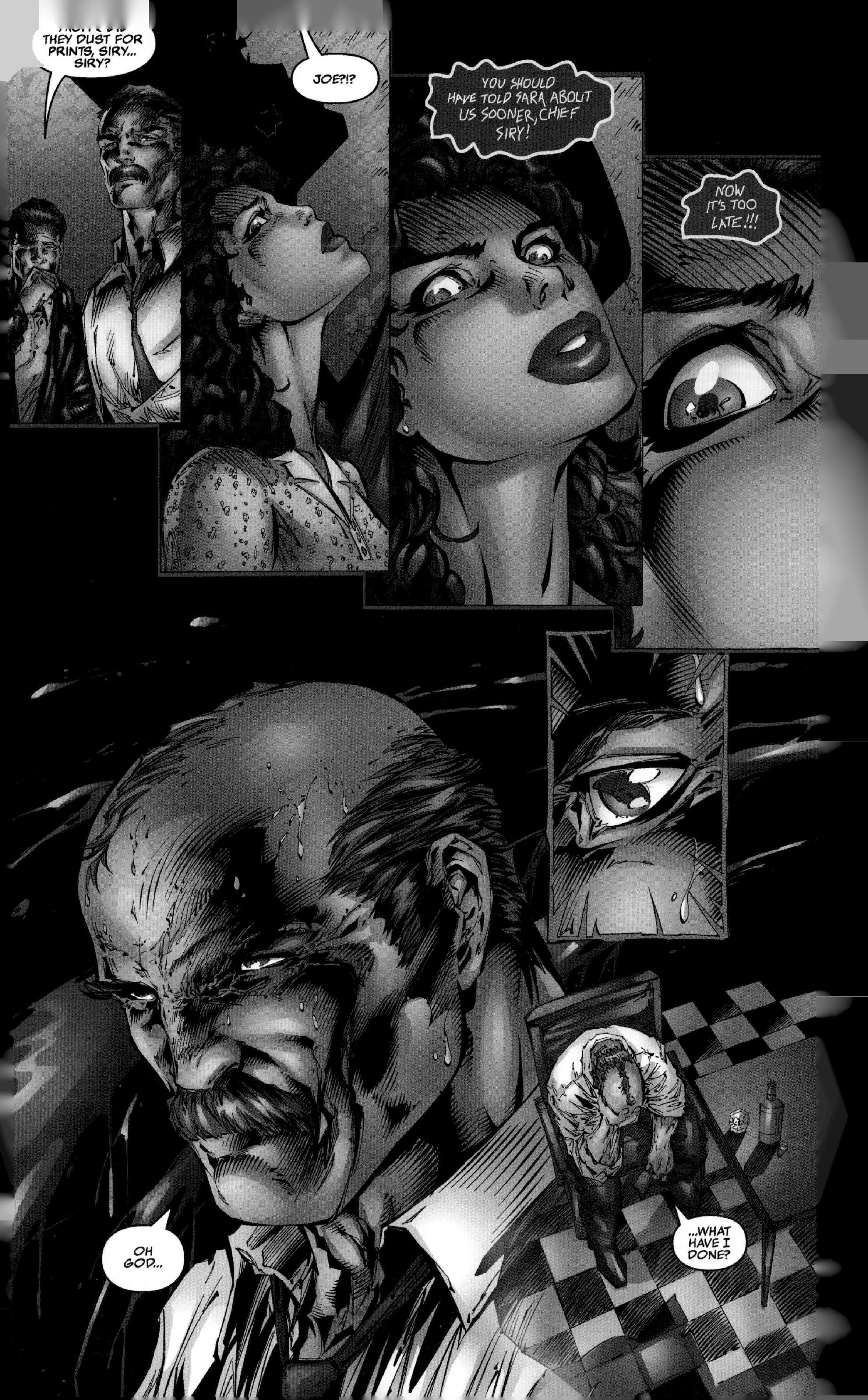
THEY DUST FOR PRINTS, SIRY... SIRY?
JOE?!?
YOU SHOULD HAVE TOLD SARA ABOUT US SOONER, CHIEF SIRY!
NOW IT'S TOO LATE!!!
OH GOD...
...WHAT HAVE I DONE?

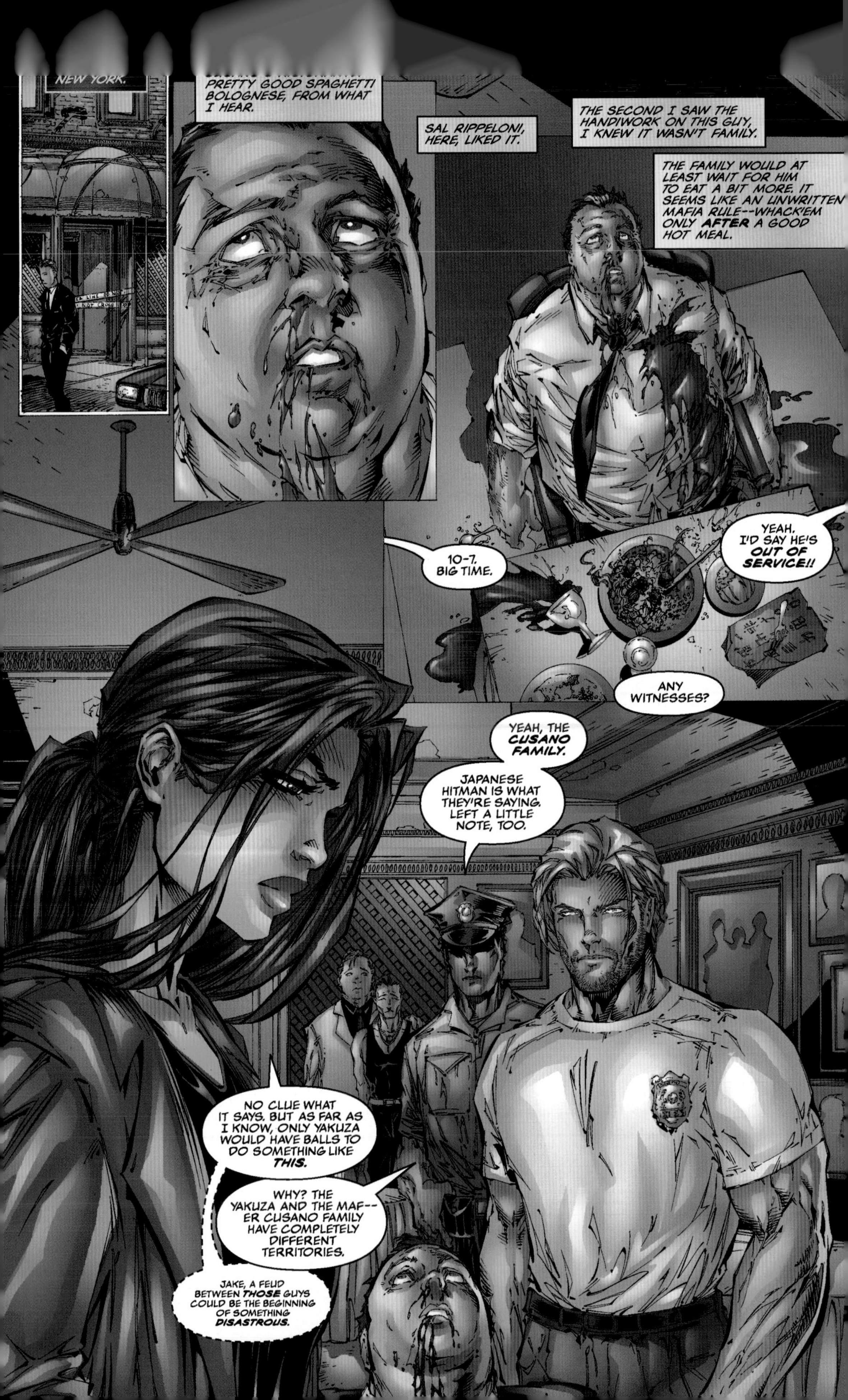
NEW YORK.
PRETTY GOOD SPAGHETTI BOLOGNESE, FROM WHAT I HEAR.
SAL RIPPELONI, HERE, LIKED IT.
THE SECOND I SAW THE HANDIWORK ON THIS GUY, I KNEW IT WASN'T FAMILY.
THE FAMILY WOULD AT LEAST WAIT FOR HIM TO EAT A BIT MORE. IT SEEMS LIKE AN UNWRITTEN MAFIA RULE--WHACK'EM ONLY AFTER A GOOD HOT MEAL.
10-7. BIG TIME.
YEAH. I'D SAY HE'S OUT OF SERVICE!!
ANY WITNESSES?
YEAH, THE CUSANO FAMILY.
JAPANESE HITMAN IS WHAT THEY'RE SAYING. LEFT A LITTLE NOTE, TOO.
NO CLUE WHAT IT SAYS. BUT AS FAR AS I KNOW, ONLY YAKUZA WOULD HAVE BALLS TO DO SOMETHING LIKE THIS.
WHY? THE YAKUZA AND THE MAF-- ER CUSANO FAMILY HAVE COMPLETELY DIFFERENT TERRITORIES.
JAKE, A FEUD BETWEEN THOSE GUYS COULD BE THE BEGINNING OF SOMETHING DISASTROUS.

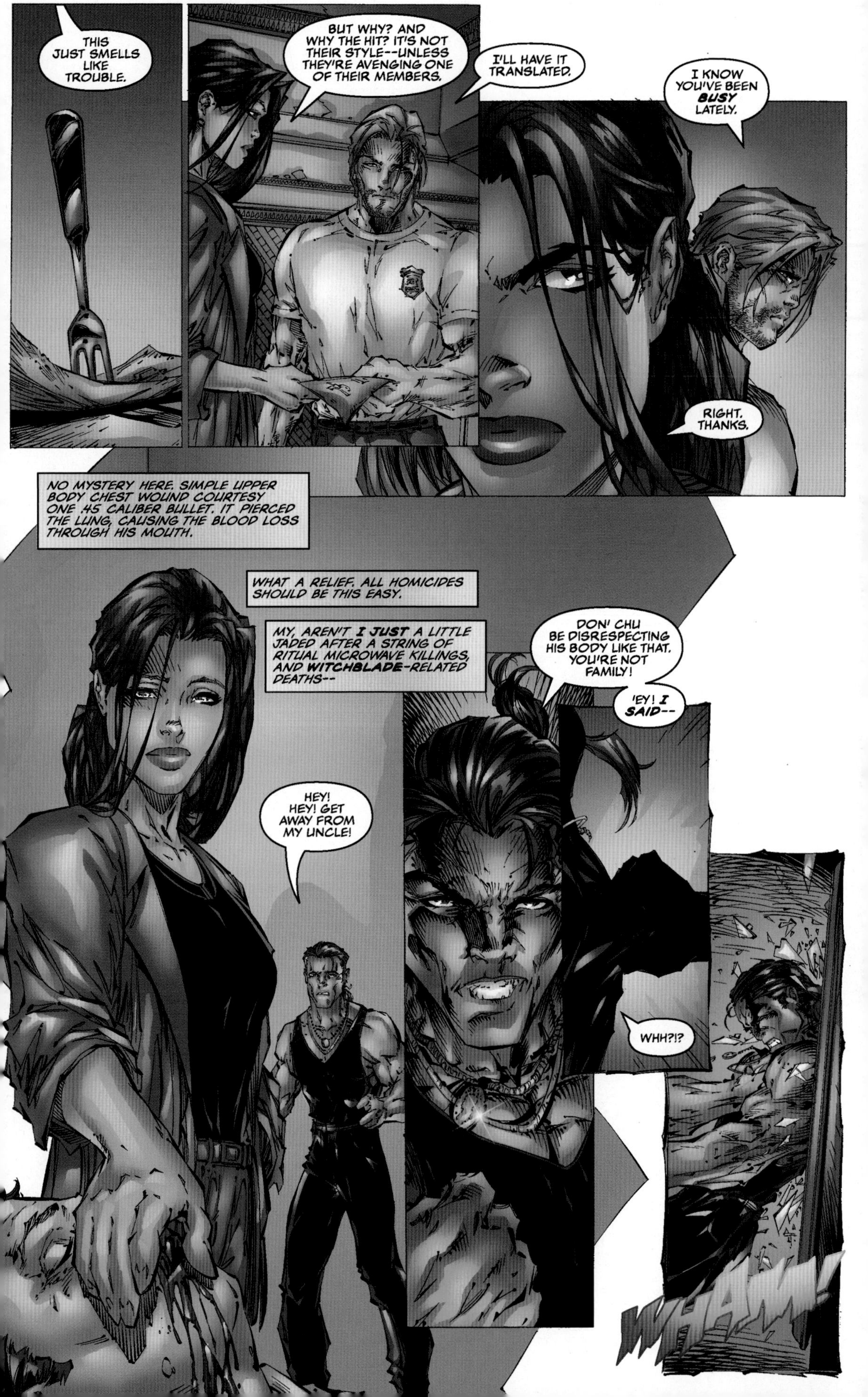
THIS JUST SMELLS LIKE TROUBLE.
BUT WHY? AND WHY THE HIT? IT'S NOT THEIR STYLE--UNLESS THEY'RE AVENGING ONE OF THEIR MEMBERS.
I'LL HAVE IT TRANSLATED.
I KNOW YOU'VE BEEN **BUSY** LATELY.
RIGHT. THANKS.
NO MYSTERY HERE. SIMPLE UPPER BODY CHEST WOUND COURTESY ONE .45 CALIBER BULLET. IT PIERCED THE LUNG, CAUSING THE BLOOD LOSS THROUGH HIS MOUTH.
WHAT A RELIEF. ALL HOMICIDES SHOULD BE THIS EASY.
MY, AREN'T **I JUST** A LITTLE JADED AFTER A STRING OF RITUAL MICROWAVE KILLINGS, AND **WITCHBLADE**-RELATED DEATHS--
HEY! HEY! GET AWAY FROM MY UNCLE!
DON' CHU BE DISRESPECTING HIS BODY LIKE THAT. YOU'RE NOT FAMILY!
'EY! **I SAID**--
WHH?!?
WHAM!

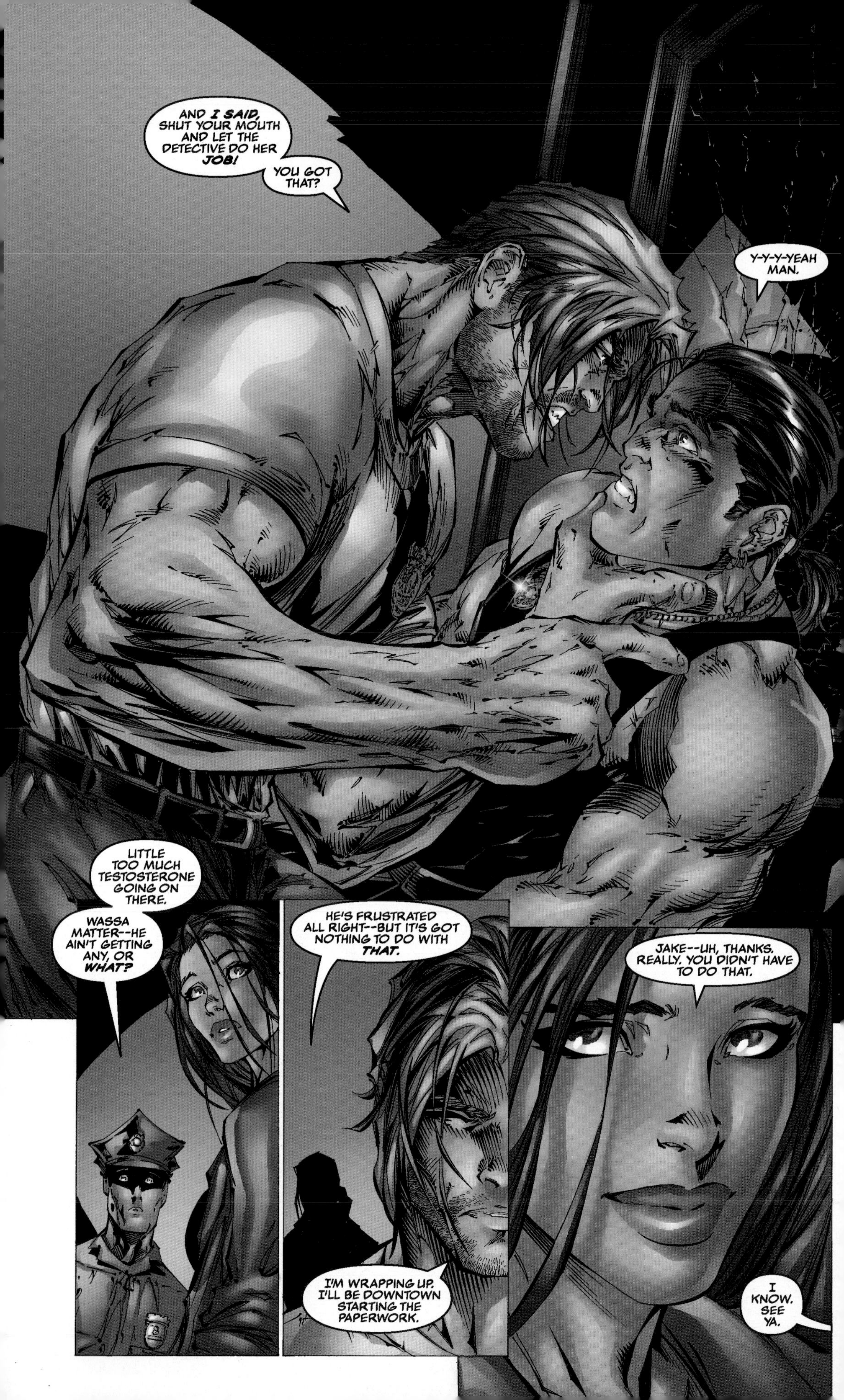
AND I SAID, SHUT YOUR MOUTH AND LET THE DETECTIVE DO HER JOB!
YOU GOT THAT?
Y-Y-Y-YEAH MAN.
LITTLE TOO MUCH TESTOSTERONE GOING ON THERE.
WASSA MATTER--HE AIN'T GETTING ANY, OR WHAT?
HE'S FRUSTRATED ALL RIGHT--BUT IT'S GOT NOTHING TO DO WITH THAT.
I'M WRAPPING UP. I'LL BE DOWNTOWN STARTING THE PAPERWORK.
JAKE--UH, THANKS. REALLY. YOU DIDN'T HAVE TO DO THAT.
I KNOW. SEE YA.

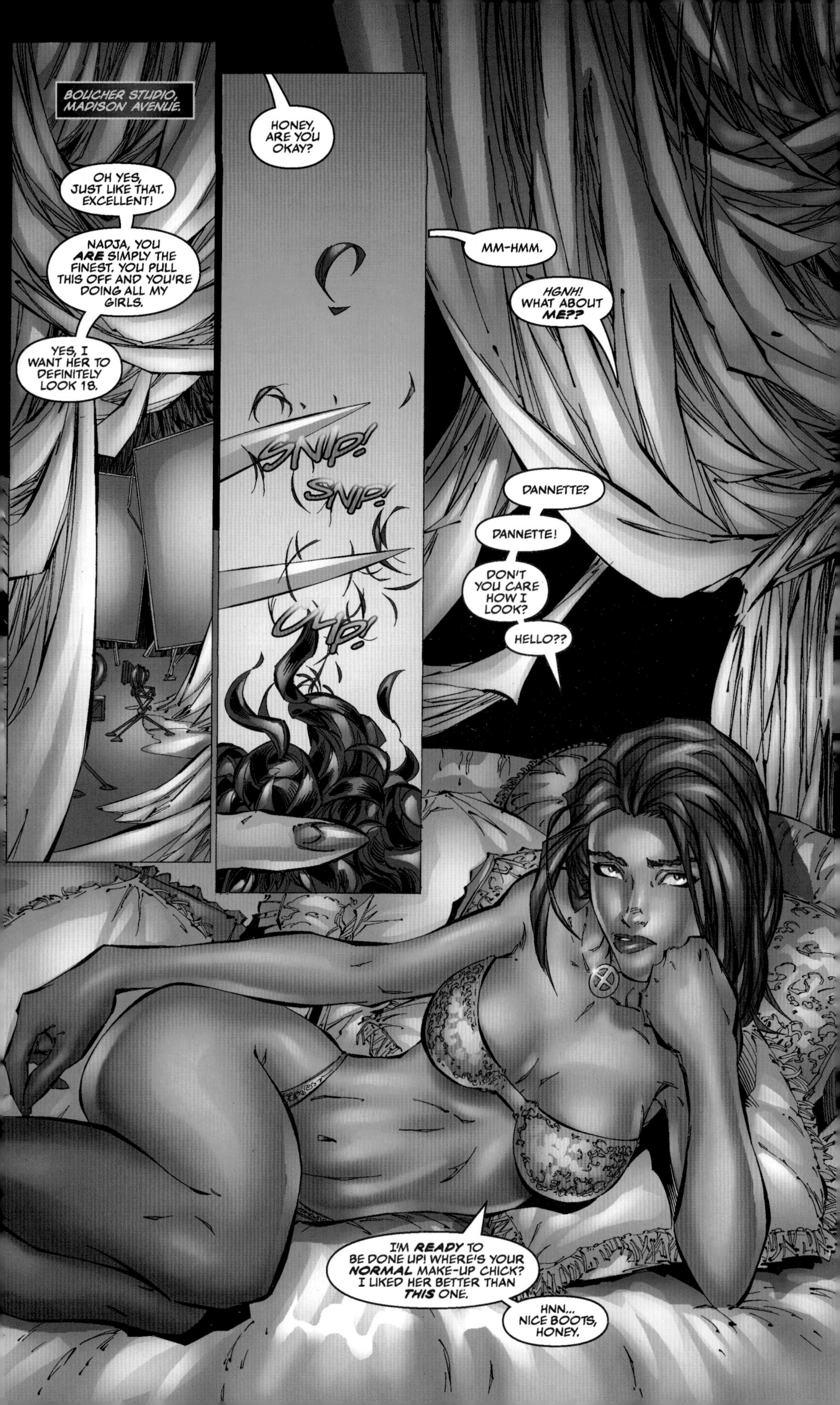

BOUCHER STUDIO, MADISON AVENUE.
OH YES, JUST LIKE THAT. EXCELLENT!
NADJA, YOU ARE SIMPLY THE FINEST. YOU PULL THIS OFF AND YOU'RE DOING ALL MY GIRLS.
YES, I WANT HER TO DEFINITELY LOOK 18.
HONEY, ARE YOU OKAY?
MM-HMM.
HGNH! WHAT ABOUT ME??
SNIP!
SNIP!
UMP!
DANNETTE?
DANNETTE!
DON'T YOU CARE HOW I LOOK?
HELLO??
I'M READY TO BE DONE UP! WHERE'S YOUR NORMAL MAKE-UP CHICK? I LIKED HER BETTER THAN THIS ONE.
HNN... NICE BOOTS, HONEY.

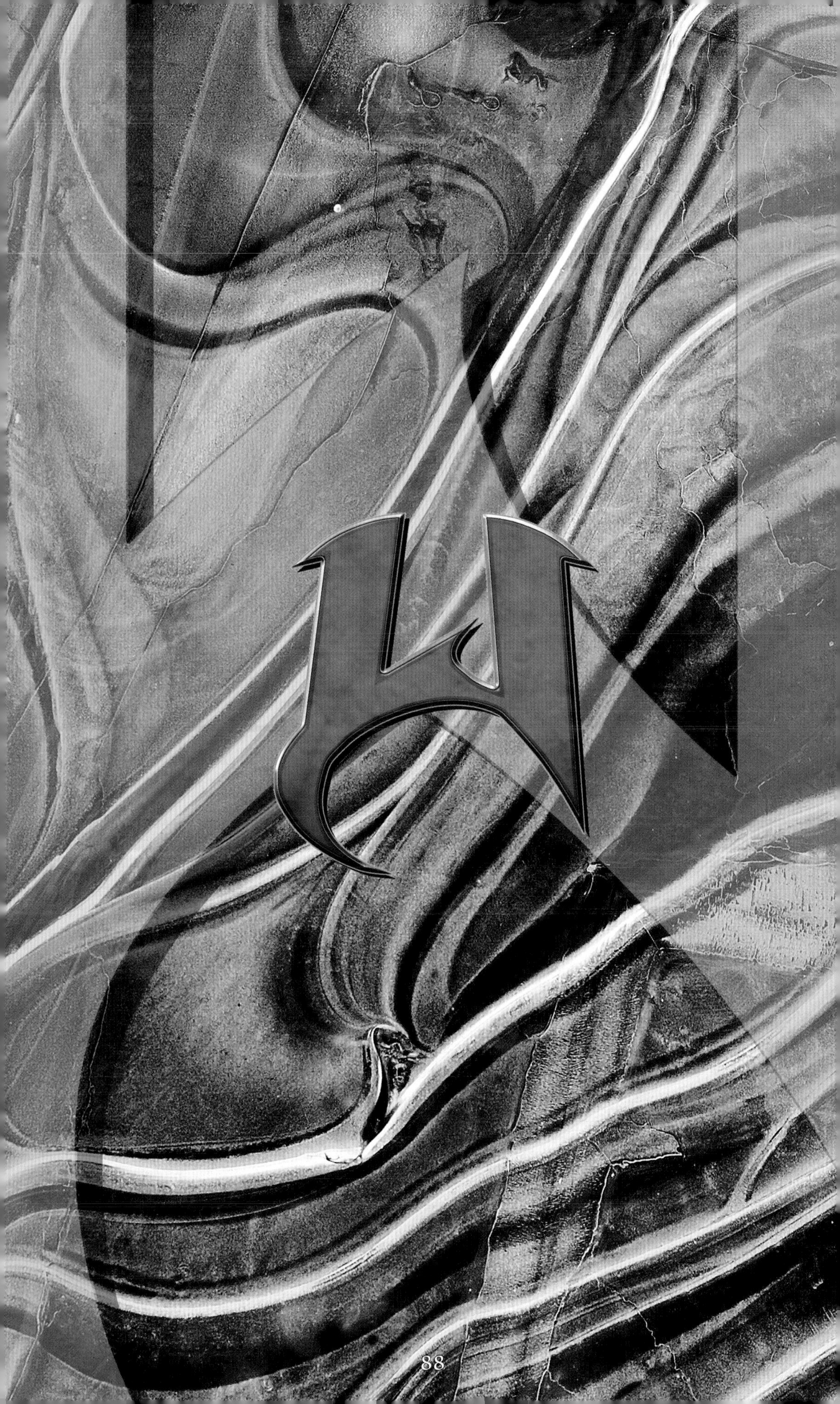

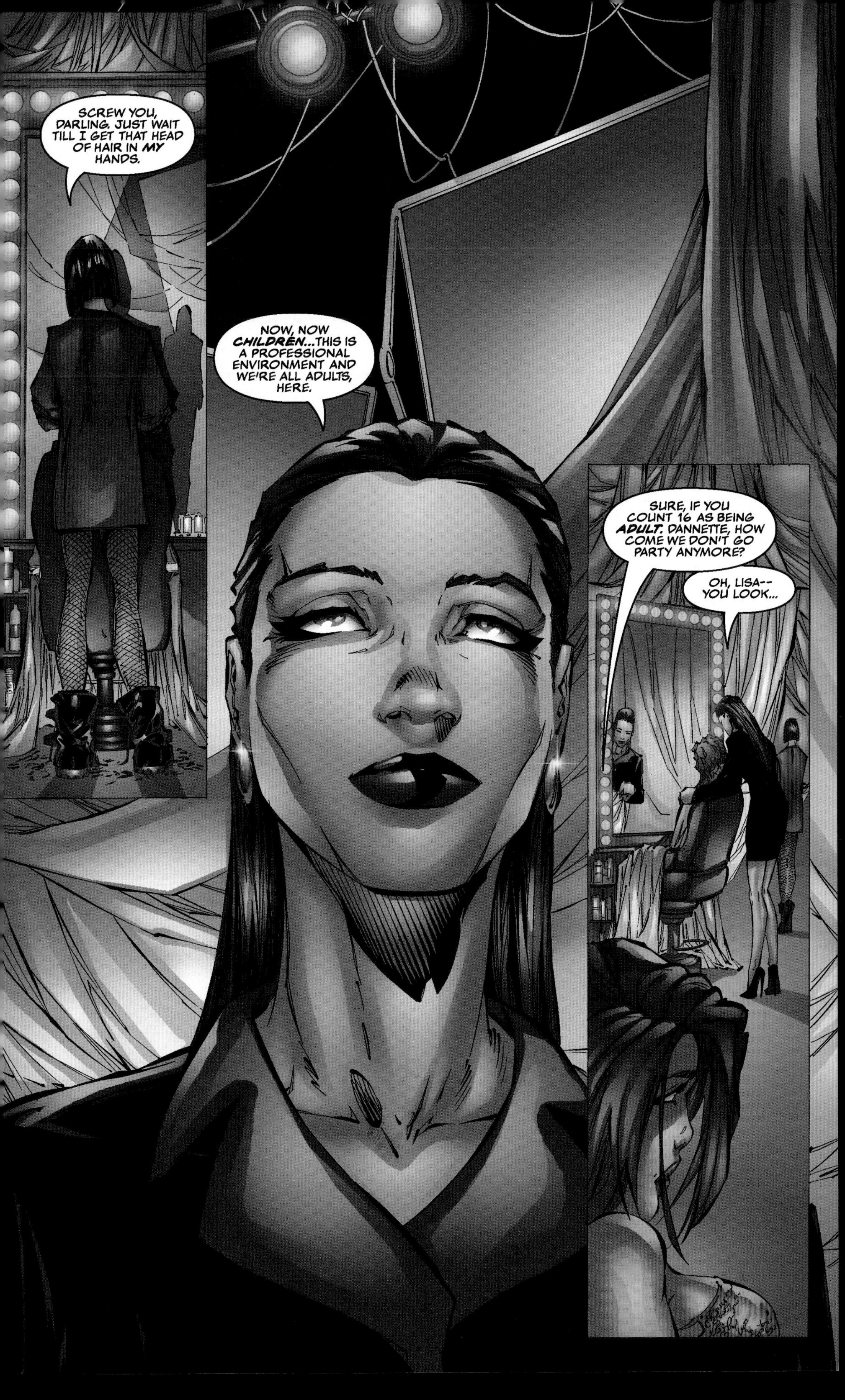
SCREW YOU, DARLING. JUST WAIT TILL I GET THAT HEAD OF HAIR IN MY HANDS.
NOW, NOW CHILDREN...THIS IS A PROFESSIONAL ENVIRONMENT AND WE'RE ALL ADULTS, HERE.
SURE, IF YOU COUNT 16 AS BEING ADULT. DANNETTE, HOW COME WE DON'T GO PARTY ANYMORE?
OH, LISA-- YOU LOOK...

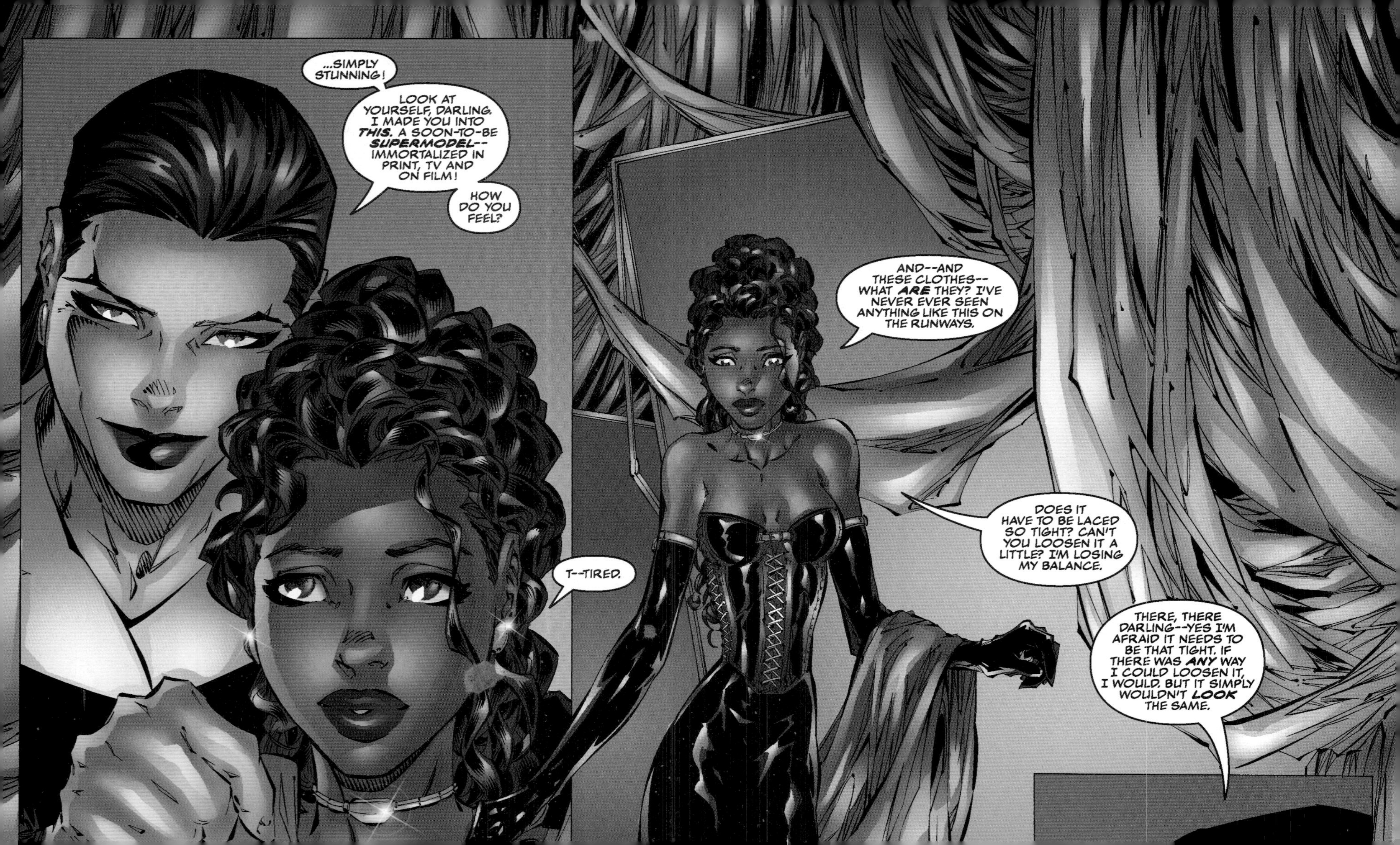
...SIMPLY STUNNING!
LOOK AT YOURSELF, DARLING. I MADE YOU INTO **THIS.** A SOON-TO-BE **SUPERMODEL**--IMMORTALIZED IN PRINT, TV AND ON FILM!
HOW DO YOU FEEL?
T--TIRED.
AND--AND THESE CLOTHES--WHAT **ARE** THEY? I'VE NEVER EVER SEEN ANYTHING LIKE THIS ON THE RUNWAYS.
DOES IT HAVE TO BE LACED SO TIGHT? CAN'T YOU LOOSEN IT A LITTLE? I'M LOSING MY BALANCE.
THERE, THERE DARLING--YES I'M AFRAID IT NEEDS TO BE THAT TIGHT. IF THERE WAS **ANY** WAY I COULD LOOSEN IT, I WOULD. BUT IT SIMPLY WOULDN'T **LOOK** THE SAME.

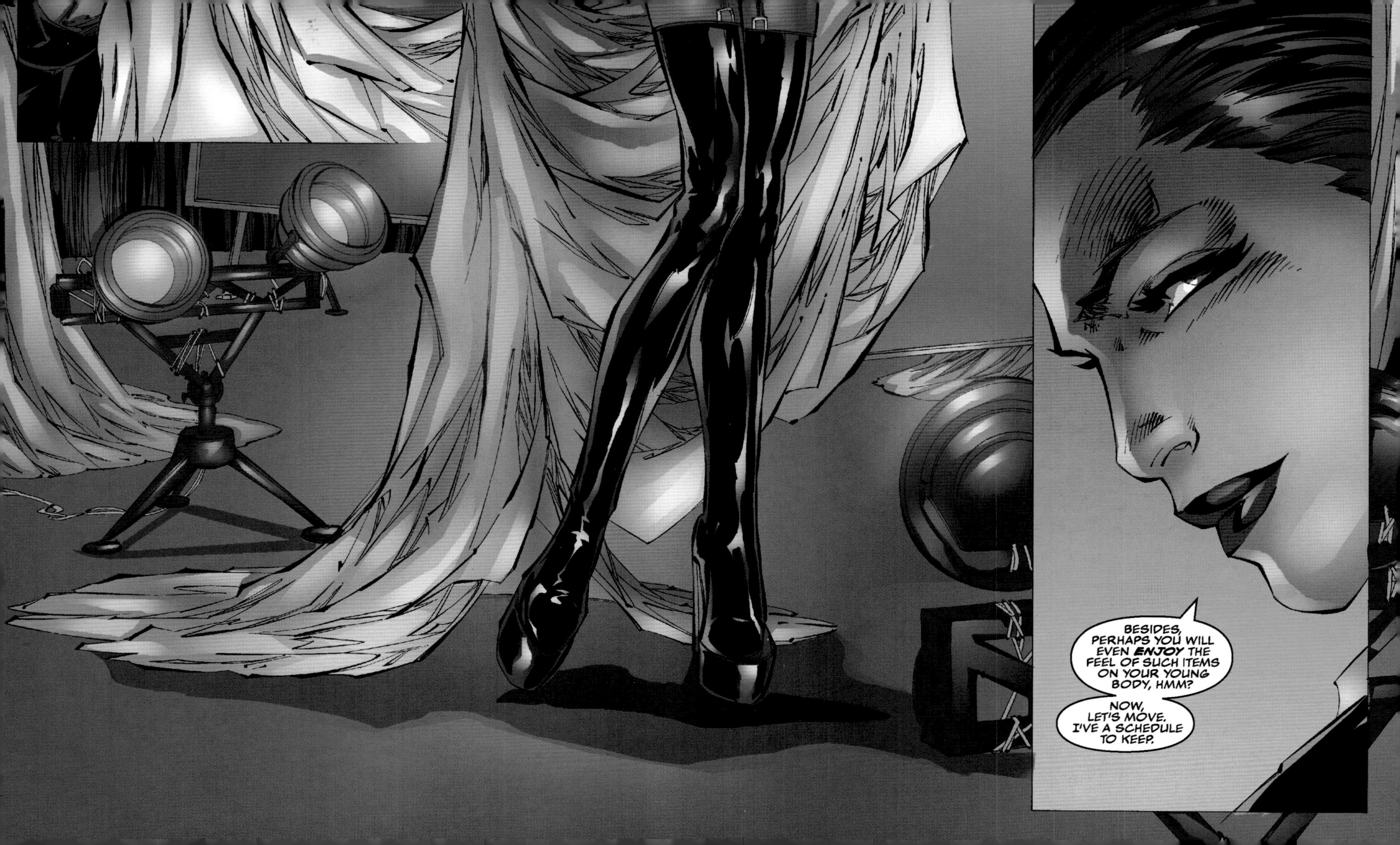
BESIDES, PERHAPS YOU WILL EVEN ENJOY THE FEEL OF SUCH ITEMS ON YOUR YOUNG BODY, HMM?
NOW, LET'S MOVE. I'VE A SCHEDULE TO KEEP.

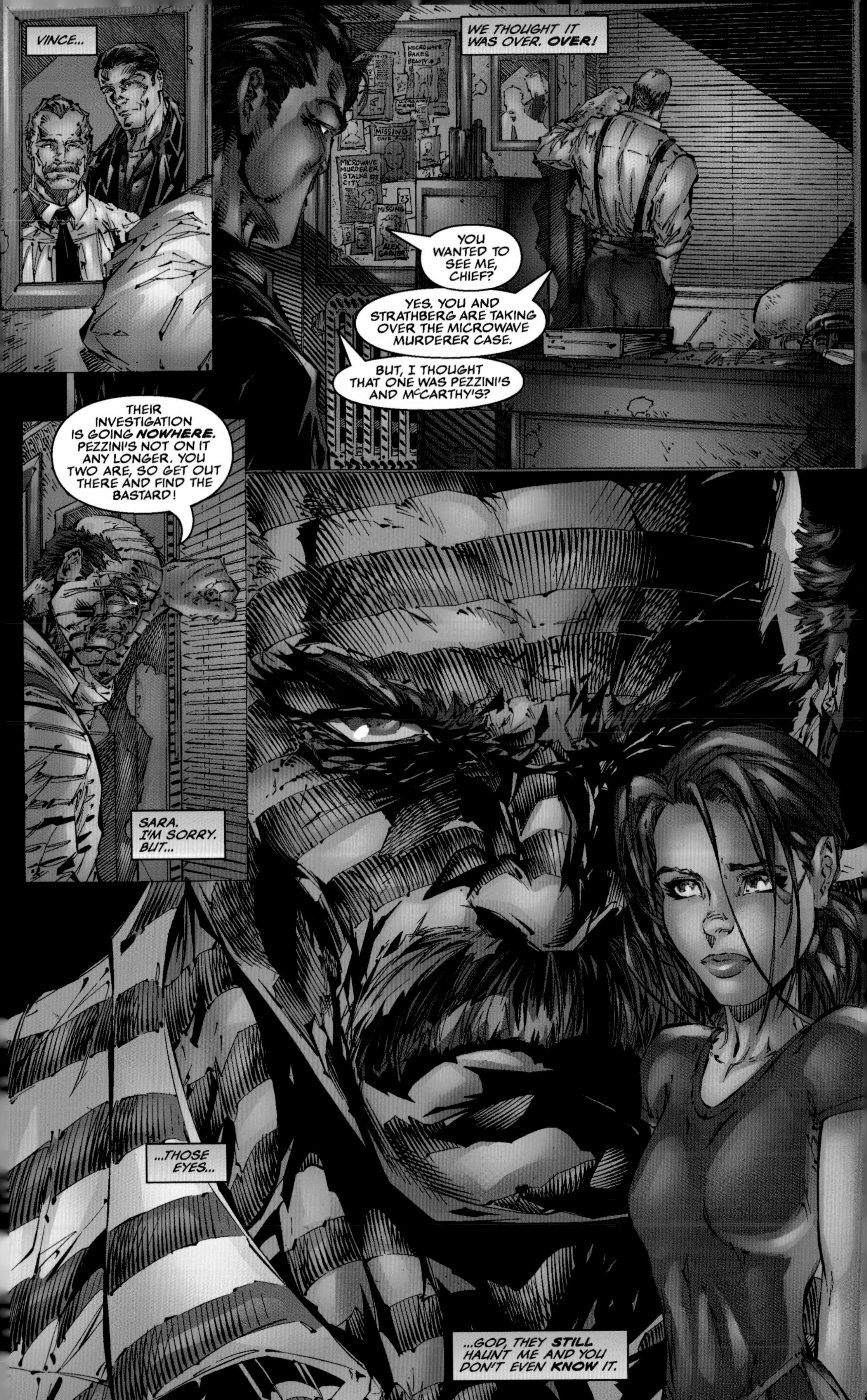
VINCE...
WE THOUGHT IT WAS OVER. **OVER!**
YOU WANTED TO SEE ME, CHIEF?
YES, YOU AND STRATHBERG ARE TAKING OVER THE MICROWAVE MURDERER CASE.
BUT, I THOUGHT THAT ONE WAS PEZZINI'S AND McCARTHY'S?
THEIR INVESTIGATION IS GOING **NOWHERE.** PEZZINI'S NOT ON IT ANY LONGER. YOU TWO ARE, SO GET OUT THERE AND FIND THE BASTARD!
SARA. I'M SORRY. BUT...
...THOSE EYES...
...GOD, THEY **STILL** HAUNT ME AND YOU DON'T EVEN **KNOW** IT.

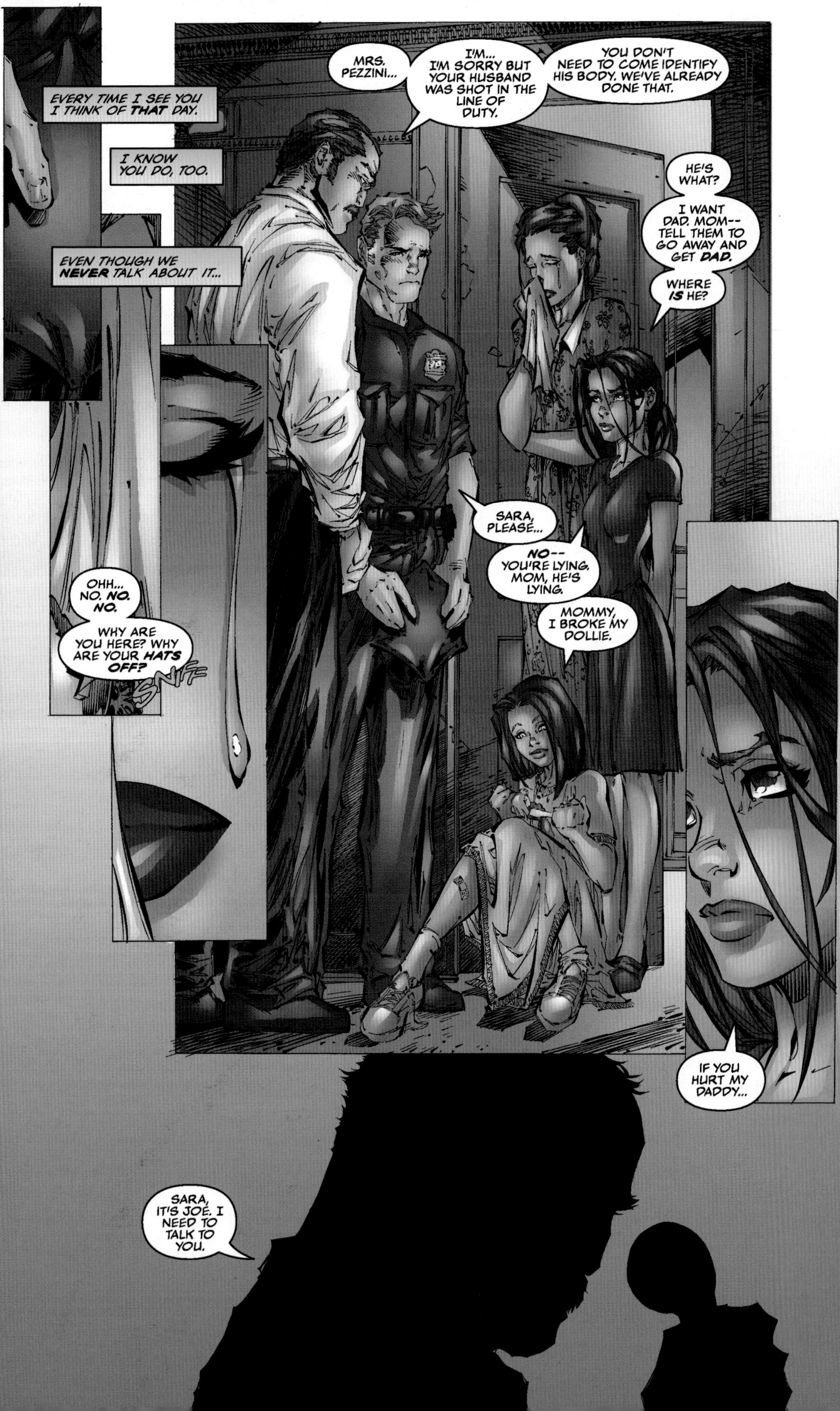

EVERY TIME I SEE YOU I THINK OF THAT DAY.
I KNOW YOU DO, TOO.
EVEN THOUGH WE NEVER TALK ABOUT IT...
MRS. PEZZINI...
I'M... I'M SORRY BUT YOUR HUSBAND WAS SHOT IN THE LINE OF DUTY.
YOU DON'T NEED TO COME IDENTIFY HIS BODY. WE'VE ALREADY DONE THAT.
HE'S WHAT?
I WANT DAD. MOM-- TELL THEM TO GO AWAY AND GET DAD.
WHERE IS HE?
OHH... NO. NO. NO.
WHY ARE YOU HERE? WHY ARE YOUR HATS OFF?
SNIFF
SARA, PLEASE...
NO-- YOU'RE LYING. MOM, HE'S LYING.
MOMMY, I BROKE MY DOLLIE.
IF YOU HURT MY DADDY...
SARA, IT'S JOE. I NEED TO TALK TO YOU.

AND, ACROSS THE EAST RIVER...
OKAY, MS. PEZZINI. NO MORE QUESTIONS. YOU'LL TELL ME WHEN *YOU'RE* READY.
FINE, THEN. BUT MEANWHILE, WE HAVE A FEW CASES TO SOLVE. *BIG* CASES.
HMM. WONDER IF THAT'S TOO STRONG--
Bbbrrrp! Bbbrrrp!
McCARTHY HERE.
JAKE, I'VE GOT SOME NEWS YOU'LL BE VERY INTERESTED IN HEARING. CAN YOU GET TO MIDTOWN?
BRUCE? HEY--YEAH, I CAN GET THERE.
I'M AT GRAND CENTRAL STATION. GET OVER HERE RIGHT AWAY. IT'S ABOUT THE MAFIA.
SURE. I'LL SEE YOU IN A FEW.
AND BRUCE, I NEED TO TALK TO YOU ABOUT A FEW THINGS TOO, OKAY?
HELLO?
BRUCE?
WELL, SARA. IF YOU WON'T TELL ME WHAT I NEED TO KNOW, MAYBE I'VE FOUND SOMEONE WHO CAN...

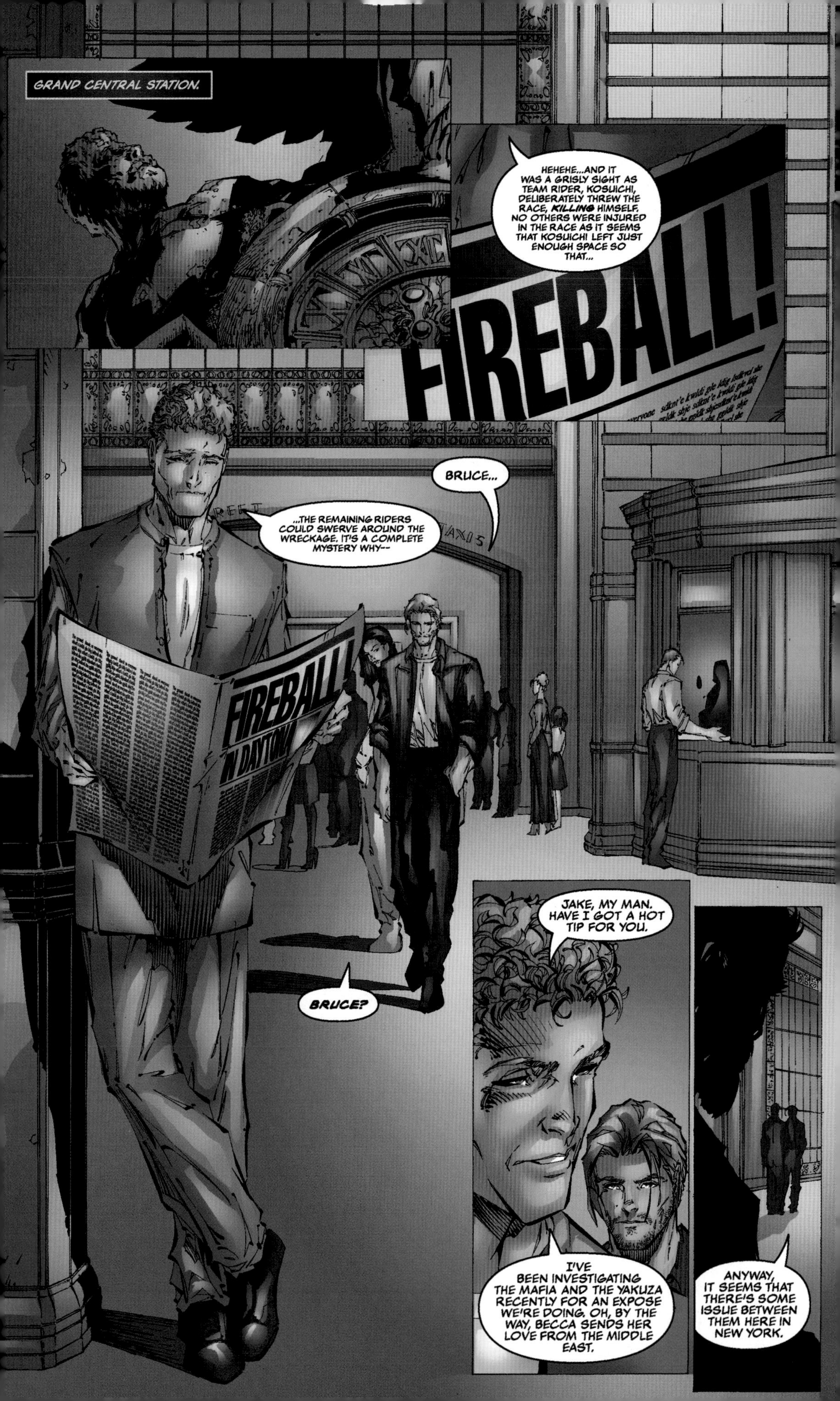
GRAND CENTRAL STATION.
HEHEHE...AND IT WAS A GRISLY SIGHT AS TEAM RIDER, KOSUICHI, DELIBERATELY THREW THE RACE, KILLING HIMSELF. NO OTHERS WERE INJURED IN THE RACE AS IT SEEMS THAT KOSUICHI LEFT JUST ENOUGH SPACE SO THAT...
FIREBALL!
BRUCE...
...THE REMAINING RIDERS COULD SWERVE AROUND THE WRECKAGE. IT'S A COMPLETE MYSTERY WHY--
FIREBALL! IN DAYTONA
BRUCE?
JAKE, MY MAN. HAVE I GOT A HOT TIP FOR YOU.
I'VE BEEN INVESTIGATING THE MAFIA AND THE YAKUZA RECENTLY FOR AN EXPOSE WE'RE DOING. OH, BY THE WAY, BECCA SENDS HER LOVE FROM THE MIDDLE EAST.
ANYWAY, IT SEEMS THAT THERE'S SOME ISSUE BETWEEN THEM HERE IN NEW YORK.

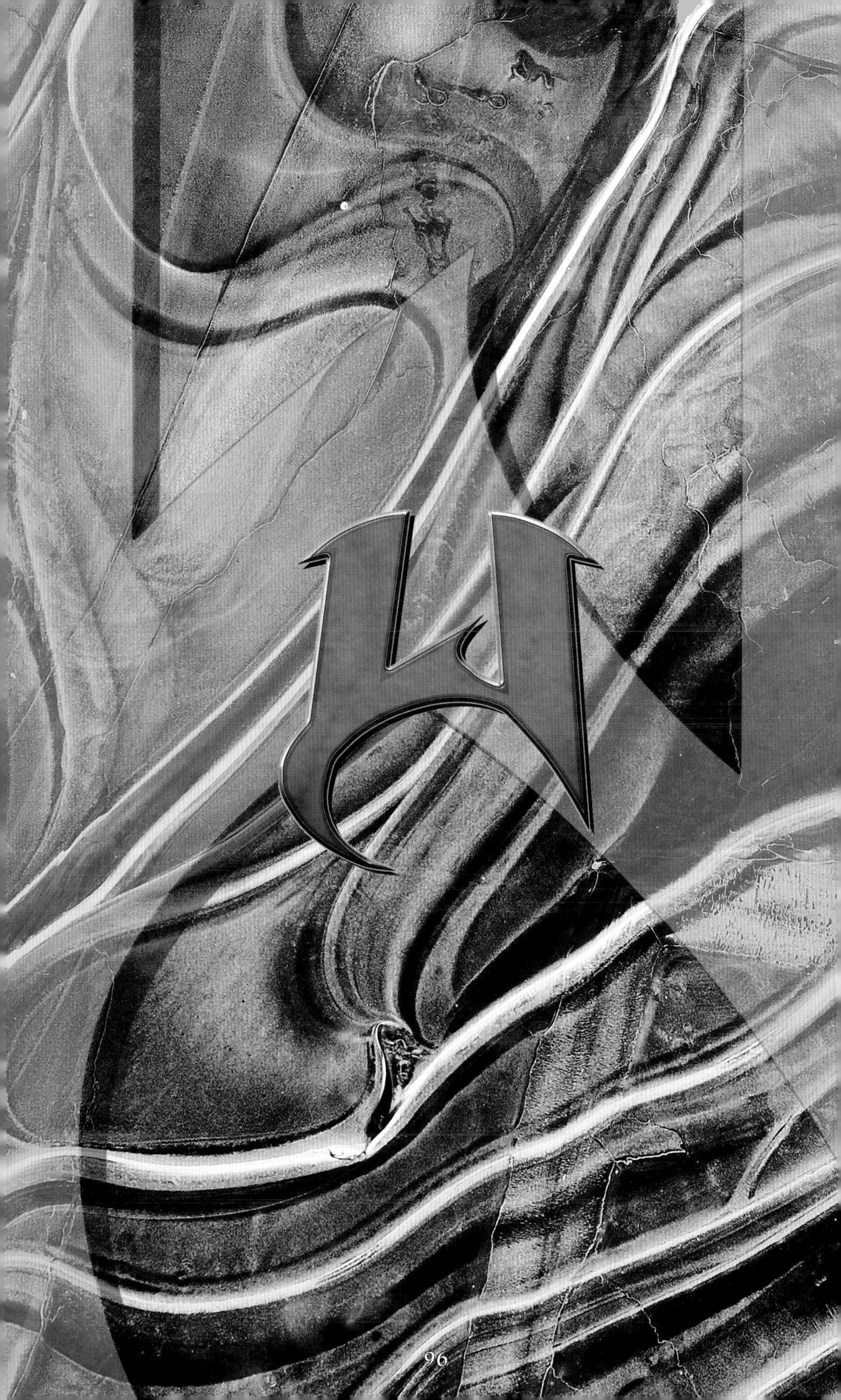

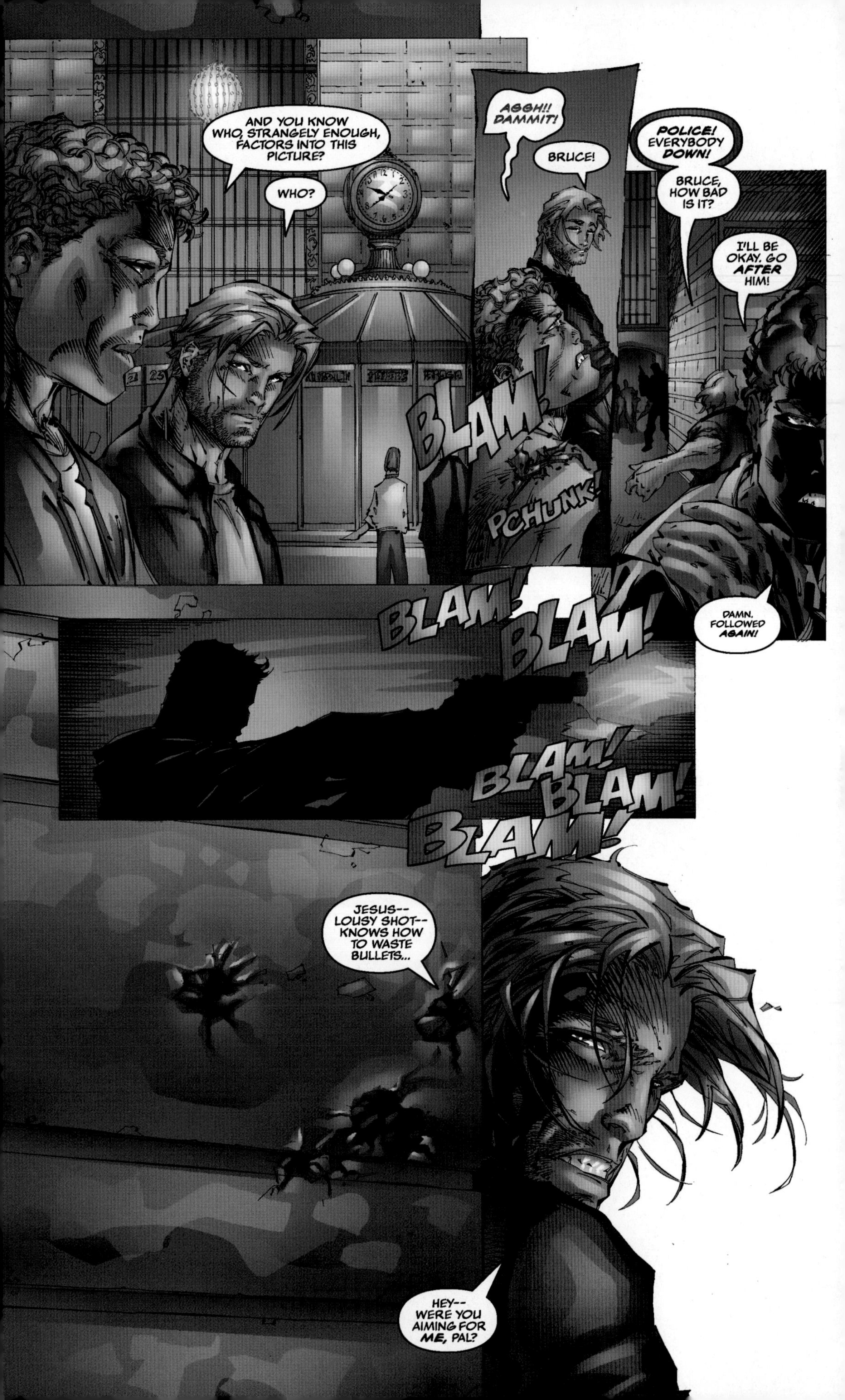
AND YOU KNOW WHO, STRANGELY ENOUGH, FACTORS INTO THIS PICTURE?
WHO?
AGGH!! DAMMIT!
BRUCE!
BLAM!
PCHUNK!
POLICE! EVERYBODY DOWN!
BRUCE, HOW BAD IS IT?
I'LL BE OKAY. GO AFTER HIM!
DAMN. FOLLOWED AGAIN!
BLAM! BLAM!
BLAM! BLAM! BLAM!
JESUS-- LOUSY SHOT-- KNOWS HOW TO WASTE BULLETS...
HEY-- WERE YOU AIMING FOR ME, PAL?

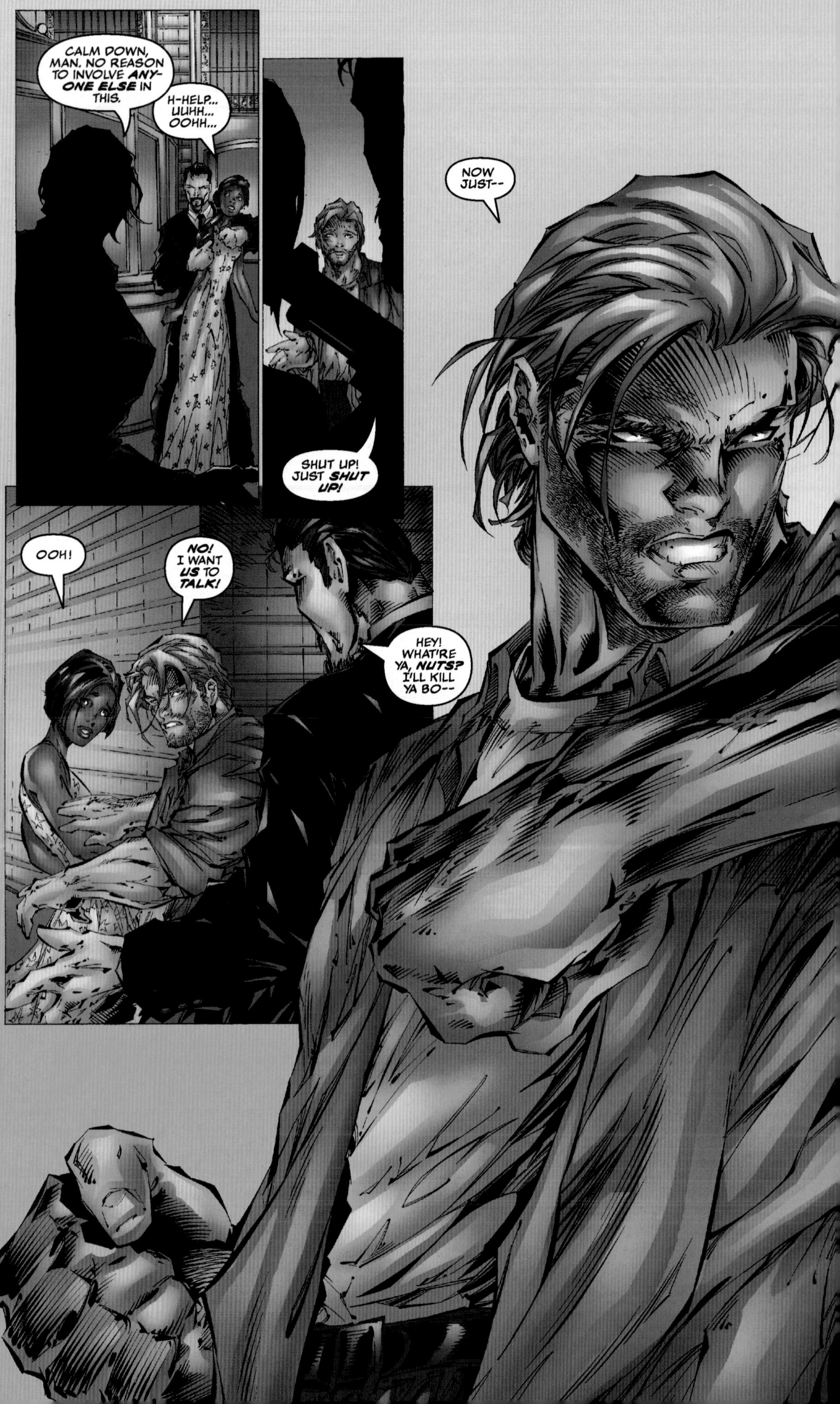
CALM DOWN, MAN. NO REASON TO INVOLVE ANY-ONE ELSE IN THIS.
H-HELP... UUHH... OOHH...
SHUT UP! JUST SHUT UP!
NOW JUST--
OOH!
NO! I WANT US TO TALK!
HEY! WHAT'RE YA, NUTS? I'LL KILL YA BO--

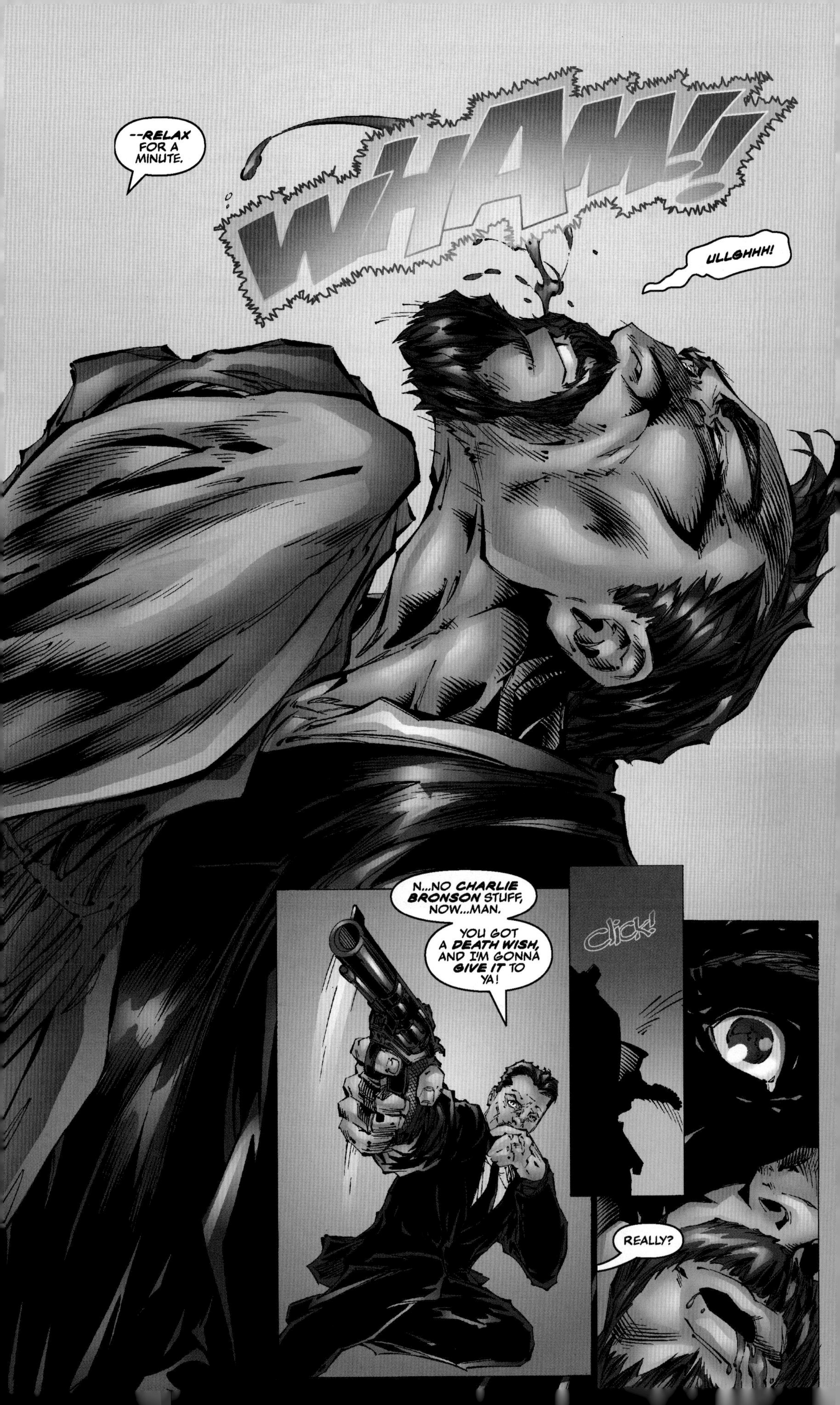
--RELAX FOR A MINUTE.
WHAM!
ULLGHHH!
N...NO CHARLIE BRONSON STUFF, NOW...MAN.
YOU GOT A DEATH WISH, AND I'M GONNA GIVE IT TO YA!
CLICK!
REALLY?

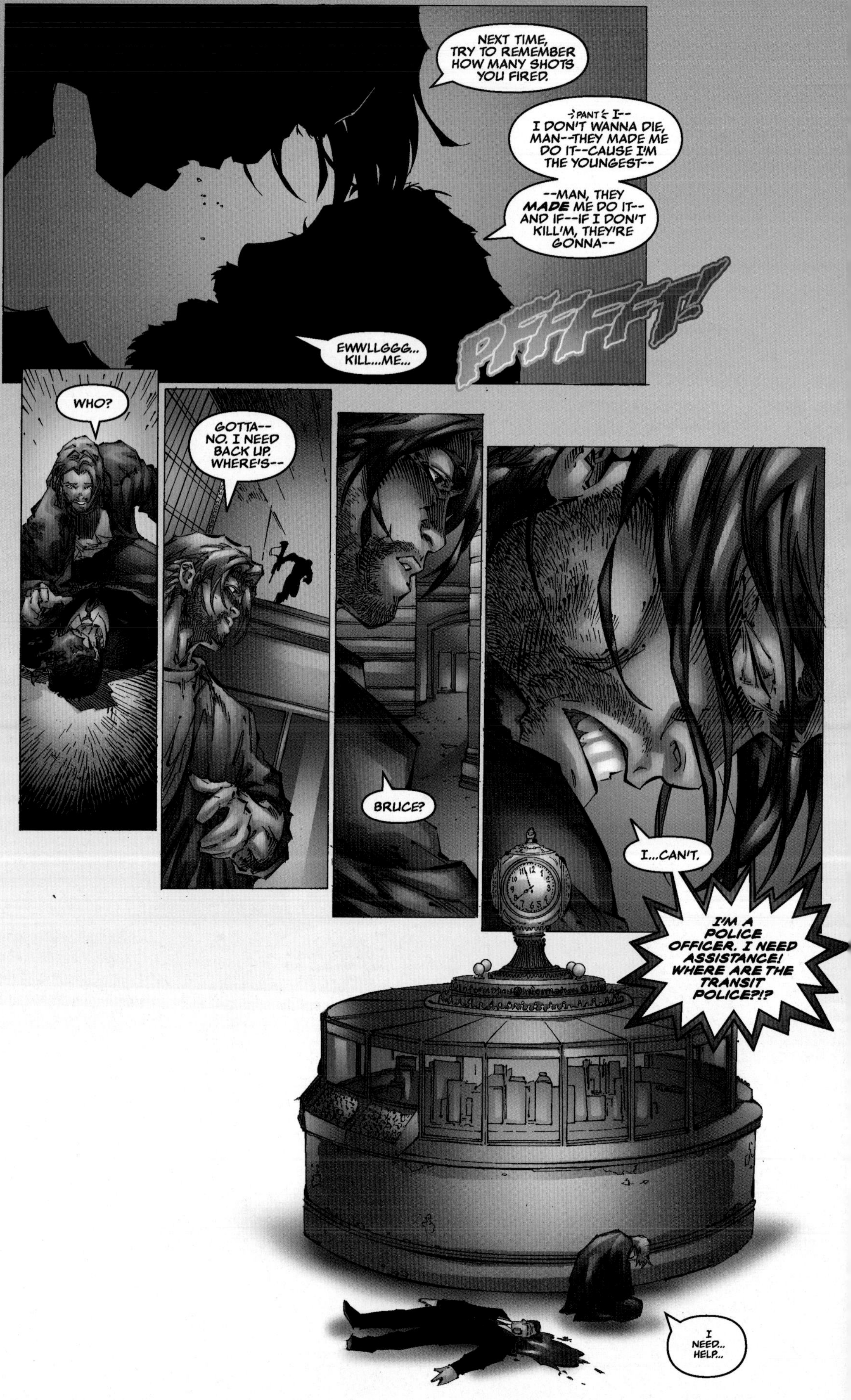
NEXT TIME, TRY TO REMEMBER HOW MANY SHOTS YOU FIRED.
PANT I-- I DON'T WANNA DIE, MAN--THEY MADE ME DO IT--CAUSE I'M THE YOUNGEST--
--MAN, THEY MADE ME DO IT-- AND IF--IF I DON'T KILL'M, THEY'RE GONNA--
PFFFFT!
EWWLLGGG... KILL...ME...
WHO?
GOTTA-- NO. I NEED BACK UP. WHERE'S--
BRUCE?
I...CAN'T.
I'M A POLICE OFFICER. I NEED ASSISTANCE! WHERE ARE THE TRANSIT POLICE?!?
I NEED... HELP...

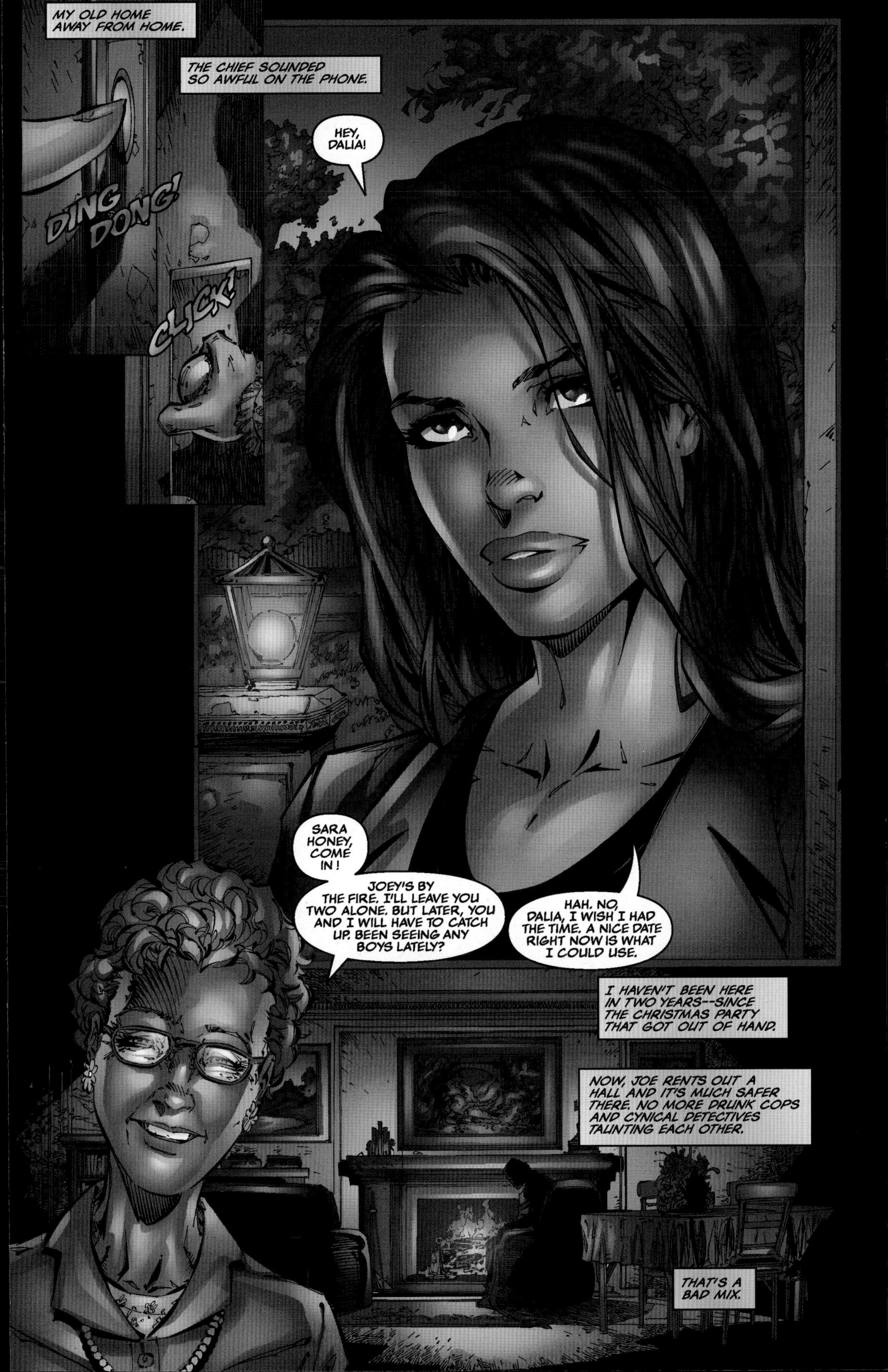
MY OLD HOME AWAY FROM HOME.
THE CHIEF SOUNDED SO AWFUL ON THE PHONE.
DING DONG!
CLICK!
HEY, DALIA!
SARA HONEY, COME IN!
JOEY'S BY THE FIRE. I'LL LEAVE YOU TWO ALONE. BUT LATER, YOU AND I WILL HAVE TO CATCH UP. BEEN SEEING ANY BOYS LATELY?
HAH. NO, DALIA, I WISH I HAD THE TIME. A NICE DATE RIGHT NOW IS WHAT I COULD USE.
I HAVEN'T BEEN HERE IN TWO YEARS--SINCE THE CHRISTMAS PARTY THAT GOT OUT OF HAND.
NOW, JOE RENTS OUT A HALL AND IT'S MUCH SAFER THERE. NO MORE DRUNK COPS AND CYNICAL DETECTIVES TAUNTING EACH OTHER.
THAT'S A BAD MIX.

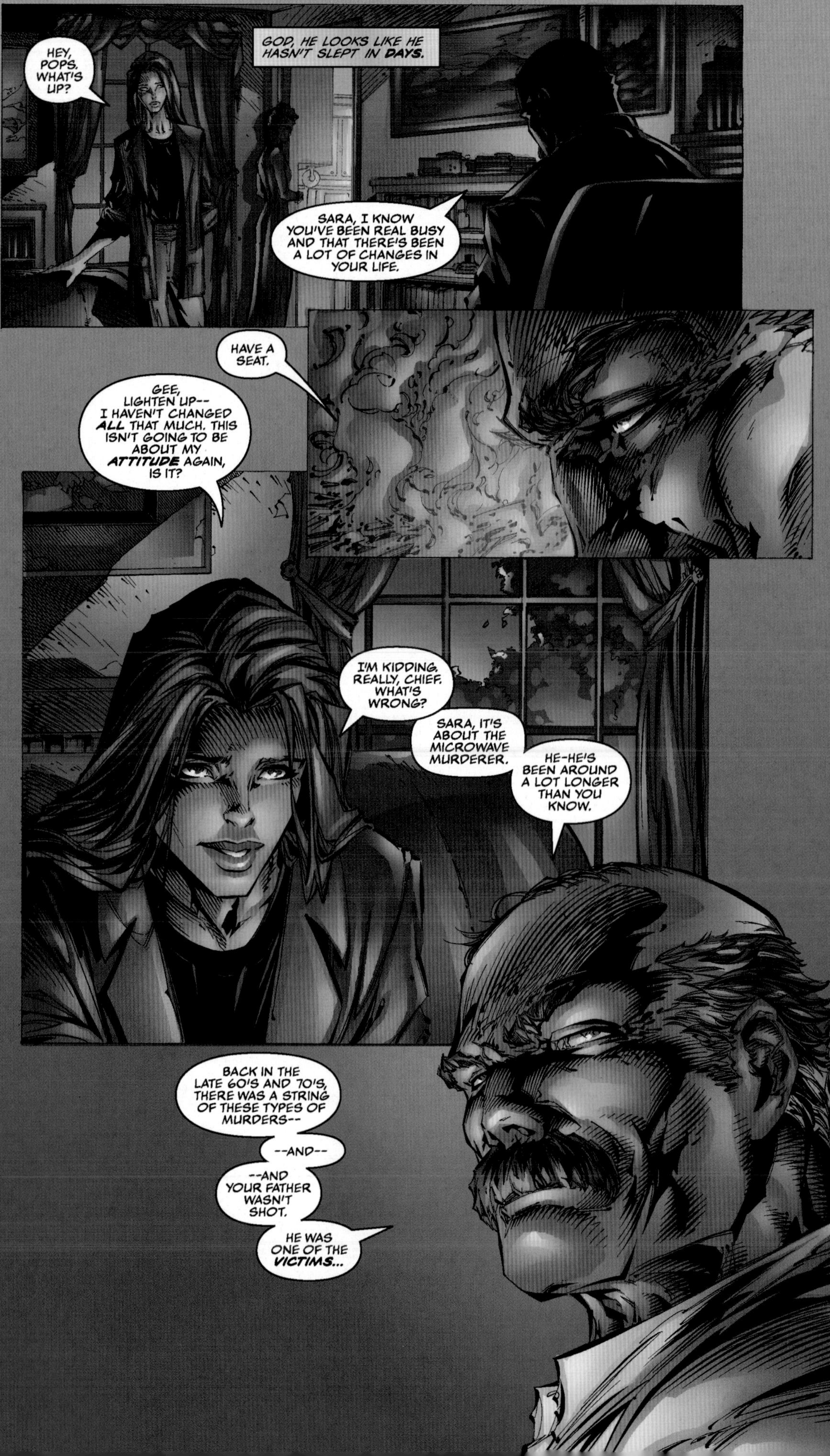
HEY, POPS. WHAT'S UP?
GOD, HE LOOKS LIKE HE HASN'T SLEPT IN DAYS.
SARA, I KNOW YOU'VE BEEN REAL BUSY AND THAT THERE'S BEEN A LOT OF CHANGES IN YOUR LIFE.
HAVE A SEAT.
GEE, LIGHTEN UP-- I HAVEN'T CHANGED ALL THAT MUCH. THIS ISN'T GOING TO BE ABOUT MY ATTITUDE AGAIN, IS IT?
I'M KIDDING. REALLY, CHIEF. WHAT'S WRONG?
SARA, IT'S ABOUT THE MICROWAVE MURDERER.
HE-HE'S BEEN AROUND A LOT LONGER THAN YOU KNOW.
BACK IN THE LATE 60'S AND 70'S, THERE WAS A STRING OF THESE TYPES OF MURDERS--
--AND--
--AND YOUR FATHER WASN'T SHOT.
HE WAS ONE OF THE VICTIMS...

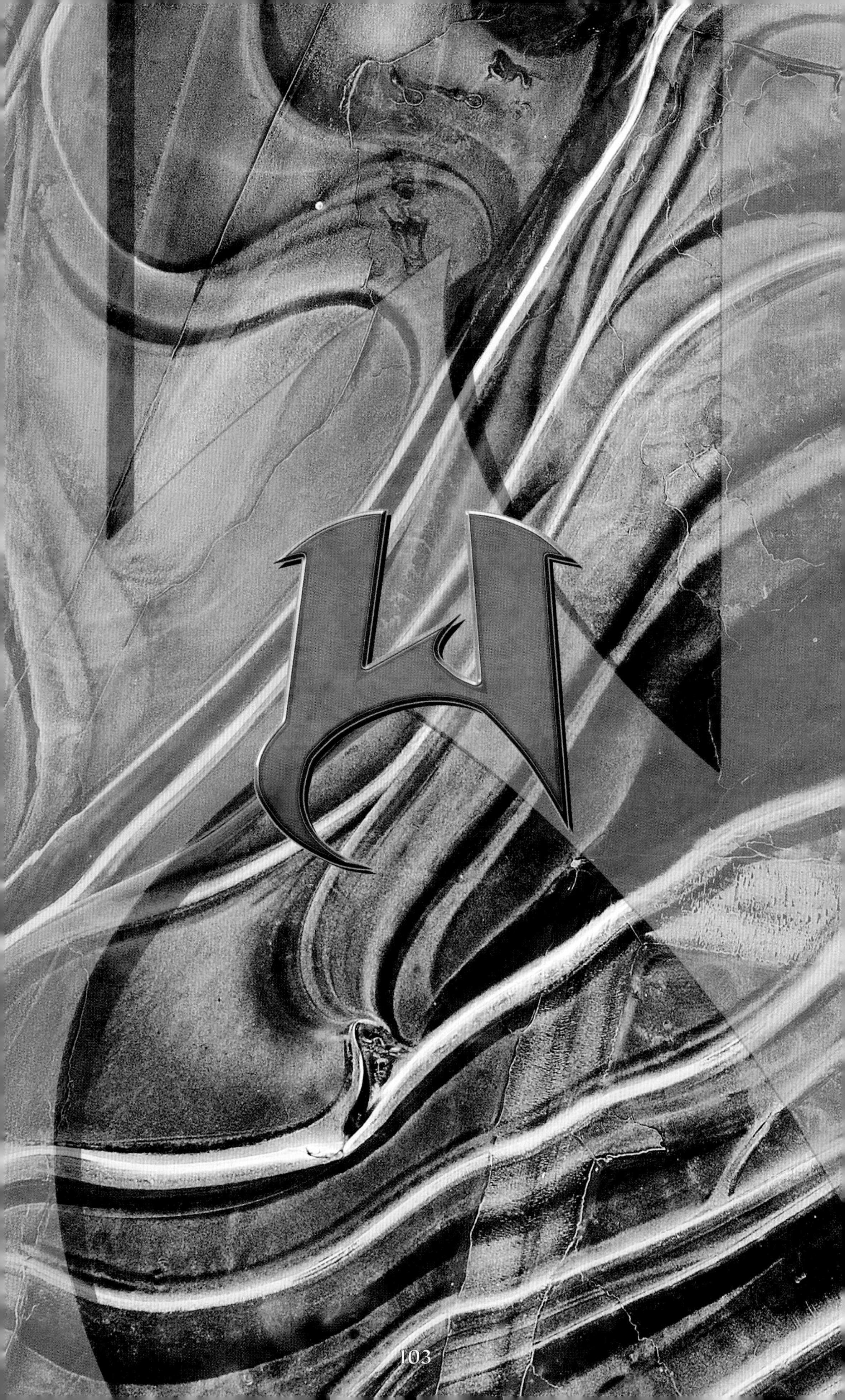

ISSUE #13

story: **David Wohl** and **Christina Z.**
pencils/co-plot: **Michael Turner**
inks: **D-Tron**
colors: **JD Smith**

ink assists: **Jeff De Los Santos, Jose "Jag" Guillen, Marsha Chen, Viet Trong**
and **Andy Kim**

lettering assists: **Robin Sphehar**

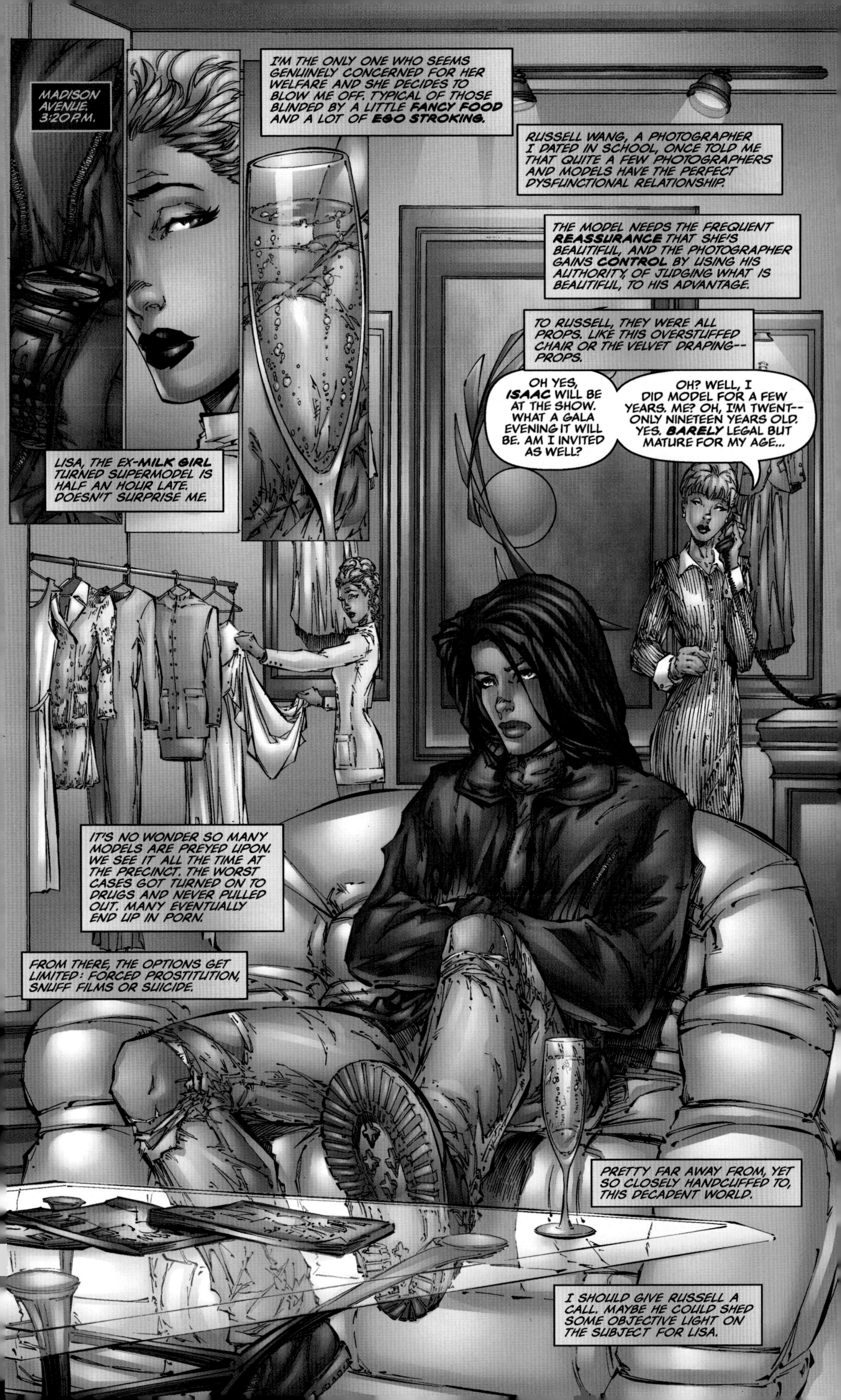

MADISON AVENUE. 3:20 P.M.
I'M THE ONLY ONE WHO SEEMS GENUINELY CONCERNED FOR HER WELFARE AND SHE DECIDES TO BLOW ME OFF. TYPICAL OF THOSE BLINDED BY A LITTLE FANCY FOOD AND A LOT OF EGO STROKING.
LISA, THE EX-MILK GIRL TURNED SUPERMODEL IS HALF AN HOUR LATE. DOESN'T SURPRISE ME.
RUSSELL WANG, A PHOTOGRAPHER I DATED IN SCHOOL, ONCE TOLD ME THAT QUITE A FEW PHOTOGRAPHERS AND MODELS HAVE THE PERFECT DYSFUNCTIONAL RELATIONSHIP.
THE MODEL NEEDS THE FREQUENT REASSURANCE THAT SHE'S BEAUTIFUL, AND THE PHOTOGRAPHER GAINS CONTROL BY USING HIS AUTHORITY, OF JUDGING WHAT IS BEAUTIFUL, TO HIS ADVANTAGE.
TO RUSSELL, THEY WERE ALL PROPS. LIKE THIS OVERSTUFFED CHAIR OR THE VELVET DRAPING-- PROPS.
OH YES, ISAAC WILL BE AT THE SHOW. WHAT A GALA EVENING IT WILL BE. AM I INVITED AS WELL?
OH? WELL, I DID MODEL FOR A FEW YEARS. ME? OH, I'M TWENT-- ONLY NINETEEN YEARS OLD. YES. BARELY LEGAL BUT MATURE FOR MY AGE...
IT'S NO WONDER SO MANY MODELS ARE PREYED UPON. WE SEE IT ALL THE TIME AT THE PRECINCT. THE WORST CASES GOT TURNED ON TO DRUGS AND NEVER PULLED OUT. MANY EVENTUALLY END UP IN PORN.
FROM THERE, THE OPTIONS GET LIMITED: FORCED PROSTITUTION, SNUFF FILMS OR SUICIDE.
PRETTY FAR AWAY FROM, YET SO CLOSELY HANDCUFFED TO, THIS DECADENT WORLD.
I SHOULD GIVE RUSSELL A CALL. MAYBE HE COULD SHED SOME OBJECTIVE LIGHT ON THE SUBJECT FOR LISA.

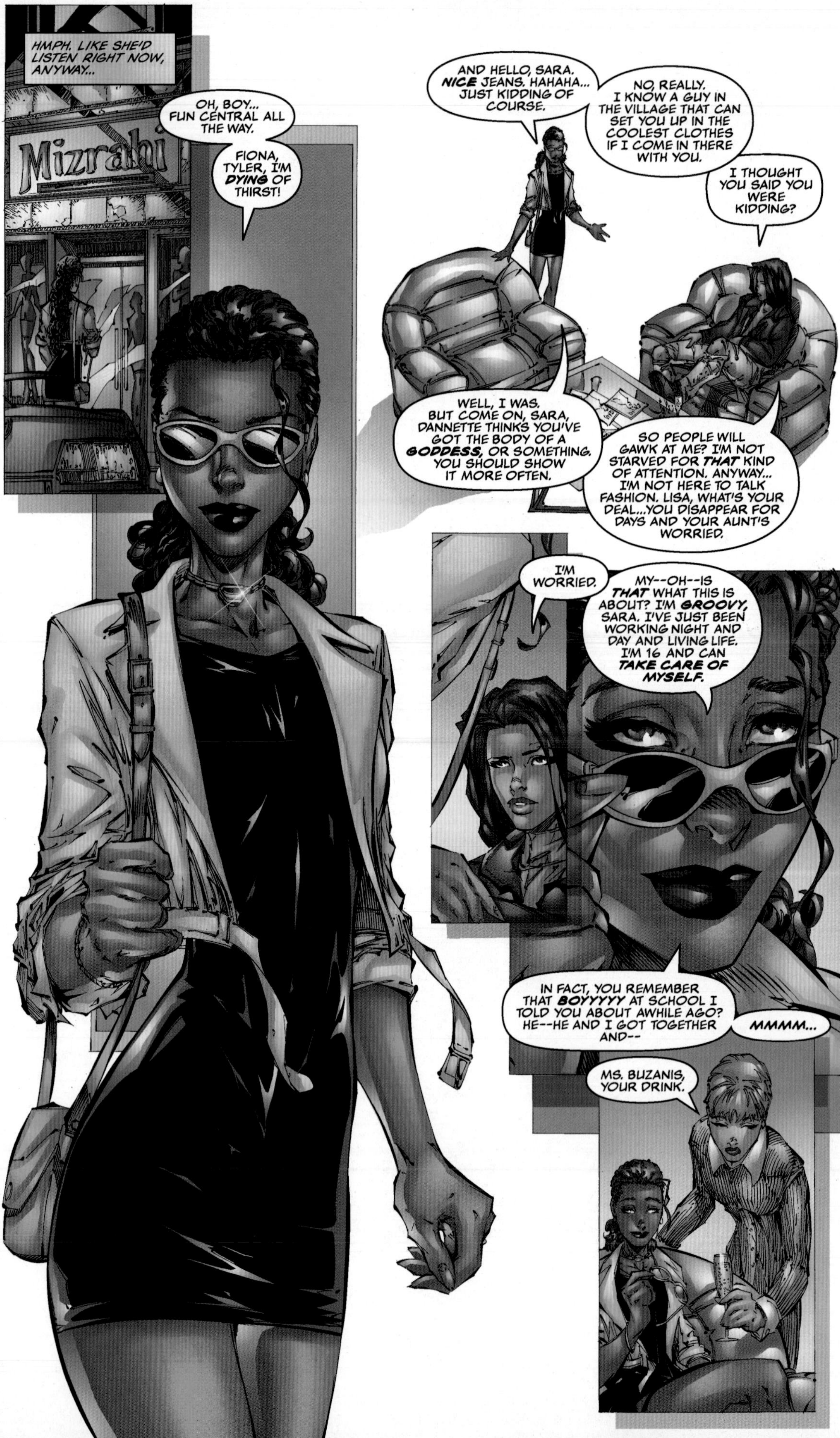
HMPH. LIKE SHE'D LISTEN RIGHT NOW, ANYWAY...
Mizrahi
OH, BOY... FUN CENTRAL ALL THE WAY.
FIONA, TYLER, I'M DYING OF THIRST!
AND HELLO, SARA. NICE JEANS. HAHAHA... JUST KIDDING OF COURSE.
NO, REALLY. I KNOW A GUY IN THE VILLAGE THAT CAN SET YOU UP IN THE COOLEST CLOTHES IF I COME IN THERE WITH YOU.
I THOUGHT YOU SAID YOU WERE KIDDING?
WELL, I WAS. BUT COME ON, SARA, DANNETTE THINKS YOU'VE GOT THE BODY OF A GODDESS, OR SOMETHING. YOU SHOULD SHOW IT MORE OFTEN.
SO PEOPLE WILL GAWK AT ME? I'M NOT STARVED FOR THAT KIND OF ATTENTION. ANYWAY... I'M NOT HERE TO TALK FASHION. LISA, WHAT'S YOUR DEAL...YOU DISAPPEAR FOR DAYS AND YOUR AUNT'S WORRIED.
I'M WORRIED.
MY--OH--IS THAT WHAT THIS IS ABOUT? I'M GROOVY, SARA. I'VE JUST BEEN WORKING NIGHT AND DAY AND LIVING LIFE. I'M 16 AND CAN TAKE CARE OF MYSELF.
IN FACT, YOU REMEMBER THAT BOYYYYY AT SCHOOL I TOLD YOU ABOUT AWHILE AGO? HE--HE AND I GOT TOGETHER AND--
MMMM...
MS. BUZANIS, YOUR DRINK.

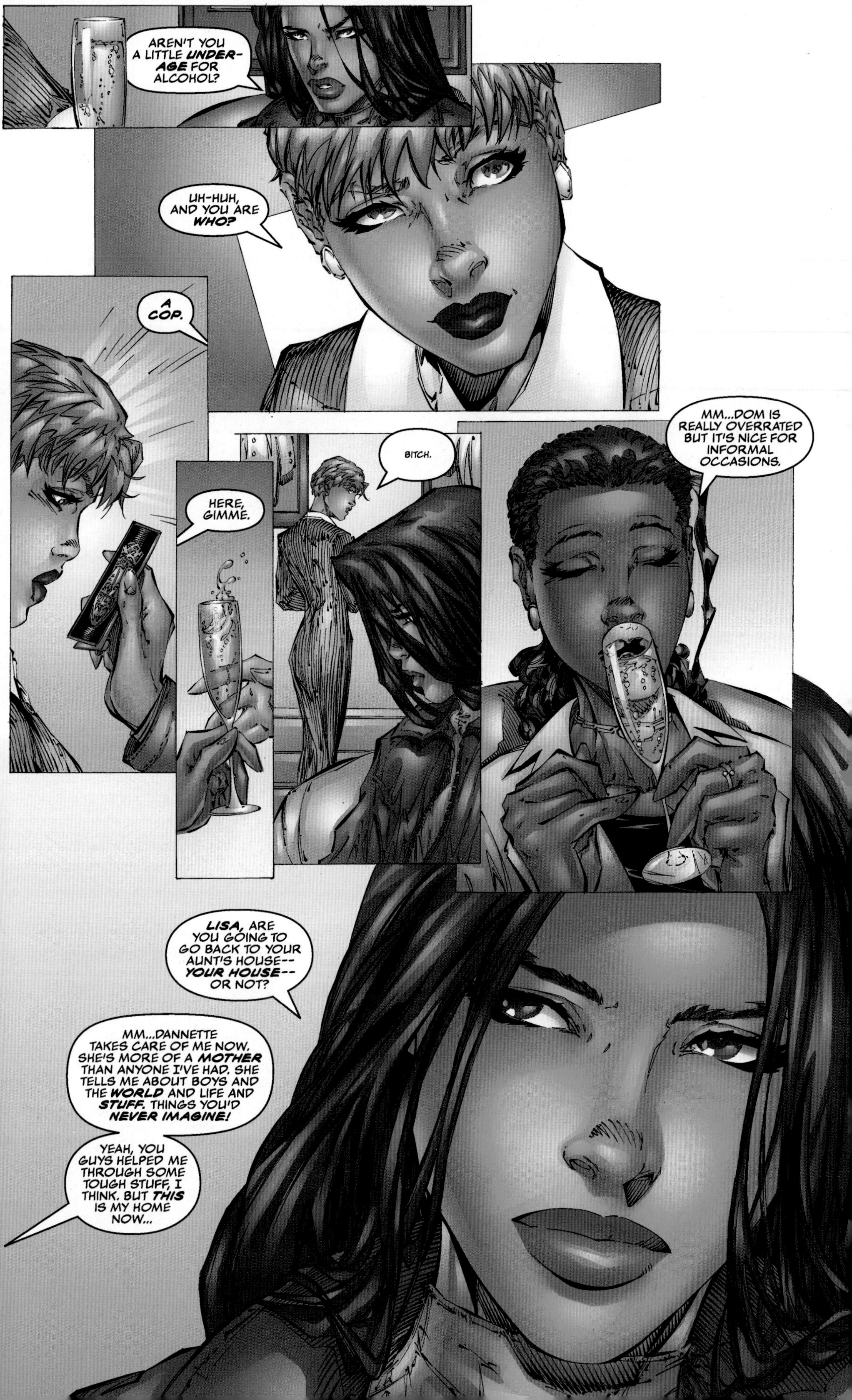

AREN'T YOU A LITTLE UNDER-AGE FOR ALCOHOL?
UH-HUH, AND YOU ARE WHO?
A COP.
HERE, GIMME.
BITCH.
MM...DOM IS REALLY OVERRATED BUT IT'S NICE FOR INFORMAL OCCASIONS.
LISA, ARE YOU GOING TO GO BACK TO YOUR AUNT'S HOUSE-- YOUR HOUSE-- OR NOT?
MM...DANNETTE TAKES CARE OF ME NOW. SHE'S MORE OF A MOTHER THAN ANYONE I'VE HAD. SHE TELLS ME ABOUT BOYS AND THE WORLD AND LIFE AND STUFF. THINGS YOU'D NEVER IMAGINE!
YEAH, YOU GUYS HELPED ME THROUGH SOME TOUGH STUFF, I THINK, BUT THIS IS MY HOME NOW...

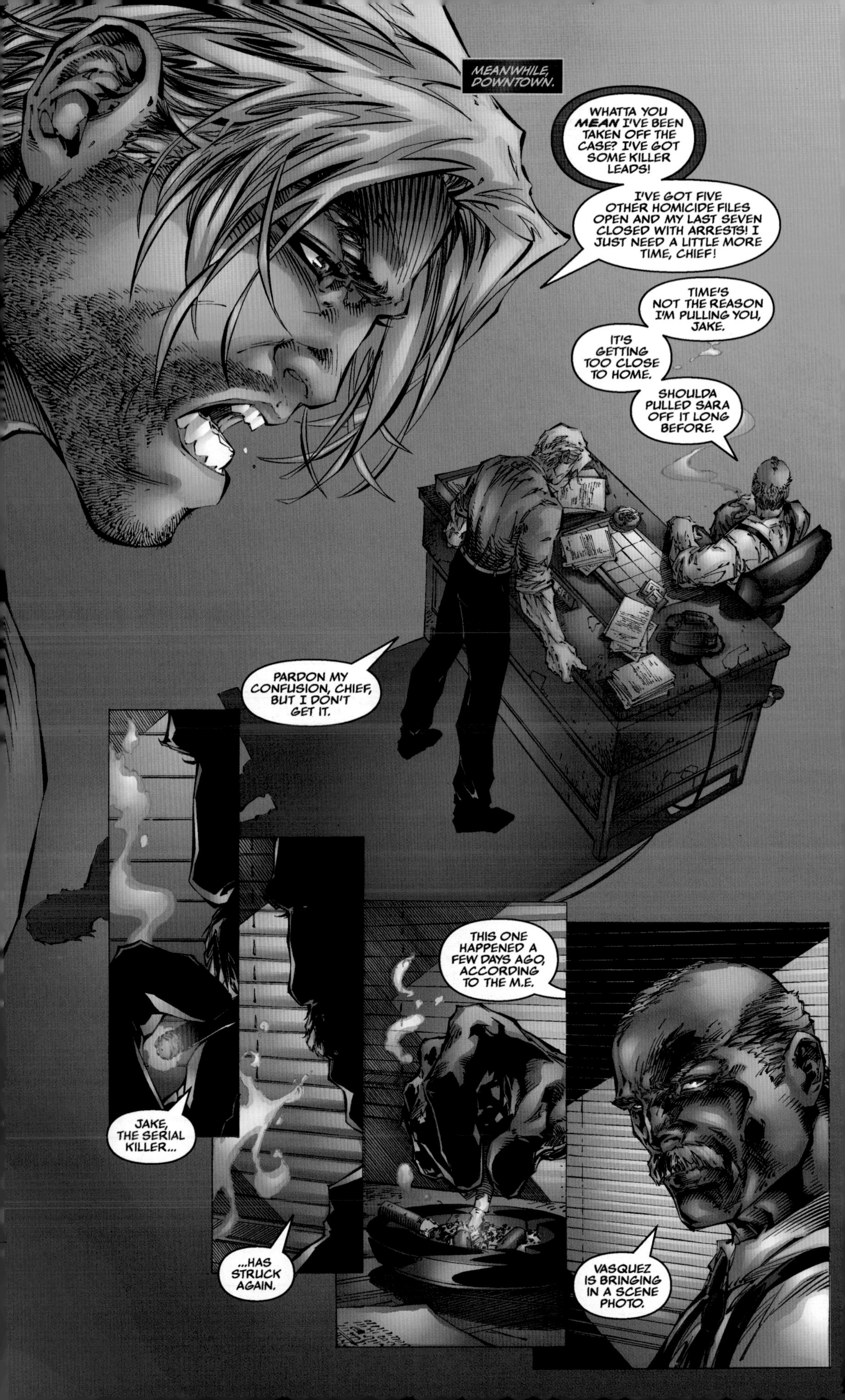
MEANWHILE, DOWNTOWN.
WHATTA YOU MEAN I'VE BEEN TAKEN OFF THE CASE? I'VE GOT SOME KILLER LEADS!
I'VE GOT FIVE OTHER HOMICIDE FILES OPEN AND MY LAST SEVEN CLOSED WITH ARRESTS! I JUST NEED A LITTLE MORE TIME, CHIEF!
TIME'S NOT THE REASON I'M PULLING YOU, JAKE.
IT'S GETTING TOO CLOSE TO HOME.
SHOULDA PULLED SARA OFF IT LONG BEFORE.
PARDON MY CONFUSION, CHIEF, BUT I DON'T GET IT.
JAKE, THE SERIAL KILLER...
...HAS STRUCK AGAIN.
THIS ONE HAPPENED A FEW DAYS AGO, ACCORDING TO THE M.E.
VASQUEZ IS BRINGING IN A SCENE PHOTO.

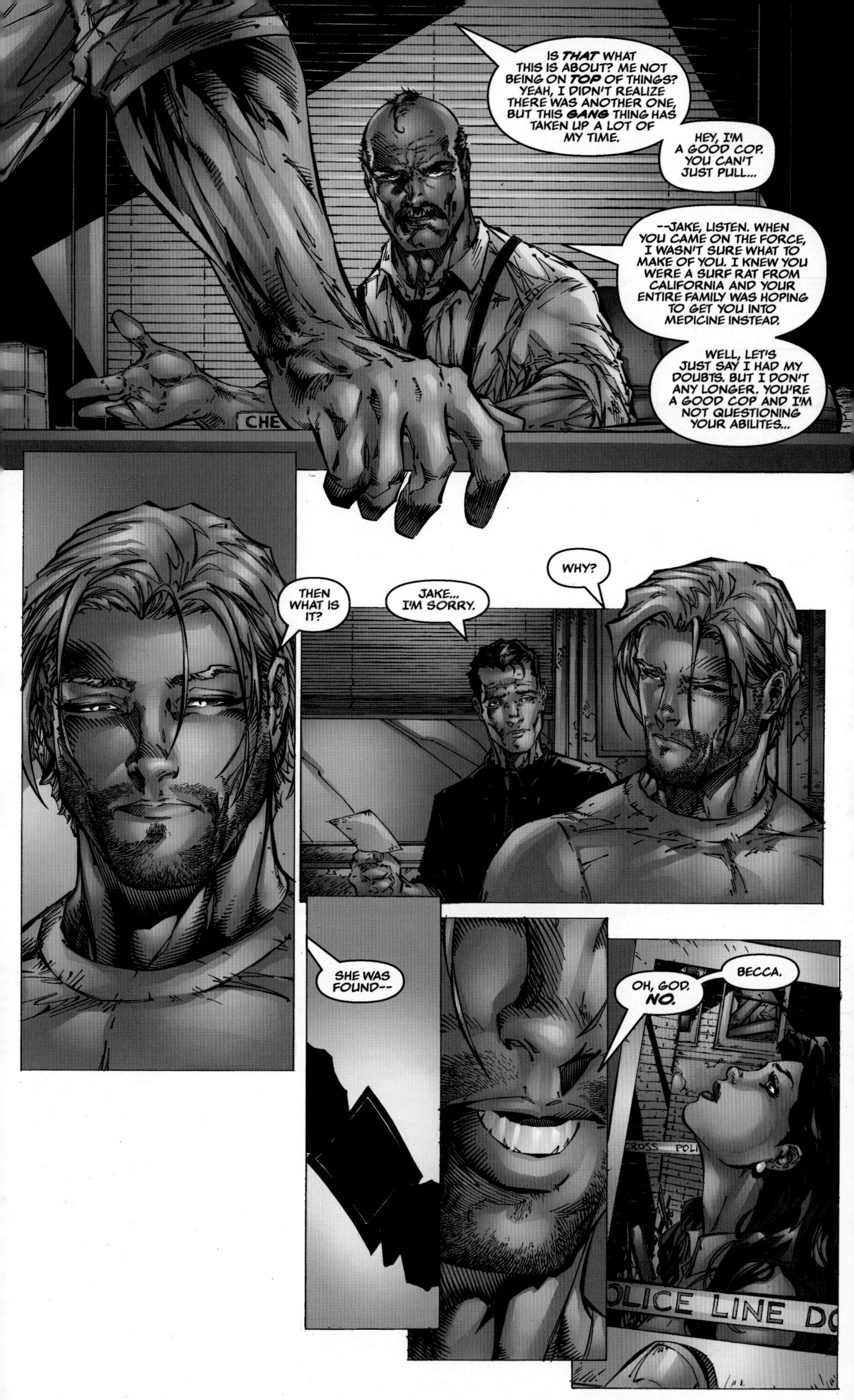

IS *THAT* WHAT THIS IS ABOUT? ME NOT BEING ON *TOP* OF THINGS? YEAH, I DIDN'T REALIZE THERE WAS ANOTHER ONE, BUT THIS *GANG* THING HAS TAKEN UP A LOT OF MY TIME.
HEY, I'M A GOOD COP. YOU CAN'T JUST PULL...
--JAKE, LISTEN. WHEN YOU CAME ON THE FORCE, I WASN'T SURE WHAT TO MAKE OF YOU. I KNEW YOU WERE A SURF RAT FROM CALIFORNIA AND YOUR ENTIRE FAMILY WAS HOPING TO GET YOU INTO MEDICINE INSTEAD.
WELL, LET'S JUST SAY I HAD MY DOUBTS. BUT I DON'T ANY LONGER. YOU'RE A GOOD COP AND I'M NOT QUESTIONING YOUR ABILITES...
CHE
THEN WHAT IS IT?
JAKE... I'M SORRY.
WHY?
SHE WAS FOUND--
BECCA.
OH, GOD. **NO.**
CROSS POLI
OLICE LINE DO

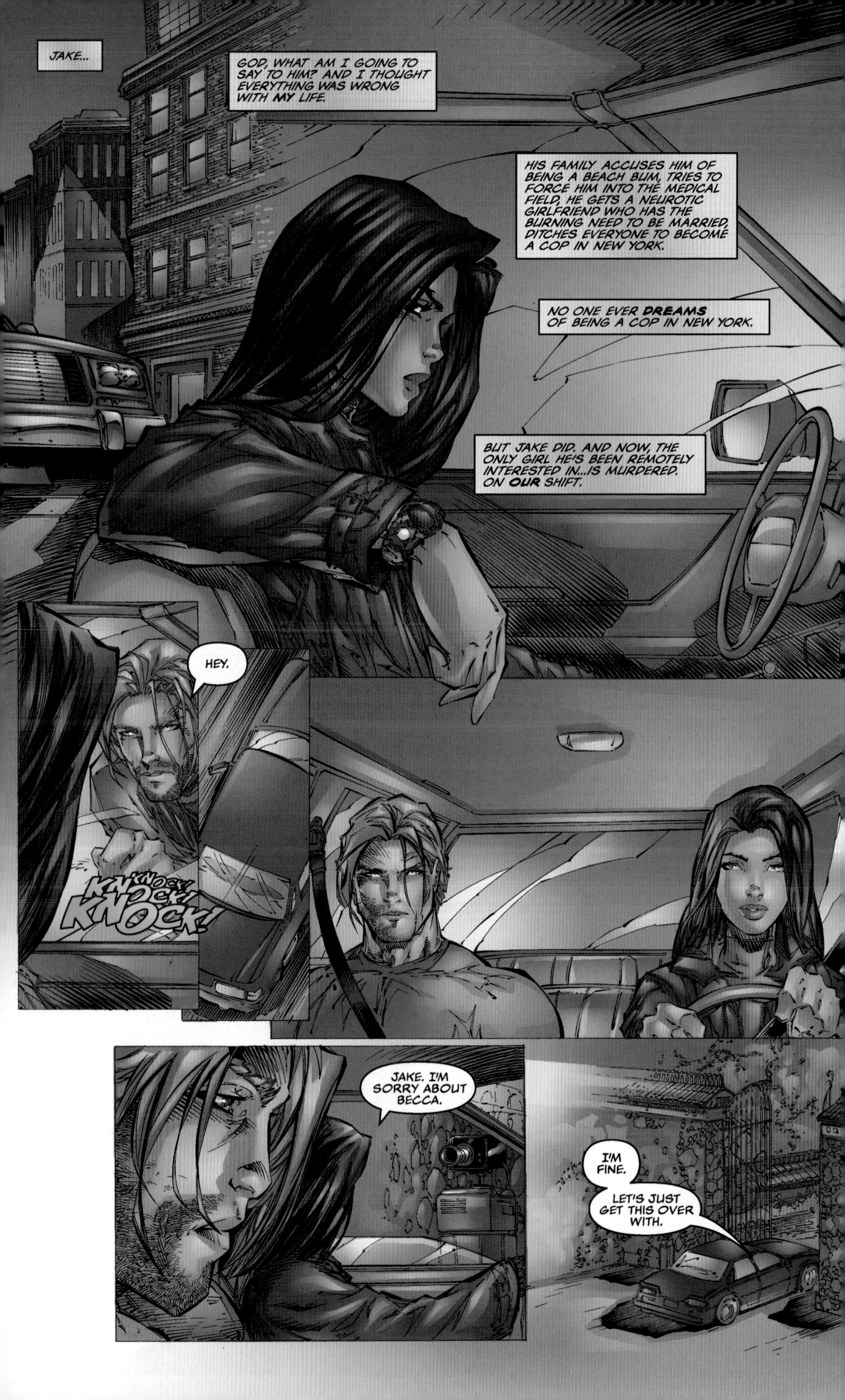
JAKE...
GOD, WHAT AM I GOING TO SAY TO HIM? AND I THOUGHT EVERYTHING WAS WRONG WITH MY LIFE.
HIS FAMILY ACCUSES HIM OF BEING A BEACH BUM, TRIES TO FORCE HIM INTO THE MEDICAL FIELD, HE GETS A NEUROTIC GIRLFRIEND WHO HAS THE BURNING NEED TO BE MARRIED, DITCHES EVERYONE TO BECOME A COP IN NEW YORK.
NO ONE EVER DREAMS OF BEING A COP IN NEW YORK.
BUT JAKE DID. AND NOW, THE ONLY GIRL HE'S BEEN REMOTELY INTERESTED IN...IS MURDERED. ON OUR SHIFT.
KNOCK! KNOCK! KNOCK!
HEY.
JAKE. I'M SORRY ABOUT BECCA.
I'M FINE.
LET'S JUST GET THIS OVER WITH.

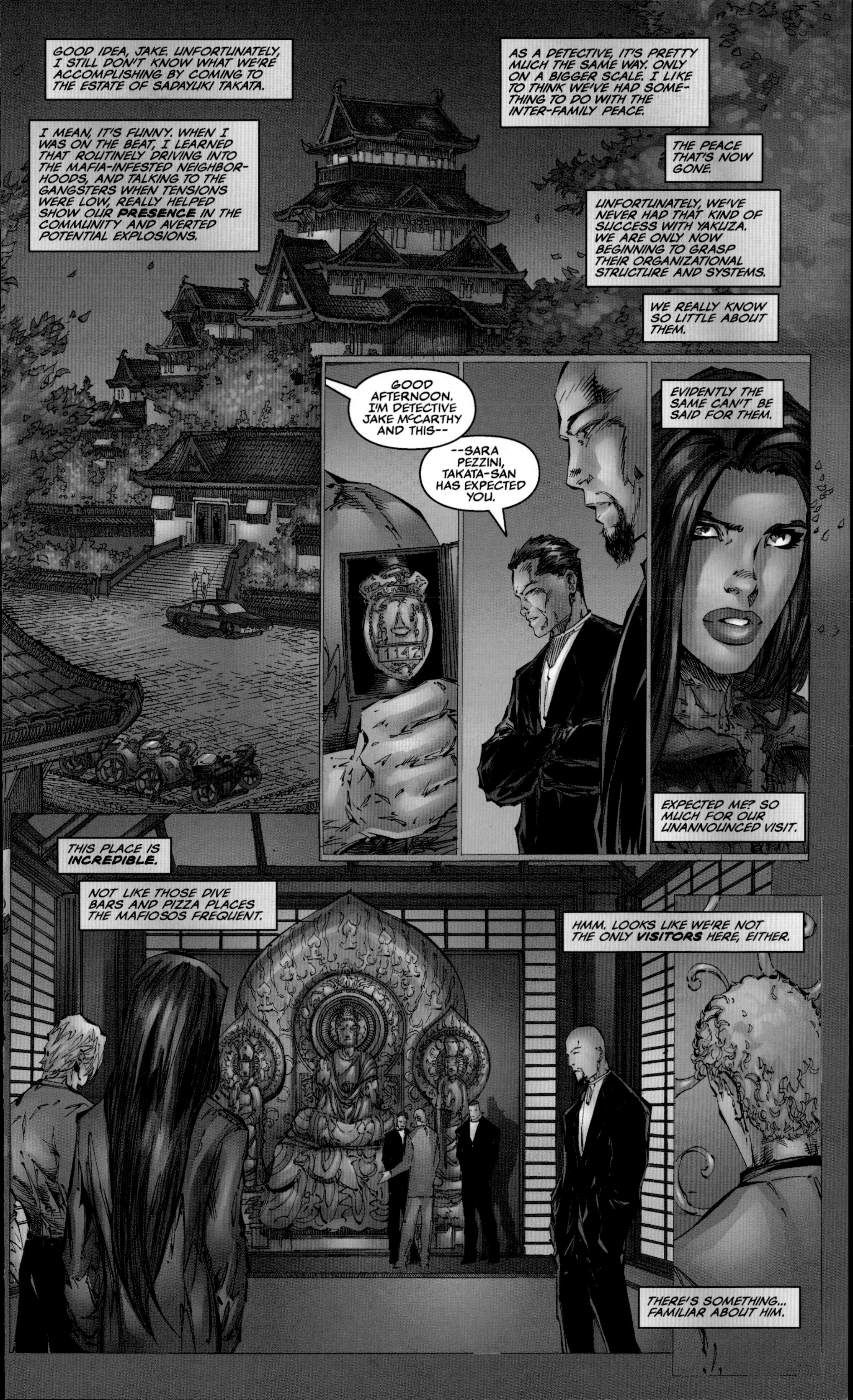
GOOD IDEA, JAKE. UNFORTUNATELY, I STILL DON'T KNOW WHAT WE'RE ACCOMPLISHING BY COMING TO THE ESTATE OF SADAYUKI TAKATA.
I MEAN, IT'S FUNNY. WHEN I WAS ON THE BEAT, I LEARNED THAT ROUTINELY DRIVING INTO THE MAFIA-INFESTED NEIGHBORHOODS, AND TALKING TO THE GANGSTERS WHEN TENSIONS WERE LOW, REALLY HELPED SHOW OUR PRESENCE IN THE COMMUNITY AND AVERTED POTENTIAL EXPLOSIONS.
AS A DETECTIVE, IT'S PRETTY MUCH THE SAME WAY. ONLY ON A BIGGER SCALE. I LIKE TO THINK WE'VE HAD SOMETHING TO DO WITH THE INTER-FAMILY PEACE.
THE PEACE THAT'S NOW GONE.
UNFORTUNATELY, WE'VE NEVER HAD THAT KIND OF SUCCESS WITH YAKUZA. WE ARE ONLY NOW BEGINNING TO GRASP THEIR ORGANIZATIONAL STRUCTURE AND SYSTEMS.
WE REALLY KNOW SO LITTLE ABOUT THEM.
GOOD AFTERNOON. I'M DETECTIVE JAKE McCARTHY AND THIS--
--SARA PEZZINI, TAKATA-SAN HAS EXPECTED YOU.
1142
EVIDENTLY THE SAME CAN'T BE SAID FOR THEM.
EXPECTED ME? SO MUCH FOR OUR UNANNOUNCED VISIT.
THIS PLACE IS INCREDIBLE.
NOT LIKE THOSE DIVE BARS AND PIZZA PLACES THE MAFIOSOS FREQUENT.
HMM. LOOKS LIKE WE'RE NOT THE ONLY VISITORS HERE, EITHER.
THERE'S SOMETHING... FAMILIAR ABOUT HIM.

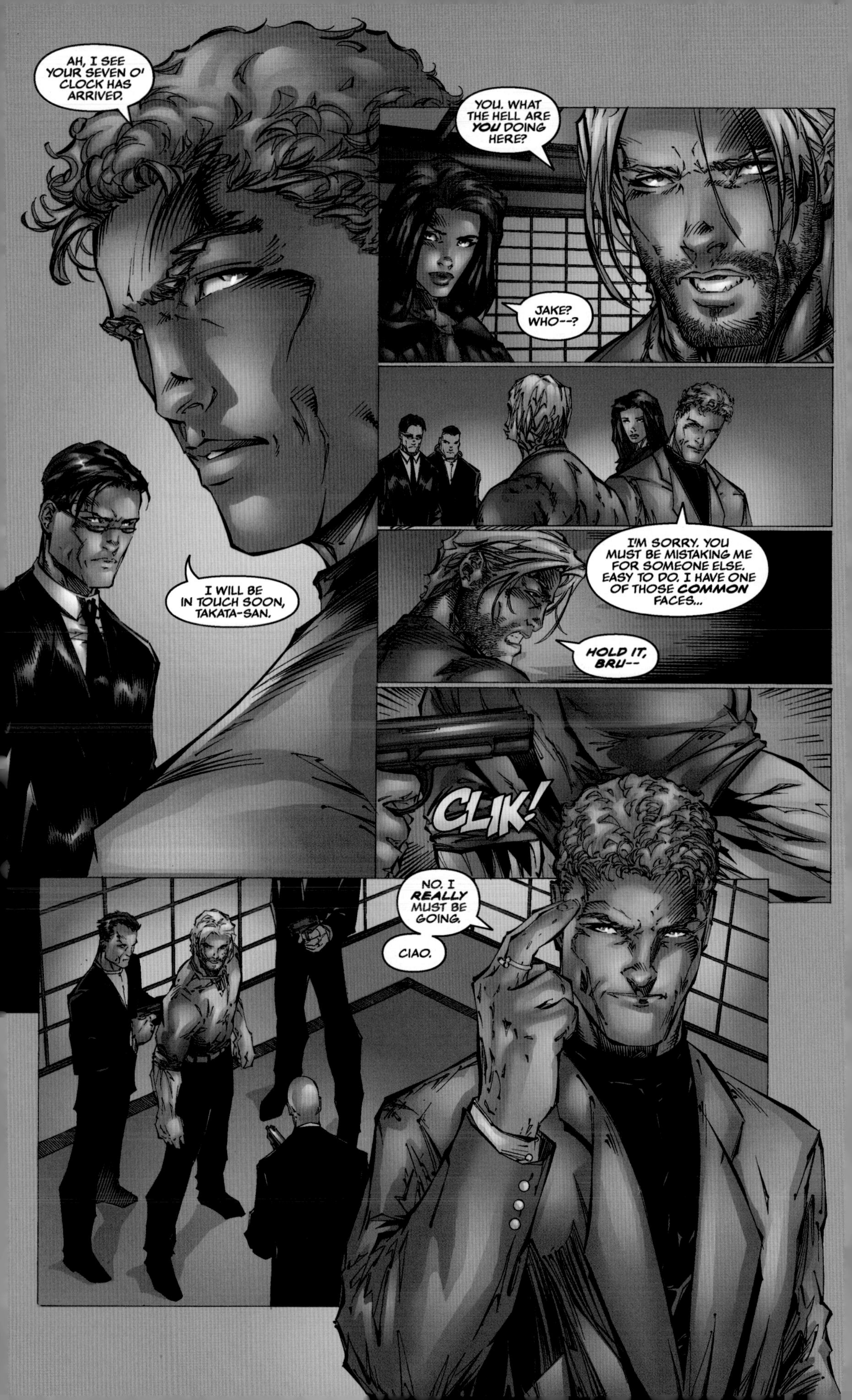
AH, I SEE YOUR SEVEN O' CLOCK HAS ARRIVED.
YOU. WHAT THE HELL ARE *YOU* DOING HERE?
JAKE? WHO--?
I WILL BE IN TOUCH SOON, TAKATA-SAN.
I'M SORRY. YOU MUST BE MISTAKING ME FOR SOMEONE ELSE. EASY TO DO. I HAVE ONE OF THOSE **COMMON** FACES...
HOLD IT, BRU--
CLIK!
NO. I ***REALLY*** MUST BE GOING.
CIAO.

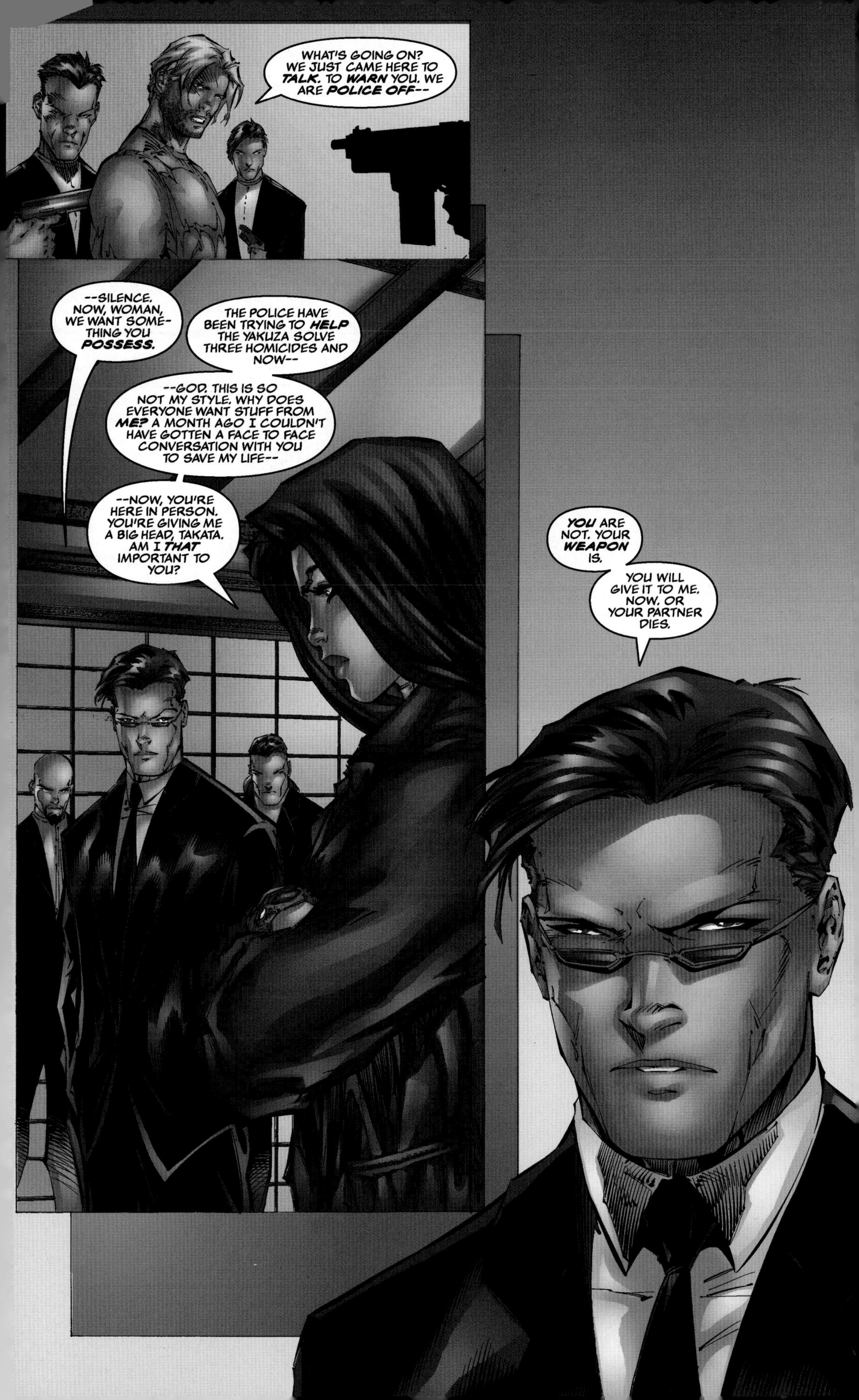
WHAT'S GOING ON? WE JUST CAME HERE TO TALK. TO WARN YOU. WE ARE POLICE OFF--
--SILENCE. NOW, WOMAN, WE WANT SOME-THING YOU POSSESS.
THE POLICE HAVE BEEN TRYING TO HELP THE YAKUZA SOLVE THREE HOMICIDES AND NOW--
--GOD. THIS IS SO NOT MY STYLE. WHY DOES EVERYONE WANT STUFF FROM ME? A MONTH AGO I COULDN'T HAVE GOTTEN A FACE TO FACE CONVERSATION WITH YOU TO SAVE MY LIFE--
--NOW, YOU'RE HERE IN PERSON. YOU'RE GIVING ME A BIG HEAD, TAKATA. AM I THAT IMPORTANT TO YOU?
YOU ARE NOT. YOUR WEAPON IS.
YOU WILL GIVE IT TO ME. NOW. OR YOUR PARTNER DIES.

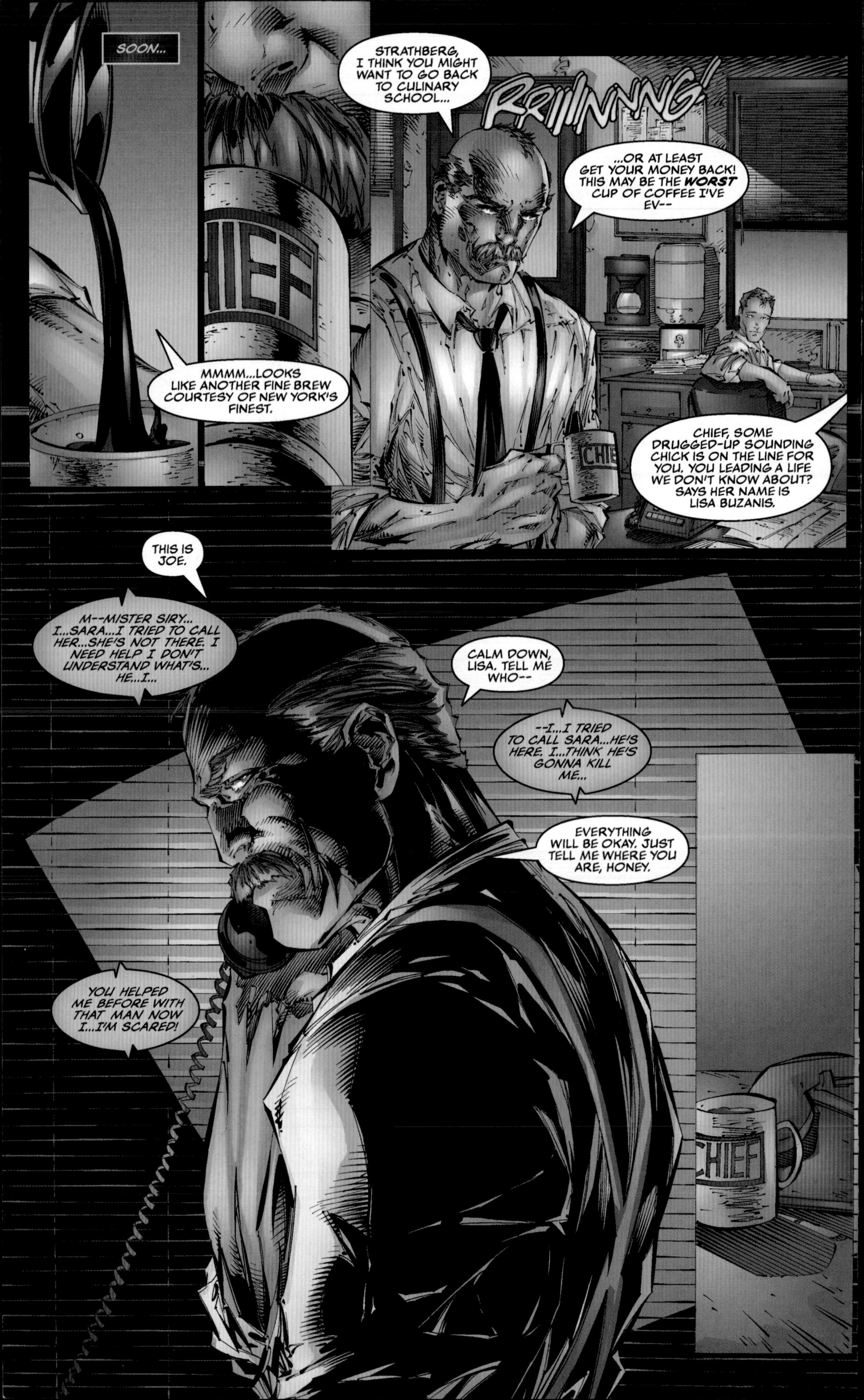
SOON...
STRATHBERG, I THINK YOU MIGHT WANT TO GO BACK TO CULINARY SCHOOL...
RRIIINNNG!
...OR AT LEAST GET YOUR MONEY BACK! THIS MAY BE THE WORST CUP OF COFFEE I'VE EV--
MMMM...LOOKS LIKE ANOTHER FINE BREW COURTESY OF NEW YORK'S FINEST.
CHIEF, SOME DRUGGED-UP SOUNDING CHICK IS ON THE LINE FOR YOU. YOU LEADING A LIFE WE DON'T KNOW ABOUT? SAYS HER NAME IS LISA BUZANIS.
THIS IS JOE.
M--MISTER SIRY... I...SARA...I TRIED TO CALL HER...SHE'S NOT THERE. I NEED HELP I DON'T UNDERSTAND WHAT'S... HE...I...
CALM DOWN, LISA. TELL ME WHO--
--I...I TRIED TO CALL SARA...HE'S HERE. I...THINK HE'S GONNA KILL ME...
EVERYTHING WILL BE OKAY. JUST TELL ME WHERE YOU ARE, HONEY.
YOU HELPED ME BEFORE WITH THAT MAN NOW I...I'M SCARED!

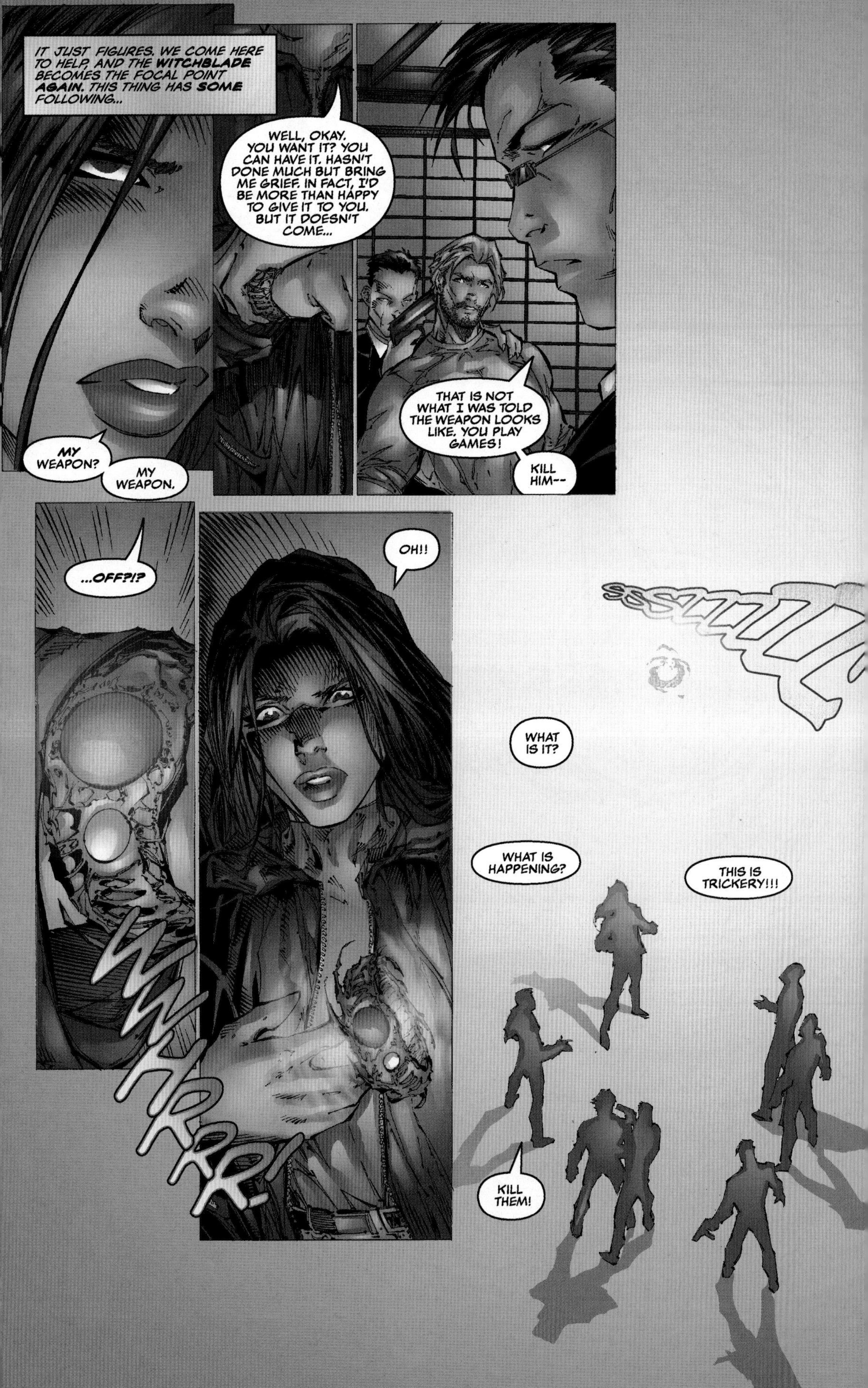
IT JUST FIGURES. WE COME HERE TO HELP, AND THE WITCHBLADE BECOMES THE FOCAL POINT AGAIN. THIS THING HAS SOME FOLLOWING...
WELL, OKAY. YOU WANT IT? YOU CAN HAVE IT. HASN'T DONE MUCH BUT BRING ME GRIEF. IN FACT, I'D BE MORE THAN HAPPY TO GIVE IT TO YOU. BUT IT DOESN'T COME...
MY WEAPON?
MY WEAPON.
THAT IS NOT WHAT I WAS TOLD THE WEAPON LOOKS LIKE. YOU PLAY GAMES!
KILL HIM--
...OFF?!?
OH!!
WWHRRR!
SSSZZZT
WHAT IS IT?
WHAT IS HAPPENING?
THIS IS TRICKERY!!!
KILL THEM!

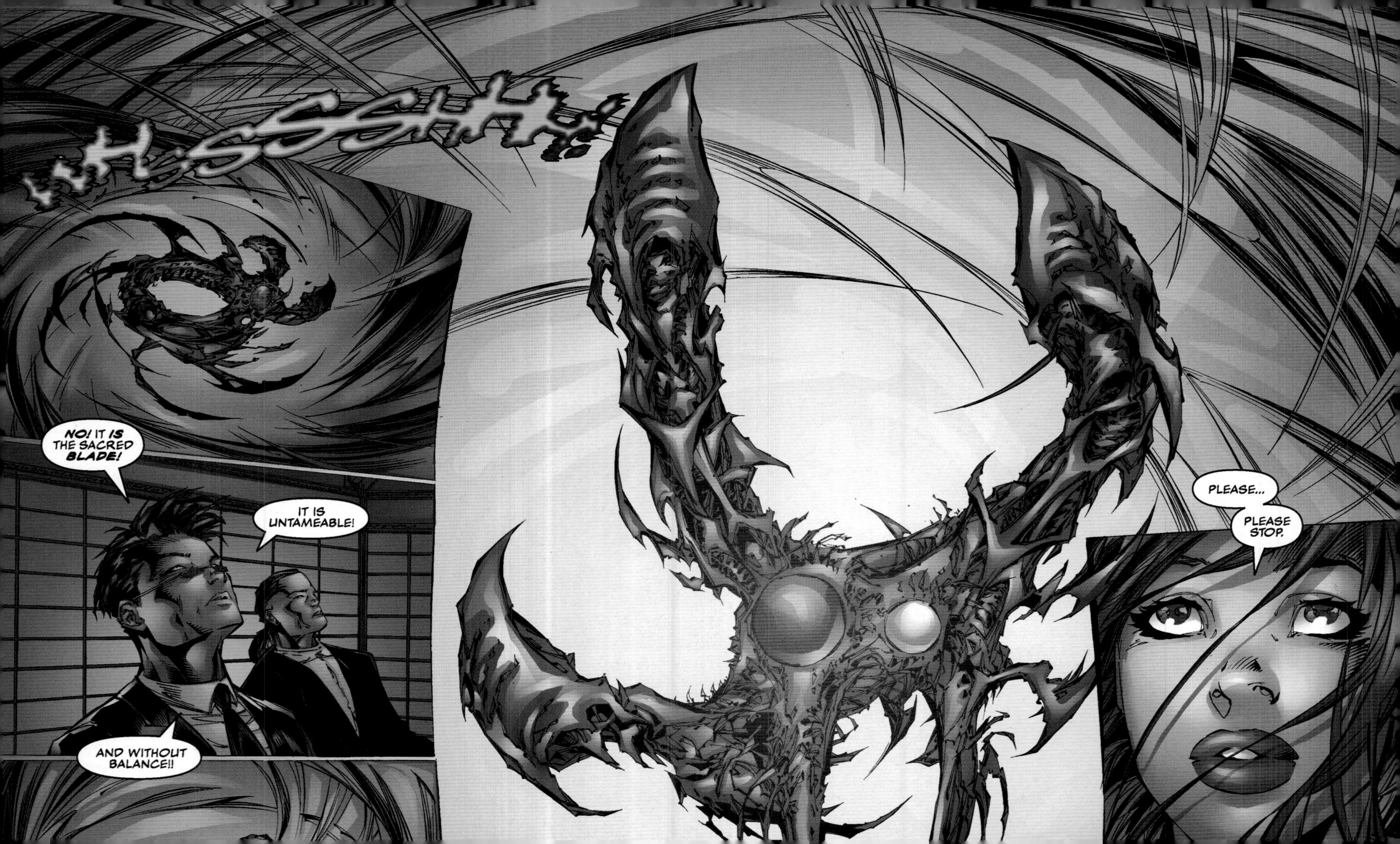
WHSSHH!
NO! IT IS THE SACRED BLADE!
IT IS UNTAMEABLE!
AND WITHOUT BALANCE!!
PLEASE...
PLEASE STOP.

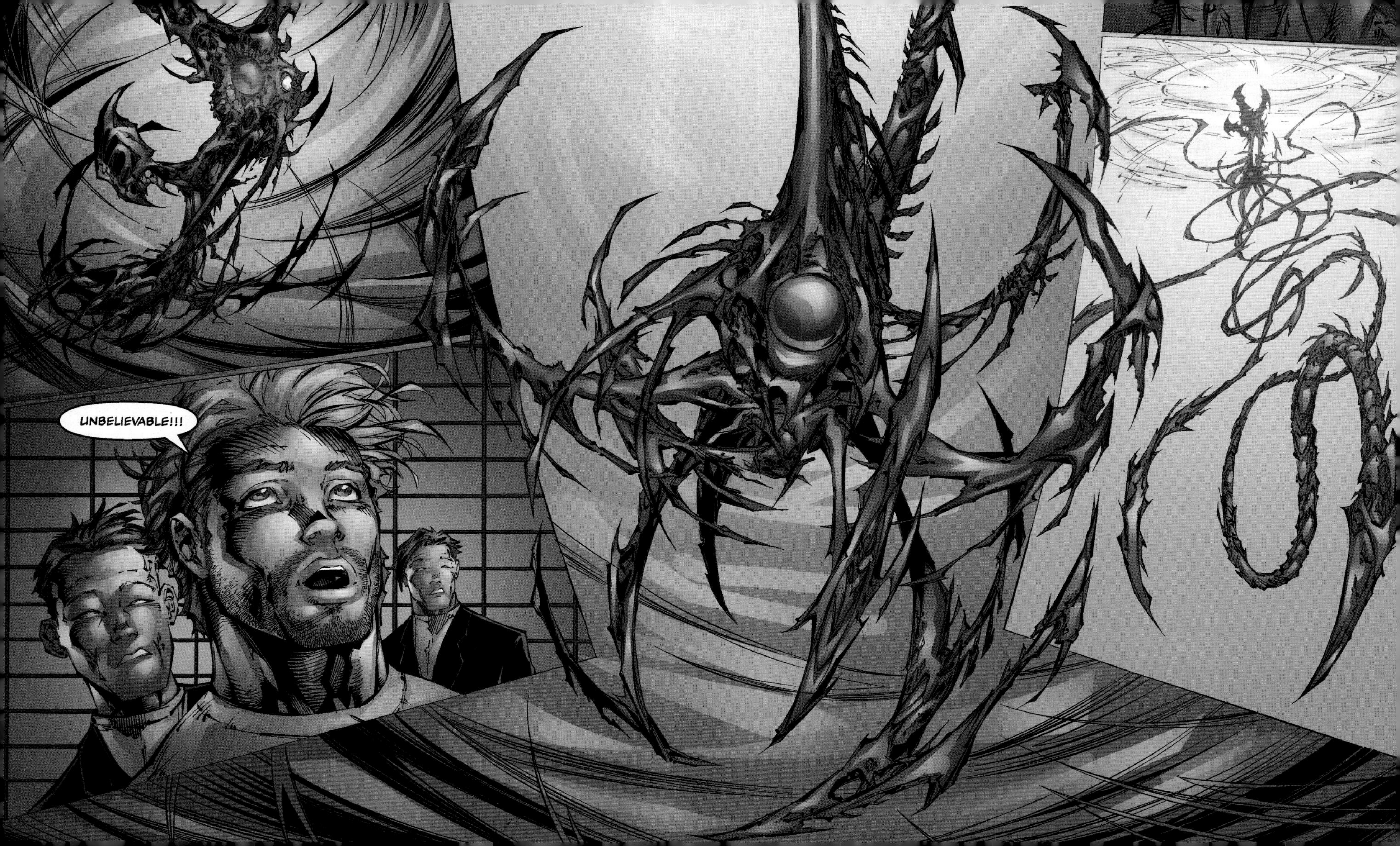
UNBELIEVABLE!!!

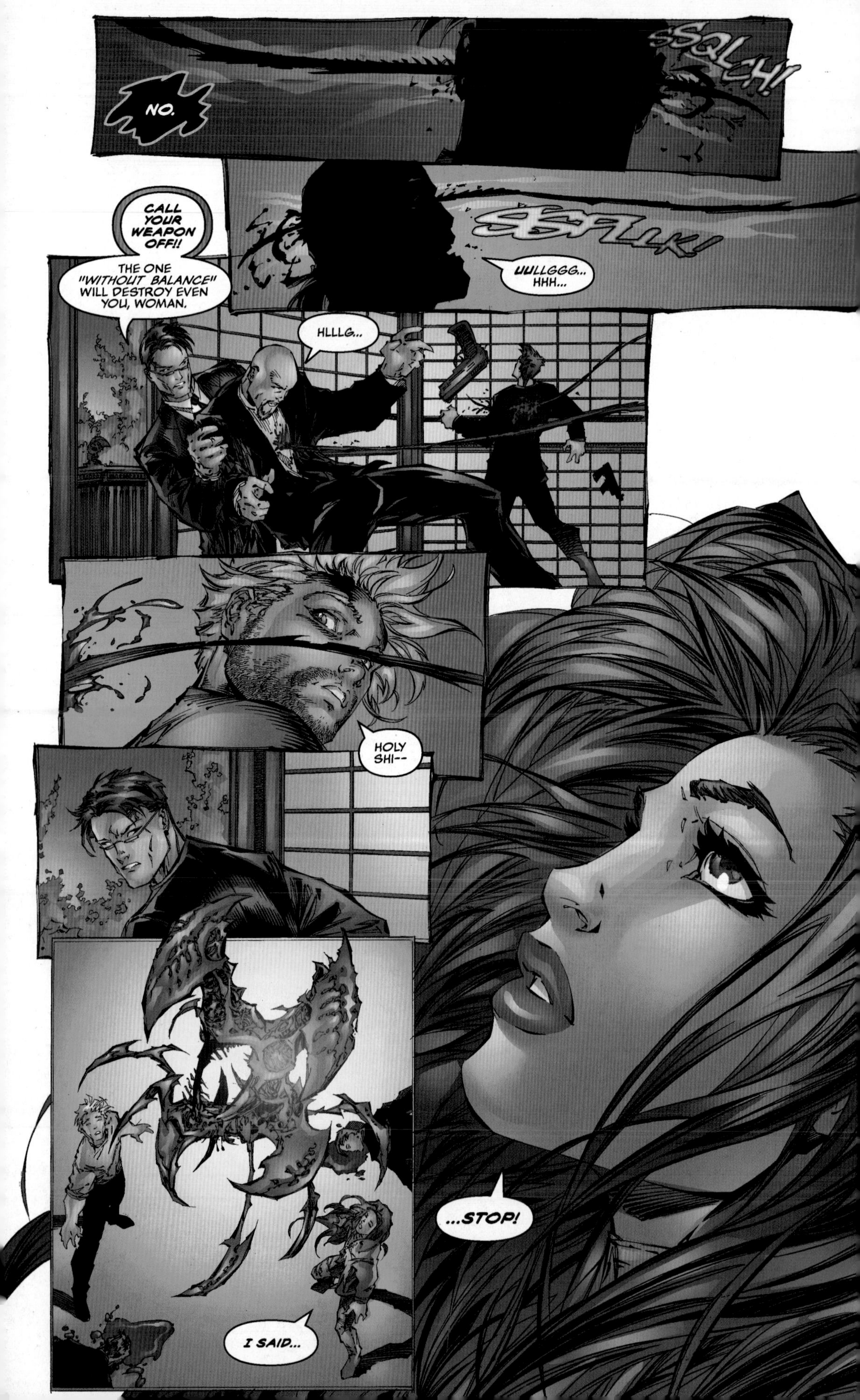
NO.
SSQLCH!
SSPLLK!
UULLGGG... HHH...
CALL YOUR WEAPON OFF!!
THE ONE "WITHOUT BALANCE" WILL DESTROY EVEN YOU, WOMAN.
HLLLG...
HOLY SHI--
I SAID...
...STOP!

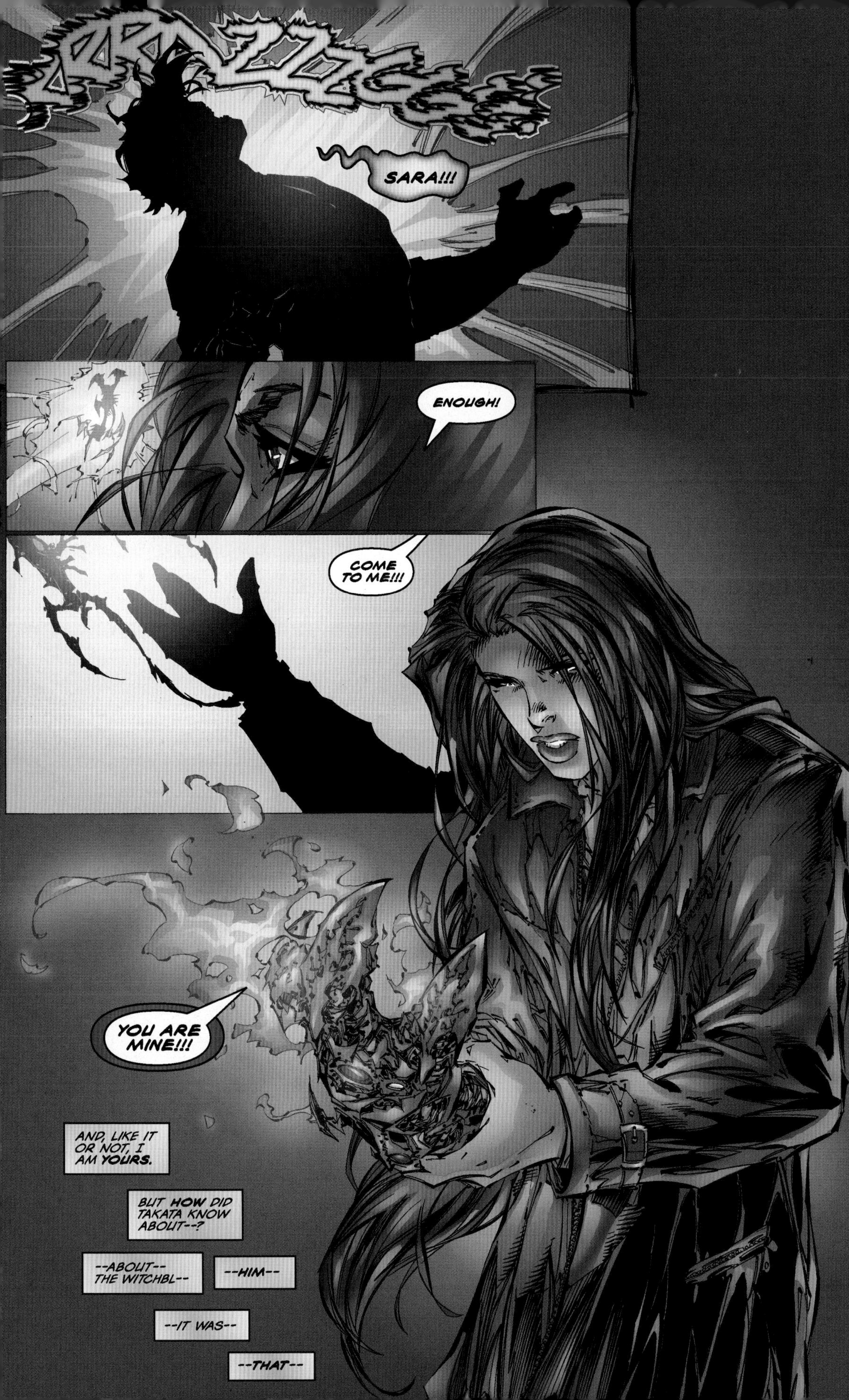

KRAZZOOOM
SARA!!!
ENOUGH!
COME TO ME!!!
YOU ARE MINE!!!
AND, LIKE IT OR NOT, I AM YOURS.
BUT HOW DID TAKATA KNOW ABOUT--?
--ABOUT-- THE WITCHBL--
--HIM--
--IT WAS--
--THAT--

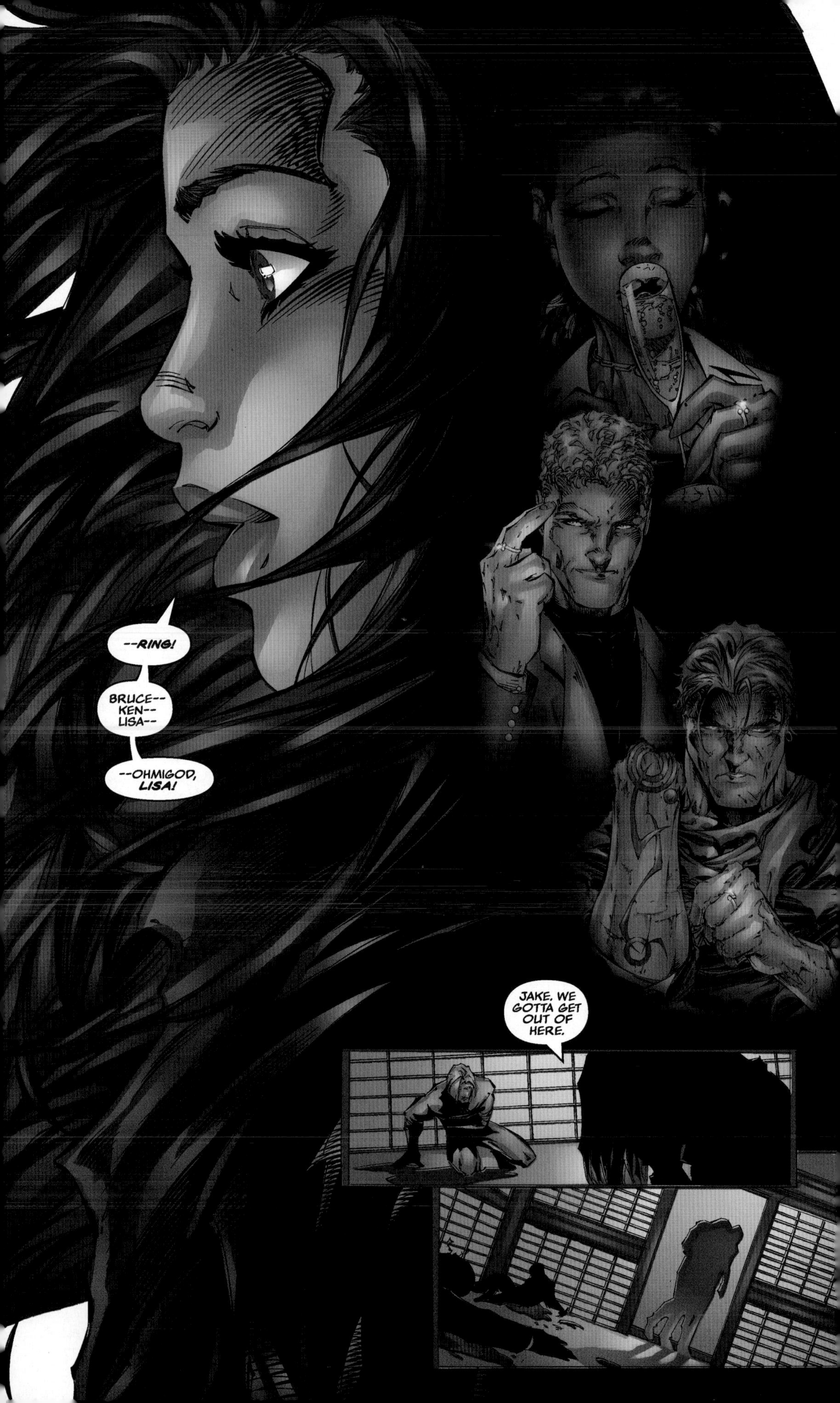
--RING!
BRUCE-- KEN-- LISA--
--OHMIGOD, LISA!
JAKE. WE GOTTA GET OUT OF HERE.

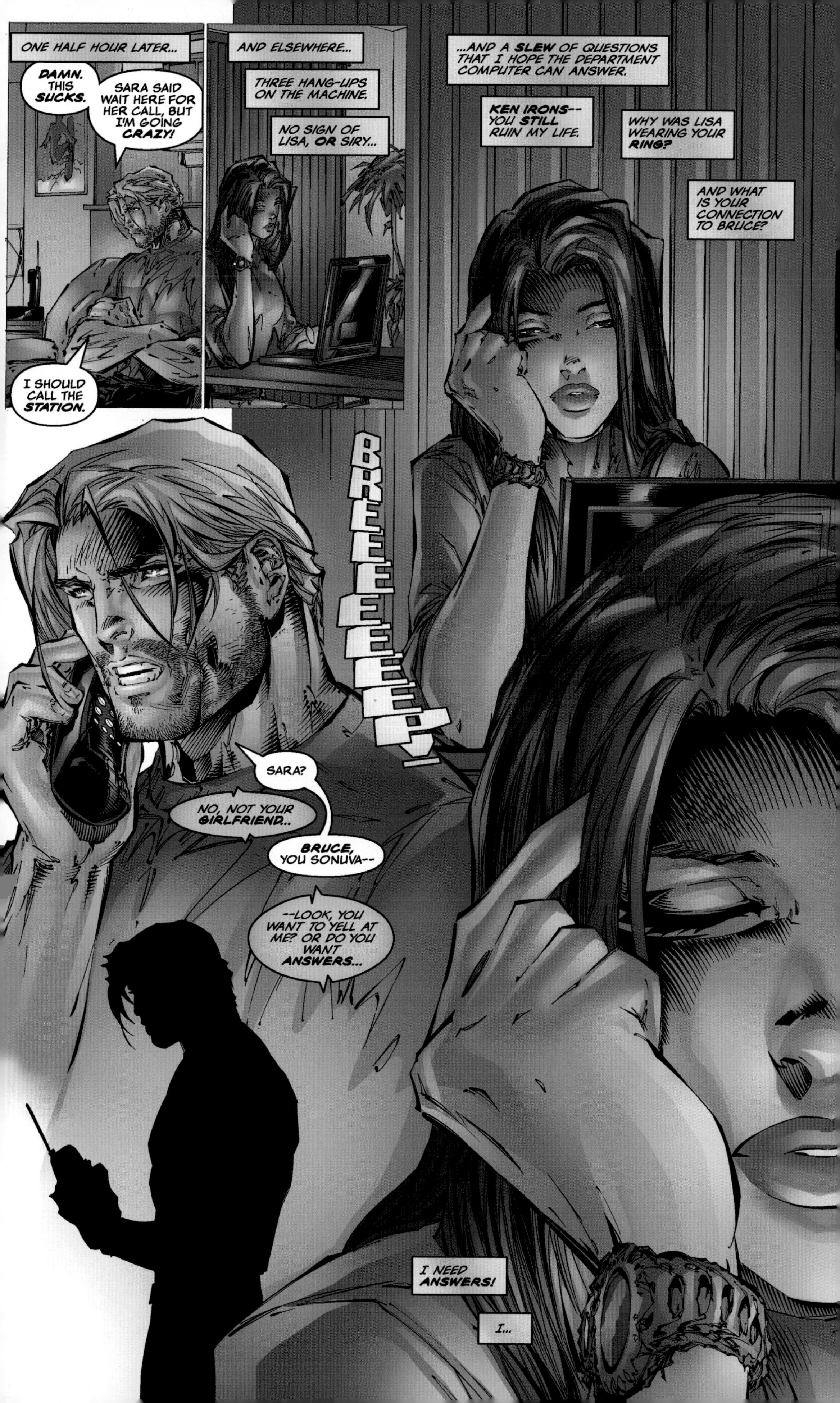
ONE HALF HOUR LATER...
DAMN. THIS SUCKS.
SARA SAID WAIT HERE FOR HER CALL, BUT I'M GOING CRAZY!
I SHOULD CALL THE STATION.
AND ELSEWHERE...
THREE HANG-UPS ON THE MACHINE.
NO SIGN OF LISA, OR SIRY...
...AND A SLEW OF QUESTIONS THAT I HOPE THE DEPARTMENT COMPUTER CAN ANSWER.
KEN IRONS-- YOU STILL RUIN MY LIFE.
WHY WAS LISA WEARING YOUR RING?
AND WHAT IS YOUR CONNECTION TO BRUCE?
BREEEEEEEP!
SARA?
NO, NOT YOUR GIRLFRIEND..
BRUCE, YOU SONUVA--
--LOOK, YOU WANT TO YELL AT ME? OR DO YOU WANT ANSWERS...
I NEED ANSWERS!
I...

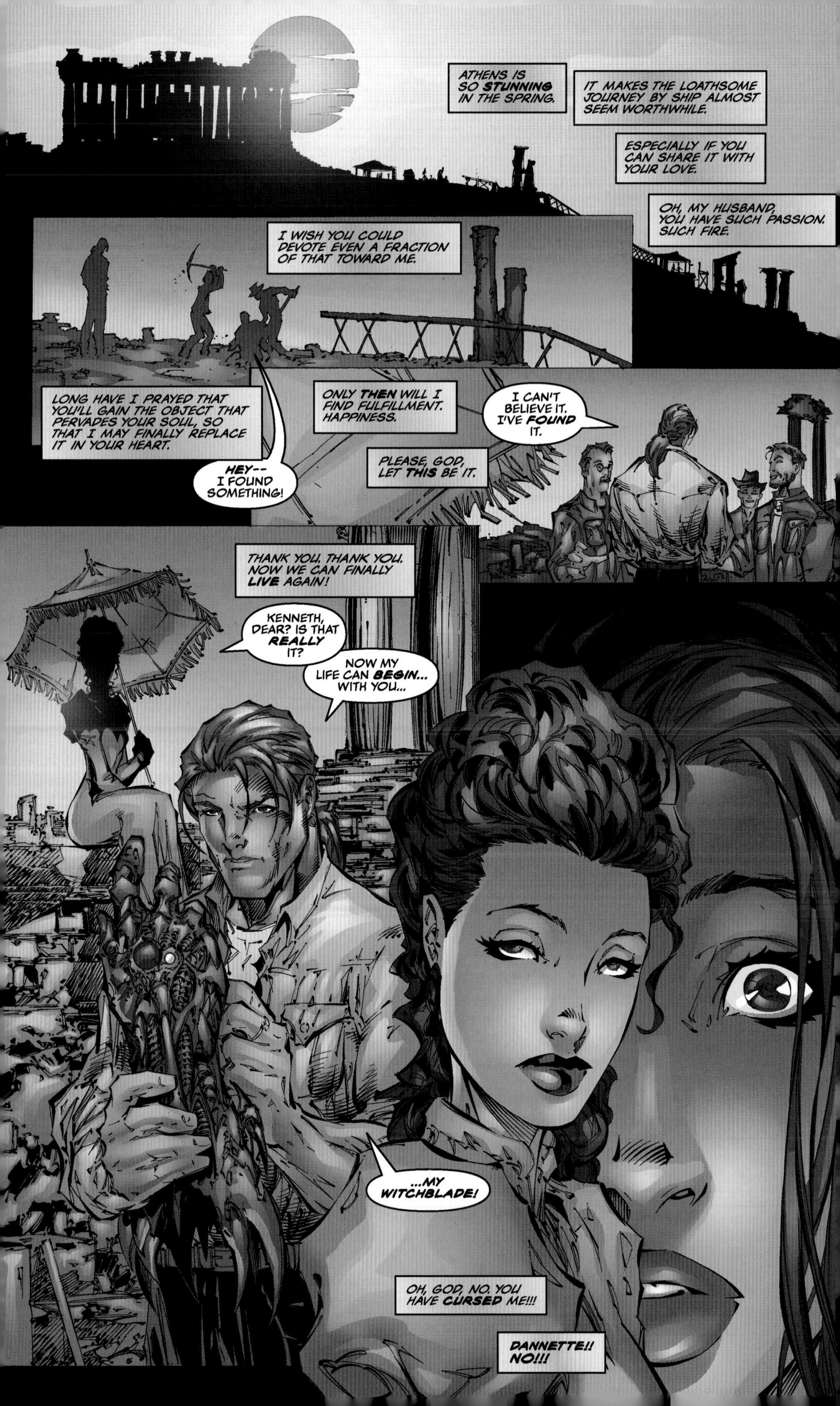

ATHENS IS SO STUNNING IN THE SPRING.
IT MAKES THE LOATHSOME JOURNEY BY SHIP ALMOST SEEM WORTHWHILE.
ESPECIALLY IF YOU CAN SHARE IT WITH YOUR LOVE.
OH, MY HUSBAND, YOU HAVE SUCH PASSION. SUCH FIRE.
I WISH YOU COULD DEVOTE EVEN A FRACTION OF THAT TOWARD ME.
LONG HAVE I PRAYED THAT YOU'LL GAIN THE OBJECT THAT PERVADES YOUR SOUL, SO THAT I MAY FINALLY REPLACE IT IN YOUR HEART.
HEY-- I FOUND SOMETHING!
ONLY THEN WILL I FIND FULFILLMENT. HAPPINESS.
PLEASE, GOD, LET THIS BE IT.
I CAN'T BELIEVE IT. I'VE FOUND IT.
THANK YOU. THANK YOU. NOW WE CAN FINALLY LIVE AGAIN!
KENNETH, DEAR? IS THAT REALLY IT?
NOW MY LIFE CAN BEGIN... WITH YOU...
...MY WITCHBLADE!
OH, GOD, NO. YOU HAVE CURSED ME!!!
DANNETTE!! NO!!!

THE TWO OF THEM ARE--WERE--OH, NO...

WHAT IS THIS?

ALL THE VICTIMS HAD THOSE RINGS?

IRONS, Ken

BODY WAS NEVER PO[...] IDENTIFIED

WHY DIDN'T I SEE THAT?

AND... MY GOD...

KEN...

...YOU'RE NOT DEAD.

...WE GOTTA TAKE A RIDE.

SARA...

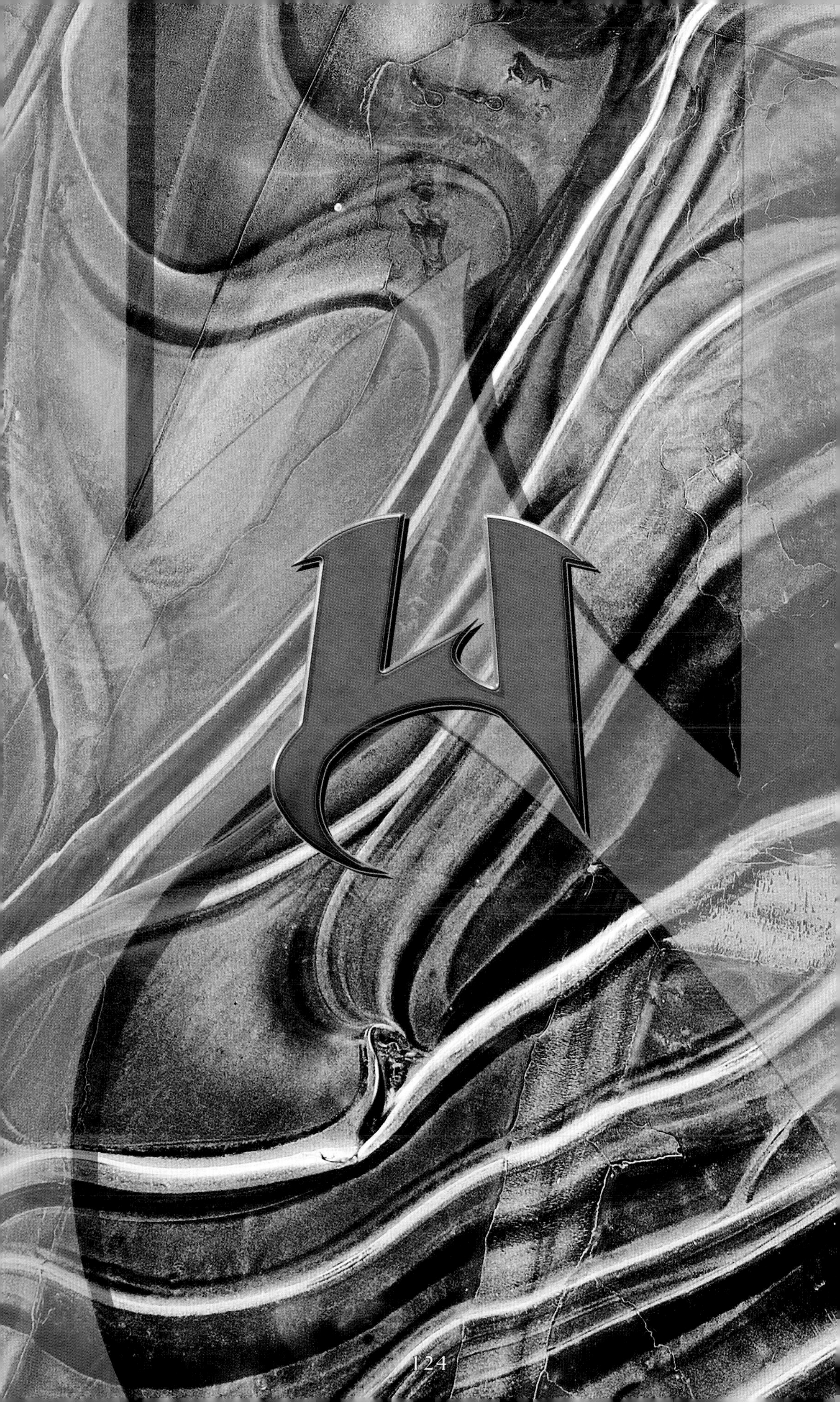

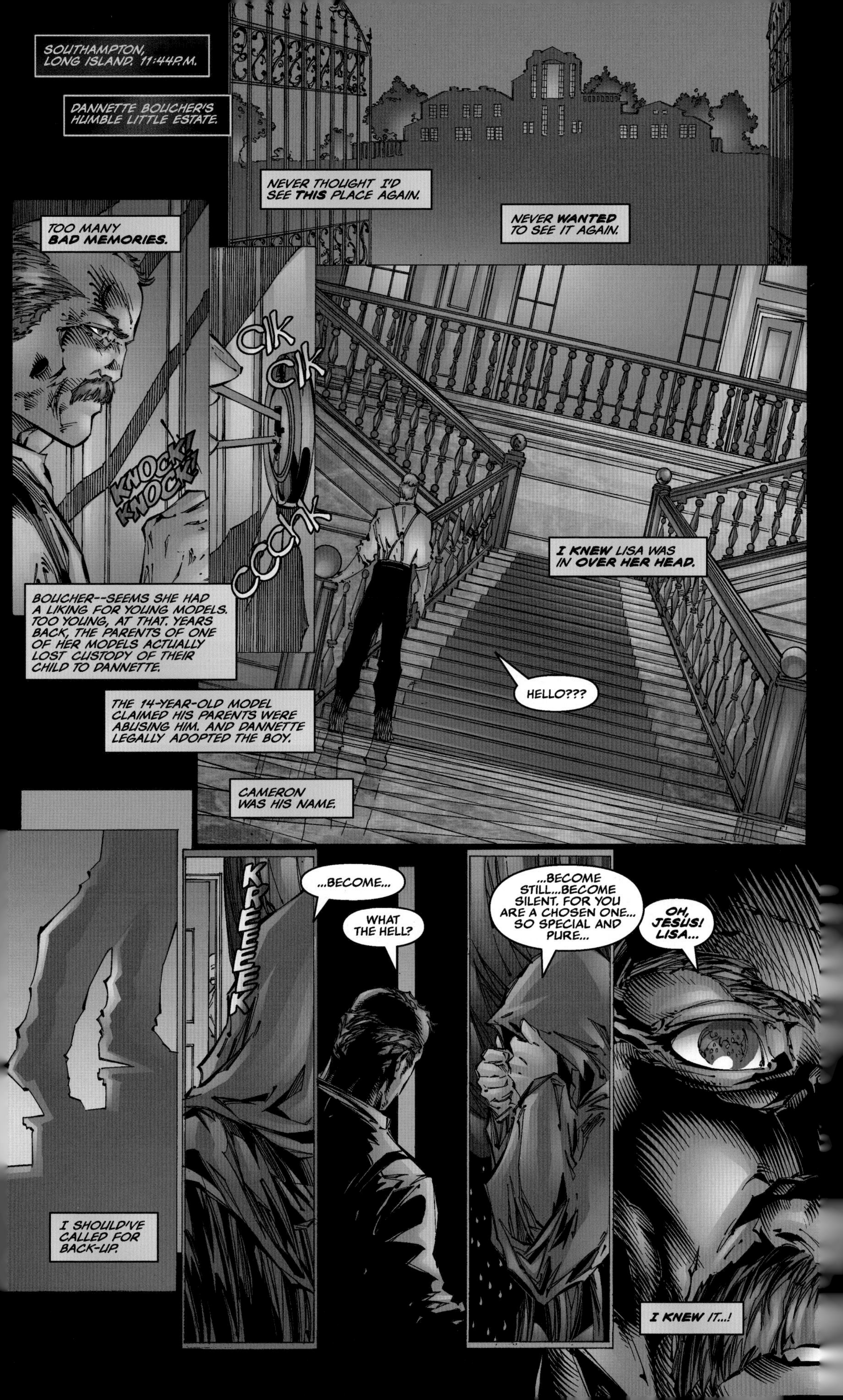
SOUTHAMPTON, LONG ISLAND. 11:44P.M.
DANNETTE BOUCHER'S HUMBLE LITTLE ESTATE.
NEVER THOUGHT I'D SEE THIS PLACE AGAIN.
NEVER WANTED TO SEE IT AGAIN.
TOO MANY BAD MEMORIES.
KNOCK! KNOCK!
CIK CIK
CCCHK
I KNEW LISA WAS IN OVER HER HEAD.
BOUCHER--SEEMS SHE HAD A LIKING FOR YOUNG MODELS. TOO YOUNG, AT THAT. YEARS BACK, THE PARENTS OF ONE OF HER MODELS ACTUALLY LOST CUSTODY OF THEIR CHILD TO DANNETTE.
HELLO???
THE 14-YEAR-OLD MODEL CLAIMED HIS PARENTS WERE ABUSING HIM. AND DANNETTE LEGALLY ADOPTED THE BOY.
CAMERON WAS HIS NAME.
I SHOULD'VE CALLED FOR BACK-UP.
KREEEEK
...BECOME...
WHAT THE HELL?
...BECOME STILL...BECOME SILENT. FOR YOU ARE A CHOSEN ONE... SO SPECIAL AND PURE...
OH, JESUS! LISA...
I KNEW IT...!

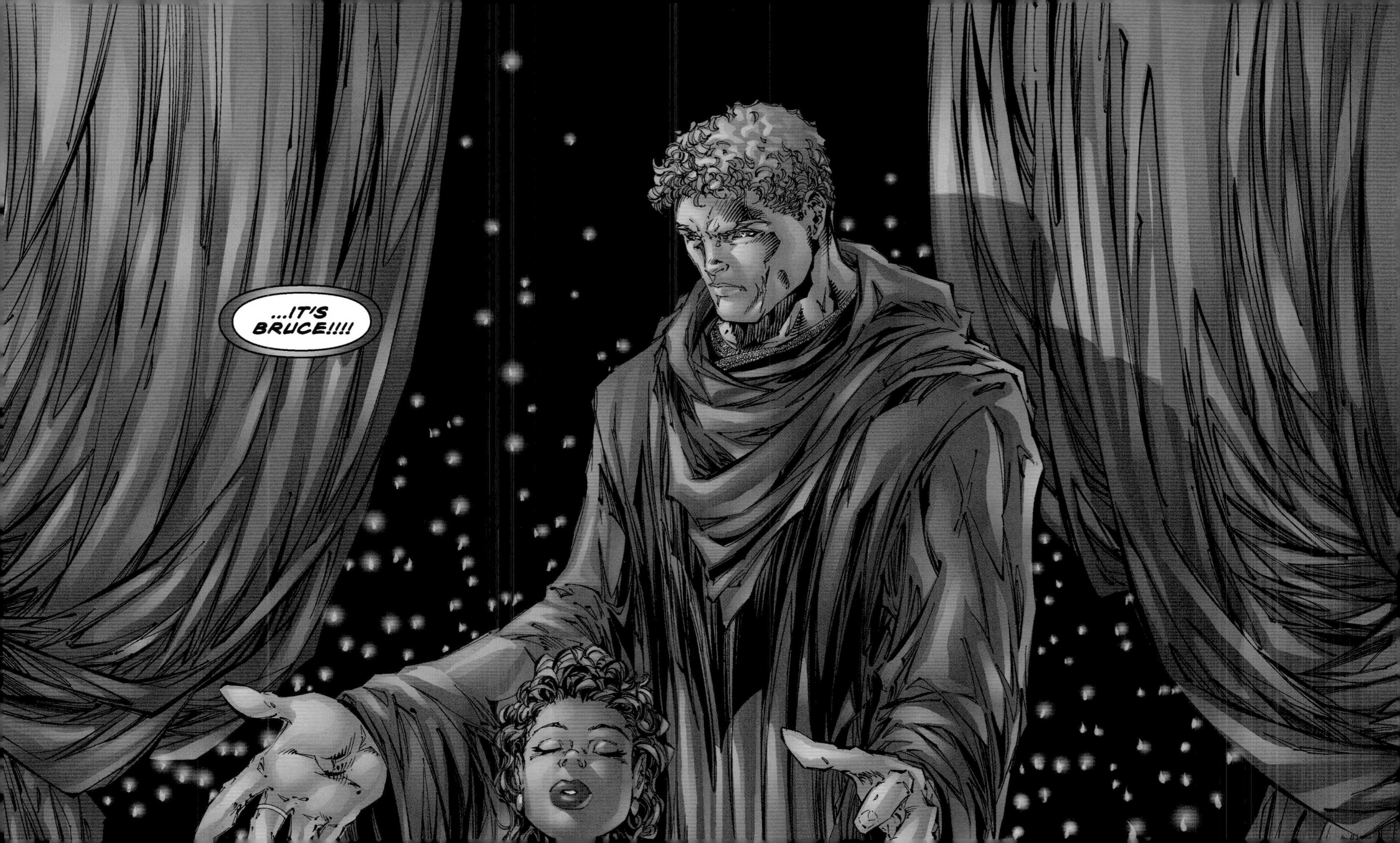
...IT'S BRUCE!!!!

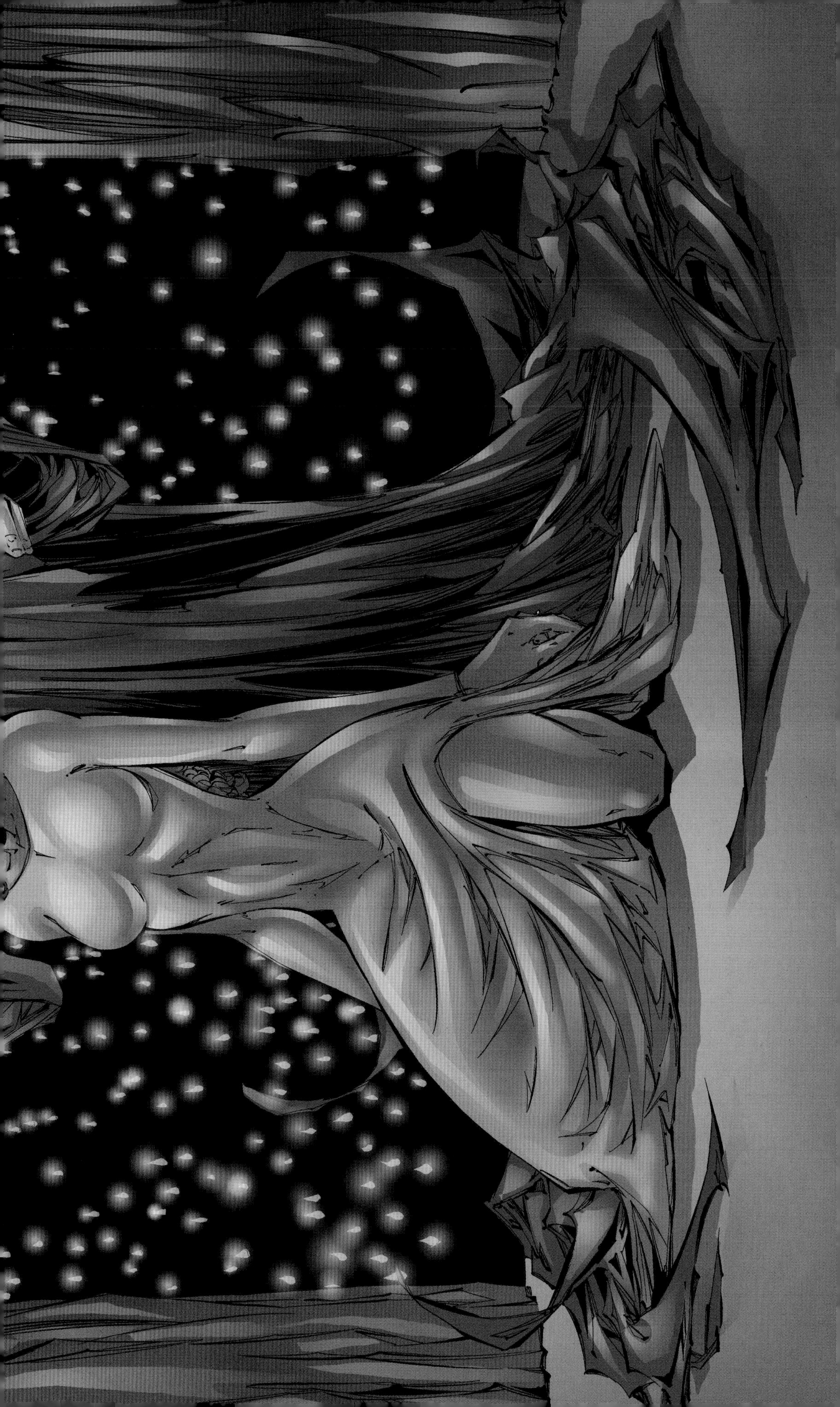

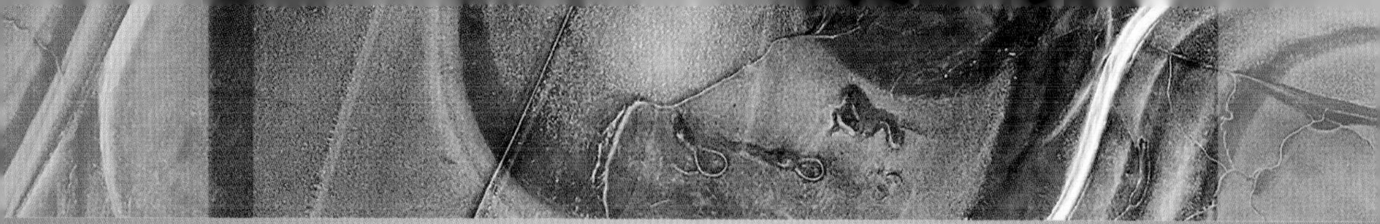

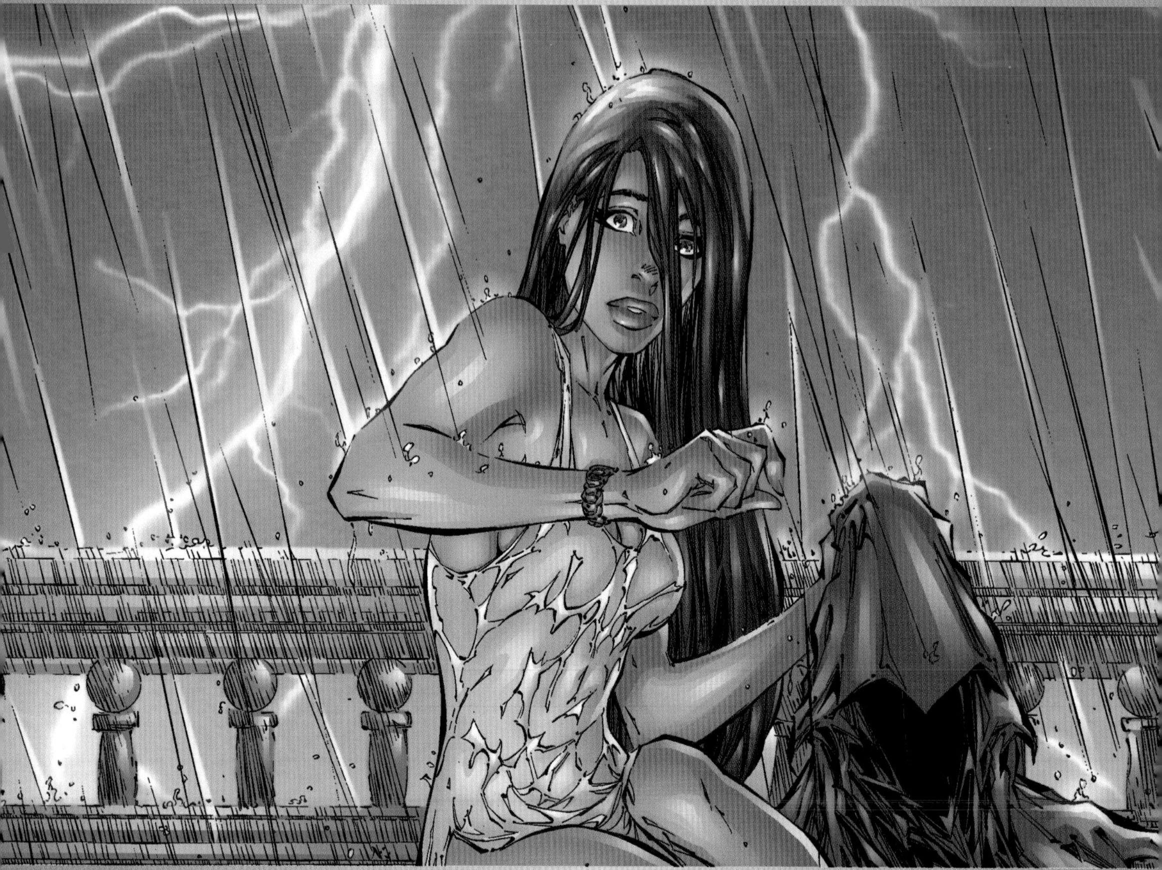

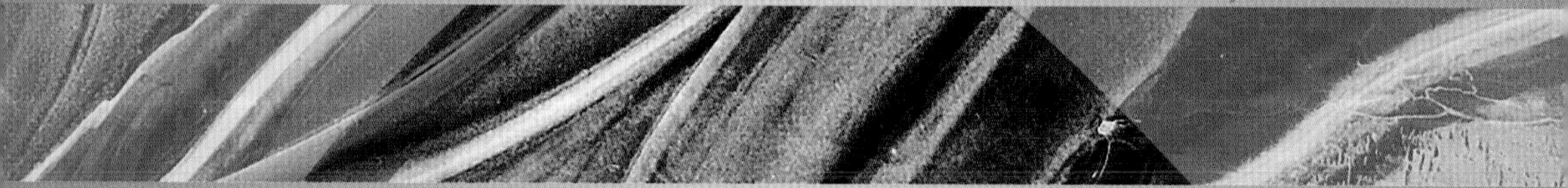

ISSUE #14

plot: **David Wohl** and **Christina Z.**
script: **Christina Z.**
pencils/co-plot: **Michael Turner**
inks: **D-Tron**
colors: **JD Smith**

ink assists: **Jeff De Los Santos, Jose "Jag" Guillen** and **Marsha Chen**

lettering assists: **Robin Sphehar**

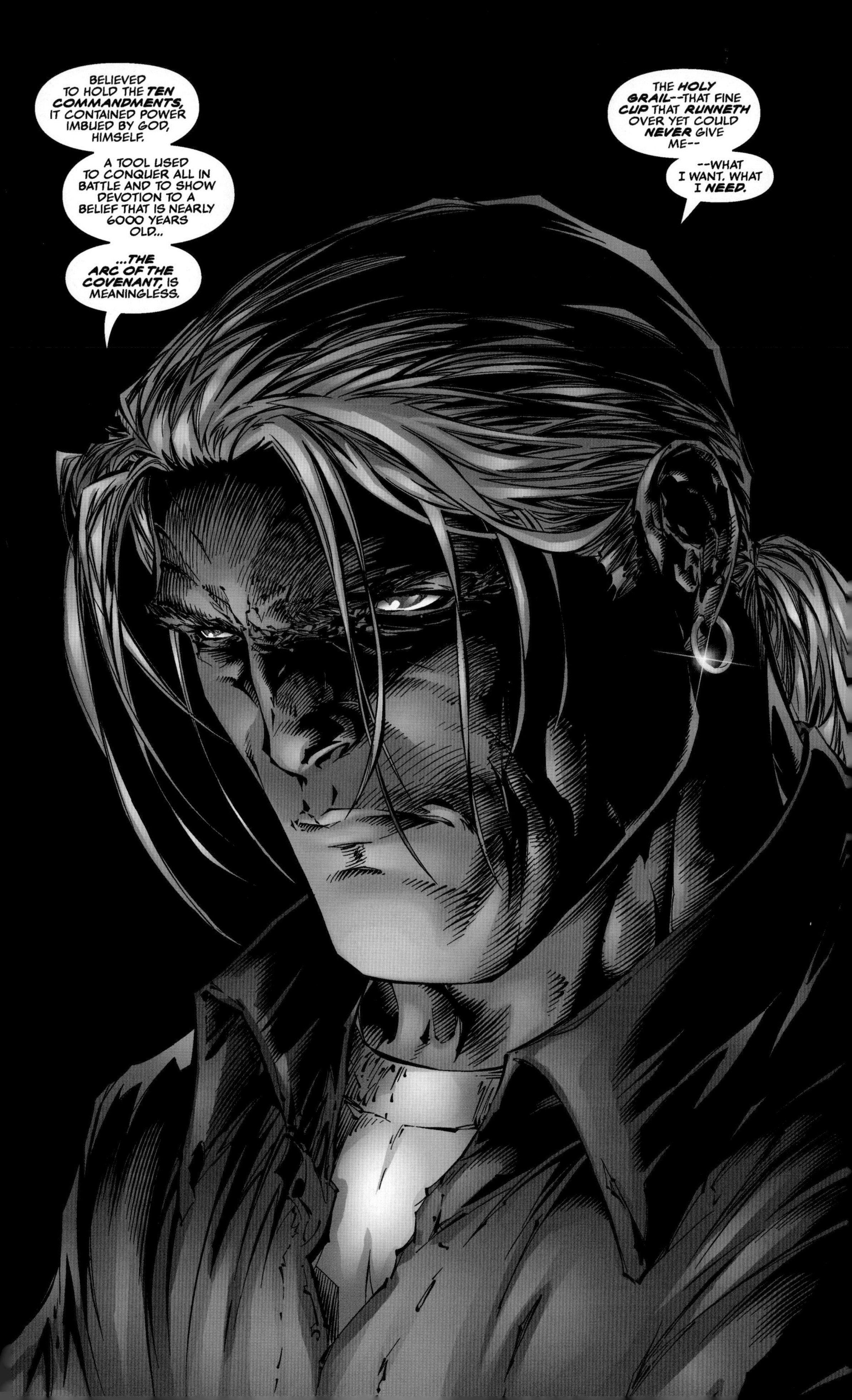
BELIEVED TO HOLD THE TEN COMMANDMENTS, IT CONTAINED POWER IMBUED BY GOD, HIMSELF.
A TOOL USED TO CONQUER ALL IN BATTLE AND TO SHOW DEVOTION TO A BELIEF THAT IS NEARLY 6000 YEARS OLD...
...THE ARC OF THE COVENANT, IS MEANINGLESS.
THE HOLY GRAIL--THAT FINE CUP THAT RUNNETH OVER YET COULD NEVER GIVE ME--
--WHAT I WANT. WHAT I NEED.

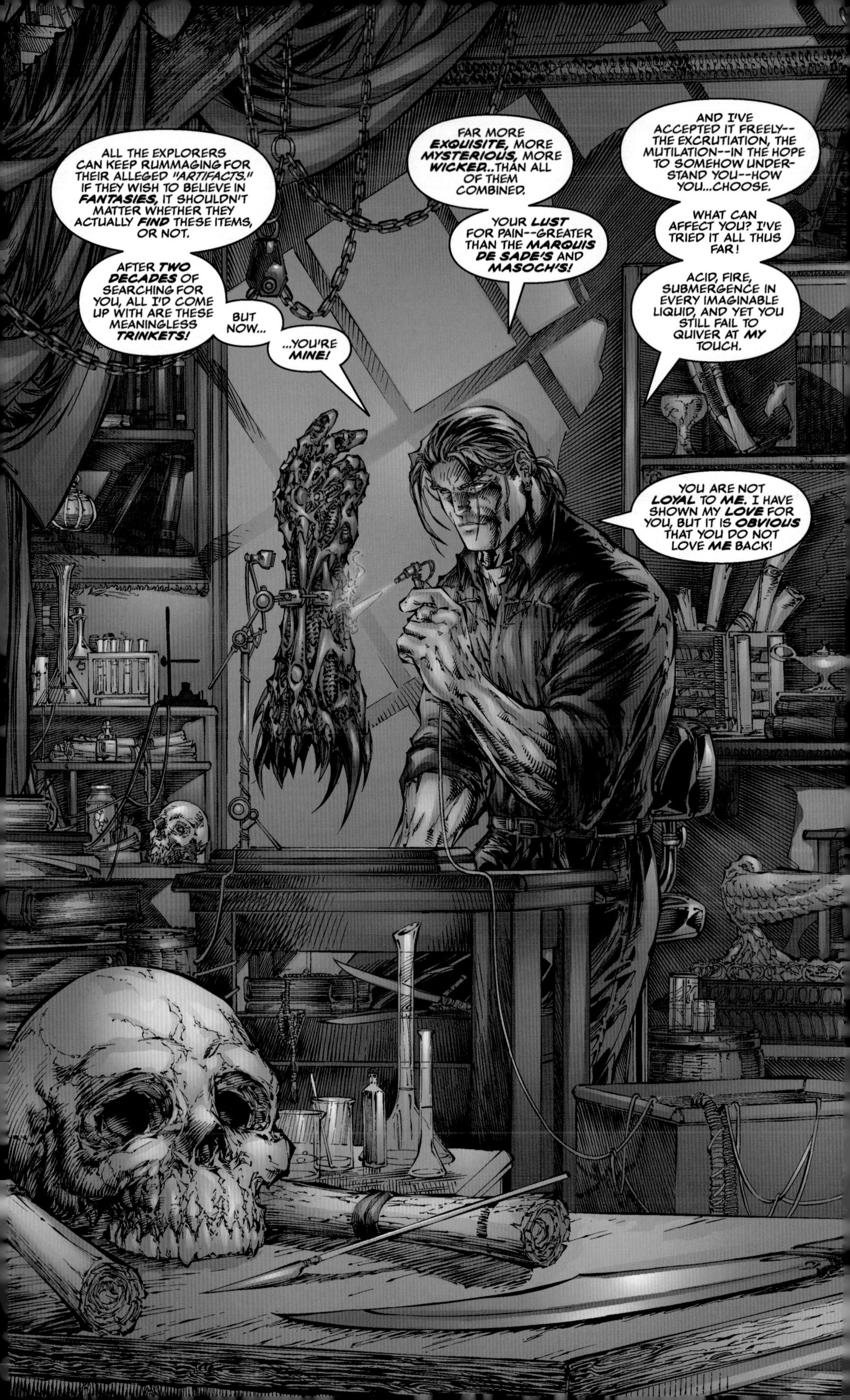
ALL THE EXPLORERS CAN KEEP RUMMAGING FOR THEIR ALLEGED "ARTIFACTS." IF THEY WISH TO BELIEVE IN FANTASIES, IT SHOULDN'T MATTER WHETHER THEY ACTUALLY FIND THESE ITEMS, OR NOT.
AFTER TWO DECADES OF SEARCHING FOR YOU, ALL I'D COME UP WITH ARE THESE MEANINGLESS TRINKETS!
BUT NOW...
...YOU'RE MINE!
FAR MORE EXQUISITE, MORE MYSTERIOUS, MORE WICKED...THAN ALL OF THEM COMBINED.
YOUR LUST FOR PAIN--GREATER THAN THE MARQUIS DE SADE'S AND MASOCH'S!
AND I'VE ACCEPTED IT FREELY-- THE EXCRUTIATION, THE MUTILATION--IN THE HOPE TO SOMEHOW UNDER-STAND YOU--HOW YOU...CHOOSE.
WHAT CAN AFFECT YOU? I'VE TRIED IT ALL THUS FAR!
ACID, FIRE, SUBMERGENCE IN EVERY IMAGINABLE LIQUID, AND YET YOU STILL FAIL TO QUIVER AT MY TOUCH.
YOU ARE NOT LOYAL TO ME. I HAVE SHOWN MY LOVE FOR YOU, BUT IT IS OBVIOUS THAT YOU DO NOT LOVE ME BACK!

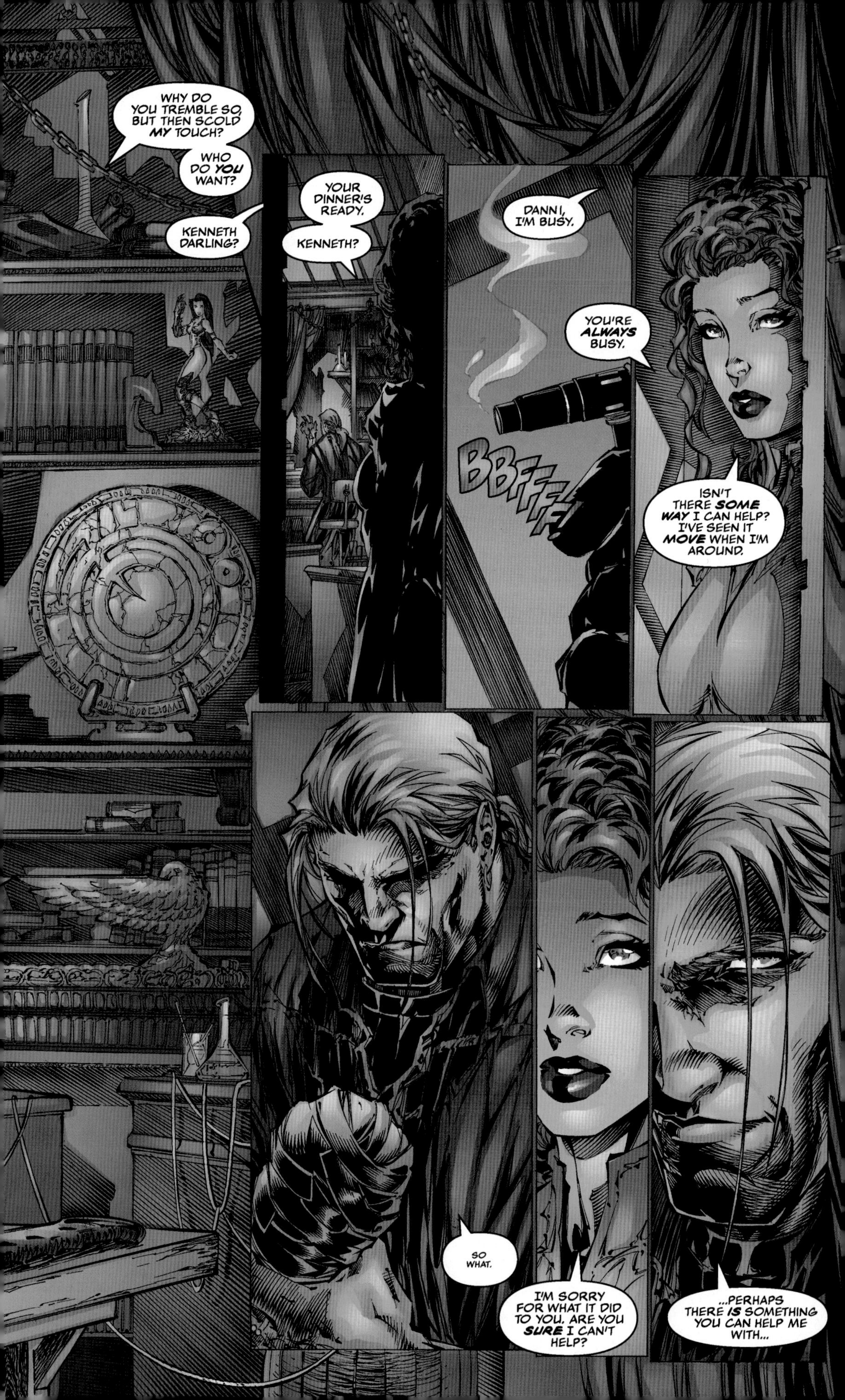
WHY DO YOU TREMBLE SO, BUT THEN SCOLD MY TOUCH?
WHO DO YOU WANT?
KENNETH DARLING?
YOUR DINNER'S READY.
KENNETH?
DANNI, I'M BUSY.
YOU'RE ALWAYS BUSY.
BBFFFF
ISN'T THERE SOME WAY I CAN HELP? I'VE SEEN IT MOVE WHEN I'M AROUND.
SO WHAT.
I'M SORRY FOR WHAT IT DID TO YOU. ARE YOU SURE I CAN'T HELP?
...PERHAPS THERE IS SOMETHING YOU CAN HELP ME WITH...

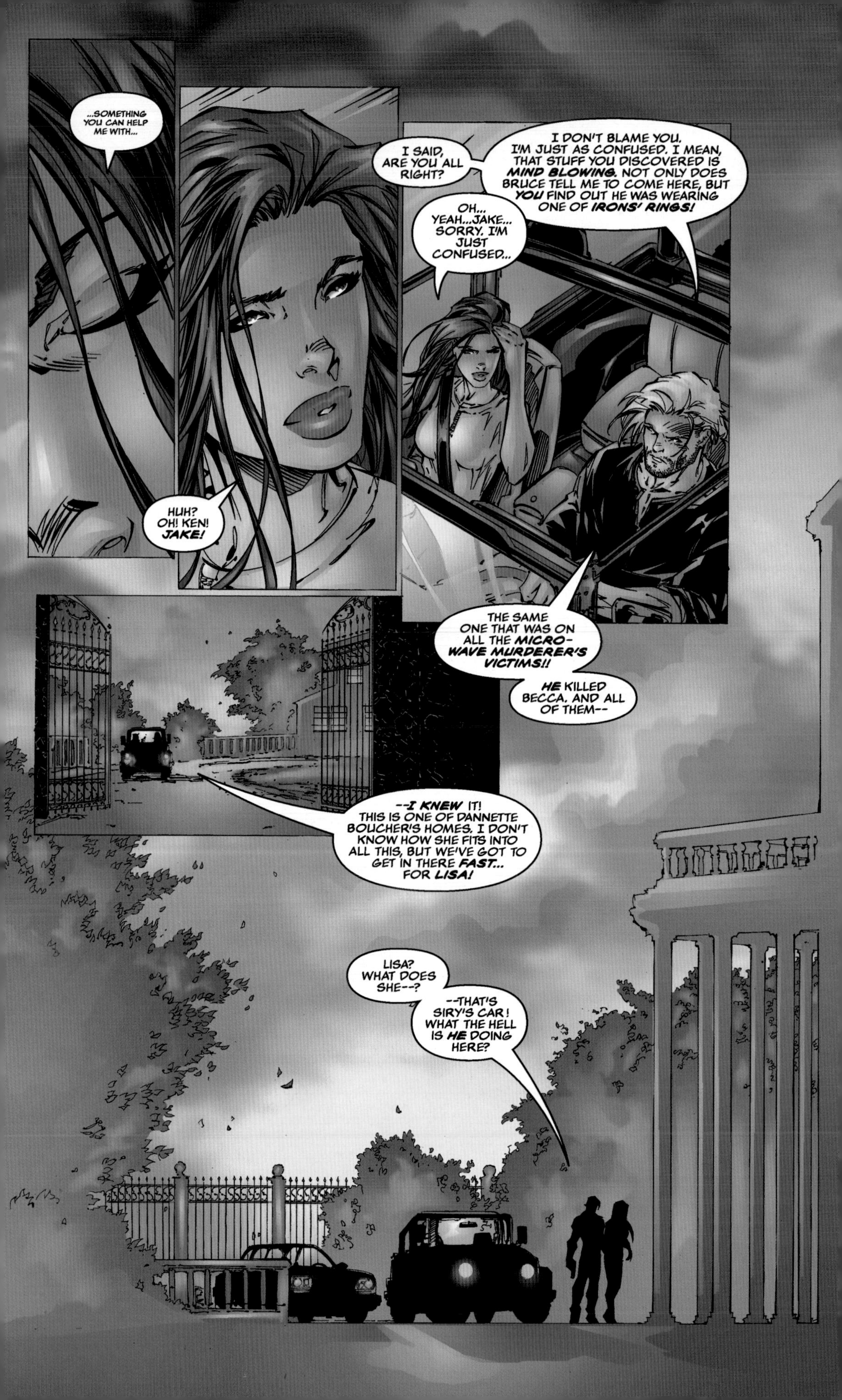

...SOMETHING YOU CAN HELP ME WITH...
HUH? OH! KEN! JAKE!
I SAID, ARE YOU ALL RIGHT?
OH... YEAH...JAKE... SORRY. I'M JUST CONFUSED...
I DON'T BLAME YOU. I'M JUST AS CONFUSED. I MEAN, THAT STUFF YOU DISCOVERED IS MIND BLOWING. NOT ONLY DOES BRUCE TELL ME TO COME HERE, BUT YOU FIND OUT HE WAS WEARING ONE OF IRONS' RINGS!
THE SAME ONE THAT WAS ON ALL THE MICRO-WAVE MURDERER'S VICTIMS!!
HE KILLED BECCA. AND ALL OF THEM--
--I KNEW IT! THIS IS ONE OF DANNETTE BOUCHER'S HOMES. I DON'T KNOW HOW SHE FITS INTO ALL THIS, BUT WE'VE GOT TO GET IN THERE FAST... FOR LISA!
LISA? WHAT DOES SHE--?
--THAT'S SIRY'S CAR! WHAT THE HELL IS HE DOING HERE?

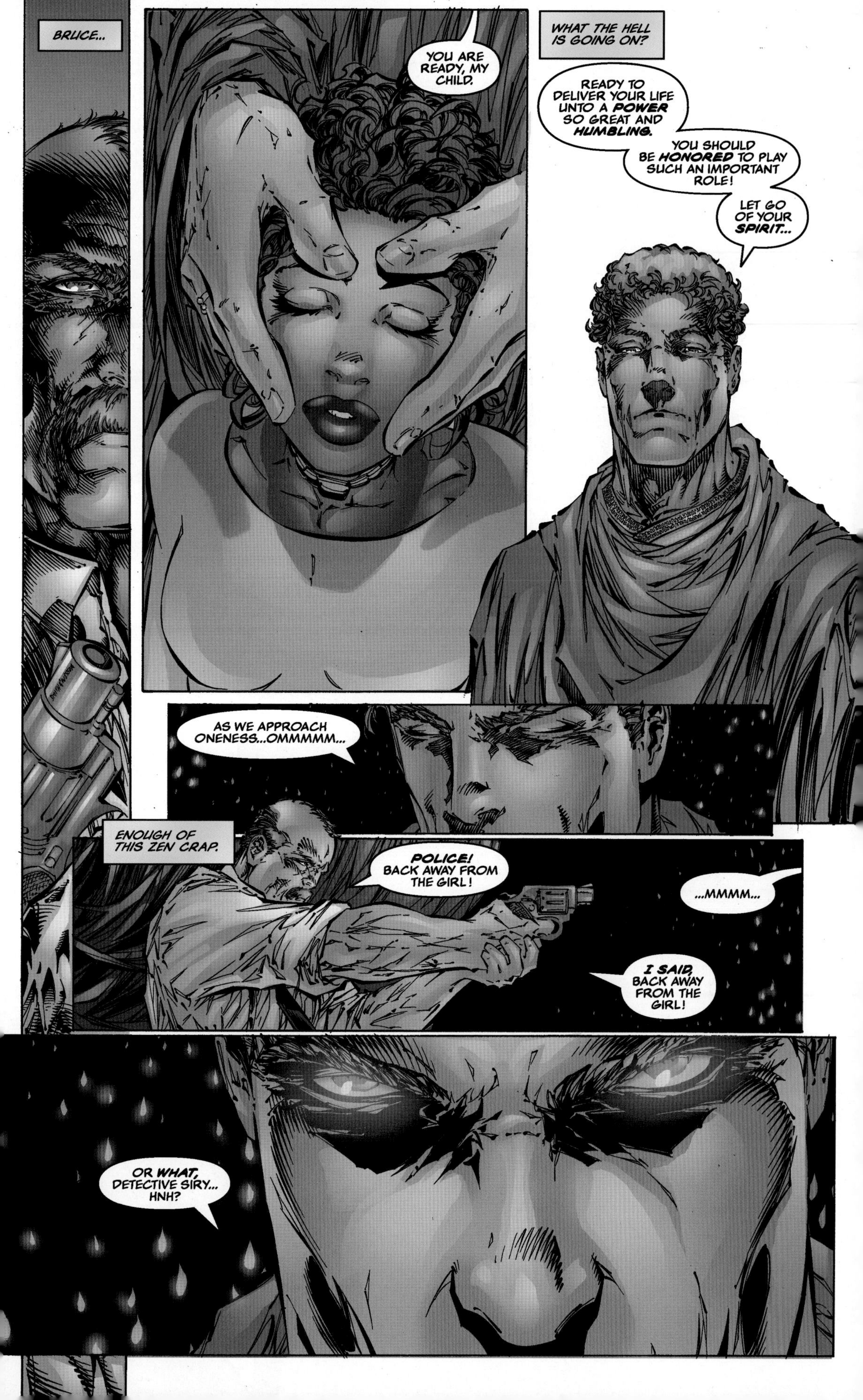
BRUCE...
YOU ARE READY, MY CHILD.
WHAT THE HELL IS GOING ON?
READY TO DELIVER YOUR LIFE UNTO A POWER SO GREAT AND HUMBLING.
YOU SHOULD BE HONORED TO PLAY SUCH AN IMPORTANT ROLE!
LET GO OF YOUR SPIRIT...
AS WE APPROACH ONENESS...OMMMMM...
ENOUGH OF THIS ZEN CRAP.
POLICE! BACK AWAY FROM THE GIRL!
...MMMM...
I SAID, BACK AWAY FROM THE GIRL!
OR WHAT, DETECTIVE SIRY... HNH?

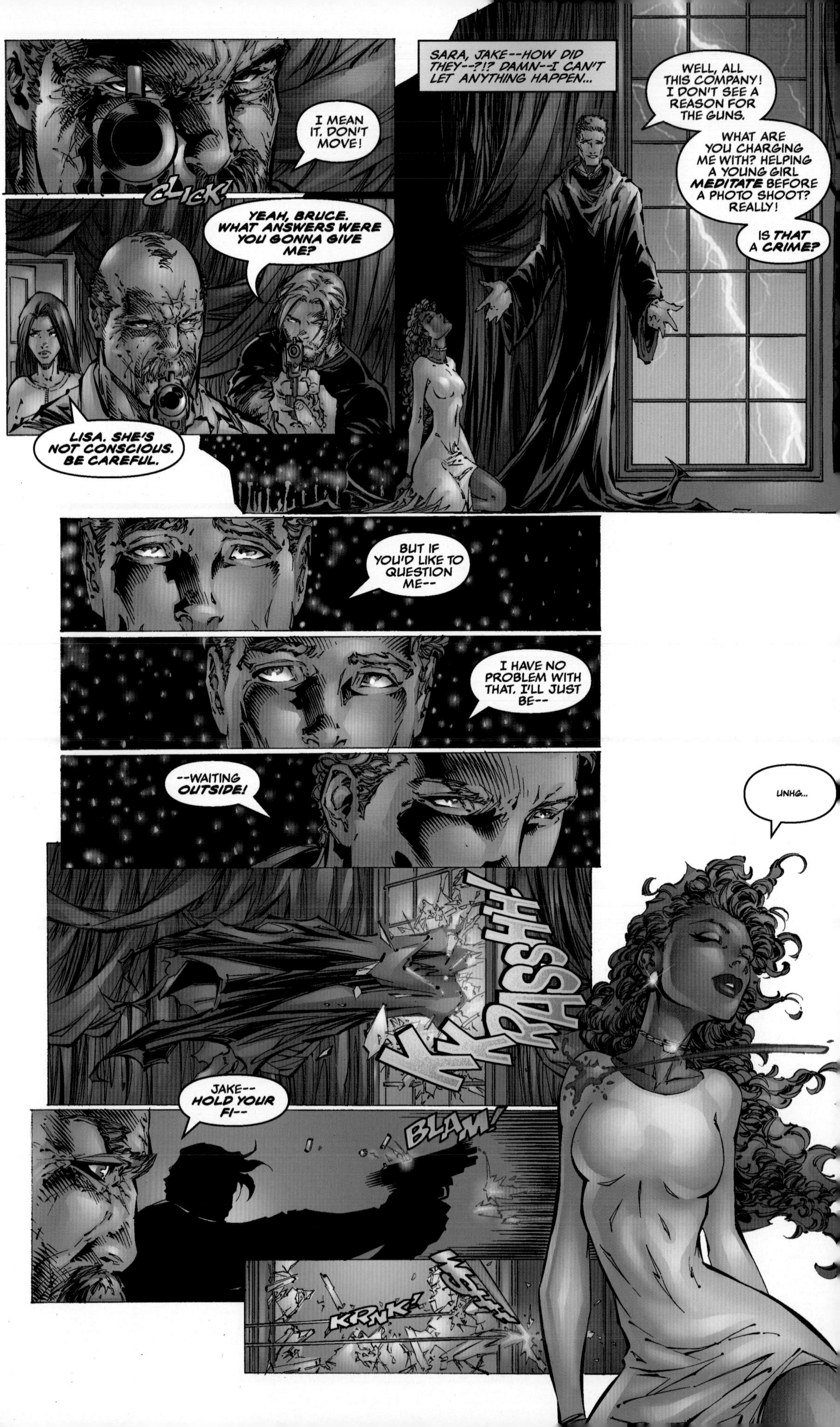
I MEAN IT. DON'T MOVE!
CLICK!
SARA, JAKE--HOW DID THEY--?!? DAMN--I CAN'T LET ANYTHING HAPPEN...
WELL, ALL THIS COMPANY! I DON'T SEE A REASON FOR THE GUNS.
WHAT ARE YOU CHARGING ME WITH? HELPING A YOUNG GIRL MEDITATE BEFORE A PHOTO SHOOT? REALLY!
IS THAT A CRIME?
YEAH, BRUCE. WHAT ANSWERS WERE YOU GONNA GIVE ME?
LISA. SHE'S NOT CONSCIOUS. BE CAREFUL.
BUT IF YOU'D LIKE TO QUESTION ME--
I HAVE NO PROBLEM WITH THAT. I'LL JUST BE--
--WAITING OUTSIDE!
UNHG...
KKRASHH!
JAKE--HOLD YOUR FI--
BLAM!
KRNK!

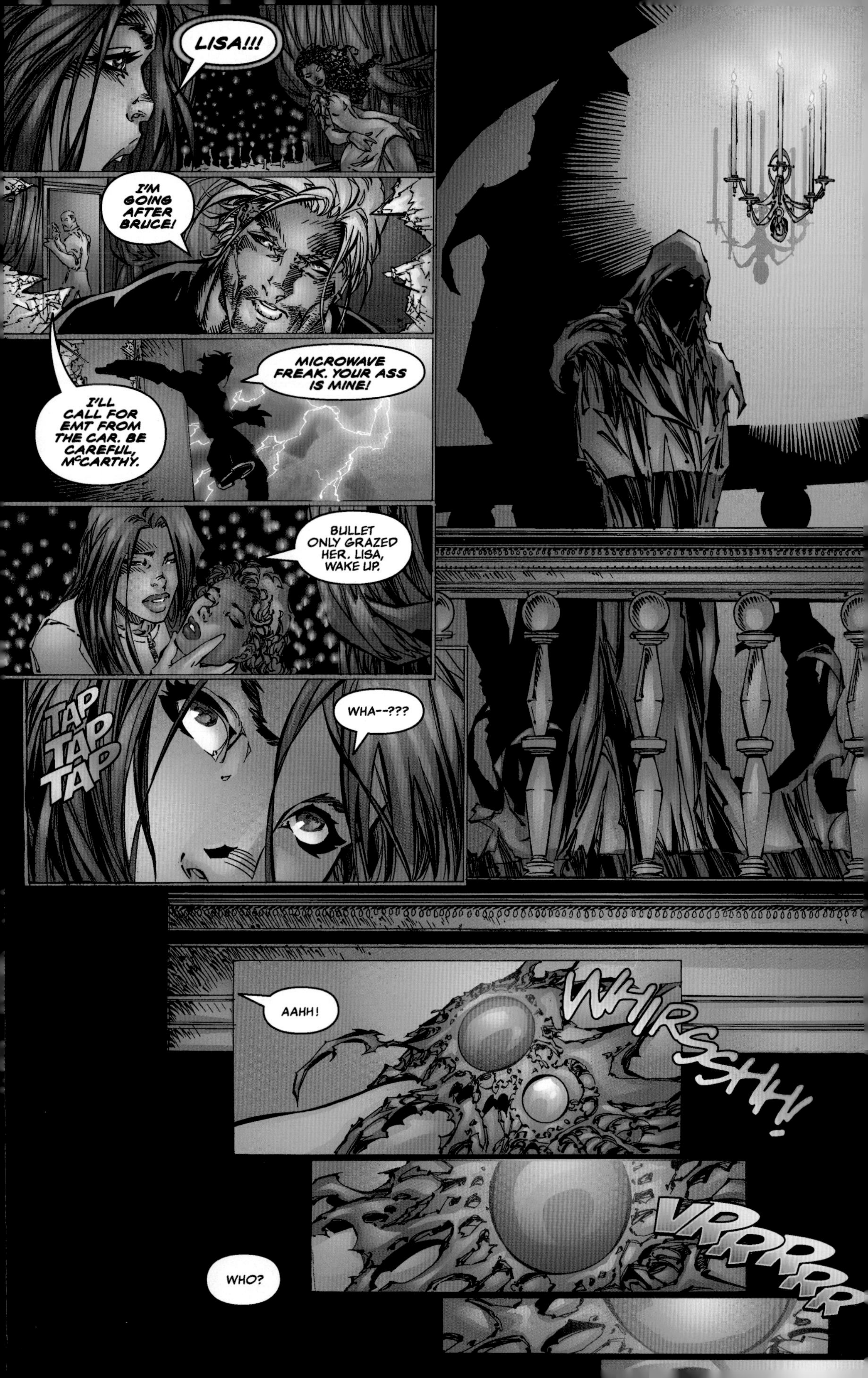
LISA!!!
I'M GOING AFTER BRUCE!
I'LL CALL FOR EMT FROM THE CAR. BE CAREFUL, McCARTHY.
MICROWAVE FREAK. YOUR ASS IS MINE!
BULLET ONLY GRAZED HER. LISA, WAKE UP.
TAP TAP TAP
WHA--???
AAHH!
WHIRSSHH!
VRRRRR
WHO?

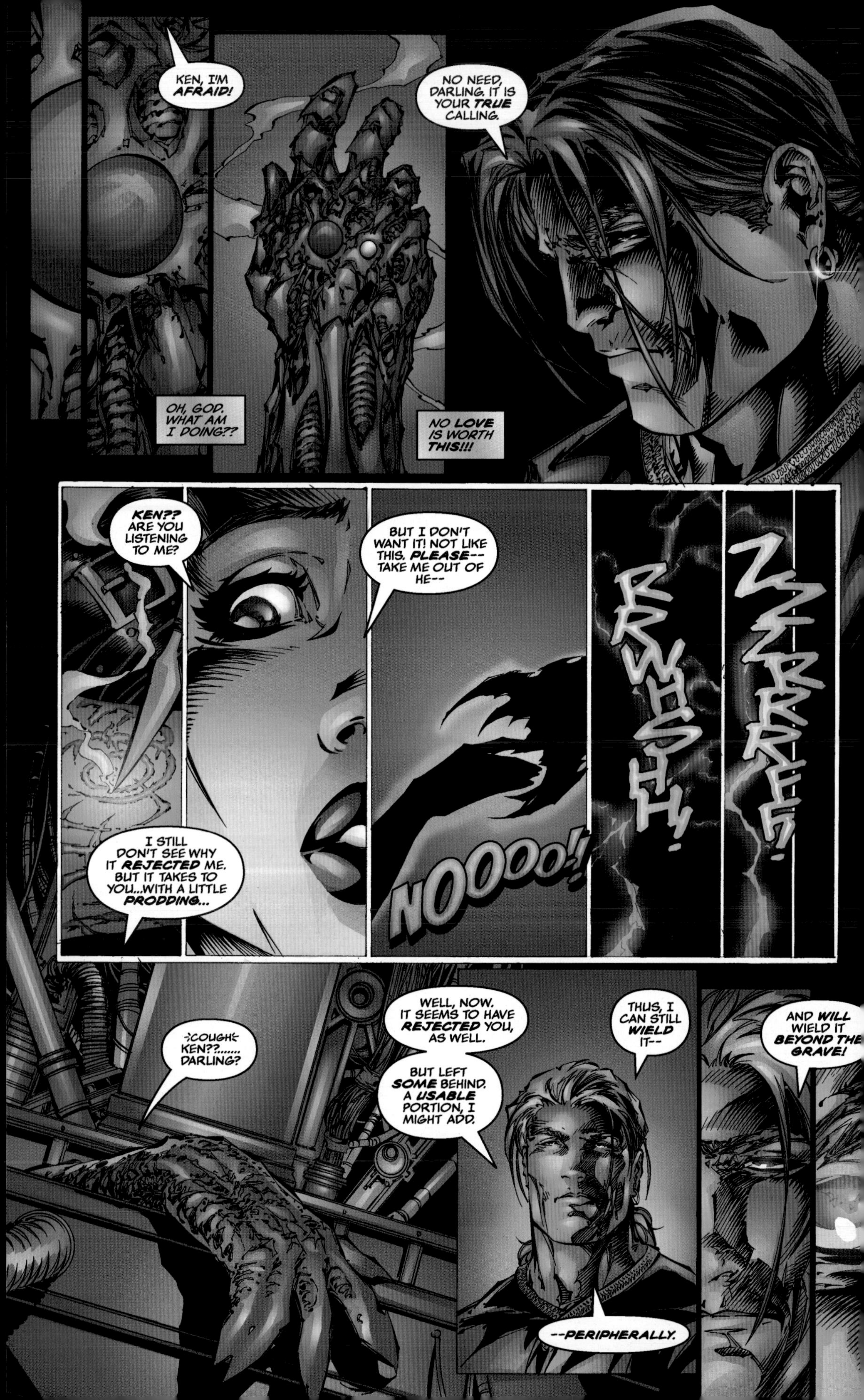

KEN, I'M AFRAID!
NO NEED, DARLING. IT IS YOUR TRUE CALLING.
OH, GOD. WHAT AM I DOING??
NO LOVE IS WORTH THIS!!!
KEN?? ARE YOU LISTENING TO ME?
I STILL DON'T SEE WHY IT REJECTED ME. BUT IT TAKES TO YOU...WITH A LITTLE PRODDING...
BUT I DON'T WANT IT! NOT LIKE THIS. PLEASE-- TAKE ME OUT OF HE--
NOOOOO!!
RRWHSHH!
ZZRRRFF!
COUGH KEN??....... DARLING?
WELL, NOW. IT SEEMS TO HAVE REJECTED YOU, AS WELL.
BUT LEFT SOME BEHIND. A USABLE PORTION, I MIGHT ADD.
THUS, I CAN STILL WIELD IT--
--PERIPHERALLY.
AND WILL WIELD IT BEYOND THE GRAVE!

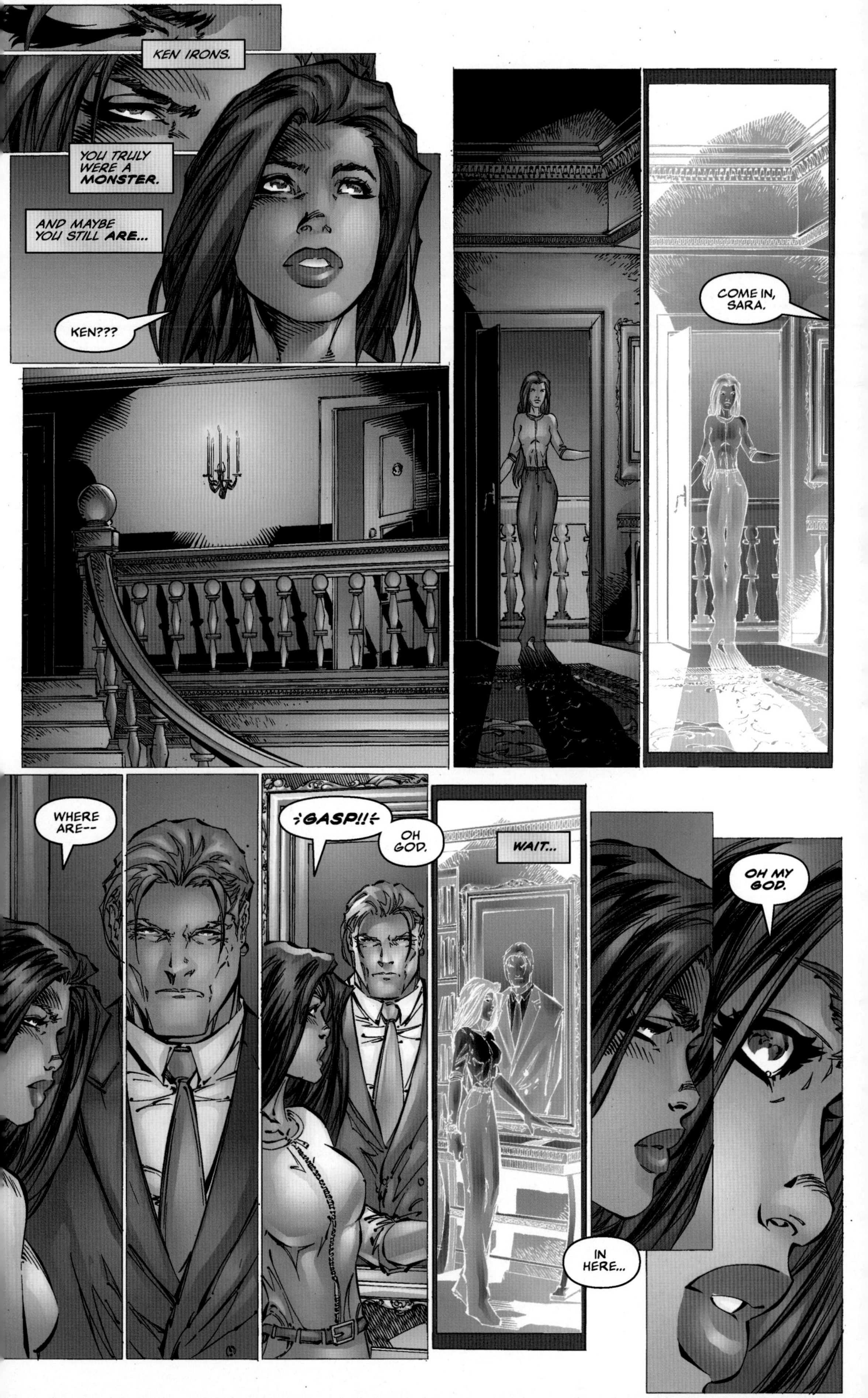

KEN IRONS.
YOU TRULY WERE A MONSTER.
AND MAYBE YOU STILL ARE...
KEN???
COME IN, SARA.
WHERE ARE--
:GASP!!:
OH GOD.
WAIT...
IN HERE...
OH MY GOD.

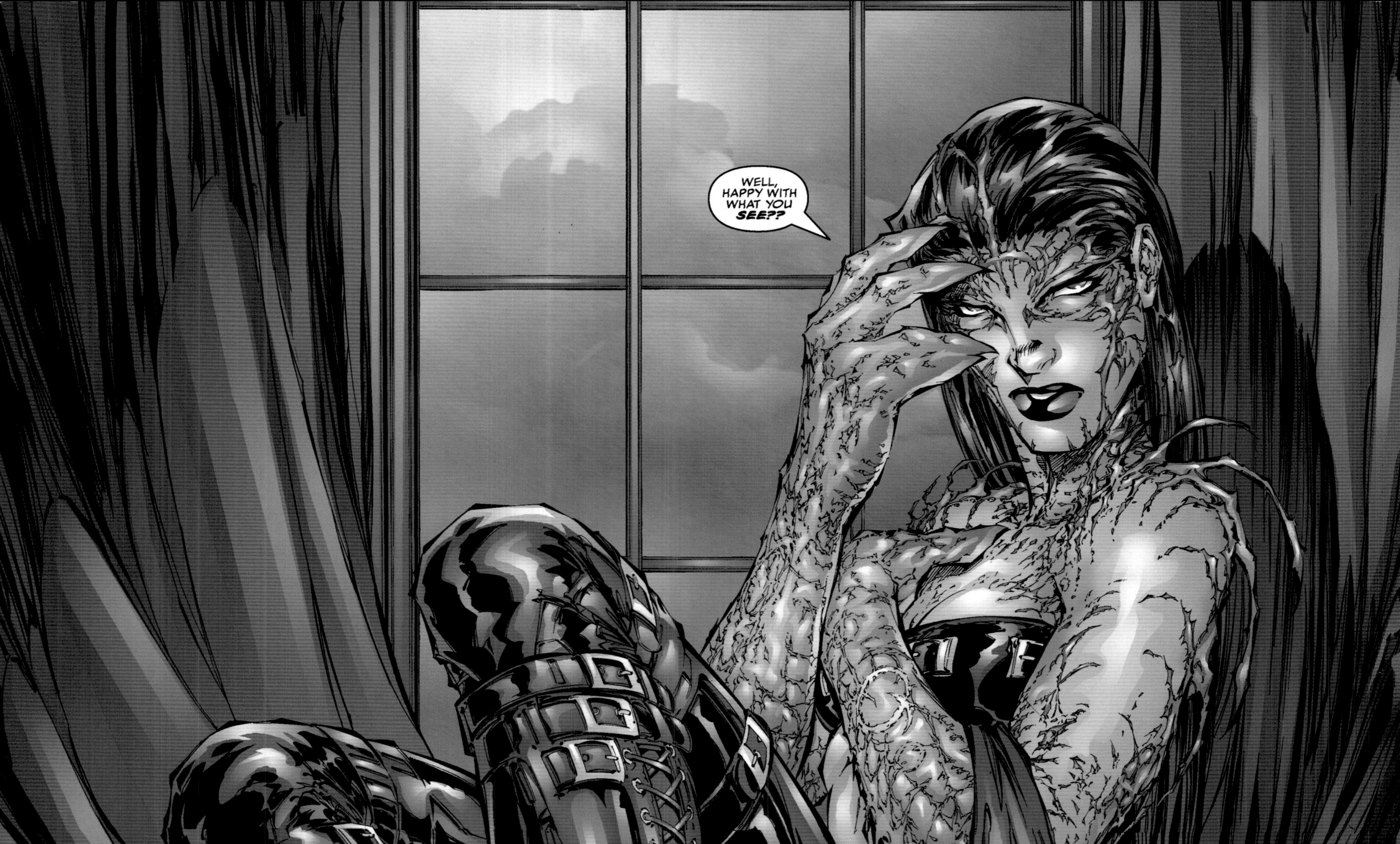
WELL, HAPPY WITH WHAT YOU SEE??

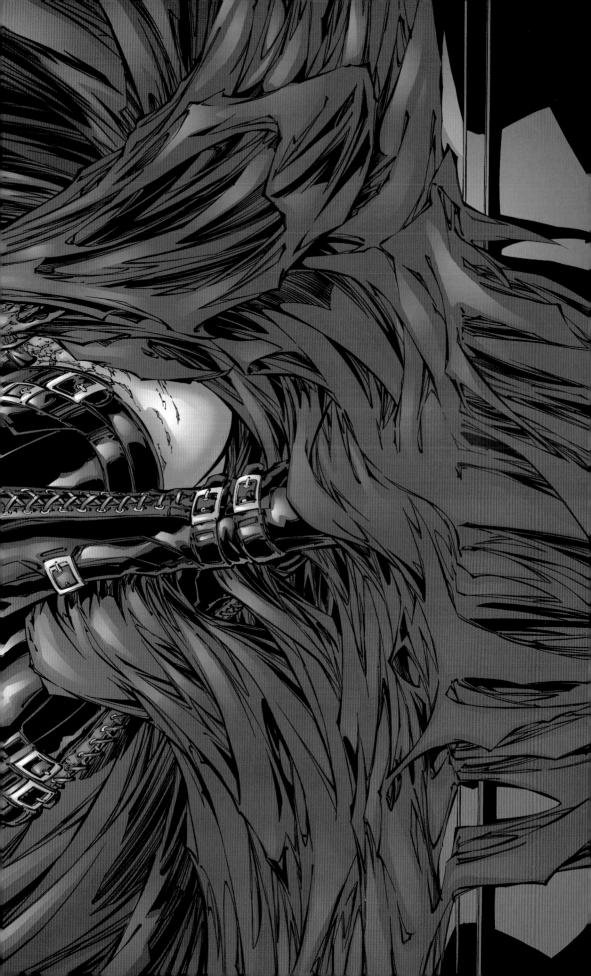

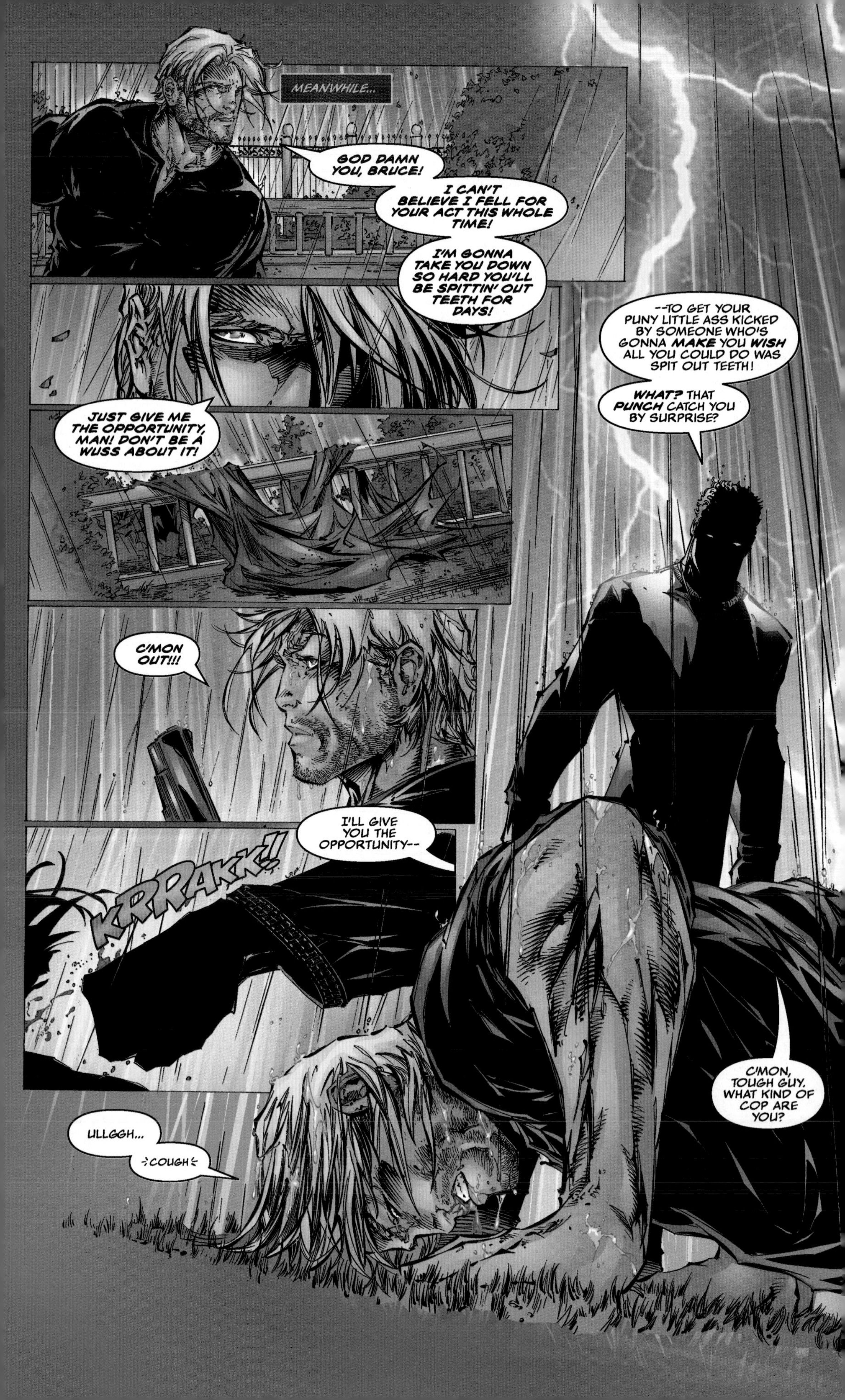

MEANWHILE...
GOD DAMN YOU, BRUCE!
I CAN'T BELIEVE I FELL FOR YOUR ACT THIS WHOLE TIME!
I'M GONNA TAKE YOU DOWN SO HARD YOU'LL BE SPITTIN' OUT TEETH FOR DAYS!
JUST GIVE ME THE OPPORTUNITY, MAN! DON'T BE A WUSS ABOUT IT!
C'MON OUT!!!
I'LL GIVE YOU THE OPPORTUNITY--
KRRAKK!!
--TO GET YOUR PUNY LITTLE ASS KICKED BY SOMEONE WHO'S GONNA MAKE YOU WISH ALL YOU COULD DO WAS SPIT OUT TEETH!
WHAT? THAT PUNCH CATCH YOU BY SURPRISE?
ULLGGH...
COUGH
C'MON, TOUGH GUY. WHAT KIND OF COP ARE YOU?

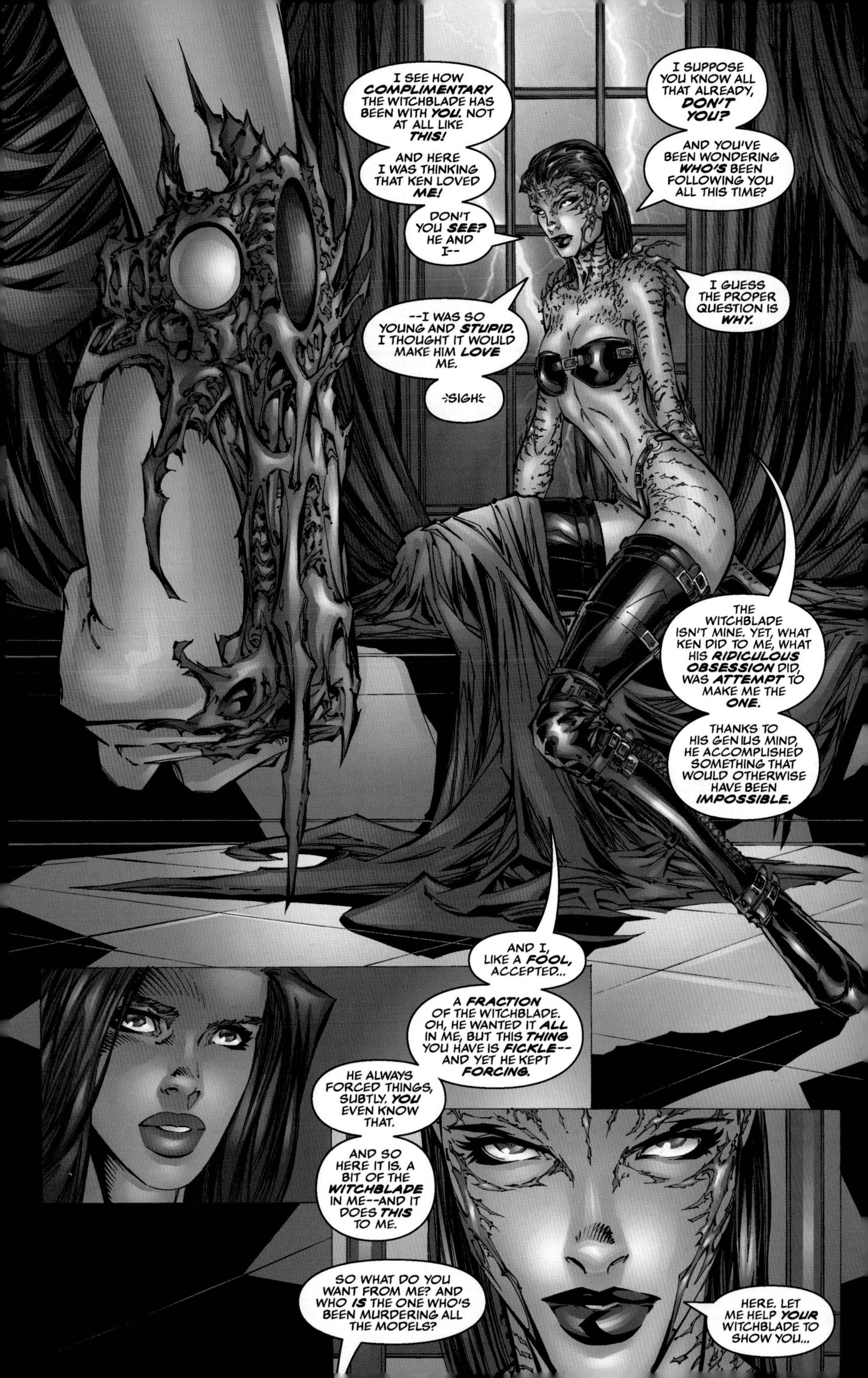
I SEE HOW COMPLIMENTARY THE WITCHBLADE HAS BEEN WITH YOU. NOT AT ALL LIKE THIS!
AND HERE I WAS THINKING THAT KEN LOVED ME!
DON'T YOU SEE? HE AND I--
--I WAS SO YOUNG AND STUPID. I THOUGHT IT WOULD MAKE HIM LOVE ME.
SIGH
I SUPPOSE YOU KNOW ALL THAT ALREADY, DON'T YOU?
AND YOU'VE BEEN WONDERING WHO'S BEEN FOLLOWING YOU ALL THIS TIME?
I GUESS THE PROPER QUESTION IS WHY.
THE WITCHBLADE ISN'T MINE. YET, WHAT KEN DID TO ME, WHAT HIS RIDICULOUS OBSESSION DID, WAS ATTEMPT TO MAKE ME THE ONE.
THANKS TO HIS GENIUS MIND, HE ACCOMPLISHED SOMETHING THAT WOULD OTHERWISE HAVE BEEN IMPOSSIBLE.
AND I, LIKE A FOOL, ACCEPTED...
A FRACTION OF THE WITCHBLADE. OH, HE WANTED IT ALL IN ME, BUT THIS THING YOU HAVE IS FICKLE-- AND YET HE KEPT FORCING.
HE ALWAYS FORCED THINGS, SUBTLY. YOU EVEN KNOW THAT.
AND SO HERE IT IS. A BIT OF THE WITCHBLADE IN ME--AND IT DOES THIS TO ME.
SO WHAT DO YOU WANT FROM ME? AND WHO IS THE ONE WHO'S BEEN MURDERING ALL THE MODELS?
HERE. LET ME HELP YOUR WITCHBLADE TO SHOW YOU...

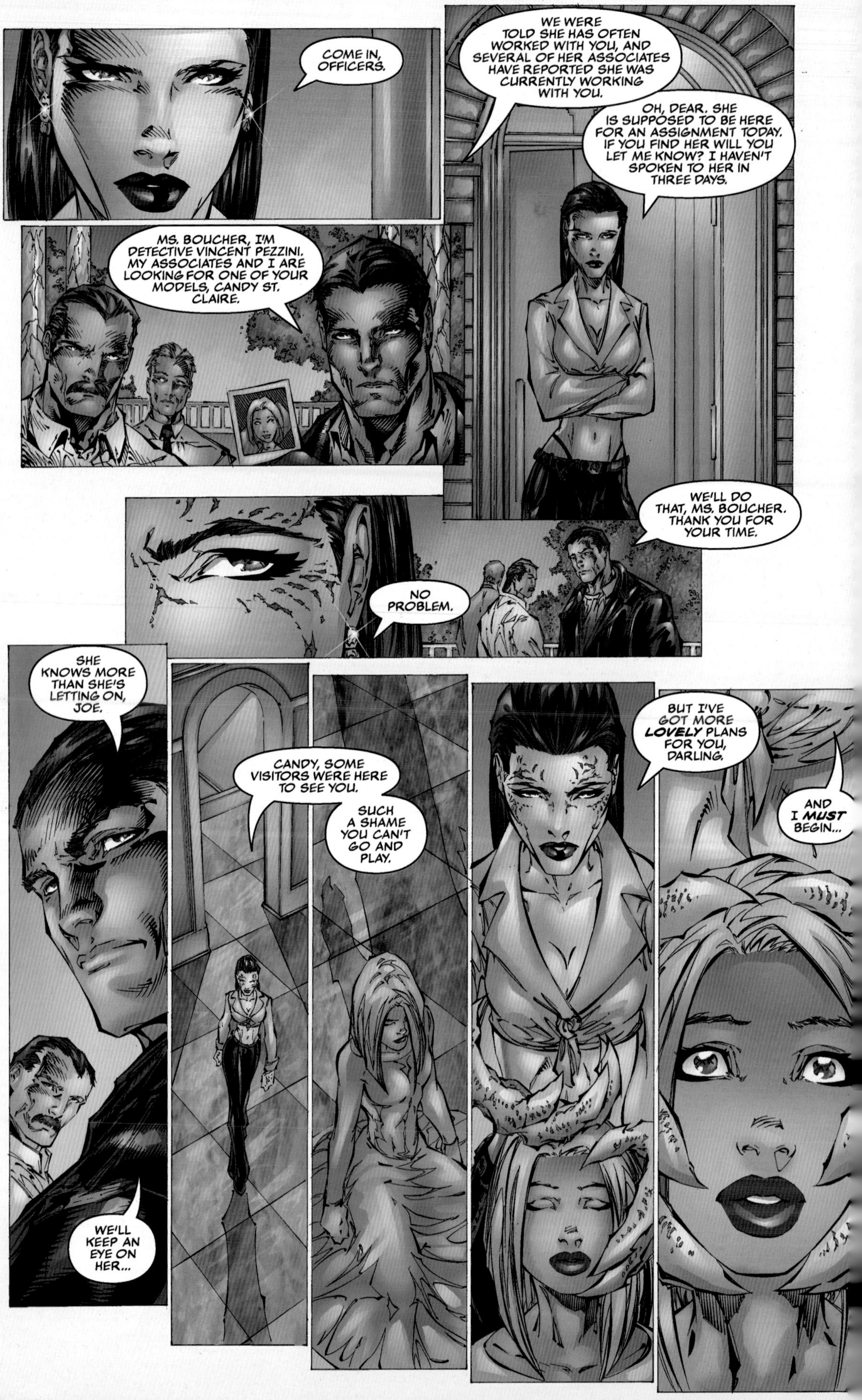
COME IN, OFFICERS.
MS. BOUCHER, I'M DETECTIVE VINCENT PEZZINI. MY ASSOCIATES AND I ARE LOOKING FOR ONE OF YOUR MODELS, CANDY ST. CLAIRE.
WE WERE TOLD SHE HAS OFTEN WORKED WITH YOU, AND SEVERAL OF HER ASSOCIATES HAVE REPORTED SHE WAS CURRENTLY WORKING WITH YOU.
OH, DEAR. SHE IS SUPPOSED TO BE HERE FOR AN ASSIGNMENT TODAY. IF YOU FIND HER WILL YOU LET ME KNOW? I HAVEN'T SPOKEN TO HER IN THREE DAYS.
WE'LL DO THAT, MS. BOUCHER. THANK YOU FOR YOUR TIME.
NO PROBLEM.
SHE KNOWS MORE THAN SHE'S LETTING ON, JOE.
WE'LL KEEP AN EYE ON HER...
CANDY, SOME VISITORS WERE HERE TO SEE YOU.
SUCH A SHAME YOU CAN'T GO AND PLAY.
BUT I'VE GOT MORE LOVELY PLANS FOR YOU, DARLING.
AND I MUST BEGIN...

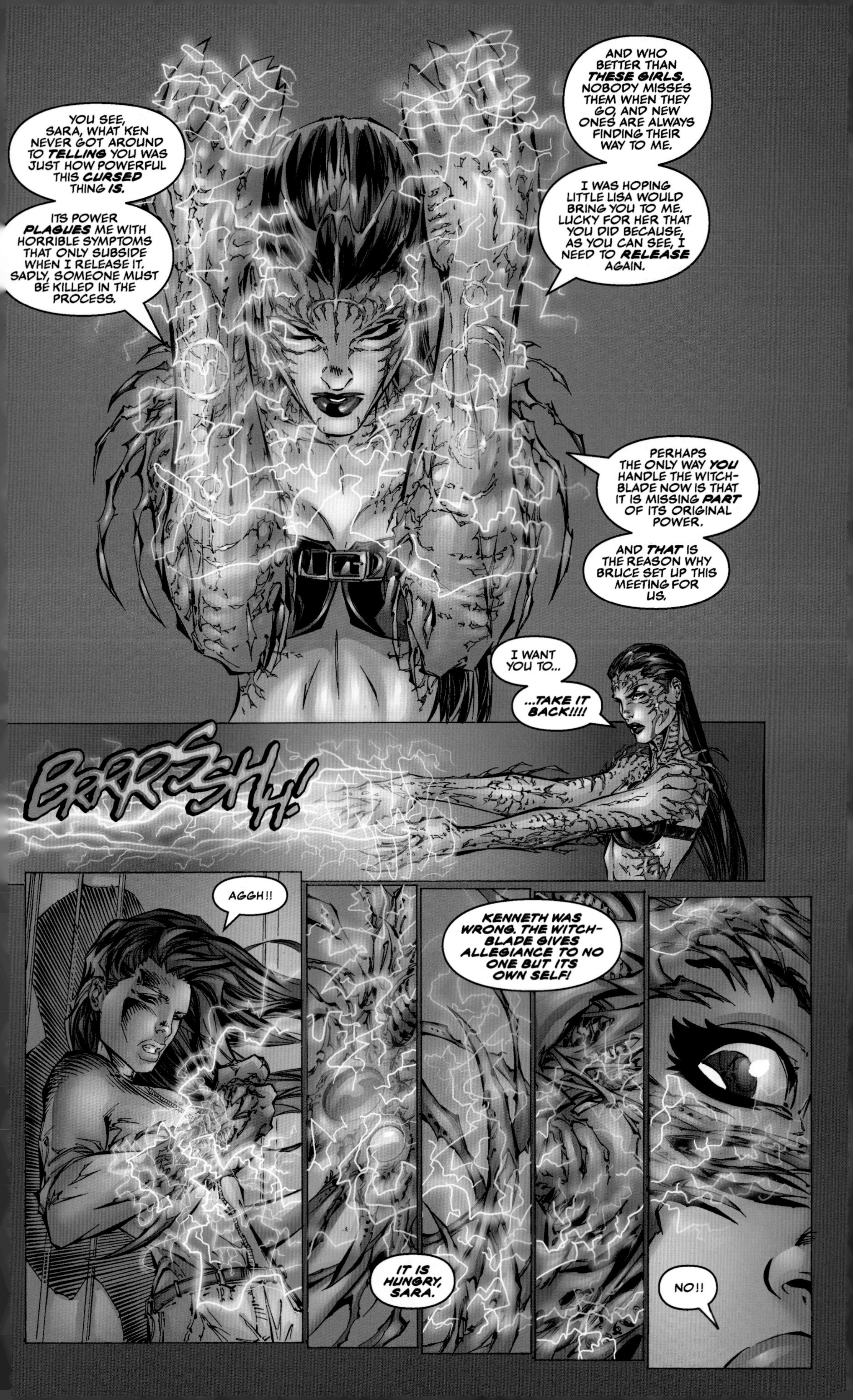
YOU SEE, SARA, WHAT KEN NEVER GOT AROUND TO TELLING YOU WAS JUST HOW POWERFUL THIS CURSED THING IS.
ITS POWER PLAGUES ME WITH HORRIBLE SYMPTOMS THAT ONLY SUBSIDE WHEN I RELEASE IT. SADLY, SOMEONE MUST BE KILLED IN THE PROCESS.
AND WHO BETTER THAN THESE GIRLS. NOBODY MISSES THEM WHEN THEY GO, AND NEW ONES ARE ALWAYS FINDING THEIR WAY TO ME.
I WAS HOPING LITTLE LISA WOULD BRING YOU TO ME. LUCKY FOR HER THAT YOU DID BECAUSE, AS YOU CAN SEE, I NEED TO RELEASE AGAIN.
PERHAPS THE ONLY WAY YOU HANDLE THE WITCH-BLADE NOW IS THAT IT IS MISSING PART OF ITS ORIGINAL POWER.
AND THAT IS THE REASON WHY BRUCE SET UP THIS MEETING FOR US.
I WANT YOU TO...
...TAKE IT BACK!!!!
BRRRSSHH!
AGGH!!
KENNETH WAS WRONG. THE WITCH-BLADE GIVES ALLEGIANCE TO NO ONE BUT ITS OWN SELF!
IT IS HUNGRY, SARA.
NO!!

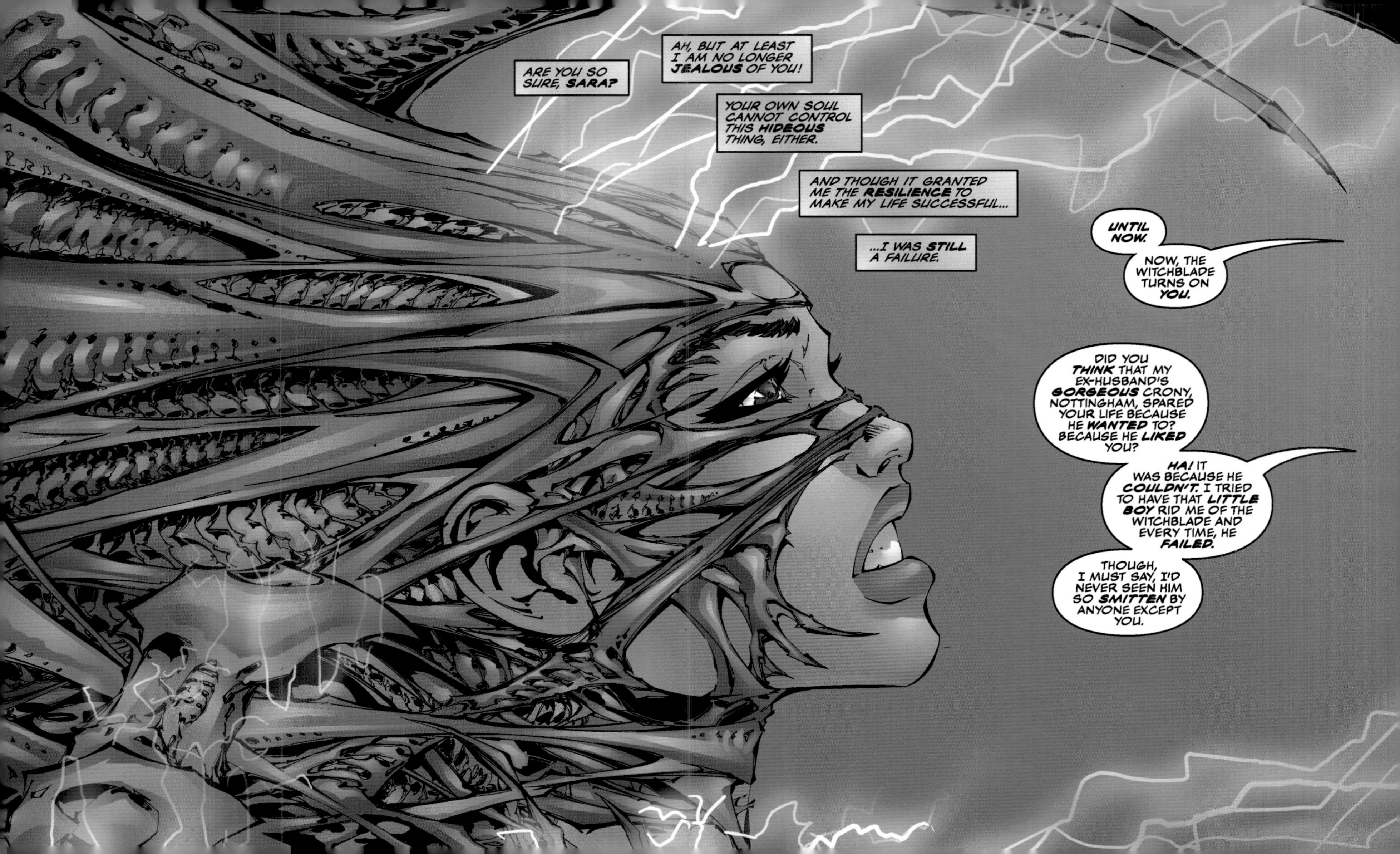
ARE YOU SO SURE, SARA?
AH, BUT AT LEAST I AM NO LONGER JEALOUS OF YOU!
YOUR OWN SOUL CANNOT CONTROL THIS HIDEOUS THING, EITHER.
AND THOUGH IT GRANTED ME THE RESILIENCE TO MAKE MY LIFE SUCCESSFUL...
...I WAS STILL A FAILURE.
UNTIL NOW.
NOW, THE WITCHBLADE TURNS ON YOU.
DID YOU THINK THAT MY EX-HUSBAND'S GORGEOUS CRONY, NOTTINGHAM, SPARED YOUR LIFE BECAUSE HE WANTED TO? BECAUSE HE LIKED YOU?
HA! IT WAS BECAUSE HE COULDN'T. I TRIED TO HAVE THAT LITTLE BOY RID ME OF THE WITCHBLADE AND EVERY TIME, HE FAILED.
THOUGH, I MUST SAY, I'D NEVER SEEN HIM SO SMITTEN BY ANYONE EXCEPT YOU.

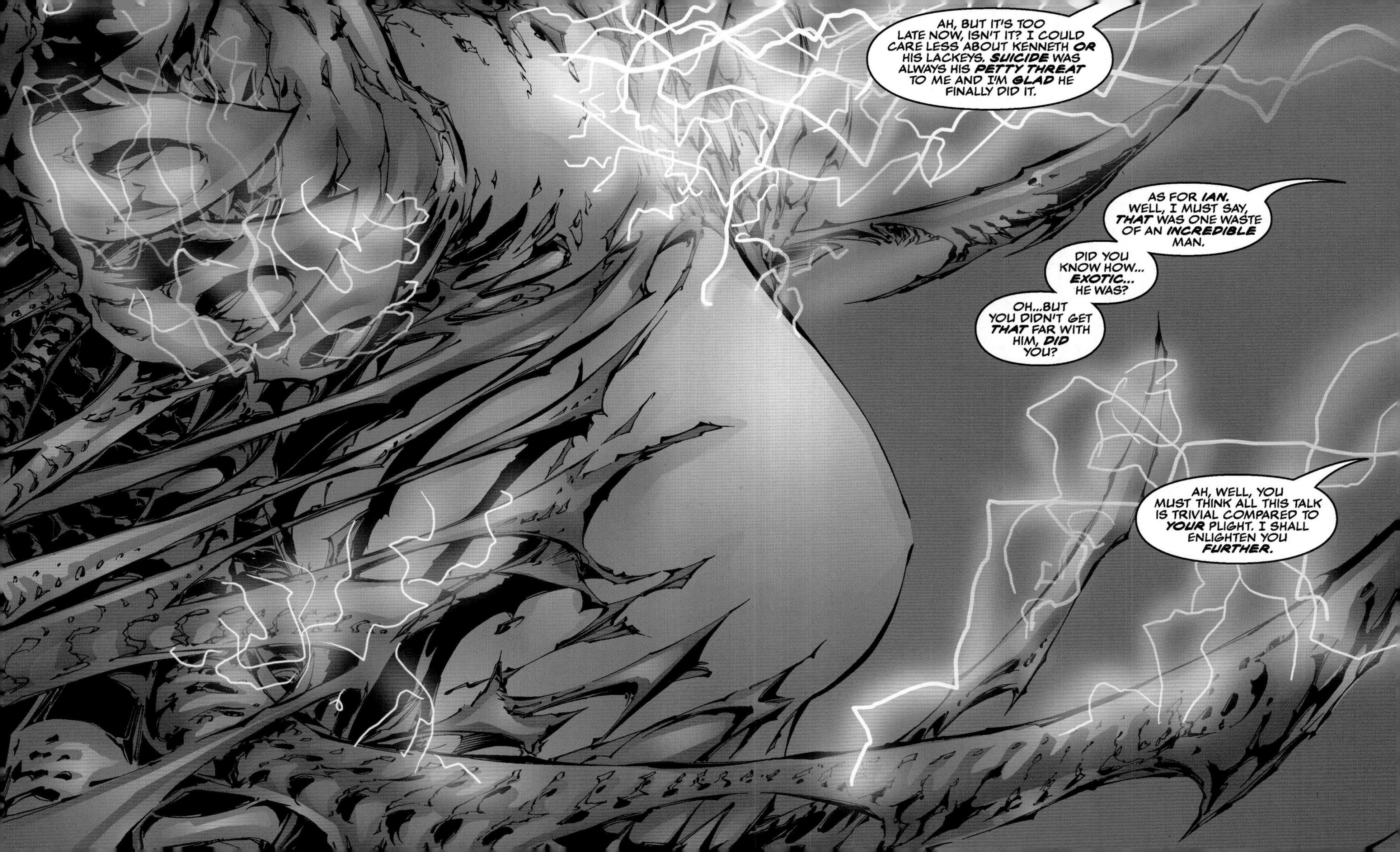
AH, BUT IT'S TOO LATE NOW, ISN'T IT? I COULD CARE LESS ABOUT KENNETH **OR** HIS LACKEYS. **SUICIDE** WAS ALWAYS HIS **PETTY THREAT** TO ME AND I'M **GLAD** HE FINALLY DID IT.
AS FOR **IAN.** WELL, I MUST SAY, **THAT** WAS ONE WASTE OF AN **INCREDIBLE** MAN.
DID YOU KNOW HOW... **EXOTIC...** HE WAS?
OH...BUT YOU DIDN'T GET **THAT** FAR WITH HIM, **DID** YOU?
AH, WELL, YOU MUST THINK ALL THIS TALK IS TRIVIAL COMPARED TO **YOUR** PLIGHT. I SHALL ENLIGHTEN YOU **FURTHER.**

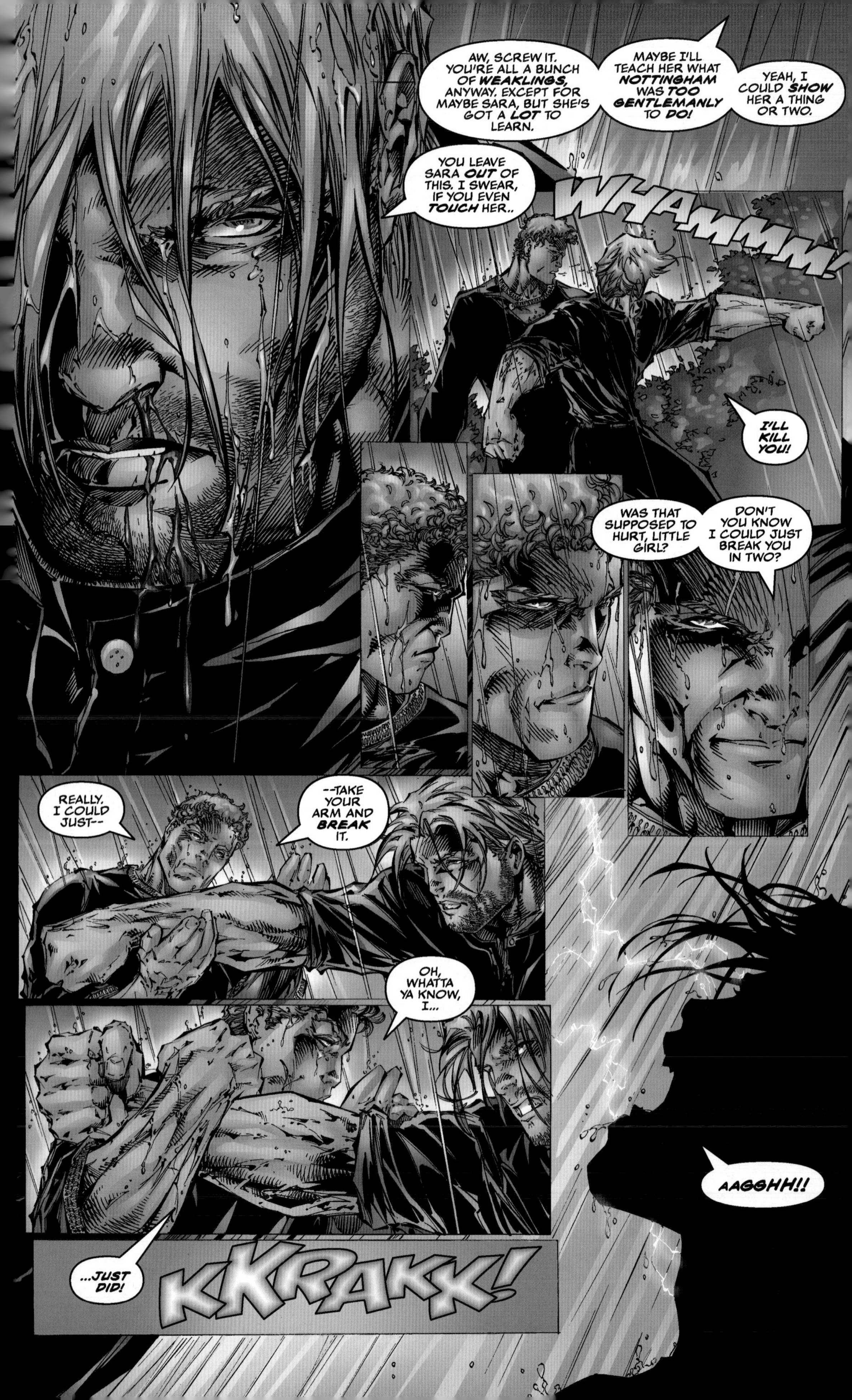
AW, SCREW IT. YOU'RE ALL A BUNCH OF WEAKLINGS, ANYWAY. EXCEPT FOR MAYBE SARA, BUT SHE'S GOT A LOT TO LEARN.
MAYBE I'LL TEACH HER WHAT NOTTINGHAM WAS TOO GENTLEMANLY TO DO!
YEAH, I COULD SHOW HER A THING OR TWO.
YOU LEAVE SARA OUT OF THIS. I SWEAR, IF YOU EVEN TOUCH HER..
WHAMMMM!
I'LL KILL YOU!
WAS THAT SUPPOSED TO HURT, LITTLE GIRL?
DON'T YOU KNOW I COULD JUST BREAK YOU IN TWO?
REALLY. I COULD JUST--
--TAKE YOUR ARM AND BREAK IT.
OH, WHATTA YA KNOW, I...
...JUST DID!
KKRAKK!
AAGGHH!!

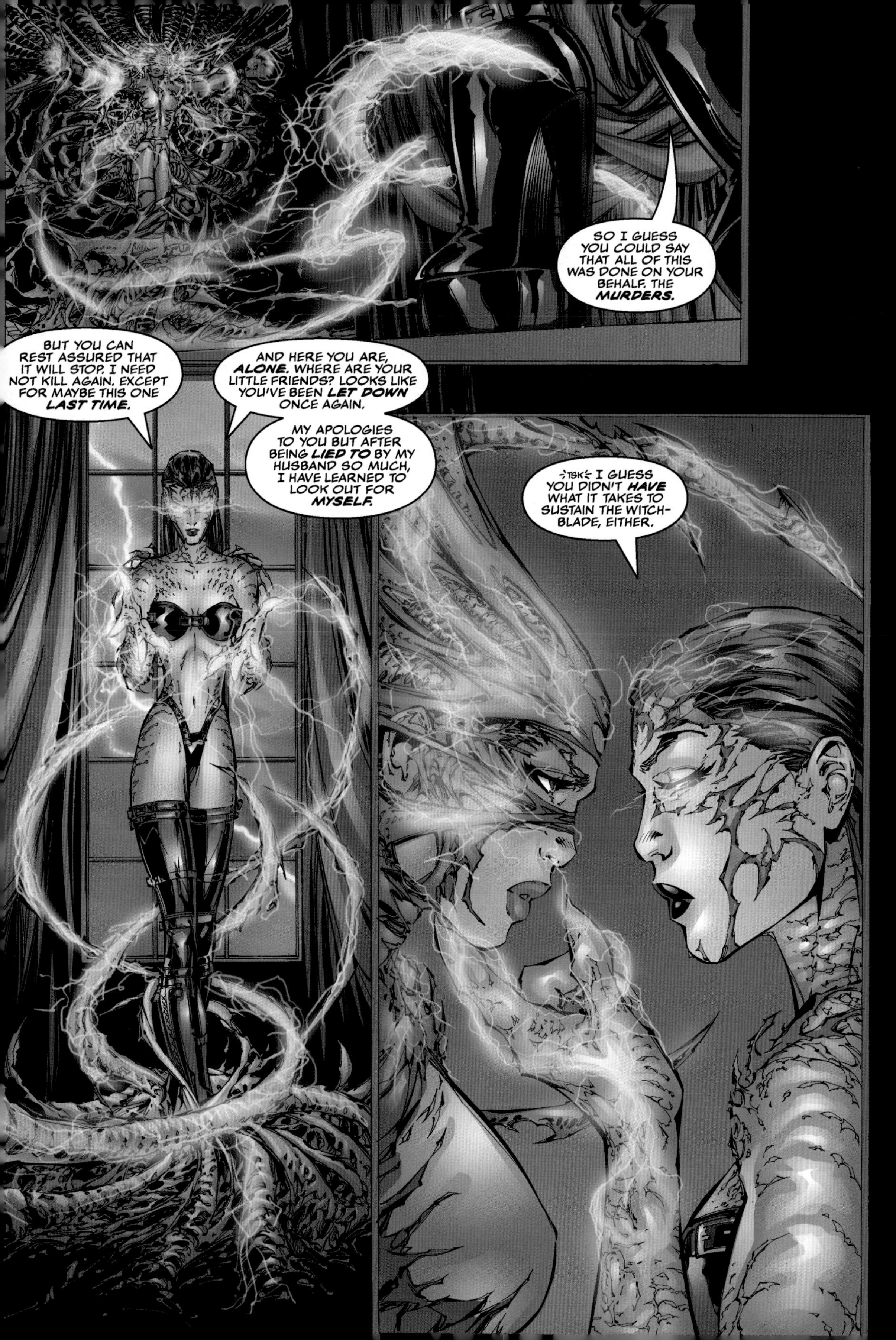

SO I GUESS YOU COULD SAY THAT ALL OF THIS WAS DONE ON YOUR BEHALF. THE MURDERS.
BUT YOU CAN REST ASSURED THAT IT WILL STOP. I NEED NOT KILL AGAIN. EXCEPT FOR MAYBE THIS ONE LAST TIME.
AND HERE YOU ARE, ALONE. WHERE ARE YOUR LITTLE FRIENDS? LOOKS LIKE YOU'VE BEEN LET DOWN ONCE AGAIN.
MY APOLOGIES TO YOU BUT AFTER BEING LIED TO BY MY HUSBAND SO MUCH, I HAVE LEARNED TO LOOK OUT FOR MYSELF.
TSK I GUESS YOU DIDN'T HAVE WHAT IT TAKES TO SUSTAIN THE WITCH-BLADE, EITHER.

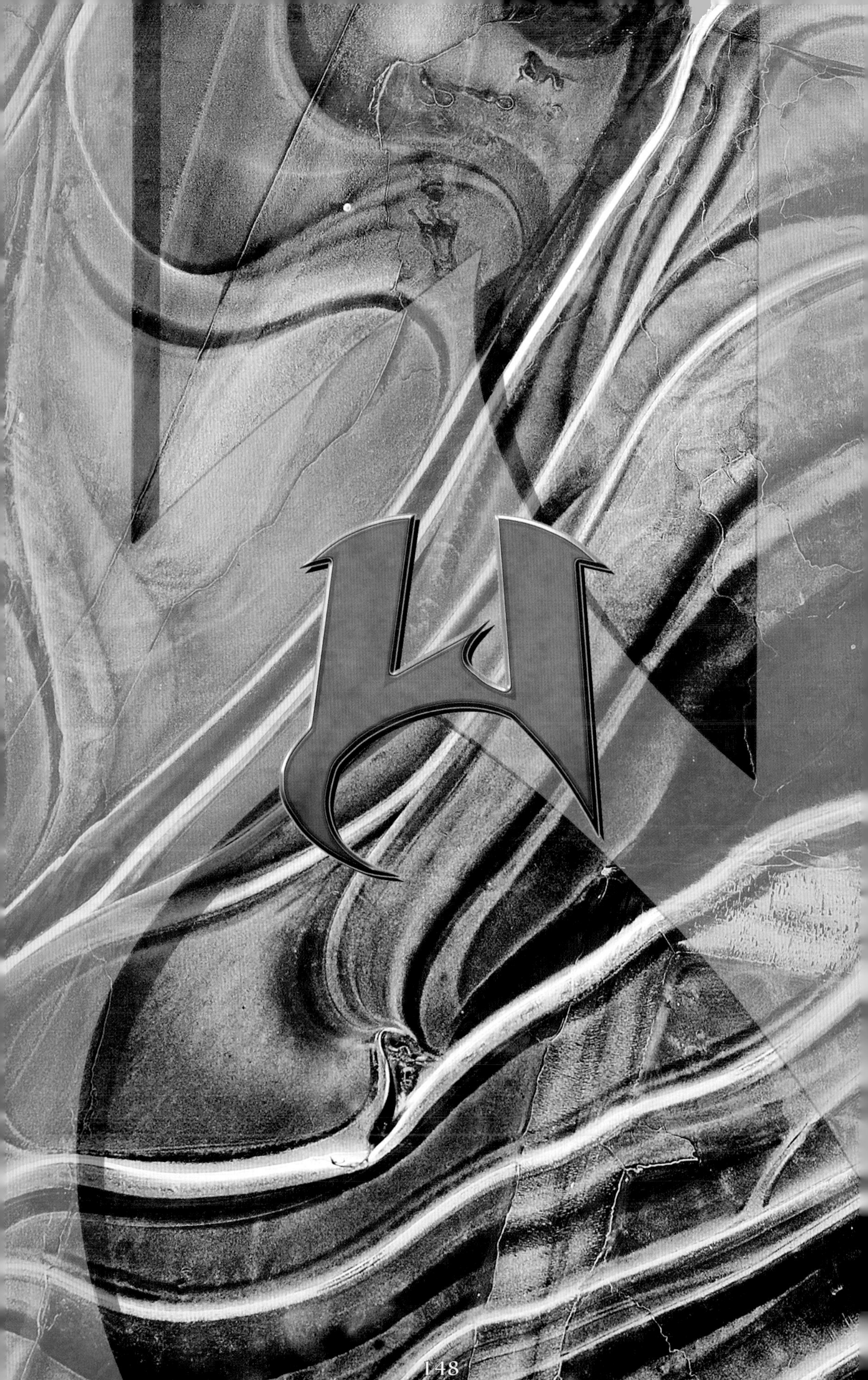

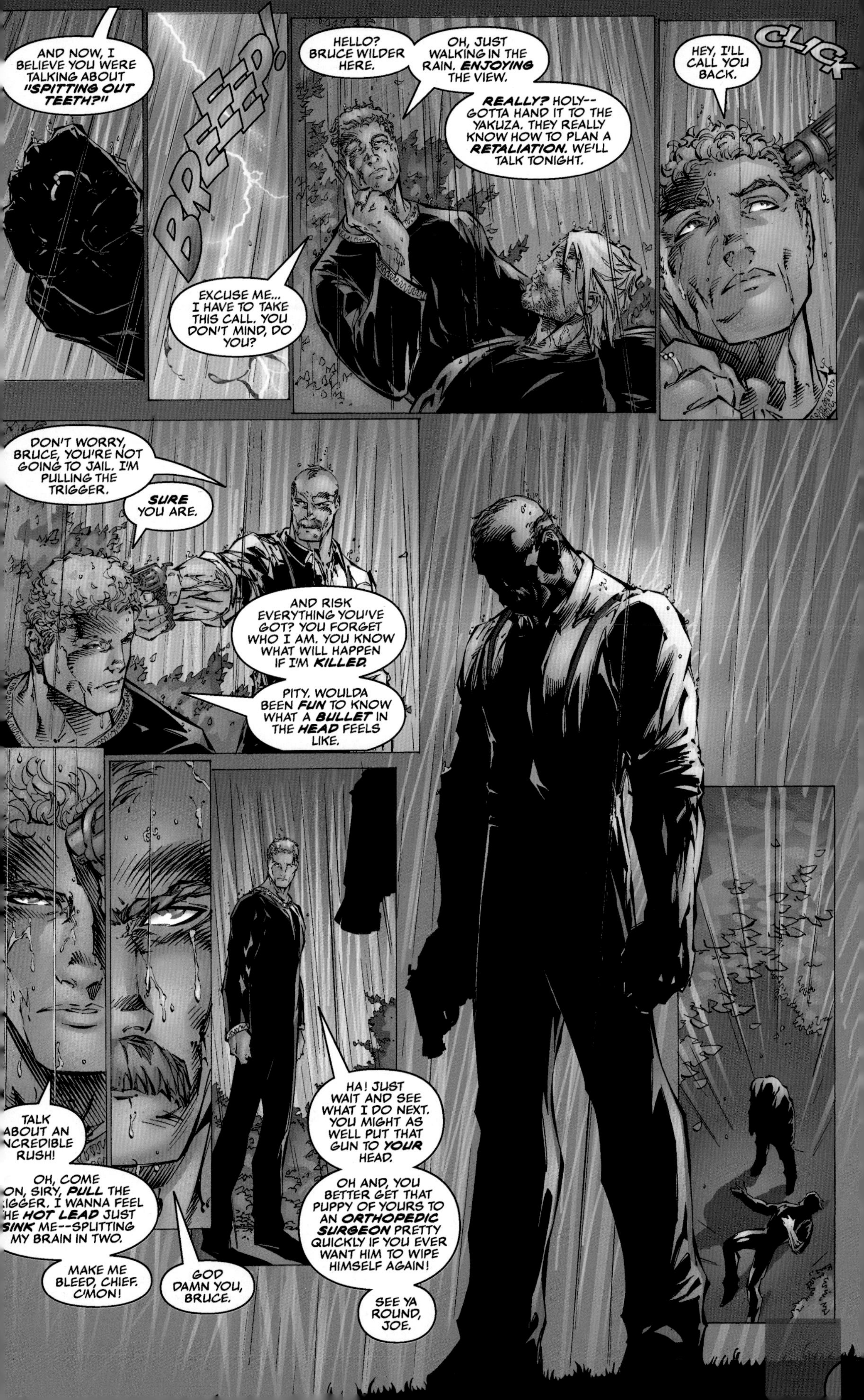

AND NOW, I BELIEVE YOU WERE TALKING ABOUT "SPITTING OUT TEETH?"
BREEEP!
EXCUSE ME... I HAVE TO TAKE THIS CALL. YOU DON'T MIND, DO YOU?
HELLO? BRUCE WILDER HERE.
OH, JUST WALKING IN THE RAIN. ENJOYING THE VIEW.
REALLY? HOLY-- GOTTA HAND IT TO THE YAKUZA. THEY REALLY KNOW HOW TO PLAN A RETALIATION. WE'LL TALK TONIGHT.
HEY, I'LL CALL YOU BACK.
CLICK
DON'T WORRY, BRUCE, YOU'RE NOT GOING TO JAIL. I'M PULLING THE TRIGGER.
SURE YOU ARE.
AND RISK EVERYTHING YOU'VE GOT? YOU FORGET WHO I AM. YOU KNOW WHAT WILL HAPPEN IF I'M KILLED.
PITY. WOULDA BEEN FUN TO KNOW WHAT A BULLET IN THE HEAD FEELS LIKE.
TALK ABOUT AN NCREDIBLE RUSH!
OH, COME ON, SIRY, PULL THE RIGGER. I WANNA FEEL HE HOT LEAD JUST SINK ME--SPLITTING MY BRAIN IN TWO.
MAKE ME BLEED, CHIEF. C'MON!
GOD DAMN YOU, BRUCE.
HA! JUST WAIT AND SEE WHAT I DO NEXT. YOU MIGHT AS WELL PUT THAT GUN TO YOUR HEAD.
OH AND, YOU BETTER GET THAT PUPPY OF YOURS TO AN ORTHOPEDIC SURGEON PRETTY QUICKLY IF YOU EVER WANT HIM TO WIPE HIMSELF AGAIN!
SEE YA ROUND, JOE.

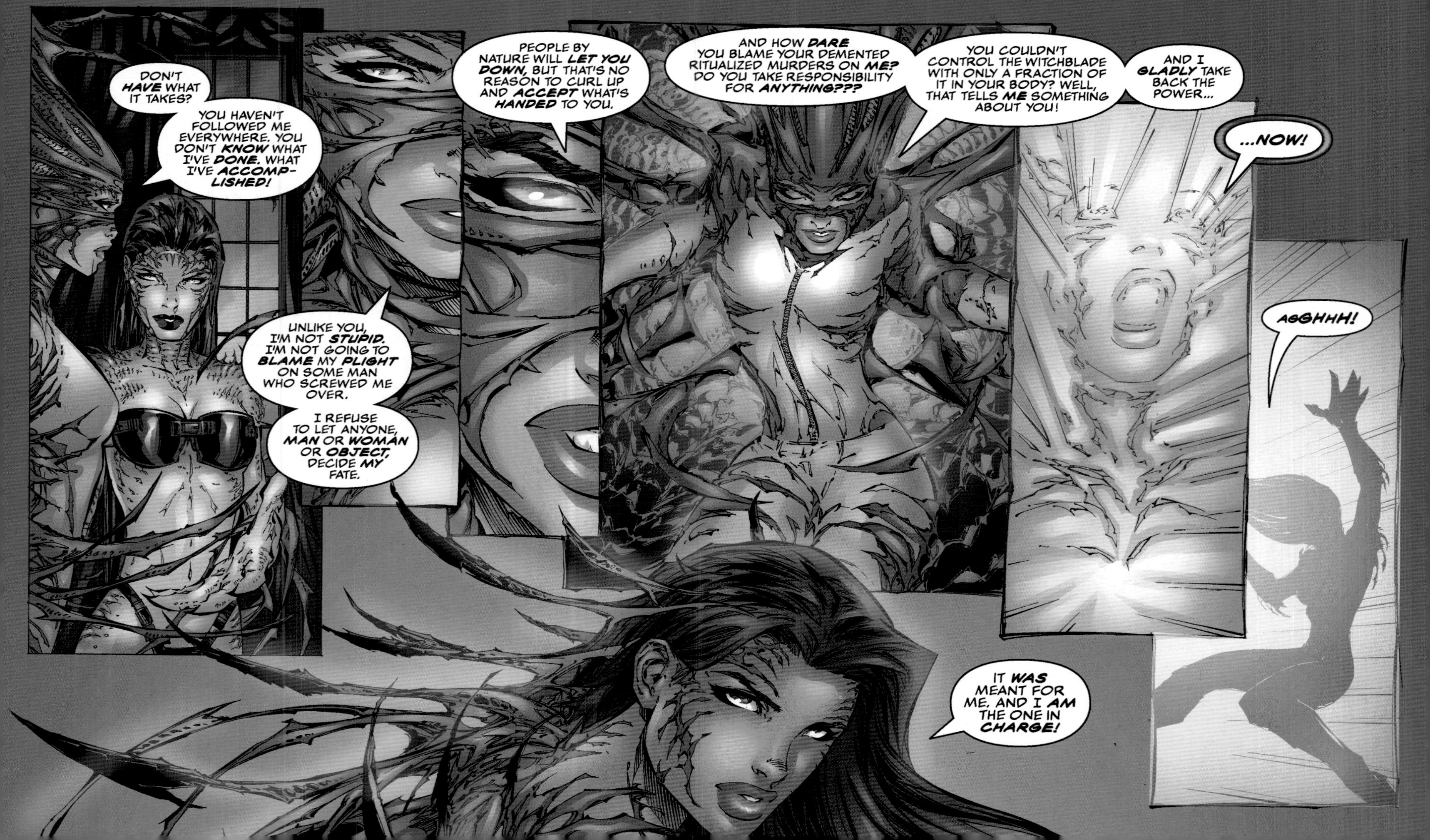
DON'T HAVE WHAT IT TAKES?
YOU HAVEN'T FOLLOWED ME EVERYWHERE. YOU DON'T KNOW WHAT I'VE DONE. WHAT I'VE ACCOMP-LISHED!
UNLIKE YOU, I'M NOT STUPID. I'M NOT GOING TO BLAME MY PLIGHT ON SOME MAN WHO SCREWED ME OVER.
I REFUSE TO LET ANYONE, MAN OR WOMAN OR OBJECT, DECIDE MY FATE.
PEOPLE BY NATURE WILL LET YOU DOWN, BUT THAT'S NO REASON TO CURL UP AND ACCEPT WHAT'S HANDED TO YOU.
AND HOW DARE YOU BLAME YOUR DEMENTED RITUALIZED MURDERS ON ME? DO YOU TAKE RESPONSIBILITY FOR ANYTHING???
YOU COULDN'T CONTROL THE WITCHBLADE WITH ONLY A FRACTION OF IT IN YOUR BODY? WELL, THAT TELLS ME SOMETHING ABOUT YOU!
AND I GLADLY TAKE BACK THE POWER...
...NOW!
AGGHHH!
IT WAS MEANT FOR ME, AND I AM THE ONE IN CHARGE!

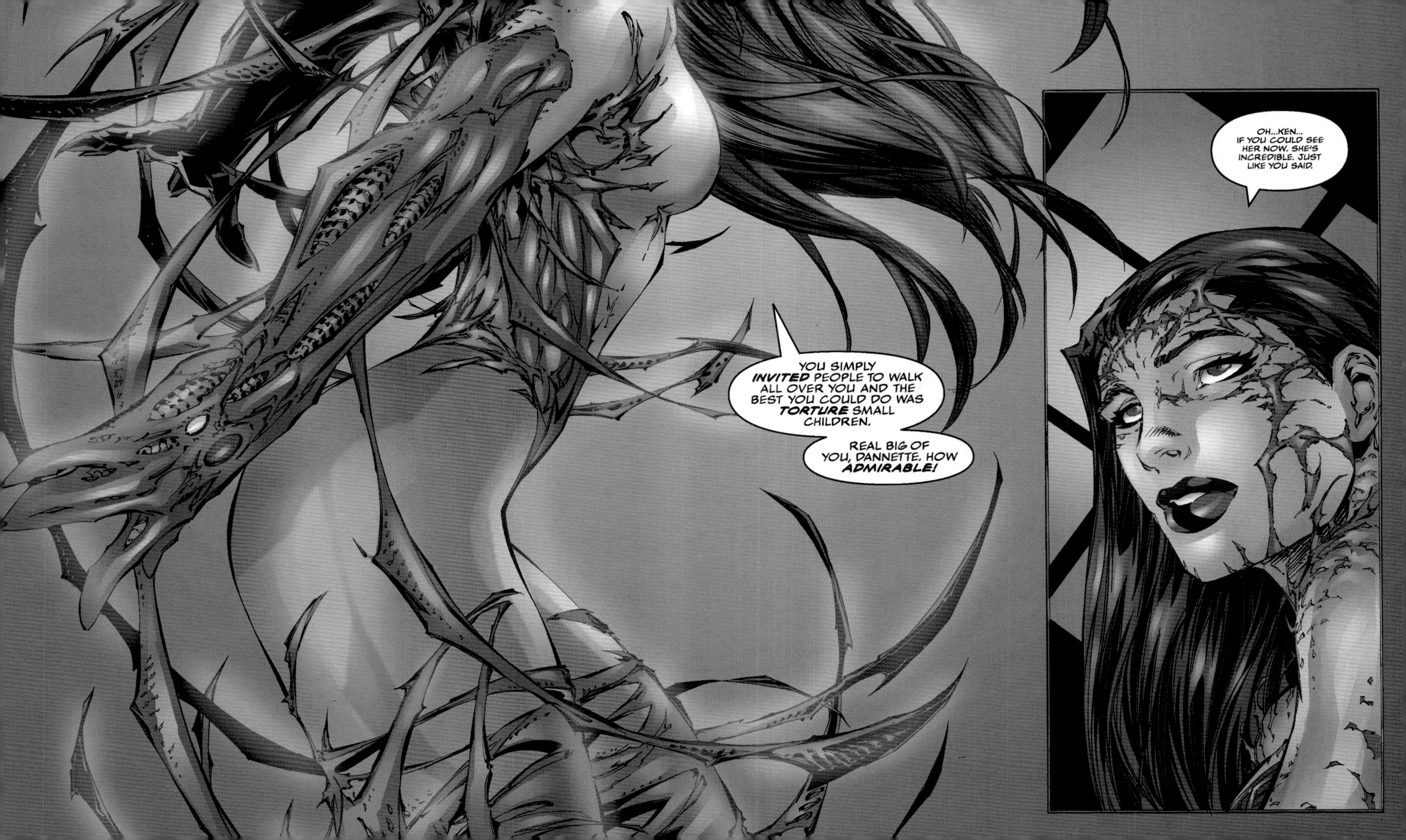
YOU SIMPLY **INVITED** PEOPLE TO WALK ALL OVER YOU AND THE BEST YOU COULD DO WAS **TORTURE** SMALL CHILDREN.
REAL BIG OF YOU, DANNETTE. HOW **ADMIRABLE!**
OH...KEN... IF YOU COULD SEE HER NOW. SHE'S INCREDIBLE. JUST LIKE YOU SAID.

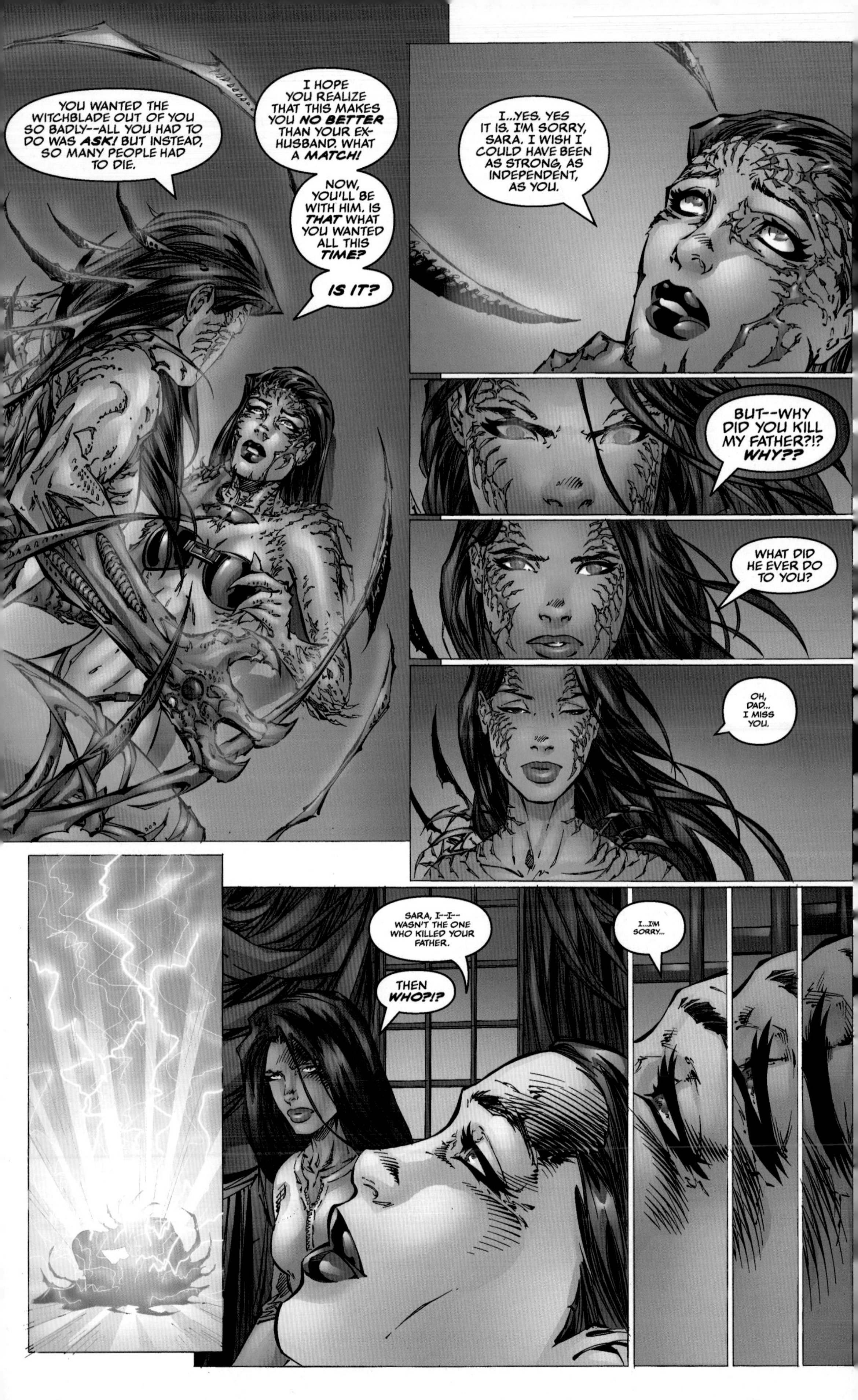
YOU WANTED THE WITCHBLADE OUT OF YOU SO BADLY--ALL YOU HAD TO DO WAS ASK! BUT INSTEAD, SO MANY PEOPLE HAD TO DIE.
I HOPE YOU REALIZE THAT THIS MAKES YOU NO BETTER THAN YOUR EX-HUSBAND. WHAT A MATCH!
NOW, YOU'LL BE WITH HIM. IS THAT WHAT YOU WANTED ALL THIS TIME?
IS IT?
I...YES. YES IT IS. I'M SORRY, SARA. I WISH I COULD HAVE BEEN AS STRONG, AS INDEPENDENT, AS YOU.
BUT--WHY DID YOU KILL MY FATHER?!? WHY??
WHAT DID HE EVER DO TO YOU?
OH, DAD... I MISS YOU.
SARA, I--I--WASN'T THE ONE WHO KILLED YOUR FATHER.
THEN WHO?!?
I...I'M SORRY...

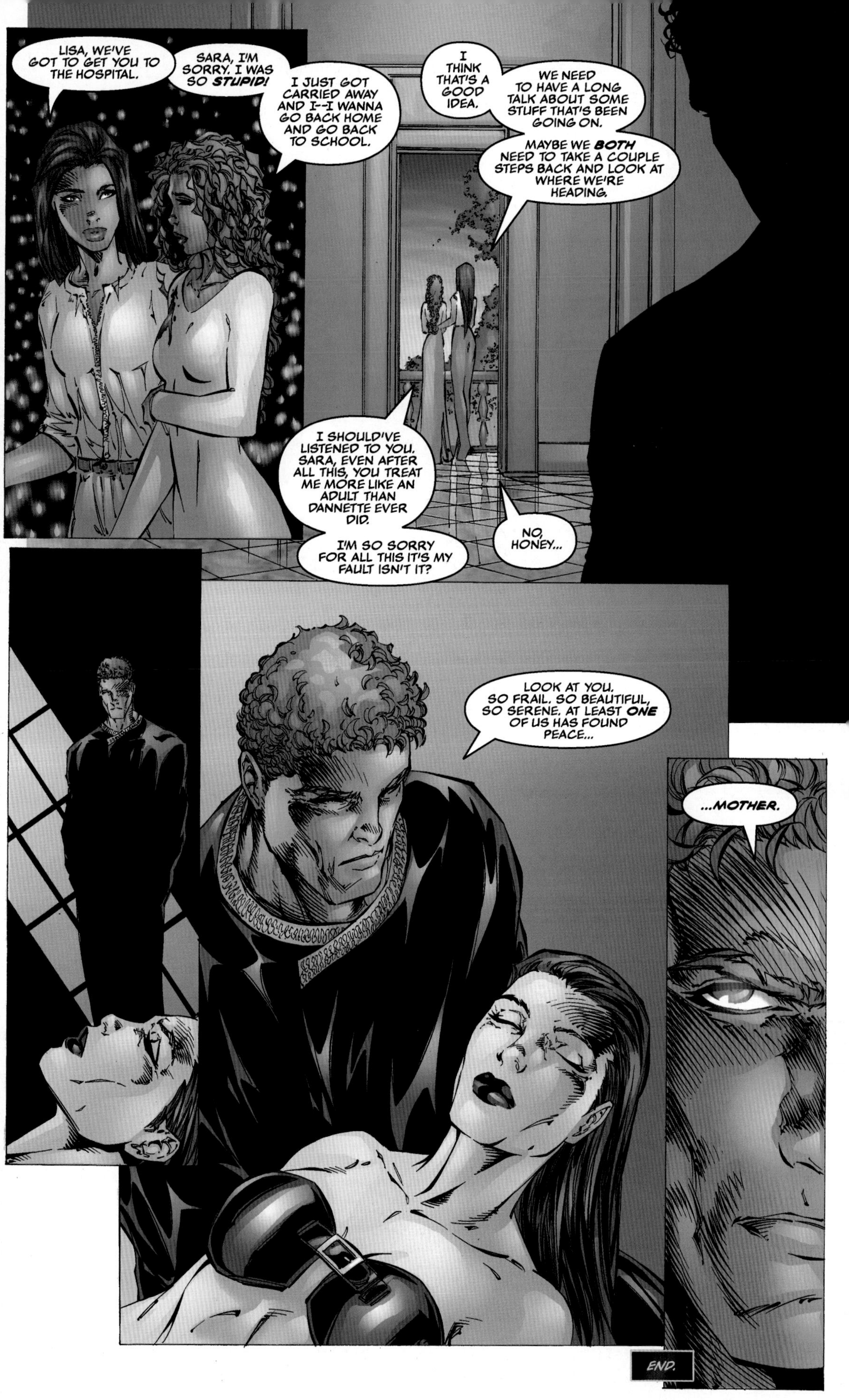
LISA, WE'VE GOT TO GET YOU TO THE HOSPITAL.
SARA, I'M SORRY. I WAS SO STUPID!
I JUST GOT CARRIED AWAY AND I--I WANNA GO BACK HOME AND GO BACK TO SCHOOL.
I THINK THAT'S A GOOD IDEA.
WE NEED TO HAVE A LONG TALK ABOUT SOME STUFF THAT'S BEEN GOING ON.
MAYBE WE BOTH NEED TO TAKE A COUPLE STEPS BACK AND LOOK AT WHERE WE'RE HEADING.
I SHOULD'VE LISTENED TO YOU, SARA, EVEN AFTER ALL THIS, YOU TREAT ME MORE LIKE AN ADULT THAN DANNETTE EVER DID.
I'M SO SORRY FOR ALL THIS IT'S MY FAULT ISN'T IT?
NO, HONEY...
LOOK AT YOU. SO FRAIL. SO BEAUTIFUL, SO SERENE. AT LEAST ONE OF US HAS FOUND PEACE...
...MOTHER.
END.

#15

ISSUE

story: **David Wohl** and **Christina Z.**
pencils/co-plot: **Michael Turner**
inks: **D-Tron**
colors: **JD Smith**

ink assists: **Jeff De Los Santos, Jose "Jag" Guillen, Marsha Chen, Viet Trong**
and **Andy Kim**

lettering assists: **Robin Sphehar**

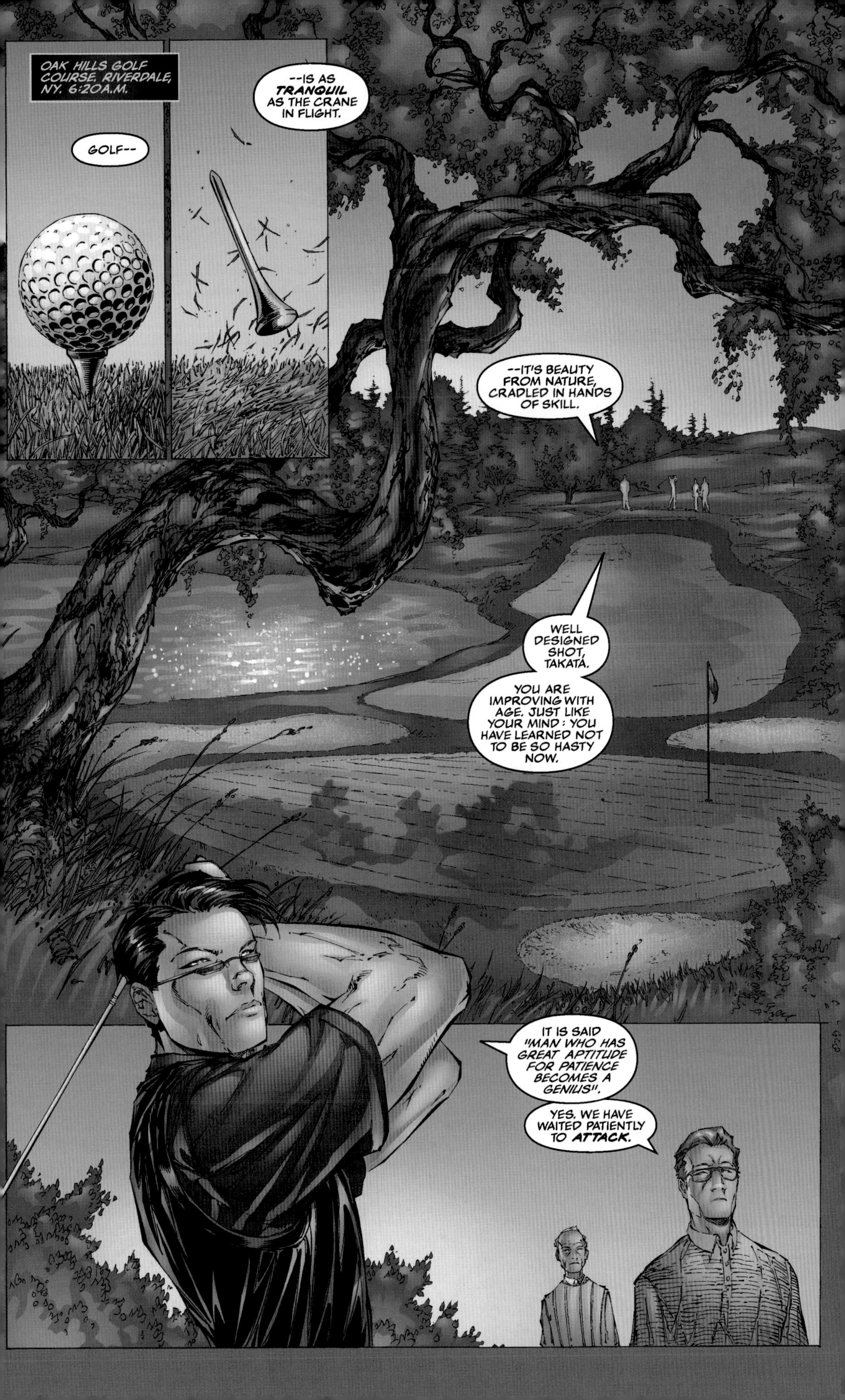
OAK HILLS GOLF COURSE. RIVERDALE, NY. 6:20A.M.
GOLF--
--IS AS TRANQUIL AS THE CRANE IN FLIGHT.
--IT'S BEAUTY FROM NATURE, CRADLED IN HANDS OF SKILL.
WELL DESIGNED SHOT, TAKATA.
YOU ARE IMPROVING WITH AGE. JUST LIKE YOUR MIND: YOU HAVE LEARNED NOT TO BE SO HASTY NOW.
IT IS SAID "MAN WHO HAS GREAT APTITUDE FOR PATIENCE BECOMES A GENIUS".
YES. WE HAVE WAITED PATIENTLY TO ATTACK.

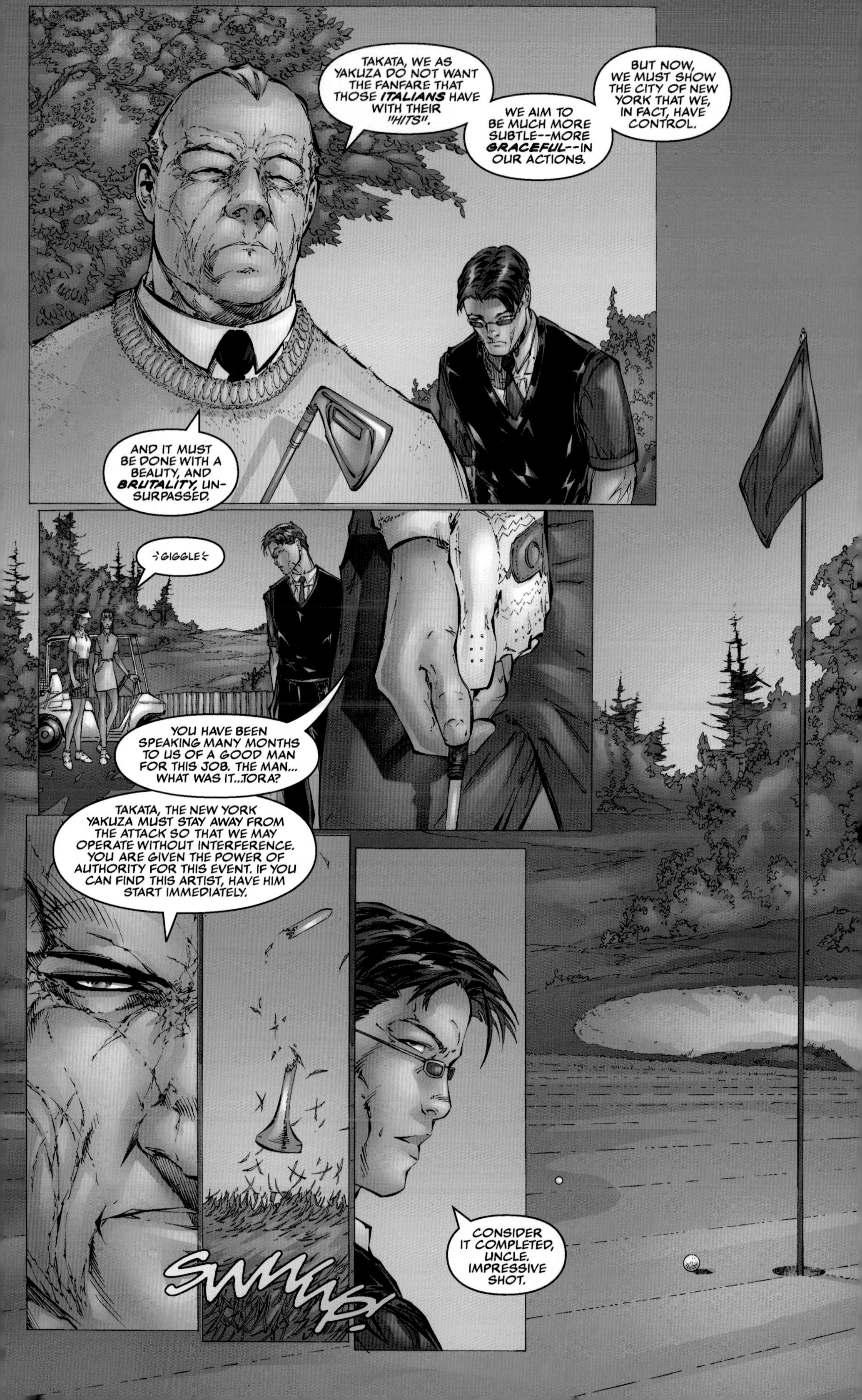
TAKATA, WE AS YAKUZA DO NOT WANT THE FANFARE THAT THOSE ITALIANS HAVE WITH THEIR "HITS".
WE AIM TO BE MUCH MORE SUBTLE--MORE GRACEFUL--IN OUR ACTIONS.
BUT NOW, WE MUST SHOW THE CITY OF NEW YORK THAT WE, IN FACT, HAVE CONTROL.
AND IT MUST BE DONE WITH A BEAUTY, AND BRUTALITY, UNSURPASSED.
GIGGLE
YOU HAVE BEEN SPEAKING MANY MONTHS TO US OF A GOOD MAN FOR THIS JOB. THE MAN... WHAT WAS IT...TORA?
TAKATA, THE NEW YORK YAKUZA MUST STAY AWAY FROM THE ATTACK SO THAT WE MAY OPERATE WITHOUT INTERFERENCE. YOU ARE GIVEN THE POWER OF AUTHORITY FOR THIS EVENT. IF YOU CAN FIND THIS ARTIST, HAVE HIM START IMMEDIATELY.
SWOOP!
CONSIDER IT COMPLETED, UNCLE. IMPRESSIVE SHOT.

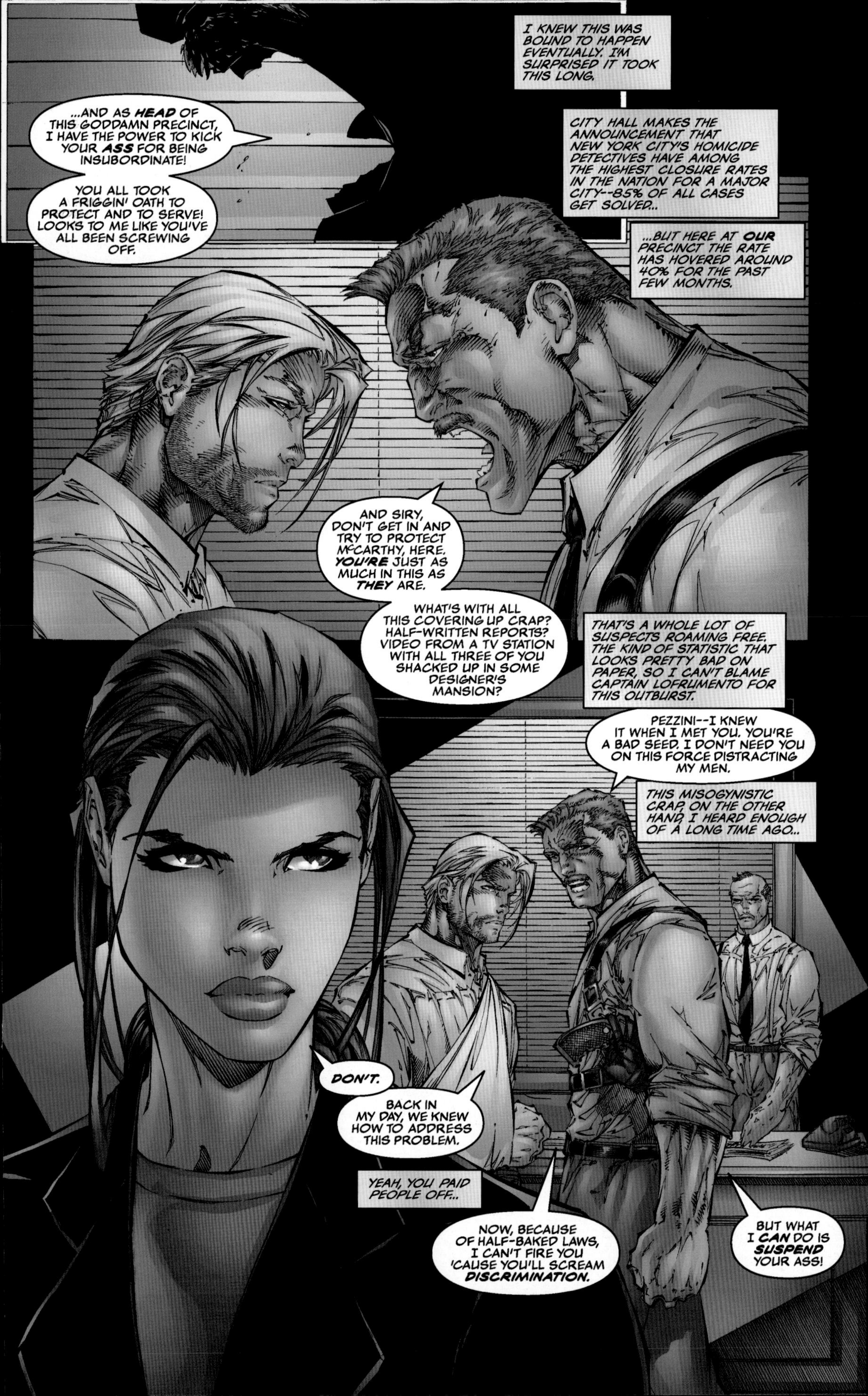
I KNEW THIS WAS BOUND TO HAPPEN EVENTUALLY. I'M SURPRISED IT TOOK THIS LONG.
...AND AS HEAD OF THIS GODDAMN PRECINCT, I HAVE THE POWER TO KICK YOUR ASS FOR BEING INSUBORDINATE!
YOU ALL TOOK A FRIGGIN' OATH TO PROTECT AND TO SERVE! LOOKS TO ME LIKE YOU'VE ALL BEEN SCREWING OFF.
CITY HALL MAKES THE ANNOUNCEMENT THAT NEW YORK CITY'S HOMICIDE DETECTIVES HAVE AMONG THE HIGHEST CLOSURE RATES IN THE NATION FOR A MAJOR CITY--85% OF ALL CASES GET SOLVED...
...BUT HERE AT OUR PRECINCT THE RATE HAS HOVERED AROUND 40% FOR THE PAST FEW MONTHS.
AND SIRY, DON'T GET IN AND TRY TO PROTECT McCARTHY, HERE. YOU'RE JUST AS MUCH IN THIS AS THEY ARE.
WHAT'S WITH ALL THIS COVERING UP CRAP? HALF-WRITTEN REPORTS? VIDEO FROM A TV STATION WITH ALL THREE OF YOU SHACKED UP IN SOME DESIGNER'S MANSION?
THAT'S A WHOLE LOT OF SUSPECTS ROAMING FREE. THE KIND OF STATISTIC THAT LOOKS PRETTY BAD ON PAPER, SO I CAN'T BLAME CAPTAIN LOFRUMENTO FOR THIS OUTBURST.
PEZZINI--I KNEW IT WHEN I MET YOU. YOU'RE A BAD SEED. I DON'T NEED YOU ON THIS FORCE DISTRACTING MY MEN.
THIS MISOGYNISTIC CRAP, ON THE OTHER HAND, I HEARD ENOUGH OF A LONG TIME AGO...
DON'T.
BACK IN MY DAY, WE KNEW HOW TO ADDRESS THIS PROBLEM.
YEAH, YOU PAID PEOPLE OFF...
NOW, BECAUSE OF HALF-BAKED LAWS, I CAN'T FIRE YOU 'CAUSE YOU'LL SCREAM DISCRIMINATION.
BUT WHAT I CAN DO IS SUSPEND YOUR ASS!

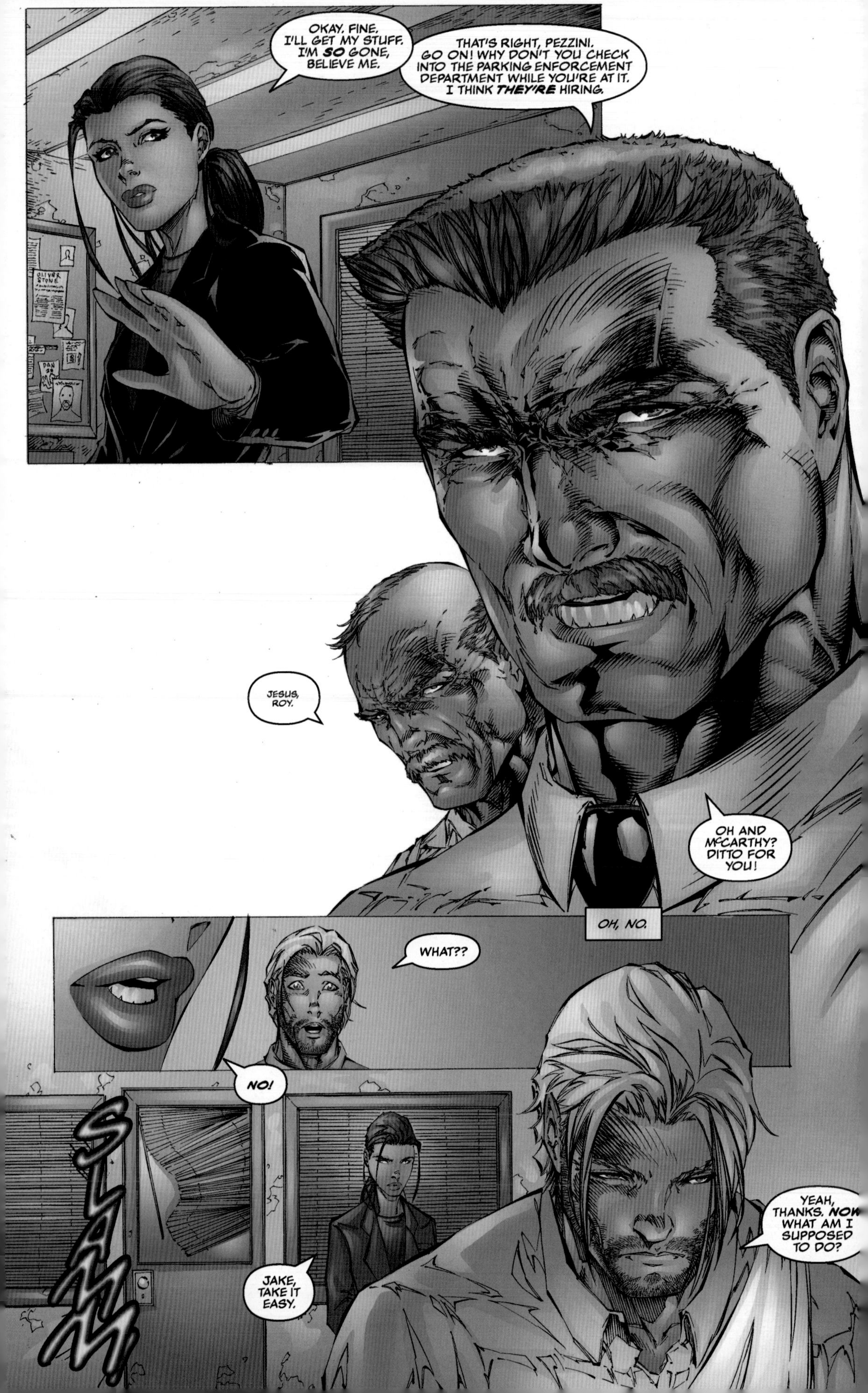
OKAY. FINE. I'LL GET MY STUFF. I'M SO GONE, BELIEVE ME.
THAT'S RIGHT, PEZZINI. GO ON! WHY DON'T YOU CHECK INTO THE PARKING ENFORCEMENT DEPARTMENT WHILE YOU'RE AT IT. I THINK THEY'RE HIRING.
JESUS, ROY.
OH AND McCARTHY? DITTO FOR YOU!
OH, NO.
WHAT??
NO!
SLAM
JAKE, TAKE IT EASY.
YEAH, THANKS. NOW WHAT AM I SUPPOSED TO DO?

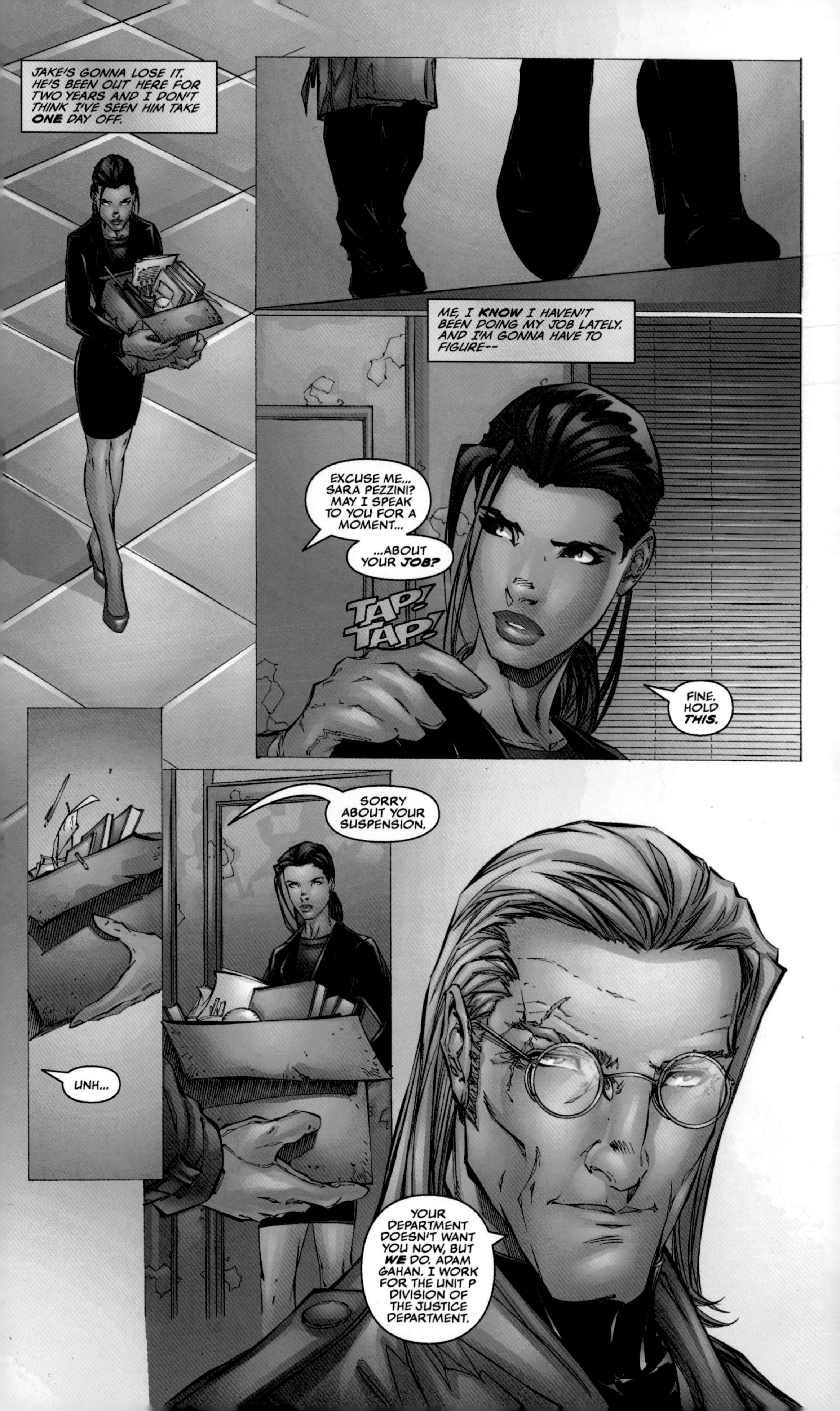
JAKE'S GONNA LOSE IT. HE'S BEEN OUT HERE FOR TWO YEARS AND I DON'T THINK I'VE SEEN HIM TAKE ONE DAY OFF.
ME, I KNOW I HAVEN'T BEEN DOING MY JOB LATELY. AND I'M GONNA HAVE TO FIGURE--
EXCUSE ME... SARA PEZZINI? MAY I SPEAK TO YOU FOR A MOMENT...
...ABOUT YOUR JOB?
TAP-TAP!
FINE. HOLD THIS.
UNH...
SORRY ABOUT YOUR SUSPENSION.
YOUR DEPARTMENT DOESN'T WANT YOU NOW, BUT WE DO. ADAM GAHAN. I WORK FOR THE UNIT P DIVISION OF THE JUSTICE DEPARTMENT.

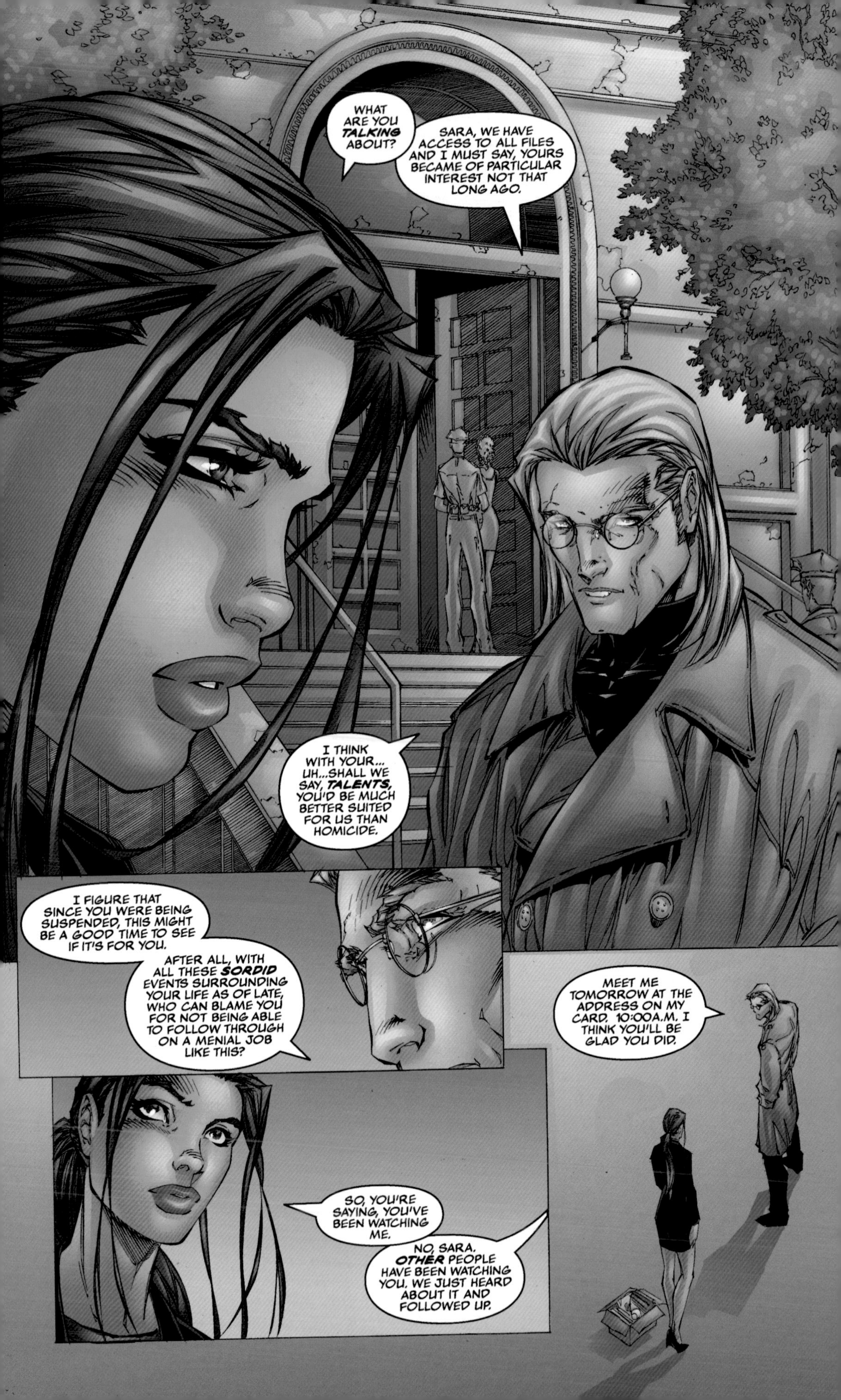
WHAT ARE YOU *TALKING* ABOUT?
SARA, WE HAVE ACCESS TO ALL FILES AND I MUST SAY, YOURS BECAME OF PARTICULAR INTEREST NOT THAT LONG AGO.
I THINK WITH YOUR... UH...SHALL WE SAY, *TALENTS*, YOU'D BE MUCH BETTER SUITED FOR US THAN HOMICIDE.
I FIGURE THAT SINCE YOU WERE BEING SUSPENDED, THIS MIGHT BE A GOOD TIME TO SEE IF IT'S FOR YOU.
AFTER ALL, WITH ALL THESE *SORDID* EVENTS SURROUNDING YOUR LIFE AS OF LATE, WHO CAN BLAME YOU FOR NOT BEING ABLE TO FOLLOW THROUGH ON A MENIAL JOB LIKE THIS?
SO, YOU'RE SAYING, YOU'VE BEEN WATCHING ME.
NO, SARA. *OTHER* PEOPLE HAVE BEEN WATCHING YOU. WE JUST HEARD ABOUT IT AND FOLLOWED UP.
MEET ME TOMORROW AT THE ADDRESS ON MY CARD. 10:00A.M. I THINK YOU'LL BE GLAD YOU DID.

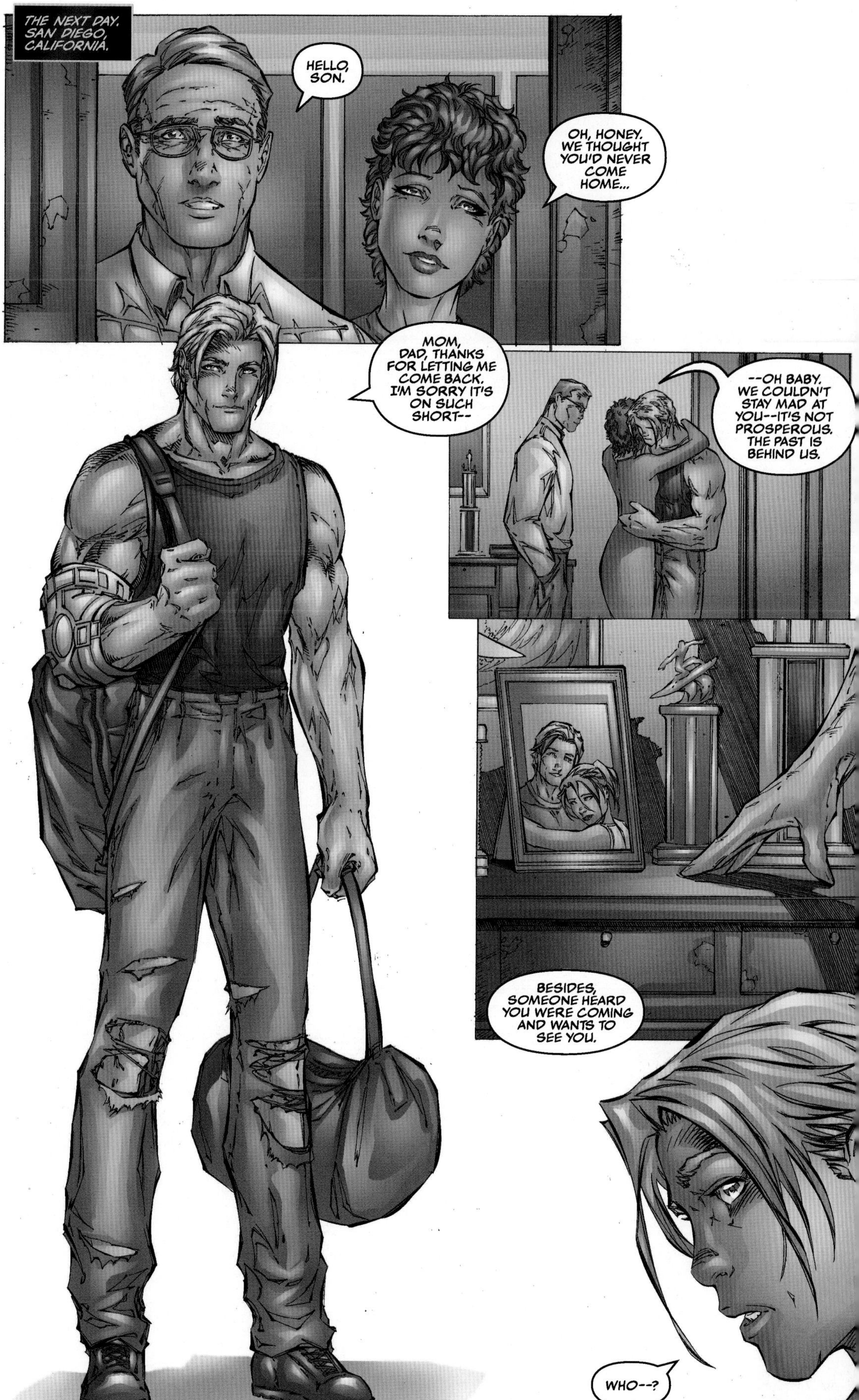

THE NEXT DAY. SAN DIEGO, CALIFORNIA.
HELLO, SON.
OH, HONEY. WE THOUGHT YOU'D NEVER COME HOME...
MOM, DAD, THANKS FOR LETTING ME COME BACK. I'M SORRY IT'S ON SUCH SHORT--
--OH BABY. WE COULDN'T STAY MAD AT YOU--IT'S NOT PROSPEROUS. THE PAST IS BEHIND US.
BESIDES, SOMEONE HEARD YOU WERE COMING AND WANTS TO SEE YOU.
WHO--?

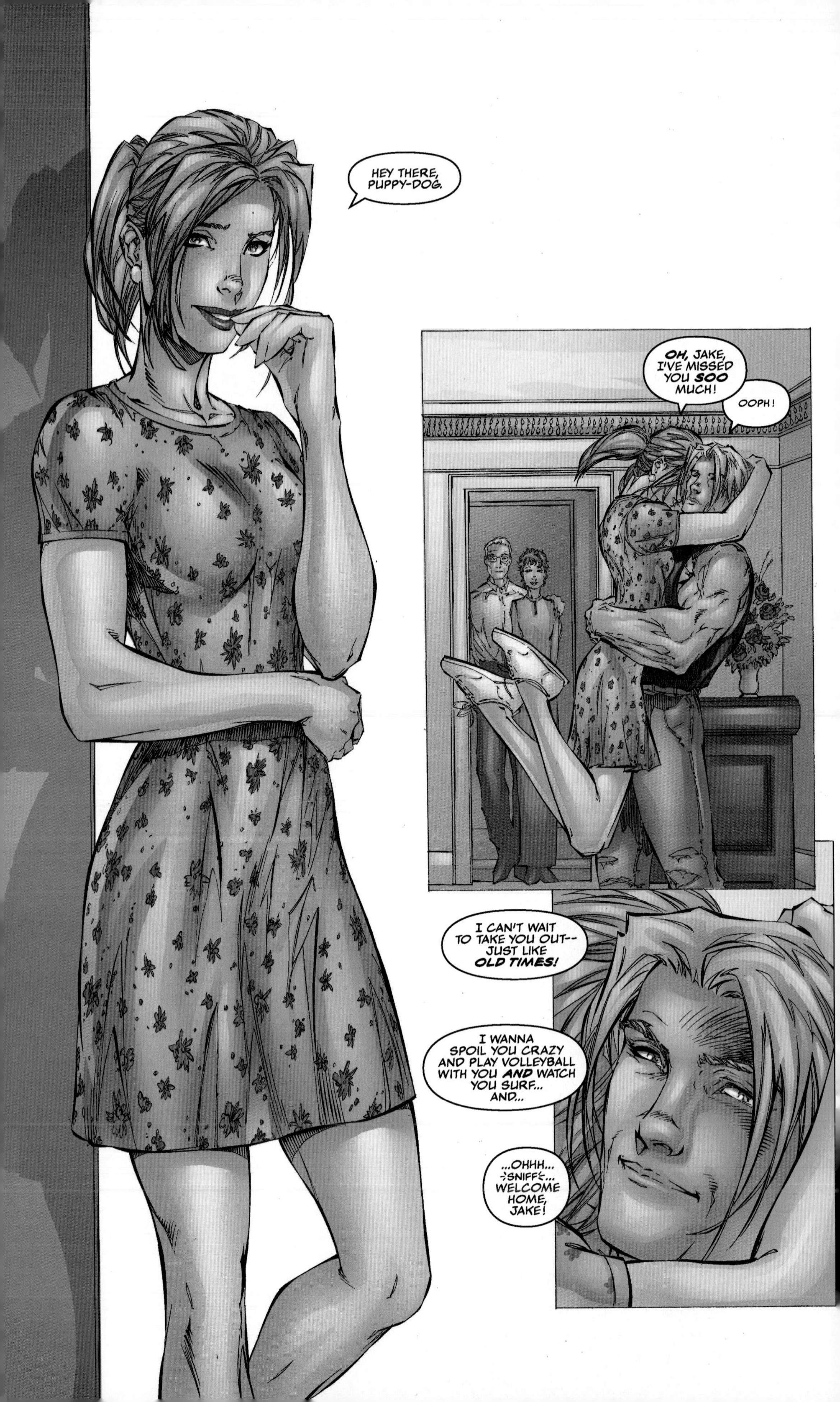
HEY THERE, PUPPY-DOG.
OH, JAKE, I'VE MISSED YOU SOO MUCH!
OOPH!
I CAN'T WAIT TO TAKE YOU OUT-- JUST LIKE OLD TIMES!
I WANNA SPOIL YOU CRAZY AND PLAY VOLLEYBALL WITH YOU AND WATCH YOU SURF... AND...
...OHHH... SNIFF... WELCOME HOME, JAKE!

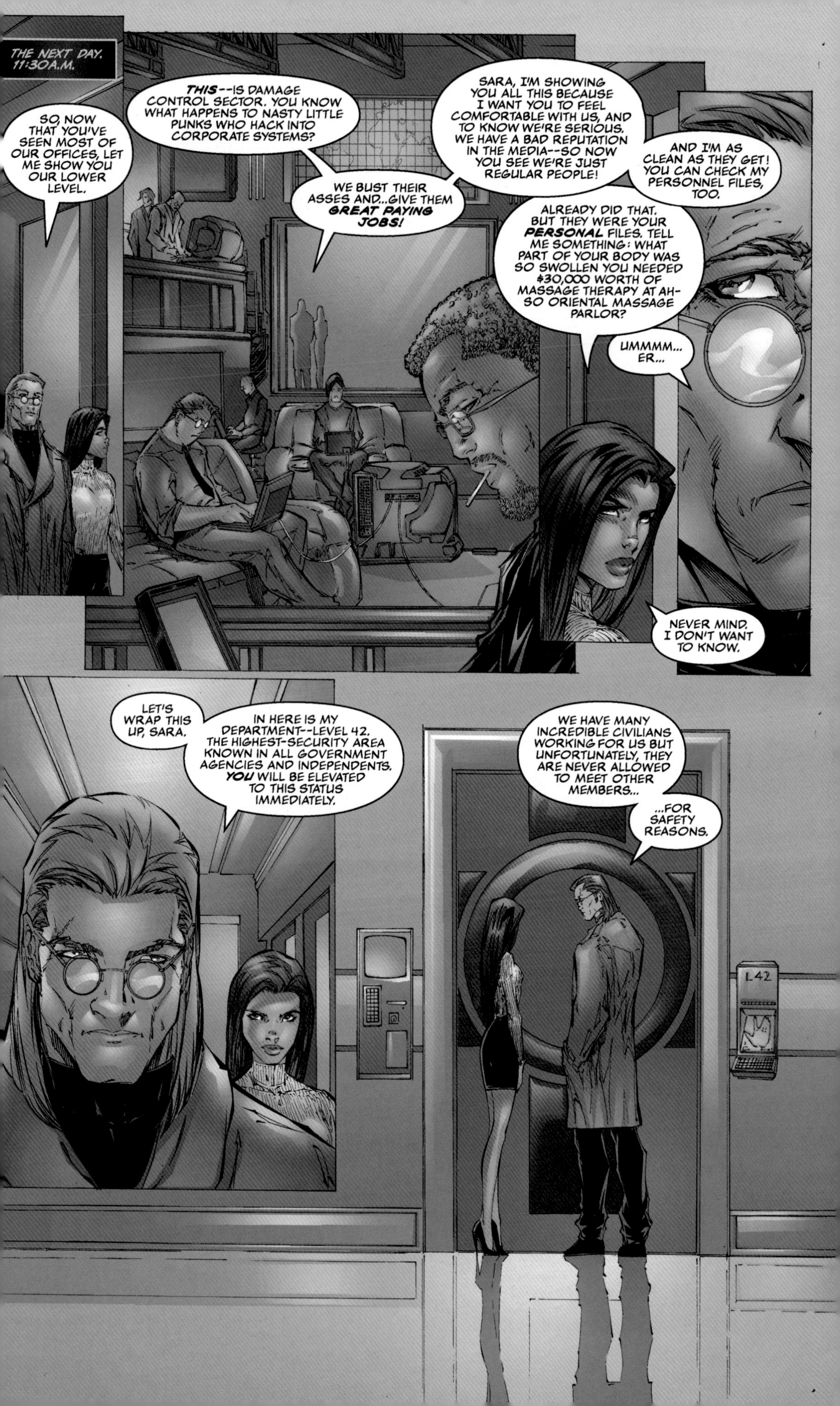
THE NEXT DAY. 11:30A.M.
SO, NOW THAT YOU'VE SEEN MOST OF OUR OFFICES, LET ME SHOW YOU OUR LOWER LEVEL.
THIS--IS DAMAGE CONTROL SECTOR. YOU KNOW WHAT HAPPENS TO NASTY LITTLE PUNKS WHO HACK INTO CORPORATE SYSTEMS?
WE BUST THEIR ASSES AND...GIVE THEM GREAT PAYING JOBS!
SARA, I'M SHOWING YOU ALL THIS BECAUSE I WANT YOU TO FEEL COMFORTABLE WITH US, AND TO KNOW WE'RE SERIOUS. WE HAVE A BAD REPUTATION IN THE MEDIA--SO NOW YOU SEE WE'RE JUST REGULAR PEOPLE!
AND I'M AS CLEAN AS THEY GET! YOU CAN CHECK MY PERSONNEL FILES, TOO.
ALREADY DID THAT. BUT THEY WERE YOUR PERSONAL FILES. TELL ME SOMETHING: WHAT PART OF YOUR BODY WAS SO SWOLLEN YOU NEEDED $30,000 WORTH OF MASSAGE THERAPY AT AH-SO ORIENTAL MASSAGE PARLOR?
UMMMM... ER...
NEVER MIND. I DON'T WANT TO KNOW.
LET'S WRAP THIS UP, SARA.
IN HERE IS MY DEPARTMENT--LEVEL 42. THE HIGHEST-SECURITY AREA KNOWN IN ALL GOVERNMENT AGENCIES AND INDEPENDENTS. YOU WILL BE ELEVATED TO THIS STATUS IMMEDIATELY.
WE HAVE MANY INCREDIBLE CIVILIANS WORKING FOR US BUT UNFORTUNATELY, THEY ARE NEVER ALLOWED TO MEET OTHER MEMBERS...
...FOR SAFETY REASONS.
L42

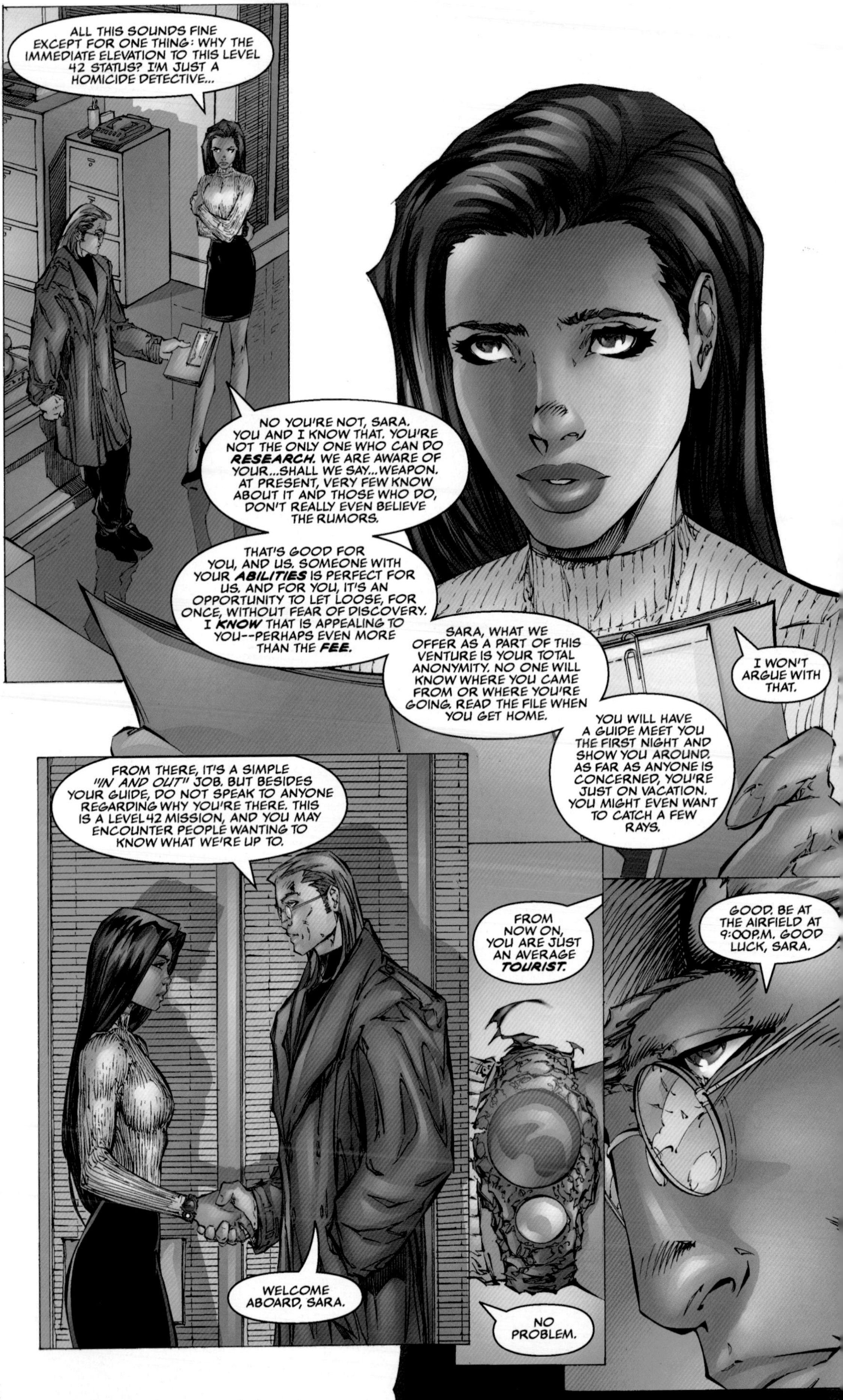

ALL THIS SOUNDS FINE EXCEPT FOR ONE THING: WHY THE IMMEDIATE ELEVATION TO THIS LEVEL 42 STATUS? I'M JUST A HOMICIDE DETECTIVE...
NO YOU'RE NOT, SARA. YOU AND I KNOW THAT. YOU'RE NOT THE ONLY ONE WHO CAN DO RESEARCH. WE ARE AWARE OF YOUR...SHALL WE SAY...WEAPON. AT PRESENT, VERY FEW KNOW ABOUT IT AND THOSE WHO DO, DON'T REALLY EVEN BELIEVE THE RUMORS.
THAT'S GOOD FOR YOU, AND US. SOMEONE WITH YOUR ABILITIES IS PERFECT FOR US. AND FOR YOU, IT'S AN OPPORTUNITY TO LET LOOSE, FOR ONCE, WITHOUT FEAR OF DISCOVERY. I KNOW THAT IS APPEALING TO YOU--PERHAPS EVEN MORE THAN THE FEE.
SARA, WHAT WE OFFER AS A PART OF THIS VENTURE IS YOUR TOTAL ANONYMITY. NO ONE WILL KNOW WHERE YOU CAME FROM OR WHERE YOU'RE GOING. READ THE FILE WHEN YOU GET HOME.
I WON'T ARGUE WITH THAT.
YOU WILL HAVE A GUIDE MEET YOU THE FIRST NIGHT AND SHOW YOU AROUND. AS FAR AS ANYONE IS CONCERNED, YOU'RE JUST ON VACATION. YOU MIGHT EVEN WANT TO CATCH A FEW RAYS.
FROM THERE, IT'S A SIMPLE "IN AND OUT" JOB. BUT BESIDES YOUR GUIDE, DO NOT SPEAK TO ANYONE REGARDING WHY YOU'RE THERE. THIS IS A LEVEL 42 MISSION, AND YOU MAY ENCOUNTER PEOPLE WANTING TO KNOW WHAT WE'RE UP TO.
WELCOME ABOARD, SARA.
FROM NOW ON, YOU ARE JUST AN AVERAGE TOURIST.
NO PROBLEM.
GOOD. BE AT THE AIRFIELD AT 9:00P.M. GOOD LUCK, SARA.

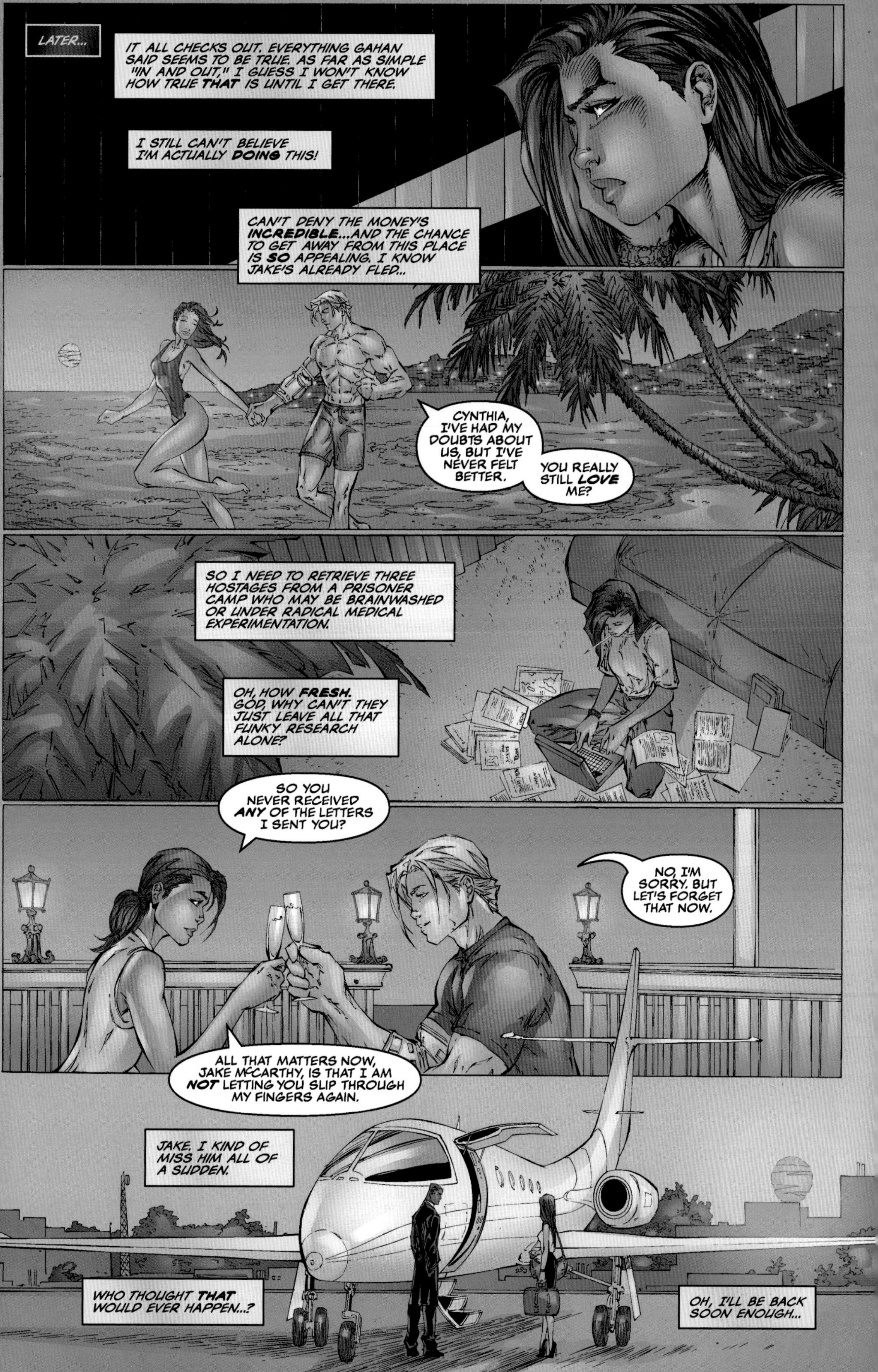
LATER...
IT ALL CHECKS OUT. EVERYTHING GAHAN SAID SEEMS TO BE TRUE. AS FAR AS SIMPLE "IN AND OUT," I GUESS I WON'T KNOW HOW TRUE THAT IS UNTIL I GET THERE.
I STILL CAN'T BELIEVE I'M ACTUALLY DOING THIS!
CAN'T DENY THE MONEY'S INCREDIBLE...AND THE CHANCE TO GET AWAY FROM THIS PLACE IS SO APPEALING. I KNOW JAKE'S ALREADY FLED...
CYNTHIA, I'VE HAD MY DOUBTS ABOUT US, BUT I'VE NEVER FELT BETTER.
YOU REALLY STILL LOVE ME?
SO I NEED TO RETRIEVE THREE HOSTAGES FROM A PRISONER CAMP WHO MAY BE BRAINWASHED OR UNDER RADICAL MEDICAL EXPERIMENTATION.
OH, HOW FRESH. GOD, WHY CAN'T THEY JUST LEAVE ALL THAT FUNKY RESEARCH ALONE?
SO YOU NEVER RECEIVED ANY OF THE LETTERS I SENT YOU?
NO, I'M SORRY. BUT LET'S FORGET THAT NOW.
ALL THAT MATTERS NOW, JAKE McCARTHY, IS THAT I AM NOT LETTING YOU SLIP THROUGH MY FINGERS AGAIN.
JAKE. I KIND OF MISS HIM ALL OF A SUDDEN.
WHO THOUGHT THAT WOULD EVER HAPPEN...?
OH, I'LL BE BACK SOON ENOUGH...

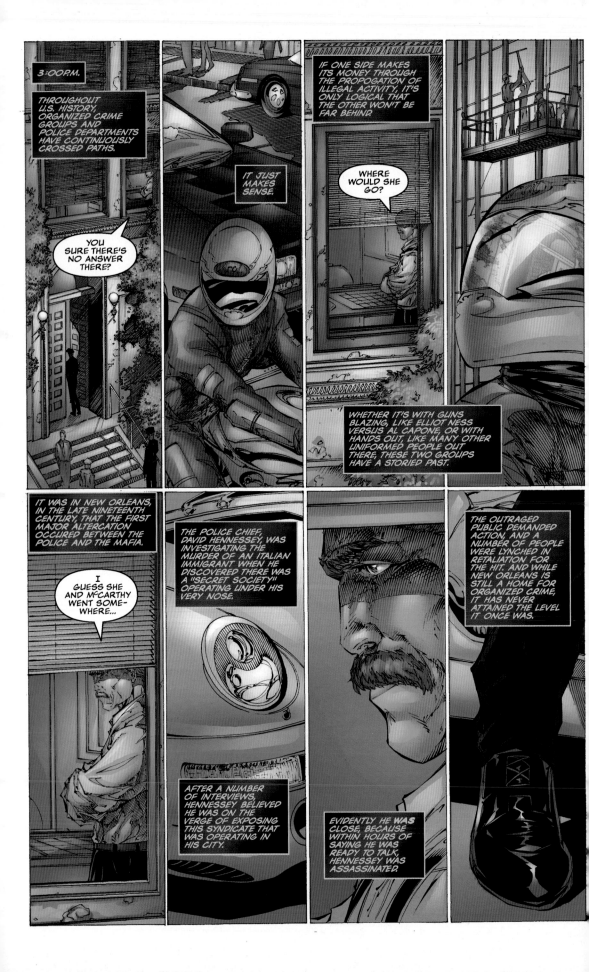

3:00 P.M.

THROUGHOUT U.S. HISTORY, ORGANIZED CRIME GROUPS AND POLICE DEPARTMENTS HAVE CONTINUOUSLY CROSSED PATHS.

YOU SURE THERE'S NO ANSWER THERE?

IT JUST MAKES SENSE.

IF ONE SIDE MAKES ITS MONEY THROUGH THE PROPAGATION OF ILLEGAL ACTIVITY, IT'S ONLY LOGICAL THAT THE OTHER WON'T BE FAR BEHIND.

WHERE WOULD SHE GO?

WHETHER IT'S WITH GUNS BLAZING, LIKE ELLIOT NESS VERSUS AL CAPONE, OR WITH HANDS OUT, LIKE MANY OTHER UNIFORMED PEOPLE OUT THERE, THESE TWO GROUPS HAVE A STORIED PAST.

IT WAS IN NEW ORLEANS, IN THE LATE NINETEENTH CENTURY, THAT THE FIRST MAJOR ALTERCATION OCCURRED BETWEEN THE POLICE AND THE MAFIA.

I GUESS SHE AND McCARTHY WENT SOME-WHERE...

THE POLICE CHIEF, DAVID HENNESSEY, WAS INVESTIGATING THE MURDER OF AN ITALIAN IMMIGRANT WHEN HE DISCOVERED THERE WAS A "SECRET SOCIETY" OPERATING UNDER HIS VERY NOSE.

AFTER A NUMBER OF INTERVIEWS, HENNESSEY BELIEVED HE WAS ON THE VERGE OF EXPOSING THIS SYNDICATE THAT WAS OPERATING IN HIS CITY.

EVIDENTLY HE WAS CLOSE, BECAUSE WITHIN HOURS OF SAYING HE WAS READY TO TALK, HENNESSEY WAS ASSASSINATED.

THE OUTRAGED PUBLIC DEMANDED ACTION, AND A NUMBER OF PEOPLE WERE LYNCHED IN RETALIATION FOR THE HIT. AND WHILE NEW ORLEANS IS STILL A HOME FOR ORGANIZED CRIME, IT HAS NEVER ATTAINED THE LEVEL IT ONCE WAS.

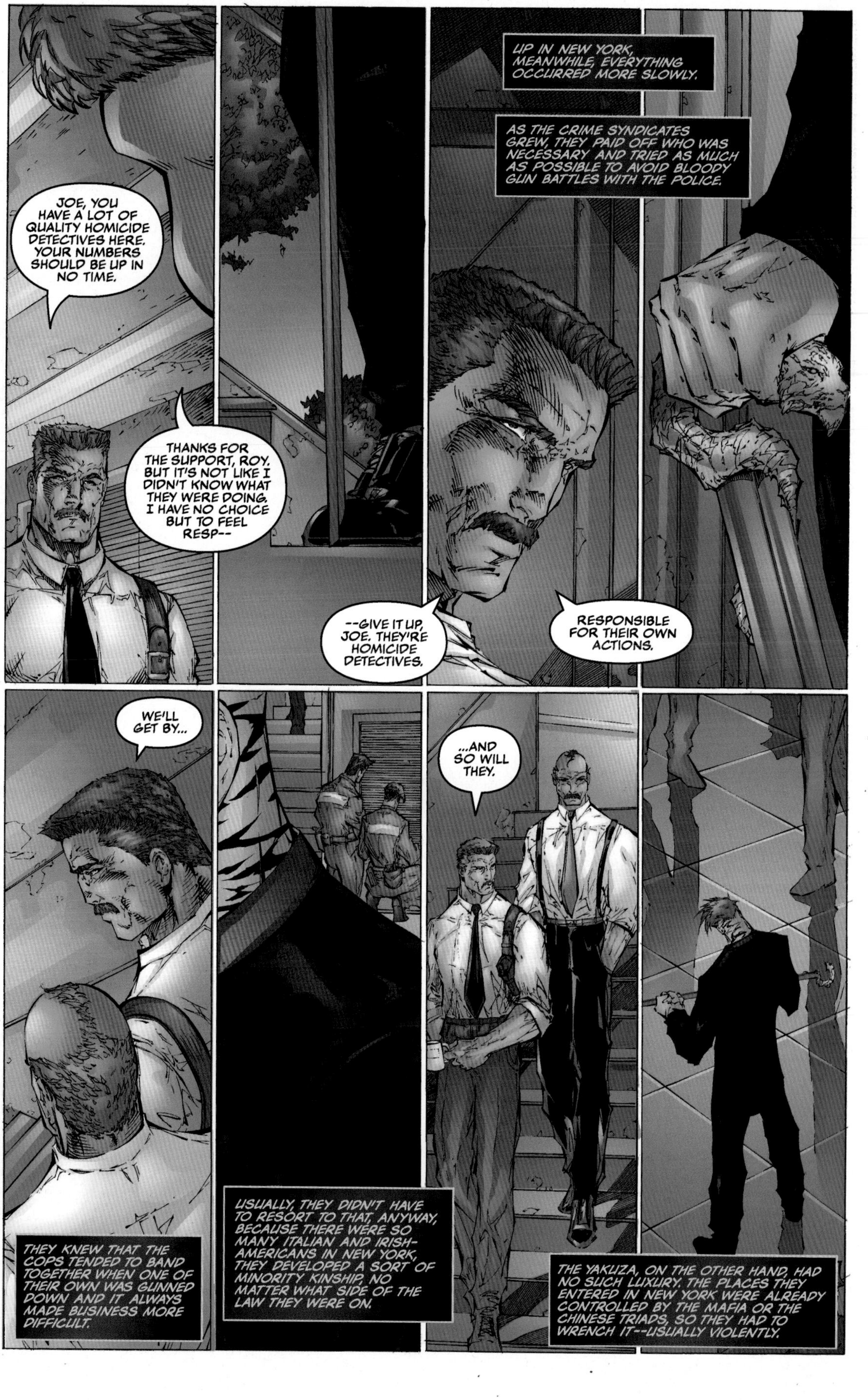

JOE, YOU HAVE A LOT OF QUALITY HOMICIDE DETECTIVES HERE. YOUR NUMBERS SHOULD BE UP IN NO TIME.
THANKS FOR THE SUPPORT, ROY. BUT IT'S NOT LIKE I DIDN'T KNOW WHAT THEY WERE DOING. I HAVE NO CHOICE BUT TO FEEL RESP--
UP IN NEW YORK, MEANWHILE, EVERYTHING OCCURRED MORE SLOWLY.
AS THE CRIME SYNDICATES GREW, THEY PAID OFF WHO WAS NECESSARY AND TRIED AS MUCH AS POSSIBLE TO AVOID BLOODY GUN BATTLES WITH THE POLICE.
--GIVE IT UP, JOE. THEY'RE HOMICIDE DETECTIVES.
RESPONSIBLE FOR THEIR OWN ACTIONS.
WE'LL GET BY...
THEY KNEW THAT THE COPS TENDED TO BAND TOGETHER WHEN ONE OF THEIR OWN WAS GUNNED DOWN AND IT ALWAYS MADE BUSINESS MORE DIFFICULT.
USUALLY, THEY DIDN'T HAVE TO RESORT TO THAT, ANYWAY, BECAUSE THERE WERE SO MANY ITALIAN AND IRISH-AMERICANS IN NEW YORK, THEY DEVELOPED A SORT OF MINORITY KINSHIP, NO MATTER WHAT SIDE OF THE LAW THEY WERE ON.
...AND SO WILL THEY.
THE YAKUZA, ON THE OTHER HAND, HAD NO SUCH LUXURY. THE PLACES THEY ENTERED IN NEW YORK WERE ALREADY CONTROLLED BY THE MAFIA OR THE CHINESE TRIADS, SO THEY HAD TO WRENCH IT--USUALLY VIOLENTLY.

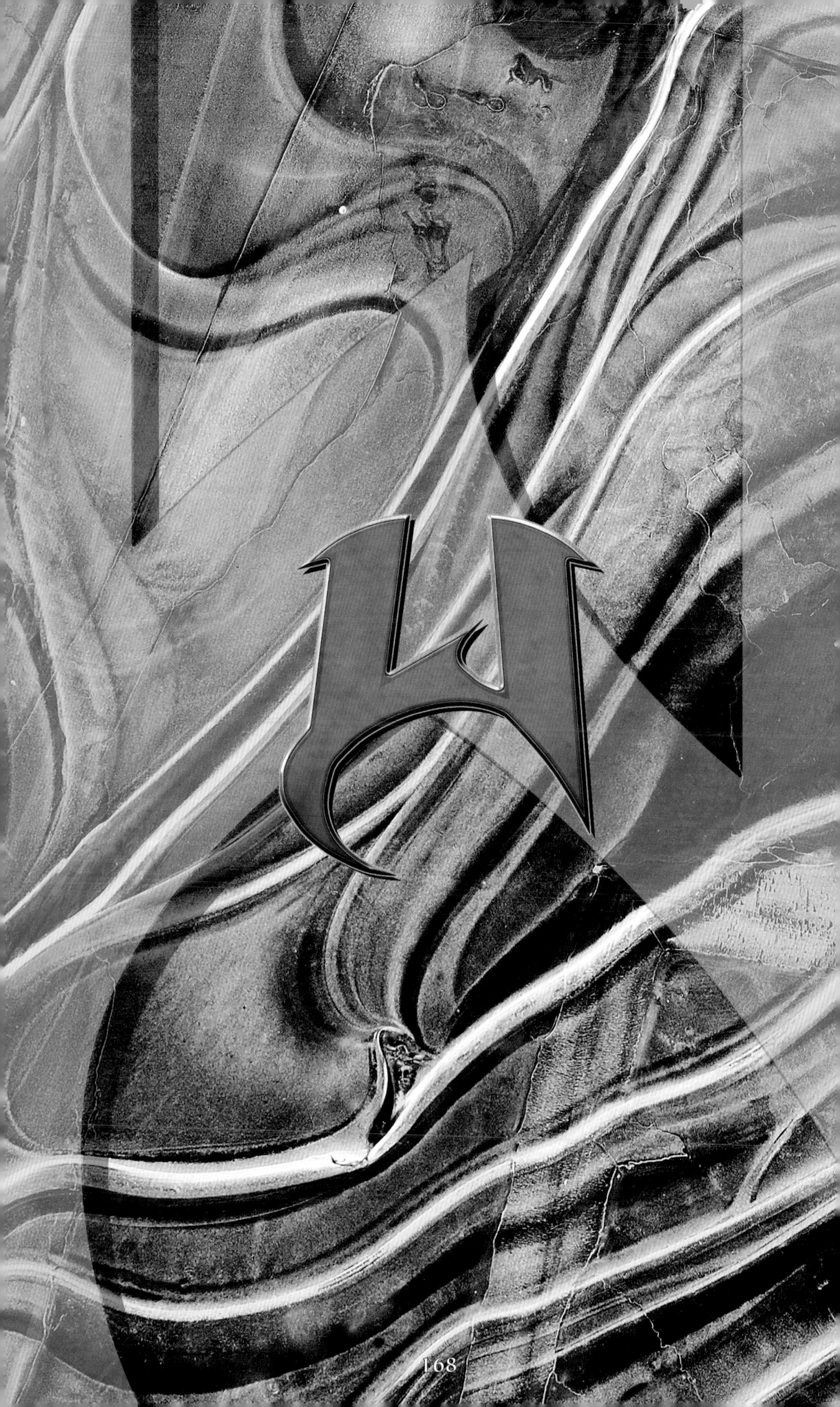

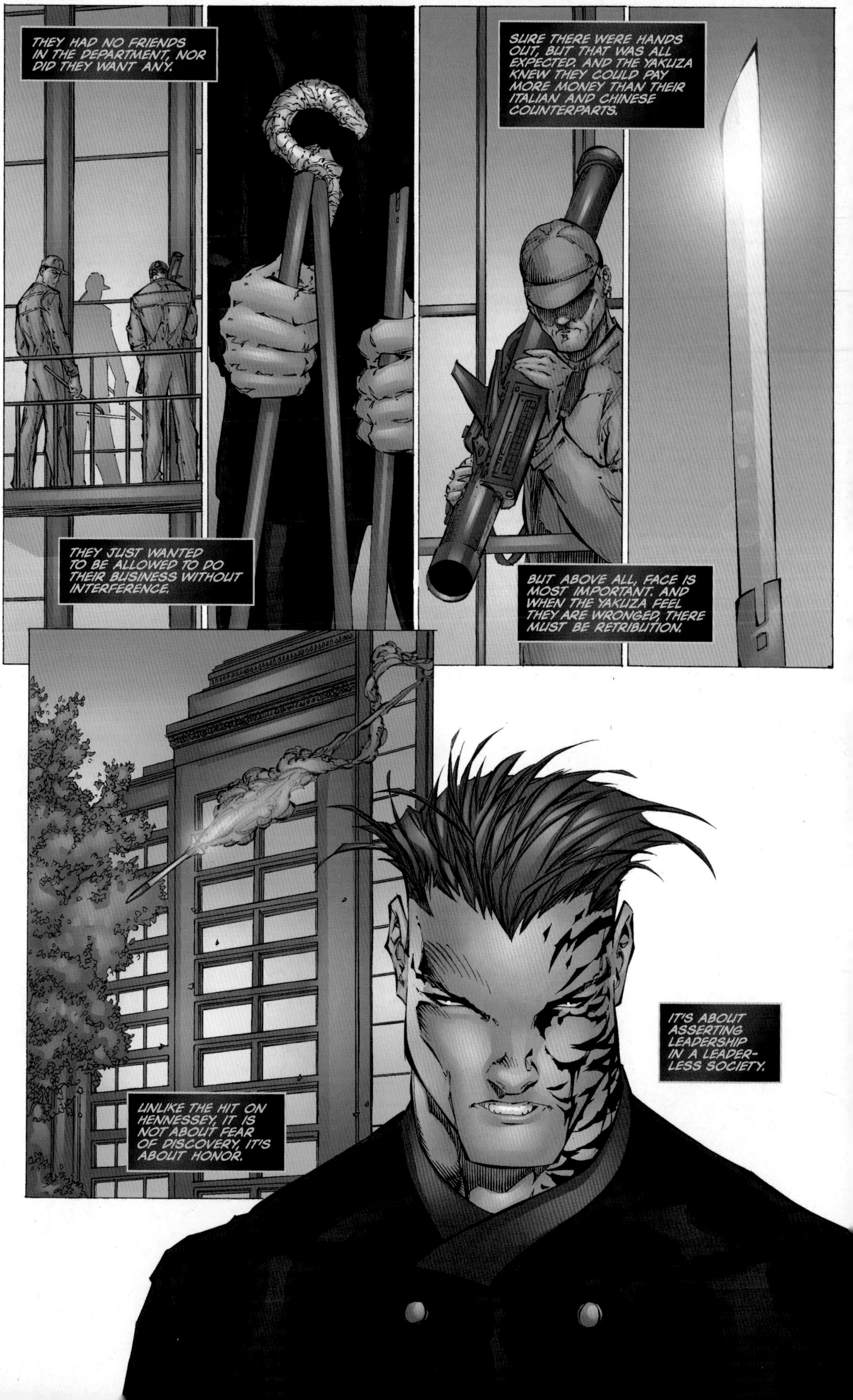
THEY HAD NO FRIENDS IN THE DEPARTMENT, NOR DID THEY WANT ANY.
THEY JUST WANTED TO BE ALLOWED TO DO THEIR BUSINESS WITHOUT INTERFERENCE.
SURE THERE WERE HANDS OUT, BUT THAT WAS ALL EXPECTED. AND THE YAKUZA KNEW THEY COULD PAY MORE MONEY THAN THEIR ITALIAN AND CHINESE COUNTERPARTS.
BUT ABOVE ALL, FACE IS MOST IMPORTANT. AND WHEN THE YAKUZA FEEL THEY ARE WRONGED, THERE MUST BE RETRIBUTION.
UNLIKE THE HIT ON HENNESSEY, IT IS NOT ABOUT FEAR OF DISCOVERY, IT'S ABOUT HONOR.
IT'S ABOUT ASSERTING LEADERSHIP IN A LEADER-LESS SOCIETY.

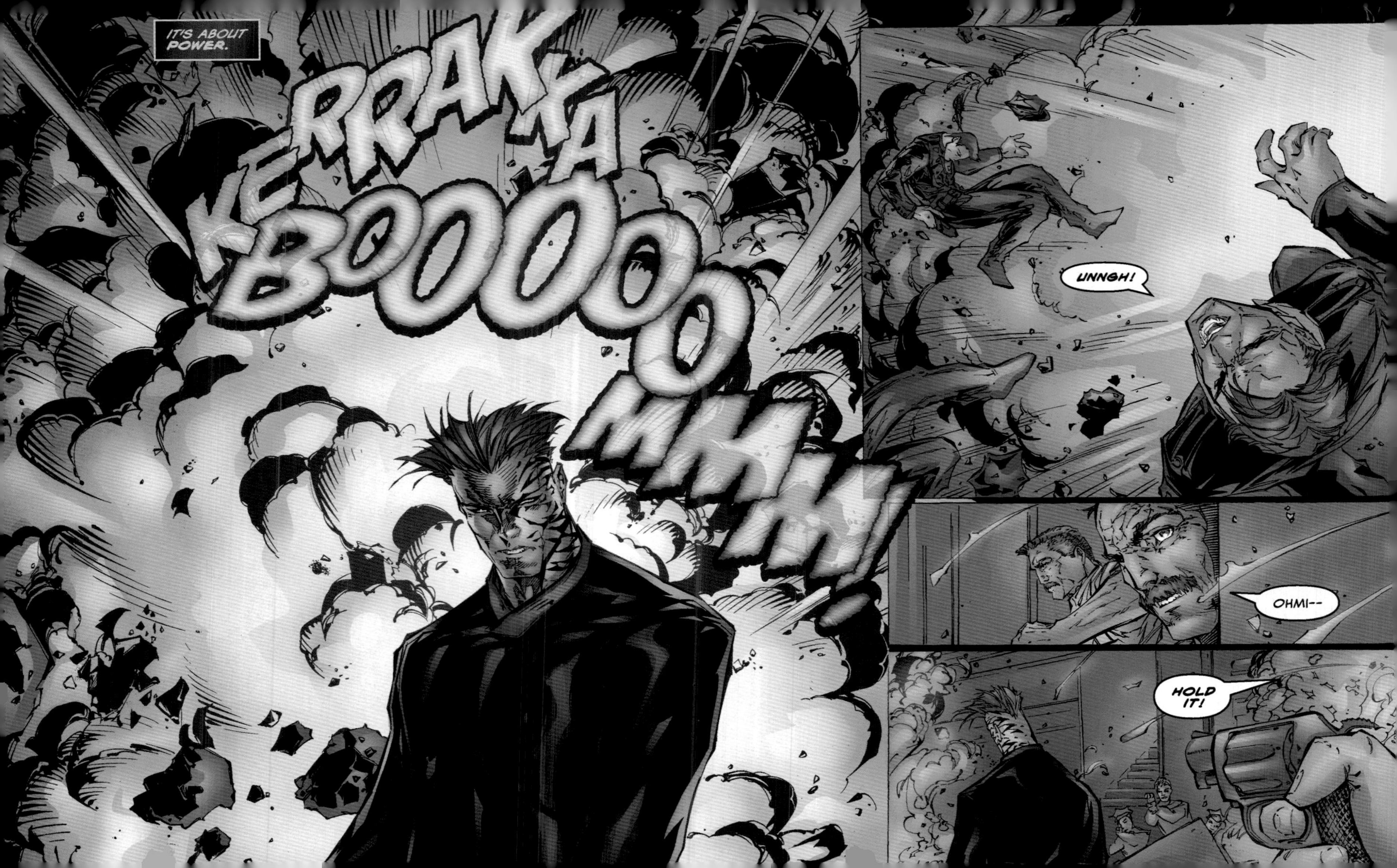
IT'S ABOUT POWER.
KERRAKKA BOOOOOOMMMM!
UNNGH!
OHMI--
HOLD IT!

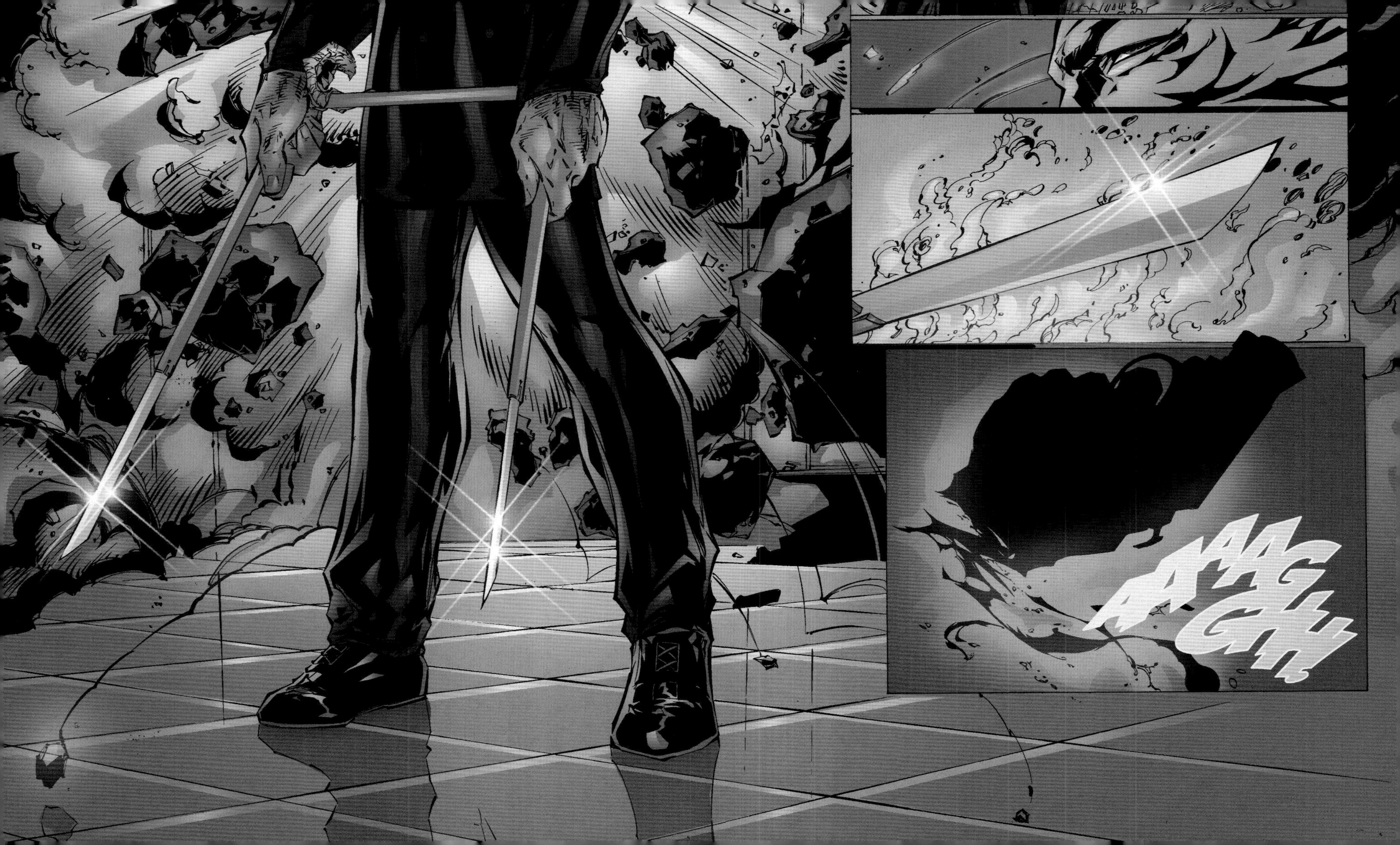
AAAAGGH!

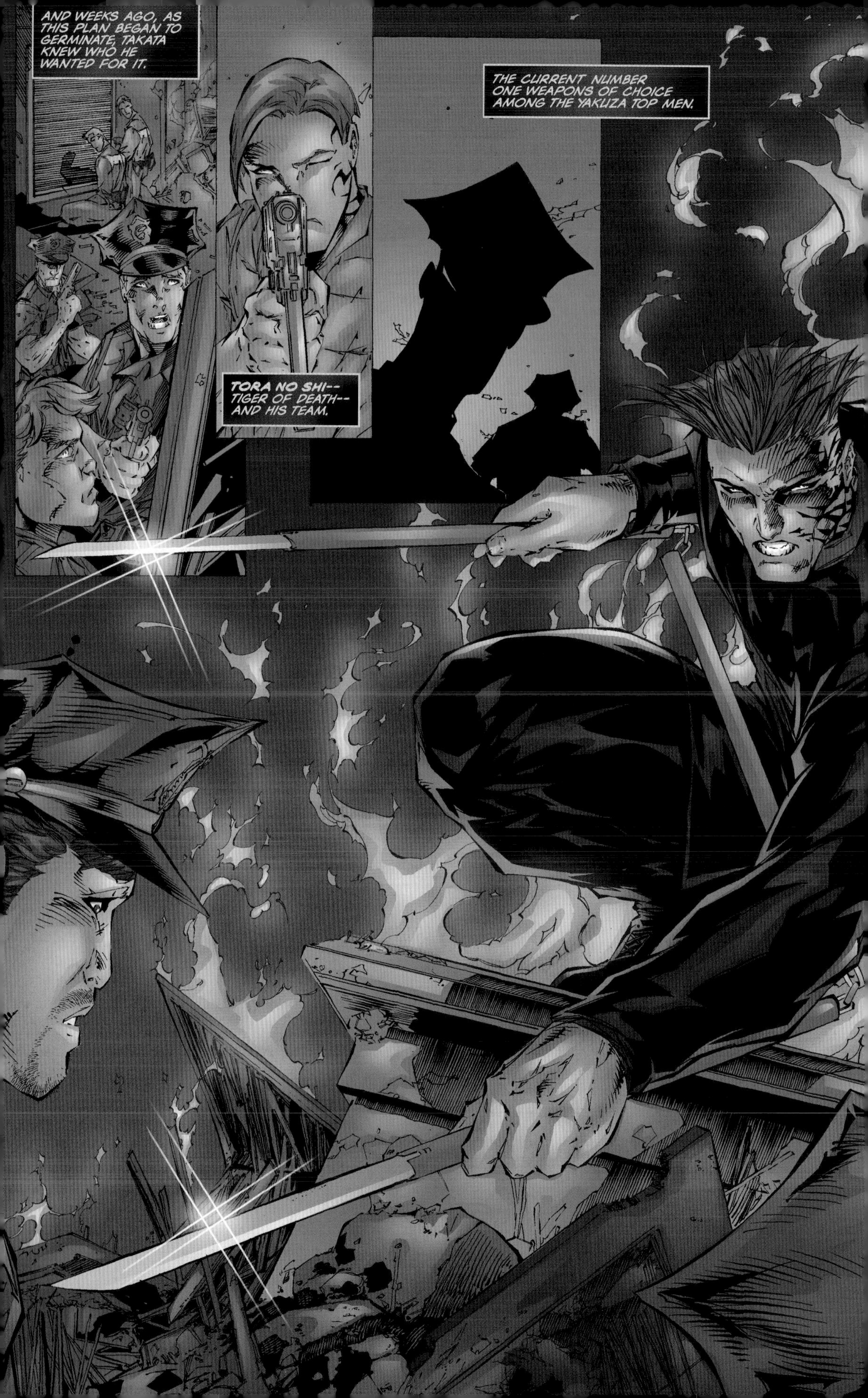
AND WEEKS AGO, AS THIS PLAN BEGAN TO GERMINATE, TAKATA KNEW WHO HE WANTED FOR IT.
TORA NO SHI-- TIGER OF DEATH-- AND HIS TEAM.
THE CURRENT NUMBER ONE WEAPONS OF CHOICE AMONG THE YAKUZA TOP MEN.

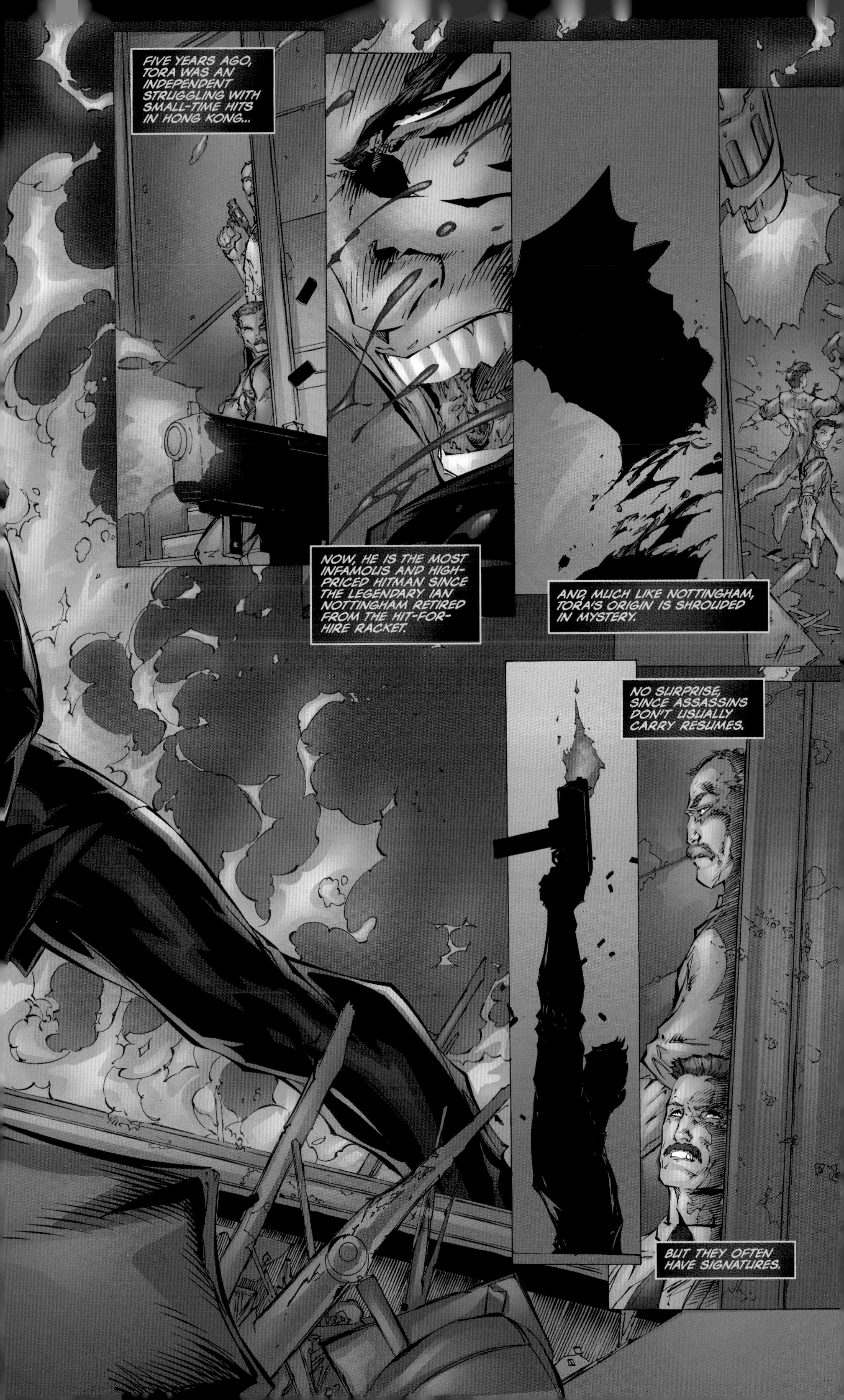
FIVE YEARS AGO, TORA WAS AN INDEPENDENT STRUGGLING WITH SMALL-TIME HITS IN HONG KONG...
NOW, HE IS THE MOST INFAMOUS AND HIGH-PRICED HITMAN SINCE THE LEGENDARY IAN NOTTINGHAM RETIRED FROM THE HIT-FOR-HIRE RACKET.
AND, MUCH LIKE NOTTINGHAM, TORA'S ORIGIN IS SHROUDED IN MYSTERY.
NO SURPRISE, SINCE ASSASSINS DON'T USUALLY CARRY RESUMES.
BUT THEY OFTEN HAVE SIGNATURES.

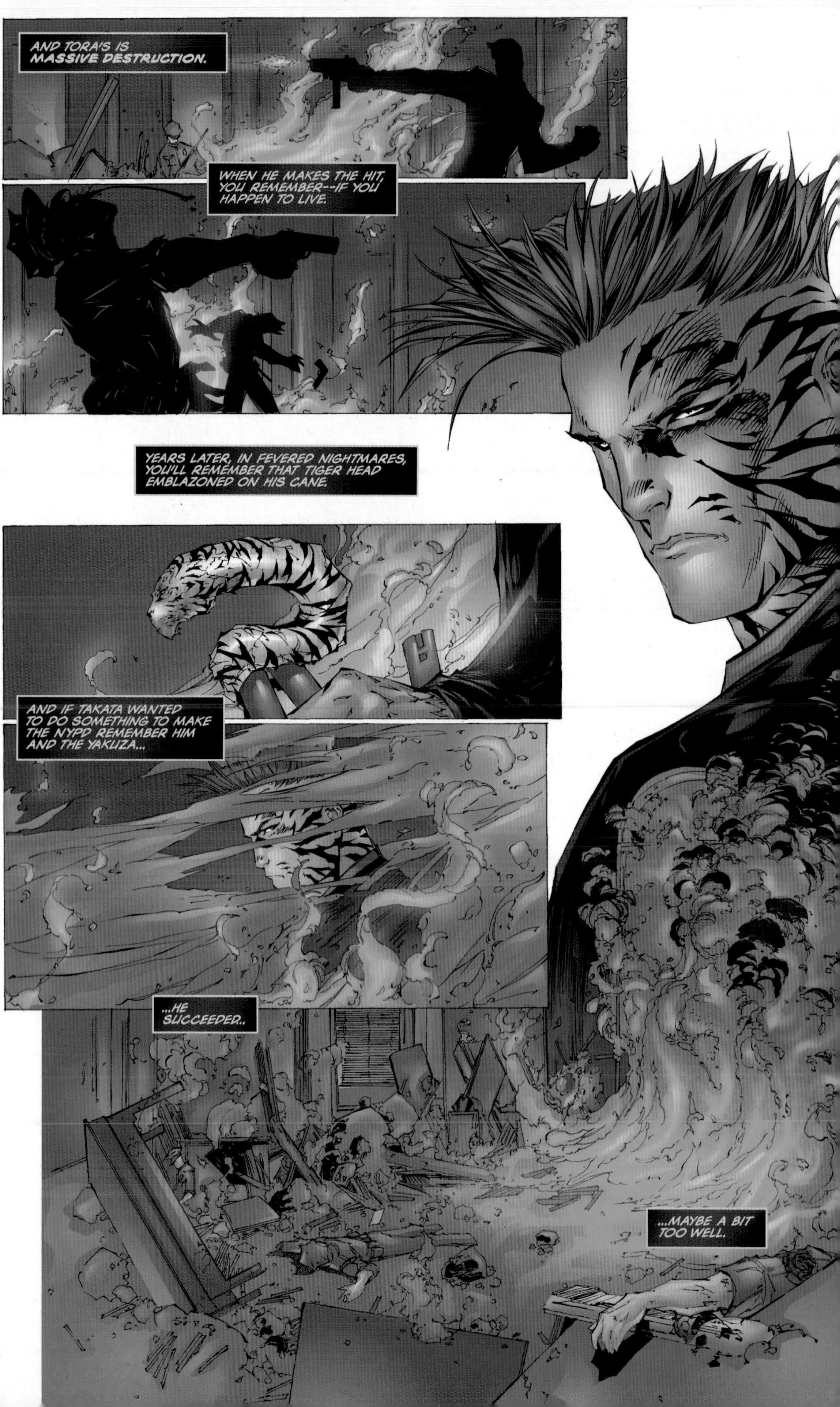
AND TORA'S IS MASSIVE DESTRUCTION.
WHEN HE MAKES THE HIT, YOU REMEMBER--IF YOU HAPPEN TO LIVE.
YEARS LATER, IN FEVERED NIGHTMARES, YOU'LL REMEMBER THAT TIGER HEAD EMBLAZONED ON HIS CANE.
AND IF TAKATA WANTED TO DO SOMETHING TO MAKE THE NYPD REMEMBER HIM AND THE YAKUZA...
...HE SUCCEEDED..
...MAYBE A BIT TOO WELL.

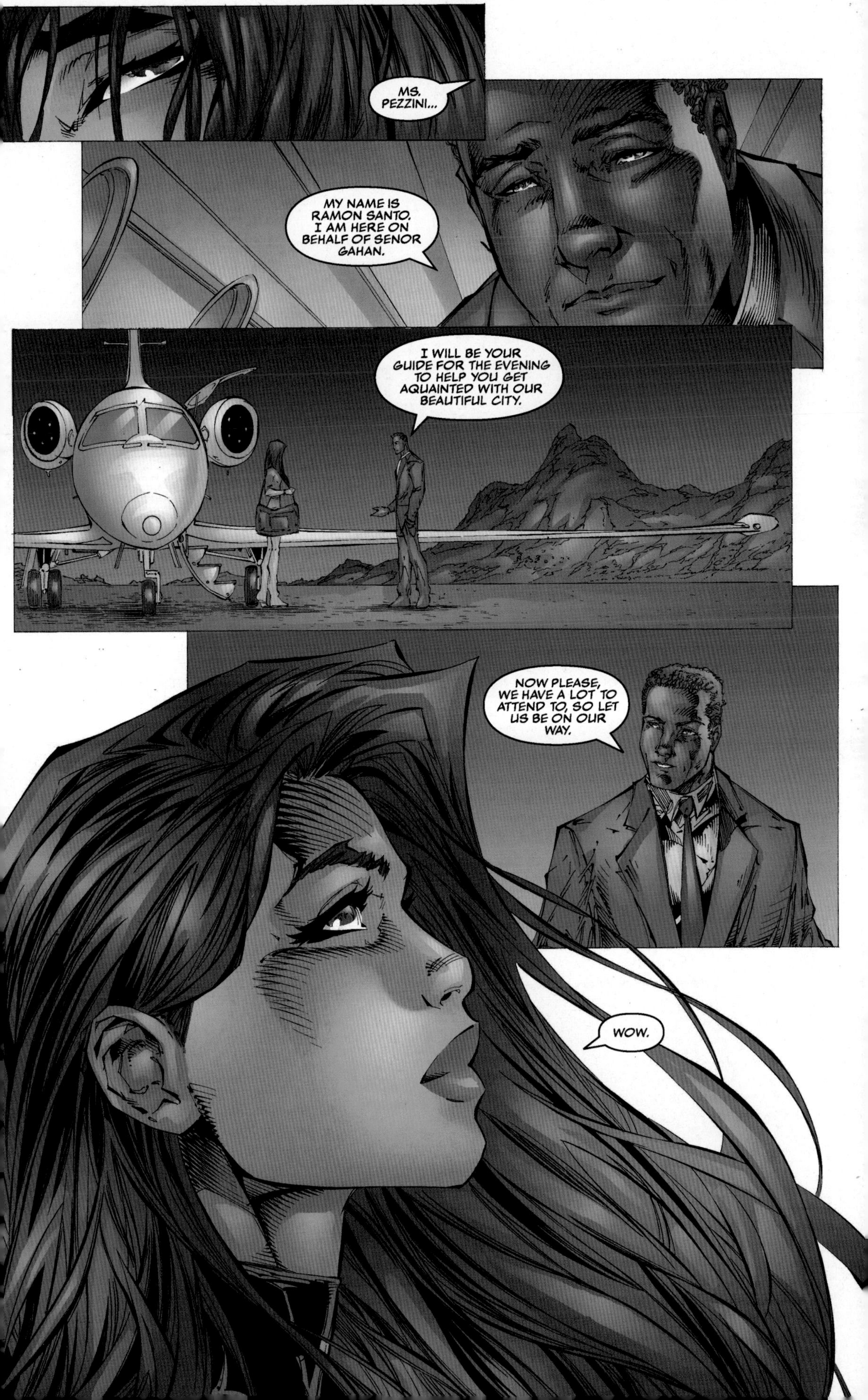
MS. PEZZINI...
MY NAME IS RAMON SANTO. I AM HERE ON BEHALF OF SENOR GAHAN.
I WILL BE YOUR GUIDE FOR THE EVENING TO HELP YOU GET AQUAINTED WITH OUR BEAUTIFUL CITY.
NOW PLEASE, WE HAVE A LOT TO ATTEND TO, SO LET US BE ON OUR WAY.
WOW.

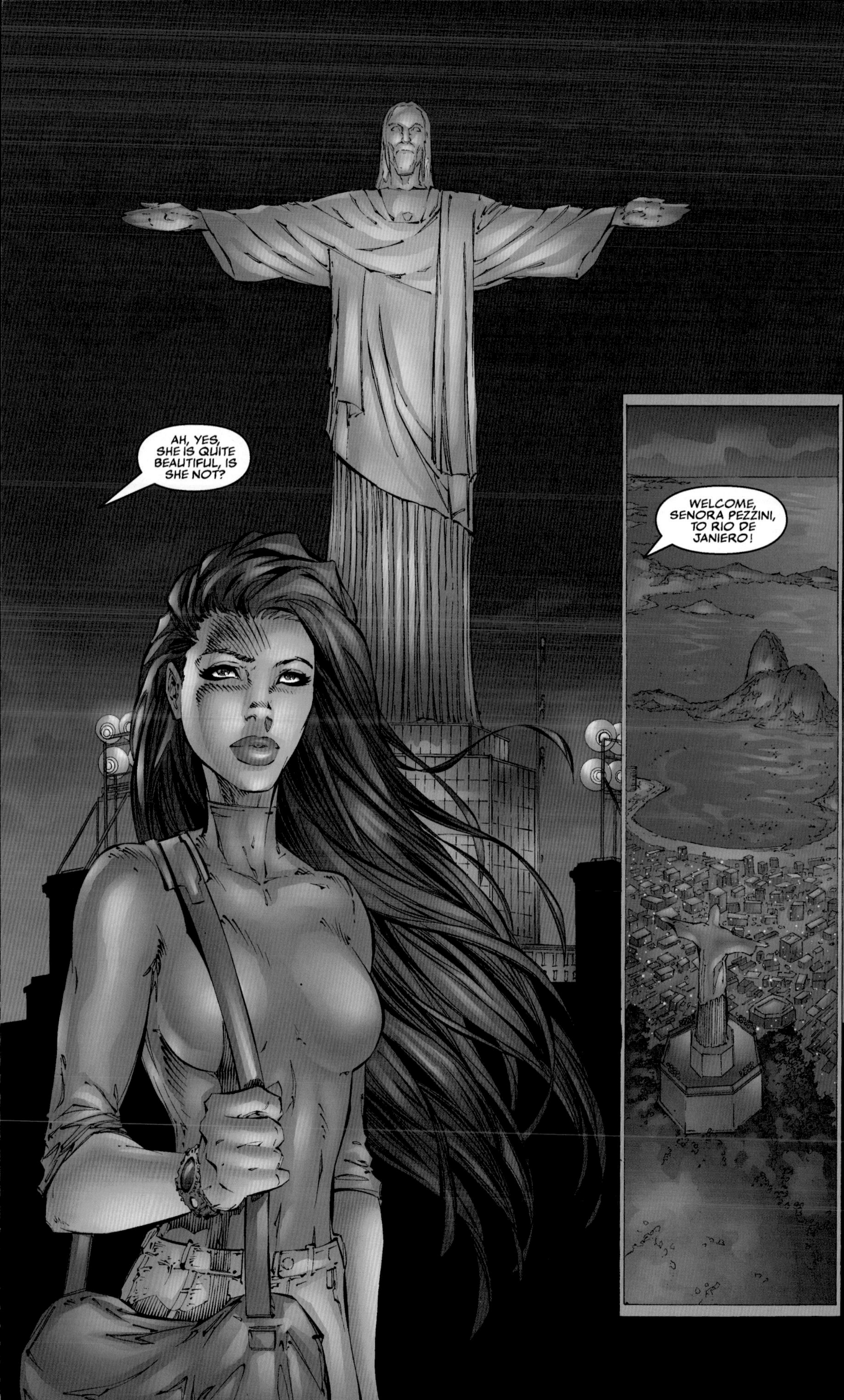
AH, YES, SHE IS QUITE BEAUTIFUL, IS SHE NOT?
WELCOME, SENORA PEZZINI, TO RIO DE JANIERO!

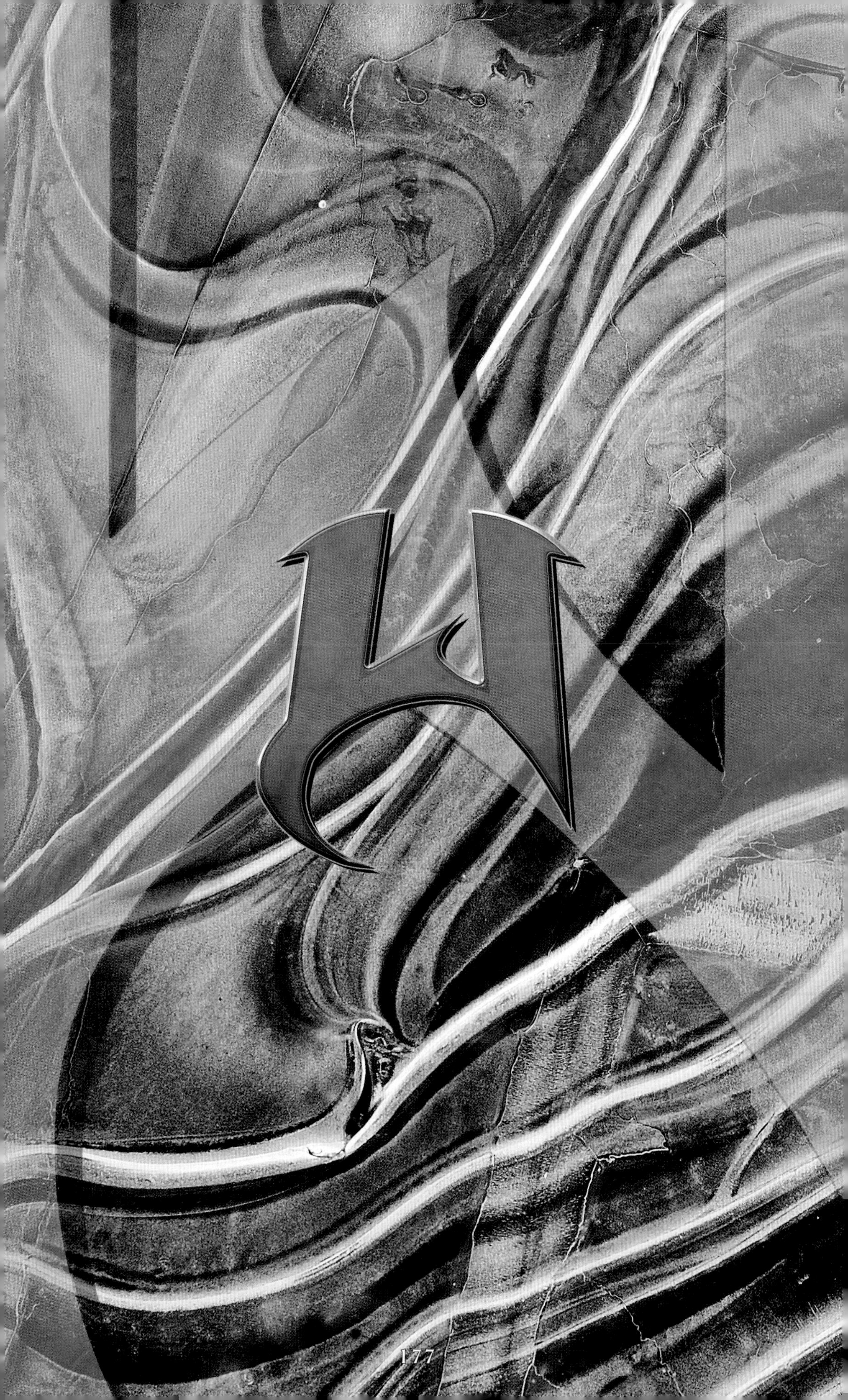

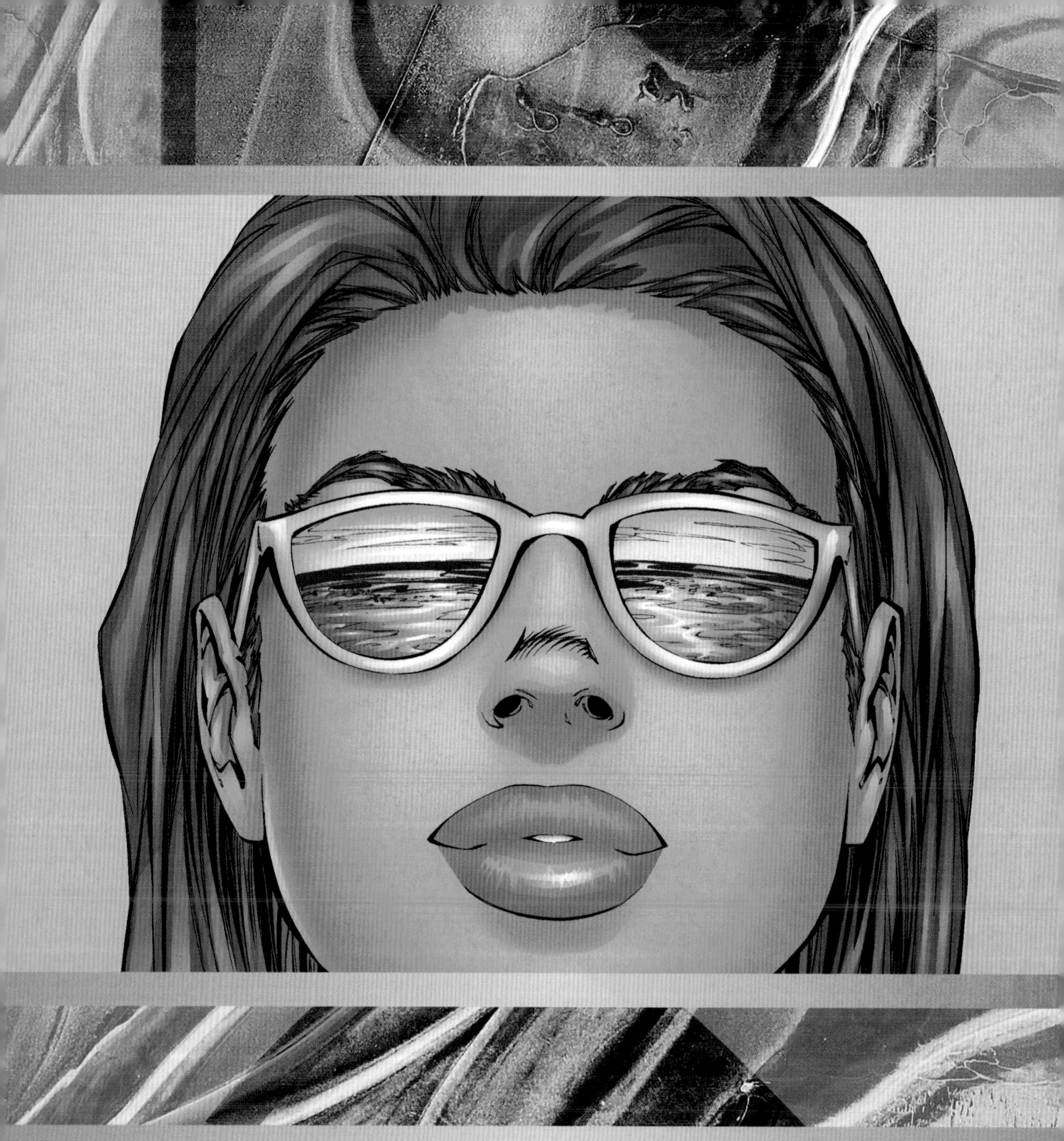

issue #16

story: **David Wohl** and **Christina Z.**
pencils/co-plot: **Michael Turner**
inks: **D-Tron**
colors: **JD Smith**

ink assists: **Jeff De Los Santos, Jose "Jag" Guillen, Marsha Chen, Viet Trong** and **Andy Kim**

background color assists: **Richard Isanove** and **Bike Kinzie**

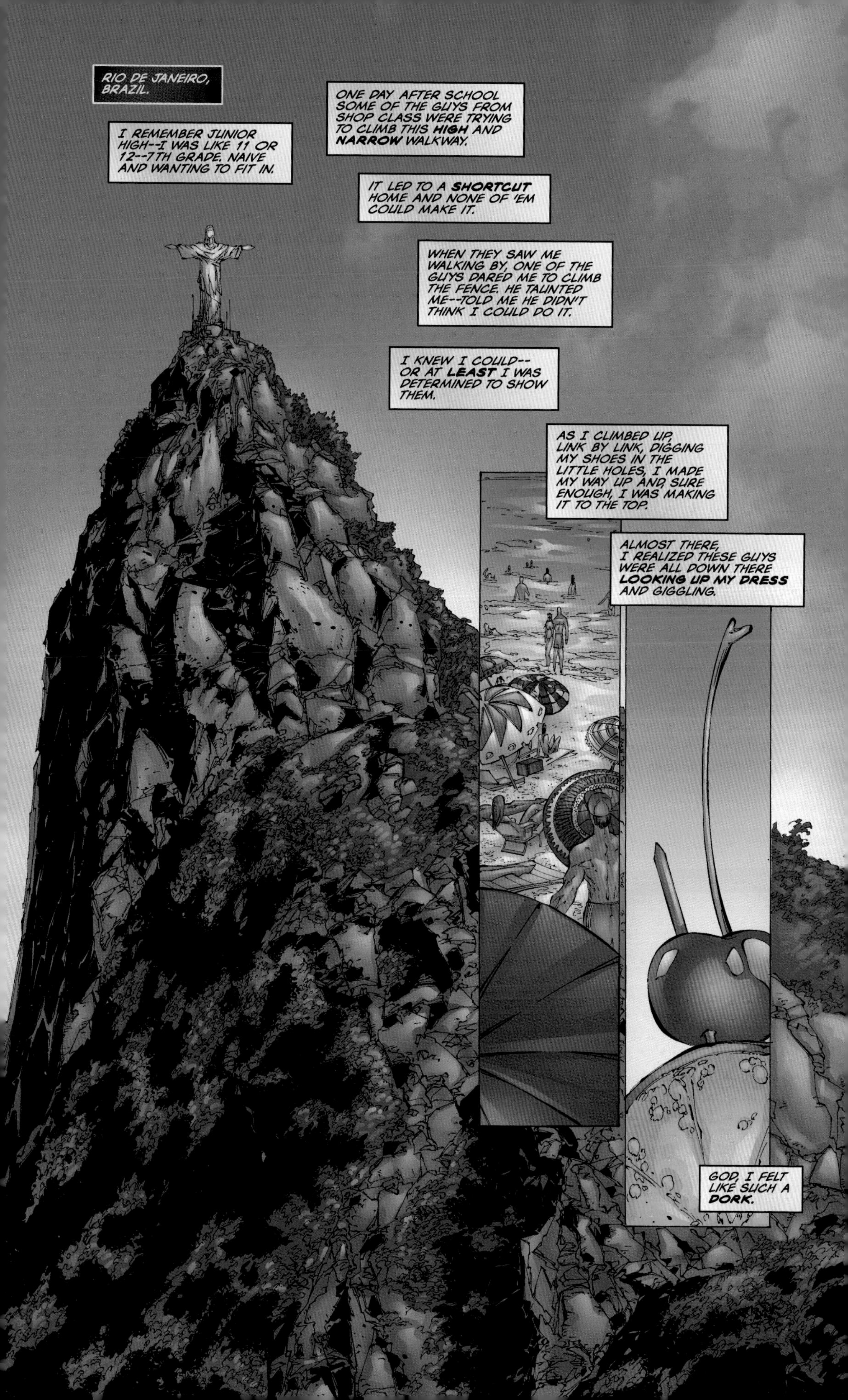
RIO DE JANEIRO, BRAZIL.
I REMEMBER JUNIOR HIGH--I WAS LIKE 11 OR 12--7TH GRADE. NAIVE AND WANTING TO FIT IN.
ONE DAY AFTER SCHOOL SOME OF THE GUYS FROM SHOP CLASS WERE TRYING TO CLIMB THIS **HIGH** AND **NARROW** WALKWAY.
IT LED TO A **SHORTCUT** HOME AND NONE OF 'EM COULD MAKE IT.
WHEN THEY SAW ME WALKING BY, ONE OF THE GUYS DARED ME TO CLIMB THE FENCE. HE TAUNTED ME--TOLD ME HE DIDN'T THINK I COULD DO IT.
I KNEW I COULD--OR AT **LEAST** I WAS DETERMINED TO SHOW THEM.
AS I CLIMBED UP, LINK BY LINK, DIGGING MY SHOES IN THE LITTLE HOLES, I MADE MY WAY UP AND SURE ENOUGH, I WAS MAKING IT TO THE TOP.
ALMOST THERE, I REALIZED THESE GUYS WERE ALL DOWN THERE **LOOKING UP MY DRESS** AND GIGGLING.
GOD, I FELT LIKE SUCH A **DORK.**

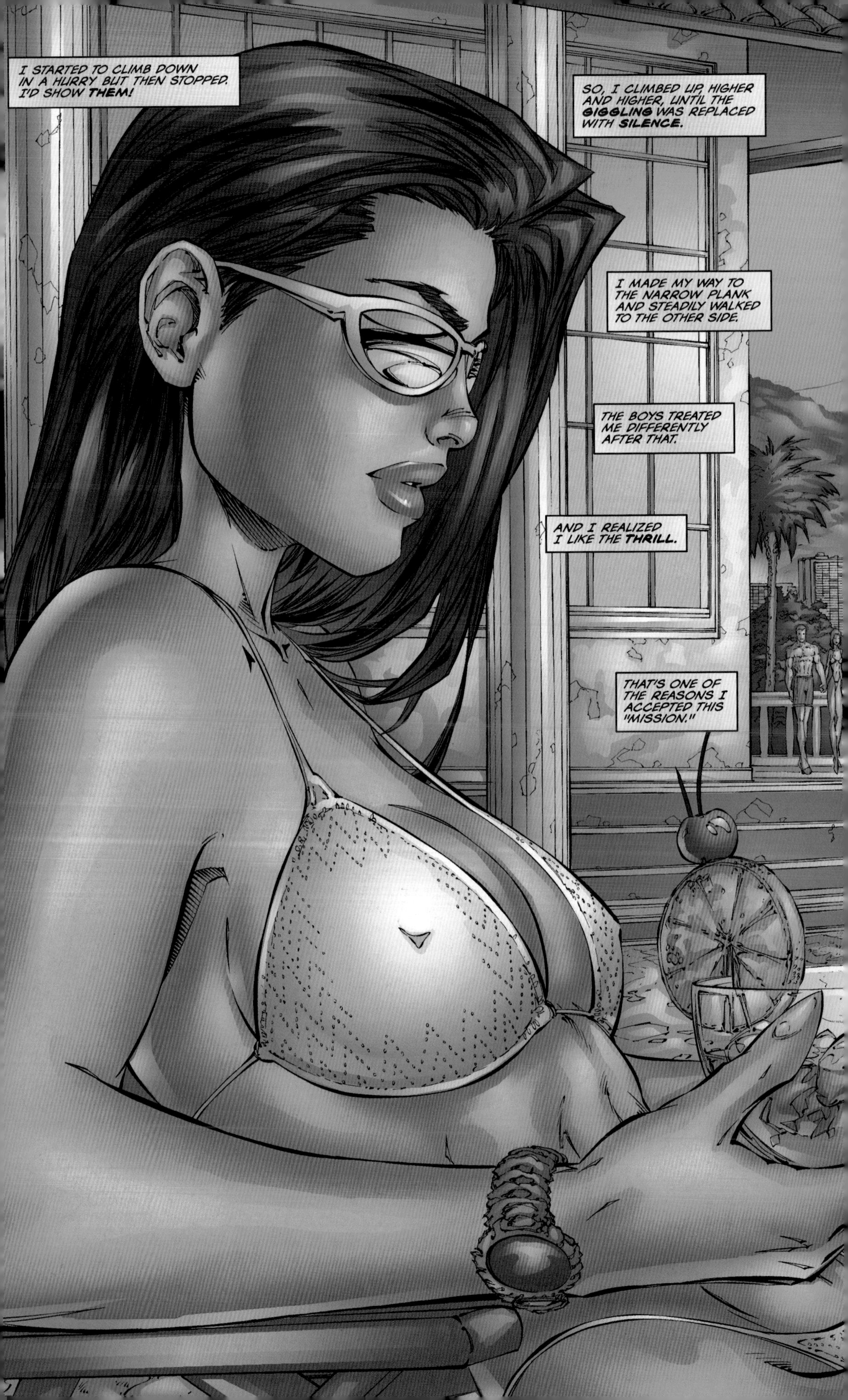
I STARTED TO CLIMB DOWN IN A HURRY BUT THEN STOPPED. I'D SHOW **THEM!**
SO, I CLIMBED UP, HIGHER AND HIGHER, UNTIL THE **GIGGLING** WAS REPLACED WITH **SILENCE**.
I MADE MY WAY TO THE NARROW PLANK AND STEADILY WALKED TO THE OTHER SIDE.
THE BOYS TREATED ME DIFFERENTLY AFTER THAT.
AND I REALIZED I LIKE THE **THRILL**.
THAT'S ONE OF THE REASONS I ACCEPTED THIS "MISSION."

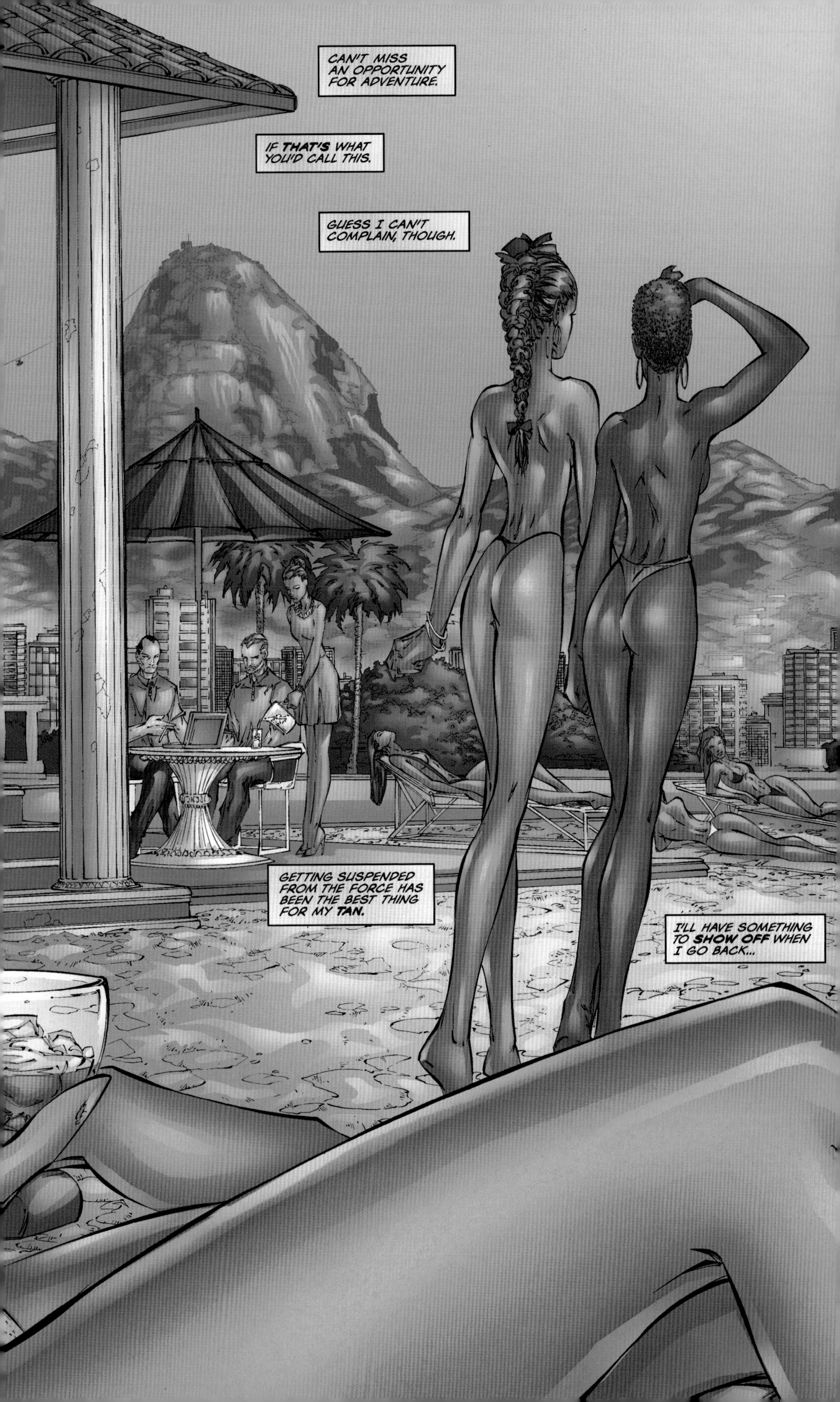
CAN'T MISS
AN OPPORTUNITY
FOR ADVENTURE.
IF **THAT'S** WHAT
YOU'D CALL THIS.
GUESS I CAN'T
COMPLAIN, THOUGH.
GETTING SUSPENDED
FROM THE FORCE HAS
BEEN THE BEST THING
FOR MY **TAN.**
I'LL HAVE SOMETHING
TO **SHOW OFF** WHEN
I GO BACK...

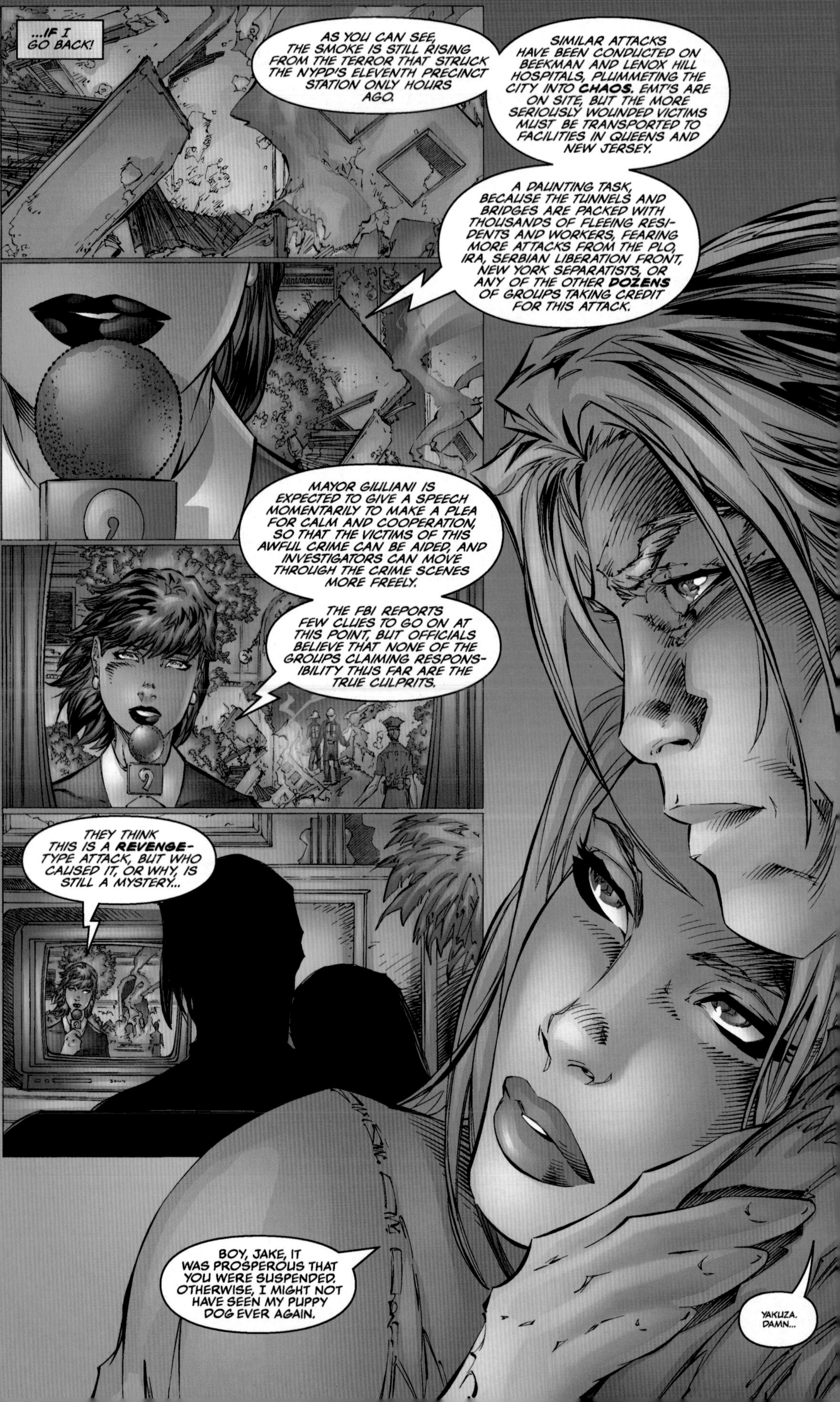

...IF I GO BACK!
AS YOU CAN SEE, THE SMOKE IS STILL RISING FROM THE TERROR THAT STRUCK THE NYPD'S ELEVENTH PRECINCT STATION ONLY HOURS AGO.
SIMILAR ATTACKS HAVE BEEN CONDUCTED ON BEEKMAN AND LENOX HILL HOSPITALS, PLUMMETING THE CITY INTO CHAOS. EMT'S ARE ON SITE, BUT THE MORE SERIOUSLY WOUNDED VICTIMS MUST BE TRANSPORTED TO FACILITIES IN QUEENS AND NEW JERSEY.
A DAUNTING TASK, BECAUSE THE TUNNELS AND BRIDGES ARE PACKED WITH THOUSANDS OF FLEEING RESI-DENTS AND WORKERS, FEARING MORE ATTACKS FROM THE PLO, IRA, SERBIAN LIBERATION FRONT, NEW YORK SEPARATISTS, OR ANY OF THE OTHER DOZENS OF GROUPS TAKING CREDIT FOR THIS ATTACK.
MAYOR GILIANI IS EXPECTED TO GIVE A SPEECH MOMENTARILY TO MAKE A PLEA FOR CALM AND COOPERATION, SO THAT THE VICTIMS OF THIS AWFUL CRIME CAN BE AIDED, AND INVESTIGATORS CAN MOVE THROUGH THE CRIME SCENES MORE FREELY.
THE FBI REPORTS FEW CLUES TO GO ON AT THIS POINT, BUT OFFICIALS BELIEVE THAT NONE OF THE GROUPS CLAIMING RESPONS-IBILITY THUS FAR ARE THE TRUE CULPRITS.
THEY THINK THIS IS A REVENGE-TYPE ATTACK, BUT WHO CAUSED IT, OR WHY, IS STILL A MYSTERY...
BOY, JAKE, IT WAS PROSPEROUS THAT YOU WERE SUSPENDED. OTHERWISE, I MIGHT NOT HAVE SEEN MY PUPPY DOG EVER AGAIN.
YAKUZA. DAMN...

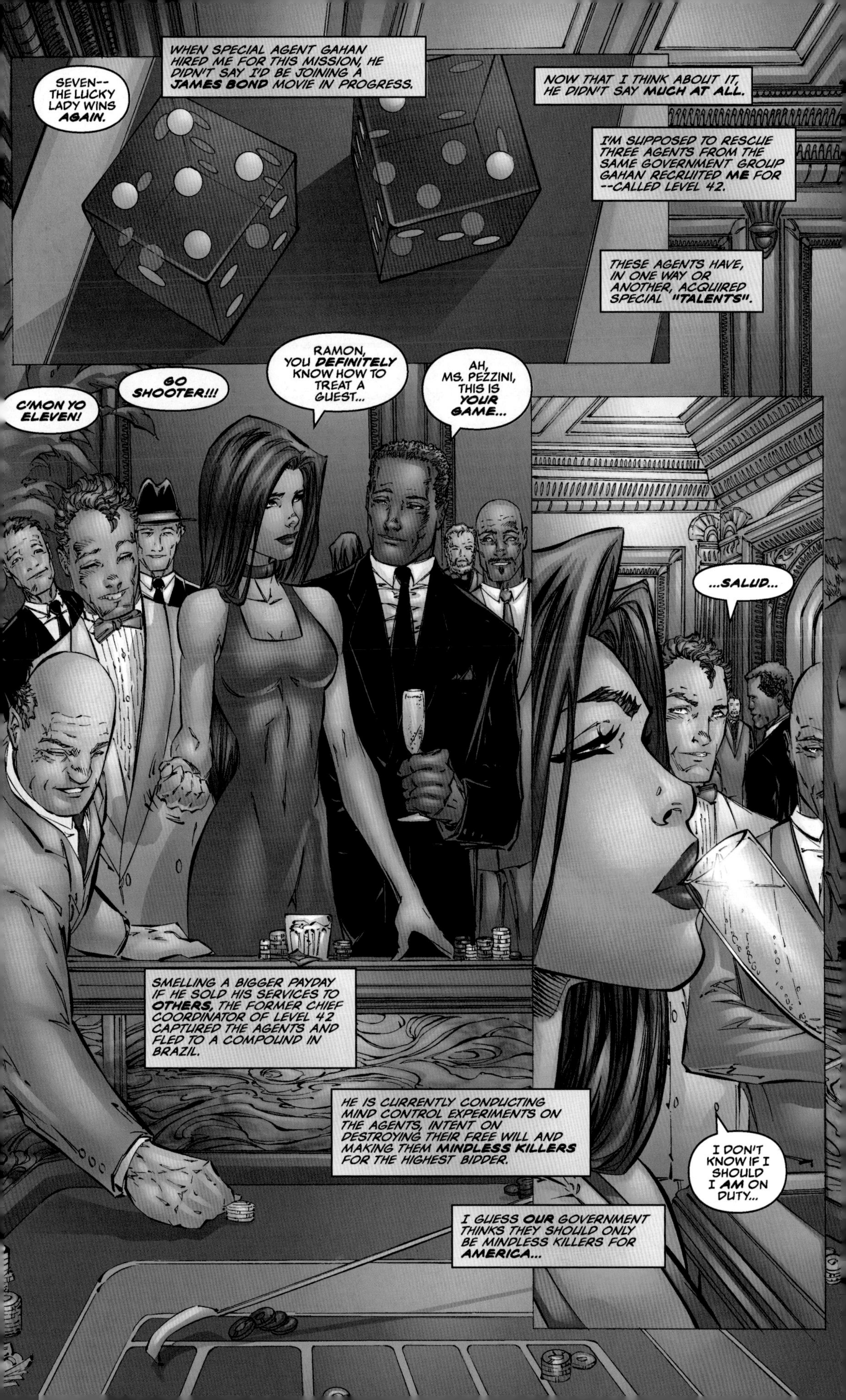
WHEN SPECIAL AGENT GAHAN HIRED ME FOR THIS MISSION, HE DIDN'T SAY I'D BE JOINING A JAMES BOND MOVIE IN PROGRESS.
SEVEN--THE LUCKY LADY WINS AGAIN.
NOW THAT I THINK ABOUT IT, HE DIDN'T SAY MUCH AT ALL.
I'M SUPPOSED TO RESCUE THREE AGENTS FROM THE SAME GOVERNMENT GROUP GAHAN RECRUITED ME FOR --CALLED LEVEL 42.
THESE AGENTS HAVE, IN ONE WAY OR ANOTHER, ACQUIRED SPECIAL "TALENTS".
C'MON YO ELEVEN!
GO SHOOTER!!!
RAMON, YOU DEFINITELY KNOW HOW TO TREAT A GUEST...
AH, MS. PEZZINI, THIS IS YOUR GAME...
SMELLING A BIGGER PAYDAY IF HE SOLD HIS SERVICES TO OTHERS, THE FORMER CHIEF COORDINATOR OF LEVEL 42 CAPTURED THE AGENTS AND FLED TO A COMPOUND IN BRAZIL.
HE IS CURRENTLY CONDUCTING MIND CONTROL EXPERIMENTS ON THE AGENTS, INTENT ON DESTROYING THEIR FREE WILL AND MAKING THEM MINDLESS KILLERS FOR THE HIGHEST BIDDER.
...SALUD...
I DON'T KNOW IF I SHOULD I AM ON DUTY...
I GUESS OUR GOVERNMENT THINKS THEY SHOULD ONLY BE MINDLESS KILLERS FOR AMERICA...

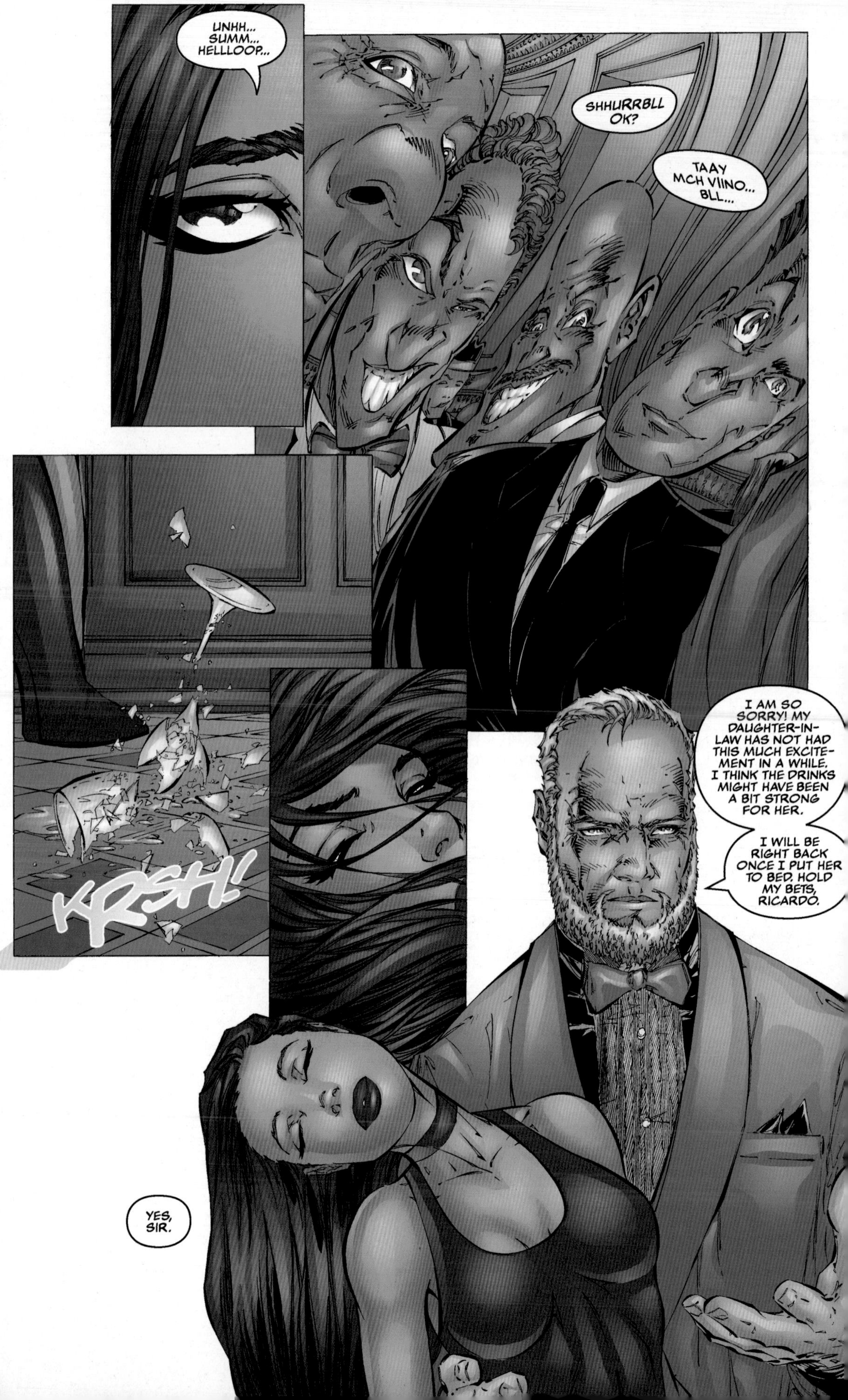
UNHH... SUMM... HELLLOOP...
SHHURRBLL OK?
TAAY MCH VIINO... BLL...
KRSH!
I AM SO SORRY! MY DAUGHTER-IN-LAW HAS NOT HAD THIS MUCH EXCITE-MENT IN A WHILE. I THINK THE DRINKS MIGHT HAVE BEEN A BIT STRONG FOR HER.
I WILL BE RIGHT BACK ONCE I PUT HER TO BED. HOLD MY BETS, RICARDO.
YES, SIR.

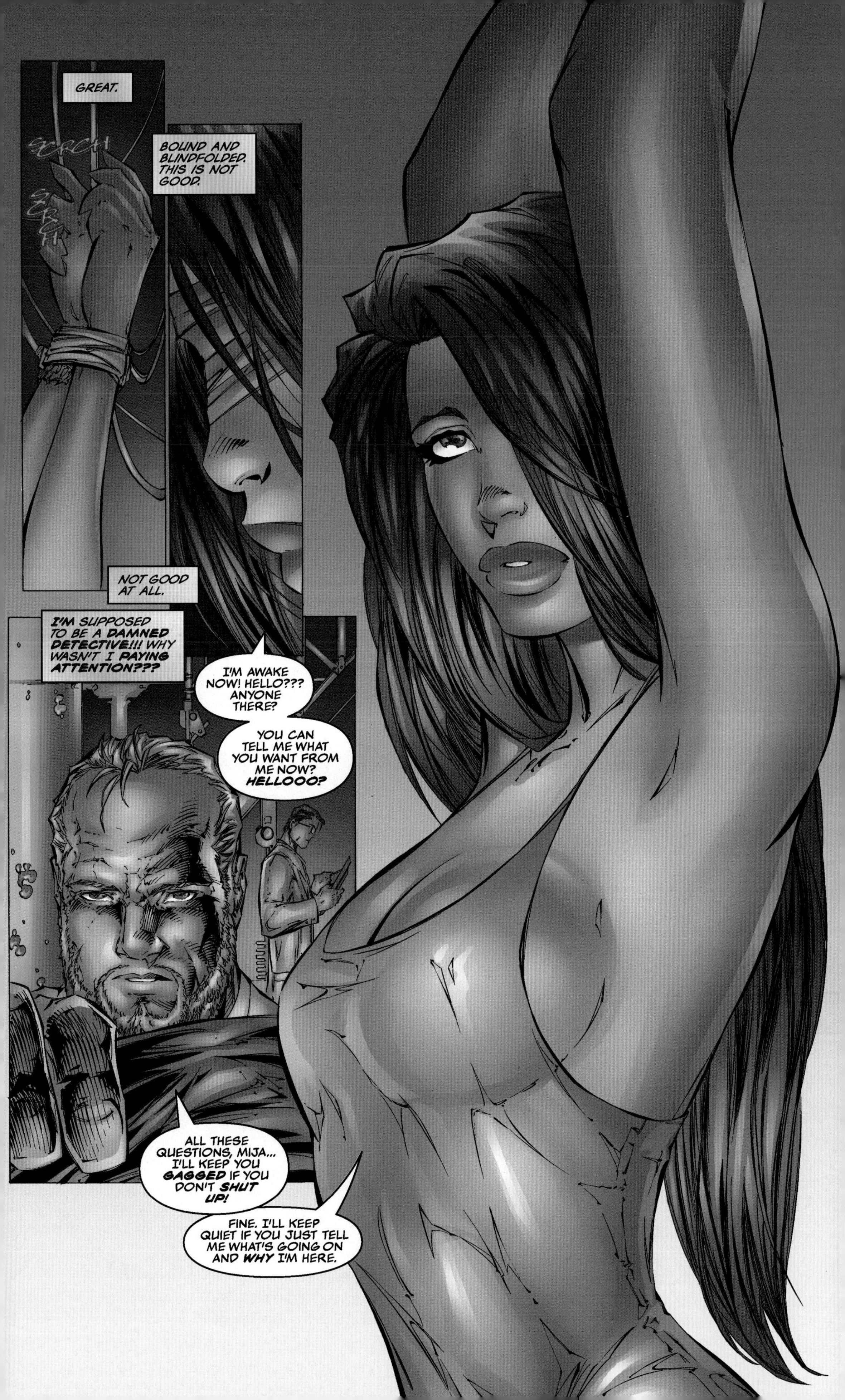
GREAT.
SCRCH
SCRCH
BOUND AND BLINDFOLDED. THIS IS NOT GOOD.
NOT GOOD AT ALL.
I'M SUPPOSED TO BE A DAMNED DETECTIVE!!! WHY WASN'T I PAYING ATTENTION???
I'M AWAKE NOW! HELLO??? ANYONE THERE?
YOU CAN TELL ME WHAT YOU WANT FROM ME NOW? HELLOOO?
ALL THESE QUESTIONS, MIJA... I'LL KEEP YOU GAGGED IF YOU DON'T SHUT UP!
FINE. I'LL KEEP QUIET IF YOU JUST TELL ME WHAT'S GOING ON AND WHY I'M HERE.

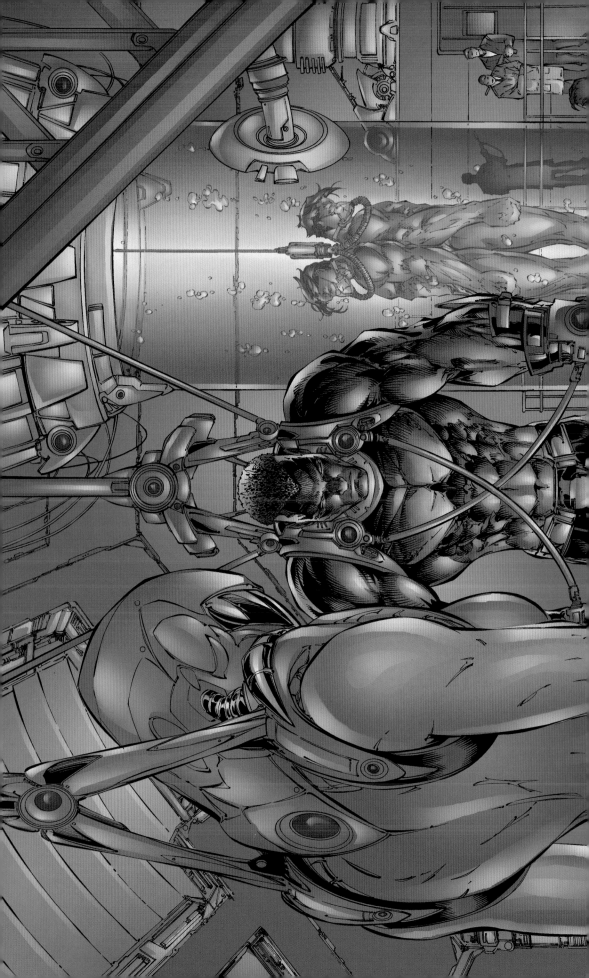

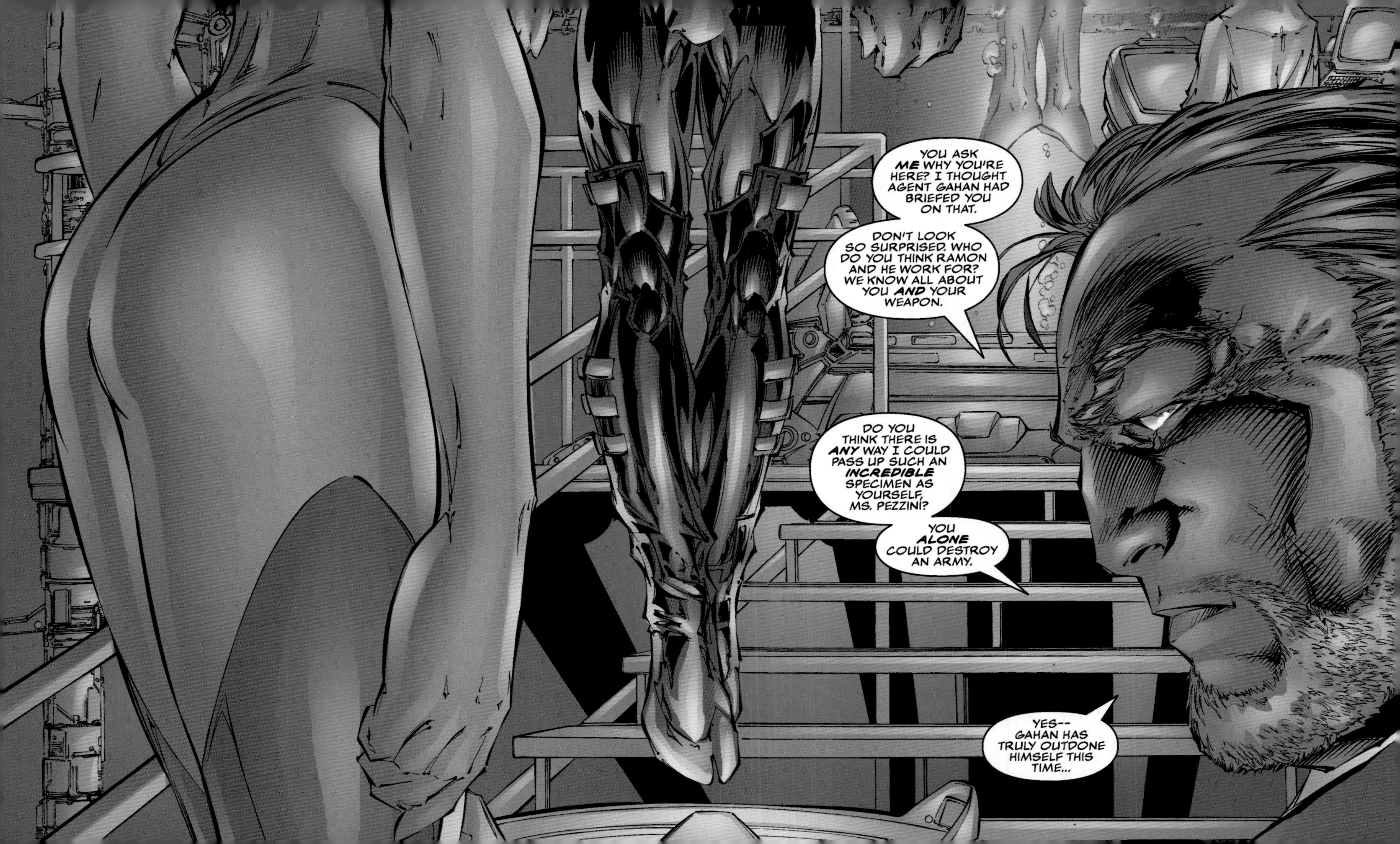
YOU ASK ME WHY YOU'RE HERE? I THOUGHT AGENT GAHAN HAD BRIEFED YOU ON THAT.
DON'T LOOK SO SURPRISED. WHO DO YOU THINK RAMON AND HE WORK FOR? WE KNOW ALL ABOUT YOU AND YOUR WEAPON.
DO YOU THINK THERE IS ANY WAY I COULD PASS UP SUCH AN INCREDIBLE SPECIMEN AS YOURSELF, MS. PEZZINI?
YOU ALONE COULD DESTROY AN ARMY.
YES-- GAHAN HAS TRULY OUTDONE HIMSELF THIS TIME...

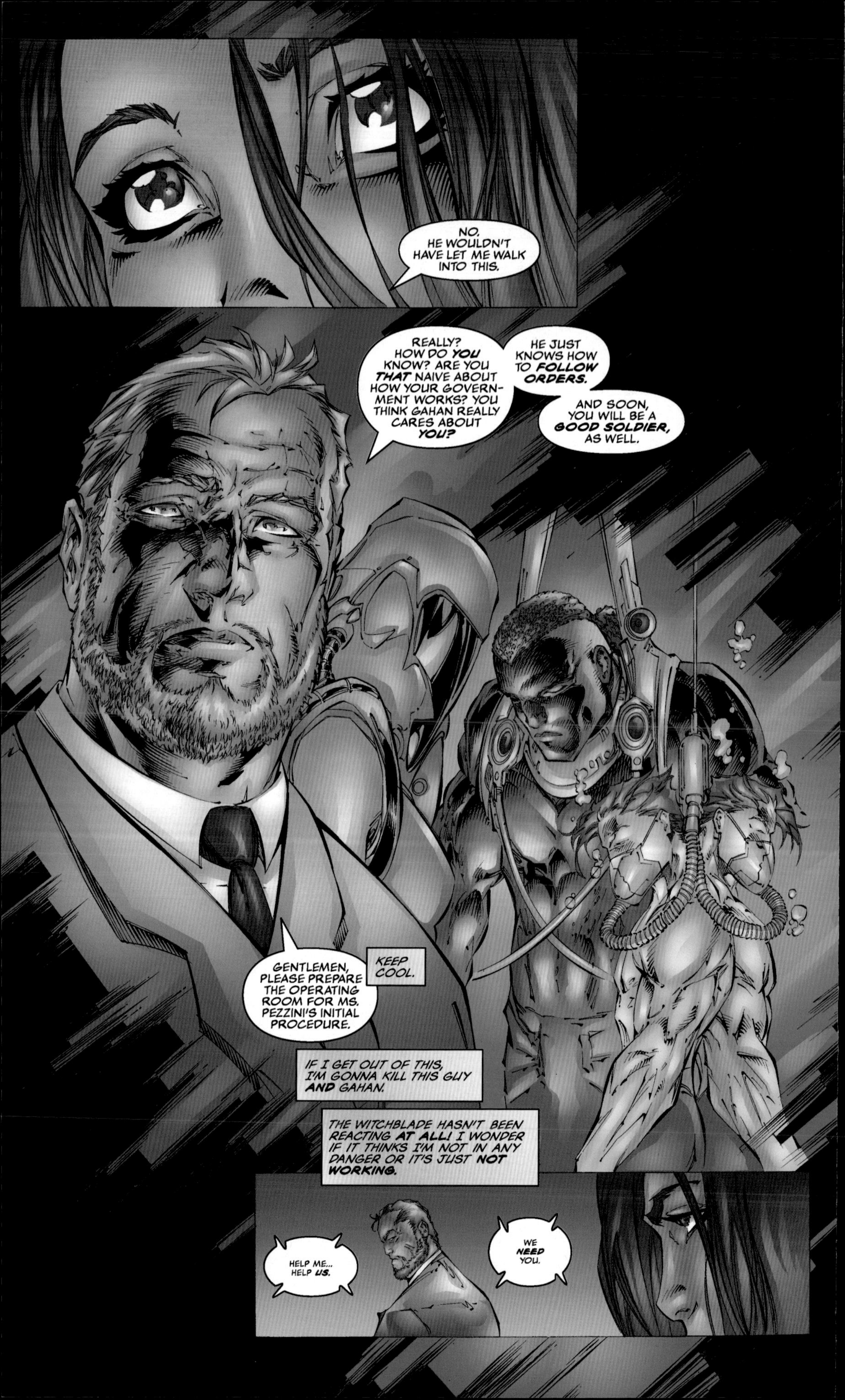
NO. HE WOULDN'T HAVE LET ME WALK INTO THIS.
REALLY? HOW DO YOU KNOW? ARE YOU THAT NAIVE ABOUT HOW YOUR GOVERNMENT WORKS? YOU THINK GAHAN REALLY CARES ABOUT YOU?
HE JUST KNOWS HOW TO FOLLOW ORDERS.
AND SOON, YOU WILL BE A GOOD SOLDIER, AS WELL.
GENTLEMEN, PLEASE PREPARE THE OPERATING ROOM FOR MS. PEZZINI'S INITIAL PROCEDURE.
KEEP COOL.
IF I GET OUT OF THIS, I'M GONNA KILL THIS GUY AND GAHAN.
THE WITCHBLADE HASN'T BEEN REACTING AT ALL! I WONDER IF IT THINKS I'M NOT IN ANY DANGER OR IT'S JUST NOT WORKING.
HELP ME... HELP US.
WE NEED YOU.

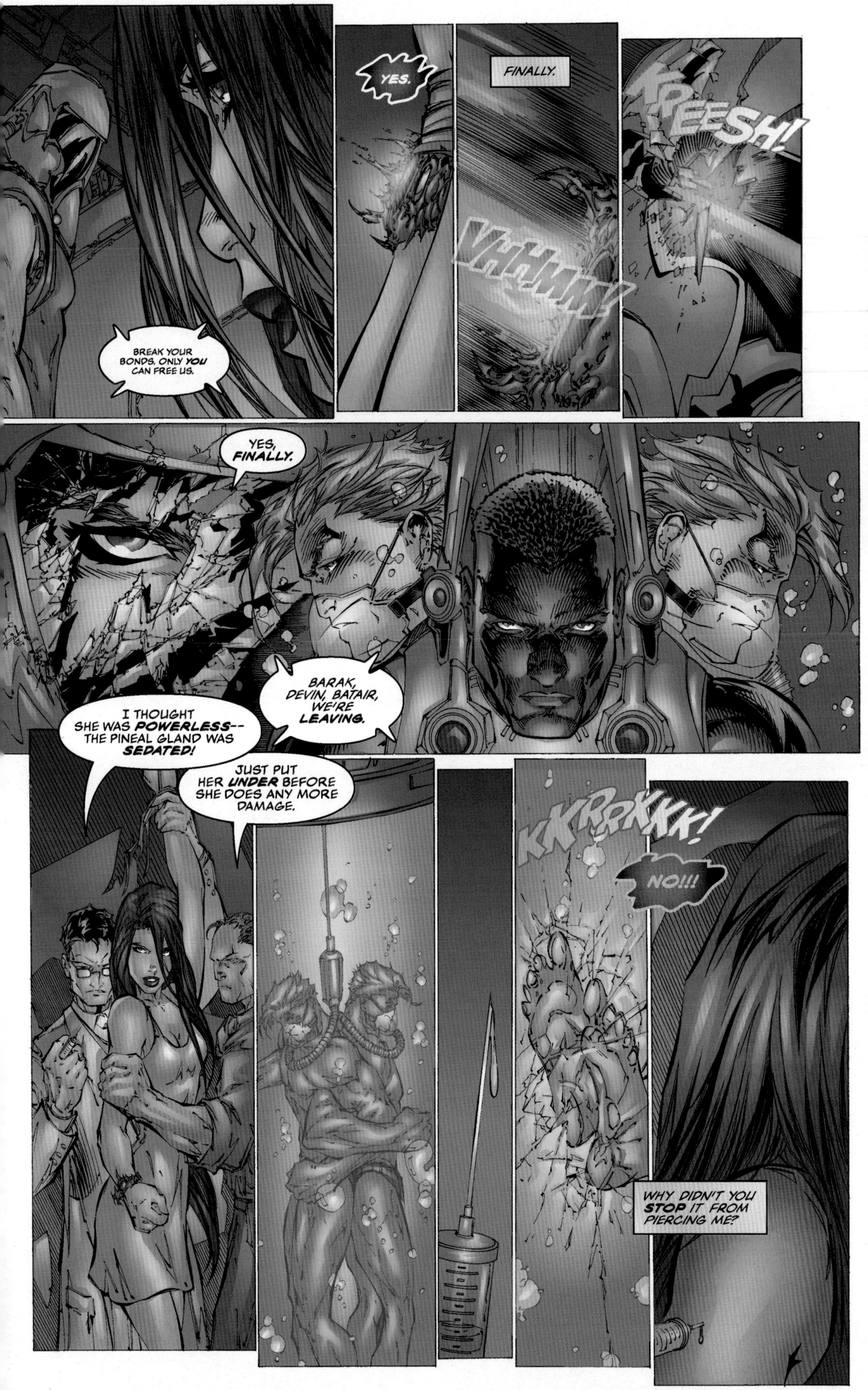
BREAK YOUR BONDS. ONLY YOU CAN FREE US.
YES.
FINALLY.
VHHMM!
KRRESH!
YES, FINALLY.
BARAK, DEVIN, BATAIR, WE'RE LEAVING.
I THOUGHT SHE WAS POWERLESS-- THE PINEAL GLAND WAS SEDATED!
JUST PUT HER UNDER BEFORE SHE DOES ANY MORE DAMAGE.
KKRRKKK!
NO!!!
WHY DIDN'T YOU STOP IT FROM PIERCING ME?

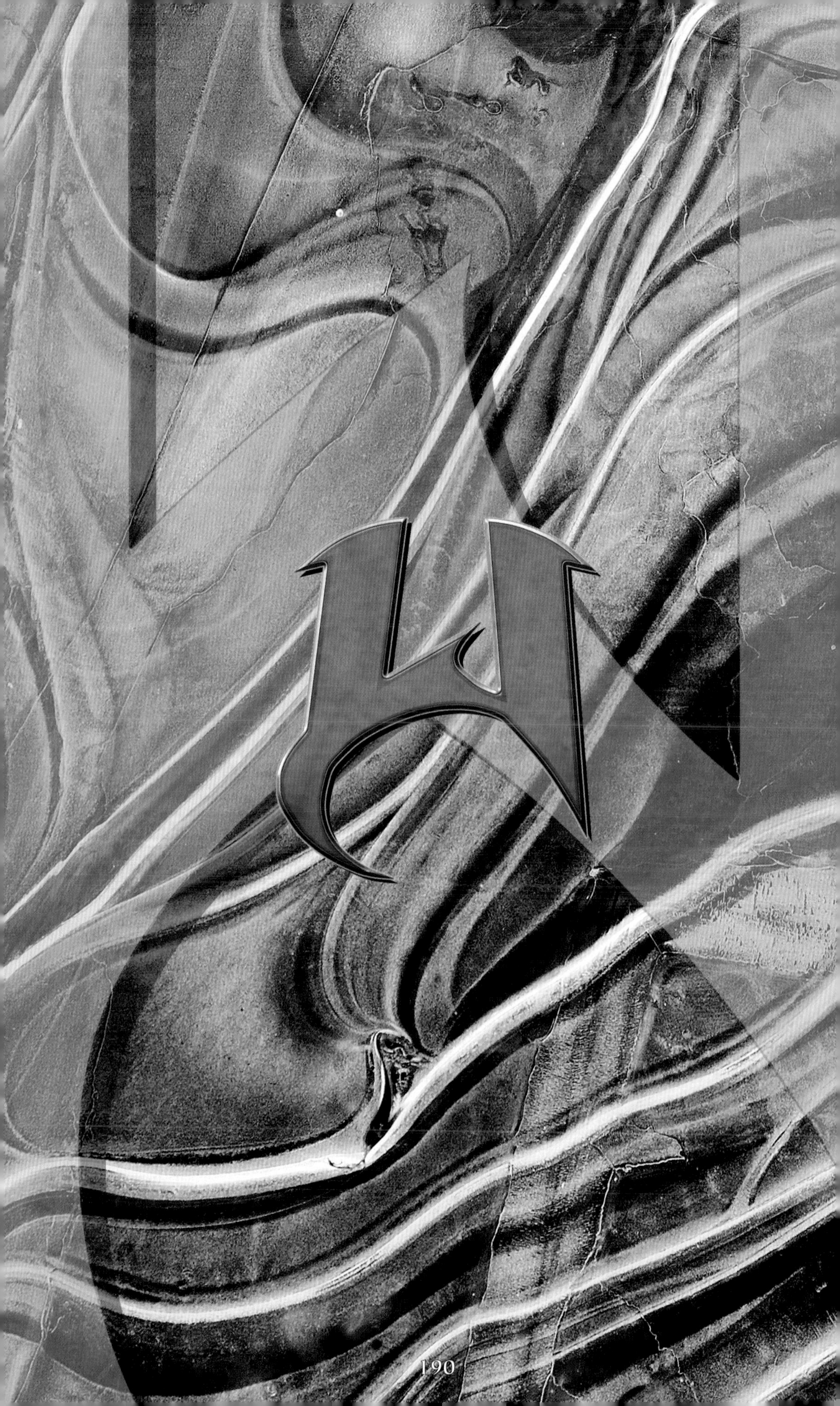

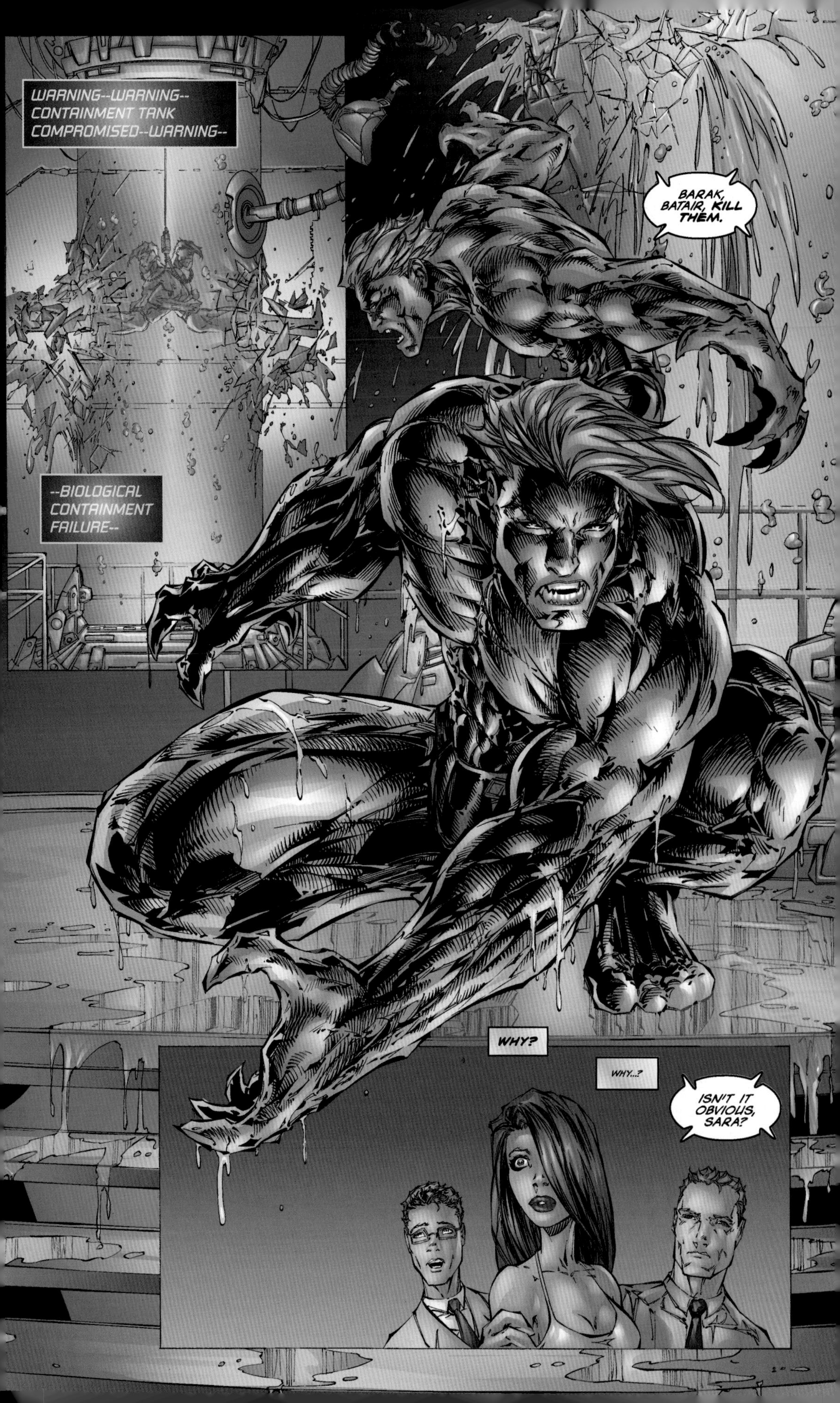
WARNING--WARNING--
CONTAINMENT TANK
COMPROMISED--WARNING--
BARAK, BATAIR, KILL THEM.
--BIOLOGICAL CONTAINMENT FAILURE--
WHY?
WHY...?
ISN'T IT OBVIOUS, SARA?

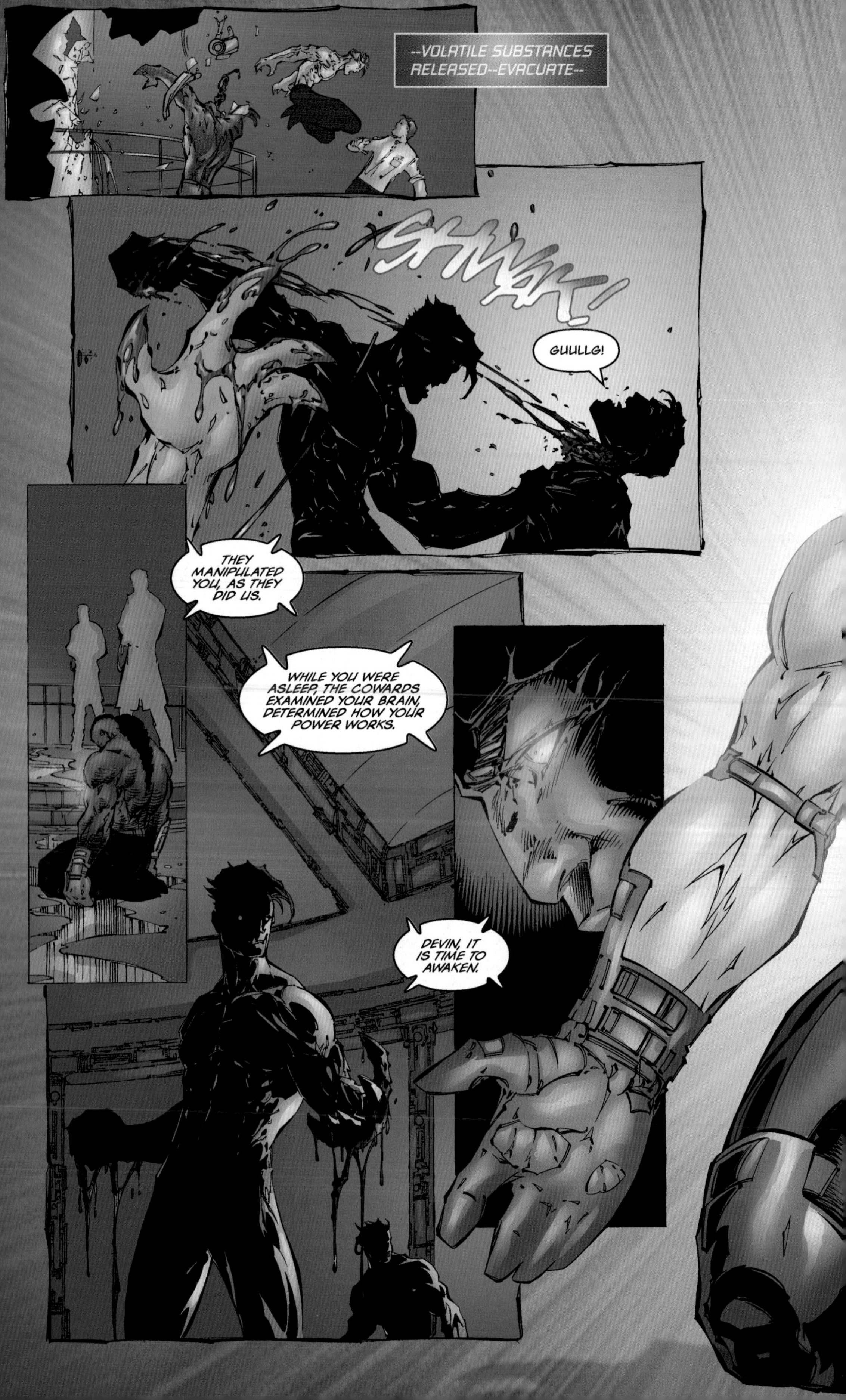
--VOLATILE SUBSTANCES RELEASED--EVACUATE--
SHUNK!
GUULLG!
THEY MANIPULATED YOU, AS THEY DID US.
WHILE YOU WERE ASLEEP, THE COWARDS EXAMINED YOUR BRAIN, DETERMINED HOW YOUR POWER WORKS.
DEVIN, IT IS TIME TO AWAKEN.

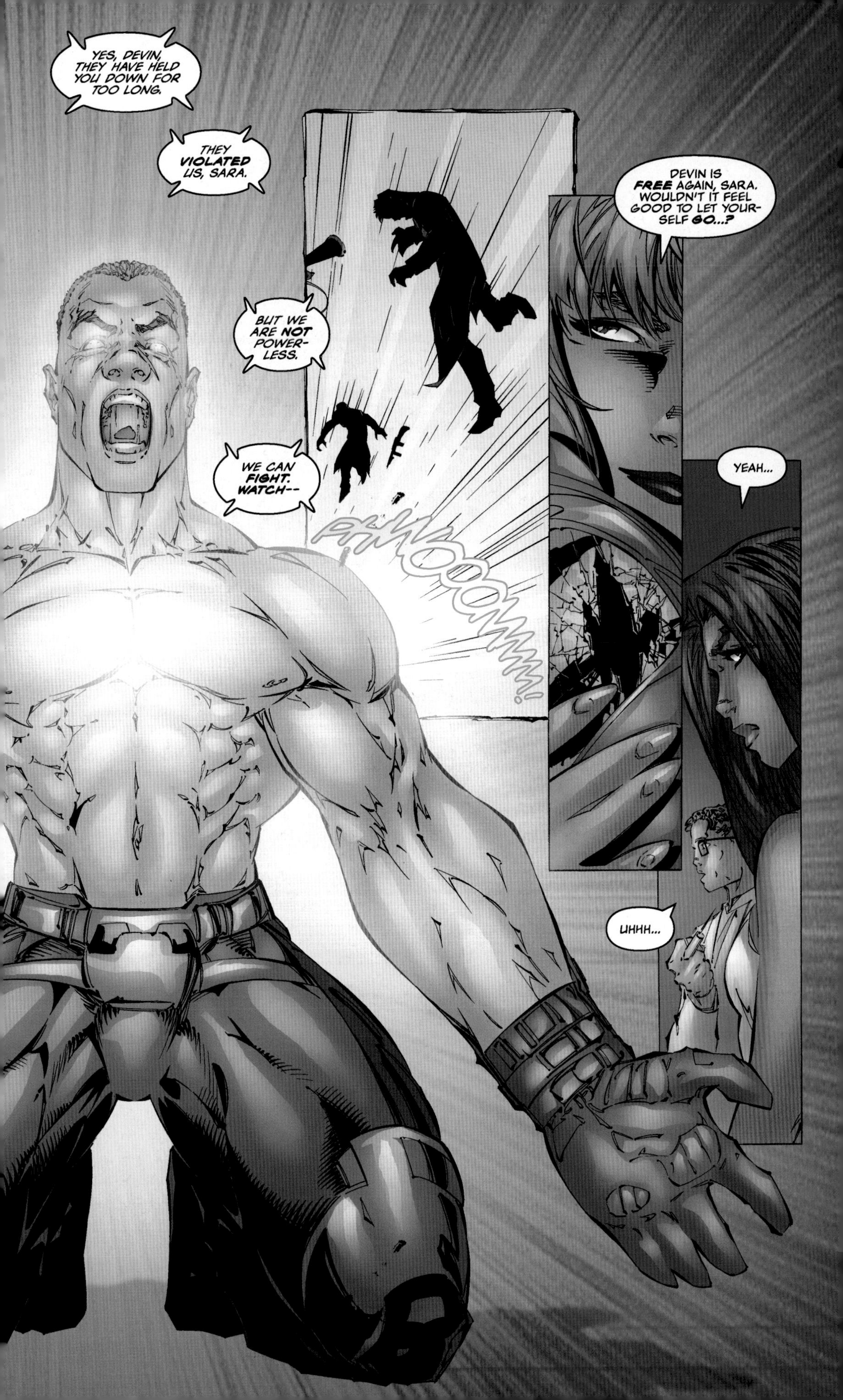
YES, DEVIN, THEY HAVE HELD YOU DOWN FOR TOO LONG.
THEY VIOLATED US, SARA.
BUT WE ARE NOT POWERLESS.
WE CAN FIGHT. WATCH--
PHWOOOOMMM!
DEVIN IS FREE AGAIN, SARA. WOULDN'T IT FEEL GOOD TO LET YOURSELF GO...?
YEAH...
UHHH...

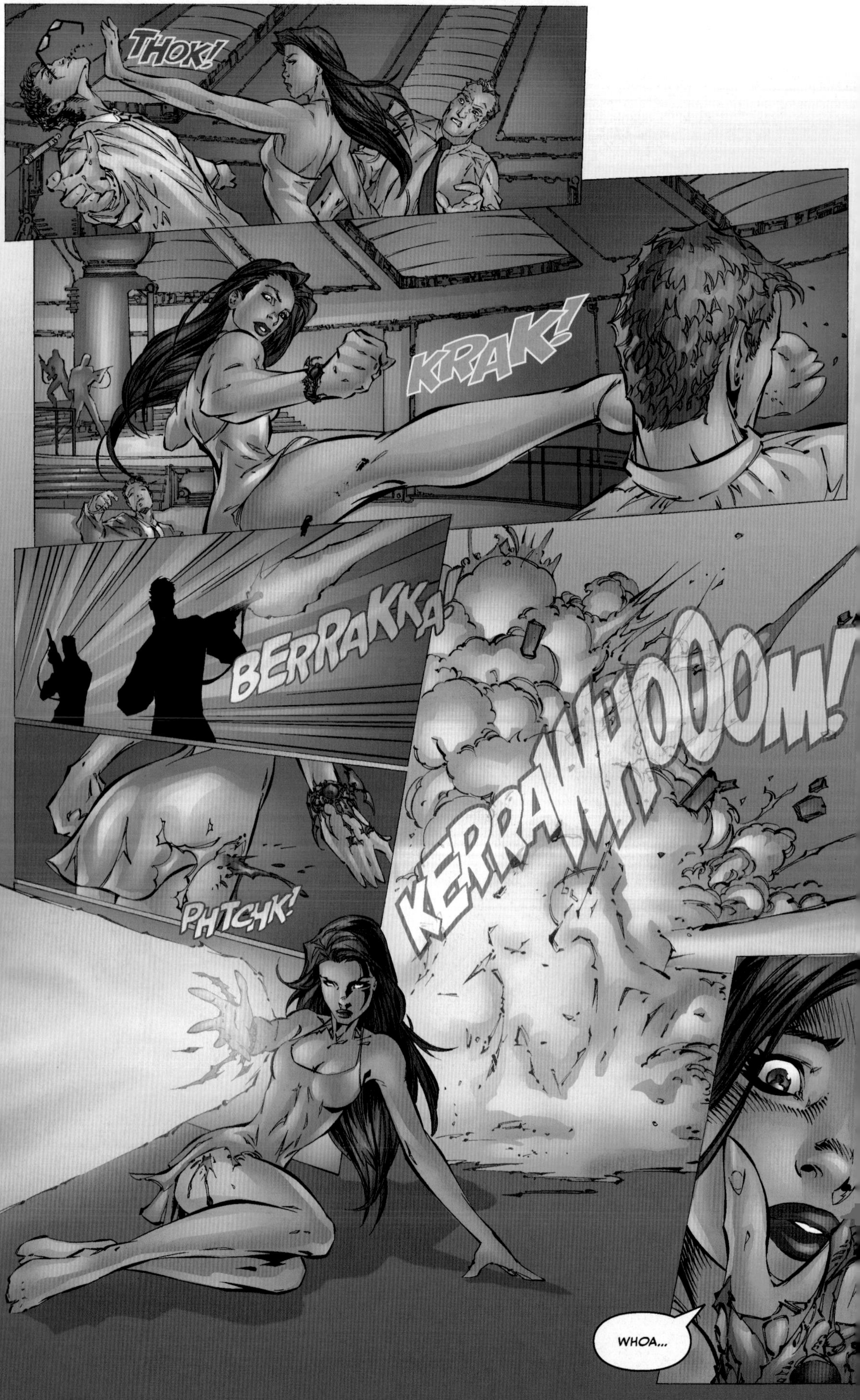
THOK!
KRAK!
BERRAKKA!
KERRAWHOOOM!
PHTCHK!
WHOA...

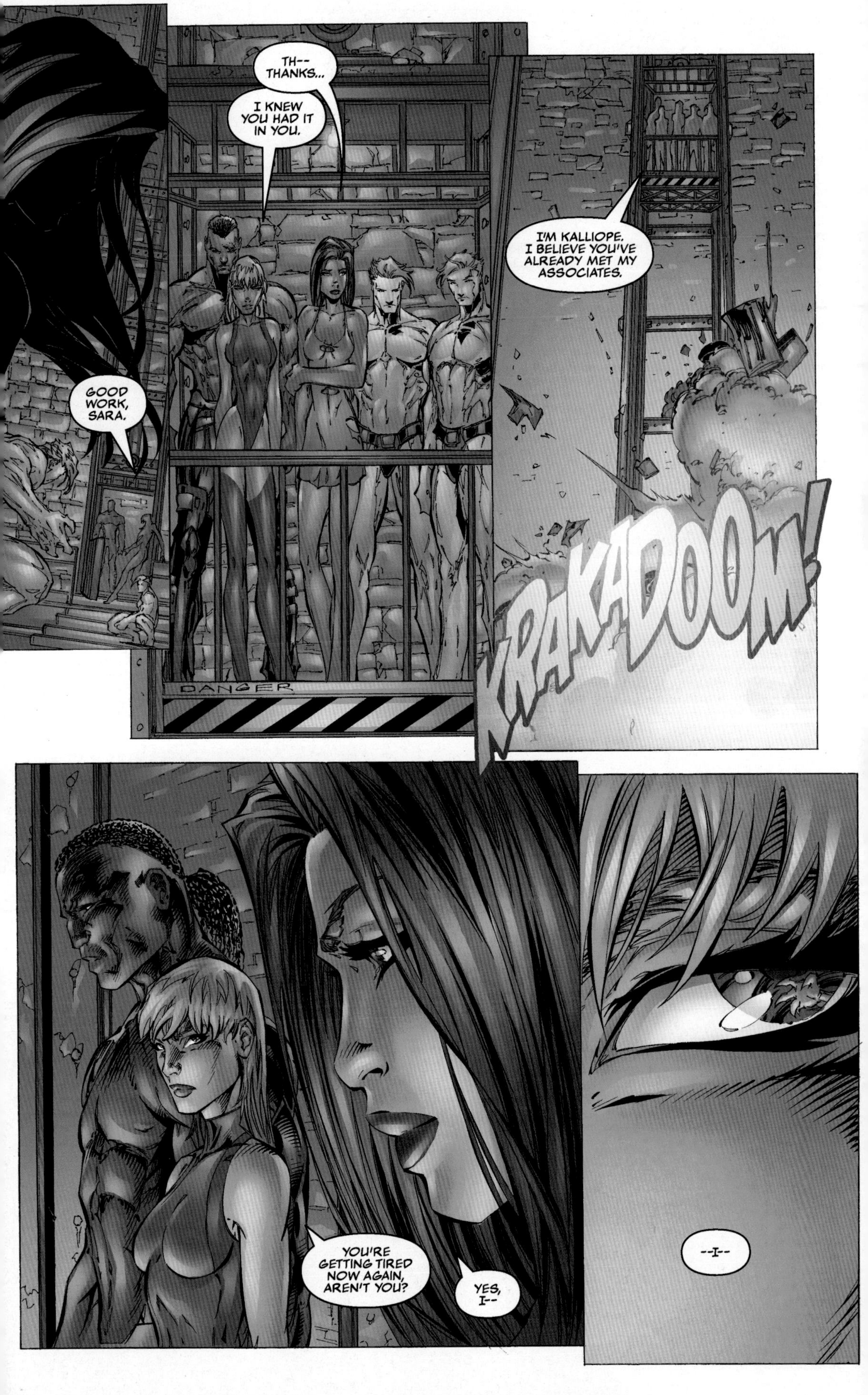
GOOD WORK, SARA.
TH-- THANKS...
I KNEW YOU HAD IT IN YOU.
DANGER
I'M KALLIOPE. I BELIEVE YOU'VE ALREADY MET MY ASSOCIATES.
KRAKADOOM!
YOU'RE GETTING TIRED NOW AGAIN, AREN'T YOU?
YES, I--
--I--

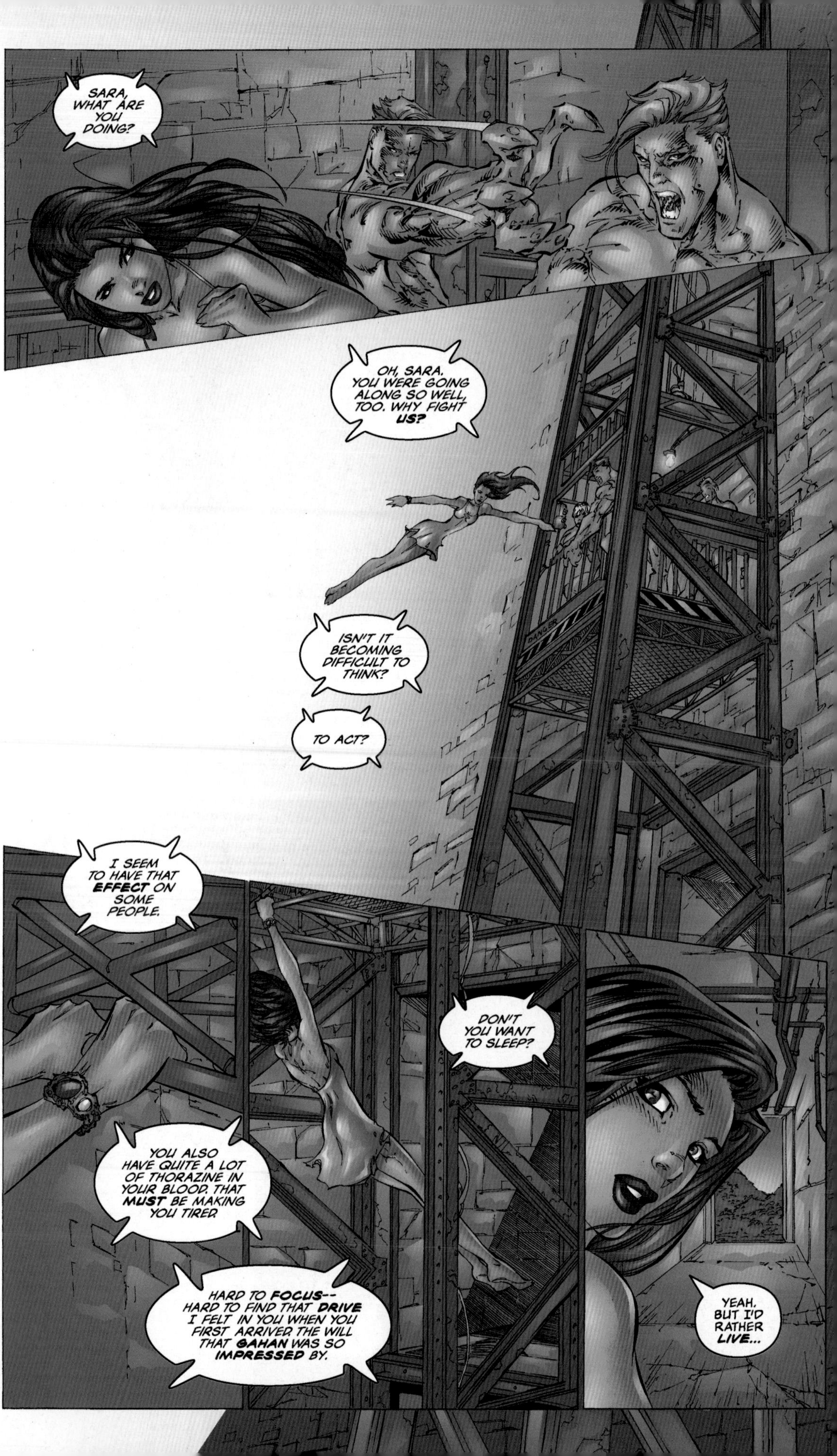
SARA, WHAT ARE YOU DOING?
OH, SARA. YOU WERE GOING ALONG SO WELL, TOO. WHY FIGHT **US?**
ISN'T IT BECOMING DIFFICULT TO THINK?
TO ACT?
DANGER
I SEEM TO HAVE THAT **EFFECT** ON SOME PEOPLE.
DON'T YOU WANT TO SLEEP?
YOU ALSO HAVE QUITE A LOT OF THORAZINE IN YOUR BLOOD. THAT **MUST** BE MAKING YOU TIRED.
HARD TO **FOCUS**-- HARD TO FIND THAT **DRIVE** I FELT IN YOU WHEN YOU FIRST ARRIVED. THE WILL THAT **GAHAN** WAS SO **IMPRESSED** BY.
YEAH, BUT I'D RATHER **LIVE...**

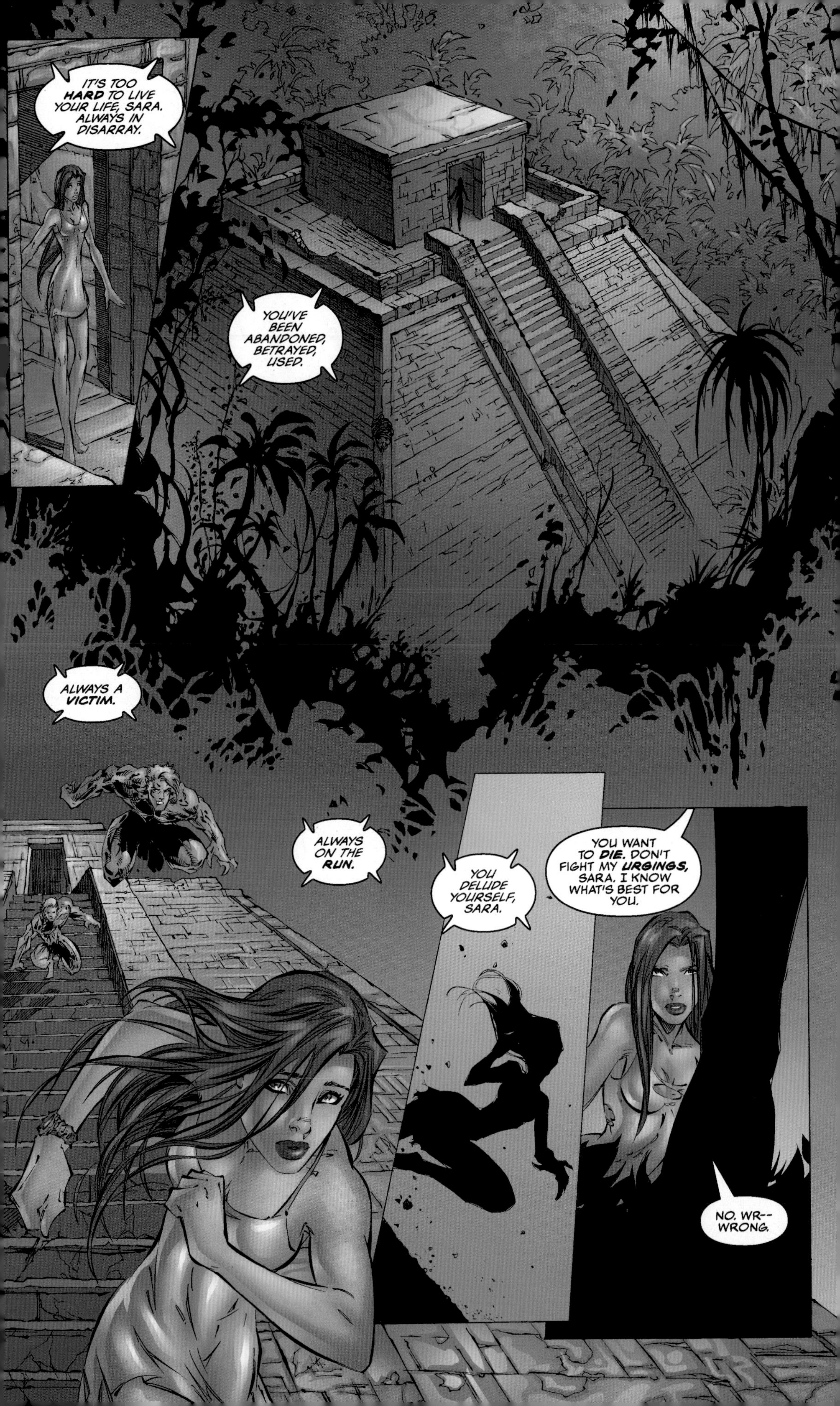
IT'S TOO HARD TO LIVE YOUR LIFE, SARA. ALWAYS IN DISARRAY.
YOU'VE BEEN ABANDONED, BETRAYED, USED.
ALWAYS A VICTIM.
ALWAYS ON THE RUN.
YOU DELUDE YOURSELF, SARA.
YOU WANT TO DIE. DON'T FIGHT MY URGINGS, SARA. I KNOW WHAT'S BEST FOR YOU.
NO. WR-- WRONG.

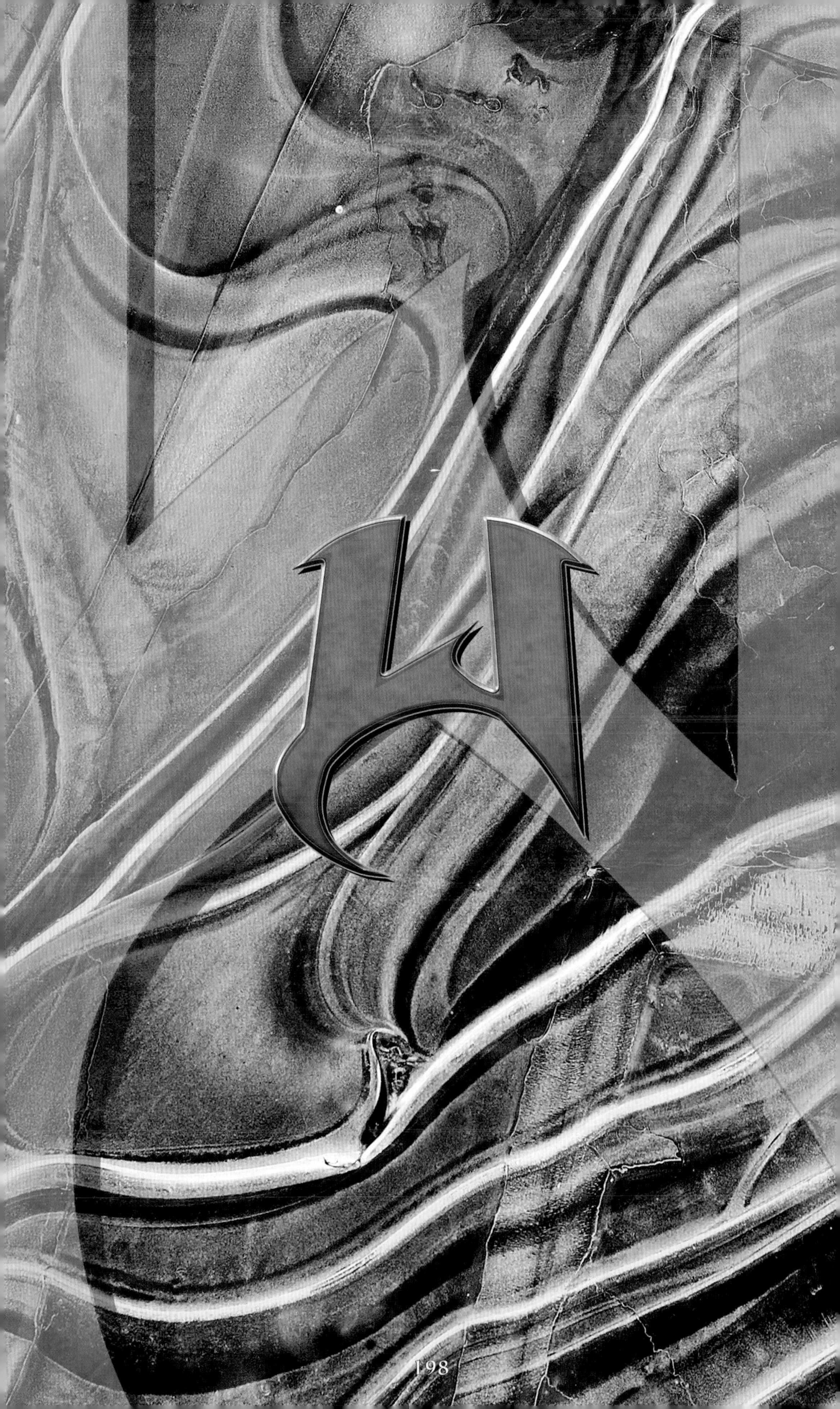

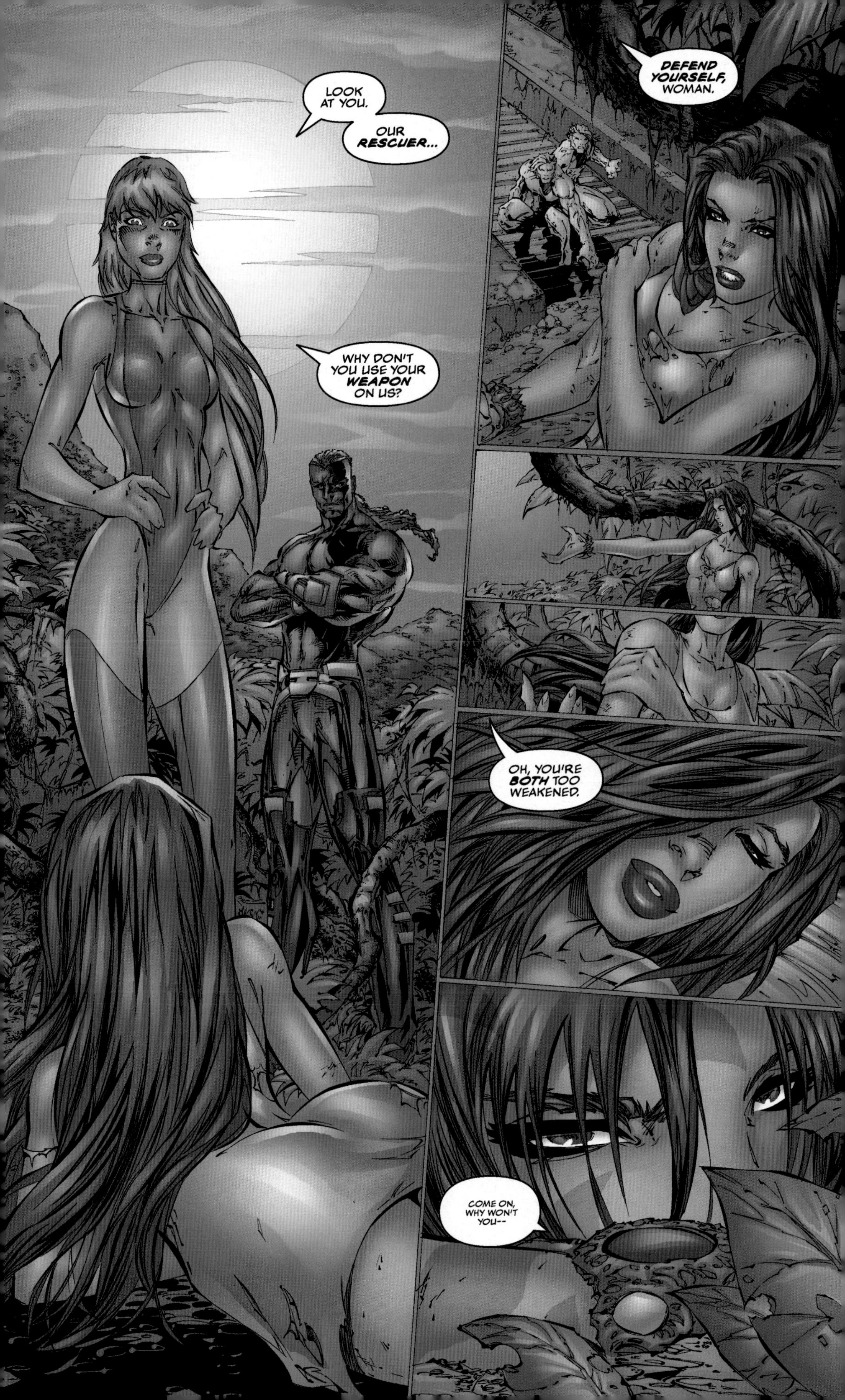
LOOK AT YOU.
OUR RESCUER...
WHY DON'T YOU USE YOUR WEAPON ON US?
DEFEND YOURSELF, WOMAN.
OH, YOU'RE BOTH TOO WEAKENED.
COME ON, WHY WON'T YOU--

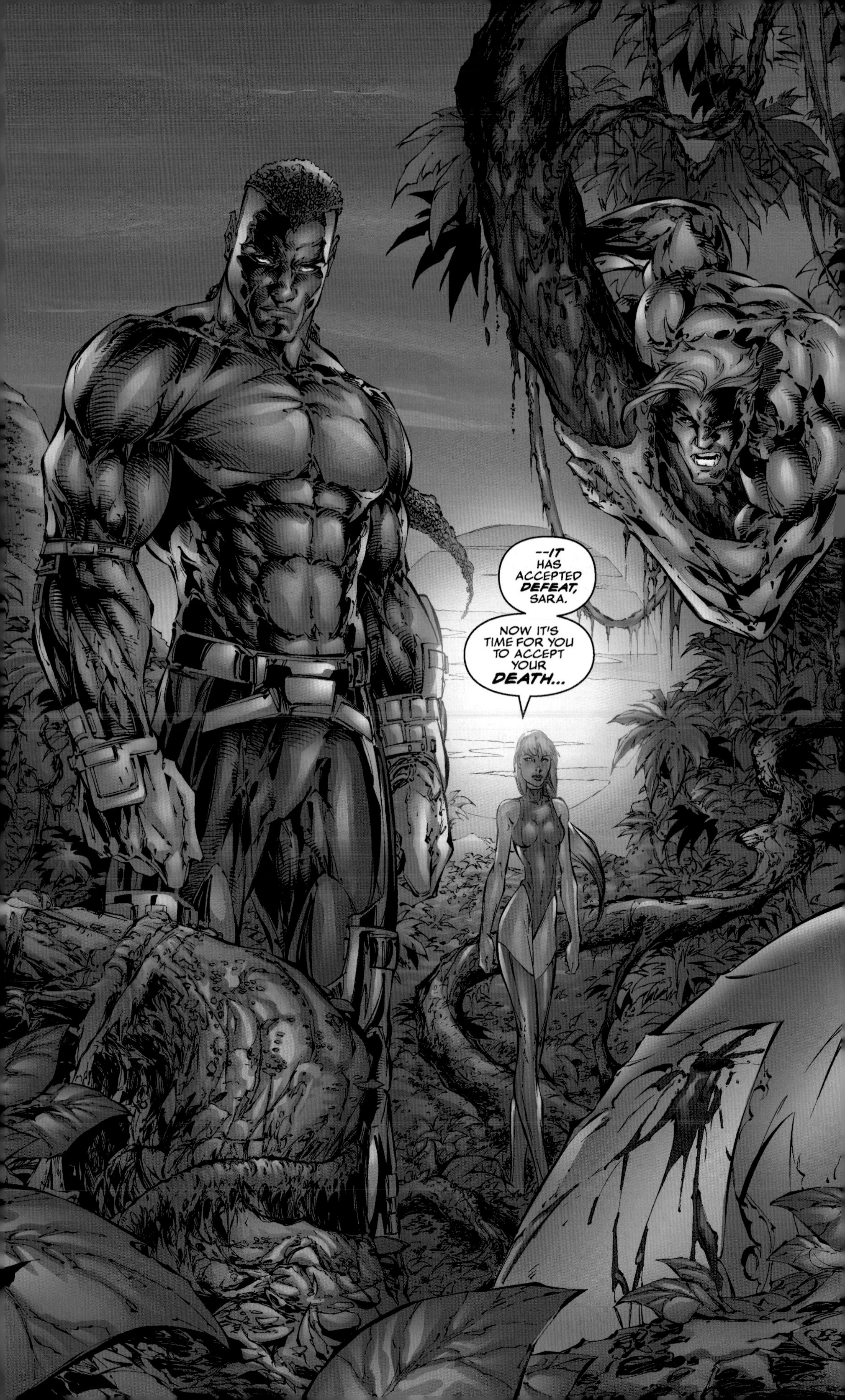
--IT HAS ACCEPTED DEFEAT, SARA.
NOW IT'S TIME FOR YOU TO ACCEPT YOUR DEATH...

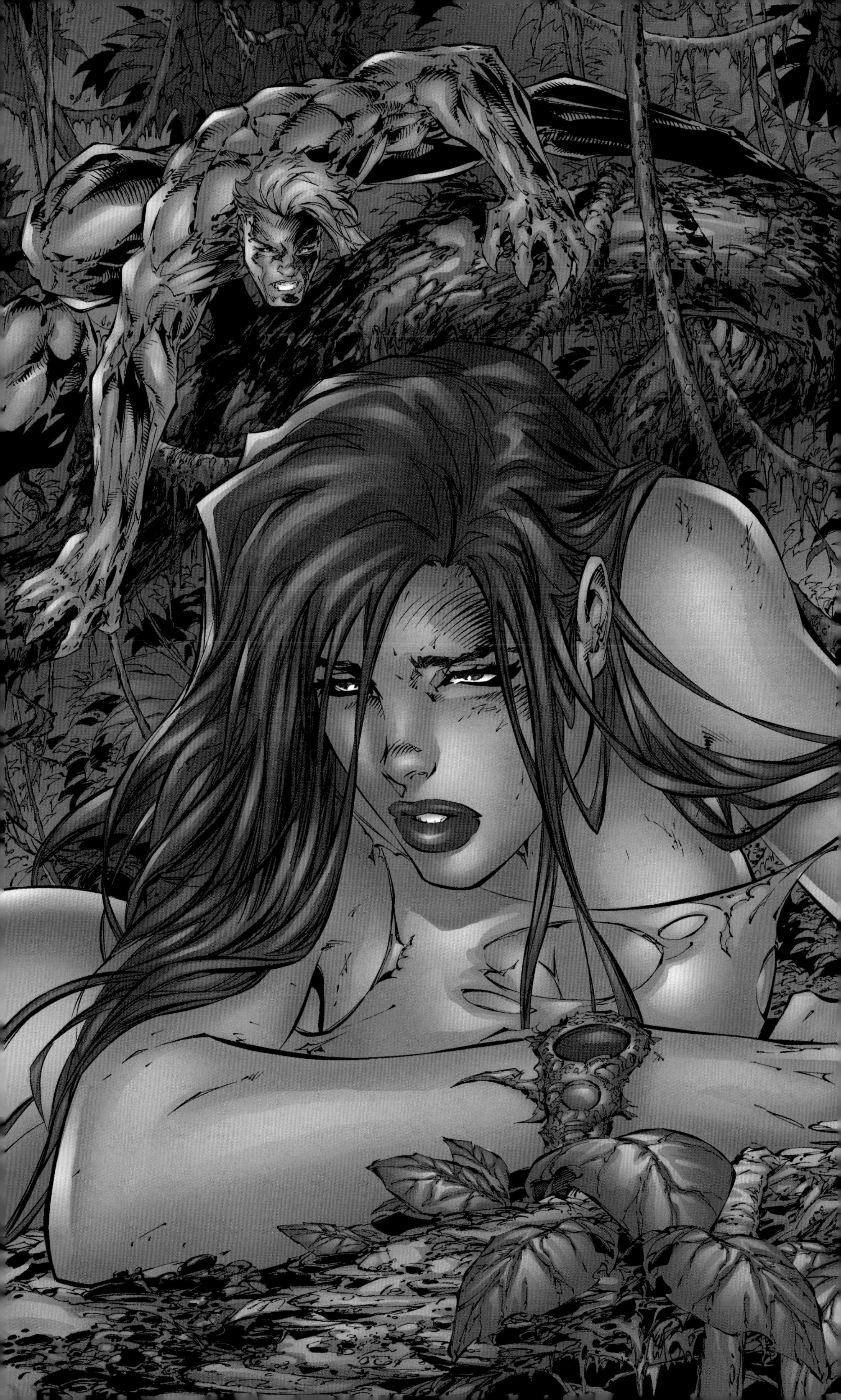

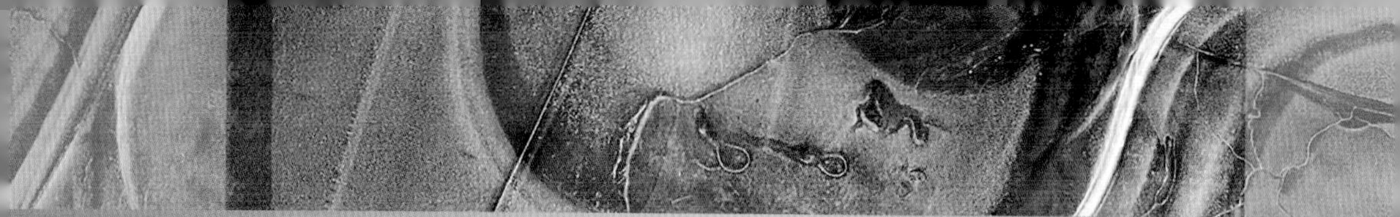

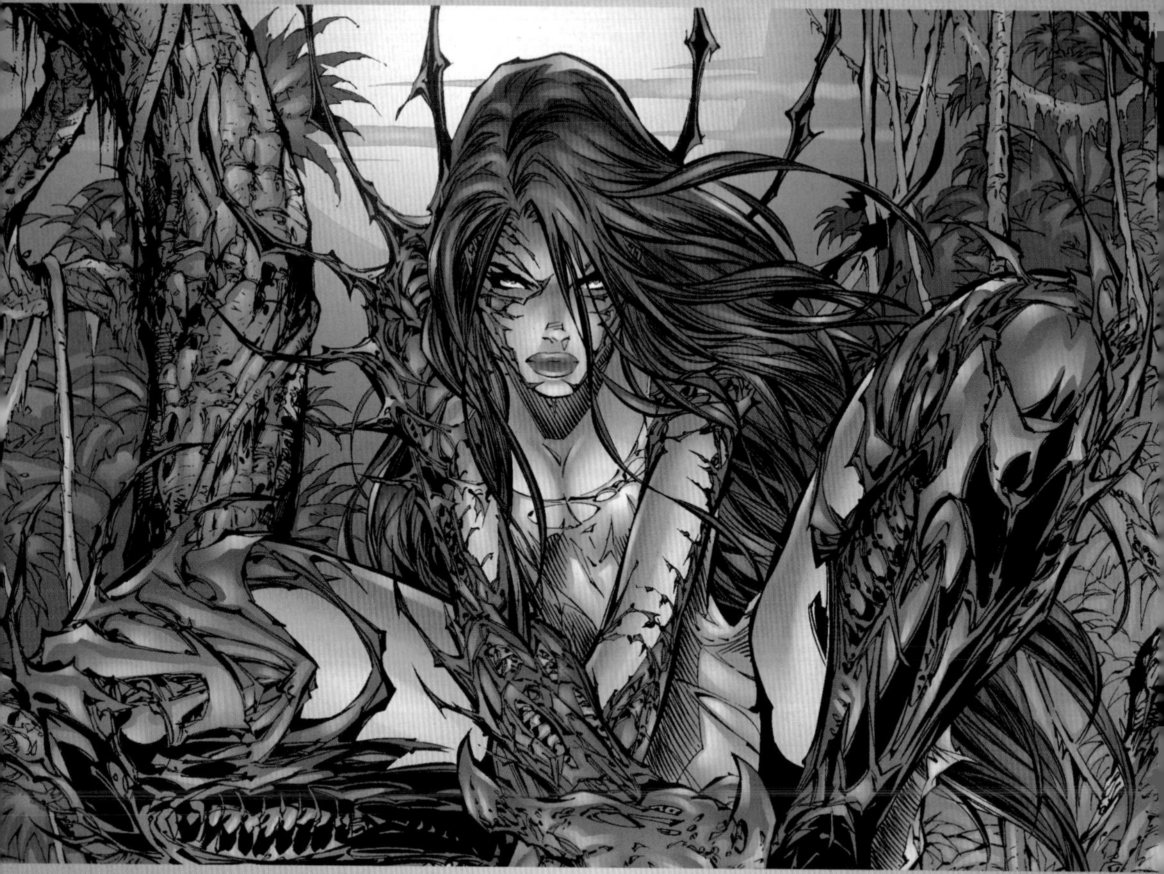

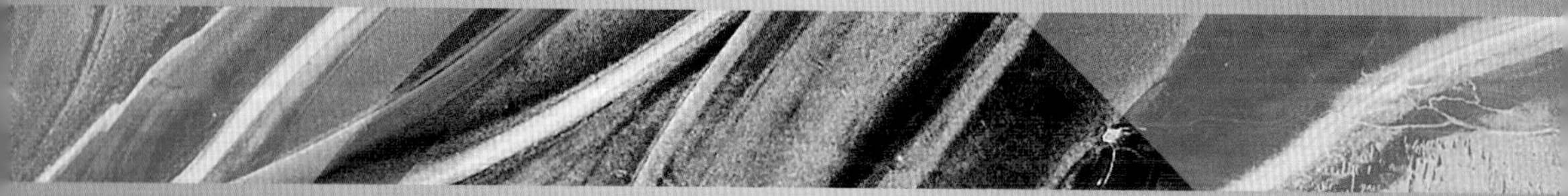

ISSUE #17

story: **David Wohl** and **Christina Z.**

pencils/co-plot: **Michael Turner**

inks: **D-Tron**

colors: **JD Smith**

ink assists: **Jeff De Los Santos, Jose "Jag" Guillen** and **Marsha Chen**

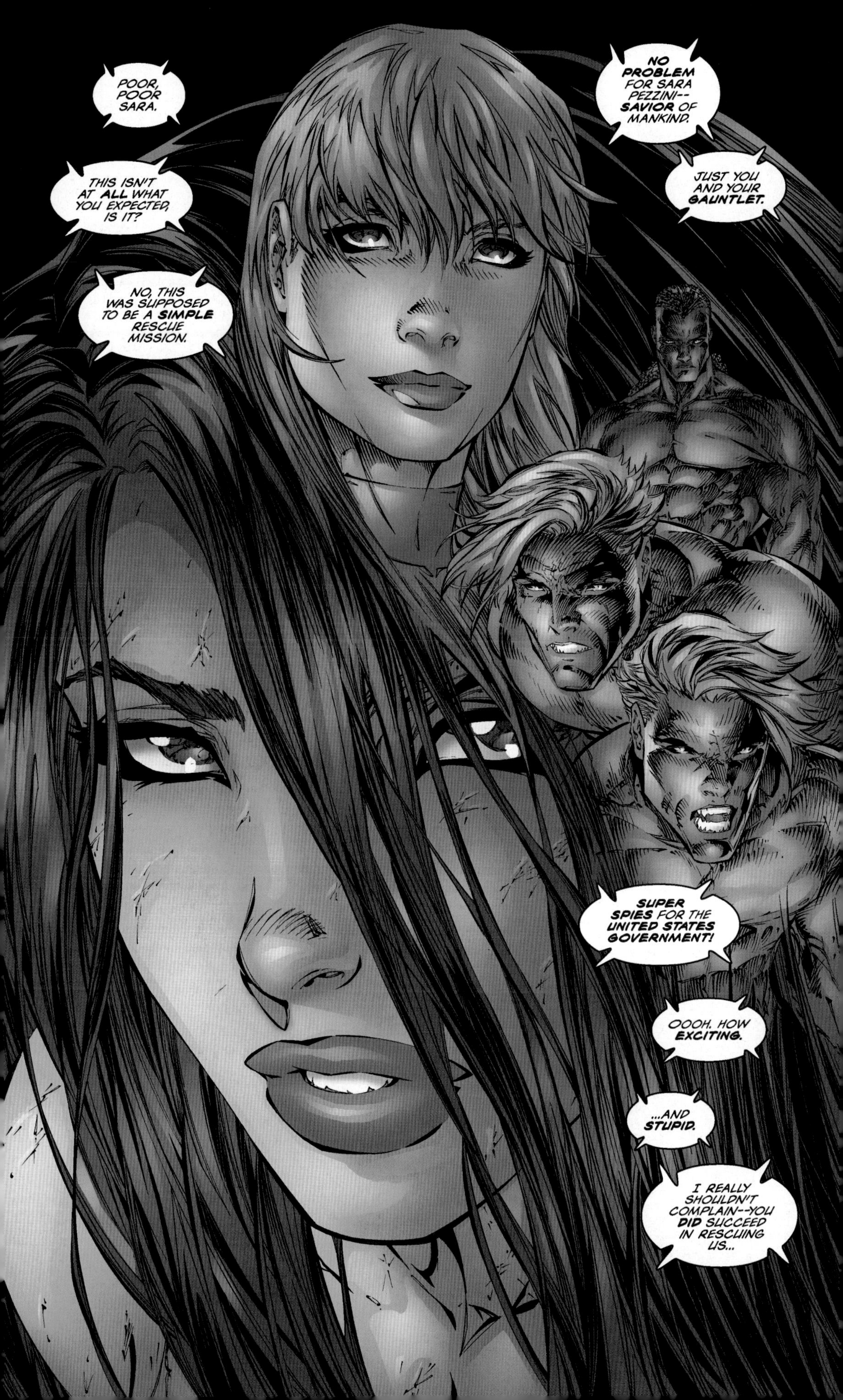
POOR, POOR SARA.
NO PROBLEM FOR SARA PEZZINI-- SAVIOR OF MANKIND.
THIS ISN'T AT ALL WHAT YOU EXPECTED, IS IT?
JUST YOU AND YOUR GAUNTLET.
NO, THIS WAS SUPPOSED TO BE A SIMPLE RESCUE MISSION.
SUPER SPIES FOR THE UNITED STATES GOVERNMENT!
OOOH, HOW EXCITING.
...AND STUPID.
I REALLY SHOULDN'T COMPLAIN--YOU DID SUCCEED IN RESCUING US...

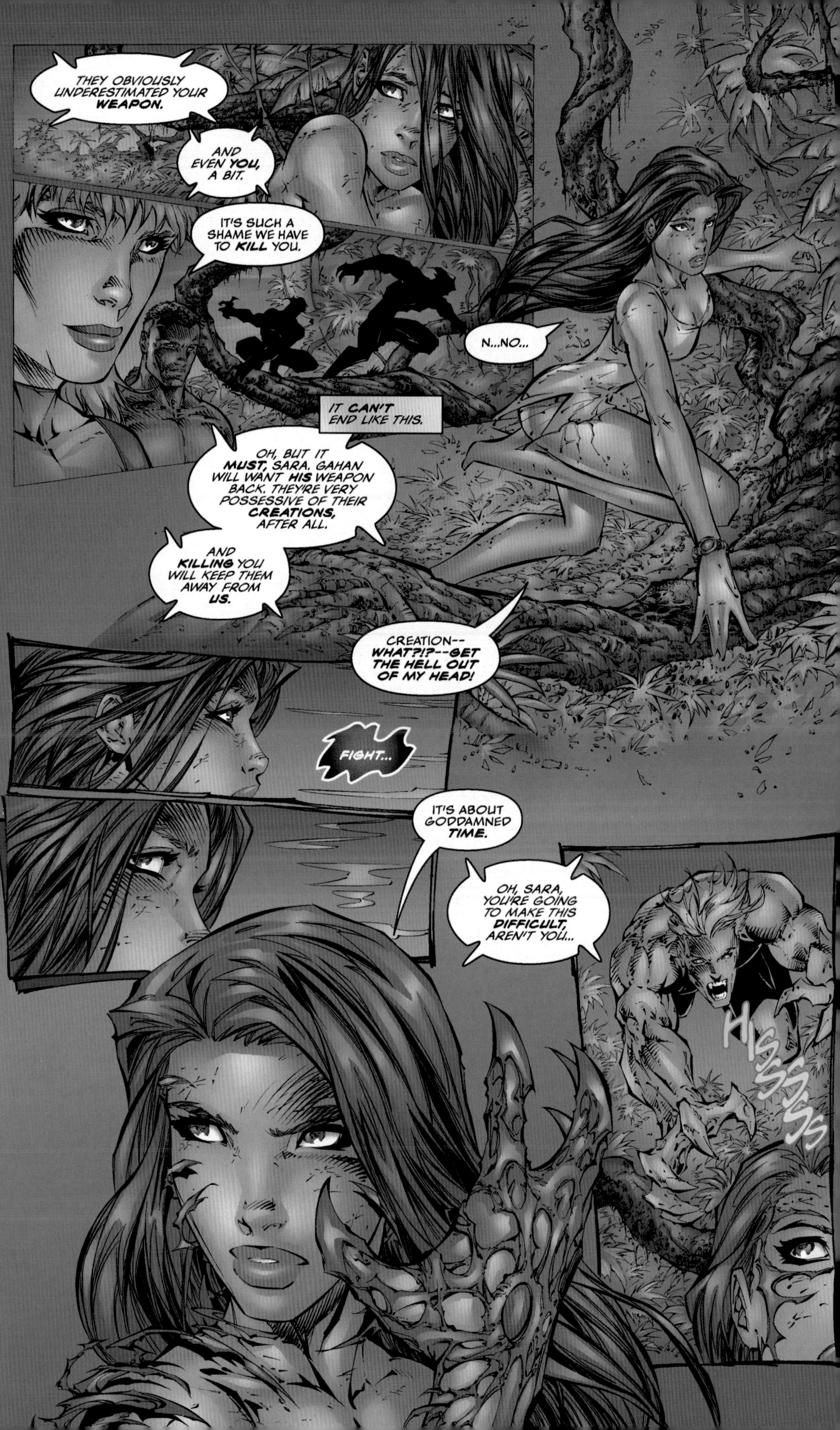
THEY OBVIOUSLY UNDERESTIMATED YOUR **WEAPON.**
AND EVEN **YOU,** A BIT.
IT'S SUCH A SHAME WE HAVE TO **KILL** YOU.
N...NO...
IT **CAN'T** END LIKE THIS.
OH, BUT IT **MUST,** SARA. GAHAN WILL WANT **HIS** WEAPON BACK. THEY'RE VERY POSSESSIVE OF THEIR **CREATIONS,** AFTER ALL.
AND **KILLING** YOU WILL KEEP THEM AWAY FROM **US.**
CREATION-- **WHAT?!?--GET THE HELL OUT OF MY HEAD!**
FIGHT...
IT'S ABOUT GODDAMNED **TIME.**
OH, SARA, YOU'RE GOING TO MAKE THIS **DIFFICULT,** AREN'T YOU...
HISSSSS

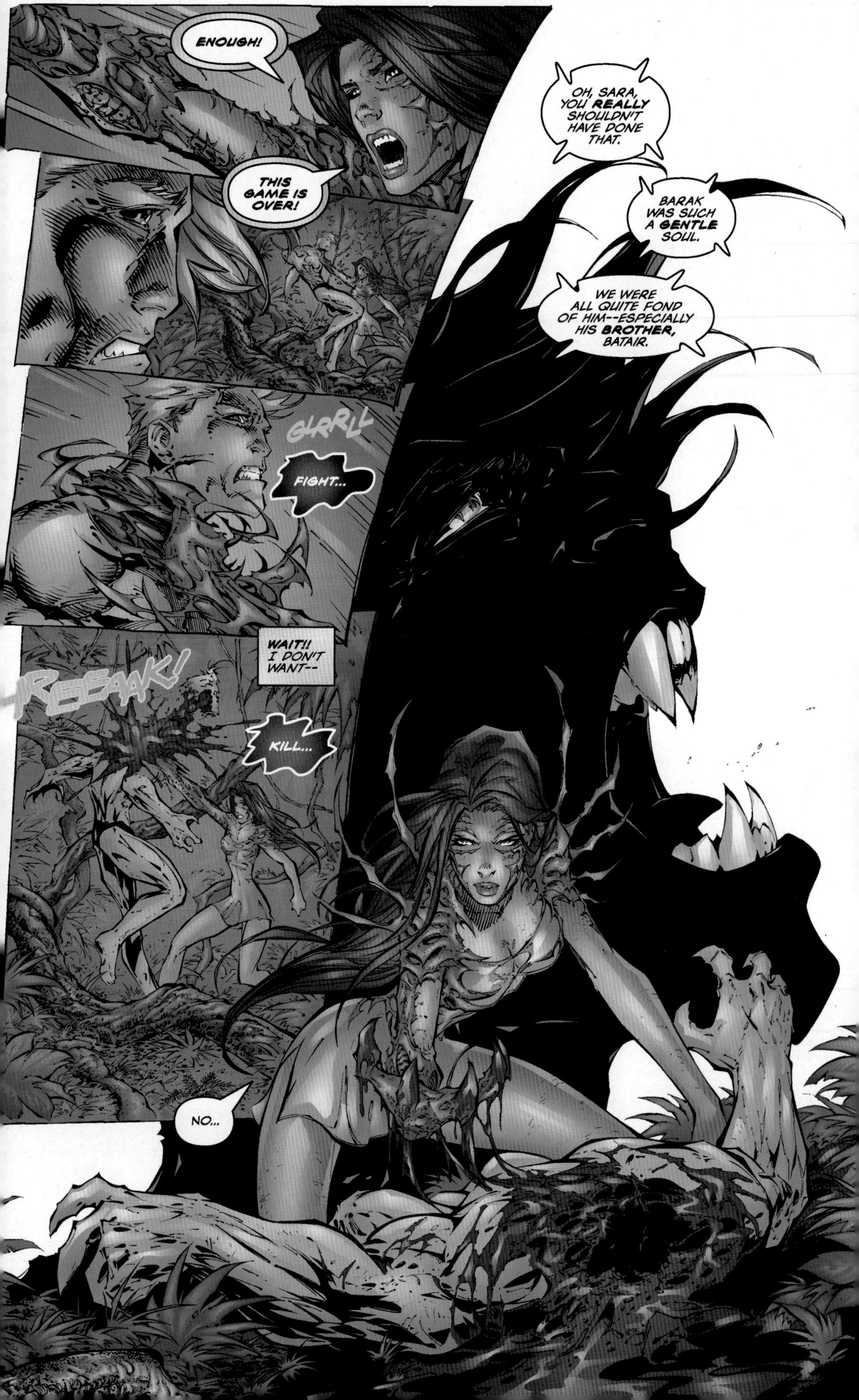
ENOUGH!
THIS GAME IS OVER!
OH, SARA, YOU REALLY SHOULDN'T HAVE DONE THAT.
BARAK WAS SUCH A GENTLE SOUL.
WE WERE ALL QUITE FOND OF HIM--ESPECIALLY HIS BROTHER, BATAIR.
GLRRLL
FIGHT...
WAIT!! I DON'T WANT--
RREEAAK!
KILL...
NO...

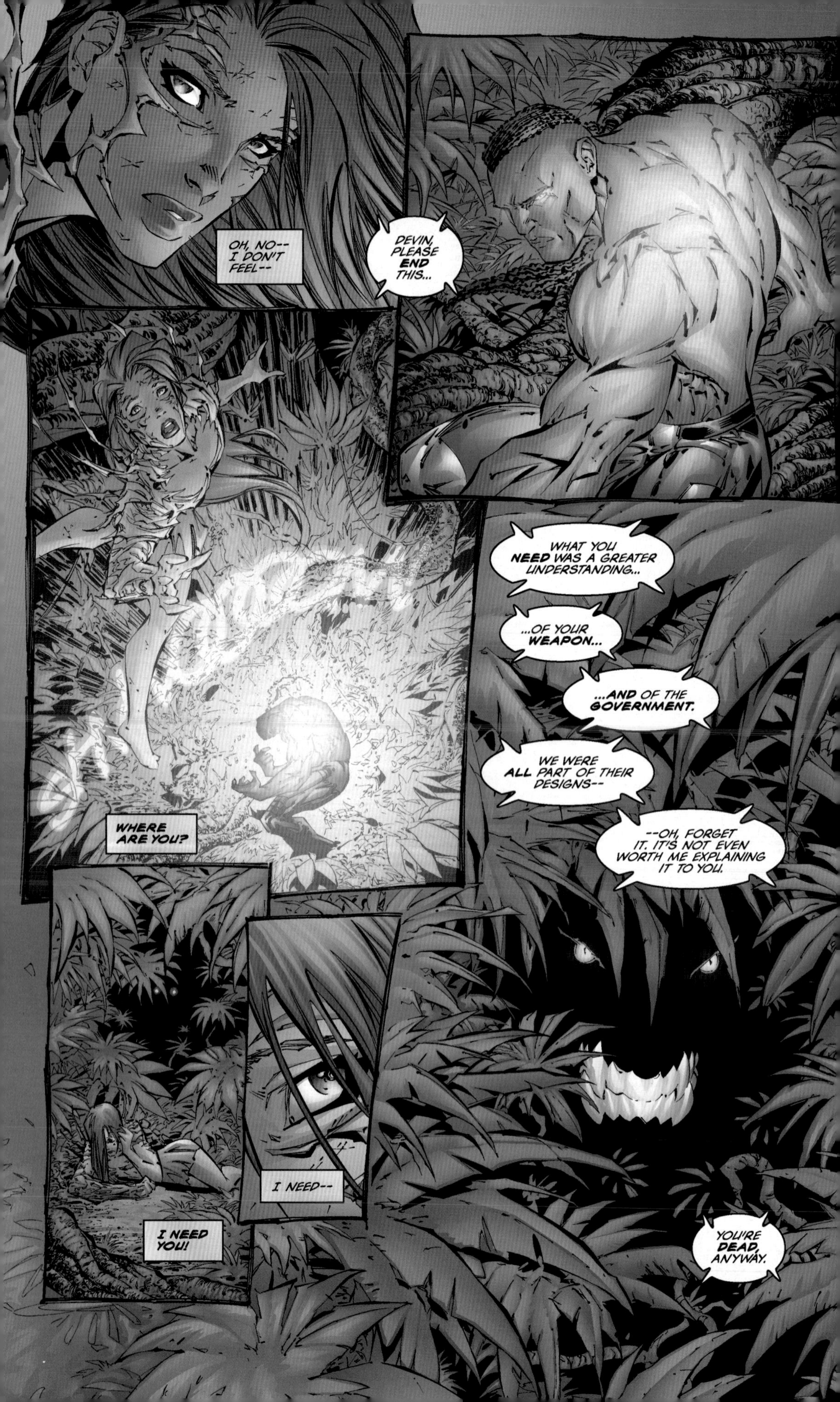

OH, NO-- I DON'T FEEL--
DEVIN, PLEASE END THIS...
WHERE ARE YOU?
WHAT YOU NEED WAS A GREATER UNDERSTANDING...
...OF YOUR WEAPON...
...AND OF THE GOVERNMENT.
WE WERE ALL PART OF THEIR DESIGNS--
--OH, FORGET IT. IT'S NOT EVEN WORTH ME EXPLAINING IT TO YOU.
I NEED--
I NEED YOU!
YOU'RE DEAD, ANYWAY.

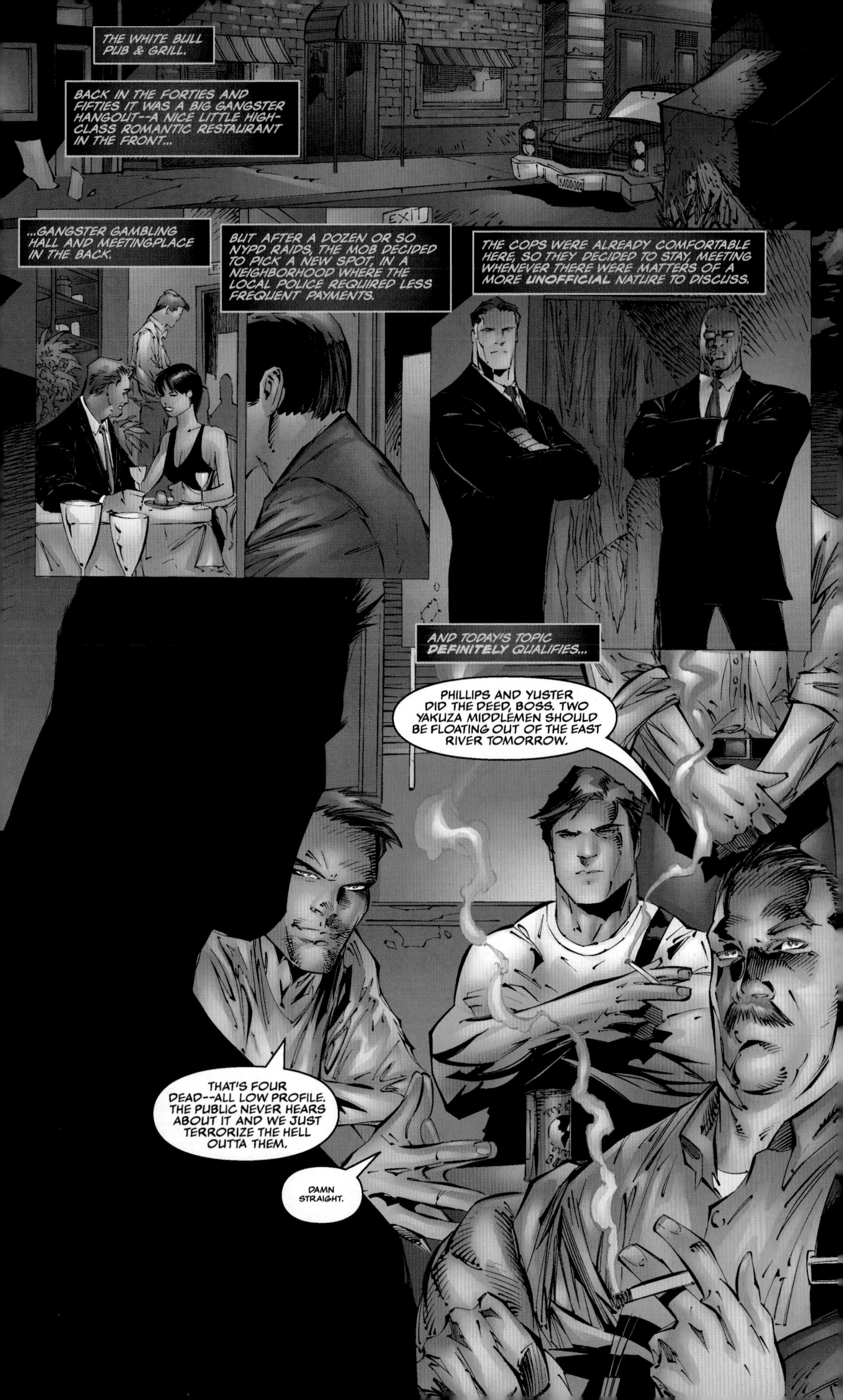
THE WHITE BULL PUB & GRILL.
BACK IN THE FORTIES AND FIFTIES IT WAS A BIG GANGSTER HANGOUT--A NICE LITTLE HIGH-CLASS ROMANTIC RESTAURANT IN THE FRONT...
EXIT
...GANGSTER GAMBLING HALL AND MEETINGPLACE IN THE BACK.
BUT AFTER A DOZEN OR SO NYPD RAIDS, THE MOB DECIDED TO PICK A NEW SPOT, IN A NEIGHBORHOOD WHERE THE LOCAL POLICE REQUIRED LESS FREQUENT PAYMENTS.
THE COPS WERE ALREADY COMFORTABLE HERE, SO THEY DECIDED TO STAY, MEETING WHENEVER THERE WERE MATTERS OF A MORE UNOFFICIAL NATURE TO DISCUSS.
AND TODAY'S TOPIC DEFINITELY QUALIFIES...
PHILLIPS AND YUSTER DID THE DEED, BOSS. TWO YAKUZA MIDDLEMEN SHOULD BE FLOATING OUT OF THE EAST RIVER TOMORROW.
THAT'S FOUR DEAD--ALL LOW PROFILE. THE PUBLIC NEVER HEARS ABOUT IT AND WE JUST TERRORIZE THE HELL OUTTA THEM.
DAMN STRAIGHT.

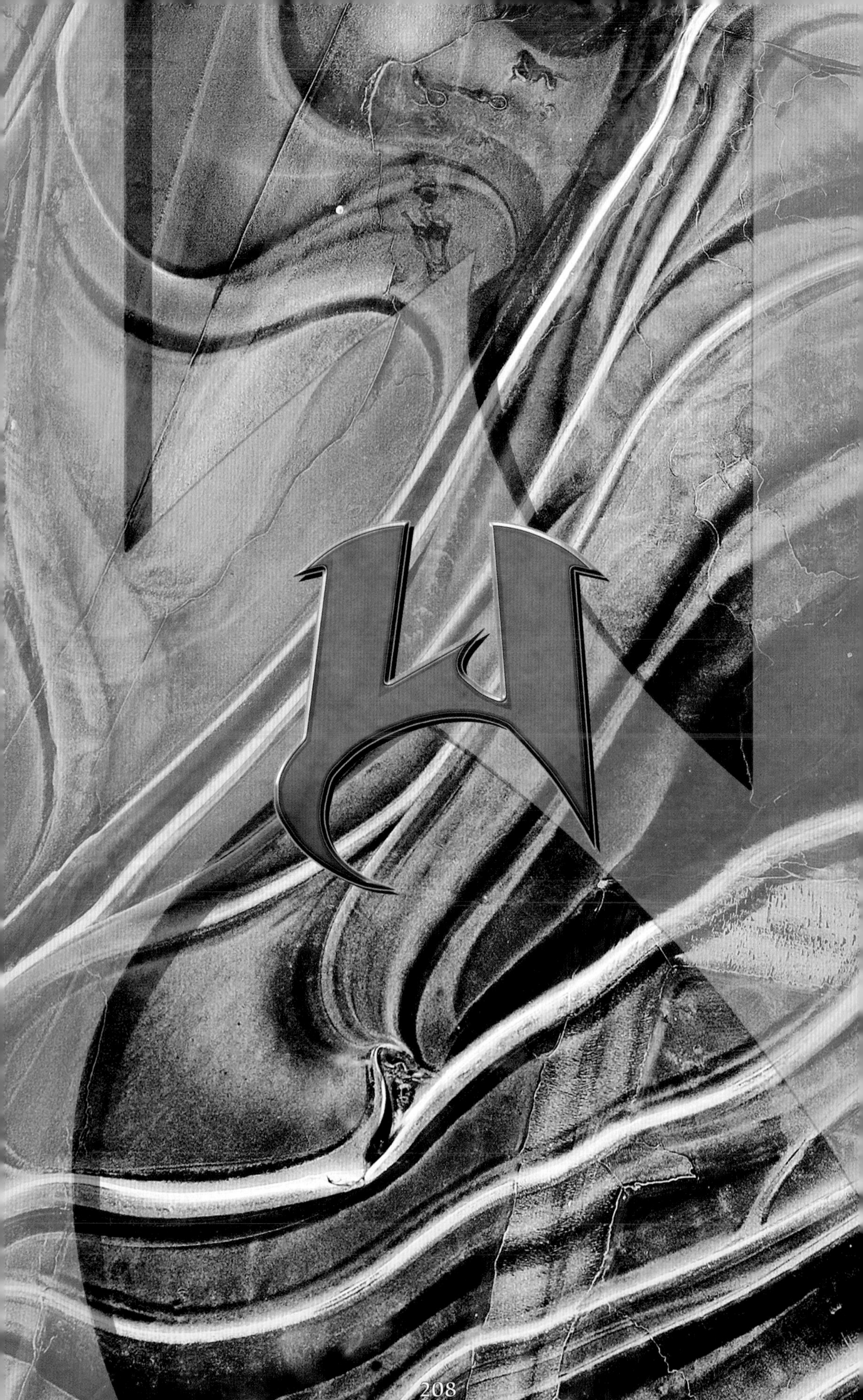

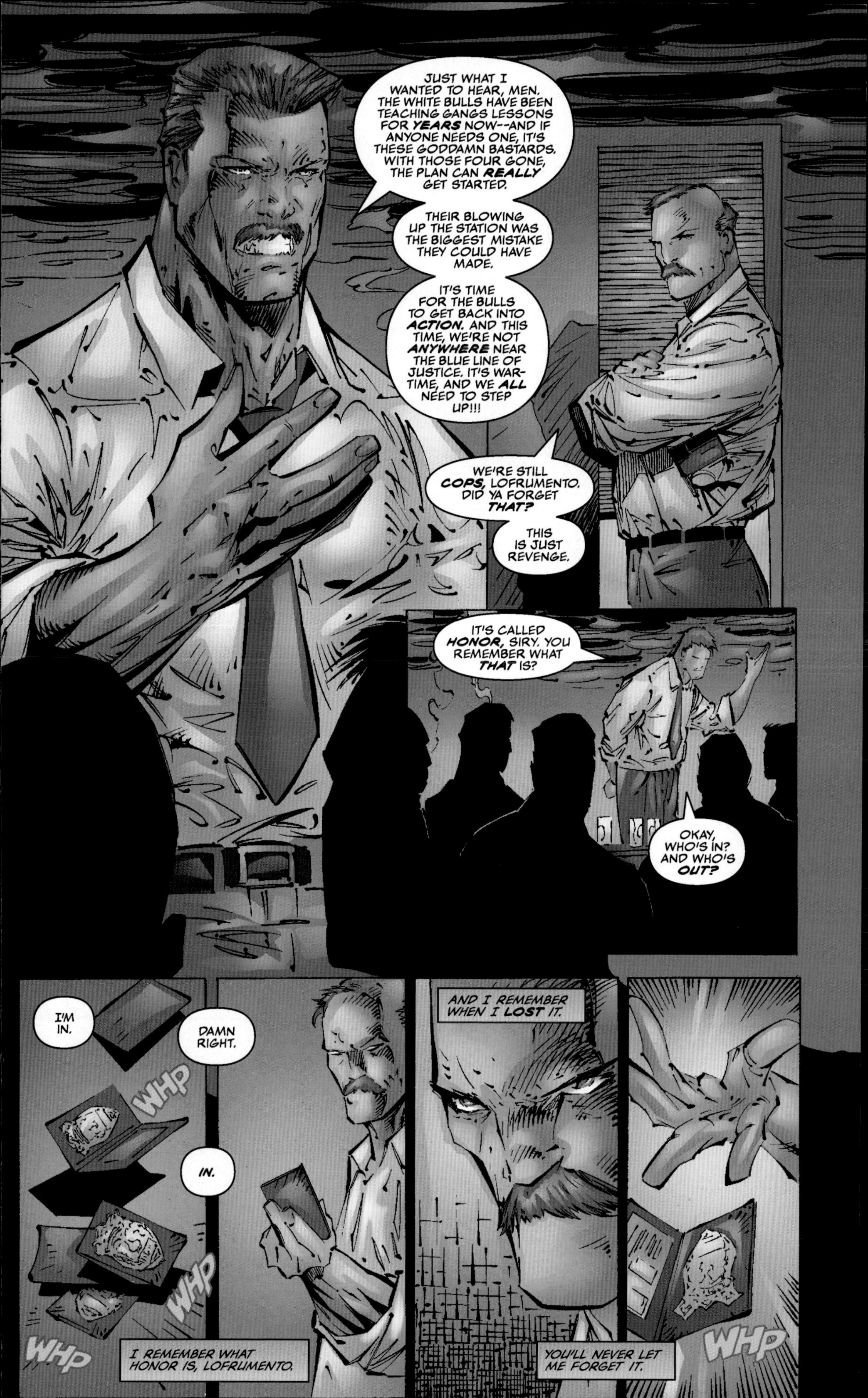

JUST WHAT I WANTED TO HEAR, MEN. THE WHITE BULLS HAVE BEEN TEACHING GANGS LESSONS FOR YEARS NOW--AND IF ANYONE NEEDS ONE, IT'S THESE GODDAMN BASTARDS. WITH THOSE FOUR GONE, THE PLAN CAN REALLY GET STARTED.
THEIR BLOWING UP THE STATION WAS THE BIGGEST MISTAKE THEY COULD HAVE MADE.
IT'S TIME FOR THE BULLS TO GET BACK INTO ACTION. AND THIS TIME, WE'RE NOT ANYWHERE NEAR THE BLUE LINE OF JUSTICE. IT'S WAR-TIME, AND WE ALL NEED TO STEP UP!!!
WE'RE STILL COPS, LOFRUMENTO. DID YA FORGET THAT?
THIS IS JUST REVENGE.
IT'S CALLED HONOR, SIRY. YOU REMEMBER WHAT THAT IS?
OKAY, WHO'S IN? AND WHO'S OUT?
I'M IN.
DAMN RIGHT.
WHP
IN.
WHP
WHP
I REMEMBER WHAT HONOR IS, LOFRUMENTO.
AND I REMEMBER WHEN I LOST IT.
YOU'LL NEVER LET ME FORGET IT.
WHP

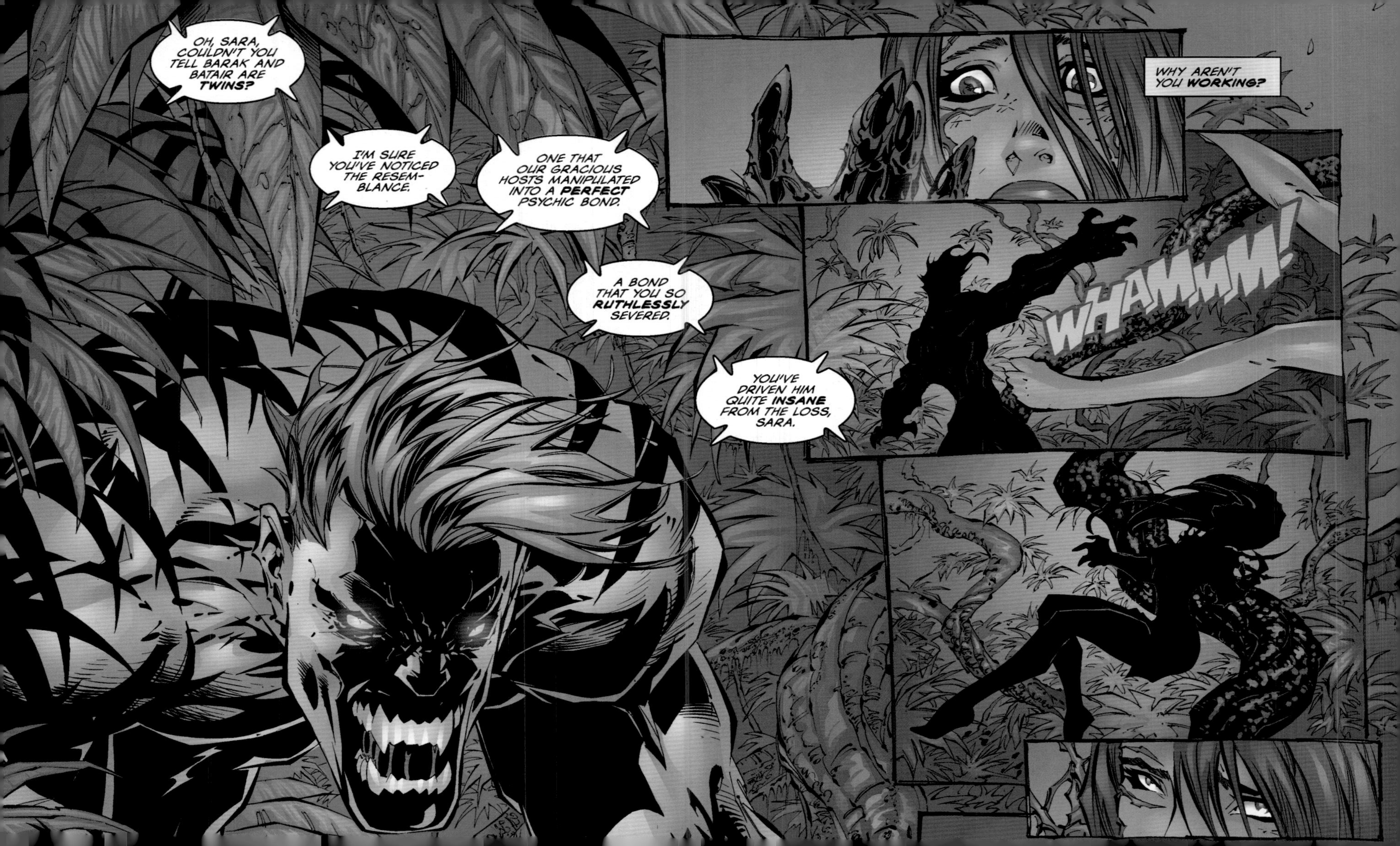
OH, SARA, COULDN'T YOU TELL BARAK AND BATAIR ARE **TWINS?**
I'M SURE YOU'VE NOTICED THE RESEM-BLANCE.
ONE THAT OUR GRACIOUS HOSTS MANIPULATED INTO A **PERFECT** PSYCHIC BOND.
A BOND THAT YOU SO **RUTHLESSLY** SEVERED.
YOU'VE DRIVEN HIM QUITE **INSANE** FROM THE LOSS, SARA.
WHY AREN'T YOU **WORKING?**
WHAMMM!

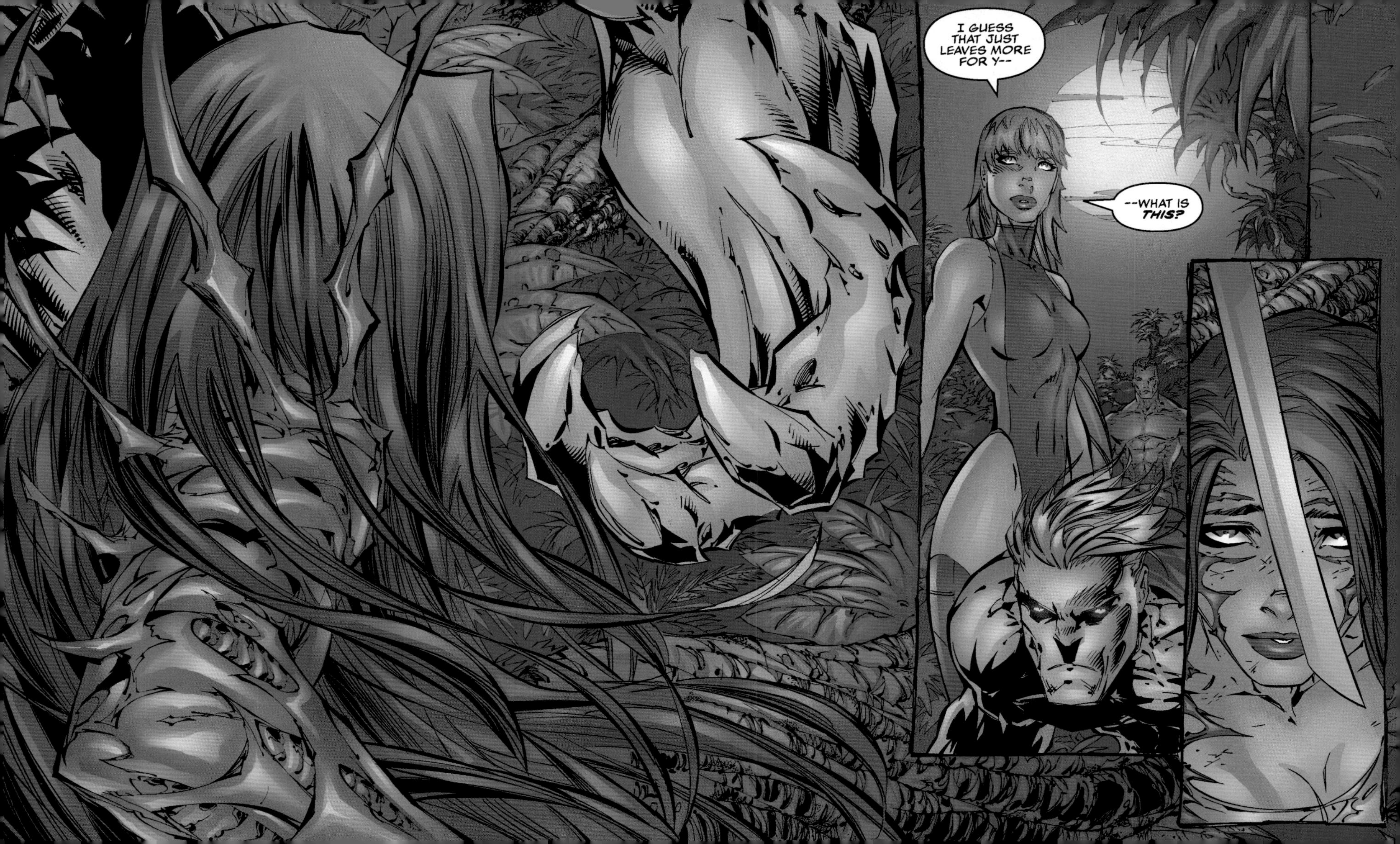
I GUESS THAT JUST LEAVES MORE FOR Y--
--WHAT IS *THIS?*

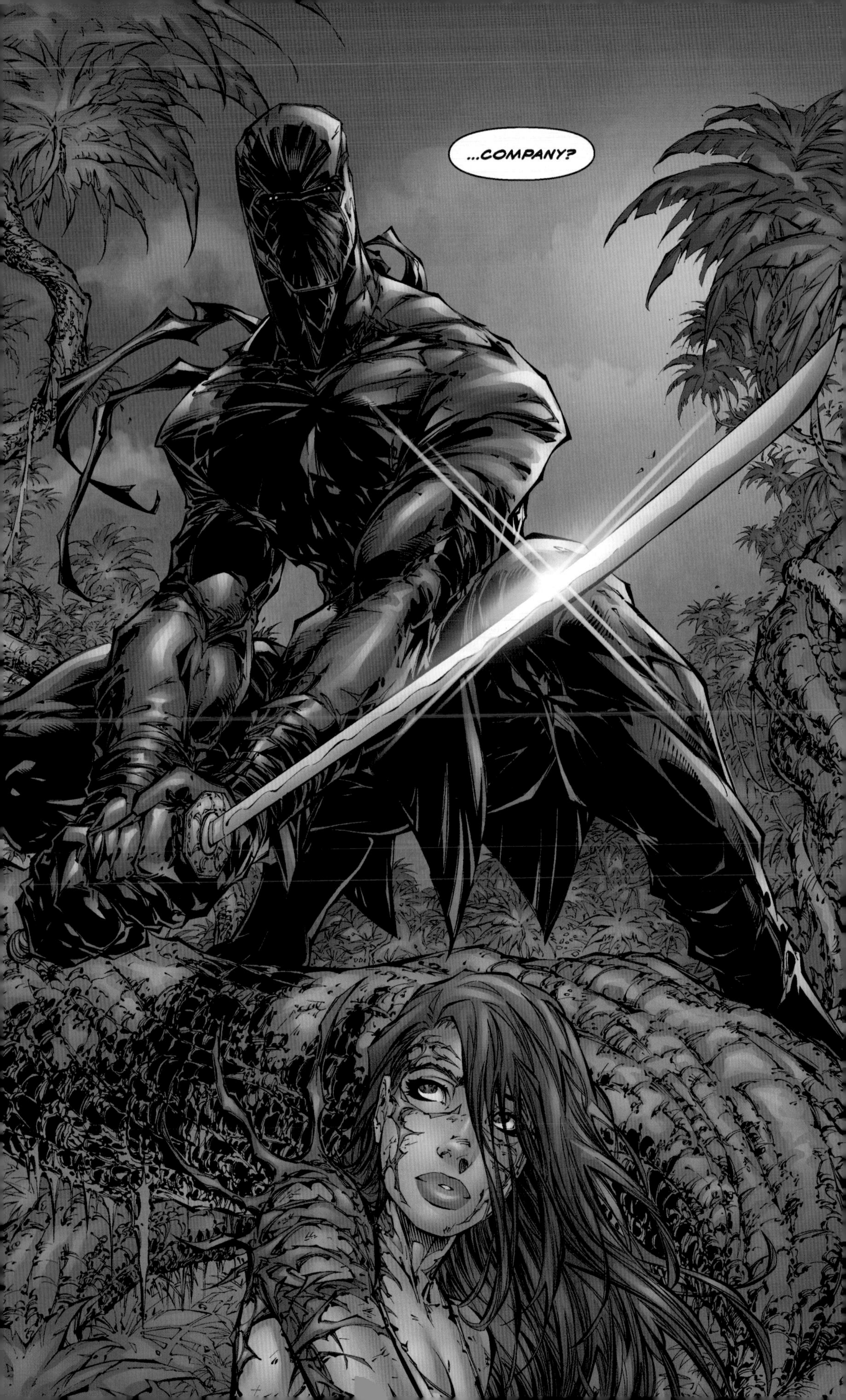
...COMPANY?

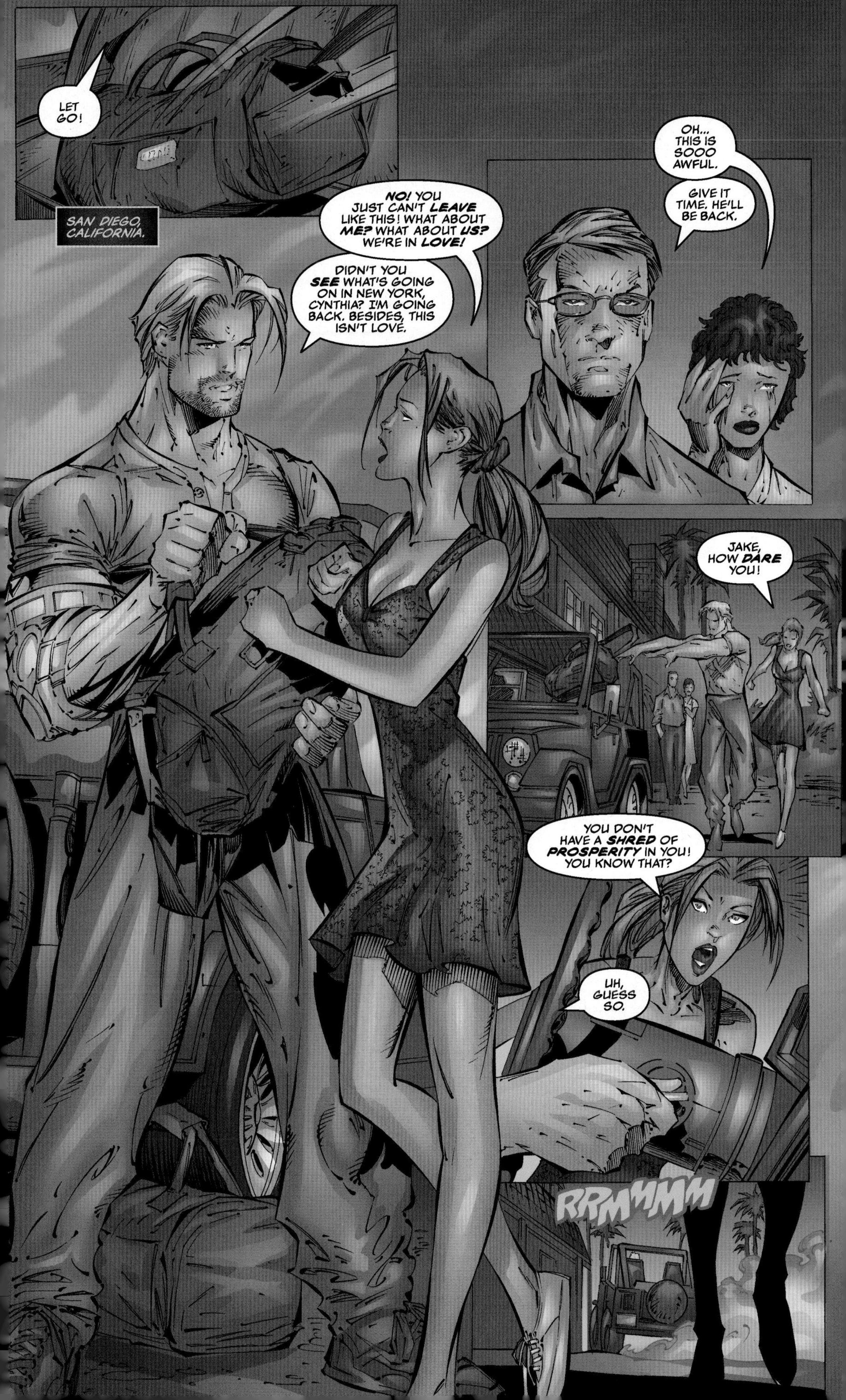
LET GO!
SAN DIEGO, CALIFORNIA.
NO! YOU JUST CAN'T LEAVE LIKE THIS! WHAT ABOUT ME? WHAT ABOUT US? WE'RE IN LOVE!
DIDN'T YOU SEE WHAT'S GOING ON IN NEW YORK, CYNTHIA? I'M GOING BACK. BESIDES, THIS ISN'T LOVE.
OH... THIS IS SOOO AWFUL.
GIVE IT TIME. HE'LL BE BACK.
JAKE, HOW DARE YOU!
YOU DON'T HAVE A SHRED OF PROSPERITY IN YOU! YOU KNOW THAT?
UH, GUESS SO.
RRMMMM

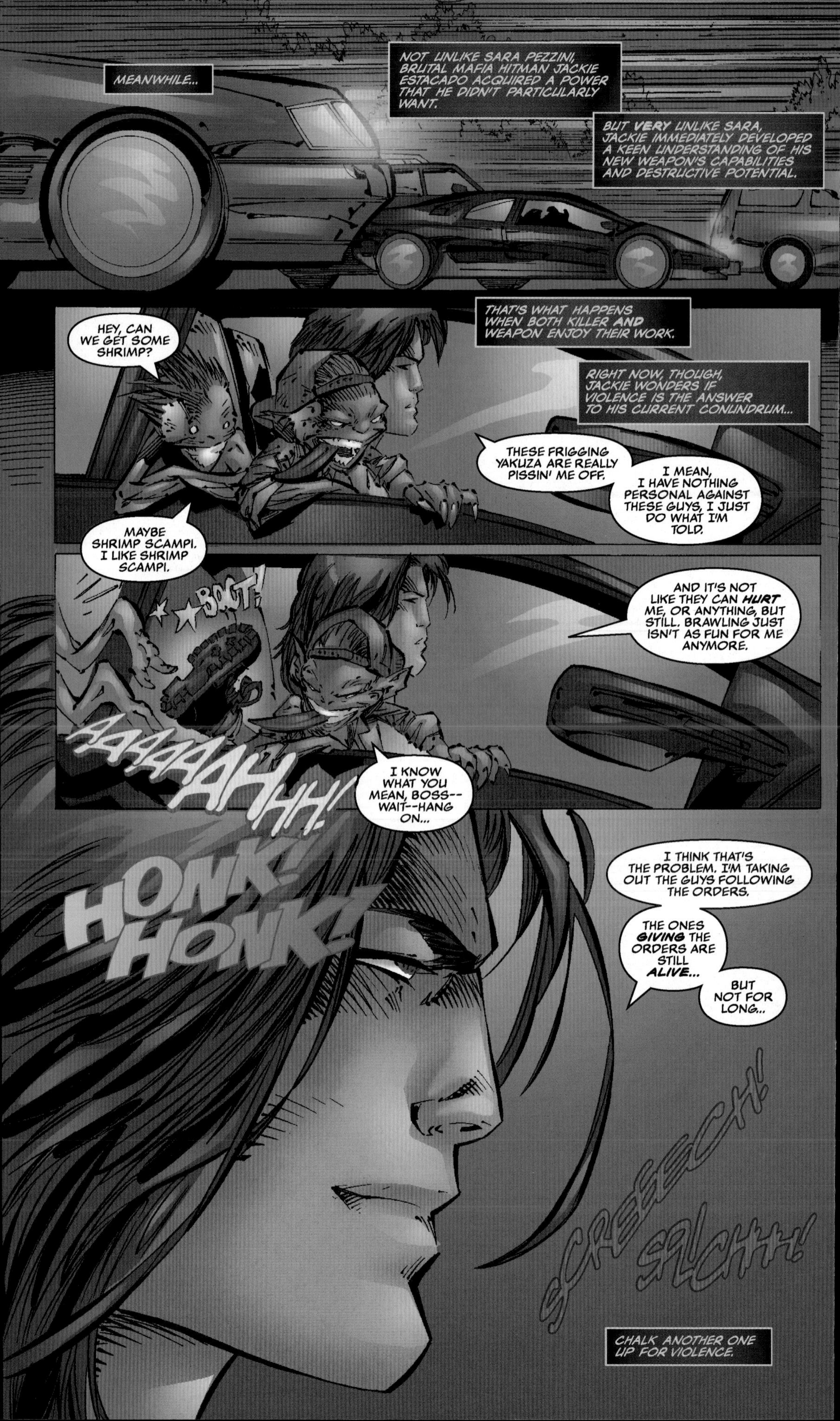
MEANWHILE...
NOT UNLIKE SARA PEZZINI, BRUTAL MAFIA HITMAN JACKIE ESTACADO ACQUIRED A POWER THAT HE DIDN'T PARTICULARLY WANT.
BUT VERY UNLIKE SARA, JACKIE IMMEDIATELY DEVELOPED A KEEN UNDERSTANDING OF HIS NEW WEAPON'S CAPABILITIES AND DESTRUCTIVE POTENTIAL.
THAT'S WHAT HAPPENS WHEN BOTH KILLER AND WEAPON ENJOY THEIR WORK.
HEY, CAN WE GET SOME SHRIMP?
RIGHT NOW, THOUGH, JACKIE WONDERS IF VIOLENCE IS THE ANSWER TO HIS CURRENT CONUNDRUM...
THESE FRIGGING YAKUZA ARE REALLY PISSIN' ME OFF.
I MEAN, I HAVE NOTHING PERSONAL AGAINST THESE GUYS, I JUST DO WHAT I'M TOLD.
MAYBE SHRIMP SCAMPI. I LIKE SHRIMP SCAMPI.
BOOT!
AND IT'S NOT LIKE THEY CAN HURT ME, OR ANYTHING, BUT STILL. BRAWLING JUST ISN'T AS FUN FOR ME ANYMORE.
AAAAAAHHH!
I KNOW WHAT YOU MEAN, BOSS-- WAIT--HANG ON...
HONK! HONK!
I THINK THAT'S THE PROBLEM. I'M TAKING OUT THE GUYS FOLLOWING THE ORDERS.
THE ONES GIVING THE ORDERS ARE STILL ALIVE...
BUT NOT FOR LONG...
SCREEEECH!
SPLCHH!
CHALK ANOTHER ONE UP FOR VIOLENCE.

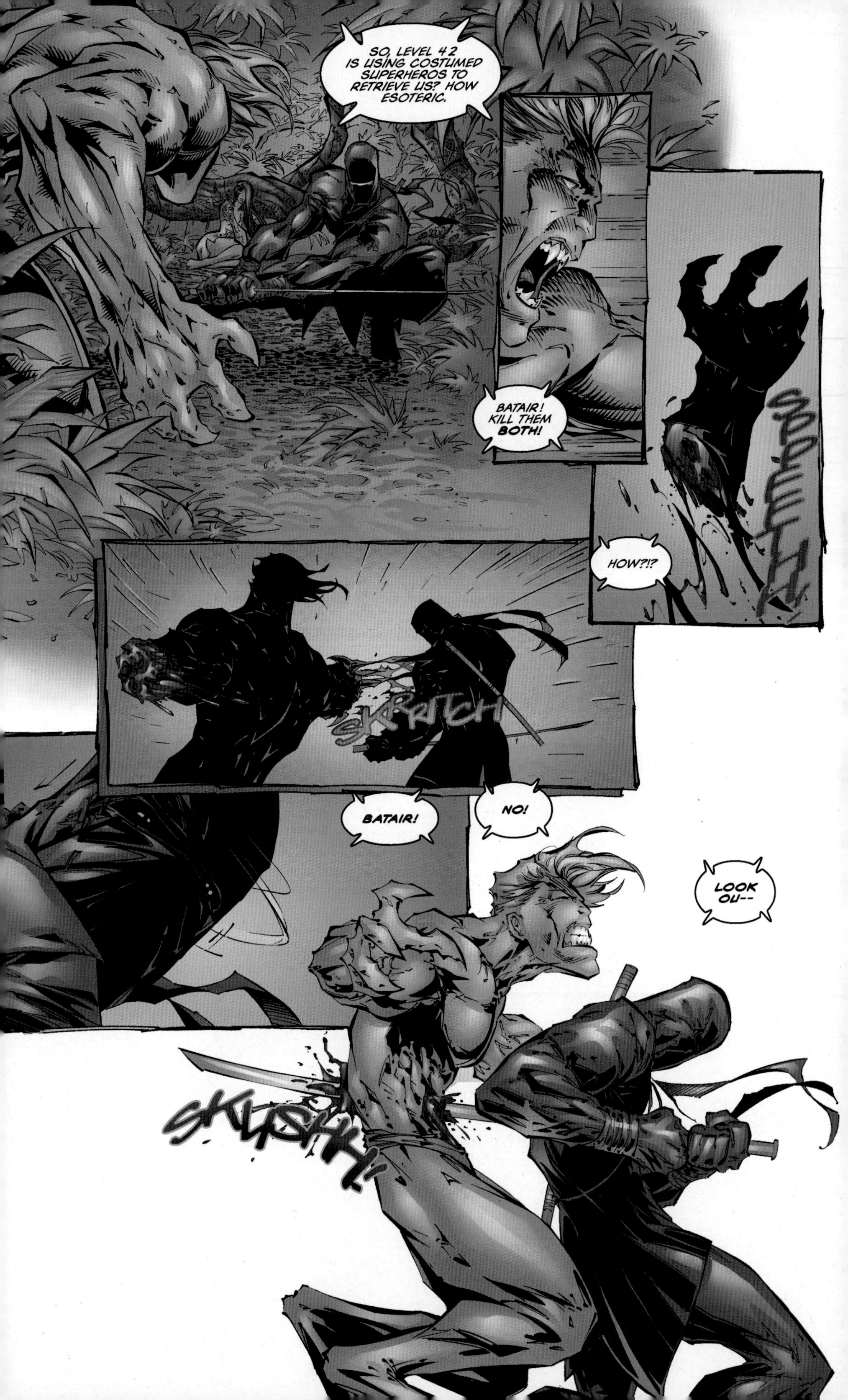
SO, LEVEL 42 IS USING COSTUMED SUPERHEROS TO RETRIEVE US? HOW ESOTERIC.
BATAIR! KILL THEM BOTH!
SPPEEHH
HOW?!?
SKRRITCH
BATAIR!
NO!
LOOK OU--
SKLSHH!

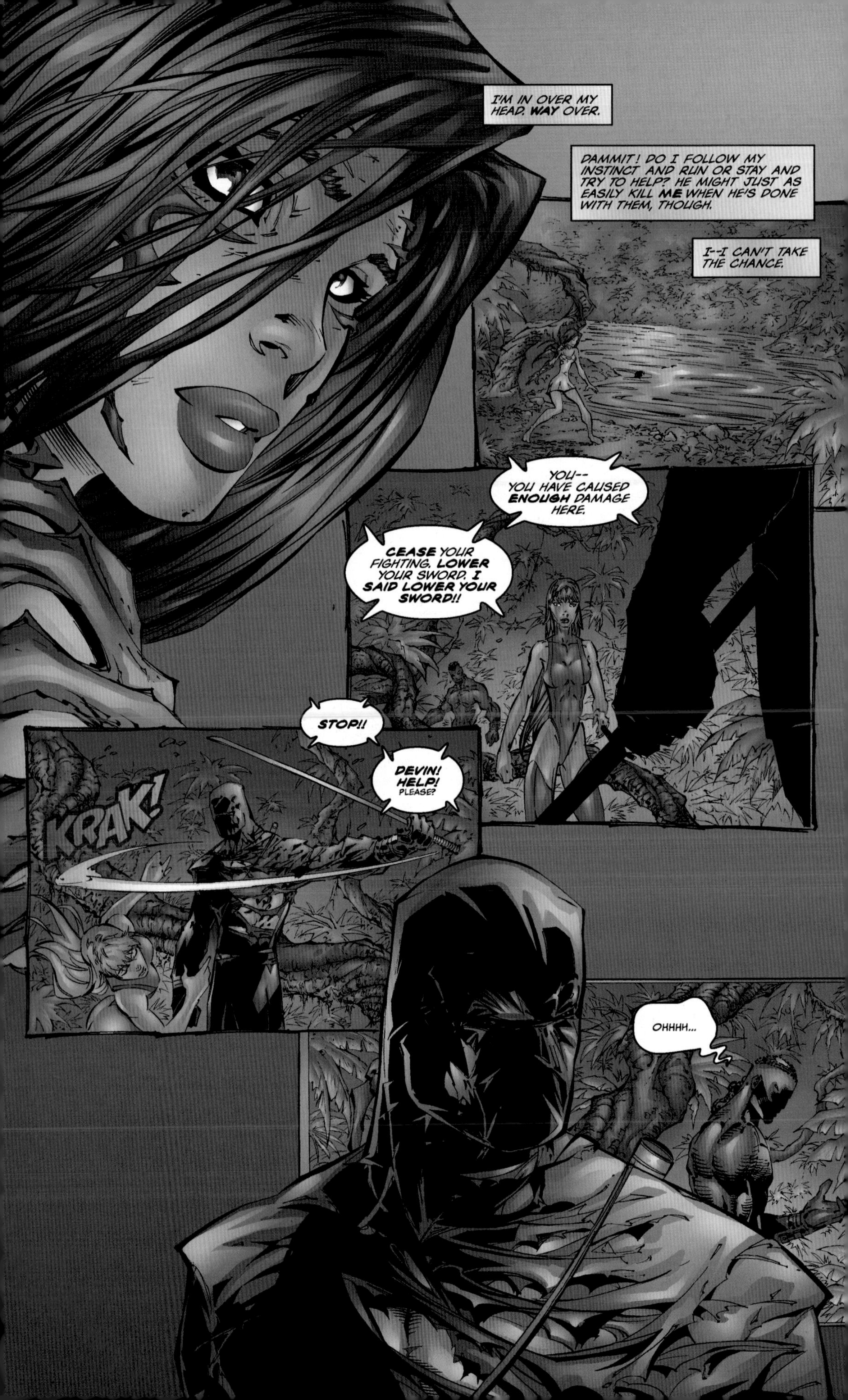
I'M IN OVER MY HEAD. **WAY** OVER.
DAMMIT! DO I FOLLOW MY INSTINCT AND RUN OR STAY AND TRY TO HELP? HE MIGHT JUST AS EASILY KILL **ME** WHEN HE'S DONE WITH THEM, THOUGH.
I--I CAN'T TAKE THE CHANCE.
YOU-- YOU HAVE CAUSED **ENOUGH** DAMAGE HERE.
CEASE YOUR FIGHTING. **LOWER** YOUR SWORD. **I SAID LOWER YOUR SWORD!!**
STOP!!
KRAK!
DEVIN! HELP! PLEASE?
OHHHH...

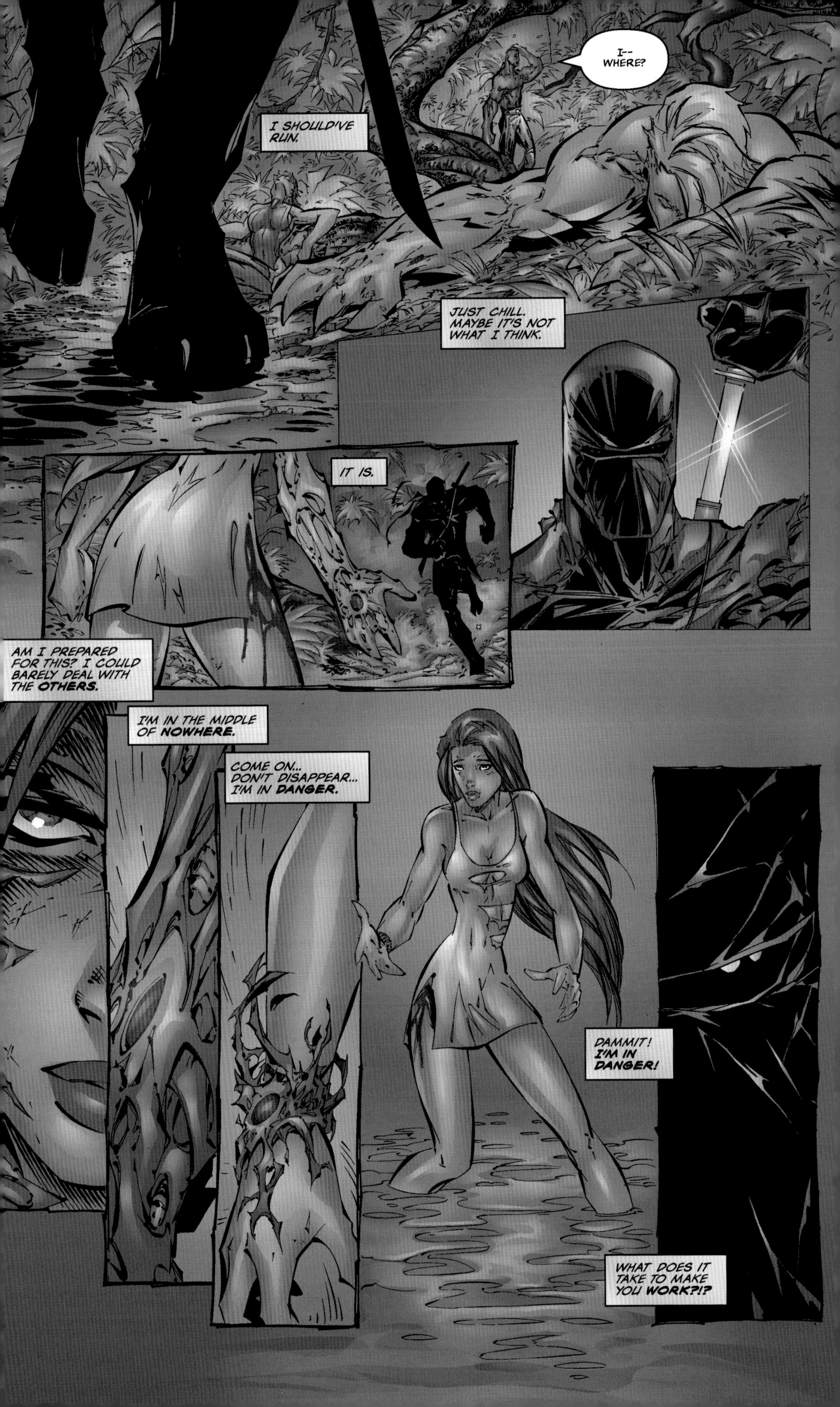
I SHOULD'VE RUN.
I-- WHERE?
JUST CHILL. MAYBE IT'S NOT WHAT I THINK.
IT IS.
AM I PREPARED FOR THIS? I COULD BARELY DEAL WITH THE OTHERS.
I'M IN THE MIDDLE OF NOWHERE.
COME ON... DON'T DISAPPEAR... I'M IN DANGER.
DAMMIT! I'M IN DANGER!
WHAT DOES IT TAKE TO MAKE YOU WORK?!?

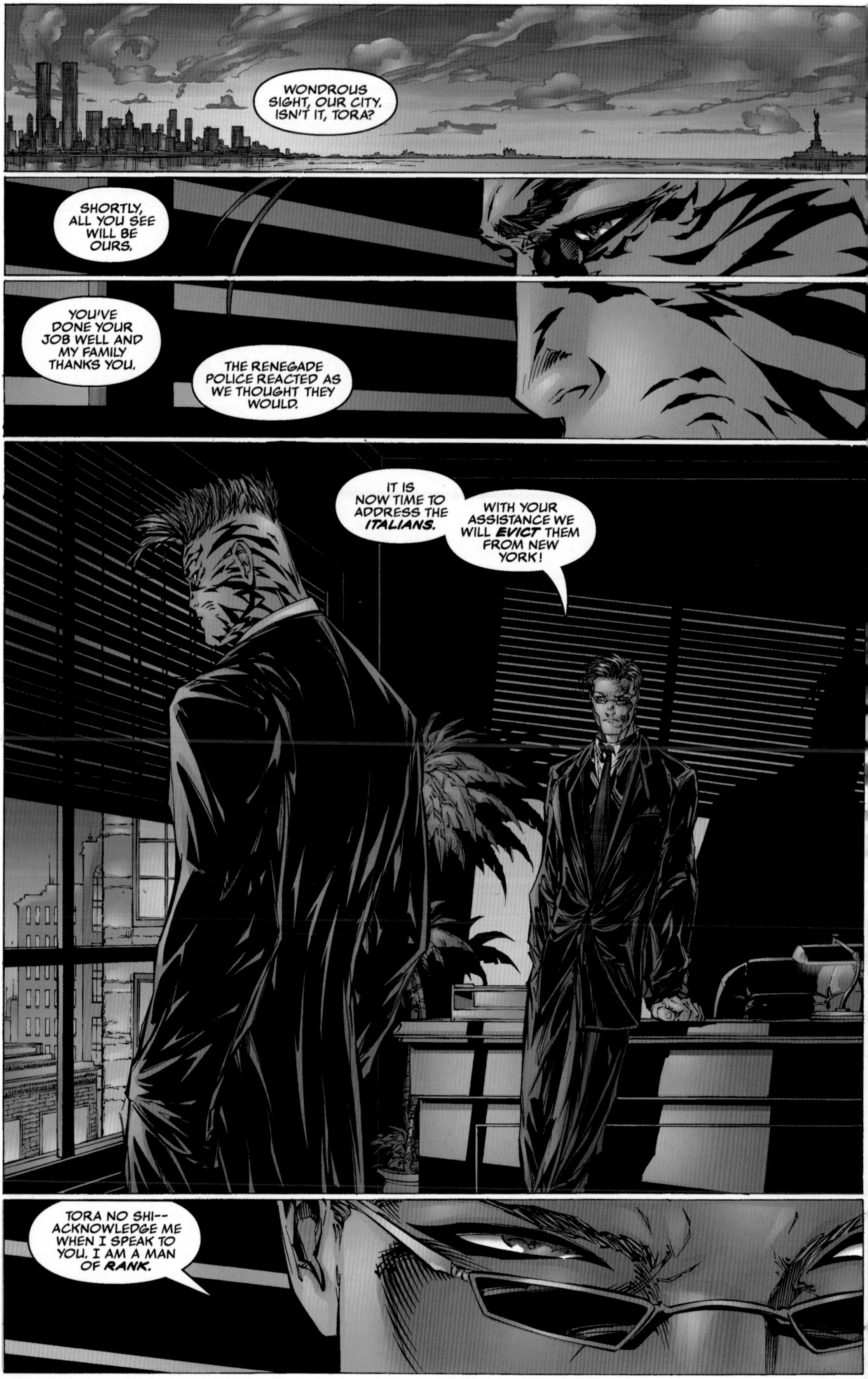
WONDROUS SIGHT, OUR CITY. ISN'T IT, TORA?
SHORTLY, ALL YOU SEE WILL BE OURS.
YOU'VE DONE YOUR JOB WELL AND MY FAMILY THANKS YOU.
THE RENEGADE POLICE REACTED AS WE THOUGHT THEY WOULD.
IT IS NOW TIME TO ADDRESS THE *ITALIANS.*
WITH YOUR ASSISTANCE WE WILL *EVICT* THEM FROM NEW YORK!
TORA NO SHI-- ACKNOWLEDGE ME WHEN I SPEAK TO YOU. I AM A MAN OF *RANK.*

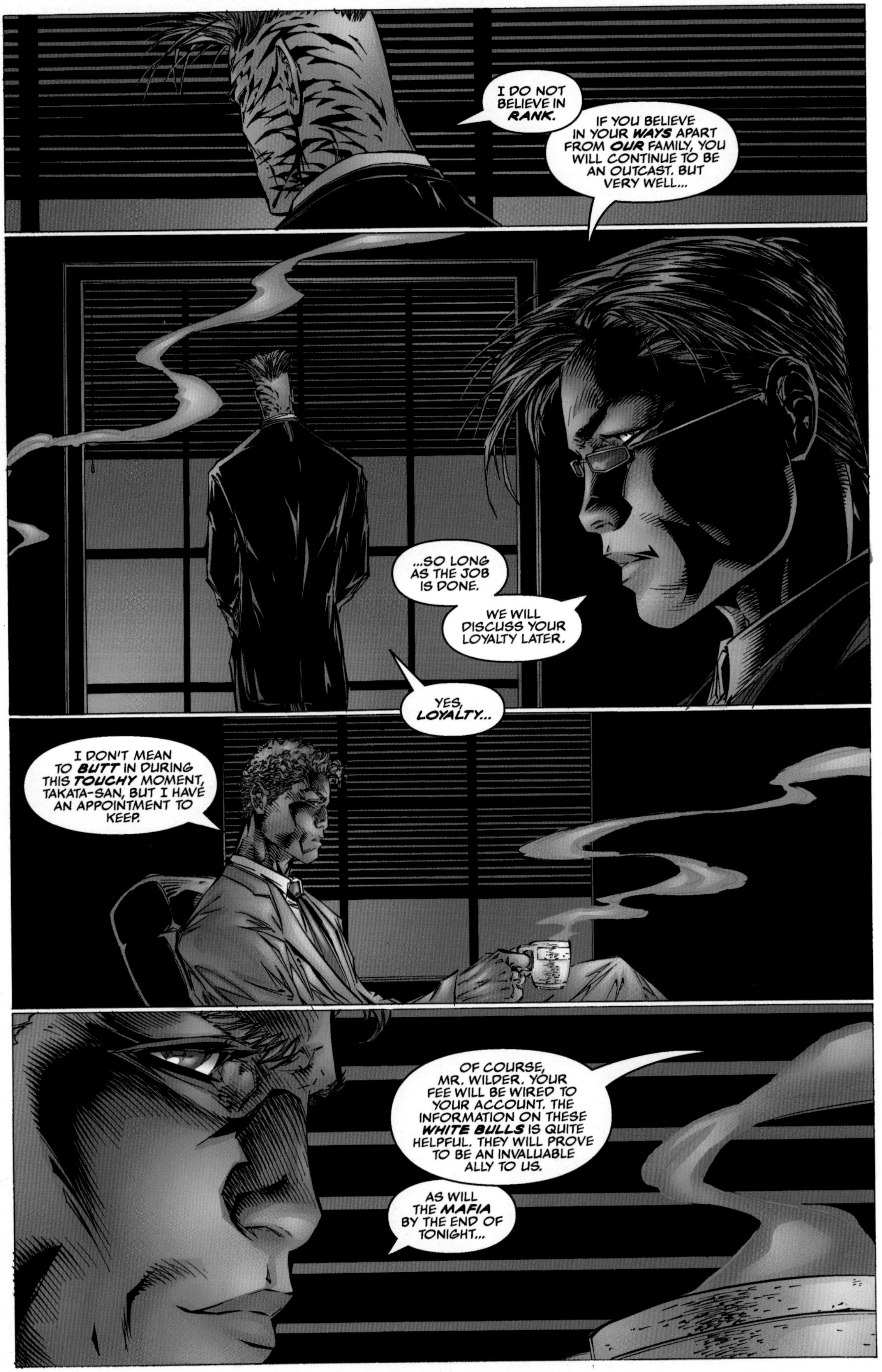

I DO NOT BELIEVE IN RANK.
IF YOU BELIEVE IN YOUR WAYS APART FROM OUR FAMILY, YOU WILL CONTINUE TO BE AN OUTCAST. BUT VERY WELL...
...SO LONG AS THE JOB IS DONE.
WE WILL DISCUSS YOUR LOYALTY LATER.
YES, LOYALTY...
I DON'T MEAN TO BUTT IN DURING THIS TOUCHY MOMENT, TAKATA-SAN, BUT I HAVE AN APPOINTMENT TO KEEP.
OF COURSE, MR. WILDER. YOUR FEE WILL BE WIRED TO YOUR ACCOUNT. THE INFORMATION ON THESE WHITE BULLS IS QUITE HELPFUL. THEY WILL PROVE TO BE AN INVALUABLE ALLY TO US.
AS WILL THE MAFIA BY THE END OF TONIGHT...

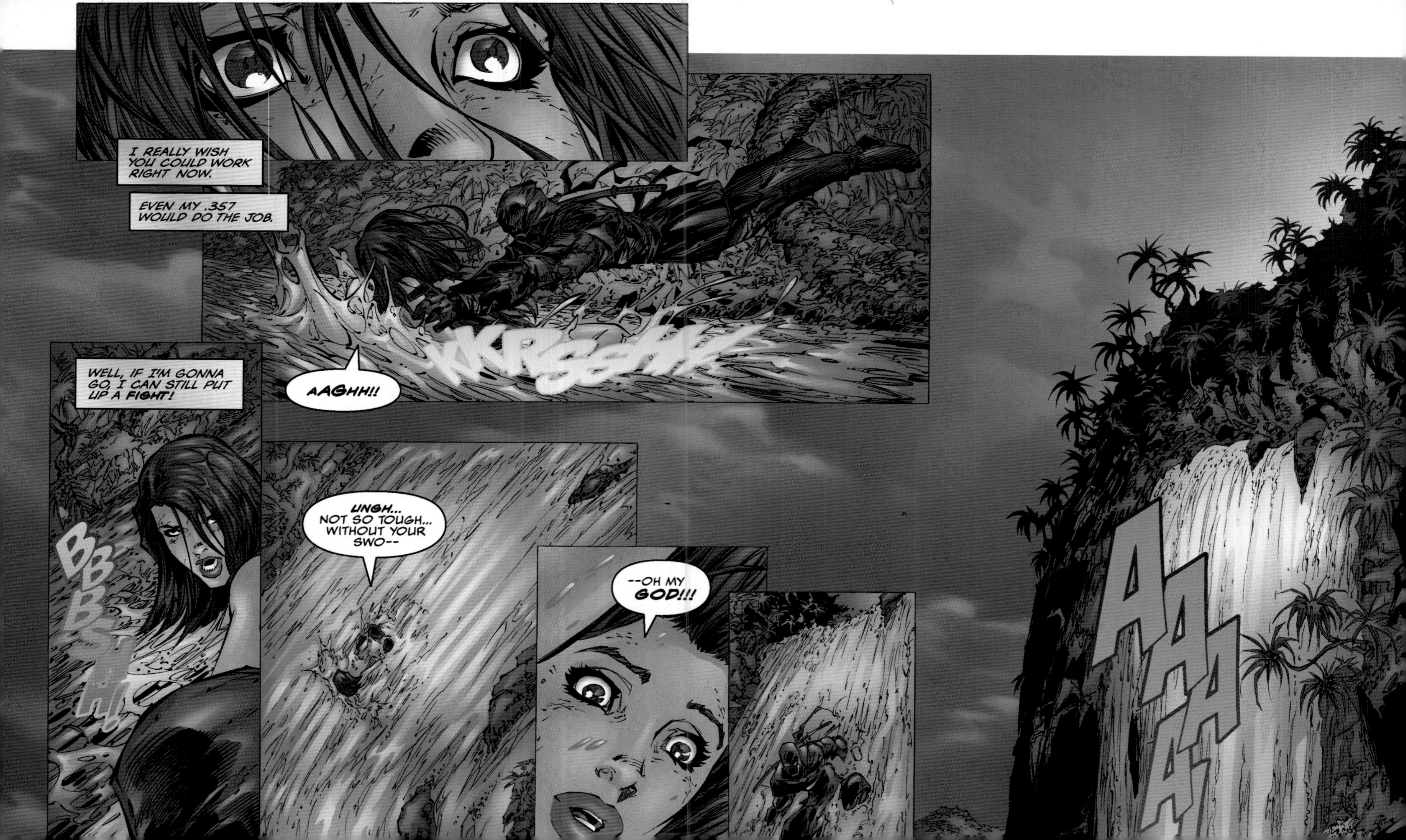
I REALLY WISH YOU COULD WORK RIGHT NOW.
EVEN MY .357 WOULD DO THE JOB.
KKRSSHH
AAGHH!!
WELL, IF I'M GONNA GO, I CAN STILL PUT UP A **FIGHT**!
BBBSSHH
UNGH... NOT SO TOUGH... WITHOUT YOUR SWO--
--OH MY **GOD!!!**
AAAAA

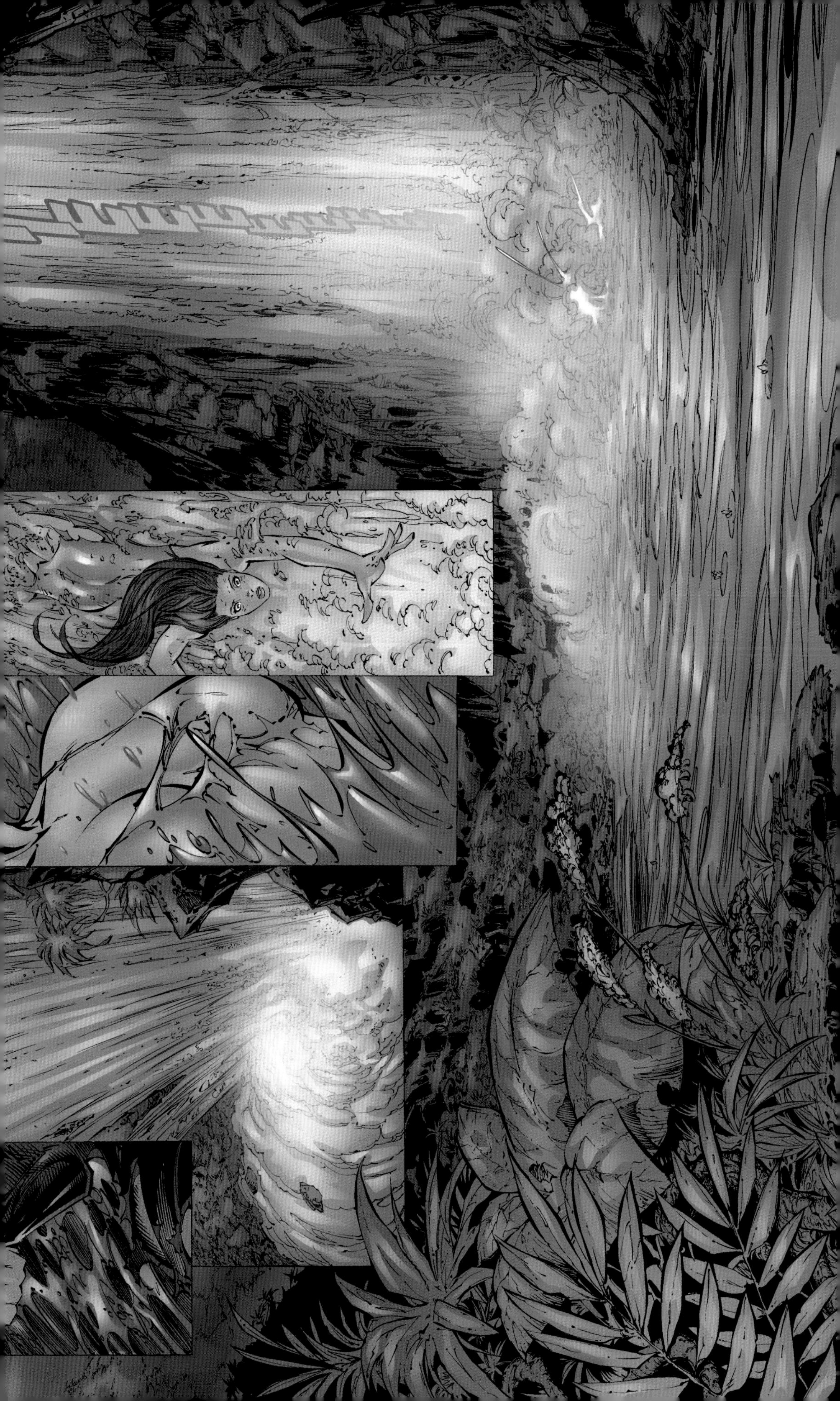

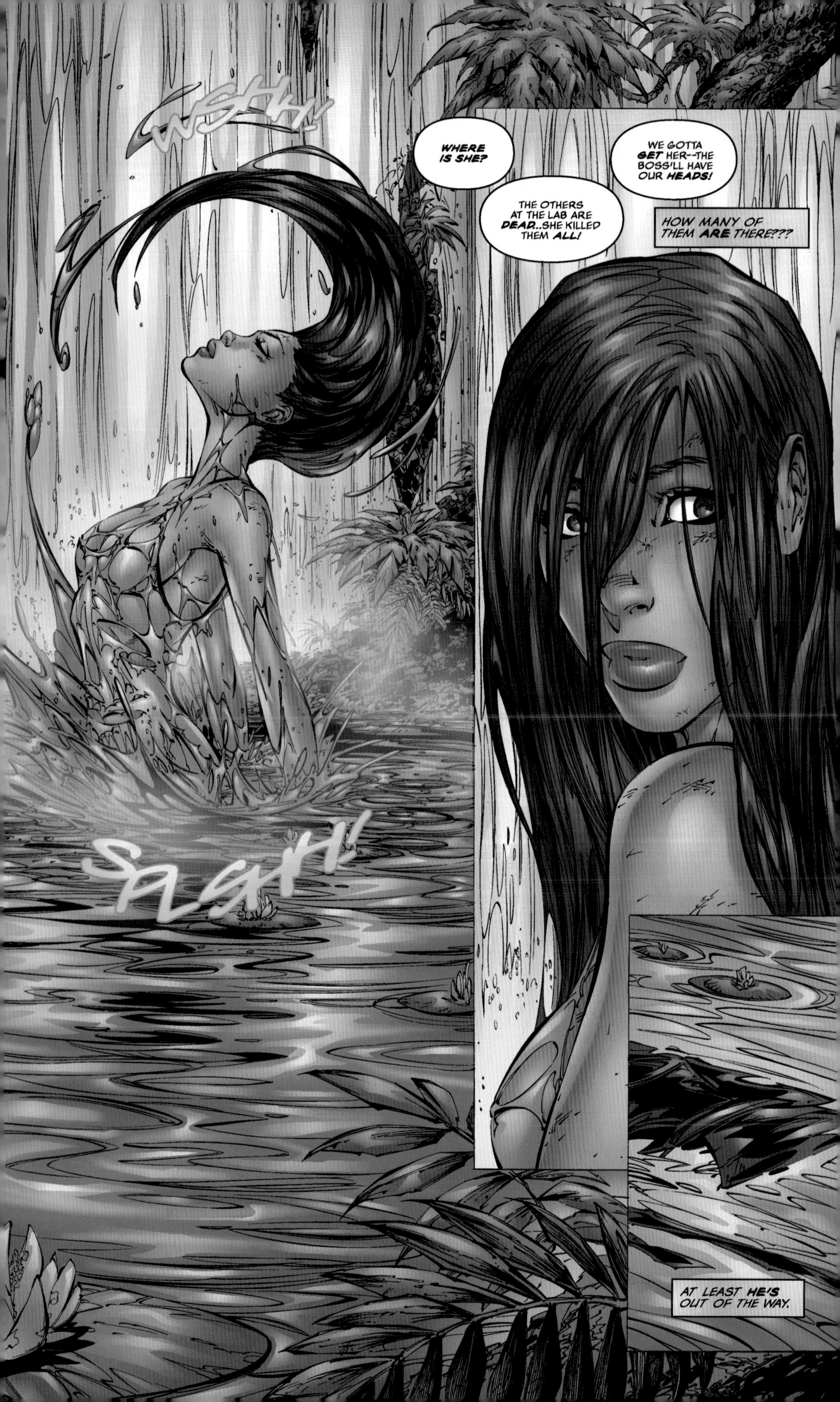
WSHH!
SPLSSH!
WHERE IS SHE?
WE GOTTA GET HER--THE BOSS'LL HAVE OUR HEADS!
THE OTHERS AT THE LAB ARE DEAD...SHE KILLED THEM ALL!
HOW MANY OF THEM ARE THERE???
AT LEAST HE'S OUT OF THE WAY.

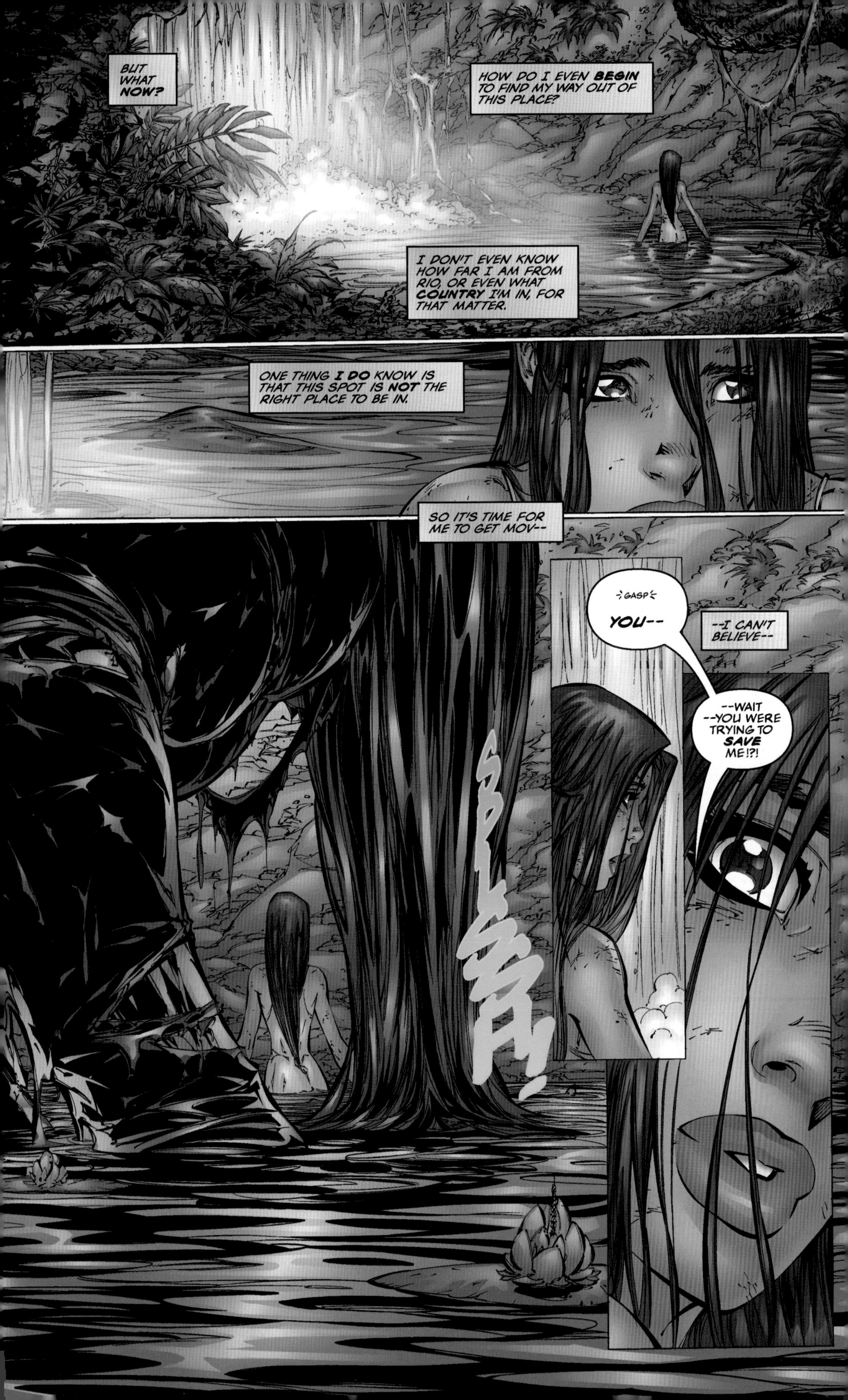
BUT WHAT NOW?
HOW DO I EVEN BEGIN TO FIND MY WAY OUT OF THIS PLACE?
I DON'T EVEN KNOW HOW FAR I AM FROM RIO, OR EVEN WHAT COUNTRY I'M IN, FOR THAT MATTER.
ONE THING I DO KNOW IS THAT THIS SPOT IS NOT THE RIGHT PLACE TO BE IN.
SO IT'S TIME FOR ME TO GET MOV--
GASP
YOU--
--I CAN'T BELIEVE--
--WAIT --YOU WERE TRYING TO SAVE ME!?!

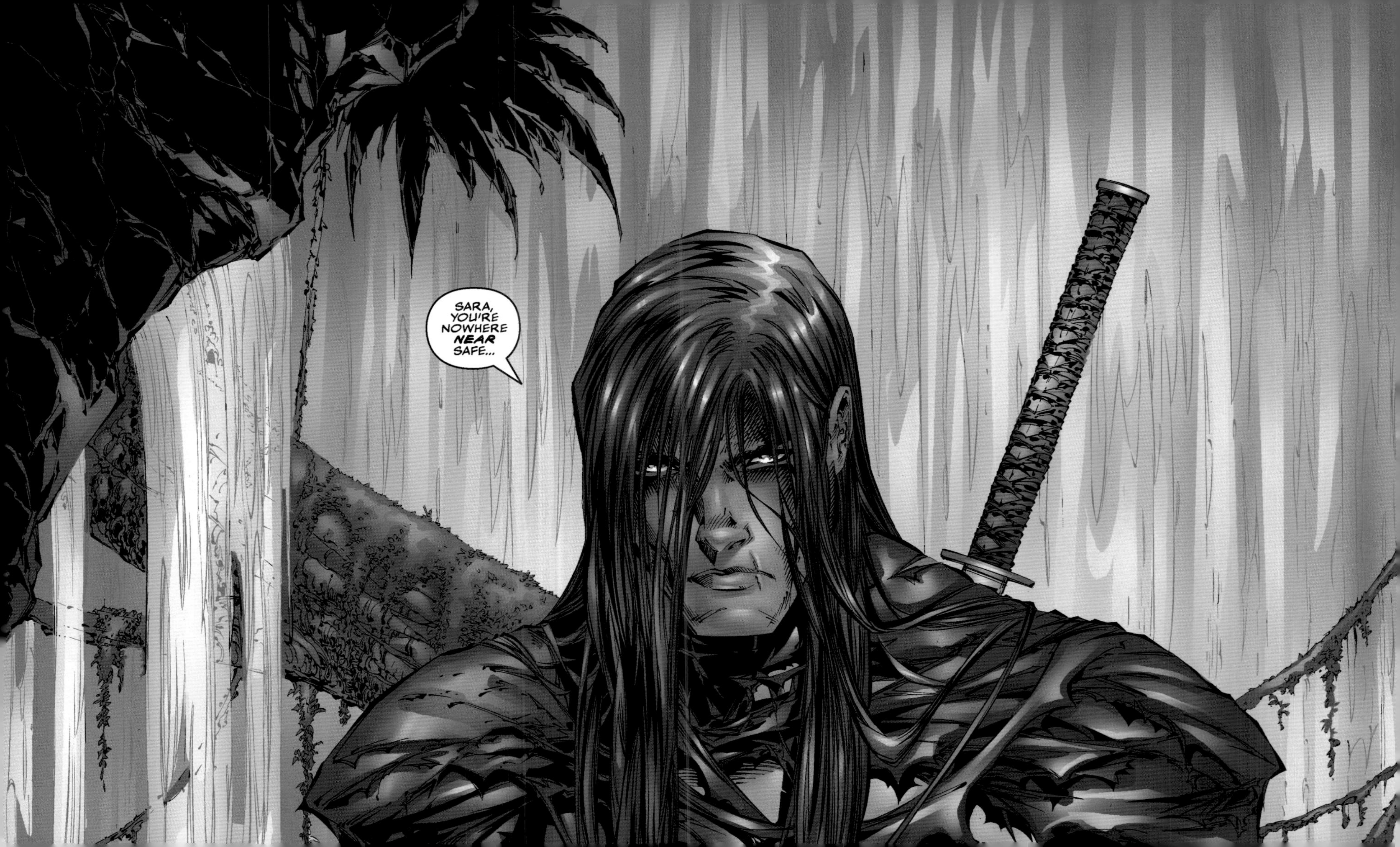
SARA, YOU'RE NOWHERE **NEAR** SAFE...

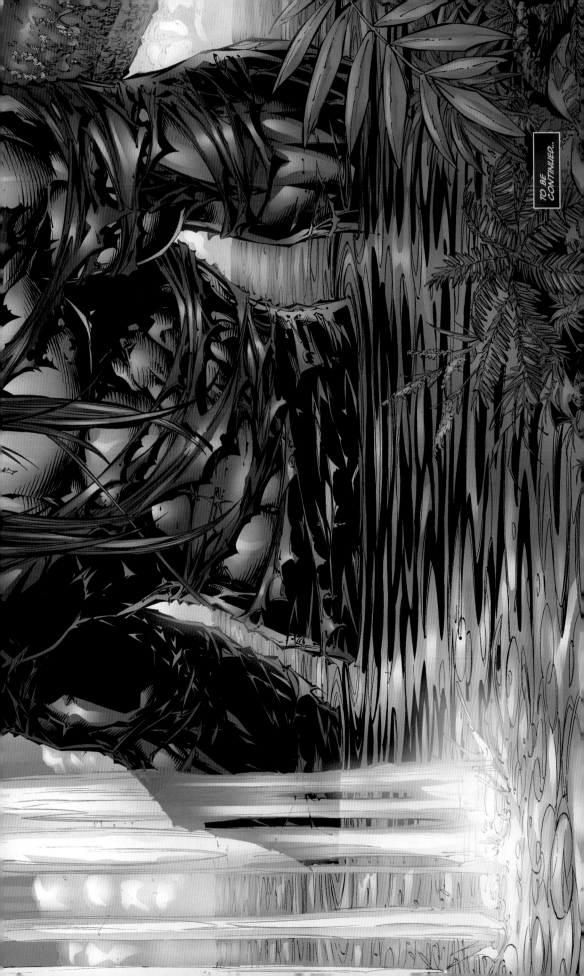

TO BE CONTINUED...

Witchblade: Origins volume 2

Cover Gallery

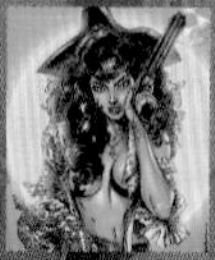

Witchblade issue #9 cover A
art by: **Tony Daniel, Kevin Conrad** and **JD Smith**

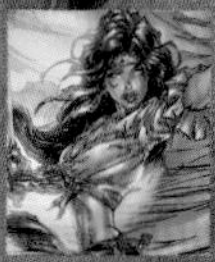

Witchblade issue #9, cover B
art by: **Michael Turner, D-Tron** and **JD Smith**

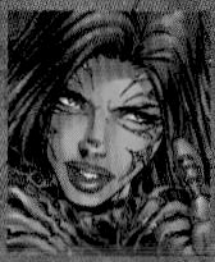

Witchblade issue #10
art by: **Michael Turner, D-Tron** and **JD Smith**

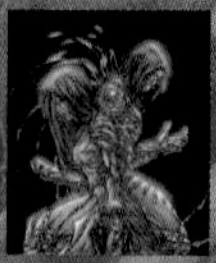

Witchblade issue #10
Dynamic forces variant
art by: **Michael Turner, D-Tron** and **JD Smith**

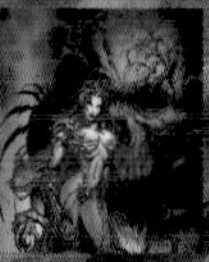

Witchblade issue #10 and *The Darkness* issue #0 variant
art by: **Marc Silvestri, Matt "Batt" Banning** and **Steve Firchow**

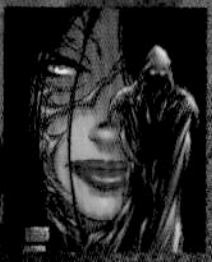

Witchblade issue #11
art by: **Michael Turner, D-Tron** and **JD Smith**

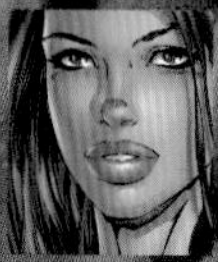

Witchblade issue #12
art by: **Michael Turner** and **JD Smith**

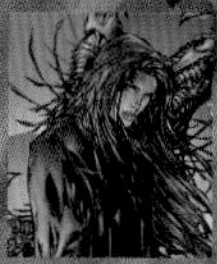

Witchblade issue #13
art by: **Michael Turner, D-Tron** and **JD Smith**

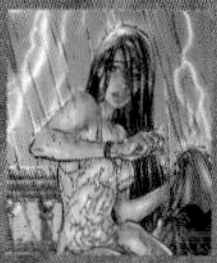

Witchblade issue #14
art by: **Michael Turner, D-Tron** and **JD Smith**

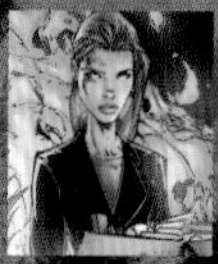

Witchblade issue #15
art by: **Michael Turner, D-Tron** and **JD Smith**

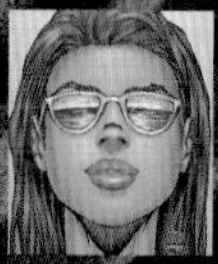

Witchblade issue #16
issue #1/2 Overstreet Fan edition variant
art by: **Michael Turner, D-Tron** and **JD Smith**

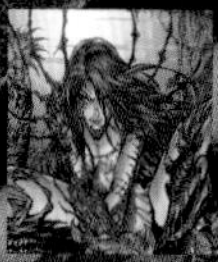

Witchblade issue #17
art by: **Michael Turner, D-Tron** and **JD Smith**

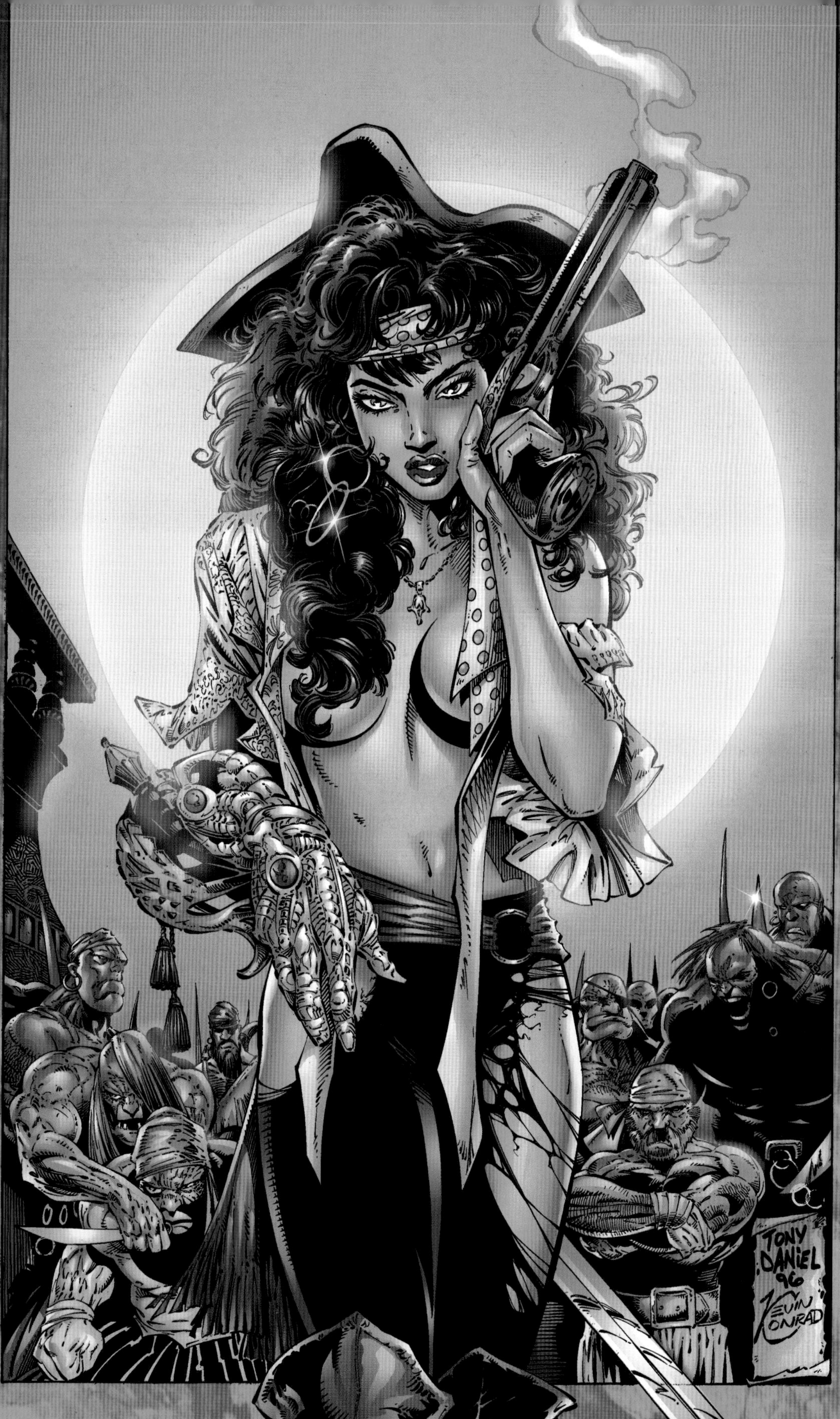
TONY DANIEL '96
KEVIN KONRAD

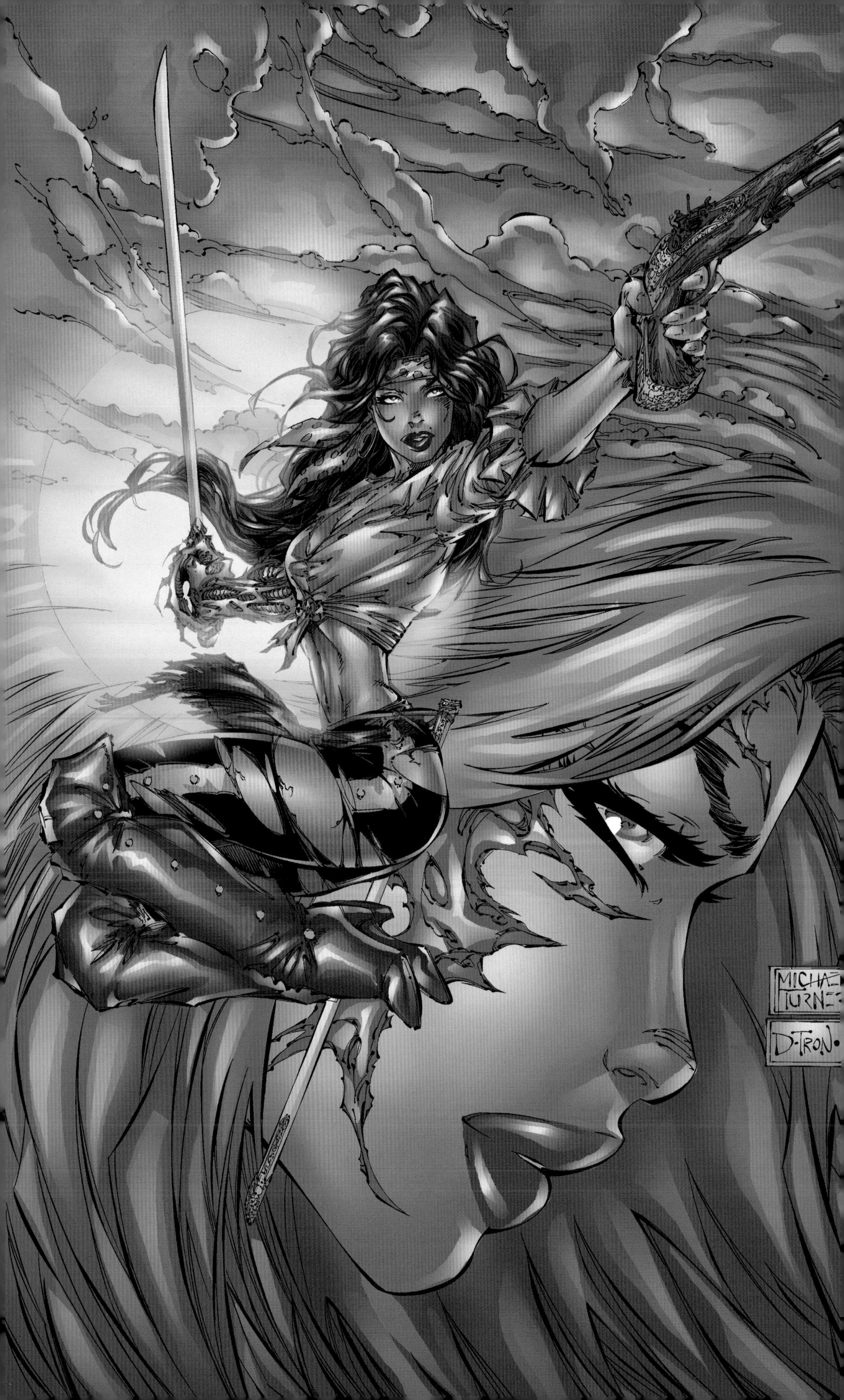

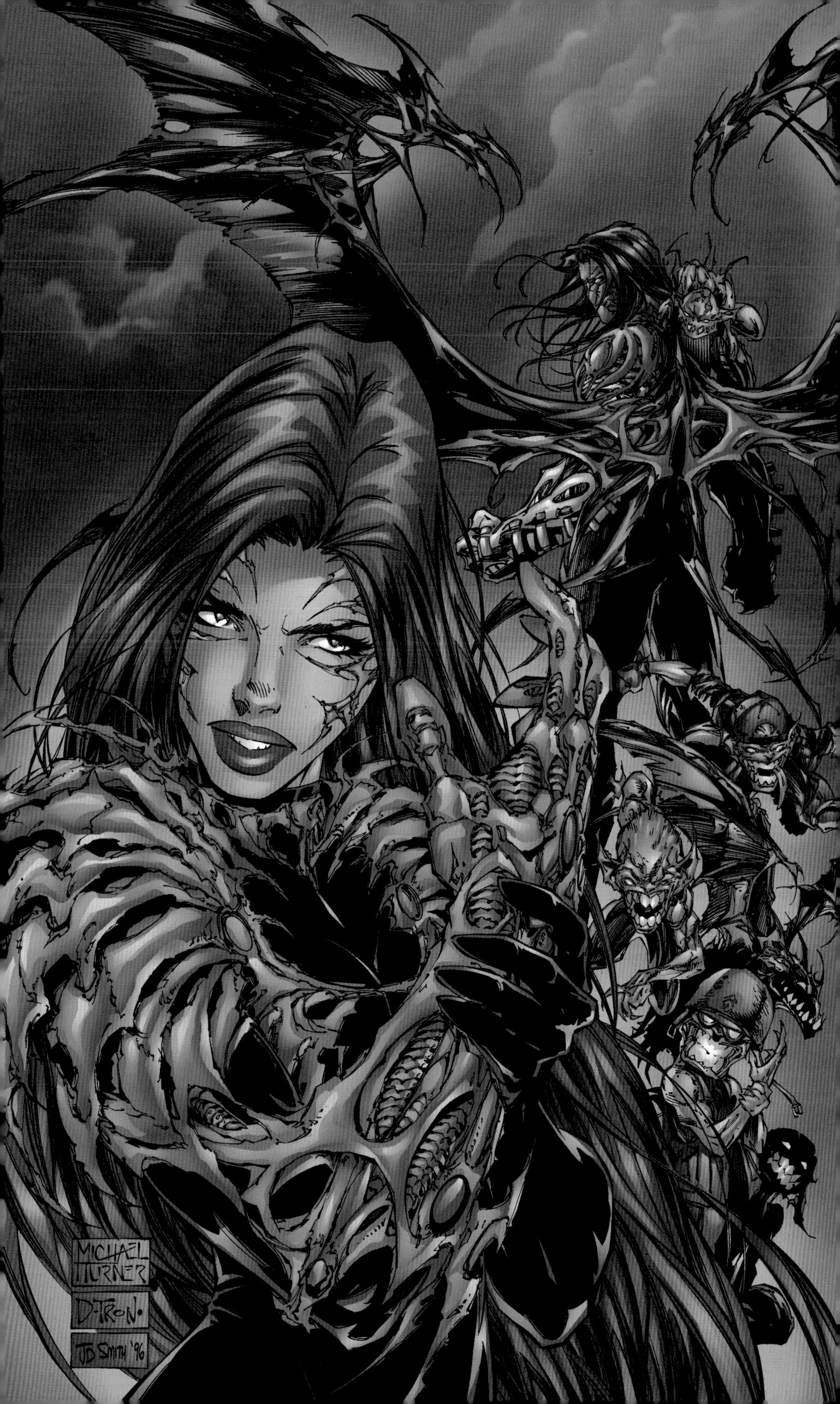
MICHAEL TURNER
D-TRON
JD SMITH '96

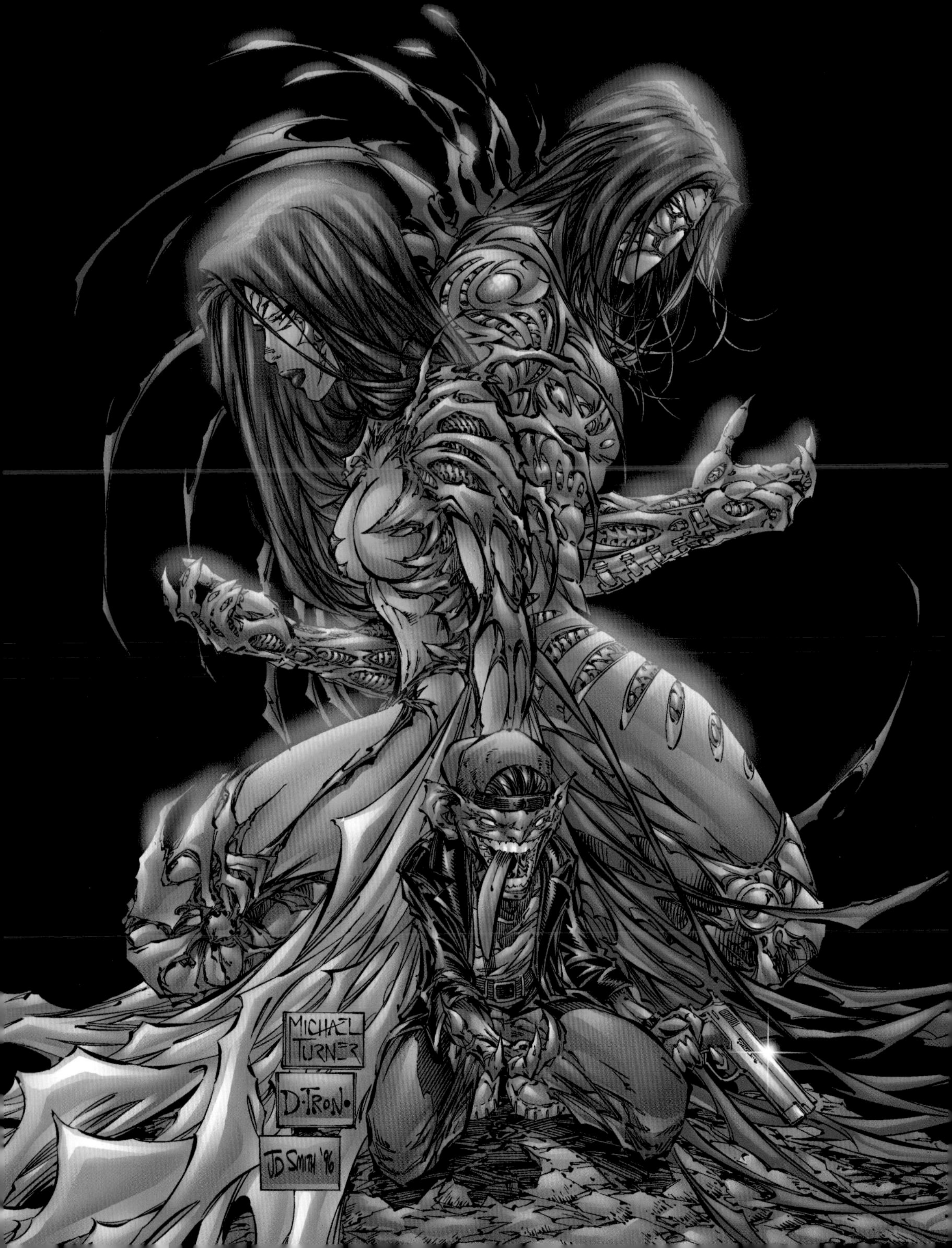
MICHAEL TURNER
D-TRON
JD SMITH '96

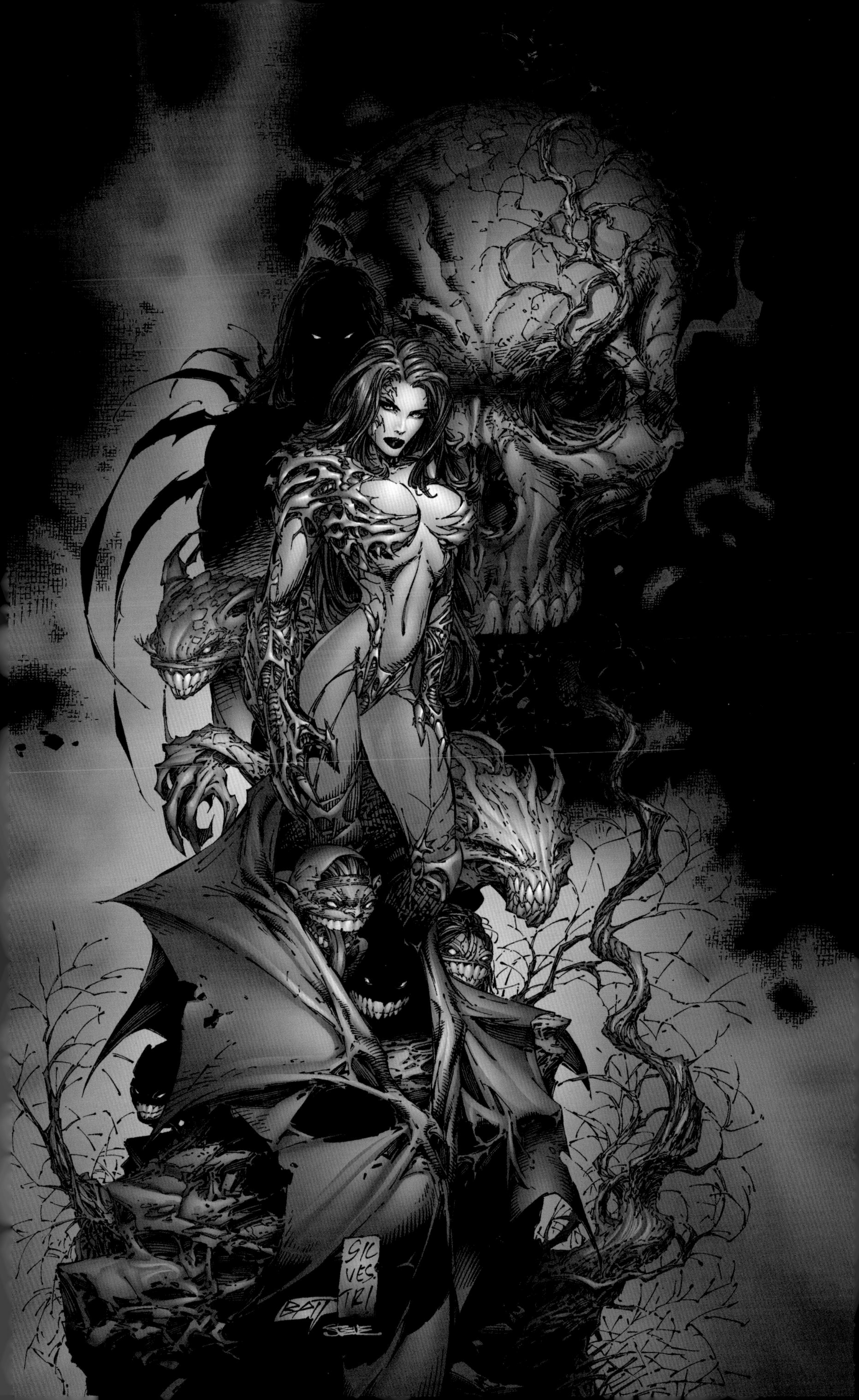
SIC
VES.
TRI

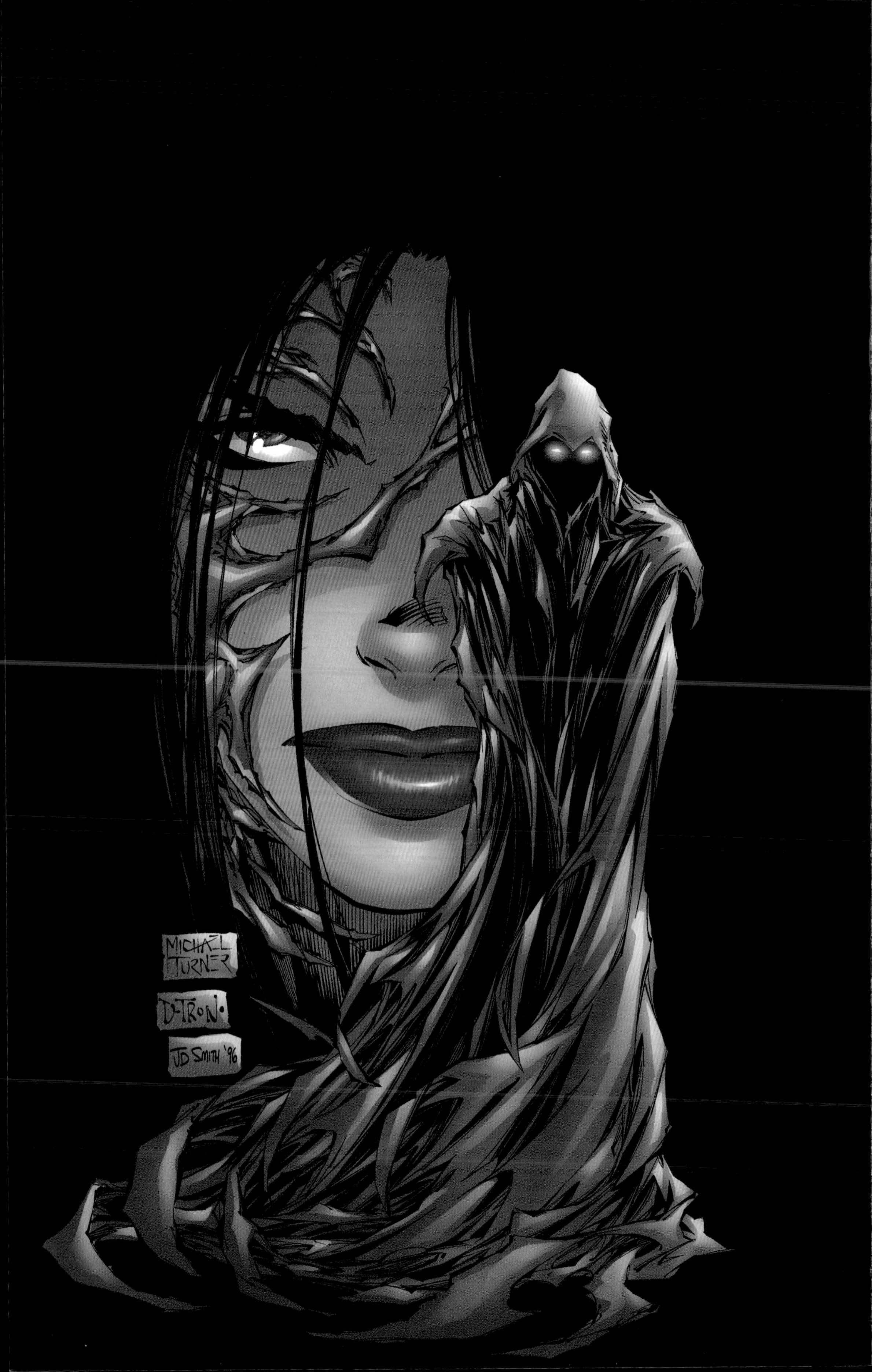
MICHAËL TURNER
D-TRON
JD SMITH '96

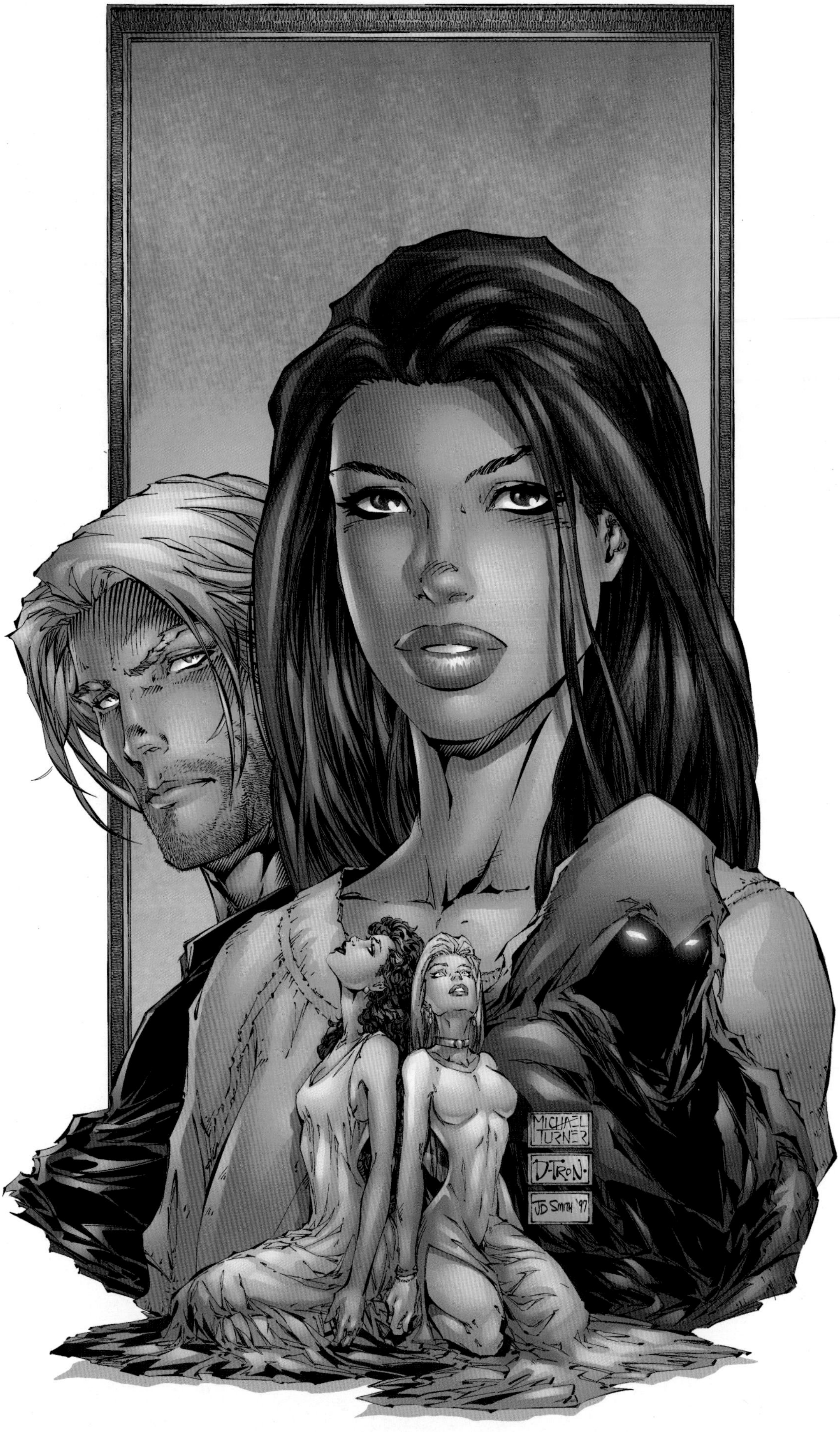
MICHAEL TURNER
D-TRON
JD SMITH '97

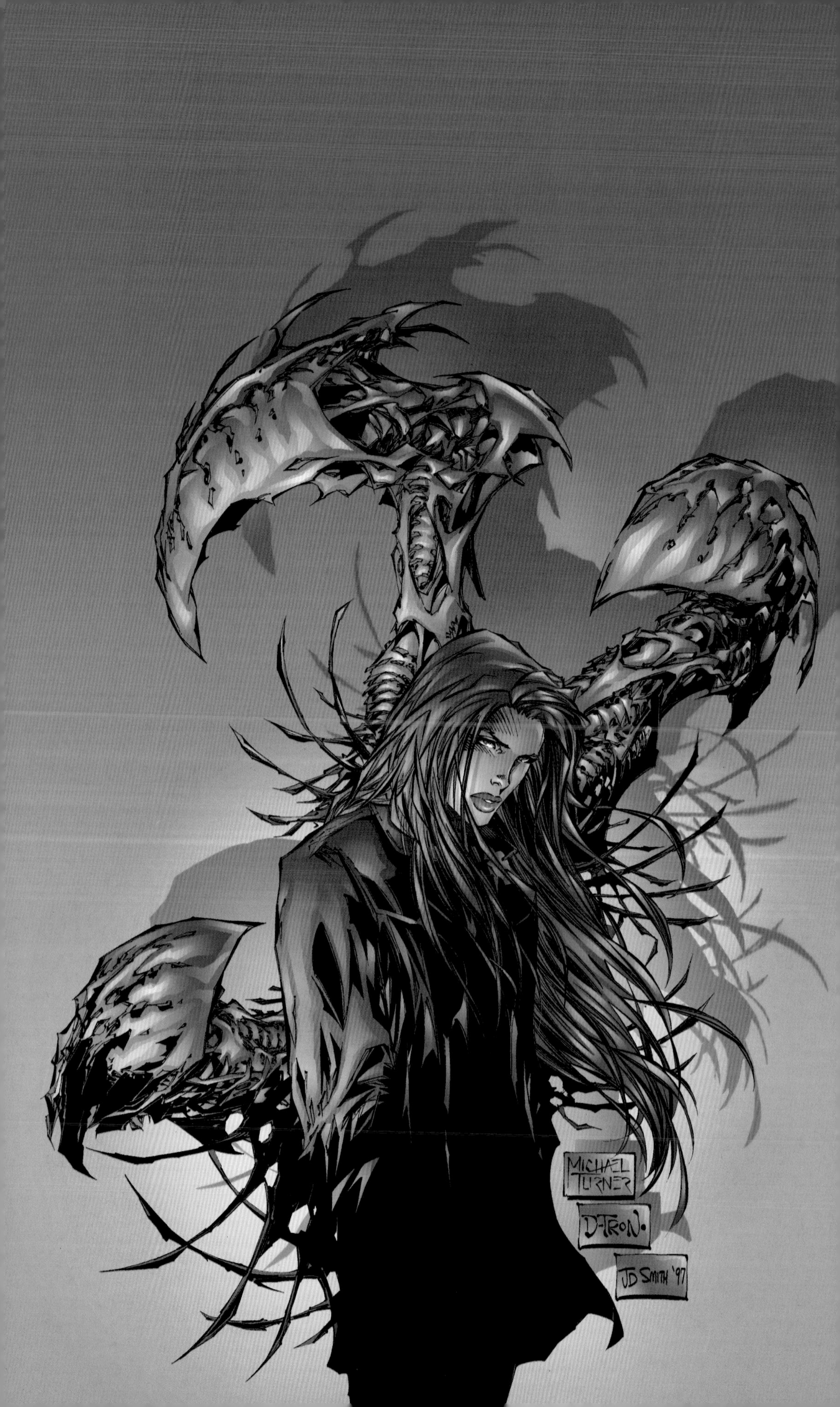
MICHAEL TURNER
D-TRON
JD SMITH '97

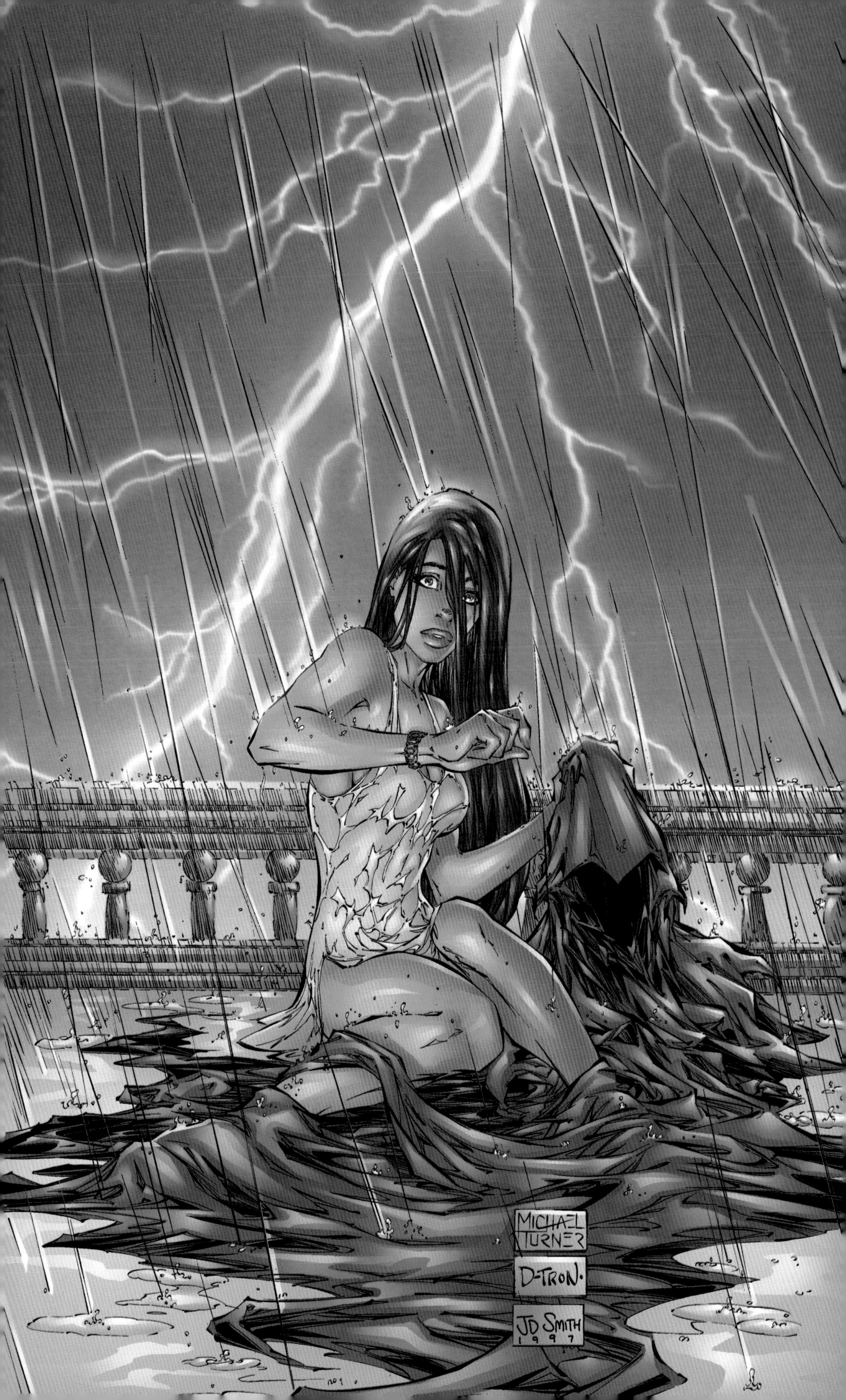
MICHAEL TURNER
D-TRON.
JD SMITH 1997

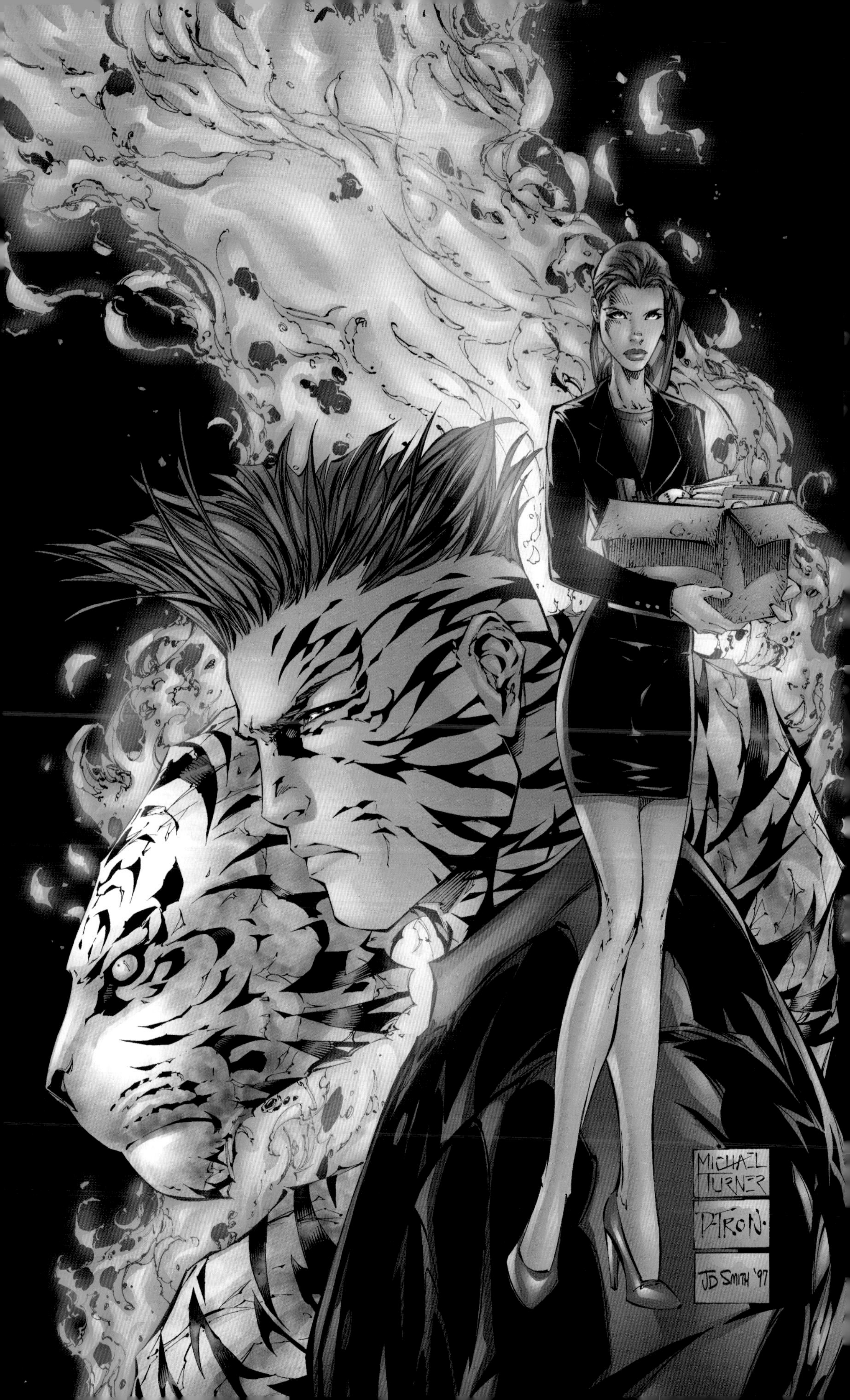
MICHAEL TURNER
D-TRON
JD SMITH '97

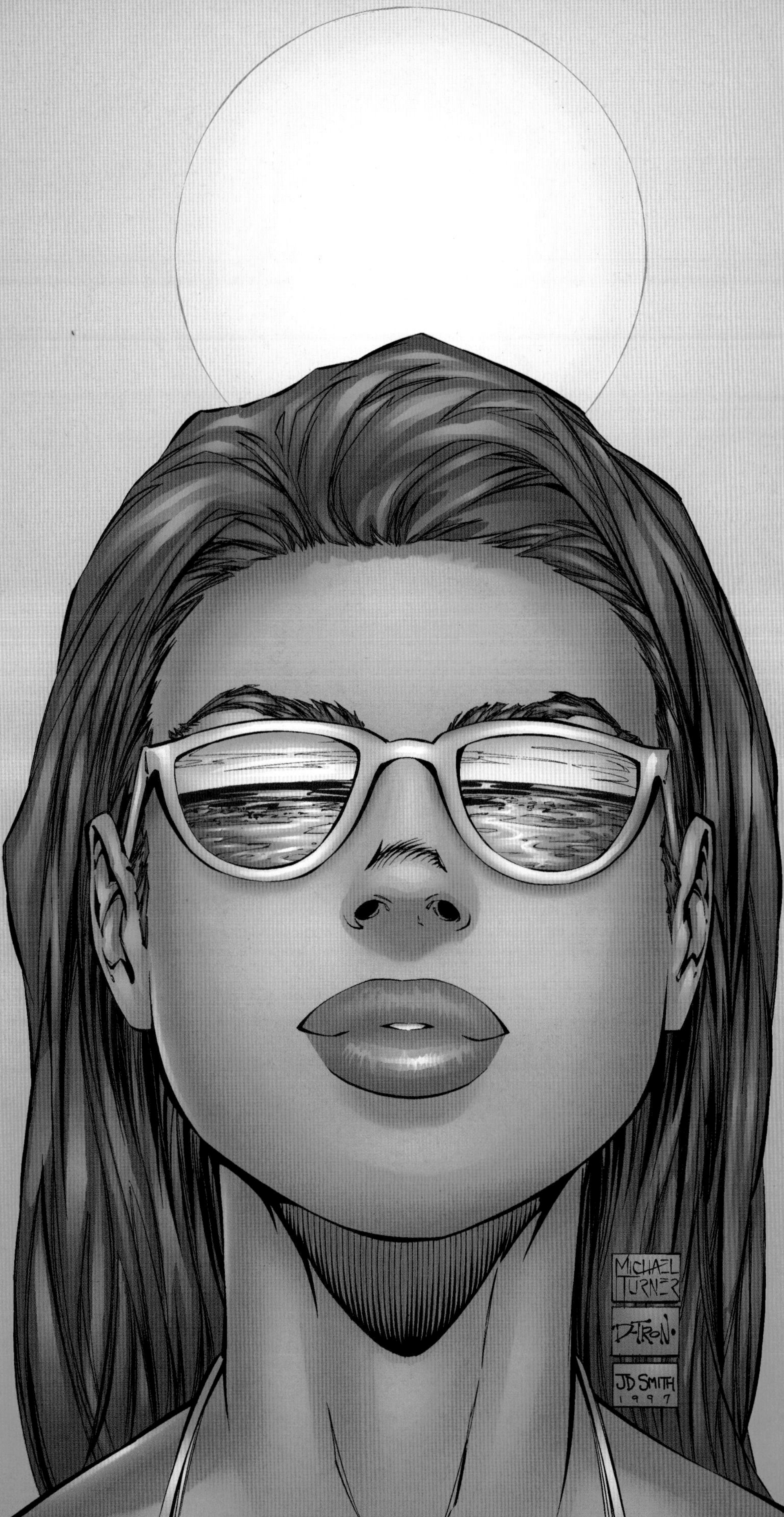
MICHAEL TURNER
D-TRON
JD SMITH 1997

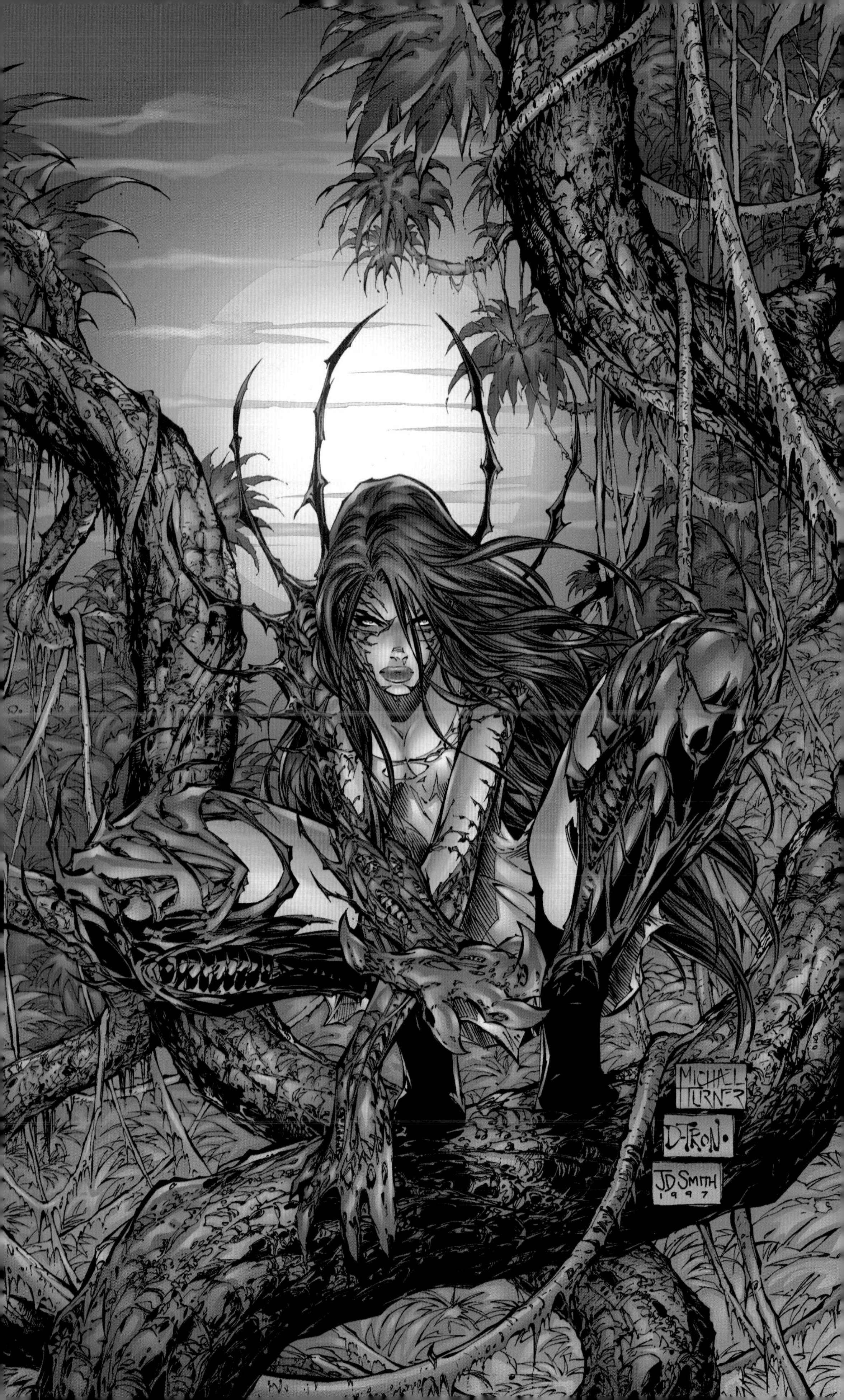
MICHAEL TURNER
D-TRON
JD SMITH 1997

Read more *Witchblade* in these trade paperback collections.

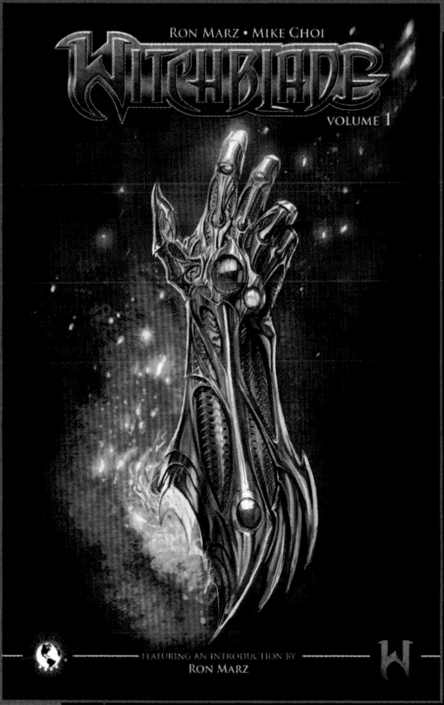

RON MARZ • MIKE CHOI
WITCHBLADE
VOLUME 1
FEATURING AN INTRODUCTION BY
RON MARZ

Witchblade

volume 1 - volume 5

written by:
Ron Marz
pencils by:
Mike Choi, Stephen Sadowski, Keu Cha, Chris Bachalo, Stjepan Sejic and more!

Get in on the ground floor of Top Cow's flagship title with these affordable trade paperback collections from Ron Marz's series re-defining run on Witchblade! Each volume collects a key story arc in the continuing adventures of Sara Pezzini and the Witchblade.

volume 1
collects issues #80-#85
(ISBN: 978-1-58240-906-1) $9.99

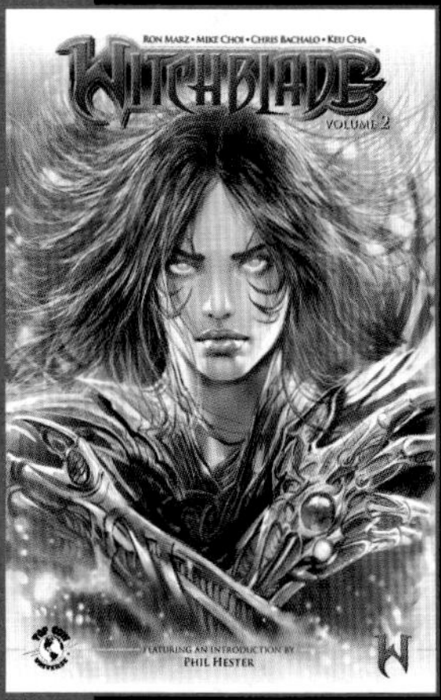

WITCHBLADE
VOLUME 2
PHIL HESTER

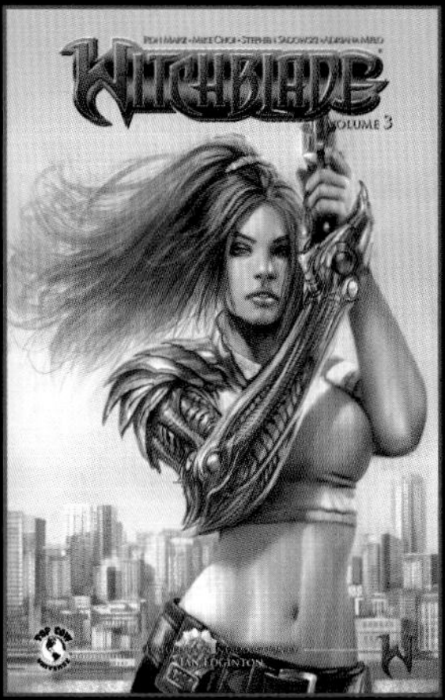

WITCHBLADE
VOLUME 3

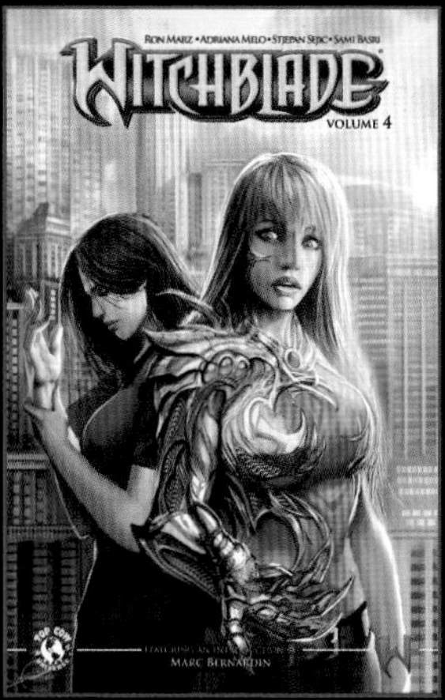

WITCHBLADE
VOLUME 4
MARC BERNARDIN

volume 2
collects issues #86-#92
(ISBN: 978-1-58240-886-6)
U.S.D. $14.99

volume 3
collects issues #93-#100
(ISBN: 978-1-58240-887-3)
U.S.D. $14.99

volume 4
collects issues #101-109
(ISBN: 978-1-58240-898-9)
U.S.D. $17.99

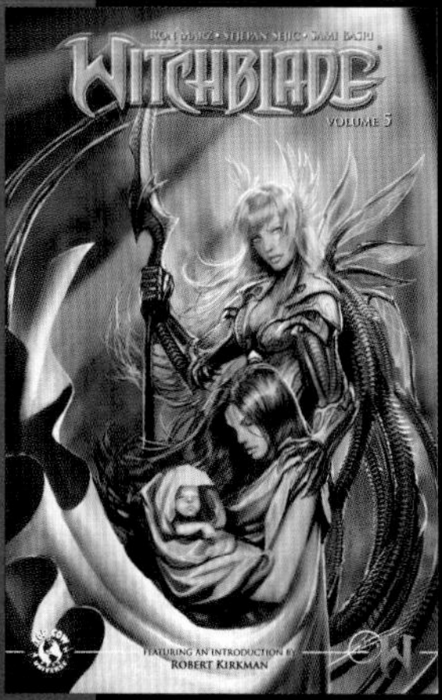

WITCHBLADE
VOLUME 5
FEATURING AN INTRODUCTION BY
ROBERT KIRKMAN

New York City Police Detective Sara Pezzini is the bearer of the Witchblade, a mysterious artifact that takes the form of a deadly and powerful gauntlet. Now Sara must try to control the Witchblade and learn its secrets, even as she investigates the city's strangest, most supernatural crimes.

volume 5
collects issues #110-115, *First Born* issues #1-3
(ISBN: 978-1-58240-899-6)
U.S.D. $17.99

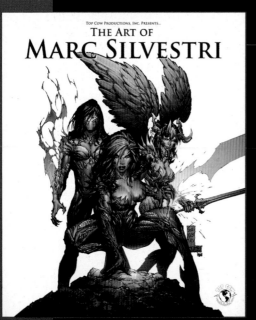